INTIMATE

Also by Elizabeth Gage

A Glimpse of Stocking
Pandora's Box
The Master Stroke
Taboo

Elizabeth Gage

INTIMATE

POCKET BOOKS

New York   London   Toronto   Sydney   Tokyo   Singapore

This book is a work of fiction. Names, characters, places and incidents are products of the author's imagination or are used fictitiously. Any resemblance to actual events or locales or persons, living or dead, is entirely coincidental.

POCKET BOOKS, a division of Simon & Schuster Inc.
1230 Avenue of the Americas, New York, NY 10020

Library of Congress Cataloging-in-Publication Data

Gage, Elizabeth.
    Intimate / Elizabeth Gage.
        p.   cm.
    ISBN: 0-671-89706-3
    I. Title.
PS3557.A327I55   1995
813'.54—dc20   94-30761
                                          CIP

First Pocket Books hardcover printing April 1995

10 9 8 7 6 5 4 3 2 1

Printed in the U.S.A.

To Maile

Acknowledgments

My heartfelt appreciation goes to Ms. Tina Gerrard and Mr. Jon Kirsh for their tireless and thorough assistance in my research. I would also like to thank Claire Zion, my editor at Pocket Books, for her valuable suggestions.

Once again I gratefully acknowledge my debt to Ernst H. Huneck, M.D., for expert advice on a host of difficult problems. And sincere thanks as always to Jay Garon, for his support and encouragement.

Elizabeth Gage

Contents

My thoughts and my discourse as madmen's are,
At random from the truth vainly expressed,
For I have sworn thee fair, and thought thee bright,
Who art as black as Hell, as dark as night.

Shakespeare, Sonnet 147

Mirror, mirror on the wall,
Who's the fairest one of all?

"Snow White"

Prologue

THE ISLAND IS CALLED XALOS. It lies in the Aegean Sea some seventy-five miles east of Athens, and an equal distance west of the Turkish coast, in the group called the Cyclades. Volcanic in origin, it supports little agriculture. Its few hundred inhabitants make their living from fishing and from the cultivation of a handful of reluctant olive orchards.

Two thousand years ago the island played an important though somewhat ambiguous role in the second Peloponnesian War, when a small but ferocious band of Spartan sailors used it as their base for an attack on the nearby Athenian garrison at Sifnos. The Spartans disguised their warships as fishing vessels and lay in wait in Xalos harbor for nearly two months before ambushing the unsuspecting Athenians and annihilating them. As it turned out, however, their victory was a Pyrrhic one, for an epidemic of cholera wiped out most of the island's population, including the Spartan occupiers, within six weeks of the decisive battle.

In the centuries since then the village has been a pawn in as many wars as the Greeks and their enemies have been able to concoct, both civil and general. It has changed hands a hundred times. But the inhabitants, whose family trees go back to the time of Aeschylus and Thucydides, have paid little attention to the tumult of political strife around them, preferring to focus their concern on tides, storms, and the unpredictable subaqueous lifestyle of the Aegean spotted bass, their chief source of livelihood.

Today the visitor to Xalos, his eye jaundiced by experience with beautiful places around the globe, is struck by the fact that the island boasts no resort hotels. Though its harbor is picturesque, its view of other Aegean islands magnificent, and its nightly sunsets equal to any in the world, it has no tourist industry whatever. A tiny hotel in the center of town, patronized by commercial travelers and the occasional live-in widow or bachelor, is the only accommodation available.

Tourists dismiss this lovely place as a spot without facilities for entertainment and therefore without interest, turning their attention elsewhere and not realizing that little Xalos remains as unspoiled as it is for a reason.

All the prime real estate that might have supported hotels, restaurants, or condominiums has been bought up in recent years by a single man and leased at low cost to the storekeepers, fishermen and villagers who live and work here. The tourist industry, so quick to swallow up every other island of natural beauty in the vicinity, has been forcibly kept away from Xalos by this man. Thus, in the late-twentieth century's version of the ancient wars for territory, the tiny island has found itself protected once again from the invading hordes by a benevolent but willful despot.

The man is rarely seen by the villagers, many of whom do not even realize he is responsible for their untroubled lives. He owns a small but luxurious house built high on a hillside overlooking the harbor. A busy man of legendary wealth, he comes here only four or five times a year, always alone, to get away from his many obligations and responsibilities. The house has no telephone, and the mail is kept for him at the village post office.

Occasionally a villager will see him walking meditatively along a cramped street or standing in silence on a parapet, hands at his sides, staring out at the Aegean. There is a man at the marina who maintains a small yacht for him, rarely used. Otherwise the owner barely exists.

On this day, in June of the year 1981, the house was not empty.

In the master bedroom, whose magnificent view of the Aegean was blocked by firmly closed curtains, a man and woman lay naked under the soft covers of a large, quiet bed, their bodies locked in the embrace of love.

The man was in his late thirties but looked younger. His body was lithe, handsome, with the hard limbs of an athlete. At the moment his thighs were curved around the woman, for he was crouched atop her. His hands held her lovingly beneath the waist, caressing her even as he pulled her harder toward him.

The woman was slim and beautiful, with creamy skin and curly reddish-blond hair tousled by the pillow beneath her head. Her eyes were closed in her excitement.

"Oh," she murmured as, with a long slow stroke, he found his way deeper inside her. "Oh, I love you."

Her arms were wrapped around him, her hands sliding up and down his back. Her legs curled about his waist. The center of her was on fire, trembling around the staff that nestled inside her.

"I love you," she repeated. "I love you. . . ."

The sound of her words seemed to strip away the last control he had over his own pleasure. He worked faster, his thrusts flaming in the quick of her. Words would no longer come. Ecstasy began to overwhelm them both.

On the bedside table, long since forgotten by the two people in the bed, was a newspaper, the *International Herald Tribune*. It was opened to an inside page, where the following headline dominated the other news:

AMERICA'S RICHEST MAN MARRIES

The story beneath the headline told of a long romance, of recent tragedy, of a child, and of a complex series of events that had led to a happy ending. It was a story that had captivated a curious world for many months and showed no sign of losing its appeal.

But the man and woman in the bed had come here to escape the public curiosity of which they were the object. At the moment nothing existed for them but each other.

The woman felt the pace of his strokes quicken, and the answering tremor deep within her loins. A musical little whimper sounded softly in her throat. She arched her back, white and pretty as a swan, and pulled him to her with eager arms. The terrible hard thing between his legs came deeper, deeper. She gasped, almost unable to bear her own delight. Then a huge spasm overtook them both, and she felt his essence come to her. She cried out her ecstasy and heard the scalded groan in his throat.

For what seemed many minutes she lay in his arms, her breath slowing, the heat of her body ebbing to precious warmth and safety. But every breath, every touch meant that she belonged to him. She smiled to feel her own surrender.

"I love you so much," she murmured. "Can this all be real? It's too good to be true."

"It's real," he said, holding her close. "I've spent my life learning to tell the difference between what's true and what isn't. You're mine now. Nothing will ever separate us again."

He was sure of his words. They contained the force of his will as well as of his understanding. He had waited a lifetime for this woman. He would never let her go.

He had lived an eventful life, even a heroic one. But it had never had meaning for him until he met her. He had given her his heart almost instantly. Then he had lost her. His entire world had been swallowed by that loss. He had lived like a ghost, exiled from his very self because of it.

Then he had found her again. Improbably, miraculously. She had come to him on the ruins of his life, and because of her his heart had awakened from its long sleep. He would never allow the world to take her from him again.

She seemed to read his thoughts, for she said, "You're right. It's not too good to be true. I belong to you. That's the only true thing."

She stood up, naked. He lay on his back, admiring her. She was so slender, so sculptured in her beauty. She was not aware of the depth of her own sensuality. He realized she could bewitch a man if she tried, spin a web around his heart so that escape was impossible.

But now she was his, and she was holding nothing back. She glanced down at him, smiling. The light of love in her eyes caught him, and he got up and went to her side. They made a stunningly perfect couple, this strong man with his Adonis-like form, and the tender, shapely woman, tall and supple, her breasts firm as his hands came to cup them.

They kissed for a long moment. Then they put on silk bathrobes—his little gift to her for this occasion—and walked out onto the terrace overlooking the harbor.

He stood with his arm around her, gazing at the sea. At this hour the waves bore a striking purplish glow, jeweled by the dying sun. Many was the time he had stood here alone, studying that shining surface and wondering about the unseen secrets that stirred beneath it.

He had spent his life learning to interpret the surfaces of things, the forces and interlockings that ruled them. To many he seemed a ruler of that world. But in the end he had learned that a man can never find himself on the surface of things. A man can amass incalculable wealth, possess a thousand women, without ever penetrating an inch beneath that surface—or coming an inch closer to his own heart.

Thus it was that his wealth had only made him seem the poorer, and his power only made him feel more helpless—until he found her again. Only now could he breathe, only now could he begin to live.

"I hate to think of it," he said.

"What?" Her question was gentle.

"How easy it was to lose you," he said, "and how hard it was to find you again. I'd give anything to have those years back."

"Darling," she said. "Maybe they weren't wasted years at all. Maybe they were necessary in their way."

Her eyes rested on the sea, the irises stealing some of its color for their own.

"Maybe," she added thoughtfully, "we were never really separated at all."

He turned to look at her. He saw that she was right. Every moment away from her had been lived under her spell, even when he had tried his hardest to forget her. Every other woman, including the most important one, had merely been a poor copy of her, a sort of mask. Like the thread of Ariadne leading Theseus through the labyrinth in the mythology of the Greeks, every other woman had merely been part of the invisible fabric that linked him to her, always her.

"I think you're right," he said. "No matter where I went or what I did, I was coming back to you. I know that now."

"Yes," she smiled. "It's good to know." She ran her hand through his hair and pulled him closer. Despite the cool freshness of the evening air, the feel of him in her arms was already beginning to send waves of wanting through her. In another instant she would kiss him, and passion would make her lead him back to the bedroom.

"I love you," she murmured, bringing his lips to hers.

He moved suddenly in her arms. At that moment a harsh, abrupt sound came from somewhere behind her. For a brief instant she tried to tell herself it came from the harbor below. But she knew already that it was the report of a gun, and dangerously nearby.

"Jordan, no."

He clung to her, a puzzled look in his eyes. Then he sank to the ground as she struggled to support him. She cried out in horror, unable to believe what she was seeing.

"No, Jordan, no . . ."

Panic seized her. She looked left and right on the terrace. She saw no one, but sensed a presence coming toward her.

Something quicker than her terror made her dart inside to the bedroom.

In a few seconds she returned. She held a pillow and a blanket. Oblivious to the danger she knew awaited her, she knelt beside the man she loved. She could not see where he was wounded. There was blood everywhere, a great deal of blood. She placed the pillow under his head.

"Oh, my God, Jordan. Jordan . . ."

The blanket was still in her hand. She touched his cheek. His eyes had gone blank now.

"Darling," she said. "Look at me. Speak to me. Please!"

She knew she was alone. There was no telephone inside. The nearest neighbor was three hundred yards away. And even if her cries could be heard from here, there was no time for them to be answered.

A voice came from the terrace behind her.

"Well, that's over."

She looked up, her face turning white. She saw a figure standing by the parapet, a gun pointing at her. The familiar face was feverish, triumphant.

"You," she said.

The lips curled in a twisted smile. "You can't run away from the past. I thought you had learned that by now."

Now the gun pointed to the limp body in her arms.

"You did this," came the voice. "You thought you could have it all. Now you see where it's gotten you."

She had pulled the blanket over Jordan. She held his head tenderly in her lap.

"Get back." The voice was harsher now. "Get back or I'll kill you, too."

She looked up. Fear made her eyes more beautiful. She shook her head.

"All right," said the intruder. "Stay where you are, then. You've asked for this. Now you're going to see the bullet go in. Then you'll know."

The gun came closer, pointing at Jordan.

"No!" she cried.

The figure looked down at her, smiling.

"What's the matter?" came the voice. "You brought this on. You thought you could hide from the truth forever. But everything has to be paid for. Are you afraid of a little justice?"

The gun was aimed carefully at Jordan's head. The hand did not shake. A finger stirred on the trigger, without haste.

"Justice," the voice repeated.

The explosion rang out over the rocky slope leading from the house to the sea. No one heard it.

Book One

MIRROR, MIRROR

1

HOLLY FLEMING THOUGHT she had seen everything.

In sixteen years as a child welfare worker on Chicago's notorious South Side, she had seen families ruined by alcohol, abandonment, poverty, drugs, hopelessness, and every form of abuse known to man. She had walked streets where life was often valued far below the price of a bag of heroin or sometimes even a carton of cigarettes.

A bright, warm-hearted spinster of thirty-nine whose paltry paycheck barely paid the rent on her cheap downtown apartment, Holly had an enormous family of needy clients who looked forward to her weekly visits as if she were a saint blessing their lives. In her years with the department she had met people who managed to respect themselves and to love each other in the midst of the most atrocious living conditions. Children above all retained their mysterious dignity and innocence, no matter what the abuse or neglect they suffered.

Perhaps it was because of those children that Holly, who no longer hoped to have a child of her own, continued her tireless pursuit of a profession that would have long since defeated a less dedicated worker, and endured daily exposure to a kind of misery unimaginable outside the urban ghetto of the modern world.

On this blustery fall morning Holly was drinking her morning coffee and flipping through her case files in preparation for the day's visits, when a colleague came to her side.

"Something new," he said, holding up a file.

Holly looked at him. His name was Keith Cassidy. He was younger than she was, and more cynical. Five years on the job had taken the youthful idealism out of him, but, unlike Holly, he had not found the core of compassion within himself that makes a social welfare worker's life bearable and fulfilling. Keith hated his work and was angling for a promotion that would get him away from client contact and into administration. In the meantime he was, if not a caring professional, at least a thorough one. He did not love his clients, but he dreaded making a mistake on a case that might hinder his hoped-for promotion. So Holly trusted him.

"What is it?" she asked.

"A family named Sundberg," he said. "Truancy and suspected child abuse. One of the neighbors called in for the fourth time. She thinks it's serious."

Holly looked at the file. It was a virtual blank. The family had only been in town for six months. There was one child, a little girl in first grade. The mother, according to the file, was a sometime cashier and receptionist. The father was not living at home. There was a boyfriend, to judge by the neighbors' reports.

"I called the little girl's school this morning," Keith said. "They said she hasn't been in school for a week. They sent a truant officer to the house, but there was nobody home. The mother's employer says she hasn't been in to work in a month. There's no phone in the house. The neighbor thinks there's something funny going on. We'd better go over there and have a look."

Holly closed the file. She knew she had a dozen other stops to make today, many of them urgent. But something about this Sundberg situation made her nervous.

"All right," she said to Keith. "The other cases can wait. Let's go."

They drove in their old state-issued sedan, with its seal on the driver's door, to the poor neighborhood where the ramshackle house was located. It was a tumble-down frame house with a shingle roof and a crumpled asphalt driveway. The shutters were loose, the gutters rusting, and the place had obviously not seen a paint job in fifteen or twenty years. The oldest, the poorest, the saddest kind of house found in this sort of community.

Keith spoke to the lady next door while Holly rang the doorbell of the Sundbergs' house. There was no answer.

At length Keith called the police. A squad car showed up within ten minutes, and the officers helped them force the front door.

They entered a foul-smelling house. Cooking smells, combined with the reek of stale cigarette smoke and the sour perfume of spilled beer, filled the place.

Holly went to the kitchen. She opened the refrigerator. It was empty except for an old apple and some brown lettuce.

There had been no mother here for some time. There was no doubt of this.

Accompanied by the police officer and Keith, Holly searched the house slowly. The living room and the master bedroom revealed nothing. The double bed was unmade. A large ashtray full of cigarette butts was on the bedside table, along with a greasy-looking glass that smelled of cheap gin.

The closet was nearly empty. It looked as though the mother had left, taking most of her clothes with her. Yet the place did not seem entirely abandoned. To Holly's practiced eye it showed mysterious signs of life. It seemed haunted, she mused, as she moved along the hall.

The child's bedroom confirmed her suspicion. The bed was neatly made up. There was a little metal table with a school notebook on it. An easel stood in the corner with a cheap watercolor paint set beside it. The little girl had no doubt been doing her homework here, until . . . until when?

At last they descended to the basement. Keith turned on the naked bulb that hung from the ceiling. There was a furnace, a hot water heater, and not much else. Some old boxes, some assorted junk, and a rocking horse.

"Well, there's no one here," Keith said. "The mother must have taken the daughter and cleared out. With the boyfriend, I imagine. Let's go."

They stood for a moment. Keith was looking around disinterestedly. The officer glanced at his watch, impatient to leave. Holly hesitated. She sensed that something was wrong here. Very wrong.

"Well?" Keith asked. "What are we waiting for?"

Holly held a finger to her lips to silence him. Then she moved quietly toward the furnace. As she did so she heard a very soft noise. At first she thought it was a mouse. She was afraid of mice, and stopped in her tracks.

Then she got an idea.

"Jill," she said, "you can come out now. Everything is all right. We're here to help you."

Again the tiny sound, a small, nervous stirring, but this time betraying a human intention.

Holly looked behind the furnace. An involuntary gasp escaped her lips.

The little girl was there. She was dressed in pajamas. She wore no socks or slippers. She was obviously suffering from malnutrition. She was filthy and emaciated. Her blond hair was too long, and the braids were unkempt.

"It's all right, honey," said Holly. "We're going to take care of you now. You're going to be fine."

The girl looked at her through blank eyes. Now that Holly was getting used to the shadows she saw welts and bruises on the child's skin. The unmistakable signature of prolonged, vicious abuse.

"My name is Holly," she said. "Holly Fleming. I'm pleased to meet you, Jill. I hope we're going to be good friends."

They took the little girl upstairs. The officer called in on his radio while Holly and Keith assessed the situation. Obviously they would have to take the little girl with them now. Attempts to contact the mother would come later.

The bedroom showed traces of food. The child had apparently gone out to buy milk and bread with her own money, until the money ran out. There was a bag of crackers with a few crumbs in the bottom. Evidently the child had tried to survive alone in the house.

There was a calendar in the kitchen with the dates crossed off. To judge by the last cross-out, the mother had been gone for four weeks. Therefore the daughter had gone to school on her own and fooled the teachers for three weeks before finally not going anymore. In some profound, childish way she must have gotten discouraged. Perhaps she was waiting at home for death. In any case, she had not confided in her teacher.

"Have you been alone a long time, Jill?" Holly asked. "Where's your mom?"

The little girl said nothing.

"Well, we're going to take you someplace where you can have something to eat and meet some nice children. Let's get you ready."

Holly had to suppress a gasp when she took the little girl's pajamas off to dress her for the trip. Her body was covered with bruises. From the swollen look of her ribcage, she might have one or more cracked ribs.

"It's all right, honey," Holly said, fighting back the tears that were coming to her eyes. "We're going to take care of you. You're going to be fine."

When the child was in the foyer with Keith, Holly returned to her bedroom to see if there was anything she had forgotten.

She noticed the easel. It bore a colorful painting of a woman.

Holly turned the page. There was another picture underneath, and others beneath that. The whole pad was filled with watercolor paintings.

Many of the pictures showed a sort of made-up mother or fairy godmother. She was tall and slim, with red hair and green eyes, and a very gentle smile. Though the other details of her appearance changed from picture to picture, she always wore a red dress. She bore no resemblance to the real mother, who had been described by the neighbors as a dark, overweight woman.

There could be little doubt that the child had painted the pictures during this hellish period of complete isolation. They must have been her only hold on sanity.

Holly went to the bedroom door to call out to her.

"Would you like to take your paintings?" Holly asked.

The little girl said nothing, but simply stared at Holly. She had said nothing since their arrival.

Holly packed the child's few possessions in a paper shopping bag. As they were leaving she went back into the bedroom, on an impulse, took one of the pictures of the fairy godmother, folded it into her briefcase, and took it with her.

They took the child to the South Side shelter, where she was processed. The police were alerted to search for the mother. Holly made an effort to take the little girl's history, but she could not get a word out of her.

The child was given a medical examination that afternoon. It revealed that she had been sexually abused, no doubt many times. The doctor shook his head with a significant frown when he showed Holly his report.

So much for the mother's boyfriend, Holly thought.

Now that the little girl had been cleaned up, and her hair washed and braided by Holly, her extraordinary beauty emerged. She had lovely alabaster skin and liquid blue eyes whose expression must once have been trusting. Now it was heartbreakingly empty.

Two days went by, in which Holly tried to keep up with her remaining cases while following the progress of the Sundberg girl's case. Then the order came in to transport the child to the old state facility for orphaned children downstate.

Holly said good-bye to Jill Sundberg on Thursday morning. One of the state custodians would drive her the three-hour journey to the orphanage, a huge and ugly facility located on the outskirts of a town whose inhabitants avoided it like the plague.

"I'll come to see you soon, Jill," Holly promised. "They'll take good care of you there. My name is Holly Fleming. Can you remember that?"

She was holding the girl by her shoulders. The girl did not protest, did not try to escape. But the look in her eyes made Holly look away. There was something uncanny, even monstrous about it. This child no longer trusted anyone. Perhaps she never would. Severe and constant abuse had stolen the human heart from her. How she would survive the remainder of her life on earth was beyond Holly.

"Can you smile for me, sweetie?" Holly asked. "Can you say good-bye?"

The child said nothing.

Holly watched in silence as the custodian put the little girl in the state car and closed the door. It was not until the car was out of sight that Holly realized her eyes were full of tears. Her hands felt cold where they had touched the little shoulders, only moments ago.

Six years old!

With that thought Holly sighed and went back to her work.

The child sat in the back seat of the state car as it drove the two-lane routes through flat corn fields toward the orphanage. The social worker beside her spoke every now and again, but the little girl did not answer.

She carried no trace of her past. The clothes she wore had been bought by Holly Fleming on a state voucher. She held a small teddy bear that Holly had paid for out of her own pocket.

The girl stared out the window in a neutral, quiet way that reassured the social worker about her probable behavior on the trip but filled her with worry about what was going on in the child's mind.

The social worker was well aware that the state shelter for homeless children had no facilities for counseling or therapy. This little girl would be thrown in with hundreds of homeless children, many of them as tough and ruthless as she was passive. How she would survive in that crucible depended entirely on her own character. Her physical wounds would heal, but the state would do nothing to treat the spiritual ones.

Halfway to their destination a detour forced them off the state route and onto a county road that took them through a small town called Ellicott. It was an average county town with perhaps about five thousand people. There was a main drag about twenty blocks long, with diagonal parking and a collection of stores and businesses.

The social worker noticed that everywhere she looked she seemed to see the name Patterson. Patterson Realty, Patterson Insurance, Patterson Construction. A typical small town, she reflected, dominated by one wealthy family that probably owned a lot of the farmland in the area.

The detour took the state car past a small graveyard. There was a funeral procession just coming to the cemetery gates, and it stopped in front of them, blocking their way. One of the cars was stopped right beside them.

It was a tiny procession, composed of no more than four vehicles, not counting the hearse. In the first car behind the hearse a man sat at the wheel with his young daughter on the seat beside him. They were both dressed in mourning. The man had dark hair and eyes, but the little girl had curly hair of a bright strawberry blond, and a healthy complexion spotted with sunny freckles that belied her funereal attire.

There was a delay in opening the cemetery gates. The two cars remained stopped alongside each other. The eyes of the little girl in mourning met those of the homeless child in the back seat of the state car. They looked at each other with the normal interest of children, unabashed by each other's strangeness.

The two girls were of approximately the same age and physical type. But the healthy girl in the car with her father was all color and light. The orphan, despite her blond hair and limpid blue eyes, already bore not only the pallor of malnutrition but the grayness of institutional life.

Suddenly Jill Sundberg's expression changed. She studied the face of the girl in the other car. Though it bore a mask of grief over the death of someone close—her mother?—there was a natural twinkle in the green eyes. This little girl had known happiness, or believed in happiness. No one had ever abused her. She was innocent.

Jill looked closely at the clear little face. As she did so something in her own face began to change. A light shone in her eyes, as though to mirror the life she saw in the other face. Something stirred inside her in a desperate effort to take her out of her own life and into that of the bright little girl in the other car. It was a silent paroxysm, and it shook her to the foundations of her being.

The other little girl's eyes widened as she looked at Jill. It was as though she were witnessing a natural phenomenon she had never seen before, something spectacular like the midnight sun or the emergence of a butterfly from its chrysalis. She turned to her father, who was looking out the front windshield, and then silently back to the other car.

By now the gates of the cemetery were open. The cars separated. The pretty little girl with her surprised face disappeared, swooping laterally out of sight.

Jill Sundberg was on her way to her future.

Inside her car, Leslie Chamberlain sat beside her father as the small procession made its way into the cemetery.

She was thinking about the little girl in the other car.

"How are you doing, honey?" her father asked.

"Fine, Daddy," she answered. "How are you?"

It had once been a joke between them. He would say "How are you, honey?" and she would reply, "And how are you?" He would repeat, "How are you?" and they would tease each other with the question until they both laughed.

But today it was serious. Leslie's mother lay inside that hearse ahead, and her father was taking her to her mother's funeral.

Leslie was six years old. She had not known her mother very well, for almost from the time she could remember, Mother had been sick. It was some sort of kidney ailment that had gotten much worse when Mother had Leslie, and had never really improved.

Mother had been in the hospital so often that it was Daddy who cooked for Leslie, shopped for her clothes, played with her, drew pictures with her, and told her stories at night when she went to bed. It was Daddy who kissed her good night and helped her say her prayers.

The two of them would greet Mommy when she came home from the hospital and take care of her until she had to go back.

Mommy—her real name was Rosemary Chamberlain—had been a nice woman, without humor but full of affectionate warmth. She cursed the illness that kept her away from her family for weeks and months at a time. But she thanked her lucky stars for her husband, Tom, who was a good and dedicated father, and whose protectiveness toward Leslie was matched by his own intuitive understanding of her.

By the time Leslie was five, the final stages of her mother's illness were coming on. When she was home Mother sat with a faraway look in her eyes. As disease pulled her further and further away from the center of the family, Tom and his daughter grew closer and closer together, as though to prepare for the imminent moment when they would be alone.

Then the mother died, on the third day of what was to be a routine visit to the hospital for tests and treatment.

Today Leslie sat beside her father, staring at the hearse in front of her.

"Dad, where's Mom now?" she asked.

He turned his eyes to her.

"She's in heaven, honey," he said.

"What will she do there?"

17

"She'll watch over you. She'll watch over both of us," he said.

"She's not there in that coffin?" Leslie asked.

"Only her body, honey. That's not your real mom. Mom was a spirit. You know that. That's why she's still with us, even now. That's what we remember."

Tom Chamberlain was a worker in the bottle factory in town. He was an ignorant man, but a sensitive one. He had adored his wife and counted on a long life with her. When illness forced her deeper and deeper into a half-human state of pain and delirium he gradually transferred his hopes to his daughter, seeing in her the infinite horizon of possibilities that was so quickly being cut off from himself and his wife.

And even today, as the child sat preoccupied on the front seat beside him, hiding her grief under her laconic questions, he could feel her natural strength and vitality. She was going to live. She was going to grow up and be normal and happy and healthy. And he was here to see that she did so. Today he could do nothing to ease the pain and loss she was feeling. But tomorrow, and from now on, he would do everything in his power to give her the normal, happy life that death was trying so cruelly to take away.

The hearse was stopping beside the open grave now. The father had not noticed the brown state car with its seal on the driver's door at the cemetery gates.

He saw his daughter looking out the window.

"What's up, Leslie? Did you see something interesting?"

"There was a little girl in that brown car."

"Ah. Someone we know?"

She didn't answer. Tom Chamberlain forgot the incident.

But Leslie was thinking about the little girl. At first the pale blue eyes behind the window of the strange car had seemed almost as dead as the body in the hearse.

Then something astonishing had happened. The little girl had come to life.

But she had done so in an odd way. As color came into her cheeks and light into her eyes, she no longer looked quite like herself.

She began to look like Leslie.

The process was accelerating, the empty blue eyes turning brighter, the little body sitting up straighter, curiosity beginning to eclipse the emptiness in the little face, as the two cars pulled apart.

But as Leslie caught a last glimpse of the little girl, she was looking out the back window at her. And it was like seeing herself, pulling away from her quickly, receding into another life that was not hers.

Leslie did not tell her father about this. His mind was on other things. He looked so sad.

But what she had seen made a deep impression on her.

The little girl who was me, she would call it, for the three or four years that she recalled the incident.

2

ON FEBRUARY 19, 1958, an accident occurred on the assembly line at the Lukas Tool Works in the small manufacturing town of Webster, Pennsylvania.

A heavy piece of cast steel weighing four thousand pounds was being positioned for welding by three workers when the assembly line crane collapsed. The piece of steel crashed to the floor of the factory, crushing the legs and back of one of the workers.

His name was Albert P. Lazarus. At age fifty-seven, he was the father of six children, four boys and two girls. He had worked for the Lukas Tool Works since graduating from the eighth grade some forty-three years earlier.

Emergency procedures were immediately taken to handle the situation. Albert Lazarus was taken by stretcher to the infirmary, where he was picked up by an ambulance and taken to the emergency ward at County Hospital. Meanwhile, a maintenance crew repaired the assembly line and brought in a new crane to lift the fallen block of steel back into place.

The repair work lasted nearly three hours. The line had been badly maintained for several years due to the pressures of production, and the specialists who repaired it now had to work under a deadline. They did their best under the circumstances, leaving the line pretty much as it had been before the accident. By late afternoon the Lukas Tool Works was back in full operation. The piece of steel that had fallen on Albert Lazarus was finished in time for shipment the next morning to its destination, a construction site in Maryland.

A total of $550 was lost in profit by the company due to the delay and the cost of repairs to the line. Reports on the accident—not the first of its kind at the Lukas plant—were sent through routine channels to management and to the company's insurance carrier.

Business at Lukas went on as usual. The incident was virtually forgotten a week after it happened.

Albert Lazarus was examined at County Hospital and found to have a crushed hipbone, two shattered femurs, and, most serious of all, irreversible damage to several lumbar vertebrae. He spent three days in the intensive care ward before being transferred to the regular orthopedic ward as a charity patient.

He would spend much of the next year in the hospital undergoing a series of operations, and the rest of his life in a wheelchair.

On May 3, three months after his accident, Lazarus and his family received official word from the Lukas Tool Works of the pension he would receive in his forced retirement. Lukas Tool Works was a nonunion shop. Lazarus had never earned more than $2 an hour in his forty-three years of service.

The pension amounted to $75 a month, payable for the next ten years. The health insurance plan underwritten by the employer paid for only the initial surgery and the first sixty days of hospitalization, with no provision made for medication, physicians' fees, further surgery, or future hospitalizations.

In short, the injured worker was unofficially consigned to abject poverty for the rest of his days. The employer, thanks to his bargain-basement insurance and pension plans, would scarcely feel the expense caused by the mishap.

On the evening of May 3 the family of Albert P. Lazarus gathered in the living room of his ramshackle house on a sooty street near the factory where he had worked away the best years of his life.

Present were Lazarus's four sons and two daughters, as well as his wife, Mary.

All four of the sons, Gerald, Clay, Ryan, and Jordan, also worked for the Lukas Tool Works. Gerald and Clay were in their midtwenties, and Ryan was thirty-two years old. Jordan, the baby among the boys, was only seventeen.

Louise, the older daughter, was a married woman in her twenties, with two young children. Her husband, Dick, also worked for the plant. She herself worked in a local food store as a clerk and stock girl.

Meg, the youngest, was a girl of sixteen, in delicate health. She had suffered a serious bout of rheumatic fever as a child, and been left with a heart murmur that limited her activity. For this reason she had been exempted from the family rule that would have sent her out to work at age sixteen, and she was hoping to finish high school and find secretarial work in town.

In the wake of Albert Lazarus's disabling accident Meg, a sweet and loyal girl, had repeatedly expressed her willingness to quit school now and go to work to help the family. But her protective older brothers would not hear of this. They felt an obscure duty to Meg not only because of her health but because of the pivotal psychological role she played in the Lazarus family. In a sense Meg, the weakest member of the group physically, was also the most spiritually developed. She was the family's moral leader and the magnet that held it together. Now that Father was bedridden and Mother had to devote herself to his physical needs, Meg's wisdom and love were more crucial than ever before.

Then there was Jordan. Born a year before Meg, and resembling her almost like a twin, though he was dark and she a freckled redhead, Jordan was the runt of the boys. He was slender of build and dreamy of manner. If Meg was the spiritual prodigy of the family, then Jordan was its artist. He had always had perfect grades in school—a feat no Lazarus boy had accomplished in generations—and his essays, drawings, and teachers' reports bore witness to an extraordinary and quickly growing mind with an inspired artistic sensibility.

In the impoverished school system of Webster, Pennsylvania, Jordan had never been given an IQ test. Had such a test been administered, and his true IQ discovered, his life might have been very different. As things stood, though, he was just another teenage plant worker, somewhat out of place among his peers but capable and thorough on the job.

Jordan Lazarus had been so slight and weak as a boy that the family had feared he might have an illness like Meg, which would have posed a danger to the family finances. His dark, burning eyes, light skin, and curly black hair gave him the look of a poet, and his father had secretly wondered whether he would ever be any good as a worker.

But adolescence had given Jordan the physical strength that ran in the family, and he had shot up to six feet in what seemed a matter of months. He was not as brawny as his brothers but wiry and tight in his build, with hard young pectorals, a deep chest, and a washboard rib cage above his long legs.

He had gone to work in the plant last June, leaving school, like his brothers before him, after the tenth grade. He was a line worker, like all the men of the family.

He never complained about leaving school to go to work in the plant. The family was poor and always had been. It was expected that all the young men would go into the plant as early as possible. Indeed, the purpose of having a large family was to produce enough young men to go into the plant and support the needs of the family.

The fact that the young men would soon create their own families, with more mouths to feed, was a problem that people in that society never seemed to quite understand. This was how the vicious cycle of large families, ramshackle houses, and lives wasted in the pursuit of rock-bottom wages was perpetuated.

The only person who objected—albeit privately—when Jordan went into the plant was Meg. She had been far closer to Jordan than any other member of the family since their earliest youth together, and felt he was wasting himself by doing what was expected of him.

"You're too good for that life, Jordie," she told him. "You're cut out for something better. Something special. I know Mother and Dad will be upset if you insist on finishing school, but they'll get used to the idea. You can't throw away your life just to make sixty dollars a week for the family. We can live without the money. You have your own destiny."

Jordan had listened politely to Meg's pleas, and even understood to some extent the logic behind them. On a private level of his personality he knew he was different from his brothers, different, in fact, from everyone he knew at school or in town. Ideas and impressions swarmed in his head at all hours of the day and night, leading far away from the predictable concerns of his peers to an unknown region that seemed to hold out its hand to him mysteriously. It was this inner world, always strange and new, that peeked out in his school papers, impressing his teachers. And it was this world that Meg sensed in her closeness with him.

But in the end Jordan could not follow Meg's advice. He was still an adolescent and dependent on the approval of his father and brothers for his self-respect. He felt he had to prove himself in the plant as a real man like the others. Completing high school would have been, in his eyes, an abandonment of his masculine responsibility to the family.

His decision was final, and Meg respected it. But ever since the September day when he went into the plant while other kids his age were going on to finish high school and perhaps go to college, Meg regarded him with a sadness that made him ill at ease. He loved her more than anyone else in the family and felt a special bond with her. Thus it irritated him that she, who understood him so well, was against the decision he had made and deplored in her heart the life he had chosen for himself.

He had been unconsciously avoiding Meg within the family ever since, and spending less time alone with her. The hours he had once spent conversing with her in her bedroom he now spent alone, walking about the town, absorbed in his own thoughts. He was waiting for her to accept the inevitability of his choice.

But now the injury to his father threw the family into a crisis that eclipsed such considerations.

Tonight, in the wake of the disastrous news about the minuscule pension the company had decided to provide Father, the family was in a state of considerable upset.

"Mother, you and the girls go into the kitchen," commanded Ryan, the second in command since his father's illness. Albert Lazarus was upstairs in his bed, groaning from the chronic pain of his ruined bones.

Mary Lazarus obediently took Meg into the kitchen. Louise followed, carrying one of her children in her arms. The Lazarus women recognized that this was a time for man talk.

As soon as they had left, Clay, the hothead of the sons, spoke up.

"We're not going to let them get away with this," he said. "I'll go down there and blow up the goddamned place myself if I have to."

Gerald agreed. "You work your life out for these pirates, and they pay you back by stiffing you on your benefits."

Ryan, a bit more reasonable than the others by nature, added, "This isn't the first time, you know. Bunny Potter, last year, when he had his accident on the line. His wife didn't get a thing from them."

"They don't care a damn for the working man," said Clay. "They just use us up and spit us out. Well, I'm not going to stand for it. Not when it's Daddy they've ruined."

"Come on, let's have a beer." Clay brought four beers and passed them around.

If the appearance of alcohol in the room signaled a first subtle sign of capitulation, no one seemed to notice. Young Jordan took a sip of the sour liquid. It tasted unpleasant to him, though he was proud to be included by his older brothers.

"What we'll do," said Clay with a hateful smile, "we'll get all the fellows together, and we'll go down there and strike the hell out of old Lukas."

"I've got a better idea," said Ryan. "We'll pull a slowdown. We'll drop the work to twenty percent until Lukas gives in."

"Listen," objected Gerald. "I asked Susan Birch about things this afternoon. Her brother-in-law's a lawyer. You can sue them for failure to meet the terms of the implied contract of employment. That line has been defective for years, and everybody knows it. Under the law they have an obligation to protect the worker or to pay for his injuries."

"Lawsuits cost money," said Ryan quietly. He took a large swig of his beer. "Besides, the company has its own high-priced lawyers. Have you boys ever heard of a worker winning a case like that?"

"All right, then, we'll strike 'em!" shouted Clay. "We'll get all the fellows together, and have a meeting. They can't go on getting away with this."

"We'll unionize!" Gerald chimed in. "We'll send representatives to the national union. They can't stop us. It's our right."

The brothers had already decided to surrender, although they did not know it yet. Their recourse to the beer went hand in hand with the empty bluster of their threats. They were genuinely outraged at the destruction of their father's health. But they came from generations of workers who viewed the company as a paternalistic monolith that could not be challenged.

The company was their livelihood. They could complain loudly about its injustices, but to do anything about it could cost them their jobs. And their jobs were their life's blood. They could not bite the hand that fed them.

Thus, even in their rantings, they had already given up.

Nothing would be done. Albert Lazarus, groaning helplessly in his bed, would have to live out his days in the agony that followed like a coda upon his four decades of backbreaking work for the Lukas Tool Works. Like millions of other workers for similar companies, Albert was the victim of an exploitation he could not see or understand clearly enough to fight. He was a little man, ground up by the company just as surely as the bulk steel it turned into manufacturing parts. His point of view meant nothing more than that of the raw materials from which the plant made its finished products. He was a mindless cog in a great impersonal wheel—and so were his sons.

So the brothers drank another beer, and another, and continued to mouth threats that gradually became mere complaints. The hour grew later. Soon it would be time to go to bed. After all, they had to be at the plant by seven tomorrow morning.

But one voice was not raised to join this chorus of impotent anger.

Jordan Lazarus, the boy of seventeen, sat with his half-finished beer and watched what was going on.

His eyes were moving with calm appraisal from one brother to the other and back again. His own face, still touched by the mildness of adolescence, was like an image frozen in the midst of its rapid metamorphosis into manly strength and purpose. The eyes were black and sparkling, with lashes almost as long as those of a girl. But their gaze, once so dreamy and preoccupied, now seemed harder, almost piercing.

He studied his brothers, easily seeing through their bluster to the capitulation and helplessness underneath. He thought of his father, a man he had admired and looked up to from his earliest boyhood, though they had never been close, for Albert Lazarus worked long hours and had no time for his youngest son.

Father would spend the rest of his life flat on his back, in an agony undiminished by the muttered complaints of his sons, or by the paltry wages they would bring in by devoting the best of their energies to the benefit of the Lukas Tool Works.

The black eyes darted from brother to brother, while the brain behind them evaluated the injustice done to a whole family by an accident that should have been avoided.

Soon the brothers were on their way upstairs to kiss their father good-night and fall into bed half-drunk, to be awakened tomorrow by Mother or Meg and stagger off to work with hangovers and lunchboxes full of sandwiches made with cheap bread and cheese.

Neither they nor their father suspected that behind the expressionless eyes of Jordan, the youngest and least important, the future of the entire family was being decided.

The next morning, when Meg Lazarus entered the room shared by Jordan and Clay, she found that Jordan's bed had not been slept in. Most of Jordan's clothes were gone, including the inexpensive black suit he wore to funerals and other formal occasions, a hand-me-down from Gerald. The threadbare cardboard suitcase that had been shared by the boys for twenty-five years was gone as well.

Meg broke the news to the family. Everyone was upset, not only because Jordan had a special place in all their hearts, but because his meager salary was needed more than ever now that Albert P. Lazarus was an invalid. Without Jordan's sixty dollars per week, the future would be hard indeed.

The older brothers went grimly to work, determined to scrimp even more so that their paltry paychecks might help the family. Louise began looking for a better job. Meg, despite the pleas of her mother, went out to look for work that very afternoon, and managed to find a job as a trainee at a local beauty salon.

Life was different for the Lazarus family, and sadder. Albert P. Lazarus was barely human now, unable to take part in family meals or conversations, and his moans filled the house at all hours. With the loss of Jordan something vital had gone out of the family. A funereal atmosphere reigned in the house. The brothers' murmured conversations alternated between grudging respect for Jordan's courage in escaping a hopeless situation, and anger that he had abandoned a sinking ship.

Then something happened.

Three weeks after Jordan's departure, a cashier's check for $2,000, drawn on an Indiana bank, was delivered to Mary Lazarus by express mail. No letter accompanied the check, but the signature of Jordan Lazarus was alongside that of the bank officer who had approved the check.

The family had barely had time to congratulate itself on Jordan's gift, and to begin disbursing it in the payment of medical bills, when, two weeks later, a second cashier's check arrived, this time for $8,500.

A month went by, then another. The family received a postcard from Jordan bearing an image of the cornfields of Indiana.

Am doing fine, the message read. *Hope you are well. I love you all.*

The grateful Lazarus family could not know that Jordan was at that moment living in a cheap furnished room in Indianapolis alongside a dozen sets of railroad tracks.

The few possessions Jordan had taken with him when he left Webster remained all he had in the world. The only change that had been made was a new suit, a fine-quality gray pinstripe to replace the hand-me-down Jordan had left home with, a new pair of Florsheim shoes, and a silk tie.

Jordan had broken two laws and made one enemy in obtaining the first $2,000 he sent to his family. The second gift of $8,500 required the breaking of two more laws, but was earned in such a manner as to regain the friendship of the erstwhile enemy.

Within the next year, $37,000 made its way from Jordan to his family. This sum went a long way toward paying Albert P. Lazarus's medical and hospitalization bills, and relieved the family of its despair over money. By this time Jordan had moved from his furnished room in Indianapolis to a small apartment in St. Louis, and increased his wardrobe to three suits and two pairs of shoes. Tapping his enormous native intelligence, he had discovered several new ways of making money, and learned how to do so without breaking the law.

He would make more enemies as time went by, but he would always manage to regain their friendship as his own power and influence increased. Something told him that one can never be truly successful by leaving a trail of enemies in one's wake. The past has a way of coming back to haunt even the smartest of men.

It would be another two and a half years before Jordan Lazarus single-handedly saved his family from the disaster wrought upon it by the Lukas Tool Works, and another ten years before Jordan himself acquired the Lukas Tool Works under the umbrella of a national corporation he was to form, based in New York City.

Ironically, during those years Jordan was too busy making money to think much about Webster, Pennsylvania, or the life he had lived there. But when his thoughts did stray to the town of his birth and the family that had raised him, he saw only one image, and took his strength from it—the face of Meg Lazarus.

3

Ellicott, Illinois
October 20, 1965

LESLIE CHAMBERLAIN WAS in the arms of a handsome prince.

His hair was dark, his eyes flashing, his smile as seductive as it was gentle. He was sweeping her away to a glorious destiny. She felt an infinite relief, for it seemed a lifetime that she had waited alone before he came to her.

She wondered what she had done to deserve this good fortune. Her heart thrilled with love. Her life alone was a thing of the past now. The man holding her to his broad chest with strong arms was her only future.

He was bearing her away quickly. The wind was rushing through her hair. She wanted to laugh with delight, but their headlong flight took her breath away. They flew faster and faster. It almost seemed that the wind would tear her from his embrace. But she hung on with all her strength. The gusts shouted in her ears, louder and louder. She answered them with her own cries of triumph. She had never felt so excited or so free. Her prince would keep her safe forever.

Then Leslie woke up.

The only thing in her arms was her pillow. The rushing wind had turned into the strident ringing of the alarm clock beside her bed.

As she sat up to turn off the alarm the dream disappeared from her memory. It left only a vague inner tingle of ecstasy and longing as she rushed to get dressed, gather her books, and catch the schoolbus. She was alone in the little house, for her father worked the night shift and would not be home from the factory until nine. She did not bother to fix herself breakfast—Daddy would probably guess this when he came home, and upbraid her later for not eating right—but worked for a frantic few moments on her makeup in the bathroom mirror before hurrying out to the corner.

She was sixteen years old. She had lived in the little town of Ellicott all her life. Her father, widowed since Leslie was a child of six, worked as a sorter and general maintenance man in the local bottle factory. She had no brothers or sisters.

Leslie rushed out of the house just in time to catch the schoolbus, which was filled with other poor children from this dilapidated side of town. The bus driver had his portable radio on as usual. The morning news was on, telling of protest demonstrations, draft card burnings, the war between India and Pakistan, and the banning of the Communist Party in Indonesia by President Sukarno.

Leslie did not hear it. She was thinking of the face she had been looking at in the mirror back home, a face whose many imperfections she had tried vainly to hide with makeup.

The face taunted her when she looked in the mirror each morning. The teeth bore braces—an enormous drain on her father's budget but an expense he had insisted on. This was no shame in itself. But the lips seemed shapeless, the nose lacking in distinction. The complexion, alas, showed the bumpy ravages of puberty. The strawberry blond hair was far too thick and curly, and had to be tied back tightly to prevent it from exploding outward like the quills of a porcupine. She was tall for her age, and skinny. She was not filling out fast enough. After her shower she would look in the mirror at her small breasts and sigh, despairing of the future.

Leslie was too young to be able to measure her good points. She could not see the fine bone structure under her adolescent face or the elegant, willowy figure soon to emerge from her thin body. Nor could she perceive the character and intelligence in her eyes.

They were beautiful, expressive eyes of a complex hazel shade, eyes that could look emerald green or pale gray or even violet depending on the light and her mood. Indeed, her moods were many, passing over her young face like silvery clouds across the moon.

Had Leslie come from a different stratum of society she might have seen her face and body in a different light. But she came from the wrong side of the tracks in this town where status was measured only by money. She had neither a fancy wardrobe nor, more importantly, an exalted reputation to conceal her gangly figure, to magnify her tiny bust, to transform her young face into a thing of beauty admired by her peers.

The society of Ellicott was divided along lines of management and labor, based on the population of the factory that gave the town its livelihood. Leslie belonged to the children of blue-collar workers and as such was looked down upon by the children of the management families. The latter included the Betancourts, the Chamblisses, the Dauers, and above all the Pattersons, who not only were major stockholders in the company that owned the factory but themselves owned a half dozen businesses in town and thousands of acres of real estate in the surrounding county.

Leslie was like a fish out of water in this rigidly structured social world. She lacked the glamour and status of the company kids, as they were called. At the same time her blue-collar peers at school did not see their own personalities or aspirations reflected in Leslie. For one thing, her grades were too good, her intelligence too high. For another, there was a quality of rebellion in Leslie, a sense that she could not breathe or blossom in this suffocating atmosphere but was made for another, wider world. This rebellion was so well hidden by her diffident teenage personality that she herself could not see it. But more than one of her teachers had detected it in her brilliant, imaginative papers and had told her proud father about it.

"She's got something," her English teacher had told her father in an informal exchange at the local grocery store. "It's not something that will do her much good in a town this small. But believe me, Tom, she's going to be appreciated when she gets into a bigger pond."

It was a time when girls were not encouraged to be ambitious, to think for themselves, or to value themselves in any other way than as eventual mates for eligible males. Leslie rebelled against this invisible constraint. Something in her champed impatiently at the bit imposed on her by her society. She wanted to be different, to be Somebody someday. The social handicap of her poverty only made her yearning the more painful.

But if Leslie had one foot in a future far from this time and place, the other was firmly planted in her adolescent desire to be accepted by her peers. Thus she was tormented by her failure to fit in. And her dreams for herself, exiled from the formless future, sought an object nearer to hand and better suited to the idealizing fantasy life of a lonely girl adrift in her puberty.

This object, painfully, beautifully, had turned out to be a handsome young man named Geoff Patterson.

Geoff was the only son of the town's most influential citizen, Leland Patterson. His friends belonged to the most popular crowd at school. They were pretty cheerleaders like Cindy Hoffman and Judy Betancourt, and basketball and baseball players like Barth Dillon, Craig Dauer, and the rest. These were all children of "good" families, and they stuck to each other like glue, bound together by an invisible set of rules and values that did not seem to have any substance in themselves but that rigidly excluded less privileged students like Leslie.

Geoff had rich, dark hair, dreamy blue eyes, and a tall, strong young body. Unlike many of his friends, he had better-than-average grades, and he was president of the class. His girlfriend, Judy Betancourt, was one of the most popular girls in school. In Leslie's eyes Geoff was the sum of all male perfections imaginable. She went to basketball games on frigid winter nights just to see him flash down the court on his long legs, pass the ball, or shoot a basket with sure hands.

Leslie knew that Geoff Patterson was not for her, and never would be. But this only made her private coveting of him the more forbidden and therefore the more exciting. She never spoke to anyone of it, fearing the ridicule such a confession might bring. But in her silence she worshiped Geoff's image. Her dawning womanhood, bringing new sensations to her body, had brought daunting waves of emotion to her mind. Adolescence had kindled a flame deep inside her that burned for the glorification of Geoff Patterson, a boy who did not know she was alive.

But today she was to find to her amazement that she had been mistaken.

Her first class of the day was algebra. It was her most interesting and embarrassing class at the same time, because Geoff Patterson was in it, as was his girlfriend, Judy. Mrs. Crabtree, the algebra teacher, was a dedicated professional who pushed hard to get the best from her students. She was irritated by the sluggish work of most of the popular kids and often singled Leslie out for answers to problems after the others had let her down. This embarrassed Leslie, for her own answers, though nearly always correct, seemed to bring ridicule from her classmates and set her apart as an outcast even more than before.

As for pretty Judy Betancourt, with her elegant name, her wealthy family, and her lissome young figure, she distinguished herself in class by showing her contempt for the subject. She never raised her hand to ask a question, and when called upon gave wrong answers in a condescending, ironic tone that seemed to endear her to her popular peers.

Today the class was to correct a quiz given yesterday on polynomial equations. Normally the same students corrected each other's papers, but recently Mrs. Crabtree had become suspicious of some of the corrections and suspected collusion among the pupils sitting across from each other. So she had shuffled the order by a row, forcing everyone to exchange papers with a stranger.

As luck would have it, Leslie's paper ended up in the hands of Geoff Patterson, who was sitting two rows away and a little behind her. Leslie was unnerved to see the name of her cherished fantasy right in front of her eyes, limned in a strong handwriting that immediately took on, for her, the luster of his exalted being.

The paper was full of mistakes, but this in no way lessened Leslie's admiration for its author. The quiz had been difficult, after all, and there was no shame in getting only 60 percent right. None of the popular kids worked hard on algebra. Besides, Geoff was probably too busy at athletic practice to devote much time to so silly a subject. Outcasts like Leslie, with nothing better to do, could while away their lonely hours working on algebra. Not important, popular people like Geoff.

The teacher was going through the problems with the class as the papers were corrected.

"How about number six?" she asked. "Who has the right answer to that?"

There was a silence. No one was sure of the right answer.

"Judy?" The teacher pointed at pretty Judy Betancourt.

The girl looked down at the paper in her hands.

"Sixteen and a half miles," she read with a slight snicker.

"Judy," the teacher sighed, "the question was about gallons of water—not miles."

"Well, you can only get so many miles to the gallon," Judy quipped. Laughter burst out in the room to acknowledge her wit.

"Geoff, what about you?" Mrs. Crabtree asked.

Geoff Patterson, who had been leaning back languidly in his seat, sat up straighter.

"Umm," he said in his deep voice, focusing his eyes on the paper in front of him. "Forty-eight and a half gallons per barrel."

"That's right," the teacher said. "Thank you."

Geoff held the paper up slightly for the others to see.

"Well, it's Leslie's paper," he said.

There was another laugh, full of mingled respect and contempt. The class knew that Leslie's answers were always right. But Leslie was not a popular girl. In drawing attention to her Geoff had been exposing her to a sort of gentle ridicule.

Judy Betancourt, from her place three seats behind Geoff, made a whispered remark that caused two of her popular girlfriends to laugh out loud. Leslie turned red, for she knew the joke was at her expense.

"Shall we go on, please, class?" asked Mrs. Crabtree with her accustomed irony. "Time waits for no man."

As she asked the next question Geoff Patterson studied the unfamiliar handwriting on the paper in his hands. It was a strangely wild and almost infantile script, with choppy *m*'s and *n*'s and tall, crazy *t*'s stumbling along among numbers scrawled in a hurried hand. It looked like the handwriting of a busy and very impatient little girl who could not be bothered to rein in her natural energy to make the figures neater.

Yet every single answer was right.

Geoff was struck by this odd combination of graphic sloppiness with intellectual clarity. He looked from the paper to Leslie, who was seated two rows in front of him. Though her back was to him, he noticed a long, very slender arm emerging from her blouse, and a shapely hand—she was left-handed—holding her pencil over the paper she was correcting.

Her hair, with its odd palette of red and gold, was wild and frizzy despite her attempts to control it. He could see the back of her neck, which was as delicate as that of a doe, and the long legs emerging from her skirt. Her whole body seemed to suggest the same mixture of cautious self-control with a bursting inner energy that shone in her handwriting.

When the class had finished correcting the quiz Geoff wrote "100%" at the top of the page. His own handwriting looked confident but bland next to Leslie's eccentric script. He passed the paper forward, and saw her glance back at him as it was given to her. Her eyes were downcast, her look embarrassed, but Geoff got a good look at her glowing green irises. It was the first time he had ever noticed them.

Later in the day Leslie was hurrying toward her locker as usual, trying to make herself invisible, when from a boisterous group of popular girls she heard a veiled expression of contempt.

"Queer . . ." she thought she heard.

She looked up to see the popular girls, with Judy Betancourt at their center. Judy's dark, pretty eyes were flashing as she looked at Leslie.

Leslie averted her eyes and hurried away. She heard sneering laughter, barely disguised as levity, echoing behind her, and she turned the corner.

Her locker was located next to the gym, in a corridor that was deserted at this time of day. She was turning the dial of the combination lock when she heard a voice say her name.

"Leslie."

Her hand froze on the dial. She turned to see Geoff Patterson walking toward her.

Only now did she realize how tall he was. Normally she saw him only from a distance, laughing with his friends or running on the basketball court. His true size was evident only at close quarters.

A faint scent of aftershave lotion mingled with his natural scent, which was precociously manly. The look in his dark eyes was whimsical.

"I enjoyed correcting your algebra paper today," he said. "That was the first time I ever saw a paper with all the right answers."

"Oh, well," Leslie said, blushing fiercely.

"I wish I could do that just once," he smiled. "Get all the right answers, I mean."

She looked away as though in search of someplace to hide, and then met his eyes again. As she did so the books in her arms came loose and crashed to the floor. The heavy *World Civilization* textbook landed right on her toe, sending an angry flare of pain through her, but she managed not to let him see it.

"Sorry," she said as he bent to help her pick up the books.

"Listen," he said, watching her fumble with the locker combination. "Could I walk you home today? I'll meet you by the soccer field right after school. Okay? There's something I've wanted to talk to you about."

Leslie could not believe her ears. Her mind reeled at the very thought of Geoff Patterson, a boy she had coveted so guiltily in her fantasies, actually speaking to her. His invitation made her feel faint, unsure any of this was really happening.

"I—all right," she said, the words starting from her mouth with a will of their own.

She spent the rest of the day on tenterhooks, feeling at every moment like Cinderella at the stroke of midnight, waiting for her coach to turn into a pumpkin.

But when three o'clock came, and she walked uncertainly to the athletic field, Geoff Patterson appeared alone and came to her side.

"You live on the east side, don't you?" he asked.

She nodded, embarrassed to have him know she lived on the poor side of town.

They walked in silence away from the school grounds, and through the little residential streets that led away from the center of town.

At the midpoint between the school and Leslie's house, a wide path ran through Cutter's Woods, a well-known local woods.

"We can go this way," she said. "It's a shortcut."

She had often taken this route home when she rode her bike to school as a girl, before self-consciousness made bike riding out of the question. It was a smooth, even path, covered with pine needles, very pleasant to walk along in warm weather like today, though impassable on wet or snowy days because of the muddy ground.

"This is nice," Geoff said. "I wish this were my own route home."

Leslie had to smile. Geoff drove his car home most days. And even if he hadn't had a car, his house was located on the other side of town, in the fancy neighborhood of the management families.

"How are you going to get home?" she asked suddenly. "I'm taking you out of your way."

"That's all right," he said simply.

She glanced up at him. His hair seemed thicker, his brows darker than she had remembered them in her fantasies. He was wearing his school jacket—he had letters in three sports—and jeans and a sweater. He seemed preoccupied as he glanced at the fragrant pine trees along the path.

Halfway through the woods he stopped her, his hand touching her shoulder.

"Leslie," he said.

She stopped and looked up at him. The woods were absolutely silent. She had never heard them this silent before.

"I . . ." Geoff began. There was a pained look in his eyes.

"Can I carry your books?" he asked, embarrassed.

She laughed and shook her head. "That's all right."

"No, I insist," he said.

She started to hand him the books. As she did so he abruptly took her in his arms and kissed her.

The books were crushed between their bodies, and Leslie's lips were pushed against her braces by the clumsiness of his kiss. But she did not care. Her whole body seemed to melt into his embrace.

After a moment the kiss ended. But Geoff held her close, his arms around her, and a different sort of tenderness suffused her as he petted her shoulder. His lips touched her forehead, her eyelids, her cheeks.

As though in slow motion the books tumbled to the pine needle carpet of the path. Geoff enfolded Leslie in his arms, and she felt the whole hard length of his body pressed close to hers. Again they kissed, this time more intimately. His tongue entered her mouth, new and strange and wonderful. It was her first real kiss.

In that instant something deep and womanly came to life in her body, and she nestled in his embrace as though she belonged there. He seemed to feel it himself, and she heard a sigh in his throat.

Then, as though shocked at what he had done, he released her.

"I'm sorry," he said, stooping to pick up her books.

"Don't be sorry," she said. "I'm not." The words sounded forward and dangerous on her lips, but it was too late to take them back.

They walked awhile in silence, he carrying her books, she trying to hide the fact that her body was floating on air.

"Why me?" she asked on an impulse.

He stopped.

"There's something about you," he said. "I—I don't . . ."

He looked at the place where they were standing. The path split into two diverging paths.

"Where does that path go?" he asked. "To the pond?"

She nodded. Fishers Pond was a popular fishing spot for local people during the day. By night it was the favorite petting place for teenagers who parked their cars on an overlook under the pines and watched the moonlight on the surface of the small pond. A lot of skinny-dipping went on there too.

"Leslie," Geoff said suddenly. "Would you meet me at the pond Friday night?"

She said nothing. This was a strange invitation. It was not exactly an invitation for a date. There was something more intimate about it, more forbidden. It was known that a boy might take his best girl to the pond on a warm night for a more intimate sort of date than merely going to the movies or for a hamburger. There was something romantic about the pond, something forbidden.

"What about Judy?" she asked.

Again that troubled look came over his eyes.

"Judy and I are just friends," he said. "Don't worry about that. Will you come? I'd like it to be our secret. I'll meet you at the pond at nine-thirty. What do you say?"

There was pleading in his eyes. The kiss they had just shared seemed to have left him off balance. As for Leslie, she was no longer on solid ground.

She felt there was something wrong about this invitation. But the fact of being taken for a walk by Geoff Patterson, not to mention being kissed by him in the solitude of these woods, took away her will to resist him. She felt that something private and wonderful had joined them today, that he prized her for something he could not find in his own life, his own friends.

For him she would take this chance.

"All right," she said.

"And don't tell anyone about it," he said. "Let it be our secret. Promise?"

She smiled. "I promise."

"I'll be in my car," he said. "Nine-thirty. See you then?"

She nodded. He took her in his arms and kissed her again.

He left her at the edge of the woods, and she walked the last half mile to her house alone.

In some forbidden part of her mind Leslie knew that the reason for Geoff's secrecy was Judy Betancourt. Geoff and Judy were going steady, and were practically betrothed. Rumor had it that they had been physically intimate for a long time—the very thought had filled Leslie with wild, guilty imaginings and childish jealousy—and that their families expected them to marry as soon as they finished high school.

Leslie had always suspected that Judy had a particular dislike for her, though the two girls, being from separate social circles, were not on speaking terms. It was just a feeling and could not be proved, but Leslie had the impression that Judy found Leslie's superior intelligence contemptible, and thought that Leslie was putting on airs by being smart in school.

In any case, it seemed obvious to Leslie that Geoff could not very well broadcast his date with her to his own friends, much less to Judy. This gave a forbidden aspect to Leslie's tryst with him, and the feeling of intrigue attracted her, blunting her worries about the fact that he had not openly invited her on a date or planned to take her someplace where they would be seen by others. Leslie was full of mixed feelings about the whole thing. But her memory of Geoff's warm embrace banished her second thoughts and filled her with guilty anticipation.

Leslie did not tell her father about her date. It was easy not to, because his night work and her busy days kept them from seeing much of each other during the week. But Tom Chamberlain suspected something when he saw her preoccupied look, the new makeup she was wearing the rest of that week, and her hesitation in choosing clothes to wear to school. No doubt, he thought, she had a crush on some boy. That would certainly not be a bad thing in itself. Leslie seemed too solitary a girl. Some contact with the opposite sex might help bring her out of her shell.

"How's school, honey?" he asked. "Everything all right?"

"Fine, Daddy," she replied with the air of adolescent impatience he was familiar with. If there was something new going on in her life, she was too much of a teenager to confide in him about it.

Tom Chamberlain smiled at his daughter. He was a perceptive man despite his lack of education and his low station in life. He saw not only his daughter's intelligence but also her prettiness. She had a natural elegance born of her well-formed limbs and the fine bone structure of her face, and also of her personality, which was full of depth and originality.

She was going to make a fine woman, a woman who would perhaps achieve great things, and who would certainly be more than desirable to the opposite sex.

It frustrated Tom to be able to see this so clearly when his pretty young daughter obviously could not. He knew she saw herself as homely and undesirable. Worse yet for him, he knew that her poor self-image had a lot to do with his own low social status in the town. A factory worker's daughter was hardly a fine catch for one of the popular boys.

And, of course, she had lost her mother so long ago that she had had to grow up without the special support and intimacy every girl has a right to expect from a mother, and cannot get from an overworked father.

Leslie had borne her lonely status with a dignity that was particular to her. She was fiercely devoted to her father, and spared his feelings by never complaining about her situation. She showed him a sunny and carefree face, clouded only by the occasional moodiness of adolescence.

Tom Chamberlain could not help wondering what burdens Leslie was placing on herself in sparing him that way. Her courage seemed tragic to him, for she was so young, so defenseless in many ways. He wished he had provided her with an easier existence. But there was no help for it.

So he kept his silence and hoped for the best. And most of all he yearned for Leslie to finish high school and to venture beyond the sterile confines of this little town with its closed society. He saved every penny he could to make a nest egg for her college expenses, and he thanked his lucky stars for her perfect 4.0 average, which, combined with his poverty, would ensure her a scholarship to college.

He wanted Leslie to know how proud he was of her, how remarkable she was as a person, and what a great future she had in store for her. But such assurances, coming from a father to an adolescent girl, mean nothing. They are just the lame encouragement of a parent whose words carry little weight at that age.

If she could just survive these painful adolescent years she would outgrow her social handicaps and begin a wonderful, confident life.

As he watched her experiment with her new makeup and try on outfit after outfit, Tom Chamberlain kept his fingers crossed for Leslie.

On Friday night Leslie saw her father off to work as usual at five-thirty. She had picked nervously at her dinner, trying to seem as normal as she could.

As soon as she was alone she took a hot shower and slaved over her makeup for what seemed a desperate eternity.

She dressed in a pleated skirt and a soft white blouse. It was, in its way, a sensual outfit, for her legs were bare, and her skin was visible under the sheer blouse. The memory of Geoff's kiss lingered in all her senses. She wanted to be a woman for him tonight; she wanted to excite him.

Absorbed by her forbidden mission, she left the house at nine-fifteen and struck out through the neighborhood streets. She found the entrance to the woods, which she had known since she was a girl, and walked in silence along the path, listening to her feet brush the carpet of pine needles.

The woods got darker and darker, but her excitement eclipsed all fear. She found the fork where the paths diverged, and headed for Fishers Pond.

There was a full moon. The woods looked silvery and touched by magic. Leslie moved faster as the path rose to the promontory above the pond.

When she arrived at her destination she saw a car. She knew it was Geoff's, the blue 1959 Chevy he drove to school every day.

She approached it cautiously. There were no other cars around. This made sense; most of the couples who would come here later were still in town at the movies, or at a hamburger joint. For a while, at least, she and Geoff would be alone.

She saw the silhouette of the driver behind the wheel. She moved closer to the car. Her senses were tingling.

The window began to roll down as she reached the car.

"Hi, Leslie."

She stopped in her tracks.

It was not Geoff. She recognized the voice as that of one of his friends, Barth Dillon, a fellow basketball player and a boy noted for his fast ways with girls.

Leslie stood with her mouth open. She was at a loss for words.

"I—I thought . . . " she stammered.

"Geoff couldn't make it," Barth said. "It was unavoidable. He sent me in his place. He didn't want you to be lonely. Why don't you get in, Leslie?"

She saw his eyes scrutinizing her appraisingly in the moonlight. She could not believe what she was seeing. The unreality of this scene spread itself back in time over her walk with Geoff in the woods, and it seemed that none of it was real. She knew how Cinderella felt when her coach horses turned into mice. The whole world was her enemy. She was defenseless and humiliated.

"Don't be embarrassed," Barth said. "Come on in. I've been looking forward to this. Geoff told me you were really passionate."

He was about to open the door when Leslie turned on her heel and fled.

"Leslie!" he called, irritation vying with amusement in his voice. "Don't be antisocial! Come back!"

But she had flung herself into the woods and did not even hear the roar of the car's engine or the distant sound of laughter. She plunged down the path.

She did not see anything between those first steps and her house. She rushed through the darkness like a girl possessed. She just wanted to get home.

When she got there she threw off her clothes and took a long hot shower. She was trembling in every limb. When she got out of the shower she put on her pajamas and got into bed, staring straight before her as though to blot out all memory. She clung desperately to the comforting fantasy that none of this had happened, that she was alone as always in her house, that Geoff Patterson did not know she was alive, that her life could go on undisturbed, if unhappy.

For a long time she lay that way. The slow tremors of her body rocked her almost like the lulling rhythms of sleep. She felt dazed.

It was not until after midnight that her tears came. When they did, they started as a trickle and became a painful stream. Sobs shook her young body.

She cried all night. When her father arrived home at nine in the morning, she was doing her homework at her desk. He commented on her red eyes, and she told him the new makeup she had bought had irritated them.

Soon he went to bed and she was alone. No more tears came, but it seemed that the sobs still resounded fatefully in the silence of her soul, nevermore to end.

She went to school on Monday, her eyes downcast. In the bus she listened to the other kids' morning conversation without hearing. The drone of the driver's radio added to her sense of unreality.

When she entered the school building, no one seemed to notice her. She hurried along the corridors toward her homeroom.

It was not until she was on her way to English class that she noticed a snicker from a trio of popular girls outside the classroom. Later in the morning a catcall came from one of the basketball players as she passed their group.

When she entered her world civilization class she turned red. On the blackboard was scrawled in large letters: LESLIE, THIS IS GEOFF. I LOVE YOU.

Leslie endured three minutes of the worst agony of her life, until the teacher came in and erased the chalked message as she prepared to teach the class.

After that first week the sounds of mockery at school ended, and Leslie was once again a part of the furniture, unnoticed by those around her. She rode to school on the bus, went to her classes, chatted with the girls she was friendly with—all of whom now seemed to know about what had happened but said nothing about it—and tried to forget. Like all those unlucky schoolchildren who at one time or another are the subject of a public misfortune or a great humiliation, she bore the stigma in her own mind far longer than it lasted in the minds of others. Her peers forgot about her shame quickly.

She never knew the cause of her chagrin. Naturally enough, no one told her that Geoff Patterson's invitation had been confided to Barth, his closest friend on the basketball team, and found its way to Judy Betancourt. Geoff had been warned in no uncertain terms that Judy would never forgive him for seeing another girl, much less a nobody like Leslie Chamberlain.

Uncertain as to what to do, Geoff had allowed himself to be influenced to stand Leslie up. When Barth had offered to go in his place, Geoff had reluctantly agreed, turning his careless adolescent mind away from the uncomfortable situation. Geoff had gone on a date with Judy as usual that Friday night, while Barth, in his borrowed car, waited for Leslie.

Leslie never learned any of these details. Nor did she ever learn what would have eased her pain a little, perhaps—that Geoff's walk with her in the woods, his kiss, and his invitation had all been sincere. Geoff had been attracted by Leslie's freshness, her intelligence, and the first signs of her budding female beauty. He had sensed something special in her, and dared to try to touch it.

When the rigid rules of his social caste decreed that he stand Leslie up and acquiesce in a conspiracy to humiliate her—a conspiracy hatched by Barth Dillon as a lark—Geoff had done what any other boy of his class and personality would have done. He went along with his friends and turned his thoughts away from Leslie. He forgot his own role in her punishment and went back to his basketball and his schoolwork and his socially ratified relationship with Judy.

He would not think of Leslie Chamberlain for a long time.

But Leslie would not forget Geoff Patterson.

4

JORDAN LAZARUS AT TWENTY-FOUR was a successful entrepreneur. Though not a millionaire, he was growing more wealthy every day, and using his money to support his family and to plan for the future.

Though he never returned to school after running away from home, Jordan did not abandon his powerful intellect. He found that his innate creative talent, combined with an unusual ability to see unexpected possibilities in situations and people, made him a shrewd judge of the business marketplace.

He supplemented this ability with a natural thoroughness, an appetite for research, and a limitless ambition that could not be daunted by frustration or disappointment. Armed with this arsenal of invaluable qualities, he entered the business world, first as an employee, then as a manager and consultant.

Within a year of his departure from home he had helped a wealthy investor to set up a series of small business franchises in a state two thousand miles from Webster, Pennsylvania. So successful was his work, and so grateful the investor, that Jordan soon accepted a similar opportunity from one of the investor's close financial friends.

By age twenty-one Jordan was a streetwise, self-educated entrepreneur. He made his living by helping businessmen blueprint new enterprises, and by assisting in the early stages of management and accounting. He was paid a flat sum for his efforts, combined with a bonus and a percentage of the profits. His honesty was matched by his cleverness in outwitting the competition. Already he was earning more money in a month than his father had made in a lifetime.

Other men trusted him naturally, for he had a disarming candor that matched his obvious intelligence and expertise. He was clearly a young man of seriousness and personal force.

And he had all the women he wanted. He had grown tall and strong, with a deep chest, long limbs, and a sparkling, roguish look in his dark eyes. His natural charm and spontaneity made them willing victims, and his caresses, as inventive as his thoughts, drove them to extremities of passion in which they seemed to surrender something of their humanity.

Jordan enjoyed the easy triumph of his looks and his personality over women. Not only did it give him a sense of power but it made him feel as though he were redressing an old grievance. All through his youth he had admired the middle-class girls of his town from afar and felt like a dirty urchin before them. Sometimes they and their boyfriends had made fun of his poor family and his hand-me-down clothes. He had been small and weak as a boy, and this had combined with his poverty to make him feel inadequate.

Now the shoe was on the other foot. Jordan had all the tools necessary to make attractive women his playthings. What his looks and charm did not accomplish, his success and money did. Women surrendered to him almost too predictably.

Despite his physical satisfaction, Jordan was a little disappointed to find that women were so easily impressed by money. The girls he had admired as a boy seemed to move in a world far above his own, a world that followed mysterious and magical rules, a world of beautiful people each of whom had her own peculiar essence. He had imagined that these people valued things, knew things, of which he in his poverty must remain forever ignorant. It was at once disappointing and convenient to find upon growing up that money was the only real moral currency of that world and the only weapon needed to make women his own.

So Jordan lived for his work. A drifter by choice as well as necessity, he did not want to be tied down to any one place. He kept his interests far-flung and did not spend much time in any one location. He was cautious enough about the law to keep his money in corporate bank accounts and to live in apartments under corporate names so that his own name was used as little as possible.

And, from his distance, he watched over his family.

His brothers no longer worked for the Lukas Tool Works. They ran a small contracting and interior design business, building kitchens and bathrooms for homeowners. It was called Prestige Contractors. They had started the business with money sent them by Jordan a year after his departure. Ryan, Clay, and Gerald did the physical work themselves, while Louise acted as receptionist and accountant. It was a successful little firm, doing business in a four-county area, and the family was now out of financial danger.

Father, of course, remained bedridden by his injuries. Mother spent most of her time reading to him, listening to the radio or watching television with him, fixing his meals, and listening to his complaints—for incapacitation had made him a complainer.

Then there was Meg.

Since Jordan left home Meg had suffered two serious attacks of heart failure, both caused by valve damage dating from the rheumatic fever she had had as a child. The second attack had left her seriously weakened, and her doctors would not allow her to indulge in normal activity.

She had to stop working with her brothers and sister at Prestige Contractors, and spent nearly all her time at home. She took care of Father when Mother needed a rest, and had a knack for calming his ill temper. Father, like everyone else in the family, could not say no to Meg.

Meg provided to the family the psychological leadership that might have come from Jordan had he remained at home. Her moral strength was as great as her body was weak. Her mother liked to say that Meg had "more heart than the rest of us put together," using an intentional play on words as she alluded to Meg's cardiac difficulties.

Meg settled family quarrels, solved dilemmas about correct behavior, and on the whole gave the family the sense of cohesion and balance that it might never have recovered after Father's accident and Jordan's departure.

But Meg was not getting any stronger since her second heart attack. She lived in terror of infection that might further damage her heart, and she was in constant pain. She needed costly medication every day and had to visit her cardiologist every second week or so. She had always been constitutionally the weakest of the family, whose other members possessed prodigious physical strength. Now her fragility was beginning to tell. Her milky, freckled complexion was pale now, and she had lost the look of the fresh colleen that had so beguiled Jordan when they were younger.

Jordan, to his everlasting chagrin, had been far away when Meg had her two attacks. He sent money both times but was unable to visit right away. He felt enraged and consumed with guilt over not being there for Meg when she needed him. Jordan rightly sensed that Meg needed him more than anyone else, and never doubted that Meg was the family member he cared most about.

After her second attack he came to the hospital to find her weak and feverish in her bed. She roused herself to greet him with a kiss, and assured him a dozen times over that she did not reproach him for being away, and that his being here now was all she needed or wanted. She knew how hard he worked for the family, and knew he had to be cautious about his whereabouts being known.

"If I had been here to keep an eye on you, this might never have happened," he said.

"Nonsense, Jordie," she insisted. "I'm being well looked after. And I'm not half as sick as everyone makes out. You just do your work and stay out of trouble, and everything will be fine."

Meg refused to allow Jordan to feel guilty about making a living to ensure the family's security. Nevertheless, there was a sadness in her when she saw him, and he knew its source.

Meg kept her favorite photo of Jordan on her bedside table. It had been taken when he was thirteen years old, and showed a delicate, almost ascetic young man with dark, curly hair and haunting dark eyes. It reminded Meg of the time when Jordan had been a sensitive boy given to drawing and story writing, a boy ill understood by his father or his strapping brothers but adored by his mother, who, however, could not pretend to understand him.

It was this young Jordan, his eyes full of poetry and yearning, that Meg had felt closest to. It was Meg who encouraged him in the private whimsy that made his vision of people and things so unusual. And it was Meg who had suffered more than the others when he had left all that behind to become a breadwinner, a man of the world.

Though Meg did not reproach Jordan for having done what he did in leaving the family, she wanted him to be true to the little boy he had once been, a natural artist whose vision was destined for original ideas far from those of his family or friends. And the more time Jordan spent on his work, the more money he made, the more Meg sensed that he was turning his back on that little boy and becoming a kind of man that was foreign to his inner destiny.

She never told Jordan this in so many words. But he could feel her gentle, loving reproach in her eyes—those beautiful blue-green eyes that glowed with a ghostly depth now that her face had grown thinner.

Meg felt that Jordan cared too much about the financial security he pursued with such deadly purpose. The accident to his father seemed to have wounded Jordan's soul almost more than it wounded his father's body. Since that day Jordan had been trying to subdue the world, perhaps even to wreak vengeance upon it for its indifference and cruelty. Meg worried that in this crusade to protect the family, Jordan was losing himself.

Jordan did not see things this way. He felt he had committed himself to a difficult task and was making a success of it through hard work and initiative. He did not want to look back on the boy he had been or be reminded of his youthful yearnings by Meg. He told himself that the money he was making was literally keeping Meg alive. He did not worship money; it was just a means to an end for him; the end was protecting his family.

And when his efforts brought him money and status and many beautiful women, he felt that he must be going in the right direction. For these were the things that men prized and coveted, that men laid down their lives and souls for. And lo, they were being given to him when he was hardly out of his teens.

With this somewhat self-serving thought Jordan dismissed the issue of his "other" self, the self beneath the active surface of his life. But when he was with Meg it was always there in her eyes and in her love, like a mirror showing him as he should have been and was not.

It made Jordan uncomfortable to feel that Meg, in some way, understood him better than he understood himself. "You make too much of me," he told her. "I'm not as special a fellow as you think. I'm a breadwinner. Let me be that. You're the visionary in this family, Meg."

She would shake her head with a sad look in her eyes. Meg seemed to be the keeper of the flame of his secret vocation, the vocation he had renounced when he went out into the world.

As a boy he had been told the Bible story of Lazarus, his illness, his death, and Jesus' resurrection of him after four days in the grave. The story had filled Jordan with a mystical sense of his purpose in life, a purpose he was not perhaps to know but that would be revealed to him one day, just as the biblical Lazarus had his fate revealed to him by Jesus.

He had dared to confide this presentiment to Meg when he was a boy. She had agreed with him entirely, and encouraged him to think of himself as a man with a great destiny.

"You're going to be somebody," she had said, looking deep into his eyes. "I know it. We can't see that somebody today, because he's in the future. But you have to strive toward him, Jordie, and never stop looking for him."

That was a long time ago. Nowadays Jordan felt that his purpose in life had been revealed to him by his work and by the obligation of protecting his family. He lived in the present and thought as little about the past as about the future.

But sometimes his old presentiment of a personal mission came back to him. Late at night, when fatigue and dreams stripped away his concrete concern with tangible advantages, he would lie in his bed—sometimes alongside a woman—and feel the old dreams wash over him, full of mystery and ineffable promise.

These dreams had played their part in his adolescent idealization of girls. And now they played a part in his disappointment in the women he knew, the women he made love to. For he had retained this capacity to dream of something more, to hope for and look for a coherence, a substance in the world and in himself that could not be measured in dollars or in power.

But these thoughts troubled Jordan Lazarus only for a few fugitive moments, dancing in his mind like chimeras before they gave way to impenetrable sleep. And then sleep gave way to the challenges of the new day, a day in which he would discover himself anew through action and initiative.

So he forgot the Jordan of the mirror, the Jordan of his youth, the Jordan he had seen reflected in Meg's eyes and to whom Meg still clung in her hopes and her undying confidence in him.

Thus the existence of Jordan Lazarus, twenty-four-year-old breadwinner and entrepreneur, remained in an uneasy equilibrium. Jordan lived for work, and tried not to see beyond his work. He had achieved his goal of taking care of his family, and tried his best to forget the inner goal of knowing himself.

He was well off financially, but had no dreams of glory or of great wealth. He was content to go on living and working as he had been doing for the past eight years. He lived in the present, absorbed in the immediate tasks at hand.

And he continued his amorous adventures, though he was increasingly bored with sexual conquest. Women offered him a sensuality that was entirely on the surface of himself, a pleasure blunted by the fact that they meant nothing to him as people.

Jordan was too busy a man to waste time regretting this lack in his love life. He had come to expect little from the female sex.

It did not occur to him that perhaps he had never yet encountered a truly subtle woman, a woman as subtle as himself or even more so.

5

HER NAME WAS REBECCA.

She met Jordan at a party in Philadelphia and was introduced to him as Mrs. Jarman. She made no secret about being married. Her husband was a prominent businessman and investor named Burke Jarman, a name Jordan had heard in his travels.

She also made no secret about her desire to go to bed with Jordan.

She was a very slim woman in her late twenties, with a catlike walk, smooth, tanned skin, and the darkest eyes Jordan had ever seen. With her flowing black hair, her long fingers, and the subtle way her tongue darted out to lick her lips occasionally, she had an animal look that was extraordinarily sexy.

Despite himself Jordan felt a stirring in his loins as he talked to her. He and Rebecca managed to extricate themselves from the rest of the guests and had a quiet drink alone. Her long brown leg emerged from the slit in her cocktail dress as she sat down. She studied him, her spike-heeled shoe dangling from a shapely foot.

"Your reputation precedes you," she said. "I didn't know that men as young as you got around quite that much. I understand you've had a hand in some big successes."

Jordan replied modestly, giving a handful of details about his background.

He barely heard what he was saying. He was falling deeper under Rebecca Jarman's sexual spell every second. She was so slim, so sleek, and so obviously interested in only one thing. He was intrigued by his own excitement and by her ability to provoke it.

She wasted no time in getting down to cases. Before eleven she gave Jordan an up-from-under look and murmured, "I have to go."

"Can I drop you?" he asked.

"That would be kind of you."

He watched her say good night to the host, a prominent member of the Philadelphia Chamber of Commerce. She shook hands with a few of the guests, then joined Jordan in the foyer. As he helped her on with her coat he noticed her slender back, revealed by the almost backless cocktail dress she had worn.

"Where to?" he asked when they were in the car.

She gave him a long, slow look. "Does it matter?" she asked.

Jordan took her to his hotel room. In the dim orange light provided by the bedside lamp, he watched her body emerge as her coat came off. Her hair was a bit tousled by the breeze, and he could feel the cool air of the street coming off her, a thin, brisk aura evaporating quickly from a very hot surface.

"Nice place you have here," she said with a mocking smile, watching him hang her coat in the closet.

He took her in his arms. She seemed to melt into him. Her body quickly found the sources of desire that had been awakened much earlier in the evening. The thighs against his, the small, firm breasts pushing against his chest, the hands moving down his ribs toward his loins, were so many provocations, joined by the tongue that slipped luxuriantly into his mouth.

Jordan had never felt so excited by a woman before. Despite himself his hands trembled as he looked for the zipper to undo her dress.

"Let me," she said.

But instead of unclothing herself, it was Jordan she began to strip. Kissing him all the while, she undid his tie and found the buttons of his shirt with sure fingers. Her hands moved over his chest with slow delectation, and slipped down to his belt. It came undone as though by magic, and she pulled down his pants.

He was hard under his shorts, and she smiled to see his sex strain under the white fabric. She pulled the elastic band down and saw the proud penis bounce out to freedom.

She slipped down the shorts, sank to her knees, and took him in her mouth while she remained fully clothed. Jordan's eyes closed. He buried his hands in her hair and smelled the lush, musky aroma of her, rising to his nostrils as a quick, knowing tongue worked its way over and under his penis.

"Mmm," she whispered, holding the hard staff in both her hands. "You're a big boy."

She suckled him gently until he began to tremble. Then she helped him out of the tumbled trousers and shorts and pushed him down on the bed. Still dressed in the clinging cocktail dress, she bent over him, sucking him harder and deeper while her hands explored every part of him.

In a very few moments Jordan was perilously close to orgasm. With difficulty he pulled free from her and watched her lie back on the bed. Her lips were wet with his own passion and hers. She looked satisfied, like a big, dark cat, and hungry for more. She smiled at him.

"I think it's time you fucked me, darling," she said.

He helped her off with the dress. She was wearing no underwear. A long, smooth body, tanned almost olive, displayed itself before him. The breasts were firm, with hard, waiting nipples. Her stomach was as flat as that of a girl. Her legs were long and shapely, already spreading to lure him closer.

Now it was Jordan's turn to taste every part of her. It was an amazing experience. She was made of a dozen different perfumes, it seemed, and every one an aphrodisiac. She moved with catlike cleverness to offer him her nipple, then her lips, then the tips of her fingers, then her breast again. And when he kissed the center of her at last, warm and fragrant, he felt once again that he was losing control of himself.

She turned him on his back and got astride him. A touch of her finger guided him inside her and she began to move, alternately cooing her pleasure and whimpering with hunger for more, more. There was an almost reptilian grace about her, as sinister as it was delightful. He felt the first stirrings of his ecstasy, saw her smile, and felt her loins move more quickly around him, sinews knowing as fingers on his sex.

There was no holding it any longer. He thrust his pelvis forward and came into her with a great eager burst. Her head flung back, eyes half-closed as her silky hair hung down her back. Her breasts stood out trembling. She gripped his chest with her knees, and she came with him, a low, mysterious moan sounding in her throat.

They stayed that way for a long moment, the woman poised over him, her back arched as he continued to throb inside her. He realized that every gesture, every smile she had bestowed on him at the party had been a prelude to this moment.

When at last he began to ebb from her, he felt compelled to compliment her.

"Thank you," he said. "You're wonderful."

There was something innocent in his words that made her smile.

"Don't thank me yet," she said. "We've only just begun."

They made love all that night, and most of the following week. Her husband was out of town, and Jordan found time away from his work to join her whenever she was free. They met at his hotel, for she said her home was not safe. Her husband was the jealous type, she added, with a contemptuous look in her eyes.

She showed Jordan things about making love that he had never thought possible. Her originality as a lover was not limited merely to varieties of position, although she was as experienced at those as any woman he had known. Nor was it her willingness to let him explore and enter her in forbidden places, though she was fearless on that score as well.

Instead it was the peculiar mixture of emotion and sensuality she gave to every caress, every contact of her body with his. Her kisses were full of meanings, specific and complicated. Her fingers seemed to speak volumes as they massaged different parts of Jordan's body, now slow and languorous, now slithering and triumphant. Even the shadows of the room, the position of the pillows became her accomplices in giving him pleasure in different tones and modalities.

Her lovemaking was less a symphony than a sort of jungle, filled with paths leading into something dark and dangerous and always surprising. She whispered little endearments as she made love, sometimes girlish and tender, sometimes unspeakably perverse.

And always there were those soft lips, that fragrant, tanned skin, the long, supple limbs curling snakelike about Jordan, teasing him with smooth caresses until, inevitably, he was inside her, giving perhaps more than he had intended, feeling her take with pleasure and give back seduction for seduction, until his body literally throbbed with wanting.

By the end of those first two weeks Jordan was obsessed with Rebecca Jarman. He could not get enough of her. He changed his plans, canceling two trips to the Midwest and cutting short an important stay in Boston so as to be near her. She was nearly always available to him, changing her own plans as necessary whenever he called her. When he asked her about her jealous husband, she shrugged off the question, telling him that she knew her husband like a book, that he was a busy man anyway, and that she could work around him.

But she warned Jordan to stay away from Burke Jarman.

"He's bad," she said. "Bad for me, bad for everybody who gets involved with him."

"Why did *you* get involved with him?" Jordan asked.

She gave him an ambiguous smile, tinged with contempt for her husband and with something like fear.

"A mistake," she said. "An error of my youth. Let's not talk about it anymore."

Jordan nodded. But she could see that her words had intrigued him.

"Promise me one thing right now," she said. "Don't ever do business with him. He'll ruin you if he can. That's the only way he knows how to do business. Will you promise me?"

Jordan agreed with a shrug. He had no intention of doing business with Burke Jarman. Indeed, he did not give the husband another thought. He lived only for Rebecca, for the next time she would appear at his door, give him that special, mysterious smile, and let her clothes slip to the floor before coming to bed.

For the first time in his life Jordan Lazarus had met a woman whose wiles were a match for his own sharp intelligence. Rebecca Jarman remained a mystery to him, and her charms increased accordingly. He did not ask himself what was going on underneath that sensuous surface of her being. He did not ask himself about her past. He even forgot his own past. He lived for the pure surface ecstasy of being with her.

The danger of being enmeshed this way by a woman was not lost on him. But it only added to his excitement.

Jordan was caught in a web, and he felt no desire to escape. Why should he, indeed? He was merely having an affair with an obviously experienced woman. There were no strings attached.

Then one day Rebecca's separate life came into her relationship with Jordan. It did so by leaving its mark on the body he had come to know and love so well.

She met him at his hotel. She seemed subdued. When he took off her dress he saw the reason why. There were large black-and-blue marks on her upper thighs and hips, and her rib cage as well. When he looked into her eyes he saw pain there.

"What happened to you?" he asked, touching delicately at the ugly marks.

"Burke," she said.

There was a pause.

"It's not the first time," she added.

She would say no more. Though Jordan was hesitant, she insisted they make love. This time there was something more candid in her lovemaking. Jordan felt sorry for her, and this increased his own tenderness. But he thought about the brutal husband who had done this to Rebecca, and a dark anger began to form at the back of his mind. For the first time he actually thought of the husband putting his hands on Rebecca, being intimate with her, having power over her. It made him jealous.

The black-and-blue marks gradually disappeared, and Jordan's torrid physical relationship with Rebecca Jarman continued. But it was not the same as before. Having touched her bruised flesh when she was in pain, Jordan appreciated her more. And, subtly, he gave more of himself to her, lost a bit more of the distance that had been so integral to their relationship.

A few weeks after the first beating episode, more bruises appeared on Rebecca's body. Again they were where outsiders could not see them—on the stomach, the hips, the rib cage.

"He likes to show me off to his business associates," Rebecca said bitterly. "He never hits me where it will show."

Jordan's jealousy now became overt anger.

"Why don't you leave him?" he asked.

She shook her head. "I can't do that," she said. "Not now, anyway. Don't make me explain. Just hold me."

Jordan did as he was told. As he felt her body in his arms, his heart went out to her. At the same time a desire to harm Burke Jarman, to get at him somehow, was born inside him.

The two feelings were inseparable. And the more Jordan saw Rebecca, the stronger each became.

A month later the breaking point came.

Rebecca met Jordan at his hotel. This time her bruises were worse. Her thighs, her ribs, even her collarbones were black and blue.

Jordan's jaw clenched in rage.

"I can't let him do this to you any more," he said. "Let me take care of him in my own way." Jordan's anger was out of control. He wanted revenge, and he wanted to take Rebecca away from her husband.

Rebecca was firm. There was fear in her eyes.

"No," she said. "You promised never to go near him. If you break your promise, I'll never see you again. Those are the rules."

Jordan shook his head. "Not exactly," he said. "I promised never to do *business* with him—not to stay away from him entirely."

Rebecca was thoughtful. For a long moment she seemed far away.

"You've just given me an idea," she said. "Maybe the way to handle Burke is for you to do business with him after all." She narrowed her eyes. "Without his knowing it, that is," she added.

Jordan raised an eyebrow. "What do you mean?"

She turned on her side to look at him. Her beautiful body coiled on the couch with the serpentine look that never failed to excite him.

"Burke is doing a deal with some cronies of his on Wall Street," she said. "It's a stock deal. A very shady one. They're going to drive the stock of a Chicago metals company down so they can get two places on the board. Normally Burke wouldn't try something that dangerous. He's very conservative. But one of his old college friends is on the board already, and is helping him set things up. The firm is called Michigan Metals. It's a solid company, but it's been in trouble, on and off, for a couple of years, due to stiff competition and some bad investments by the board. That's how this all got started."

Jordan looked into her eyes. "How did you find out about this?" he asked.

"I overheard Burke talking to one of his cronies about it on the phone last month," she said. "Since then I've made it my business to listen in whenever I could. At first I wasn't sure I understood what they were planning. But last week Burke had a long conversation with his pal on the Michigan Metals board. I realized what was at stake. Burke is investing a million dollars of his own money in this. He would never risk such an amount unless it was a sure thing."

Jordan was impressed. A million dollars was indeed too much to risk.

"Where do I fit in?" he asked.

"For a period of about forty-eight hours," she said, "the stock of Michigan Metals will be at an all-time low. Say, five dollars a share instead of forty. After that, the stock will shoot up, because Burke and his friends are going to announce a major reorganization and stock repurchase as soon as they get on the board. Now, if you get in on the buying during that forty-eight-hour period, you can make eight dollars for every dollar you invest. And when it's all over, you'll be a major shareholder in one of the strongest metals firms in the Midwest."

Jordan looked skeptical. "There are laws against stock manipulations like that," he said. "You can go to jail if you get caught."

"Not you," she said. "You're not in on the deal. No one can connect you to Burke or his friends. You're not involved in collusion. You're simply investing in a troubled stock at the right moment. You see, you're not taking any risk."

Jordan considered the truth of her words.

"When is all this to take place?" he asked.

"A week from Monday," she said. "Burke and his friends are going to put a lot of pressure on the stock late next week and drive it down to rock-bottom first thing Monday morning. That's the moment."

Jordan looked skeptical.

"I've never liked playing the stock market," he said. "The risk is too great. Something might go wrong, even in a deal like this."

She shook her head. "Burke never takes risks. He wouldn't be in this unless he and his friends had the stock sewed up. With their combined power and money, they can't miss. Now, wouldn't you like to get rich off him? Without having to work for your payoff?"

A liquid, sexual look came into her eyes.

"Wouldn't you like to make a million dollars off my husband?" she asked.

Jordan now saw what she was offering him. Revenge against her husband and a way of punishing him indirectly for what he had done to her. She wanted to make Burke Jarman a financial cuckold, as he was already a marital one. Jordan would not have to do business directly with Burke but would make a fortune off him without Burke's knowing it.

"All you have to do is invest a substantial amount—say, two hundred thousand—early Monday morning," she said, "and you'll be a millionaire from that deal alone by the end of the week."

Jordan looked thoughtful. He could use a million dollars. It would allow him to go through with some ambitious plans he had in the works, plans that required ready cash he did not presently have. It was a lot of money for almost no effort and almost no risk. The deal was hard to resist.

Rebecca Jarman slithered into his embrace and slipped a long, hungry tongue into his mouth. His sex hardened instantly at her touch.

"Wouldn't you like to screw him?" she asked.

She moved her loins over him. A slim hand found its way between his legs. A whimper of anticipation sounded in her throat.

"You've got his wife," she said. "Take his money, too."

Jordan's breath came short. It was a seductive proposal.

"Come on," she prodded, beginning to move atop him. "Say you'll do it. For me."

Jordan gave a long sigh. What was two hundred thousand dollars, after all, compared to the feel of this woman's body against his? The risk, indeed, heightened the pleasure he was feeling right now.

"All right," he said.

"Mmm." She began to move quickly against him, excited by their plan. Her panties were coming off already, and she guided his finger to the slippery center of her. "That's right . . ."

She undid his zipper and took hold of him. He was hot and ready for love. The hard thing in her hands left no doubt of that.

A moment later she had guided him inside her. His first thrusts were so urgent that she feared he would waste his pleasure before she was ready for him.

She looked at his face. His eyes were closed. She could see the spell she had cast on him.

Only at that moment did she really feel the rod inside her, and begin to enjoy herself.

The story Rebecca had told Jordan about Michigan Metals was a lie. In reality Burke Jarman and his friends were not driving the stock of Michigan Metals down in order to assume places on the company's board. Their aim was to bankrupt the company outright and buy its skeleton for a song, wiping out its debt in the process. With the help of a few influential friends, they would build a new company on the ruins of Michigan Metals, a company whose board would be composed entirely of their own cronies.

Jordan Lazarus's $200,000 would be lost money within hours after he invested it. Burke Jarman was simply using Jordan as a source of easy money to buy worthless shares and help bankrupt the victim company.

It had been Rebecca's job to rope Jordan in. Once the deal was done,

Rebecca would blow Jordan off with a phony story about a slip-up in the deal, an unexpected bail-out by the company's top stockholders. She would claim that the bankruptcy had come as a complete surprise to her husband as well as the others, and had hurt them as badly as it had hurt Jordan.

Rebecca was sure that Jordan, besotted by her sexually, would believe her story. The hungry look in his eyes had left no doubt she had him right where she wanted him. An overconfident young man of only twenty-four, he was no match for her in sophistication or cunning. Her seduction of him had been a work of art. A few self-inflicted blows—she bruised easily, she knew—had been all she needed to convince Jordan that she was the victim of a brutal husband. Her skill as a lover, and as a liar, had done the rest.

Unfortunately for Burke Jarman and his wife, things did not turn out the way they had planned.

On the following Monday morning, just as feverish selling had driven the price of Michigan Metals stock to a new low of $3.60 per share, the SEC suddenly froze all trading on the beleaguered stock and launched an investigation into the suspicious activity behind the stock's sudden drop.

The SEC investigators were either very clever or possessed inside information that guided them in their inquiry. Forty-eight hours after the investigation began, seven major shareholders of Michigan Metals were indicted for illicit stock manipulation and fraud. Among them was Burke Jarman.

Thanks to the prompt investigation and the emergency stockholders' meeting, Michigan Metals was saved from bankruptcy. As a matter of fact, in the following two weeks the company's fortunes took a strong upturn. By the time Burke Jarman and his cronies went to trial, Michigan Metals' stock had risen to from $3.60 to $30 per share. Thanks to some shrewd investments made by the board, the price rose to $44.50 by early summer and had reached a seven-year high of $66.20 by September.

Burke Jarman pleaded *nolo contendere* to the charges against him and spent a year in a minimum-security federal prison. No sooner was he under indictment than he launched a search for the man or men who had denounced his secret plan to the SEC.

That search revealed that Jordan Lazarus had had no part in the betrayal.

For one thing, Lazarus had never known the real plan behind Rebecca's blandishments. But far more importantly, as a thorough search of the stockholders' directory showed, Lazarus had never invested a dime in Michigan Metals—either because he failed to get his investment in before the SEC freeze, or because he failed to get together the money he promised Rebecca he would raise for the deal.

Jordan Lazarus was simply a little fish that had gotten away. Perhaps, indeed, he had been too small-time a mark for Rebecca to waste her time on. That had been her mistake, and Burke's.

Burke Jarman decided he would never know how Michigan Metals had survived. There was nothing for him to do but finish out his prison term and go back to his former life.

Then the unexpected happened.

Three months after Burke Jarman entered prison, the sum of $250,000 was deposited in Rebecca Jarman's private savings account. Burke Jarman found out about this from a bank officer who, in return for a consideration, routinely kept him personally advised of sudden changes in his wife's account.

Burke Jarman sent two of his most trusted henchmen to find Rebecca and get an explanation from her. The two men were told to torture the truth out of Rebecca if necessary.

By the time the two men arrived at the Jarman residence in Philadelphia, Rebecca was gone. So were her clothes, her jewelry, and the $250,000 from her personal bank account.

Rebecca Jarman was never seen in the United States again. Nor was she ever known by the same name. She assumed a new identity and simply disappeared. Or so Burke Jarman assumed, for he never stopped looking for her.

As for Jordan Lazarus, he spent a few pleasant months watching the stock of Michigan Metals steadily rise and counting the money he had made off the debacle that had sent Burke Jarman to jail.

For Jordan had invested in Michigan Metals after all.

Seeing through Rebecca Jarman's seduction, Jordan had done a thorough study of her husband's past business dealings and current associates. Jarman had bankrupted companies before. Jordan was convinced that was what he was up to now with Michigan Metals.

Unbeknownst to either Rebecca or her husband, it was Jordan who—anonymously—informed the beleaguered top executives of Michigan Metals that a group of investors was trying to drive the company into bankruptcy. This news reached the SEC almost immediately.

Having alerted the target company to what was afoot, Jordan had bought $500,000 worth of common stock in Michigan Metals—all the liquid assets he possessed and all he could borrow—at the price of $3.60 per share. When the company survived, Jordan's stock went up, and up again. Now at $72.15 per share, his investment was worth $10 million.

Burke Jarman never knew of the money Jordan had in Michigan Metals, because Jordan did not invest it himself. The investment was made by a trusted friend who owed Jordan a favor. Even now Jordan's name appeared nowhere in the Michigan Metals stockholders' directory.

The red-hot $250,000 that appeared so unexpectedly in Rebecca Jarman's bank account came from none other than Jordan Lazarus. That the check was a cashier's check, signed by an anonymous donor, did not protect Rebecca in the eyes of her suspicious husband. The very fact of receiving so much cash convinced him she was a traitor. Her abrupt departure completed the convincing.

As for Rebecca herself, she was too busy running for her life to wonder where the mysterious $250,000 had come from. It was not until six months later, safe in a tiny resort town on the coast of Peru, that she saw the fine irony in the amount of the anonymous gift—the $200,000 she had originally asked for, plus a small bonus—and decided the donor might have been Jordan. She toasted him silently with her piña colada and acknowledged that he had taught her something about sex as well as about life.

Jordan had outwitted the Jarmans, husband and wife, with a vengeance.

The Michigan Metals deal changed Jordan Lazarus from a successful small businessman to an ambitious, powerful entrepreneur.

Canny investments of the money he had made increased Jordan's net worth to $20 million by the end of the following year. Three years after that, thanks to some adventures in the bond market and a favorable oil deal, he was worth nearly $40 million.

But more important than the money Jordan Lazarus had made was the lesson he had learned.

When she proposed her stock deal, Rebecca Jarman had her sexual hooks firmly planted in Jordan. It had taken an enormous effort of will for Jordan to overcome his fascination with her long enough to become suspicious of the fact that she was trying to get money out of him—in exchange for a promise of sexual favors.

From this foothold on lucidity Jordan had fashioned his victory over Burke Jarman and his revenge on Rebecca. Because of Jordan she would never again help her husband screw an unsuspecting lover. Indeed, she would flee her husband for the rest of her life. And perhaps, one day, Burke Jarman would find her. Jordan did not like to think what would happen to Rebecca that day.

Thanks to that crucial display of clearheadedness at a critical moment, Jordan was now a far wealthier man than before, and a far more ambitious one. He was on his way to financial adventures far beyond his earlier dreams, thanks to the nest egg provided him by Burke Jarman and his sensual wife. Armed with $40 million, his powerful intellect was a weapon Wall Street would not be able to resist.

But most of all, Jordan had learned a valuable lesson.

Never trust a woman.

Jordan would never forget this lesson.

6

ON MARCH 21, 1970, Leslie Chamberlain returned home to spend her spring vacation with her father.

She was a junior at Cornell, majoring in journalism and advertising. The honors scholarship she had been granted upon admission to the university paid for her tuition, books, and room and board, provided that she maintain a 3.25 grade point average. Leslie's average was 4.0.

She was considered one of the most promising students in the journalism school, and was a great favorite among her peers as well as her professors. The head of her department thought her the most brilliant student he had ever had—though he was careful not to tell her so to her face.

Tom Chamberlain always looked forward to his daughter's visits, the more so because they were necessarily brief. Leslie had spent her first two college summers doing internship work at a major advertising agency in New York City, and was able to return home only for a few days at a time.

With each visit Leslie looked more beautiful, more confident, and more happy. Just as Tom Chamberlain had hoped, college and freedom from the little town of her birth had made her blossom. She seemed to glow before his eyes, and her fiery hair, whose wildness once seemed such a detriment, now added to her luster. Her complexion was rosy, her body taller now, and delicate despite her energetic manner. She wore her clothes with a natural elegance and simplicity that was striking. She looked more entrancing in blue jeans and a sweater than other women in designer creations. Her freckled complexion, without makeup, was like a summer morning.

She cooked for him, took him for drives along the endless county roads between the cornfields, and spent her evenings playing gin rummy with him, watching one of his favorite television programs, or just talking.

Sometimes they sat in wordless intimacy as the musical calls of the spring birds echoed from the fields outside the house. At such moments Tom Chamberlain wondered how well he really knew his daughter. He realized that Leslie treated him with a daughterly protectiveness in which there was little of the vulnerable child she had once been. She was a strong woman, growing up fast, and she had been hobnobbing with some pretty sophisticated people these last two and a half years. She seemed more concerned with making her father comfortable and at ease than in confiding her own problems to him. If there were any problems, that is.

One evening he found himself gazing into her eyes, which looked positively orange in the sunset, and felt he had to say something.

"Honey," he said, "do you ever feel lonely? I mean, your mother and all . . ."

She smiled. She knew how bad he felt about her motherless life.

"Daddy," she said, "I've never been lonely for a minute. I've been lucky, right from the start. Lucky to have you." And she squeezed his hand with real tenderness.

There was a pause. Tom Chamberlain was uncomfortable in being reassured by her when he felt he should be the one doing the reassuring.

It was Leslie who broke the spell.

"What was she like?" she asked.

Her father sighed and looked at the sunset reflected in her eyes.

"She was quiet," he said, "but ambitious. Oh, I don't mean that she wanted to be rich, or wanted us to be looked up to here in town. But she set high standards for herself. She wanted to fulfill her potential as a person. And she wanted the same thing for me."

Seeing the pensive look in his eyes, Leslie asked, "Did you feel you let her down?"

He seemed surprised.

"Me? Oh, no," he smiled. "She didn't mind my being a working man. It's something else I'm talking about. She wanted us to be happy in a special way. She didn't want life to just pass us by."

He looked at Leslie. "That's why you meant so much to her," he said. "When you came along, it was like a dream come true. You were—I'm not sure how to put this—you were the last piece of the puzzle that made our love complete. It was as though we had been meant to be three, not two, right from the start. But not just any three. It had to be you, honey. Just as you were."

He leaned forward, concentrating. "I'll never forget the way she used to look at you, to talk to you. When she made you clothes, there was so much love in her fingers. When she fed you, it was as though she was nourishing her own soul. From the minute you were born, she bloomed. Just bloomed. I felt I had only known half of her before that time. You made her complete."

Then his face darkened.

"That's why it hurt so much when she got sick," he said. "She was just starting to really live. Everything about our life was a beginning. You can't imagine . . . It felt so unnatural, so unjust for her to take sick just at that time. I'll never forget how sad she was. How defeated . . ."

He got up suddenly and went to look for his photo album. Dusk had fallen quickly over the cornfields like a purple cloak. Leslie sat alone at the kitchen table, toying with her half-empty cup of coffee and hearing the echo of his words. She had never heard such passion in her father's voice as just now.

A moment later he returned with the album and turned on the lamp over the kitchen table. The light made Leslie blink.

He was flipping through the pages of the album with practiced fingers. She reflected that he must spend many hours with this old album in his spare time.

He stopped at a picture of her mother with Leslie as a toddler.

"There," he said. "That's the way she looked just before she got sick. She had you, she had me . . . She was on top of the world. You can see it in her eyes."

Leslie leaned forward to look at the photograph. She had seen it many times in the past when she had idly looked through the album. But it seemed different in the light of what her father had just said. Indeed, she could see a look of passionate feminine fulfillment in her mother's still-young face. It brought sudden tears to Leslie's eyes.

Her father did not see her emotion, for he was looking more closely at the photograph, an expression of surprised concentration on his face.

"Isn't that the damnedest thing," he said.

"What, Daddy?" she asked.

"I never realized it before," he said, "but you've grown up to look so much like her."

Leslie looked at the photo again.

"Not so much on the outside," he said. "But inside . . ."

She saw that he was right. Though physically she herself owed perhaps more to her father's side of the family than to her mother's, there was a sort of spiritual likeness to the image in the photograph. Now that Leslie had grown up, she had the same look of pride and purpose that shone so brightly in her mother's face at that brief moment of great happiness.

It made her dizzy to see her eighteen-month-old self, a mischievous toddler still unformed by life, alongside the woman who would soon be taken from her by death, but whom she would grow many years later to resemble "on the inside." And to feel the eye and the love of her father behind that camera, a young man thrilled with his little family and unaware of the disaster that was to overtake it so soon . . .

"She would have been so proud of you," Tom Chamberlain was saying. The expression on his face was desolate, consumed by memory and by loss.

Leslie looked at the photograph for another long moment. Her tears had disappeared, and in their place she felt gratitude for the gift fate had granted her in the form of her father's love.

"I'm proud of you, Dad," she said, kissing his cheek as she closed the album.

On the third day after her homecoming something unexpected happened to Leslie.

She had forgotten to bring enough blouses for the vacation, and was shopping in town. She was coming out of the old local clothing store, a bag in her hand, when a deep voice stopped her.

"Fancy meeting you here."

She looked up to see a handsome face that had once been all too familiar to her. It was Geoff Patterson. He had grown from a lanky teenager into a muscled, tall young man who looked extremely handsome in his three-piece suit as the noonday sun glistened down on him.

"Well, it's been a long time," Leslie smiled, extending a hand. "I'm surprised you remember me, Geoff."

"How could I forget?" he asked. "If you don't mind my saying so, you've grown into a beautiful young woman. What are you doing these days?"

"I'm in college," she said. "Cornell. I'm majoring in journalism and advertising. How about you?"

He shrugged. "Working for my Dad," he said. "And wondering what to do with the rest of my life."

She said nothing. She was taking him in quickly, evaluating the changes both in him and in herself since they last spoke—which seemed a lifetime ago. He was more grown up, to be sure, and far more handsome. But there was a yearning, a dissatisfaction in his eyes that clashed somehow with his prosperous look.

"Listen," he said. "I can't let you slip out of my grasp this way, after so many years. Won't you have lunch with me?" He looked at his watch. "I was just on my way to Crandall's. Why don't you join me?"

Crandall's was the only local restaurant that served real hot lunches with all the trimmings. It had long been a favorite gathering place for Ellicott businessmen as well as for the ladies of the town, who wore their nicer dresses for social lunches complete with frozen daiquiris, gossip, and status-seeking.

Leslie smiled. She had nowhere to go, and shopping had made her hungry.

"I'm not sure I'm dressed for Crandall's," she said, pointing to her jeans and blouse. Geoff looked at her with undisguised admiration.

"I'm not sure Crandall's is up to your standards," he said. "But let's give it a try. Shall we?"

"I'd love to," she said.

Over lunch they brought each other up-to-date on their lives. It was a somewhat uncomfortable moment for both, because they had barely known each other in high school, but were forced by the occasion to behave like old friends, which they were not.

Yet each was interested in the other, and in what had happened over the past several years—though for different reasons.

Geoff Patterson could not take his eyes off Leslie. She had developed from a pretty but unformed adolescent into a stunningly beautiful young woman. With her thick strawberry blond hair and sparkling eyes, she had an air of bright, indefatigable energy. Yet it was alloyed by a sort of dreamy tenderness that made her intensely attractive. She was at once girlish and ladylike, youthfully sprightly and yet deeply feminine. Geoff's heart went out to her instantly. He knew he would not forget that face, having seen it this once.

At his invitation she ordered a glass of white wine. He ordered a beer. As she told him the story of her college career he was impressed by her obvious intelligence and ambition. More yet, there was an integrity about her that colored everything she said and only increased her attractiveness.

Somehow, with her composite air of sophistication and naturalness, touching her glass of wine, she was more intriguing than any woman Geoff had ever known. She was like a rare flower blossoming before his eyes, the more exotic because she had left the small world of his hometown and he had not. Yet she came from that town, just as he did, and was therefore familiar to him, even homey.

The combination was too much for Geoff Patterson. He was in love.

He was also a little embarrassed about the disparity in their stories. Leslie was full of her new life, her plans for the future. She had already made exciting discoveries and conceived new ambitions, while he was merely following a path laid out for him by his social position in this small town where nothing really changed. She seemed like a radiant princess of the future, while he was mired in the past.

Yet he was so attracted to her that he dared to try to hang on to her.

"Listen," he said as they left the restaurant. "Will you have dinner with me? It may sound crazy, but I've missed you all these years, and I would give anything to get to know you better. How about it? Friday night? We'll go dancing, too, if you like."

His grin was infectious, but it was obvious he was very serious, perhaps more serious than he himself realized.

"Don't say no," he smiled. "Please?"

Leslie looked into his eyes.

"I didn't think you were an eligible young man," she said. "What about you and Judy?"

She was referring to Judy Betancourt, the girl Geoff had gone steady with through high school. Frankly, Leslie was surprised Geoff wasn't already married to Judy. People of their society usually married young and started families right away.

"Oh, that's ancient history," Geoff said offhandedly. "We're just friends now. Judy has her own life."

He was lying. Judy Betancourt had been waiting since before high school graduation for him to propose to her, and considered herself unofficially engaged to him. As a matter of fact, his failure to propose was a bone of contention not only between himself and Judy but between him and his parents, who had had an understanding with the Betancourts for years about the future matrimony of their children, and who were embarrassed by Geoff's delaying tactics.

Now Geoff realized in a glorious instant why he had been delaying all this time. Judy, though only twenty-one, had lost her fresh adolescent looks and was beginning to resemble her older sisters, women with rather frumpy figures, weak chins, and lackluster personalities. These faults had been invisible back in high school, when Judy's social status, family name, and confident demeanor had made her seem desirable.

Now, as he sat here, he mentally compared Judy, an ordinary small-town girl good for little but to raise a brood of children and fix up her hair for church socials, to the bewitching, complex creature sitting opposite him at the intimate table. Leslie was like a rare jewel, full of unsuspected surprises. She had all the freshness of youth, combined with an indefatigable energy that seemed to plunge bravely into the future. One look at her made poor Judy Betancourt seem like an ugly stepsister by comparison.

And there was one thing more. Geoff had known Judy's body intimately for years. She was an old shoe to him now, and a less attractive one now that she was losing the firm flesh of adolescence. Whereas Leslie, whom he had barely noticed in high school, had grown up into a young woman of great beauty. Beginning in her lean limbs and lovely face, that beauty reached its crescendo in the combination of openness and inner mystery that made her so magnetic. Enchanted by what he saw on her surface, Geoff was even more hypnotized by the thought of what he could not see.

Geoff had made up his mind.

"Well?" he asked.

She was looking at him with an odd, speculative look in her eyes.

"It's interesting to be asked out by you," she said. "It happened once before. We had an almost-date, you and I, back in high school."

He looked puzzled.

She smiled. "Don't you remember?"

He shook his head. "I'm sure I would have remembered," he said. "I can't see how I could have forgotten you. . . ."

There was a pause.

Leslie shrugged. "Never mind," she said. "That's ancient history, too."

"Well?" he asked. "How about Friday?"

"I'm going out to dinner with my father Friday night," Leslie said.

"Thursday, then," Geoff insisted. "Or tomorrow. How about tomorrow?"
She hesitated.
"All right," she said. "Tomorrow night."

The next night they had their promised date. Geoff took Leslie to dinner at the country club, which boasted the only restaurant in town with any elegance. After their meal they danced to the music of the local trio that played at the club on weekend nights.

He fell further under her spell during that evening, and asked her out again. She accepted.

He took her dancing again, and this time they stayed out later. They talked about themselves and their dreams. They walked in the moonlight. They gazed at the stars, joined by an intimacy made the more piquant by their long separation.

By the time her spring vacation was coming to an end, Geoff had made up his mind to marry Leslie Chamberlain.

He bought an engagement ring at the jewelry store in town—the jeweler was a friend and fellow Elk with his father, and had to be sworn to secrecy—and had it in his pocket when he met Leslie for their next date.

He was convinced she would accept him. Despite her sophistication, she was still a very natural and even vulnerable girl. Though her horizons might be a bit wider than his own, he knew that, as far as Ellicott was concerned, she was still worlds below him. His family was the best in town, while she had come from the other side of the tracks, the motherless child of a factory hand. How could her future as a college student compare with the chance to be his wife, to join his family, to rule over town as its most desirable and admired woman? To have his children . . .

In his mind's eye he studied her beautiful face. On their last two dates she had allowed him to kiss her. He had felt embarrassed as a schoolboy and more sexually excited than he had ever been in his life, as he held her in his arms and felt her lips part to receive him. He dared not go further. She was like a nymph of the night, too magical to reveal all her secrets at once, and soon to escape him forever unless he dared to promise her everything right now.

She filled him with a wanting bordering on desperation. She was completely new, completely unexpected, while everything else in his life had become bland and routine and predictable.

He dared now to hope that, in accepting his ring, she would also give herself to him physically. So that before she returned to school he would know the charms of her entrancing body as well as her personality.

He would convince her to quit school after this year, of course. Or they would marry immediately after her graduation. They would go on a long honeymoon, to northern Michigan or Wisconsin, or even to the Bahamas.

Then she would return as his wife to have his children. Her dreams of a career would be forgotten. Life with Geoff, the original local hero, would make her cup run over.

On Thursday night he spent dinner trying to screw up his courage to show her the ring. Something about her happy demeanor, enjoying his company but excited to get back to college, sapped his strength, and he did not dare to propose to her.

After dinner he drove her to Fishers Pond, the popular parking spot he remembered from his high school days. The moon was shining on the surface of the water like a talisman urging him to forget his fears.

"Do you know this place?" he asked.

"Sort of," she said. "I used to come here in the daytime as a girl and throw stones in the water. I knew people came here to park at night, but I never thought that was for me."

"You're here now," he said, bringing her face to his.

They kissed for what seemed a long time. Geoff felt like a boy again, with all the uncontrollable sexual ferment of adolescence as well as the old ability to dream, to idealize beautiful girls. And Leslie was the most beautiful of them all.

With a final burst of resolve he dared to show her the ring.

"Leslie," he said, "I've been doing a lot of thinking. Will you marry me?"

She looked at the ring. Something stirred in her eyes.

"Isn't this a bit sudden?" she asked.

"No," he said. "I've been thinking about you all these years. And meeting you now made up my mind for me. I love you. You're the only girl for me. Please say yes, Leslie."

She seemed lost in thought. The seriousness of the occasion shadowed her face, making her look more beautiful than ever before.

She handed the box back to him. His heart sank.

"I'll give you your answer tomorrow night," she said. "This is an important decision. I don't want to make it lightly."

Geoff spent the next day in an agony of anticipation. He was convinced Leslie was his. The very fact that she had agreed to think it over proved that she was tempted. Today she must be weighing his proposal in her mind, perhaps talking it over with her father. The father would of course take Geoff's part. What retired factory hand would not want Geoff Patterson for a son-in-law?

Morning became noon, then afternoon, with excruciating slowness. Geoff needed all his self-control to keep from calling Leslie during the day. Being kept dangling this way was literally driving him mad.

He was drinking a cocktail with his parents, and trying not to look at his watch, when the phone rang.

It was Leslie.

"I'm sorry for the inconvenience, Geoff," she said, "but some unexpected family has shown up, and I have to make dinner for them. I hate to miss dinner . . ."

"Well, that's all right," Geoff said disappointedly. "But I am going to see you tonight, aren't I?"

"Of course," she laughed. "Tell you what. I'll meet you later—you know where."

"You mean, by the pond?"

"It will be more romantic that way," she promised. "Meet me where we were last night. About nine-thirty?"

"I'm not sure I can hold out that long. What have you—I mean, can you give me a hint as to what your answer will be?"

"Nine-thirty," she replied brightly. "See you then."

"I'll be there." He hung up the phone and spent the rest of the evening in his room, waiting on tenterhooks.

At the appointed hour Geoff drove his car to the spot by the lake where he had parked with Leslie the night before. There was no one else there. Perhaps this was because it was a weeknight. Or perhaps the high school kids had found another place for their petting. He did not know.

He turned off the engine and waited.

Ten minutes later, on a romantic impulse, he got out of the car and stood gazing at the surface of the pond. The moon shone on its surface, right where it had been last night. The sight of the dark water filled him with mystery and longing.

A leaf rustled quietly behind him. He was too lost in his fantasies to hear it.

Suddenly a pair of soft hands closed over his eyes from behind.

"Guess who?" a voice whispered.

He felt a tremor deep in his loins as the hands caressed his cheeks. His sex strained madly under his pants. This was it, the moment he had been waiting for.

He turned quickly and seized her, gripping her with all his might. He kissed her, his tongue slipping deep into her mouth. His hands slid down her back to the soft globes beneath her waist, pulling her hard onto him.

"Oh, Leslie," he groaned. "You've got to say yes. Don't say no. Please . . ."

He had taken the engagement ring out of his pocket, and slipped it into her hand.

"I'm begging you," he said. "Be my wife." And again he hugged her close.

At these words he realized that the body in his arms did not seem quite as unfamiliar as he had thought. Nor was her kiss as exotic as he recalled it from last night. He pulled back to let the moonlight illuminate her face.

His breath caught in his throat.

In his arms was Judy Betancourt.

In the bright moonlight he clearly saw the look on her face. In that terrible instant it began to dawn on him what had happened. They had been in on it together . . .

"Thanks," Judy said, "But no thanks—big spender."

With a quick motion she threw the engagement ring far out over the water. Together they listened to the remote plop it made in breaking the surface.

Judy turned on her heel and walked away.

For a long time Geoff Patterson stood looking at the lake where his ring now lay, and back at the trees on shore, into which Judy had disappeared. Then he got into his car and drove to Leslie's house.

Leslie's father greeted him politely and told him Leslie had taken the six-thirty train back to Cornell.

7

Detroit, Michigan
Spring 1971

THE STREETS WENT BY PAST the rainy windshield. The wiper blades slid almost silently back and forth, a languid counterpoint to the warm rain.

The hands on the steering wheel were delicate but purposeful. A map was open on the empty passenger's seat. The eyes darted from the street signs passing one by one to the streets marked on the map.

The community was not familiar to the young woman behind the wheel. But her destination was clear in her mind. Little had been left to chance.

The registration tag on the steering column read, *Fleming, Jill,* with an Ohio address.

She stopped at a traffic light and watched a mother cross by the crosswalk with a very young boy. He paused to ask his mother a question, pulling at her hand. She urged him hurriedly toward the other side but smiled gently as she did so.

As the light turned green, a car with a man behind the wheel shot quickly into position beside her car, and paused before passing her. The man was studying her intently in that split second, noticing her young face and long hair. He gave her an ambiguous look and disappeared.

She continued on her way. She glanced at the directions she had written on a sheet of paper, and again at the map on the passenger's seat. She handled the car easily, and neither her breathing nor her face showed the effect of her uncertainty about where she was or the interview ahead of her.

She had long since learned to dominate such thoughts and to focus her mind so powerfully on the task at hand that all extraneous feelings were annihilated.

Another stoplight came. This time she saw a family in a sedan. The father, a young man, was at the wheel. There were two little boys in the back seat. The mother had an infant in her arms. The father turned to the back seat to say something to the boys; he cast a furtive glance at the attractive driver alongside him.

She did not acknowledge his look. She thought briefly of what it must be like to have a family that one loves. She had never had the experience. No human being had ever been close to her. This gave her a precious distance from people and a sort of objectivity about them, which she knew was not possessed by those who loved their families and were sometimes cruelly exploited by them.

She was alone in the world. Always had been, and perhaps always would be.

She drove on another half mile, her beautiful face being noticed by drivers, pedestrians, and one police officer in his prowl car. She left a wake of desire behind her, and she knew it. But today she was looking ahead, not behind.

She arrived at her destination five minutes ahead of schedule. The sign rose up behind the gates, CONTINENTAL PRODUCTS, INC. She told the security guard her business, and was buzzed in and told where to park her car.

When she had found a space she turned off the engine and twisted the rearview mirror to look at her face. The eyes were blue, with an iridescent, crystalline quality, dangerous to look at for too long. Her cheeks were white and creamy, though she tanned easily. The cheekbones were a trifle salient, for she kept herself very thin. The eyebrows were naturally fine, the nose straight, the lips sensual in a restrained and sometimes girlish way.

It was a face that withheld its trumps. It did not advertise its purpose. For this reason, when observed at rest, it suggested a quiet mystery. This made strangers turn their heads when she passed, and forced those who knew her to think about her more than was good for them.

She pushed an errant lock of her fine blond hair from her cheek. With a last look at her face she pushed the mirror away and got out of the car. Watched in her every step by the parking guard, she moved without hurry toward the main building.

Her interviewer was named Roger Phelan. He had been with Continental Products for twelve years, and had risen to head of personnel after four. He was not an ambitious man. He was in essence a petty functionary, and he knew it.

But he was a good judge of people. He had a sharp eye for the slackness of character, the subliminal lack of honesty that separated good employees from those who were sure to wash out. He could spot the right combination of healthy self-interest and goodwill that would make a loyal and productive worker. Perhaps it was his own lack of personal ambition that made him so lucid in seeing ambition in others. He had a frumpy young wife, two little boys aged seven and nine, and a matchbox house in a modest subdivision two miles from work. He walked to and from the office, whatever the weather. He was thirty-eight years old, tall, and wore glasses for his tired eyes.

He heard a knock at the door and looked up from his file to see a young woman enter the room. She was in her early twenties, and pretty. He registered the fact objectively. He had seen many pretty girls in this office. Some he had hired, others he had passed over. It was easy to spot those who lacked talent and intended to trade on their good looks for influence and perhaps a romance with the right boss. Roger Phelan saw through them immediately.

"Miss Fleming," he said with a tight smile, "I've had a chance to look over your file. Your credentials seem excellent to me. What got you interested in Continental Products?"

The girl gave him a brief, noncommittal look, and then smiled.

"I'm sorry—do you mind if I put on my glasses?" she asked.

He nodded. She took a pair of glasses out of her purse and put them on. As she did so she dropped the purse on the floor. She reached to pick it up, retrieving two or three items that had fallen out. When she met his eyes again her face had changed remarkably. She seemed embarrassed, innocent, and quite intelligent.

"I apologize," she said. "I can't see a foot in front of my face without them. I don't really like the way they make me look. But I had to put them on, because I couldn't see you."

He nodded, still a bit off balance from the transformation the glasses had wrought in her appearance. She was sitting with her legs crossed. A strand of her wispy hair fell across her cheek. She looked attractively honest and even a trifle messy.

"I read about Continental in the business press," she said. "My interest is middle management. I'm not the most creative person in the world, but I am—well, thorough. And I'm dependable, if I say so myself. I've heard that Continental is an open company, and that it's a fair company where women are concerned. I think I can work my way up to a management level of responsibility, and—well, I guess that's it."

She smiled diffidently. Her words had impressed Roger Phelan. Obviously she was honest. She seemed unable to dissemble. Yet she respected herself and was not without ambition. Her intelligence shone clearly in the blue eyes behind her glasses. She looked like a hard worker if not a natural leader.

"Well, let me tell you a little about Continental," he said.

He went through his usual spiel about the company, its needs, its past successes and future direction. She interrupted him every few sentences to ask a question. Always an intelligent question, and one that showed she had done her homework. As they spoke he glanced down at her dossier. Her SAT scores in high school had been 1440, her CTS 92. She was a brain.

After fifteen minutes he had made up his mind.

"Well, Miss Fleming," he said, "I think I can speak for all of us when I say that Continental is interested in you if you're interested in us. We have an opening in the marketing department—assistant marketing analyst. The salary is competitive. There will be a few formalities, a few people to meet. But I'd like to see you start tomorrow—if you're interested, that is."

Her face had lit up. "Really?" she said.

In that instant she looked like a little girl.

"Really." He smiled, standing up.

They shook hands. Her palm was sweaty. Evidently she had been more nervous than she looked during the interview.

"I'm awfully grateful," she said. "I didn't really think—that is, I wasn't sure I had much of a chance. But I won't let you down. I promise you that."

"Wonderful," Roger Phelan said. "I'll start processing your forms this afternoon then. Glad to have you with us."

She left the office, darting a bright smile over her shoulder at him as she went. He did not notice the shapely thighs stirring under her skirt or the small, firm breasts outlined by her blouse. It was her pretty face that impressed him, with its innocent openness piquantly accentuated by the glasses she had put on. Pretty girls had no effect on Roger Phelan. But that girlish enthusiasm of hers, combined with her obvious intelligence, had predisposed him in her favor. He was convinced she would make a fine employee.

He went back to his desk and sat down. He looked out the window for a moment, a wistful smile playing over his thin features.

She was back in the parking lot already. The rain was still falling, but her umbrella had kept her dry. She turned the key and let the car warm up. She looked at herself in the mirror. The glasses were off now, back in her purse.

She had come prepared for anything. But the look in the personnel director's eyes had told her right off that the glasses and the innocent, puzzled personality were what was required. She had played the role to perfection, noticing in the first few seconds his vulnerability to it.

She could have played any role she liked in that office, depending on the man behind the desk. The nubile, seductive maiden. The daughterly vixen. The cold librarian. The power-hungry man-eater. Anything. All she needed were those first few seconds to size up a man, and she could play him from there like a master.

Roger Phelan was impervious to surface female charms. She had seen that right off. He prided himself on his perception of commitment. He was experienced and cold. He could spot ambition right off and distinguish it from mere self-interest. So she had given him what he wanted. She had given him honesty.

And it had worked.

But this had been only the first step. Roger Phelan was merely the palace guard. Getting past him had been the prerequisite for her real task.

She looked at the company stockholders' magazine she had brought with her in the car. There were portrait photos of the major executives spread through the magazine. She turned the pages slowly, listening to the hum of the car's engine. She paused at the photo of a slightly overweight, red-faced man in middle age, whose broad smile camouflaged a weak chin.

Harley Schrader, read the caption. Regional Sales Manager.

She turned the pages slowly, watching the executives' faces pass before her, most lit by all-American smiles that effectively hid their private personalities. She paused again when she came to a photo of a handsome man in his late forties with a strong jaw and slightly cruel features. The text under the photo read, Roy English. Vice President in Charge of Finance.

She raised an eyebrow, noting the eyes in the photograph. They looked wise. Wiser than Roger Phelan, because Roy English operated at a much higher level. He would see a lot.

The same was true of all his peers in senior management. They were clever, ruthless men, or they would not have reached their high positions. A lot of bodies must be buried in the wake of their success.

But she did not fear them. Instead they were like mechanical bears in a shooting gallery, parading their bluster before a rifle poised to shoot them down. If their ruthlessness made them dangerous, their pride was the Achilles' heel that made them vulnerable to her.

She knew what to do. The only question was where to start.

With this thought Jill Fleming drove to her new home, a small apartment in a modest neighborhood a few miles from the company, and got a good long sleep in preparation for her first day of work.

8

EARL "BUD" OWENS SAT BEHIND the executive desk in his office at Ogilvie, Thorpe, and Owens, one of the biggest and most successful advertising agencies in Chicago.

Bud Owens was an advertising executive of the old school. His business degree was twenty years old, and he had worked his way up in advertising through the ranks. He had done layout and copy from the lowest level to the highest, and made himself an expert in demographics and market research as the times demanded it.

Bud Owens had made his way to the top slowly, without friends, without influence in high places. It had taken him twelve years to get a senior position at Ogilvie and Thorpe, and it was only after his backbreaking work on several key accounts had made the firm $15 million that he became a partner.

He was proud of his achievements, but he still had a chip on his shoulder from the hard years he had spent in the trenches. He resented the "ninety-day wonders" the colleges and universities were turning out, journalism and business majors who had never worked on a real account but considered themselves experts in all the newest theories of marketing, management, and sales. He had seen dozens of them come and go at his agency, and enjoyed firing them when they washed out. He gave them their pink slip with a little sermon about hard work being worth a lot more than fancy degrees and good intentions.

Today Bud Owens had just such a person before him—this time a job applicant. Her name was Leslie Chamberlain, and she had just graduated with honors from Cornell. Her faculty adviser, Professor James Nesbitt, was a classmate of Bud's from college and a onetime colleague in the business.

Bud Owens looked from the attractive young woman across the desk to the file before him. Then he closed the file and leaned back in his chair.

"I said I would see you personally," Mr. Owens said, "because I respect Jim Nesbitt, and I've worked with him in the past. He knows his stuff, and he knows talent. He says you're the best young mind he's seen in years. I believe what he says."

His look darkened.

"But I'm going to level with you, Miss Chamberlain," he said. "I don't like college talent. I've seen it come and go in my years here. College kids think advertising is going to be a lark. When they see how hard the work is, they move on to something easier."

Leslie said nothing. She simply looked at him with her candid, intelligent eyes.

"And another thing," he added with open hostility. "I don't have much confidence in members of your sex. Not in this business, anyway. No matter how dedicated they are, how competent, they end up in a romance that distracts them from their work. And sooner or later the romance leads to termination—by way of marriage, children, resignation, or whatever. Advertising is a field that demands one hundred percent of your time and your commitment. You don't rise to the top overnight. You have to pay your dues. It takes years. It's not a field for amateurs."

Leslie said nothing. Her expression was neutral, as though refusing to take the bait he was offering her.

"Well?" he asked irritably. "Have you heard what I've been saying?"

"Yes, sir," she said. "I have."

"What do you have to say for yourself?" he demanded.

She raised an eyebrow. "One hundred percent is one hundred percent," she said. "If that's what you require, that's what I'll give. If you're not satisfied with my work, just let me know. That's all I can promise you—the best I have."

Bud Owens was perplexed. He had been prepared to dislike this girl, even to hate her, from the minute she walked into this room with her fresh face, her beautiful body, and her classy college dossier. But her display of courage in listening to him, and in not trying to duck his justifiable mistrust, had impressed him. And there was obvious intelligence behind those complicated eyes of hers. He could not deny this.

"Well, that may not be enough," he said suspiciously.

She was still looking him straight in the eye.

"As for the question of my sex," she added, "there's not much I can say in an interview to allay your misgivings. If that's the way you feel about women, you might be better off hiring a man. I'll make my way somewhere else if I have to."

She fell silent. Frowning, he looked from her watchful eyes to the beautiful body under her crisp business suit. She was all sincerity and ambition and talent. Somehow this aggravated him no end. As an experienced judge of people Bud Owens knew she could be valuable to the firm. But he hated to go against his own prejudices. Time and hard-won success had made him set in his ways.

He looked at her for another long moment, weighing his choices. Then he got up, went to a large filing cabinet behind his desk, and removed a thick portfolio from it. He placed the portfolio on the desk before her.

"Take a look," he said.

Leslie opened the folder. She saw a collection of print advertisements for a large kitchen appliance company named Aurora Appliance Corp.

"Are you familiar with them?" Bud Owens asked.

Leslie nodded. "Of course. They've been around a long time. As far as I know, their products are well built and dependable. My father has had an Aurora refrigerator for as long as I can remember."

Bud Owens smiled, pointing to one of the ads. "Like the ad says."

Leslie looked down at the folder. The top advertisement was familiar to her. It had been used by the Aurora Appliance Corporation for at least twenty or thirty years. It showed a homespun-looking wife in her kitchen, wearing an apron. She was handing bag lunches to her children with a loving smile on her face. The whole thing had a rather dated Norman Rockwell look to it.

The slogan printed across the bottom of the ad was: AURORA APPLIANCE CORP. WHERE DEPENDABILITY IS A TRADITION.

"What do you think?" Bud Owens asked.

Leslie frowned. "It's very old-fashioned," she said. "I don't think they've changed this layout, or the slogan, since I've been alive. They're an old company."

"And it shows in their sales," Bud Owens said. "Their market share is now sixteen percent. Twenty years ago it was forty percent. They've come down in the world, to put it mildly. Do you want to know what keeps them going?"

Leslie's brow furrowed. "Customer loyalty?" she asked dubiously.

He smiled. "Not exactly, but a variation on that idea. The simple fact is that their appliances are the best you can buy. They outperform the competition two to one in longevity and in service costs. Their warranty is the best in the business. In a sense you may be right. If Grandma had an Aurora stove, it could be that Mom and Granddaughter heard her praise it. But it's more likely that they're smart shoppers who bought Aurora for the quality."

"But the company's market share has gone downhill," Leslie said.

"That's not hard to understand, is it?" he asked.

She looked at the ads. "I guess not," she said. "These ads are really antiquated. No one tries to sell products this way anymore. Look at that mother in the photograph. Mothers today have to work. They don't wear aprons and pass out bag lunches to their kids in the morning."

Bud Owens smiled and closed the folder.

"Now you know what we're up against," he said.

Leslie looked up at him. The intelligence in her eyes already bore the spark of a new challenge.

"The chairman of the board is named Barton Hatcher the Fourth," he said. "The company is privately owned by the Hatcher family. It was founded by Hatcher's great-grandfather seventy-five years ago, in the town of Aurora, Minnesota. It's stayed right there ever since. These are very old-fashioned people, dyed-in-the-wool country Republicans. They don't like change. They're very wealthy, and they haven't particularly cared that Aurora sales have been steadily going down. Not until the market share dropped below eighteen percent, that is. Now they're concerned."

"Well," Leslie said, "it should be a simple matter to design an up-to-date campaign."

He shook his head. "You don't know Barton Hatcher," he said.

Then he smiled. "But you're going to."

Leslie raised an eyebrow. "What do you mean?"

"As of this moment you are in charge of the Aurora Appliance account," Bud Owens said with ill-concealed sadism. "It's your baby."

Leslie took a deep breath. "Well," she said. "Thank you. I guess."

"You won't thank me when you know what you're dealing with," he said. "We've had Aurora for three years. In that time they have refused every new idea for advertising, promotion, or marketing that we've submitted. They've forced us to stick with the same old ads. And now they're threatening to take the account to another agency, because we're not getting the results they want. Most of our top executives have tried to deal with them, and have ended up with ulcers. Aurora is the most inflexible account we've ever had. Now it's up to you. If you succeed, it will be a great feather in your cap. If you fail . . ."

"We lose the account," Leslie said.

He nodded complacently.

She thought over her dilemma. This was a no-lose situation for Bud Owens. He obviously did not like Leslie and resented her college background and her credentials. If she worked on the account and failed, it would confirm him in his lack of confidence in her. If she succeeded, he would take the credit as the man who hired her and gave her the account.

The latter result would of course be to her advantage.

Bud Owens could follow the train of Leslie's thought by looking into her candid eyes. He knew she was intrigued by the challenge. But he also knew something she did not. Ogilvie, Thorpe, and Owens had all but given up on the Aurora account as of the last executive meeting. It was taken for granted that Barton Hatcher would soon take his business elsewhere. The top executives at Ogilvie, Thorpe were frankly delighted by the prospect of getting rid of Hatcher and his white elephant. Bud Owens was under no pressure to save the account, for it was considered a lost cause.

So Bud Owens watched with some amusement as the fresh young woman before him warmed to the challenge he had faced her with.

"All right," she said, standing up. "When do I start?"

"There's no time like the present," he said. "I'll have Arlene find you a temporary office. And," he added, pointing to the portfolio full of advertisements, "you can take that with you."

Leslie gave him a brittle smile and held out her hand. "I appreciate your hiring me, sir," she said. "I'll do my best."

"Good," he said, shaking her hand. "We'll find out whether your best is good enough."

She could feel his eyes studying her as she left the office.

Now she knew what a sacrificial lamb feels like.

9

LESLIE CLOSETED HERSELF with the Aurora Appliance account for two weeks. She ate little, and slept less, during that time. She could see that in handling an account for a hidebound traditional company opposed to new ideas, the Ogilvie, Thorpe, and Owens Agency had saddled itself with a monster.

Modern advertising could hardly help a client who did not want its help. Yet Aurora expected Ogilvie, Thorpe, and Owens to increase sales, and would change agencies if it failed. It all seemed impossible. Yet Leslie's quick mind told her there was more here than met the eye. Something crucial had not yet been tried.

After her first week on the job she had a bright idea. She called Wes Glaser, the previous Aurora account executive, and asked him to have lunch with her.

"I had an idea, and I just wanted to check it out with you," she said.

"Shoot," Wes smiled. He was a friendly man, and frankly delighted to be off the account. He seemed sympathetic.

"I think the company needs to change its name," Leslie said. " 'Aurora Appliance Corp.' sounds hopelessly dated. It's an eyesore just to put it in a print ad. If you update the name, you update the company. A lot of other companies have done it recently, including huge corporations like Exxon and Citgo. I think it would be a great idea."

Wes laughed out loud.

Leslie looked at him. "What's the matter?"

"You need to come back to earth," he said. "Old man Hatcher won't hear of a single change in the copy for his print ads, and that's twenty-five years old. If you ask him to change the name of the goddamned company, he'll get himself a new agency before you can say Jack Robinson. The company name, like the company itself, is a tradition with him and his family. No, Leslie, you've got to think smaller. Remember who you're dealing with, for God's sake. We're talking pride here."

"Foolish pride," Leslie said ruminatively.

"Anyway," Wes said, taking a sip of his coffee. "Anything else you wanted to run past me?"

In that instant, despite his amiable personality, Leslie could feel his condescension. He must think she was a brainless beginner even to have suggested such an impolitic idea. He would probably be joking about her naïveté with his male colleagues on the golf course this week.

She could also feel him noticing her body. She had worn a dress instead of a business suit today, and it showed off her figure to good advantage. She wondered if Wes, or any other account executive, could take her work seriously, since she was a woman.

For an instant she felt the frustration of her predicament. Then, as though by an inspiration, she saw an opportunity in it.

"Thanks for talking to me, Wes," she said. "I'm going to have to run. Sorry."

"Don't mention it," he smiled, watching her get up. "Anytime."

Anytime at all, he mused, noticing the way her legs moved under her dress as she walked out of the lunchroom.

No one at Ogilvie, Thorpe heard any more from Leslie about her drawing-board plans for Aurora Appliance. She kept them a dark secret.

Bud Owens and his colleagues assumed that her silence reflected her disarray. The Aurora account was an adman's nightmare, an impossibility. Bud Owens had saddled Leslie with it simply in order to take her down a peg and to throw cold water on her illusions about her talent.

Thus he was surprised to hear, a month after she had been hired, that she had invited Barton Hatcher and the Aurora advertising department to a meeting at Ogilvie, Thorpe headquarters to present a campaign proposal to them.

"What are you doing?" he asked over the office phone. "Are you going in cold? Don't you want to talk over what you have with the rest of us?"

"I'd prefer it to be a surprise, if you don't mind," she said. "After all, you dropped this thing in my lap. You might as well let me run with the ball."

"It's your funeral," Bud Owens smiled. "See you at the meeting."

And he sat back comfortably, looking forward to the funeral of Leslie Chamberlain's hopes.

The meeting took place on August 10. It was a hot day, and the air conditioning at the office was a welcome relief to the executives and their guests.

The contingent from Aurora arrived like a small army in lockstep. Barton Hatcher, a tall, impressive man with thick white hair and an imperious demeanor, entered surrounded by vice presidents and advertising executives. He greeted Bud Owens coldly, spoke a few quiet words to his associates, sat down, and pulled out a cigar, which was lit for him by one of his executives.

"May we begin?" he asked.

Leslie stood up and moved to the front of the conference room. She was wearing a light dress to suit the season. Her straight young shoulders and firm breasts stood out under the bright fabric, and her legs, tanned by recent trips to the Oak Street beach, made a lush contrast to the dress. She looked awfully young but not as vulnerable as some in the room might have expected.

"Gentlemen," she said, "welcome to our meeting. Mr. Hatcher and associates, welcome again to Ogilvie, Thorpe, and Owens. I'd like to show you our proposal for a major new ad campaign on behalf of Aurora Appliance, and a couple of special suggestions we've conceived for your company."

The Aurora executives were looking at Leslie skeptically. They were disturbed by her sex but more so by her youth. The best senior minds at Ogilvie, Thorpe had so far failed to come up with a slogan Aurora could accept. Was Ogilvie, Thorpe farming out this important account to beginners?

Without appearing to notice these hostile looks, Leslie moved to a large television screen at the front of the room. She lowered the lights and turned on a videocassette player beside the television set.

As music played in the background, an advertisement for Aurora kitchen appliances appeared on the screen. An attractive young woman, dressed in a business suit with a ruffled silk blouse, walked into a beautifully appointed kitchen, already putting down her briefcase and taking off her jacket. She turned on her stove, quickly removed a dish of food from the refrigerator, popped it into the microwave oven, turned on the coffeemaker, and set the toaster oven to preheat.

The message of the ad was clear. This was a young working woman, just home from the office, who was quickly preparing a meal. She looked bright, breezy, and more than a little sensual as she turned on appliances in her silky blouse. Close-ups of her shapely hands showed her turning knobs, starting things up, getting things moving. She radiated youthful energy and happiness, as well as an undeniable feminine attractiveness.

A voice-over announcer said, "Why work in the kitchen when the kitchen can work for you? You work hard all day, and when you come home, you want to have fun. That's where Aurora comes in."

A dissolve in the film indicated the passage of time, and the beautiful young woman was shown in her dining room having a romantic glass of wine with her handsome husband. Her dinner had been prepared in short order, thanks to her own planning and to the efficiency of her beautiful Aurora kitchen appliances. As the music played softly, the look of expectancy in her eyes left little doubt that she and her husband had romantic plans for the evening.

The camera lingered on her sensual eyes as a slogan came across the screen: AURORA LIFESTYLES. WE GET YOU OUT OF THE KITCHEN AND INTO YOUR LIFE.

The commercial faded out.

Leslie turned to an easel that had been set up alongside the television screen. She folded back the sheet covering it. Inside was a print advertisement showing the same youthful, slender, frankly sexy girl, moving through her kitchen in a business suit with ruffled blouse to meet her husband, while sparkling Aurora appliances gleamed in the background.

The same slogan, WE GET YOU OUT OF THE KITCHEN AND INTO YOUR LIFE, was the banner headline of the ad.

Leslie turned to her audience.

"The radio campaign will make the same point through dialogue between the young wife and her husband, and through music," Leslie said. "The message is clear. Today's working woman has no time to waste in the kitchen. She devotes her life to her profession and to her husband. She wants action and fulfillment, not drudgery. The kitchen is a means to an end to her. And Aurora products, known for their dependability, are the best way to keep her out of the kitchen and in her exciting life."

A hand was raised by one of the Aurora ad executives.

"What is this 'Aurora Lifestyles'?" he asked skeptically.

"That's the biggest surprise," Leslie said. "Aurora Lifestyles is not only the name of this new campaign and of the new image for Aurora products. It is the new name we are suggesting for the company itself."

There was a sharp collective intake of breath around the room. What Leslie had just suggested was pure heresy. The Ogilvie, Thorpe executives turned pale. The Aurora people cringed, expecting their leader to either die of apoplexy on the spot or fire them all within the hour. No one could believe what they were hearing.

Leslie herself was looking expectantly at Barton Hatcher, who sat impassively, the smoke from his cigar making hazy plumes in the air above his head.

The silence continued, leaden as that of a tomb, while those present tried to collect themselves. Leslie did not say a word.

At last one of the Aurora executives leaned toward Hatcher.

"Mr. Hatcher," he whispered, "I think we'd better discuss this . . ."

"Be quiet," Barton Hatcher said. The executive cringed like a puppy and fell silent, looking down at his briefcase.

The silence deepened, almost unbearable. Everyone in the room felt as though Barton Hatcher had just been slapped in the face by the pretty young girl before them. They were already preparing to protest the fact that such an inexperienced beginner could have been entrusted with such a sensitive account. They assumed she would be fired immediately after this meeting, along with whoever had been so foolish as to hire her. Anticipating the wrath of their boss, they looked forward to rising in unison to approve his summary rejection of Ogilvie, Thorpe in favor of another agency.

At last Barton Hatcher spoke. His voice was quiet but commanding.

"Gentlemen," he said, "I like it."

A shock wave went through the room. The executives could not believe their ears. They looked at each other and at Barton Hatcher. His eyes were on Leslie.

"It has style," he said. "That's something we've been sorely lacking for some time now. Yes, I like it. I like it fine."

"What about the new company name, Mr. Hatcher?" someone asked tremulously.

"Yes, sir," chimed in another. "We've always kept our name intact."

"Nonsense," Hatcher said, his voice booming suddenly. "We were never against a new name—as long as it was an improvement on the old one. If it isn't broke, don't fix it. That's my motto. Now, this young lady—what did you say your name was?"

"Chamberlain, sir. Leslie Chamberlain," Leslie said.

"Miss Chamberlain is not asking us to give anything up," Hatcher said. "Aurora is still the name. It's just a different accent now. Aurora Lifestyles instead of Aurora Appliance Corp. I think it's perfect. It's up-to-date. It has a nice ring to it. What's the matter with you fellows? Can't you recognize something good when it hits you in the face?"

Voices rang out around the table.

"Of course, Mr. Hatcher."

"You're absolutely right, Mr. Hatcher."

"That's just what I was thinking, Mr. Hatcher."

Before the echoes could die down Barton Hatcher had stood up. His assistants leaped to their feet like a group of windup toys.

"Well," he said, "I have things to do. I'll leave you fellows to iron out the details." He turned to Bud Owens. "I'm glad you people finally came up with something we could use," he said. "I was getting worried there for a while." He nodded at Leslie. "Looks like some new blood was what we needed all along," he concluded. "Good work."

He held out his hand. Bud Owens, still pale from what had just happened, shook it with a weak smile.

"Glad you feel that way, sir," he said.

"And Miss—what did you say your name was?" Hatcher boomed across the room at Leslie, who was still standing beside the easel.

"Chamberlain, sir," said Bud Owens. "Leslie Chamberlain."

"Miss Chamberlain," Hatcher said, "you've done a fine job, and I congratulate you. I want you to have dinner with me tonight before I leave for home. If that's convenient."

"Certainly, sir," Leslie said.

"Good," Hatcher concluded. "Now, if there's nothing else, gentlemen, I'll take my leave."

He swept from the room, surrounded by his lieutenants.

Bud Owens was left with his stunned staff. Leslie was standing at the front of the room, smiling quietly.

Bud moved to Leslie's side. Her expression infuriated him. She looked like the cat that had eaten the canary. But he could hardly criticize her. She had literally accomplished the impossible for his agency.

"Well, I guess you showed us something," he said. "Congratulations." The praise sounded like it hurt him.

"You said a hundred percent," Leslie smiled. "That's what I gave. I'm glad it worked out."

Bud shook his head, still incredulous. "So am I," he said. "So am I."

That evening Leslie met Barton Hatcher at an elegant French restaurant on North Clark Street. She wore an evening dress of traditional cut, with long sleeves and a somewhat low-cut bodice, enough to show off the girlish swell of her breasts without being too forward. It was a carefully chosen outfit, designed to show off her sensuality and wholesomeness in one statement. And it worked, as the admiring look in Barton Hatcher's eyes confirmed.

He had ordered champagne, and smiled as the waiter poured it. He touched his glass to Leslie's.

"Well, my dear," he said, "I guess we showed them, didn't we?"

Leslie grinned, sipping her champagne. "I guess we did at that," she said.

Barton Hatcher sat back and admired the brilliant girl whose campaign was sure to lift his company out of its doldrums and put it right back where it belonged.

Leslie Chamberlain was no stranger to him. He had met her three and a half weeks ago, when she had first outlined her plan to him in strictest confidentiality. She had come to his small Minnesota town to show him the plan personally. "I've been assigned to your account," she had said, "and I've been told you were opposed to certain kinds of changes in your company's image. I thought I'd confirm it in person before proceeding with what I have in mind."

On that first day Hatcher had been struck by Leslie's fresh, all-American beauty. She had told him about her own small-town background, and mentioned the Aurora appliances that had been part of her life in her own home and at her grandmother's house. She showed an extraordinary familiarity with the problems his company faced in the marketplace, as well as a great respect for the superiority of the Aurora product line.

Coming from this candid young woman, so sincere and down-to-earth, the bold suggestion of a new campaign and a new company name had not shocked Barton Hatcher. Instead, it had impressed him with its originality. And Leslie had impressed him with her honesty. Almost at once he had begun to think of her as a welcome change from the male executives at Ogilvie, Thorpe, whose ideas he decided had been too weak, too predictable to help his company. Rewriting history inside his own ego, he saw himself as a flexible executive who had always been open to new ideas, and those around him as the stodgy stick-in-the-muds who were trapped in old ways of thinking.

Leslie soon won him over, and they began to plan her big presentation as a sort of father-daughter conspiracy designed to impress and win over the others, the skeptics—instead of a presentation to win over Hatcher himself.

When the great day came, it was with secretive pleasure that Hatcher and Leslie pretended not to know each other. Hatcher enjoyed his pretense of loudly asking for Leslie's name to be repeated.

Tonight he was delighted not only with the exciting changes planned for his company—changes that were long overdue, he told himself—but also with the beautiful young woman who had melted his aged heart even as she convinced him of her campaign's value.

She reminded him greatly of his late wife, Claire, who had been a ravishing debutante in Minnesota when he married her fifty years ago. He had noticed this resemblance from the first day Leslie came to see him. It had predisposed him in her favor even as it filled him with nostalgic longing for the wife he had loved so dearly.

Barton Hatcher had not remarried after losing his wife. As time passed after her death, he found his mental image of her reverting from the old woman she was at the end to the pert, young small-town debutante he had courted and married so long ago. The remembered romance of their courtship made his own waning years on earth more bearable and even pleasant.

He kept a life-size portrait of the youthful Claire in the reception area at Aurora, and would not listen to any suggestion that it be replaced by something less personal. He venerated his wife's memory, for she was the only human being he had ever trusted or truly taken seriously. In the portrait she wore the mauve satin dress that had always been his favorite, the color harmonizing beautifully with her green eyes.

Meeting Leslie Chamberlain had been almost like seeing his late wife come back from the grave, smiling at him through sparkling eyes, charming him with her small-town candor and her sharp intelligence. Moreover, Leslie respected his loyalty to the land of his birth. She had come from a similar place herself. She made him feel he belonged more than ever to Aurora, Minnesota, and did not have to leave it behind to compete in the modern world.

Now he raised his glass to Leslie. "Let's be honest, my dear," he said. "Not we. *You* showed them."

Leslie smiled. She had become oddly close to Barton Hatcher during these past weeks. Almost like a daughter. He genuinely liked her, and she felt a real affection for his gruff ways and his attachment to his small town.

As she thought back over the past weeks, she wondered which of the strategies she had used had had the most effect. Was it the new company name? The slogan? Her gesture in going to Hatcher personally?

Or was it the research she had done on his private life and his marriage before meeting him? Based on that careful research she had done her hair to match that of his late wife in his favorite portrait and worn a mauve dress the day she first appeared at his office.

Who could tell?

When one gives a hundred percent, every detail can count.

10

Detroit, Michigan
July 1971

ROY ENGLISH WAS A POWERFUL executive who was used to getting his own way.

He had been with Continental Products for ten years. Before that he had been a vice president at a construction and design firm owned by his former wife's father. When Roy divorced his wife, he quit his job, not wanting it to be said that he needed his wife's father for anything.

He was a proud man and a hard worker. In the first two years with Continental he had made himself indispensable, impressing the board with dozens of creative suggestions about marketing, new products, finance, and management. The then president, Hughes Dillard, had made Roy his protégé, and when Dillard retired to take a place on the board, Roy became vice president in charge of finance and, by common consent, the most powerful man in the company.

Roy was as ruthless toward his peers as he was loyal to the company. For this reason his new bosses made him their ax man. When an executive's skills seemed to be eroding, or his personal life was interfering with his work, or he had simply "peaked" professionally and could no longer be counted on for the kind of productivity a competitive company needs, Roy English was turned loose on him.

It was Roy who examined the man's performance, spied on his personal life if necessary, made a cold and heartless report to the board and, in the end, was given the job of firing the unlucky victim. The latter was not a task Roy particularly enjoyed; nor did it displease him. He never fired a man who didn't deserve it. When he saw the look of disgrace and supplication in his victim's eyes, it gave him a little thrill of power. For he knew his own performance would never suffer like that of the men around him. He would always be on top.

Roy's friend Harley Schrader had made the move with him from the earlier company. The two had been college friends and had remained confidants and golf partners ever since. They knew each other better than either knew anybody else. Harley was not an ambitious man like Roy. He was a competent manager but without original ideas.

It was Roy who had introduced Harley to his wife, Jean, a girl who had formerly been Roy's own girlfriend—a fact Harley seemed to accept with good grace, for he had made countless affectionate jokes about it since his marriage.

Harley had been repeatedly and inexcusably unfaithful to Jean over the years, a fact Roy knew about because he kept an eye on Harley for the company just as he kept an eye on everybody else.

Both men were womanizers, but in different ways. Harley tended to like sleazy women, party girls, the camp followers who were always available to businessmen at conventions and sales meetings in far-flung cities.

Roy disapproved of the kind of woman Harley liked—the painted, loose-moraled, opportunist type without any integrity of personality.

Roy was himself a man of high moral principle. He had been brought up in a religious background, and though he had left religion behind a long time ago, he had retained a sense of honor and of responsibility that made him take his work seriously and frown on moral or sexual slackness in others.

Roy had had his share of women, naturally. As a bachelor he had sown a great many wild oats. He was very good-looking in a somewhat brutal sort of way. A collegiate swimmer, he had turned to weight lifting after college. He had a tall, wiry body, cold gray eyes, an inscrutable manner, dark hair graying slightly at the temples, and a face tanned by the sun of the golf course.

As a lover he was careful, thorough, and cruel. Women loved him for this.

He had cheated on his wife only twice—both times with women he genuinely liked. After his divorce he had gone back to playing the field. But he paid no attention to the always available secretaries and junior executive women who tried to get their hooks into him. For one thing, he knew the type so well from his long years in business that he knew what they were thinking before they themselves did. He had no interest in being a woman's meal ticket.

He dated women from other companies, women he met at parties, sometimes total strangers. He had a taste for blonds, was a "leg man," and preferred slim women—he did not like fat, for it seemed to connote moral slackness.

At the moment he had two lady friends between whom he divided his bedroom charms—an attractive restaurant hostess from downtown and a materials buyer for a tool company in the suburbs. Both were married, and both doted on him.

But he was growing tired of them both, and tired of work as well. Business was in a period of monotony, with nothing new happening. Roy had been divorced for ten years. He was forty-four, in the prime of his manhood and his brilliant business career—but unfulfilled. He reigned supreme at Continental, and would probably become president after a couple of retirements, power shifts on the board, and terminations had taken place.

But Roy English was not excited by this eventuality. His whole life felt stale. Continental Products bored him, and he bored himself.

Roy was in need of a challenge.

Thus he was quick to take notice when, suddenly, a challenge came his way.

One day when he was visiting the marketing department on his usual rounds he noticed a new girl. She was working at her desk, and not looking at him, so he asked the manager who she was.

"Jill Fleming," he was told. "Been here a month. Not bad, so far." The manager raised an eyebrow to signify that the girl was a looker but had shown no overt signs of sleeping around.

Roy said nothing. The girl's looks were not very striking from a distance. She had sandy blond hair and a creamy complexion. She was very slender and somewhat delicate looking. He could not see her eyes, for they were looking down at her desk. As he was gazing at her she suddenly looked up at him. Their eyes met, and a slight smile curled her lips. She tossed her head softly to remove a lock of hair from her cheek, and looked back down at her work.

Roy paid no more attention to her. He left the department and went back to his office.

A week later he was walking into the main building from the parking lot when he noticed an attractive young woman walking ahead of him. She was carrying a briefcase. Her hair, looking somewhat more blond now, flowed over her slim shoulders in long waves. Her legs moved quickly, for she was on her way to work, but there was a sort of languor hidden somewhere in the long thighs. Roy caught up with her at the door and opened it for her.

She acknowledged his gesture with a brief look. He recognized her as the new girl from marketing. Close up she looked extraordinarily young, almost like a schoolgirl. There was something fresh and sweet about her that made her seem almost too young to be working in such a place.

She did not speak. He walked behind her to the elevators, again noticing the slim, girlish legs and rounded hips under her skirt. He got into the elevator with her. Her fragrance was fine and natural, without a trace of perfume. He saw the outline of firm young breasts under her blouse.

After this second encounter Roy found that her image returned to his mind three or four times before at last fading. Once, late at night in his bed, he thought of her just before falling asleep. Later he felt he had dreamed about her, though he could not recall precisely how.

But he stayed away from marketing, almost deliberately.

The following Sunday was the company picnic. Roy was there as usual, playing in the softball game and exchanging greetings with his colleagues and their families.

He saw a group of young employees throwing a Frisbee back and forth on the lawn at the park. One of them, a young woman wearing shorts and a halter top, had the most delicate-looking body he had seen on a woman in a long time. Her slim wrists and ankles, soft, slender neck, her back and haunches, were all like those of a girl. She smiled gently as she played with her friends.

When they had finished she passed close by him. It was the girl from marketing, Jill Fleming. He had taken the trouble to look up her name in the company directory during the past week.

"Hello," he said.

"Hello," she replied with a pretty smile. She was polite but not familiar. She did not seem to recognize him.

After that day he thought about her a lot. The mental image of her in her shorts and halter had something almost indecently innocent about it. He still saw the lush, sandy hair dancing about her shoulders as she threw the Frisbee, saw the slender legs jump as she ran to catch it.

Among her female peers she had looked like a goddess of youth. Their made-up faces, their tarnished personalities, their thick thighs and sagging cheeks made them look like lady wrestlers compared to this delicate feminine sprite.

On the Monday after the picnic Roy found an excuse to go down to marketing. He talked to the manager about some insignificant ongoing business, and took pains to get a look at Jill. She was hard at work at her desk, concentrating on something before her, and did not look up. Her hair fell forward over her shoulders. Something about her studious posture, the limpid blue eyes with their long lashes downcast as she studied her work, made her seem heartbreakingly innocent.

Listening to the manager's prattle, and watching the new girl out of the corner of his eye while the mental image of her in her shorts and halter danced in his memory, Roy made his decision.

He waited for her to get off work that evening and stopped her in the corridor.

"I don't believe we've met," he said. "I'm Roy English. Ned pointed you out to me the other day when I visited your department. Welcome to the company."

She smiled. "Thanks. It's nice to meet you." Her voice was naturally sweet and mellifluous.

Roy assumed the girl had heard of him and was afraid of him. Everybody in the company was afraid of Roy English. Yet it required an effort for him to muster his usual arrogance as he asked her out.

"How about dinner sometime?" he asked. "I'd like to get to know you better."

He had delivered his usual line quickly, almost as though to get it over with before his courage flagged. He was watching her face as she listened to him. Her eyes met his.

"No, thanks," she said. "Thanks very much for the offer, though. Nice to meet you."

And she turned on a sprightly heel and walked away from him.

Roy was reeling, not so much from her refusal as from the sound of her voice and the look in her eyes. The voice combined firmness with a girlish lilt that harmonized powerfully with his fantasies about her. The eyes had looked at him with a limpid candor that was full of self-respect. She was young, innocent—and yet strong. She had refused him like a good girl who has been brought up by her mother to know how to turn off predatory males. And now she was walking into the elevator, her slim ankles and calves peeking at him from beneath the hem of her skirt.

As the doors shut she turned around, and her big blue eyes glanced at him one last time, without interest.

She was gone.

Roy was impressed. More than impressed.

A week later he asked her out again. It was the day after an executive meeting in which he had had to give a report on a high-level reorganization being done under his direction. His picture was in the company newsletter that day. He knew that the Fleming girl, like everyone else, would be particularly aware of him this week.

He contrived to meet her in the parking lot at day's end.

"Hello again," he said.

"Hello." Her expression was as cool as before. There was a sort of kindness in her eyes, but for others, for herself—not for Roy English. This impression of a private life full of smiles, affection, laughter perhaps, from which he was shut out, created a strange longing in Roy.

"I hope I didn't give the wrong impression the other day," he said. "I just wanted to . . ."

"Not at all," she said. "I just don't believe in mixing business with pleasure."

"Then let's make it a business dinner," he said. "I won't ask a thing about you. We'll talk only about marketing." He smiled, trying to be charming.

"I'm very flattered," she said. "But no thanks."

And again she turned on her heel and walked away, her pretty young body smiling its beautiful shape at him even as her strong will shut him out of her life.

Roy went home and drank two stiff martinis. He had not been rebuffed this way in fifteen years. His power and position forced even those women who did not like him to treat him with consideration.

The liquor made his loins thrill with something between sexual desire and hatred. He called one of his two lady friends, met her at a motel, and had brutal, unsatisfying sex with her.

"You're a tiger tonight," she said, pleased by his passion. "What's gotten into you?"

He could not answer her with the truth. It was too humiliating.

He thought his situation over for another ten days. He wondered if the stale plateau he had reached in his life was what had made him vulnerable to this gentle young girl, or whether it was something about the forthright look in her eyes that had seduced him. Or perhaps it was simply her refusal. Perhaps the challenge put in his path had gotten his blood up.

But whenever he fought for lucidity about her, all he saw was her tender young body, the small breasts, the rounded hips, the beautiful slim thighs disappearing under her skirts to the magic place where her sex waited—a sex that was not for him.

Roy English was out of his element. No woman had meant anything to him since his courtship with his wife, many years ago. Women were nothing but fleshly arenas for the satisfaction of his lust.

But his heart went out to young Jill Fleming. And with his heart went a kind of desire he could neither understand nor control. Against his better judgment, he went to her department to ask her out for a third time.

The other employees cringed as usual when they saw him coming. But Jill greeted him warmly.

"Good to see you," she said. "What can we do for you?"

"I'd like to speak to you for a moment."

He took her outside into the corridor.

"I've been thinking about what you said," he said. "I understand your position. And I think you're right. But I have to know: was it me you were saying no to, or your boss?"

She looked thoughtful.

"I think I explained myself pretty well last week," she said.

"Listen," he insisted. "Just have dinner with me. I'm not asking you to compromise yourself in any way. I like you. I admire you. Can't we just have dinner?"

She gave him a long, unreadable look.

"Thanks," she said, "but no thanks."

Her eyes sparkled like jewels in the fluorescent light of the corridor. Her cheeks seemed more pale than before. Something inside him began to collapse. It was all he could do to stop himself from kissing her right there.

"Please," he said. The word hurt him more than anything he had said to a woman in years. He was aghast at his own weakness.

She glanced at the office door. "I have to go," she said. "I'm very flattered, really. Good-bye."

And she moved away along the wall, sideways so as to escape his imprisoning presence. Her body seemed smaller than ever as she slipped away. She looked like a cheerleader, a Girl Scout, someone's daughter, a feminine Peter Pan, full of an ingenue sexuality as fresh as spring.

And as he watched her recede from him Roy felt as though something precious, something he could not live without, was slipping away with her.

After that third rebuff, Roy did not ask her out again. His pride would not let him. But he did not stop thinking about her. In his mind he went over the few words she had spoken to him, the look in her eyes, the sight of her body.

Something about her took Roy back to his adolescence, when his own inexperience had caused him to fantasize about girls in an almost straitlaced way. In those days he had let his thoughts linger on their skirts, their soft purses, the way their bare arms disappeared inside the sleeves of their blouses. He had been almost more entranced by this clean outer surface of girls than he was by his more pungent fantasies of the private parts of their bodies.

That had been an era when youthful wonder had still been more powerful than knowledge, when adult experience had not yet tarnished the mystery of the opposite sex. It was a time when he could take a girl on a date, look at her shining face in the front seat of his car, and savor the fact that he was going to kiss her—or try to, anyway—but had not yet done so. There was a sort of halo around girls in those days, a halo afforded by his own youth and his romantic exultation. It made girls magical. In later years, when women offered their bodies to him so routinely, usually expecting some sort of advantage in return, that magic of femininity was lost.

Roy lay awake at night thinking about Jill and pondering the youthful wanting she had kindled in him. He found he could no longer sleep well, and he was losing his appetite. Just like a boy in love, he told himself with bitter amusement.

He was not about to give in to these feelings. So he grabbed on to their opposite. He tried to focus his mind on her in a purely corporate way. He arranged to have a chat with Jill's supervisor, without revealing that he was personally interested in her. He managed to give the impression that he was checking up on Roger Phelan, whose work as personnel director he wanted to monitor.

The supervisor, a man named Ned Joiner, reported with some pride that Jill was a model employee. Not only was she pulling her weight but she had personally solved a thorny marketing problem concerning the company's western outlets.

"I told her about it but didn't assign it to her," Ned said. "Two weeks later she told me she had been working on it in her spare time, and showed me her solution, all mapped out on paper, with figures to match. I showed it to the boys upstairs, and they implemented it immediately." He smiled. "It did all of us a lot of good, and particularly my department," he said. "Oh, Jill is a crackerjack. No doubt about that."

Roy was interested in this news but not particularly pleased. Secretly he had hoped that the Fleming girl might have had some problems in her work, or at least not been so brilliant. He had hoped he could intimidate her in some subtle way, based on the competition within her department and her lack of job security within it. He did not think of this expedient as sexual harassment but rather as a last-ditch way to get her to soften toward him.

But now he realized that in her work she was just as firm and confident as in her personal life. She had a justifiable pride in her work to go along with her personal backbone. In other words, she had all the armor necessary to make her invulnerable to Roy's authority as well as his blandishments.

Roy thought this whole business over for another two weeks. They were two of the most difficult weeks of his life. He had never wanted anything as badly as he wanted this girl. And there was no doubt in his mind that she did not want him, and perhaps even hated him.

Roy was fighting against a private demon more terrible than any he had ever faced before.

And this time the heart of stone that had seen him so far through life was leaving him in the lurch.

11

LESLIE WAS A MINOR CELEBRITY at Ogilvie, Thorpe, and Owens.

Since her triumphant and shocking success with the Aurora Lifestyles account she had assumed the role of a prodigy in her new job.

Her success had brought her a new title—assistant accounts manager—a sizable raise in salary, and a combination of respect, envy, and admiration from other ad executives, who were as impressed by her creativity and initiative as they were annoyed by her youth and beauty.

Leslie was surprised and disappointed to find that her hard work did not seem to entitle her to friendly relationships with her executive peers. Most of the older executives were rather cold to her, giving her a wide berth as she passed through the corridors of Ogilvie, Thorpe. A few treated her with ill-concealed condescension, and only one or two bothered to congratulate her on her success.

Some of the younger males asked her out on dates. She accepted a few but was shocked when their protestations of admiration for her executive ability led to fumbling wrestling matches of the crudest kind. After that she made a firm rule to avoid social contact with her peers. She was less hurt than amused by what had happened, but she began concealing an increasing loneliness under her bright, friendly demeanor.

She was working ten- and twelve-hour days now. Every time she scored a success she was given a new account to handle. The company, impressed by her talent, was trying to get the most out of her—and perhaps challenging her to prove she was not a flash in the pan.

Leslie was tempted to refuse some of the extra load, and to reproach Bud Owens to his face for allowing her to be so overworked. But in an obscure way she sensed that Bud was waiting for just such a complaint from her. So she deliberately kept her silence, worked harder than ever, and brought success after success to the company. Despite the coolness of the top executives, her reputation as the most brilliant mind at Ogilvie, Thorpe grew with each passing month.

She managed to go home to see her father only once in those first months of work, and then only for a brief weekend. She enjoyed the relaxation and her closeness with her dad, but already she had the uncomfortable feeling that her past was slipping away from her and becoming less relevant somehow. The town of her birth seemed cut off from her by time and by her own development as a person. The family friends and neighbors she saw seemed provincial to her and somehow wrapped up in themselves, unconnected to the real world of fast action and challenge in which she now lived.

Her father saw this, and graciously made room for a new relationship in which Leslie could be more and more independent while still counting on his support. He knew she was now a far more cosmopolitan person than he. Her achievements were already far beyond anything he had done or even dreamed of doing in his life. But she still needed his love and understanding, and he provided both unstintingly. They made the most of their brief time together, and she continued to telephone him from Chicago at least once a week, letting him fill her ears with his routine news and thinking about the past he represented, with all its joys and sorrows.

Leslie was on a cutting edge between her past and her future, driven forward by her own hard work toward new challenges and new accomplishments. It was an uncomfortable position, because her identity was being left behind. Were it not for the fact that her energy and intellect made her a match for so many of the daunting new tasks before her, she would have felt dangerously confused. Thus, for the time being at least, Leslie became a sort of workaholic, a person whose sense of her own self was inseparable from her performance in the workplace.

On a brisk Monday in early October Leslie was rushing through a schedule even more grueling than her normal one. She had had a morning meeting with a new client and a lunch with Bud Owens and two other higher-ups in which she had to report on her current work. She was on her way to an afternoon meeting with one of the agency's most important clients, a meeting in which she had to present a complex and expensive campaign. She could already see that she would be working tonight on the layouts she had failed to finish last night. It was going to be a busy week.

She was hurrying into the elevator, her mind on the afternoon facing her, when she bumped headlong into someone coming out. She felt a sharp rap against her forehead. At the same instant her briefcase crashed to the floor and burst open, scattering memos, layouts, and plan sheets all over the floor.

"I'm terribly sorry," she heard a deep male voice say. "Are you hurt?"

She touched her forehead. There didn't seem to be any damage, though the place she had hit was tender.

The man was already bending down to help her gather her tumbled papers. She did not notice the elevator door closing as she hurriedly scooped up the materials.

"It was my fault," he was saying. "I wasn't looking where I was going."

"No, it was my fault," Leslie corrected him firmly. "I was late coming back from lunch, and I was rushing. I'm really sorry . . ."

They stood up at the same instant, their hands filled with her papers and layouts. The man was tall, dressed in a dark suit. The first thing Leslie noticed about him was his eyes. They were dark and very handsome. They were looking at her with concern and a slightly knowing glint of amusement.

The second thing she noticed about him was the red spot on his chin where she had crashed into him. There was no blood, thank heaven, but he looked as though he had taken a solid blow from her forehead.

Around these central details, the probing eyes and the red mark on the chin, the rest of his face crystallized. The brows were dark and a bit roguish, the cheeks tanned, the jaw square, the neck very strong-looking. He was tall, at least six feet two, and powerfully built. He was smiling down at her with undisguised admiration.

"It can't be your fault," he said. "You look like a lady who knows her way around here. And I'm a stranger."

Leslie said nothing. His eyes were caressing her in a peculiarly knowing way. She found this presumptuous, and did not return his smile.

"Well, now that that's established," he said, "this might be a good time to ask directions. I'm trying to find my way to Austin Bailey's office. So far without much luck."

"Austin Bailey?" Leslie asked. "He's in the financial section. Top floor, at the end of the hall. I'm not sure of the number . . ."

"That's close enough," the stranger said. "Thank you. And sorry about the accident."

"Yes . . . Sorry . . ." Leslie was pushing the elevator button, eager to make her departure and get back to work.

There was a pause while they waited for the elevator. Leslie hurriedly stuffed the papers back in her briefcase. She could feel the stranger appraising her with the same glimmer of amusement in his eyes. It made her uncomfortable, and she waited impatiently for the elevator to arrive.

"Sure you're not hurt?" he asked, apparently enjoying their forced interval together.

"I'm fine," Leslie insisted. "And you?"

"None the worse for wear," he said.

At last the elevator arrived, and five or six hurried people got out. Leslie and the stranger got in. Leslie reached to push the button for her floor, but his hand got there before hers, and their fingers touched for an instant.

"Which is yours?" he asked, pushing 6 for himself.

"Four," she said, still feeling a tingle in her fingers from the touch of his hand.

The elevator seemed to crawl upward forever. When it reached the fourth floor Leslie gave the stranger a neutral look and hurried out to her office.

Her afternoon meeting was more difficult than she had expected. The client, a manufacturer of convenience foods, flatly refused the campaign Leslie had worked so hard to put together over the past month, though he had approved the concept enthusiastically at their initial meetings. His objections seemed to make little sense, and it was hard for Leslie to understand what changes he wanted in the approach.

The meeting broke up after a lot of inconclusive wrangling. Leslie was very tired by now, and looking forward to going home for a hot bath before she got to work on her unfinished layouts. She wished the weekend were here. The work week seemed to loom before her like a mine field, hostile and unpredictable.

Overloaded with her briefcase and two large portfolios, she took the elevator downstairs. When the doors opened on the ground floor she began to hurry out, then bumped into someone. Her brows rose in embarrassment when she saw who it was.

"We meet again."

The stranger she had bumped into after lunch was standing in the corridor, smiling at her. To her horror she saw a small bandage on his chin, at the spot where her forehead had struck him earlier.

"Oh—yes," she said, trying to muster the same expression of cool indifference she had given him before. But as she looked at his handsome face she suddenly realized it had not been entirely out of her thoughts all afternoon. Underneath her hard work the stranger's dark eyes had been scrutinizing her, questioning her, all day.

"Still feeling all right?" he asked. "Not dizzy from that bump on the head?"

She shook her head.

"Since fate seems determined to make us bump into each other," he said, "we should at least know who we're bumping into. My name is Tony Dorrance. I'm a regional sales manager with Price-Davis, in Atlanta. Nice to meet you."

"Leslie Chamberlain." she said. "I work here. I'm an account executive."

"Pleased to meet you, Leslie," he said.

There was a moment's silence as the other Ogilvie, Thorpe workers streamed past them on their way to the parking lot. Leslie felt oddly immobilized by the stranger's steady gaze. The black eyes were hypnotic. There was laughter in them, but also something else, something atrociously knowing and exploratory. She wanted to get away from him, but something kept her riveted to the spot. A wave of fatigue came over her. She could not even break the gaze that joined them.

"Well, since I've practically injured you twice now," he said, "I think we should stop fighting this thing, don't you? Fate wants us to meet; let's do it on an amicable footing, then. Will you have dinner with me?"

Leslie tried again to muster a cool smile that would not come.

"I can't," she said. "I'm busy. But thanks for asking."

"I'm busy myself," he said. "I have a dinner with two of your associates upstairs. But it would be a simple matter for me to tell them I injured myself coming out of the elevator"—he gestured to the bandage—"and that I can't make it. Who are you dining with?"

She looked at the bandage with a sort of fascination. So she had done that to him. She had actually hurt him. The badge of his wound seemed strangely attractive against his tanned face.

"I—have to work," she said, not lying as cleverly as she would have wished. "I just can't make it."

"Can't you start work an hour later?" he asked. "I won't take up much of your time."

"It can't wait," she said firmly. "But thanks anyway."

"Let me at least walk you to your car," he insisted.

Not knowing how to get rid of him, she turned to go to the parking lot. He walked beside her in silence, each of his firm strides matching two of her own. She felt small and somewhat ridiculous, hurrying along while he easily kept pace with her.

By the time they reached her car his silence had become a challenge. She did not know how to get rid of him.

"Volkswagen," he remarked, looking at the little car. "A nice car. Probably gives you a lot of mileage for the money."

She had taken out her keys but turned to face him before putting the key in the lock.

"Look," she said, "Mr.—what did you say your name was?"

"Dorrance," he said. "But call me Tony."

"Look, Mr. Dorrance, you're very nice to accompany me to my car, and I'm awfully sorry that I cut your chin. But if it's all right with you, I have places to go. Can't we just say good-bye?"

Her tone was firm, but there was a note of nervous supplication in it that he did not fail to notice.

"I can't just let you go," he said. "Not looking the way you do. You're so pretty . . ."

Leslie was taken aback by this. The look in his eyes had changed. It was candid and tender, and there was something sad about it.

"Don't walk out of my life as quickly as you walked in," he said. "You've made my day by bumping into me. If you disappear like Cinderella, I won't know what to do with myself."

A pause.

"I don't get up here very often," he said. "I'm only here this time because the regular fellow is ill. I'm just doing the boss a favor. I might not get back for months."

He looked stricken.

"Don't condemn me to go home alone and think about you every night for the next three months without at least remembering your smile," he said.

Another pause.

"Just dinner?" he pleaded. "One hour? I can live on that hour for a long time, Leslie."

She looked at him. The sound of her first name on his lips was so caressing that his use of it did not seem presumptuous.

"Please?" he asked her.

She sighed, giving in. "All right," she said. "But it's for one hour. No more. I really do have things to do."

"Of course you do," he smiled, steering her toward his own car.

He took her to an intimate restaurant in Lincoln Park where the leisurely service hardly promised an end to the meal within an hour.

But somehow Leslie did not want it to end. For something happened at that dinner that had never happened to her before.

Tony Dorrance talked easily about himself. He came from an impoverished background much like Leslie's, but he had turned out very differently. Where Leslie was controlled and cautious, Tony was joyful and almost reckless in his confidence. This quality showed itself in his every word and gesture. He had left his past behind him, worked his way through college, and held a variety of jobs before becoming a high-level executive at Price-Davis, one of the best known communications firms in the country. He told her he was being groomed for a vice presidency in marketing, but he was turned off by the idea of being tied to a desk. In his present work he traveled all over the world, and loved it.

"I'm not cut out for board meetings and corporate politics," he said. "I'd rather just do the job and live my own life as I choose."

Leslie nodded. "I know what you mean," she said.

He listened with a peculiar intentness, watching her closely as she told him briefly about her hard work in college, her interview with Bud Owens, and the Aurora Lifestyles coup that had led to her present, highly responsible job.

"It's a fascinating story," Tony Dorrance said. "You've had some hard knocks, emotionally as well as financially. But I can tell you've risen above it all. You're a real doer." He smiled good-naturedly. "I don't know whether I feel quite adequate in the company of a person of your seriousness."

"Oh, not at all," Leslie said. She suspected that Tony Dorrance was an intensely serious person underneath his devil-may-care exterior.

"I can see that you respect yourself," he said. "You don't let people push you into things you don't want."

She said nothing. She knew this was true.

"And you're patient, deep inside," he went on. "You're not going to settle for second-best for yourself. You're waiting for the right thing to come along."

This speech sounded odd to Leslie. She wondered whether he was flattering her inconsequentially.

"But in the meantime, you're a little lonely," he said. "You choose your friends carefully. So carefully, I'll bet, that you don't have many."

She said nothing. He had hit the mark. Her one failure in her working life had been social. Not only did she have little in the way of a romantic life, she did not even have any close friends. Work had occupied all her time and energy.

She deflected the question. "What about you?"

"Oh, I have lots of friends," he said. "Hundreds. I'm a great collector of friends. But not a single close one. That's par for the course with a guy like me. The more acquaintances you collect, the more alone you are."

There was a long silence. Leslie twirled the wineglass in her hand. She could feel his eyes on her. She could think of nothing to say.

It was Tony who broke the spell.

"You are extraordinarily beautiful," he said.

She blushed. "That's quite a compliment," she said. "After a day at the office like today, I feel like something the cat dragged in."

"I don't mean that," he said. "Not so much your face, though it's a beautiful one. Or your body—though that's very special, too. It's the look in your eyes. The way you respect yourself. That's so rare. I saw it right away, when you came out of the elevator."

He laughed. "In that split second before you clipped me on the jaw," he added.

Leslie was silent. She was reflecting that Tony Dorrance was without a doubt the handsomest man she had ever met. And it was not only his tanned, strong face or his powerful body that made him handsome. It was a sort of controlled wildness in him, combined with a deep inner confidence she herself had never possessed. He had no fear of life. This made him—why deny it?—very attractive, very sexy.

At that moment Leslie felt something begin to weaken inside her. She wanted to get out of here and away from him as quickly as possible.

At the same time she wanted this evening never to end.

"Look at the time," he said. "I've kept you over the limit. Does that mean our coach is going to turn into a pumpkin?"

"It means I've got to go," Leslie said with a smile. "Thank you for dinner—and for the conversation."

In silence he took her to his car and drove her to back to the parking lot at Ogilvie, Thorpe. He helped her out and stood with her in the darkness while she took out her keys.

"I have to go back home this evening," he said. "I won't be back this way for a long time—officially, anyway. But next Thursday I have to fly to Denver for a conference." He reached out and took her hand, as though to shake it. But he held it tenderly in his own. "I could get back here Friday night on my way home. What would you think of that?"

She looked up at him, confusion in her eyes. He smiled, touched her chin, and tipped her head to his before she could stop him.

His kiss broke down a barrier inside her whose existence she had not realized. She had never been kissed like this before. It literally reduced her to jelly, sapping her will, muddling her mind and sending shock waves through her senses. Her hands found their way to his shoulders, then his neck, with a will of their own. Her body was sending its own sensual messages to him, leaving her mind far behind.

The arms pulling her quickly to him were full of passion and yet controlled. It was that control, harnessing hot desire, that excited her more than anything else. He seemed to know his own body and its needs far better than Leslie had ever known herself.

Their kiss ended lingeringly. The taste of him on her lips was like a potion. Her hands were still around his neck.

"May I pick you up right here?" he asked. "Then I'll feel as though the week away had never happened. As though I had never been away from you at all. All right?"

Limp in his arms, Leslie nodded, unable to hide the gleam of anticipation in her eyes.

"Five o'clock?" he asked. "Right after work?"

She shook her head. "Six o'clock," she smiled, touching his bandaged chin. "I work long hours."

"Six, then." He held the door open for her. She got in, turned on the engine, and opened the window. "I'll miss you, Leslie."

He leaned down to kiss her again. She felt his hand on her cheek as their kiss deepened. His tongue was inside her mouth, holding her with a powerful intimacy. Her fingers trembled on the steering wheel.

She pulled the car out. He stood back, a shadowy figure in the shadows, silhouetted by the parking lot lights. She could not see his face. Only the tall outline of his body, and a hint of his smile.

As she rolled up the window, she knew she was going to go to bed with him next Friday night.

She also knew, only too well, that this would be her first time.

12

ROY ENGLISH WAS in a state of grief.

He had endured six weeks without seeing Jill Fleming.

In those six weeks he had felt his fantasies about her deepen into something that felt dangerously like love. He was sleeping poorly, lying awake nights thinking about Jill. He had lost his appetite and was losing weight. He felt consumed by his obsession with her.

And he knew she wanted no part of him. With each passing day this knowledge hurt a little bit more, like the twisting of a private screw in his gut.

In his solitude he had been through every stage of a rejected lover's torment. He had written Jill notes, intending to send them by office mail. He had torn up the notes when he saw the pathetic tone of supplication in them.

He had thought of a thousand ways to approach her. He had thought of sending her flowers, candy, letters, presents. He had rejected all these plans as showing too much weakness on his part. But he had not been able to shake off the terrible yearning behind them.

He had picked up the phone a hundred times to call Jill, and hung it up again. Twice he had actually dialed her number and heard her voice say "Hello?" on the other end of the line. He had hung up in despair, almost certain she knew who was calling.

In his consternation he had thought of using his power within the company to force her to be nice to him. In a few words he could easily explain that her coldness toward him could cost her her job.

But sexual harassment was beneath Roy; it was one of the sleazy male behaviors that he had the most contempt for. He had always believed a man should have enough balls to do his seducing on his own.

He had finally settled into the pattern of the jilted male. He went about his daily business sadly, bereft of energy. He looked at his haunted eyes in the mirror every morning and tried to forget his pain. He had stopped seeing his two regular girlfriends. He felt sexually frozen. He was going through the motions of life, waiting to feel better. And he was avoiding not only the marketing department but most of the populated corridors of Continental, because he could not bear the thought of seeing young Jill Fleming and being reminded of his despair.

But it was she who came to him.

He was at his desk, talking to a regional manager on the phone and doodling on his pad, when he saw her enter his outer office. She caught his eye and smiled. He told the manager to hold the line, and leaned over in his chair to see through the door better.

Jill was handing something to his executive secretary. She turned to leave. As she did so she saw Roy through the open door and gave him a little wave.

Roy's hand shook as he spoke into the telephone.

"Lonny, let me get back to you in five minutes," he said.

He hung up the phone and stuck his head through the door into the outer office.

"What was that all about?" he asked his secretary.

"I beg your pardon, sir?" she asked.

"The girl who was just here," he said. "What did she want?"

"Girl?" The secretary looked perplexed.

Roy felt his temperature rise. He was about to repeat his question.

"Oh, that girl," the secretary said. "She was just giving me a piece of our mail that was misrouted."

"Oh," Roy said.

He went back into his office and closed the door. He assumed, correctly, that his secretary would interpret his curiosity about the visitor as a sign of his usual finickiness about every detail of the office. It was in character for Roy to inquire about a stranger entering the office.

Behind his desk Roy was on tenterhooks. He was assailed by schoolboyish feelings that Jill had at least accepted him to the extent of recognizing his existence. She had smiled. She had even waved!

Perhaps her appearance here was a sign, he mused. Perhaps he was being given one last chance.

He had to take that chance.

He arranged to cross her path in the company lunchroom the next day and asked if he could sit down at the same table.

She smiled.

"Of course," she said.

He dared to strike up a conversation. He asked about her work in her department. She chatted amiably about marketing, about her boss.

Roy told her he had heard about her plan for the western markets. She thanked him politely for his interest. She was gratified and proud that her plan had been accepted.

Roy began to talk about himself. He talked about his role in the company, his history there, the company he had been with before. Jill asked a polite question or two, and this encouraged him. He told her about his ex-wife, their childlessness. He tried rather fumblingly to let her read between the lines that he was not a married executive looking to play around, but rather, an unattached, lonely man who genuinely admired her.

At the end of their lunch he said, "Thanks for letting me join you. I've enjoyed myself."

She was sitting with her coffee cup in her hand, looking at him through those inscrutable blue eyes of hers, neither unfriendly nor encouraging.

"Do you still feel the same way you did before about going out with me?" he asked.

Her smile faded.

"You're a very nice man," she said. "I'm sorry if I seemed rude before. I didn't mean to hurt your feelings."

"Does that mean you'll go out with me?" Roy asked.

She shook her head in an amused way.

"No," she said. "But I've enjoyed talking to you."

She got up and left briskly.

Left alone, Roy burned with loneliness. Yet he felt he was in a somewhat better position than before.

He clung to the tiny advantage she had given him. He saw her again at lunchtime. Sometimes she was with friends, and he could not join her. He looked at her female companions with haggard sexual interest, as though they bore a trace of her attractiveness from their mere proximity to her. Then he turned away, thinking only of Jill.

At other times she was alone, and he came and sat down with her.

He learned little about her during these lunches, but he told more and more about himself. He told her about his youth, about his early ideals, about the bitterness and loneliness the business world had enforced on him. He tried to impress her with his sensitivity but wondered whether he was only displaying a self-pity that was turning her off.

She listened attentively, even sympathetically. But she never let down that invisible barrier between them. Once she mentioned casually that she was not entirely comfortable in her neighborhood. She had seen tough-looking people on the street there, she said, and she was considering moving. Roy told her about other neighborhoods that would be more suited to her. She listened with interest, but said she was too busy with work to think about moving just now.

With the question of her neighborhood in mind, Roy dared to follow her home one night in his car. He watched her drive into the neighborhood, which was not in fact as safe as it might be. He saw her park on the street before her apartment building, which had no parking lot. He watched her let herself in through the front door. He sat longingly in his car, seeing her light go on upstairs, and her silhouette pass across the closed shade.

Rubbing his eyes in confusion, he thought of her taking her clothes off up there, taking a shower, sitting in her pajamas or robe, perhaps even sleeping nude. He felt his breath come short in the silence of his car. Then, humiliated, he went home.

He tried to stay away, but he couldn't. Sometimes on the very day when he had had an amicable lunch with her, he found himself following her home and sitting in his car like a forlorn lover outside her apartment building. He thought he was losing his grip on reality. His renewed relationship with her had spoiled his attempt to live without her, made him more obsessed with her than ever.

This could not go on much longer, he told himself. He could not stand it.

Then something happened.

On a rainy Monday night Roy followed Jill home for what seemed the hundredth time.

As usual she found a parking space less than a block from her building. She got out of her car and moved along the sidewalk with her briefcase.

Then all at once a man appeared from nowhere and started talking to her. Something told Roy right away that the man was not a friend. She seemed to be backing away from him. Roy got quietly out of his car. At that instant he heard Jill cry out.

"Help!"

In the next few seconds Roy ran to her side. He saw the stranger backing Jill up against the fence with a menacing posture. He had hold of her purse, and was about to strike her.

"Let her go," Roy said, grasping the man by the shoulder.

The man turned with sudden violence. Roy tried to grab hold of him, but the man produced a weapon of some kind—Roy never saw it—and struck Roy hard across the cheekbone. Roy crumpled to the sidewalk, dazed.

Jill was bending over him.

"Are you all right?" she asked.

Roy was looking at her.

"Did he take your purse?" he asked.

"No," she said. "He ran away. Come with me."

She took him inside her apartment and sat him down on her couch. There was blood running down his cheek, which had swelled already from the hard blow he had taken.

"Let me get some warm water," she said.

She hurried away, throwing off her raincoat as she went. He saw the dress she was wearing, a pale knit that hugged her delicate body tightly. Her hair flowed over her shoulders as she moved.

While she was gone he looked at her apartment. It was small but tastefully decorated. The couch was overstuffed, there was a rocking chair, a stereo with records of madrigals, motets, and Renaissance music. There were books on the shelves, including novels, and some technical books about marketing. There were cloth wall hangings instead of pictures. The whole place had a homey and private air.

By the time Jill returned with a bowl of water and a washcloth the ache in Roy's cheek was getting worse, but the flow of blood was already lessening.

"Here," she said quietly, beginning to wash off the blood. He looked at her helplessly, more disarmed by her touch than by the blow he had suffered.

"I told you this neighborhood is getting dangerous," she said. "I should have moved out a long time ago. Now I will."

Roy said nothing. He was smiling despite himself at her incredible beauty.

"Say," she said suddenly. "What were you doing here, anyway?"

He looked at her for a long moment.

"I followed you," he said.

She furrowed her brow. She seemed on the verge of anger.

"It wasn't the first time," Roy said in a helpless tone. "I've followed you before. Ever since we started having lunch together. Since you wouldn't see me, I—felt I had to be close to you in some way. Even that way."

There was a long, painful pause. She was looking at him with an expression somewhere between pity and reproach.

He shrugged. A charming smile came over his hard features.

"I'm crazy about you," he said. "I couldn't help myself."

Now she looked at him, studying his bruised cheek, his handsome face, and the sheepish expression on it.

She smiled.

"I give up," she said.

And she bent forward to kiss him.

13

*I*RONICALLY, JORDAN LAZARUS'S PROBLEMS began when he first discovered something great.

In the five years following his multimillion-dollar victory over Rebecca Jarman and her husband, Jordan had become a conglomerator in his own right. He had acquired some twenty companies scattered around the United States and Canada, most of them midsized manufacturing firms that produced consumer items for homes or offices. Jordan was modest in his acquisitions but aggressive in his development of each company he took over. As a result the conglomerate, which he named Lazarus International, Inc., became a public company with sales of over half a billion dollars, and Jordan's personal fortune grew by millions each year.

Jordan had long since solved the problem of his own financial survival and that of his family. He was well on his way to becoming a major player in the corporate world. His approach to his career was conservative. He avoided risk and innovation, preferring to choose solid building blocks for his empire and to form them into a solid structure that would continue to grow in the future.

He made one small exception to this rule. In early 1967 he acquired, on a whim, a former animal feed company in Ohio, which had now become a small producer of livestock medicines. Over the following four years Jordan managed to build this tumble-down little company into a growing veterinary pharmaceutical firm with a foothold on decent profits and a fine future.

This was thanks to one man. His name was Leo Kaminsky. He was a sloppy, unkempt young biochemical engineer who had flunked out of his doctoral program in pharmacology and gone to work for Baxter Feeds—that was the name of the company—four years earlier, after being fired from a major chemical supply firm.

During his initial visits to the company Jordan had heard crazy stories about Leo's mad-scientist working methods and his wild inventions. He had visited Leo in his laboratory—a chaotic place filled with animal cages, test tubes, and vials of sinister-looking substances—and even gone to his home, an apartment that smelled worse than the laboratory and was a lot messier.

Leo had been kicked out of his Ph.D. program because of his utter inability to follow an assignment to the desired end. He always went on a tangent, following his own instinct. When the end result was worthless he seemed unfazed. He was also unconcerned when given failing grades on his research projects and finally flunking out of the program altogether.

Leo was a skinny, bespectacled boy from the Bronx who had won every science fair he had ever entered, scored 800 on his math SATs, never had a friend in school, never known anything outside science. He loved animals and devoted himself to them. But he did not understand people. Most of his contacts with them were disastrous.

The president of Baxter Feeds had taken Leo on as a favor to Leo's parents, who were old friends of his. He paid Leo a small salary and expected nothing of him.

Then, almost by accident, Leo developed a vaccine in his laboratory against one of the most destructive livestock diseases. Leo was an expert on the immune system of hoofed animals and was working on dozens of projects, none of which had come any closer to completion in the last two years. Now, suddenly, he had a success.

It was at this point that Jordan Lazarus acquired Baxter Feeds and changed the company name to Veterinary Pharmaceuticals, Inc. It became a small but growing subsidiary of Lazarus International, Inc.

Jordan kept Leo on with a raise in salary and found a way to ingratiate himself with him. Since Leo's peculiarity was his inability to follow a project to its end, Jordan encouraged him to do just that—go off on one tangent after another, away from common procedures in pharmacology and toward the unknown.

The two men became friends. Jordan got Leo to clean up, eat right, and do some mild exercise. The men went running together. Jordan was the dream boss for Leo. He let him go his own way. He had dinner with him at regular intervals to discuss where Leo's work was leading. Jordan had to educate himself in the arcana of pharmacology to understand what Leo was talking about, but he managed to keep track.

Jordan Lazarus had acquired an eccentric new employee about whom he had a sixth sense. As for Leo Kaminsky, he had acquired the first real friend of his life.

One day in early May, two years after Jordan had acquired Leo's company, the event Jordan had been awaiting happened. Leo came up with something important.

"I've managed to create a preventive medication for heart trouble in livestock," Leo told Jordan. "I don't suppose you know it, but hardening of the arteries is one of the major killers of beef. So are stroke and heart failure."

Leo showed Jordan the technical specifications of his new drug. It was a new chemical combination of certain amines and inorganic salts that had a radical effect on the absorption of cholesterol in the blood. With the proper modifications it could not only prevent heart disease but actually act as a treatment for congestive heart failure in livestock.

Jordan encouraged Leo to keep working on the project. The results were more than encouraging. The experiments Leo performed in his laboratory had stunning results. The animals receiving the new drug were 90 percent less likely to develop heart disease than the control groups, and in many animals the drug could actually arrest heart trouble that was already advanced.

A month later Jordan asked Leo, "Do you think there is an application to humans here?"

Leo looked at him dazedly. He had never thought of that angle.

"Well, I don't know," he mused. "The metabolism is so different. Human serum cholesterol chemistry, and the specifics of the anion exchange resin . . . with inorganic salts, the absorption quotients . . ."

Leo was off in his own world again. Jordan could not begin to follow the drift of his ruminations. But he told Leo how much confidence he had in his ideas, and gave him an unlimited budget for his experiments.

Within six months after Jordan's initial suggestion Leo informed Jordan that his experimental drug, if applied properly to suit human metabolism, could well prevent hypertension, hardening of the arteries, stroke, and heart failure. He gave Jordan the good news in a mixture of incomprehensible technical jargon and dreamy, fractured language, but Jordan got the message.

"Leo, I'm very proud of you," Jordan said. "I want you to keep working on this with all your strength. From now on you'll have carte blanche—all the money and facilities you need. But I want you to promise me something. This project must be a secret between you and me. No one else must know where it is leading."

Warming to the challenge of a great quest for the sake of his only friend, Leo went to work with a fervor he had never possessed before.

And Jordan Lazarus kept up with him every step of the way. He visited Leo's laboratory at least once a week, sometimes rolling up his sleeves to help Leo with the actual laboratory work. He diverted more than $2 million from other companies and investments and poured it into Leo's project.

And he mentally counted the incalculable millions, even billions of dollars that would accrue to the company that patented a drug capable of preventing heart disease in humans.

By the end of the first year of full-time work on the project, the results were exciting indeed. Leo had done amazingly subtle comparisons of the blood chemistry of humans and livestock and was well on the way to synthesizing a special formula of his drug that might achieve equal or even superior results with human beings.

Jordan pulled out all the stops. He overextended himself financially in procuring research facilities for Leo. He worked long hours studying the legal and procedural ramifications of an experimental program involving human subjects. There was a lot of work ahead, and it would have to be as strictly controlled legally as it was experimentally. But before long, with luck, Jordan and Leo would be able to apply for a patent on the most revolutionary cardiac medication to be developed since digitalis.

But before Jordan could pursue this exciting final stage of his project, trouble came from an unexpected direction.

It was now four years since Jordan first met Leo Kaminsky, and nearly two since Leo had begun work on his top-secret project. On a frigid Thursday in early November Jordan received a visit from two representatives of Considine Industries, one of the largest corporations in America and an international conglomerate with subsidiaries in forty countries. One of the emissaries was an attorney, the other a high-level executive. Both were middle-aged and prosperous-looking.

"We understand your R and D people are working on something very exciting," the executive told Jordan.

Jordan looked at them cautiously.

"How did you find out about this?" he asked.

"Word gets around," the executive said. "Anyway, Mr. Considine takes a personal interest in research that affects heart patients, because he himself suffers from heart disease. A mild form, of course," he added carefully.

"Well," Jordan said, "we're working on many things. But we're only testing on animals. We have a long way to go before we produce something for humans."

As he spoke he was making a mental note to triple the security around Leo's entire operation.

"We have a proposition for you, and we think you're going to like it," said the lawyer. "Considine Industries would like to offer you the full range of its resources to speed up the development of this product. In return Considine would like to jointly patent the product with you, at such time as application for a patent is possible."

Jordan looked at the two men. He took care to seem impressed, even a bit in awe of the great Considine corporation.

"That's an interesting offer," he said. "Why don't you put it in writing and let my legal department look at it?"

"Delighted." The visitors took their leave with shaking of hands and smiles all around.

A week later Jordan's legal specialists received the detailed offer. As Jordan had suspected, it had a catch. The patent for any eventual product developed by Leo would be owned exclusively by Considine Industries. Lazarus International would get neither the credit for the invention nor the almost incalculable financial benefit of its long-term sales potential. A small royalty for "considerations" would be Jordan's only recompense for developing the product from scratch.

Jordan had his lawyers send a routine refusal to the conglomerate. At the same time he instituted massive security measures on Leo Kaminsky's entire operation. No one would be allowed anywhere near Leo or his work without top security clearance administered by a special staff.

Jordan assumed that was the end of the matter. He stopped worrying about Considine Industries, and turned his attention back to Leo and his experiments.

Within a week of his refusal, Jordan Lazarus became aware that Considine Industries was not so easily put off.

On Monday he received cables from his plastics company in Alberta, his appliance firm in Scranton, and his retailing chain in Florida that the banks that had handled their loans were all threatening to foreclose.

On Tuesday he learned that his shipping firm in New Jersey was being radically underpriced by a competitor, as were his precision parts manufacturers in Virginia and his electronics firm in New Mexico.

On Thursday he learned that several of his manufacturing plants in the West were threatened by union troubles.

Within one short week, most of the key businesses Jordan Lazarus owned were under the heaviest financial pressure they had ever experienced. And, as a consultation with his attorneys confirmed, the pressure in every case was coming from banks or other entities directly or indirectly owned by Considine Industries.

Jordan had a long talk with his attorneys. They advised him to make a deal with Considine on terms more acceptable to Jordan. This was a bad time to enter a financial dogfight with a powerful conglomerate. The recent oil crisis had adversely affected smaller companies throughout the country, and Jordan's fledgling business empire was overextended enough as it was, given the millions he had poured into Leo Kaminsky's experiments.

But Jordan decided to stick by his guns.

"Let them do their worst," he said. "I don't intimidate that easily."

It was as though Victor Considine himself had heard Jordan's challenging words. Within the next week the pressure increased, in a new and much more threatening way.

Movement on Lazarus International stock on Wall Street suddenly became hectic. The price fluctuated wildly for a few days, then shot up to an inappropriate $51.82 per share and stayed there.

Three days later a cash tender offer for Lazarus stock in the amount of $75 per share was published in a full-page advertisement in *The Wall Street Journal.* Considine Industries or its subsidiaries had managed to accumulate 32 percent of Lazarus International stock, and were angling to acquire a 51 percent majority.

"What's going on?" Jordan asked his chief stock specialist.

"We're in deep trouble," the analyst said. "They're going to take us over."

"How can they get away with it?" Jordan asked.

"Well, under the current laws they can make a tender offer to your stockholders at whatever price they like. Unless you have the financial resources to fight them off, you're stuck. They acquire a majority of the stock, and they own your company. Your management will be reporting to them."

And our inventions will belong to them as well, Jordan mused.

"Isn't there some way we can hold them off?" Jordan asked.

"You can seek help from a friendly conglomerate to fight off Considine," the analyst said. "A white knight, as they're beginning to be called nowadays. But then you'll have the white knight sitting on your board of directors—and I don't think you want that."

"What else?" Jordan asked.

"Well, there are various strategies you can employ to make it financially unfavorable for the raider to take you over." The analyst described numerous legal and quasi-legal ploys that would in a few short years have nicknames like "scorched earth," "poison pill," "minefield," and "booby trap." These were increasingly popular methods of deterring takeovers, but they were all financial in nature. And Jordan could see already that Victor Considine's interest in Lazarus International was personal.

"I think we can forget all that," Jordan said. "What's left?"

"You can try to convince your stockholders not to sell. That will be a tall order, when you consider that Considine is offering seventy-five dollars a share for stock that is only worth fifty at the most. The price is too good to resist. Nevertheless, you can delay your stockholders' meeting as long as possible and try to come up with some sort of incentive in the meantime, some good reason for them to hold on to their stock."

Jordan was concentrating hard.

"What sort of incentive?" he asked.

The analyst shrugged.

"Well," he said, "you can try to perfect that drug and bring it to market before the stockholders' meeting in March. Or at least convince your stockholders that the drug is nearing a marketable form, and that it is in their own interest to hang on to their stock instead of selling."

At this Jordan sat up straight. Yes, that was the solution. Since Leo Kaminsky had started this whole problem, perhaps Leo could bring it to a successful conclusion.

Jordan had a long meeting with Leo that night. Without cluttering Leo's ivory tower mind with money problems, he told him his entire corporation might soon be taken over by strangers if Leo could not create a patentable formula in a very short time.

When Leo understood that a takeover would mean he would be working for strangers, and would lose Jordan as a friend and intimate coworker, he promised to redouble his efforts. But in order to convince the Food and Drug Administration to allow Lazarus International to begin testing Leo's drug on humans, it would be necessary to have FDA approval of the experiments, therefore FDA approval of the formula itself.

There would not be time. Jordan could feel it in his bones. He also saw that Considine was counting on this very fact. Since Lazarus International was not yet ready to patent its experimental product, the perfect way to get control of the product was to acquire Lazarus International entirely. That was just what Considine was doing.

After twenty-four hours spent in deep thought, Jordan called his attorneys and financial specialists together.

"We're going the route you suggested yesterday," he said. "I want the stockholders' meeting put off from January to March. During that interval I'll try to come up with something that will convince our stockholders to stick with us. Meanwhile, I want you to institute litigation against Considine with the SEC to have the takeover declared illegal. It won't work, but it may gain us more time."

Jordan dismissed the financial specialists, and all the attorneys but one, a man approximately his own age named Dan McLaughlin, the only attorney Jordan trusted completely, and the man he had put in charge of the Considine problem from the outset.

"Dan," Jordan said, "what can you tell me about Victor Considine?"

Dan opened his briefcase and found a manila folder.

"He's a widower," he said. "His wife died ten years ago—of heart disease, as a matter of fact. She was the heiress to a manufacturing fortune. Considine had used her money as well as his own to start his empire. He's a shark of the highest order. Anybody who stood in his way, he put out of business. He's been sued a hundred times over for unethical practices, but he has good lawyers and deep pockets. He plays rough. In the last ten years, thanks to the tax laws, he's become an aggressive conglomerator. He takes over smaller companies and then, as often as not, resells them. His corporate assets are in the billions. Give him another ten years and he may be as big as Chrysler."

"Tell me about the personal side."

"He lives with his daughter. She's his only child. He plays golf, of course. He vacations two weeks a year on a small island off North Carolina. He plays poker two nights a week. Other than that he's a recluse. He has almost no social life. He has no live-in servants. The house is cleaned when he's out. He sees only his daughter. She cooks his meals."

Jordan nodded, interested.

"Tell me about the daughter."

"She's a college graduate. Swarthmore and Harvard. She had a few discipline problems in school—hushed up, of course—but high grades. She's very intelligent. The story is that she had a fiancé after college, and the father broke up the romance. He's very possessive. After his wife died he became more so. He hardly lets the daughter out of his sight."

He pushed pictures of father and daughter across the conference room table to Jordan. Victor Considine was a florid, overweight man with a moon face and cruel little eyes. Even in the photograph he looked dangerous. His flushed complexion also suggested heart disease.

"What's his own prognosis?" Jordan asked.

"Not very good," the lawyer said. "He suffers from chronic heart failure and hardening of the arteries. He's only fifty-nine. I doubt that he'll live another ten years—unless something is done to reverse the deterioration of the blood vessels. He's an ideal candidate for stroke or massive coronary."

Jordan nodded. He could see why Victor Considine wanted control of Leo's formula as soon as possible, and would stop at nothing to get it.

Jordan turned to the photograph of the daughter, Barbara. She was not pretty. She had thick, dark brows, a pale complexion, and a melancholy look. But she had large and very beautiful eyes, which seemed marooned in the middle of her plain face. Barbara looked about twenty-seven or twenty-eight.

"Well?" asked the lawyer. "What do we do?"

"We play for time," Jordan said. "And we look for a new angle."

As he said these words he glanced significantly at the photo of young Barbara Considine.

14

Detroit, Michigan

ROY ENGLISH WAS BESOTTED.

Since his first night with Jill Fleming, he had not stopped seeing her. And when he was not with her, he thought about her obsessively. Just as she ruled his body and his desire when she was with him, she ruled his fantasies when they were apart.

He saw her at least four times a week, sometimes more. He took her to dinner, and then to his spacious condominium. He had helped her pick out a new apartment for herself in a much better part of the city, but he never spent much time there, for he did not want to compromise her with her landlady or neighbors.

He would pick her up there. She would open the door and invite him in for a drink. She was always dressed in a manner that surprised him. Clean pastel skirts, fresh blouses, often a light sweater that accentuated her girlish look. Sometimes a dark low-cut evening dress that made her look sexy in an oddly innocent way. Sometimes, for their weekend outings, jeans and sandals, or white shorts and a halter, the outfit that had so charmed him at the company picnic last June.

She had an uncanny way of knowing which outfit would inflame him the most. Though her attire might look routine and even innocent to an outsider, it grabbed Roy like a magnet from the instant he saw her. It was as though she had a direct link to fantasies of which he was unaware, fantasies that sprang irresistibly into life at her image.

He would take her in his arms before even hanging up his coat, before she could get him a drink. Her body seemed to melt pliantly into his own. Already he was hard against her, and breathless with desire, so that she had to tell him to "simmer down" while she served him a drink.

All the way through dinner he struggled with the wanting that made it difficult for him to concentrate on what she was saying. He barely noticed his surroundings or what he ate. He watched Jill's hands, her eyes, her hair as she talked, and he thought about the soft young body under those clothes, the body that would be his when they got home.

And, near the end of dinner, she would look at him with a shy smile and say, "A little bird is telling me your mind is on something else."

He would hurry her home, fumble for his keys, get her inside the door of his place, and bury his face against her breast.

He would strip her quickly, falling to his knees to nuzzle the sweet sex between her legs as soon as he had helped her off with her skirt. Her fingers were in his hair, gently caressing. The center of her undulated almost imperceptibly against his face.

When she was naked he picked her up to take her to the bedroom. Her lightness amazed him. She was like a child, a sprite possessed of the sensual gifts and interests of a mature woman.

She enjoyed watching his own hard body emerge from his clothes, and sometimes amused herself by taking off his garments slowly and touching his naked flesh as it appeared.

Her hands were shy as they took hold of him, caressed him, played with him. Delicate hands, but sure in their instinct for what would make him hotter. A finger ran slowly between his buttocks, cradling the balls for an instant before sliding to the tip of the throbbing penis. Her tongue darted across his nipple, her knees squeezed at his ribs, her breasts stirred against his lips as she kissed his forehead.

Soon she was straddling him like a marvelous naked little rider, and he was inside her, thrusting deeper and deeper, watching her back arch and her eyes close. Her hands were pressed to his chest, fingers trembling against his pectorals, when the last wave began to come.

"Oh," she sighed, her face turned up so that her hair danced down her back. "Oh . . ."

And all at once, irresistible, his seed erupted into her. It seemed to ignite her somehow, for she tensed, a catlike purr sounded in her throat, and he felt the rhythmic grip of her secret sinews around his sex, squeezing gently to welcome the warm white stream of his passion.

The varieties of her seductiveness astonished Roy. She seemed to sense the invisible drift of his fantasies, the specific tonality of his desire each time they met, and she adjusted herself to it inventively, so that he was forced to surrender a new part of himself as they made love.

Once when he came to take her out for lunch and saw her wearing a pastel miniskirt, he picked her up in his arms like a child, feeling the coolness of her thighs against his bare arms, and smelling the springlike freshness of her hair. She shifted herself slightly so he could feel her panties under his hand, and murmured, "Let's go you-know-where first." And, beside himself with desire, he took her to his apartment. She let him take the skirt and blouse off, let him watch her slender body show itself to him as the clothes came off. She saw how excited she was making him, and lingered over the moment, the now-familiar look of amused sympathy in her eyes.

Once he came into his bedroom only minutes after they had gotten home, and found her crouched on the bed on her haunches like a cat, wearing only her bra, her hands extended in front of her, the slender legs curled beneath her, the beautiful globes of her buttocks pointed coyly behind her. The sight of her this way seemed to strike a chord inside him, as though that precise image had been in his mind all along.

And it always ended with him inside her, pumping away in delighted abandon as her smooth young sex caressed him, teased him with its undulations to new and hotter heights of passion until the slender legs curled around him, he pulled her harder onto the long shaft, and the hot spasm of his passion carried them both away.

Yet somehow, in these slippery extremities of pleasure, she always kept her mystery. Often she looked like an innocent child stripped cruelly, even indecently, of her coverings. The sweet little loins, the flat, girlish tummy, the slender legs, even the shapely feet and toes, all seemed terribly vulnerable, and thus incredibly naked, as he feasted his eyes on her.

*   *   *

She had a small pink mark just beneath her navel, only an inch from the sweet triangle between her legs.

"What's this?" he asked the first time he noticed it, touching the spot.

"That?" she smiled. "Just a birthmark."

He looked at it more closely. Nestled in the creamy expanse of her naked skin, it had the look of a tiny fruit, like an apple or a berry. It was very delicate, even beautiful in its way.

"Don't you like it?" she asked.

"Of course I like it," he replied.

He was not speaking to reassure her. The mark had something lovely, something provocative about it. Placed as it was so near to the warm center of her, it stood out on her naked skin like a sort of symbol representing the forbidden fruit that waited so nearby. There was something endearing about this little imperfection that made his heart go out to her.

Slowly he bent to kiss the little mark. When his lips touched it he felt the fragrance of her sex, so close to his lips. He ran a finger around her navel and touched the mark with his fingertip.

He was hard again, his penis straining and throbbing as the mark peeked up at him from her pelvis.

"It's pretty," he said. "It's . . ."

She was smiling up at him.

"Kiss me, silly," she said.

And he did.

A few moments later he had spread her legs and was inside her again. This time he knew the little mark was pressed to his own skin, moistened by him as he worked atop her. This thought was in his mind as orgasm came so quickly he could not control it.

After that day she would often lie before him in the afterglow of their passion, and his eye would stray to the little mark. His hand, drawn mysteriously, would touch it; he would feel the moisture of lovemaking on her skin. Desire would thrill almost painfully inside him as he touched this occult insignia of her charm. And he would bend down to kiss it, his tongue already frantic to taste more of her.

The more intimate he became with her, the less he felt he understood her. This entranced him, for he had always understood other women only too well. It was as though she hid on her own surface, like a sexual will-o'-the-wisp, while that very surface sent invisible tendrils into his own depths, literally turning him inside out. The experience created a kind of rapture that left Roy weak and obsessed.

Once he saw her picture in the company newsletter, after the success of something she had conceived for her department, and he realized from the picture that she looked like any other girl in her early twenties. This surprised him, because in his own imagination she had long since assumed the figure of a mystical nymph, unique and incomparable, putting all others to shame.

Similarly, he noticed to his surprise one day, as he saw her standing beside another girl from her department, that she was actually rather tall, five feet six or seven. Again he was astonished, for in his mind it had always been her tininess, the delicate smallness of her body, that had entranced him.

He renounced understanding this contradiction between the Jill he loved and the normal, physical girl she was to an outsider. The creature who owned his heart came from outside the world, and was meant for him only and for his desire.

He had read somewhere that in physical possession one possesses, ironically, nothing. Never was this more true than with Jill. The more he had of her, the more he wanted her. His desire fed itself on its own satisfaction, grew more delightful and uncontrollable with every passing week, and finally drove him to a state of permanent intoxication, a sort of living trance.

It was because of this mystery of Jill, this privacy she retained even at their hottest moments together, that Roy soon conceived the idea of marrying her.

By a curious contradiction, however, it was because of her mystery that Roy also hesitated to ask her to marry him. In withholding nothing of herself, Jill withheld everything. He felt he did not really know her. He was afraid there would be a rude awakening if he proposed to her.

But he could not live without her. Nor could he risk letting her wander the world unattached, for the idea of another man touching her drove him almost mad with jealousy. She was his girl, his child, his woman. He could never share her with anyone else.

The very thought that she might have had a sexual past before meeting him—reasonable enough, to be sure—filled him with a pain so exquisite that he forced the thought from his mind every time it occurred to him. He dared not confront this simple reality, for it was like a poison inimical to his love and even to his sanity.

Roy struggled with himself for several weeks before getting up his courage. Then he bought a costly diamond engagement ring, presented it to Jill at her own apartment, and asked her to marry him.

He was hurt, but not entirely surprised, when she told him she needed time. "It's an important decision," she said. "It wouldn't be fair to you, or to me, if I made it hastily."

Though wounded that she had not accepted him right off, Roy was filled with pride at this latest evidence of her self-respect.

She saw that her refusal had hurt him, and a little gleam entered her eyes. "Let's go you-know-where," she whispered.

And a half hour later, holding her naked body in his arms, Roy was grateful for what he had of her, and told himself he could be patient in waiting for the rest.

At around this time Roy noticed that Jill had begun to suggest he was selling himself short within the company.

He had been in a position to go after the presidency five years ago but had opted to wait, for fear that too sudden a move might predispose certain board members against him. He had wanted the company to feel sure of his indispensability before making a move.

But Jill pointed out, rightly enough, that he was stalled in the position of enforcer and troubleshooter, while other men, less able men, were making the key decisions and taking home higher salaries. Roy was far superior to these men in vision and talent but lagged behind them in ambition. It was time for him to redress the balance.

Roy had to admit she was right. He realized that in the last few years his life had been stalled in more ways than one. His wife was just a memory, he was childless, he was tired of his women, and somehow his ambition had fallen into the same funk.

But now everything was different. He had met Jill. He was on the point of marrying her. He felt like a new man, capable of actions as exciting as the new emotions he had been feeling since Jill entered his life.

He decided to act on her suggestion. As fall gave way to a frigid Detroit winter he began to send out signals that at the next board meeting he wanted the presidency to be reevaluated. Bob Perkins, the current president, was dead weight, and everybody knew it. The second in line, Baird Galloway, was a stick figure. Roy was the real power broker inside the company.

The ripples began to be felt. Bob Perkins was sending out feelers to other companies, because he could feel his power slipping away as Roy made his move. As for Baird Galloway, he did his best to garner allies on the board, but he knew that he had never been as crucial to the company as Roy. The result of a head-to-head fight for power was a foregone conclusion. So Baird too began to test his contacts at other companies.

Roy watched this progress with detached interest. He was only mildly stimulated by the idea of assuming control of the company—not anywhere near as excited as he was by the prospect of marrying Jill, bringing her under his own roof for good, sequestering her from the evils of the world of men, and enjoying her charms for the rest of his life.

So distracted was Roy by his passion that it never occurred to him, not even once, that the two things—Jill's "thinking over" his proposal and her suggestion that he become president—were connected.

At the right time and under the influence of the right woman, even a man as cunning as Roy English can fail to see what is staring him in the face.

15

VICTOR CONSIDINE WAS HAVING BREAKFAST in his Fifth Avenue duplex.

Considine was a portly man, despite his many golf outings, for he liked to eat a lot.

His daughter put a platter of fried eggs, bacon, hashed brown potatoes, and toast in front of him. His medication was in a tiny china bowl beside his orange juice.

"The doctor says you shouldn't be eating so many eggs," his daughter said. "It isn't good for you."

"Nonsense," he said contemptuously. "Eggs and bacon is the healthiest food there is. My mother ate eggs and bacon every day of her life, and she's ninety-five now."

He glanced at his daughter. "Serve yourself," he said with an edge in his voice.

She brought a plate of eggs and bacon to the table for herself. She ate it without appetite. He was busy reading *The Wall Street Journal* and paid no attention to her. But after he had finished he looked sharply at her plate. It was almost empty.

"That's a good girl," he said.

Victor Considine believed in three square meals a day. For himself, for his wife when she was alive, and for his daughter.

With the ability to compartmentalize thinking that is so common to powerful men, Considine saw no connection between his meat-and-potatoes lifestyle, inherited from his ancestors, and his heart problems. He saw heart trouble as a mere piece of bad luck, or at most as a congenital defect. He ate his rich, fatty foods and drank his daily martinis and beer without compunction. These were his rightful pleasures. It was unthinkable to him that they could be inimical to his health. When his doctors said otherwise, he reflected sagely that doctors knew nothing. He, Victor Considine, could buy and sell them and their opinions with his hard-earned millions.

He paid no attention to his daughter as she cleaned up the dishes. There was no cook in the duplex. The daughter prepared all her father's meals herself.

Barbara was a slightly plump young woman of twenty-eight, not portly like her father, but not as thin as she would have liked to be. Her dark hair was expensively done, but somehow it always looked dull and inelegant. She had a clear complexion, but she had inherited her father's round cheeks and her mother's weak chin, and the combination was not a good one.

However, she had large and extremely beautiful eyes, which shone with intelligence and vulnerability, giving her plain but honest face an air of feminine distinction. When one looked at her straight on and caught the beam of those luminous eyes, she was very attractive.

"Did you take your medication?" she asked listlessly.

"Yes, I took my medication," her father chimed with brutal sarcasm. "Can't a man have a moment's peace?" He did not like to be reminded of his health problems. Deep inside he was terrified of heart attacks, for he had seen his father drop dead of one when he, Victor, was only eleven years old. The memory of his father's stricken face losing all its color, the hectic arrival of the ambulance, the anguished waiting with his mother for the bad news had stayed with him all his life.

"Did you buy a dress for the party?" he asked, changing the subject.

He was referring to a dinner he was giving for some business leaders at the Union Club that evening. He always expected Barbara to act as hostess on such occasions.

"Yes, I got it."

"Where did you buy it?"

"St. Laurent's."

"How much did you pay?"

"Seven hundred dollars," she said, her timid voice betraying a small note of rebellion.

"You got robbed," he announced. "Or I should say, *I* got robbed. You women have no idea of the value of money. Go on, then, get it and show me. Put it on. Hurry! I haven't got all day."

She hurried to her bedroom and put on the dress. When she returned he looked at her critically.

"Not so bad," he said. "Not bad at all. Since they're going to hold me up like a bunch of pirates, I might as well get value for money. Are you going to have your hair done?"

She nodded. "This morning."

"Good." He was looking away already. His interest was on the newspaper. Barbara had not moved.

"Doesn't it remind you of something?" she asked.

He looked up blankly. "No. Should it?"

"Mother's dress," she smiled. "The one she wore for your thirtieth anniversary. It had sleeves just like this, and the color was almost the same."

He smiled, a reverent smile for his late wife. Then he frowned, looking at his daughter.

"Ah, but she knew how to carry off a dress like that," he said.

Then he looked away. "You can go now."

She went and took off the dress. Her eyes had filled with tears at his remark but were dry now. She came back to clear up after him. He kissed her on his way out the door. She left the dishes in the sink. The servants would arrive as soon as he was gone. Victor Considine could not bear the sight of a servant in his house. He hated having them underfoot when he was home. He demanded absolute privacy. For thirty years he had allowed servants in the house only after he had left for work.

After her father was gone Barbara went into the bathroom. She took off her clothes. She turned on the shower. While the water warmed she looked at herself in the mirror. Then she knelt down before the toilet and vomited up the breakfast she had eaten twenty minutes before. The spasms hurt her stomach and her throat, but when she had flushed the toilet she felt much better.

An hour and a half later she was at the hairdresser. While her hair was washed and permed she read two reports on new Considine subsidiaries. Then she went to Considine headquarters on Sixth Avenue and put in a long afternoon at the office.

Barbara Considine was her father's chief executive assistant, his "eyes and ears," as he liked to call her. She had no official title and was paid a pittance for her work, receiving only a tiny allowance by her father for her personal needs. But she enjoyed his complete trust. He never decided anything important without speaking to her first. The irony of their relationship was that he depended on her utterly while never granting her his respect.

Barbara was intelligent and thorough, and she had genuine business vision. More than once she had seen opportunities in marketplaces her father's best experts had overlooked. And when she targeted a company or a new arena of competition, she was ruthless in her methods of attack. In this she was her father's daughter. She had inherited his cunning and his zest for power, but her vision was wider, subtler than his own.

Had she been anyone but who she was, Barbara would probably have become president of a major company. But such was her dependence on her father that she languished as his assistant, doing yeoman work and giving brilliant advice for which she was never thanked.

Considine liked to call Barbara "the son I never had." This was a left-handed compliment, referring to her intelligence and competence, but also a brutal insult, for it referred to her unmarried status, her unattractiveness, and her lack of success with the opposite sex.

The afternoon was exhausting for Barbara, perhaps because she had been feeling tired lately anyway and was preoccupied by tonight's dinner. The role of hostess was torture to her. She hated being sociable to people, the more so because throughout her youth she had had to swallow people's catty remarks about her wallflower ways and, more recently, her failure to get married. With the passing years she had become more and more shy and retiring.

Barbara would have given anything to spend tonight at the office, studying reports, projections, and productivity graphs. Being sociable to business associates was something for which she had neither talent nor inclination. Her stumbling efforts to be a sparkling hostess only made her look more like a clumsy spinster.

She took an hour off late in the afternoon to go to the Union Club and make sure all the preparations for the evening were in order. She left work a half hour early so as to get dressed for dinner.

At seven-thirty she and her father took a limousine together to the Union Club. She remembered the name of every businessman and politician who had been invited. This was another of Barbara's talents, her perfect memory. She greeted them all with friendly remarks about their families or companies, and she drew a smile from each. If that smile was tinged with pity for her loneliness and her submission to her father, she tried not to notice it.

It was nine-thirty, and the party was in full swing, when something unexpected happened.

Barbara was dancing with a president of a Considine steel subsidiary when a handsome stranger cut in on her partner.

"Do you mind terribly?" he asked. The man who had been dancing with Barbara melted tactfully away, and she was in the arms of the stranger.

She looked into his eyes. He seemed familiar, though she was sure they had never met. She knew for certain that he was not invited to this party.

"How did you get in here?" she asked through her polite smile.

"I crashed the party," he said. "It's a habit of mine, I'm afraid. I'm most comfortable where I'm not wanted. My own friends bore me."

Still he looked familiar. But as she tried to place the face she was struck by its attractiveness. He was a terribly handsome man. He might be thirty, or even older, but he did not look a day over twenty-five. Only his air of confidence and authority betrayed his age.

There was something whimsical about him, almost adolescent, that was alloyed with its exact opposite, a daunting manly power. He had long, beautiful eyelashes but dark, piercing eyes, a strong brow, and a square jaw. The hand holding hers was strong as steel, yet it cradled her palm as though she were made of the finest china.

He was looking at her with a hypnotic expression of appraisal and interest.

"Do you always cheerlead these affairs?" he asked.

She nodded. "It's my job," she said. "One of my jobs, I should say."

"You're a good daughter."

A quick, ambiguous look glimmered in her eyes at his words, and was gone.

"So you know who I am," she said.

"Everyone knows Barbara Considine," he smiled. "Why, I saw your picture in *Fortune* just last month. You looked very pretty."

"What did you say your name was?" she asked.

"I didn't," he said. "I'll get around to that in a moment."

He stewarded her with perfect grace through the waltzing couples to an empty salon adjacent to the ballroom. It was like a scene from a movie, this lilting exit from the crowded dance floor, and she had to smile at his forwardness and mastery.

They stood together in the dimly lit room.

"I know about you," he said.

Barbara stood back a pace. She had turned pale.

"What do you mean?" she asked.

"I know you're a good person," he said. "Being a good daughter is one thing, but being a good person is another. I saw it in your eyes on the dance floor. And I can see it now."

She still seemed shaken by his words.

"I—don't know what you're talking about," she said.

Very gently he began to pull her to him. She wanted to escape him, for his words and manner had upset her. But those dark eyes were on her now, their expression at once intoxicating and oddly reassuring. He made her want to take a chance, to match him in daring and confidence.

Against her better judgment Barbara let him kiss her. His kiss was soft and respectful. As their lips parted she leaned back, feeling rather pleased with herself. She, Barbara Considine, had kissed a handsome stranger. The moment could not be more romantic if she were at a masked ball.

But something magnetic in his arms and in his eyes drew her back to him. This time his kiss was intimate. It sent thrills of excitement up and down her spine. A little gasp of surprise sounded in her throat. His tongue explored her boldly, stoking her senses to a heat of passion she had never experienced before. When he released her she was as limp as a rag doll in his arms.

She looked at him dazedly. The half-light cast dramatic shadows over his chiseled face. His handsomeness was princely, almost unreal.

He was gazing at her affectionately.

"They say nice girls kiss the best," he said. "I could tell you were a nice girl."

Despite the languor in her senses she managed to pull back from him.

"What did you say your name was?" she asked.

"Let me keep my mystery for just a minute more," he replied.

Now he held her by her shoulders, studying her.

"You have the most beautiful eyes," he said. "In this light they're even more lovely."

He pulled her to him. This time she tried to stop him, but it was no use. Her body was like putty in his hands. He held her softly. She lay her head against his chest.

She knew something about this was wrong, very wrong. She was the last woman in the world a total stranger would want to kiss. She knew she was off-putting and matronly in her demeanor. She knew her clothes, no matter how costly, always made her look frumpy and undesirable.

Her debut, ten years ago, had been an embarrassment and a disaster. Everyone had known that not a single young man in society of any consequence wanted her.

Ever since that awful day she had kept herself aloof from young men. Her mother had stubbornly tried to match her with various eligible bachelors. But her father, after her mother's death, had acquiesced in her isolation, for he enjoyed the comfort of having her at his beck and call. He did not need an heir. He was too selfish to care about passing along his fortune to a son.

So Barbara had been alone with her disappointment, her self-loathing, and her father's cruelty, all these years. Being taken into a secluded salon by a handsome stranger and kissed was beyond anything she had ever dreamed for herself. It made her suspicious, but it also weakened something deep inside her, dismantling some of her most basic defenses.

She allowed herself to loll in his embrace. She really did not care who he was, or what he was after. She intended to enjoy this moment. She did not expect it to last.

"You've been unhappy," he said. "I can feel that. Why are you unhappy?"

Tears started in her eyes. His voice was full of intuition.

"Don't ask that," she said.

"All right." He hugged her closer. They swayed in the shadows. The sound of the orchestra wafted into the room with delicious vagueness, like a melody from another world.

"You never think about yourself," he murmured. "That's your problem, isn't it? You just work for others all the time. Never a moment stolen for your own happiness."

She held him by both arms. "How do you see so much?" she asked.

"I don't see anything," he said. "This is between you and yourself."

There was a pause.

"Too often our minds are not open enough to new ideas," he said. "For instance, you and I could leave this party right now. We could fly to a little place I know near Cape Cod. We'd be there long before midnight. It's a lovely little hotel, with a suite overlooking the ocean. We could have champagne in that little suite, just you and I . . ."

Barbara's eyes had half-closed despite herself.

"It would be warm," he said. "Cozy. There's a fireplace. Just the two of us . . ."

"Why are you saying these things?" she asked.

"Because I want to be with you," he said. "I'm serious. Why don't you come with me tonight? No one will know."

My father will know. The words rang loudly in her head.

"I can't," she protested. "I can't do that."

He held her closer. His hands were about her waist. He kissed her cheek, her eyes, her neck. He allowed the hard power of his pelvis to push against her woman's flesh. The movement made her moan.

"You can do anything you want," he said. "You're a free woman."

The pressure of his body against her own was making her faint with desire. She could not seem to catch her breath.

"Let's go," he said.

"I can't," she moaned. "I don't even know your name."

"If I tell you my name, will you promise it won't make a difference?" he asked, kissing her slowly.

"Mmm," she answered, her eyes closed in delight.

"Will you leave with me then?" he asked.

"Mm." Barbara was too physically beside herself to answer.

"My name is Jordan," he said.

Slowly, as from a great distance, the truth came to her. And with it came the hard rampart of defense she had lived with for so many years.

Her eyes opened wide.

"Lazarus," she said.

He was looking at her steadily. He said nothing. His eyes held her like a magnet, their gaze almost but not quite attenuating her strong will.

"Jordan Lazarus," she said.

She pulled back in his embrace. Somehow the thrill lingering in all her senses only increased her shame and her anger. She slapped his face.

"Get out of here," she said, "before I have you thrown out. You don't belong here."

"Neither do you," he said. "I can see that. Why don't you come away with me, and hear my side of things? Then you'll understand."

"I understand right now," she said. "Get out of here."

"Listen," he insisted, holding her by her shoulders. "What your father is doing is wrong. You know that already. Just come with me and hear me out. I want you to understand how many people he's going to hurt if he gets away with what he's trying to do."

"What *you're* doing is wrong," she said.

He pulled her to him and kissed her again. She pushed at his arms and chest, trying to free herself. But in her very desperation there was desire, and he could feel it. He could also feel a vast, infinite pain coiled in every part of her body, and he wondered at its source.

But she had extricated herself, and stepped hurriedly back from him.

"Leave now," she said, "or I'll call the security people and have you thrown out. And I'll tell my father what you did."

Jordan smiled.

"All right," he said. "I'll leave. But think over what I've said. Think over what's passed between us tonight. Don't forget me. Please."

And he was gone.

Barbara was trembling with anger at his presumption and his falseness. But even her rage and shame were colored by the lingering storm of excitement in her senses.

She had sent Jordan Lazarus away from her. But she would not forget him.

She decided not to tell her father what had happened.

This was her own private business.

In the limousine on the way home Victor Considine thought his daughter seemed nervous. He asked her what was the matter with her. She said she had a headache.

"You don't eat enough," he said. "That's your problem."

When she was safe at home Barbara Considine took a long hot shower. She was almost reluctant to feel the soap and water wash away all the traces of Jordan Lazarus's touch. Her flesh tingled as she cleansed herself.

When she got out of the shower she looked at her naked body in the mirror. It was really not so bad to look at, after all. The breasts were full, the rib cage slim, the arms and legs only slightly overweight. A good diet and some exercise would help. It was her clothes that were making her look so bad. The right wardrobe consultant could make a world of difference.

She put on her nightgown. She moved fearfully into her bedroom. The servantless house was silent. She got into bed and opened the novel she was reading. She read the same paragraph several times, unable to concentrate on the words. The image of Jordan Lazarus danced before her mind's eye, paralyzing her. A strange dread took slow possession of her.

She was almost ready to turn out the light when a voice rang out, robust and peremptory, from the other bedroom.

"Barbara," her father called. "Come to bed."

Her heart sinking, Barbara got up to go to him.

16

LESLIE CHAMBERLAIN LAY NAKED in the strange bed, waiting.

The sheet brushed against her nipples, which were taut and eager. She felt the soft fabric on her arms, the tops of her thighs, her toes, and a faint tickle on the curly tuft of hair at the center of her. She had never felt so naked in her life, or so utterly absorbed in the hot expectancy of her flesh.

Her mind played over the last two months, and she remembered pleasures she had never dreamed possible for a woman's body. More than this, she recalled emotions unlike anything she had ever felt before. She tried to give it all a sense of perspective, a rational frame, but it was impossible. At this very moment she was outside herself, carried away by the wave that had overtaken her life. And there was nothing she could do now but wait, wait for that door to open, for the shadow to enter this room, to enter her body and her heart.

After what seemed an eternity of anticipation she heard a key turn in the lock. The door opened just enough to let a tall male figure in, then closed behind him. Darkness covered her thrillingly.

There was a moment's silence. Then she heard his murmur.

"Are you here, babe?"

She stirred in the bed, her flesh already on fire.

"I'm here, Tony."

She heard the muted sounds of him removing his clothes, an exotic rustle that made her senses tingle.

He came to the bed. She knew he was naked now. She could smell the fresh, pungent scent of his masculinity, unclothed and ready for love.

Gently he pulled back the sheet, slipped in beside her, and touched her lips with his own.

A sigh sounded in Leslie's throat. She put her arms around him.

And already, invited by her own desire, he was covering her with himself, the feel of him making her tremble with desire.

"I love you," she murmured.

He smiled against her cheek.

"You took the words right out of my mouth," he said, kissing her again.

His tongue slipped between her lips, which opened eagerly to receive him. His finger touched her cheek and moved downward, grazing her breasts, her stomach, her navel, on its way to the center of her.

Her legs spread, and a shy hand came from nowhere to guide him to her. She heard him groan as she took hold of him. In an instant he was at the waiting door of her passion. She was hot and slippery, and the feel of her was so delightful that it was hard for him to control himself.

He poised himself over her, savoring the impassioned look in her eyes. Then, in a movement that thrilled him as much as her, he slipped slowly to his hilt inside her.

His eyes closed in pleasure. He was amazed at how quickly she had learned as a lover since their first tryst only two months ago. Her body surrounded him smoothly, teasing him with sweet undulations to a fever pitch of wanting. The long thighs were wrapped lovingly around his hips, the subtle hands touching his waist and slipping downward to caress him, to pull him deeper into her.

She had not lost her girlish freshness since that first night. On the contrary, she was spontaneous and innocent in her lovemaking. The fingers running up and down his thighs were almost childlike in their exploration. Her body was made for love, and she had only needed to get past the barrier of her virginity to open sensual doors in herself that must have been cruelly locked for a long time.

Seduced by the girlish daring of her hands, her lips, he began to work deeper into her. She was so beautiful, so sensual . . .

"Love me," she murmured, moving beneath him. "Oh, love me, Tony." Her head flung this way and that, splaying her curly hair over the pillow. Her fingernails dug into his back. He saw her breasts shudder under his thrusts.

It was all too much. A hot wave surged forward from deep inside him. He grasped her shoulders and looked into her eyes. They were barely open, for she was crazed by excitement, but the jewellike irises were fixed on him with a hypnotic intensity.

He gave himself in a great burst, feeling the white-hot stream of his pleasure flow into her. His entire body was on fire. There was something exotic and almost forbidden about the paroxysm shaking him. He felt he was giving more of himself to her than he had ever given to a woman before, and thus, in a way, losing something of himself. The feeling unnerved him even as it filled him with unbearable delight.

Drained, he lay covering her. She cradled him to her breast, still feeling his sex inside her. They lay for what seemed a long time, feeling their bodies relax into the sweet afterglow of love.

Decidedly, Tony mused, she was a special girl. He had not been wrong about her that first day, when he had fought so hard to get her just to have dinner with him. Underneath her fresh, brisk exterior, so controlled, so responsible, there was a deeply passionate woman.

Almost too passionate.

At length he ebbed from her and held her in his arms, kissing her softly.

"I love you so much," he said.

"Mmm," she purred. "That goes double."

"How did I get through all those years without you?" he asked. "I must have been sleepwalking."

"I know what you mean," she murmured. She started to say something more but was so seduced by the nearness of him that she stopped talking and covered his face with kisses.

Then she lay back, admiring his body.

"But I knew the first time I laid eyes on you, coming out of that elevator, that you were something special," he said. "And it turned out I was right."

She blushed to recall their first date. It had changed her whole life. Throughout their dinner together Leslie had fought vainly to hide what was going on inside her. It was Tony who had done most of the talking, for she was tongue-tied by her own emotions. But her eyes had spoken volumes to him. And at the end of the evening, when they left the restaurant, there was no doubt in either's mind as to what was to happen next.

She had surprised herself in bed with him. Not only had her virginal body given up its fragile veil willingly, eagerly, but she had awakened to a woman's pleasure with a hot abandon that stunned and thrilled her. She wondered whether this was a quality in herself that she had long denied, or whether it was Tony, with his flashing smile, his calm understanding, and his masterful lovemaking, who had stoked such a passion in her.

She had never found out the answer to that question. They had been lovers for two months now, Tony flying in from half a dozen different directions depending on where his work took him each week. Their meetings had been like unpredictable adventures, with Tony squiring Leslie to unfamiliar restaurants, parts of the city she had never seen before, an amusement park whose existence she had not suspected. The whole landscape seemed changed by his spontaneity. It was a world that Leslie, with her concentration on work, had never seen before.

And, of course, there were the quiet little hotels where they registered as man and wife.

Each time their lovemaking was more overpowering and intense than the last. It was like a sensual dream that grew more intoxicating all the time. Leslie would have been shocked at herself had Tony's own pleasure not been so obvious, and the protective warmth of his arms so reassuring.

She held him close now, feeling the familiar contours of his body.

"You know something?" he asked.

"What?" Her face was buried in his chest, her hands running through his hair.

"You're still a mystery to me," he said.

"What do you mean?" she asked.

He sat up to look at her. Despite himself he sighed to see the long, sinuous line of her naked thighs.

"I don't understand," he said, "how someone as passionate as you could have remained hidden under that crisp, ladylike exterior all those years."

She laughed, her knee covering his thigh with a soft whispering sound. Then she took his hand, kissed it softly, and placed it on her breast.

"That's easy," she said. "I hadn't met you yet."

He smiled at her compliment. But his eyes were thoughtful.

"I like flattery," he said, "but there's more to it than that. I think you're such a great worker, and such a lady, because you've always been passionate. All that bottled-up energy was what made you such a stickler toward yourself and others."

She lay pressing his hand quietly against her breast, and thinking about the truth of his words. Yes, she had been holding something in all these years. And she had never really understood what it was.

"Maybe," he said slowly, "your mother's death hit you a little harder than you realized. Maybe losing her left a scar you didn't notice all this time."

Leslie was thoughtful. She had never articulated this notion to herself before. She had always thought of herself as a happy person, even a carefree one. Her mother's death had always seemed more like a historical event, a fact of life that she accepted, than a wound that could cause lingering pain.

She murmured, "What makes you so smart?"

"I lost my own mother," he said. "That's a scar I'm all too familiar with."

Moved more than she realized by his sudden avowal—he had told her almost nothing about his past during their few weeks together—she felt her eyes mist. A surge of maternal protectiveness flowed through her.

"Oh, Tony," she said. "Why haven't you told me about this?"

"It's ancient history," he said, patting her gently. "I only brought it up to illustrate a point. I may look like a dim-witted traveling executive, but I do have a brain."

She got up on her knees and crouched beside him.

"Tell me about it," she said. "Tell me about your family. I want to know, Tony."

He shook his head.

"Not now," he said. "In time you'll hear the whole story. But when you do, you'll understand why I don't want to talk about it yet. It would spoil the time we're having now. Or at least cast a shadow over it. And nothing is going to spoil this moment for me. I've waited a lifetime for it—and for you."

He studied her, lying naked beside him. She looked sleek and feline, unbearably attractive.

"Kiss me," he said.

Their lips met. She felt his tongue slip into her mouth, sweetly at first, then hot with the sudden male hunger she had come to know so well these past weeks.

Desire surged inside her. She moved to straddle him, still kissing him deeply.

Her knees were holding him by his waist. She could feel the male sex straining beneath her, eager to touch her. She arched her back and let her hands slowly move down his chest, along his stomach and between his legs. Her fingers took hold of him with soft triumph as a smile curled her lips. She felt like a seductress. The wisdom of her body, full of its own newfound pleasure, was telling her what to do.

She heard him sigh. The hot thing in her hands seemed to belong to her, to exist only for her. She began to caress it.

His hands clenched in the bedsheets as she squatted over him, her long legs squeezing his thighs. His eyes were closed. He strained rhythmically, and his sex moistened her fingers.

She reflected that her relationship with this handsome, sexy man did not take root in her mind, as did all the other relationships she had with those around her. It began in her woman's body, awakened to love by him. And thus it was infinitely more profound, more complete. He had made her a woman, and now she knew him as she had never known anyone else.

With this thought she guided him boldly inside her. She felt him arch upward, and ground her hips to work him to his hilt in the quick of her.

He started moving right away. She gloried in the excitement of the hard staff working deep at the core of her, provoked in its frantic urgency by her own soft body. She was thrilled to be able to make this thing want her so badly.

Amazed at her own abandon, she let her hips move to join his thrusts. The hot ache inside her grew and grew, and in a very short time she was no longer thinking at all.

His hands came up to cup her breasts, the thumbs rubbing at her nipples. Her fingernails clawed softly across his chest, leaving pink trails of desire in their passage. He worked harder beneath her.

She did not hear her voice saying, "Love me, Tony. Love me." Nor did she hear his answering sighs and moans.

For a last instant she savored him that way, her body proclaiming its triumph over the whole essence of her. Then she felt his hands come to her hips to pull her harder onto him, and pleasure overcame her completely. The deepest part of her was two instead of one, a wild commingling of forces almost inhuman in their intensity.

She whimpered softly, an animal murmur of love that drew the last wave from him. She felt him leap hot and liquid in her loins.

The spasm seemed to go on and on, joining them in a great shuddering upheaval. She thought she could not stand the sheer force of it, the pleasure, an instant longer. Then, almost mercifully, it was over and she was limp in his arms.

"Oh," she murmured. "Oh, Tony . . ."

He held her close.

"Ssshhh," he said, kissing her brow, her cheek. "Don't say anything now."

She lay beside him in silence, drained and happy.

After a while she got up to go to the bathroom. She went in and closed the door. The light made her blink. She looked at herself in the mirror.

Her eyes opened wide in surprise. She barely resembled herself. Her hair, tousled by love, seemed to be on fire. Her eyes looked drugged by passion. Worse yet, they glowed with an untamed, almost insolent satisfaction. The drug inside her, the drug that was Tony, had had its full effect. She was no longer the controlled young woman she had been two months ago. She was a new creature, one whose desires she could not know in advance, one whose actions she could not perhaps control.

One part of Leslie was proud of this metamorphosis. She felt that her past life had been shallow, superficial, because she had never known herself sexually. She had flattered herself that she knew who she was, that she respected herself and deserved to be taken seriously. But that view of herself had been colored by her inexperience. It had been a girl's self-image. Now she knew the needs and the pleasures of an adult woman. Now she knew what life was really about.

But another part of her, still conservative, was alarmed by what it saw in the mirror. She knew she was head over heels in love. It was all happening too fast. Too much of herself had sacrificed itself already on the altar of her desire for Tony. She was not sure what was left inside her. She no longer knew herself.

But there was a link between these two selves that fought for control of Leslie's mind and heart. That link was her pride in her own independence.

Despite the danger of this unexpected love, she enjoyed the feeling of being a consenting adult, a woman who made her own decision to enter into this exciting new relationship. She felt grown up, responsible, and strong. More importantly, she was daring. She was in control of her own life, and she had chosen to fall in love. She was taking a chance with her own identity. The feeling was exhilarating. She was learning how to be a woman. She had put it off long enough.

From the handful of hints Tony had given her about himself, she knew that he had been through personal struggles far more painful than her own. But he had emerged as a more open person, a person whose private cares did not keep him from a passionate *joie de vivre* that Leslie, more conservative, had always lacked. Thus her admiration for him was as powerful as her obsession with his charms. She wanted to match his own courage with her own, by loving him with all of herself, by risking everything for him.

When she emerged from the bathroom she found him sitting on the edge of the bed, still naked. He was smoking a cigarette. He looked languid and incongruously domestic as he looked up at her.

"Come here," he said, patting the bed by his side.

She came to him and sat down. Her whole body was still tingling from their lovemaking. She wished he would take her again, now, before she had even a moment to think. The wild, impudent part of her gloried in their shared nakedness, as though they were skinny-dipping, getting away with a naughty crime. Nevertheless, the other part of her, the cautious remnant, hung back, needing desperately to feel that he still wanted her, still respected her.

She tried to find casual, easy words to say to him. But she was tongue-tied. The Jekyll-and-Hyde feeling she had had while looking in the bathroom mirror had left her dizzy.

"There's something I've been meaning to ask you," he said.

"What?" she asked.

He touched her shoulder softly, then ran a finger into the tangled, fragrant wildness of her hair.

"Will you marry me?" Tony asked.

Leslie's breath caught in her throat. With his own question he was answering the one that had been tormenting her all this time without her realizing it. He seemed to have read her mind just now, as she stood in the bathroom doing a painful balancing act between the two parts of herself.

For a brief instant Leslie felt more confused than ever. This was a man she had only known two months. And in those two months she had been so seduced by his charm that she had not troubled to get to know him the way an ordinary woman knows her suitor. She had gloried on the surface of his body and his personality like a daring skater on thin ice, her pleasure feeding itself from the very danger of her position. She wondered whether her own emotions were to be trusted.

But now, as she sat naked beside him, her body proclaimed its intimacy with him and mocked at the fearful warnings of her cautious mind, as though its scruples were an outmoded thing of the past. She was a new woman now, beyond such childish fears.

In the end it was her heart that carried the day, bringing words to her lips that she would never forget as long as she lived.

"Yes, Tony. Oh, yes."

17

New York City

DURING THE THREE WEEKS after his meeting with Barbara Considine, Jordan Lazarus did everything humanly possible to prevent the hostile takeover of Lazarus International by Considine Industries.

He consulted his legal department, hoping there was a way to defeat Considine in the courts, or at least to stall the monster conglomerate through protracted litigation.

He sent an urgent message to his stockholders, explaining that the short-term benefit to be gained financially by a cash tender offer from Considine Industries would bring long-term disaster.

He contacted investment bankers and friendly corporations, looking for someone to cut a deal with him to hold off Considine. But none of them felt they could match the enormous price being offered by Considine.

He consulted patent lawyers, hoping that in some way Leo Kaminsky's groundbreaking work could be protected from the assault on the company for which Leo worked. But they told him that Leo's work was not ready to be patented yet. The concept was too revolutionary and too untested to be submitted to the federal patent office.

Victor Considine had been very clever. Since the product he wanted was not ready to be patented, the quickest way for him to acquire it was to acquire the company researching it. And since this company belonged to a growing conglomerate, he would acquire the whole conglomerate. Few business moguls had the awesome power to pay so much for what they wanted. Victor Considine was one.

Armed with his patent attorneys' advice, Jordan consulted with Leo Kaminsky about the possibility of using the new drug on humans. Leo was optimistic. He showed Jordan complex biological and pharmacological charts demonstrating that the blood chemistry of humans could accommodate the concept he had in mind.

But Leo could not promise a result soon. He could only continue his research in his own time and in his own eccentric manner.

Jordan Lazarus realized that his fledgling business empire was in the gravest possible danger. He had no weapons against a man with the financial power of Victor Considine. Sooner or later the stockholders' meeting would have to take place. It was foolish to imagine that the Lazarus shareholders would be able to resist a tender offer of $75 for shares that were worth only $50 at the most. They would sell, and Lazarus International as a free business entity would cease to exist. Jordan himself would be a man without a company. His life's work would have come to nothing.

Jordan could not let this happen.

Desperate measures were called for.

During those tempestuous weeks Barbara Considine did not forget Jordan Lazarus.

He did not let her forget. She received a dozen white roses the morning after the reception at the Union Club, and a dozen roses daily afterward.

Jordan telephoned her office nearly every day. Barbara's secretary, instructed to field the calls by saying that Barbara was in a meeting, passed on the messages. Barbara returned none of the calls.

Jordan responded by sending her notes. He invited her to join him for lunch, to meet him for a walk, to have dinner with him. She threw all the notes away.

But even as she held Jordan off with the weapon of her strong will, Barbara Considine did a lot of thinking about him.

She had recognized Jordan Lazarus's name instantly the night he kissed her on the terrace at the Union Club, because she was aware of the upcoming takeover of Lazarus International by Considine Industries, and knew about its inception. She was aware of her father's terror of the heart failure that was threatening him, and his intense interest in drug companies and cardiac drug research. It had been only natural for him to take an interest in the Lazarus corporation's new researches once his corporate spies had told him about them.

Barbara now took the trouble to fill herself in on the case. She read the files compiled by her father's spies. Though she was not an expert on pharmacology, she quickly realized that Jordan Lazarus's research people were on to something very important. But their formula was still in the experimental stage, had not been tested on humans, and was not ready to be patented.

This explained her father's eagerness to acquire Lazarus International and the gigantic tender offer he was making to Jordan's stockholders.

It also explained why Jordan had tried so brazenly to enlist her help against her father. Jordan must realize that if he could simply hang on to his company long enough for his research to bear fruit, he could come into possession of a drug industry gold mine, a patent that could make him untold millions of dollars.

An intelligent woman who knew herself as well as could be expected after her unhappy and twisted life, Barbara Considine could see where things stood. Jordan Lazarus felt nothing for her, except perhaps pity. He lacked a weapon to fight off her father. So he had come to her as a last resort. He would not have sought her out unless he was desperate.

She was nothing but a tool to Jordan Lazarus, a means to an end. His kisses, so intoxicating, had been as false as his smiles, his admiring words, his tender show of respect.

Lazarus was smart. He had undoubtedly done his homework on Victor Considine. He realized that Considine confided in his daughter and rarely took an important step of any kind without her advice. Lazarus was gambling that in influencing Barbara he could influence her father.

Barbara found herself in a difficult bind. On one hand she could not betray her father. All her life she had been in awe of him, as was her mother before her. The three of them had lived as though no one else existed in the world. After her mother's death Barbara had lived alone with her father in a sort of thrall. She was utterly intimidated by his every glance or glower. The sound of his voice demolished her will.

So confused was she by her feelings for him that even today, at age twenty-eight, she was not consciously aware of when their incestuous relationship had started. It was a fact of life for her, a thing she took for granted. Each time it happened—and it happened twice or three times a week—Barbara took leave of herself and became like a zombie. She submitted numbly to her father's will, and barely remembered afterward that anything had happened between them.

She was too morally and psychologically wounded by her father to do anything but give in to him. As long as he was alive, she was his slave. This fact was inescapable.

Therefore she knew she could not betray her father for Jordan's sake.

On the other hand, something in Jordan Lazarus's smile, in his kisses, had kindled a flame inside Barbara that could not be denied, a flame that made her hunger for something beyond the sterile, empty life she had been leading all these years. She had tried to deny it at first, but now it was burning out of control. It filled her not only with contempt and loathing for her own life but also with a taste for freedom.

Barbara was torn cruelly between these two extremes. Her loyalty to her father was all she had ever known. But her attraction to Jordan Lazarus was like an unsuspected future opening before her, a future beyond her wildest dreams.

Each day her conflict grew more painful. And each day she received, once more, an invitation from Jordan. A call, a letter, a message, like so many daggers plunged into the heart of her old life.

Barbara stuck to her routine with all the force of her strong will. She

worked hard at the office all day, impressing everyone as usual with her concentration on work and her complete professionalism.

But inside she was walking a tightrope from which she must surely tumble
to her destruction unless something came to her rescue.

A week before Christmas Barbara was to travel to White Plains, where she
had to be present as her father's representative at a reception for businessmen
in the Alhambra Hotel. Her father had another meeting out of town that
same evening, and she was to convey his regrets, have consultations with
certain important businessmen whose names he had given her, and return
home to tell him the results. She would stay overnight at the hotel and return
to Manhattan the next afternoon.

On the morning of the meeting she went to an expensive dress shop on
Fifth Avenue to check the alterations on the dress she was to wear that
evening.

In the dressing room, clad in only her slip and bra before the mirror, she
thought of Jordan as usual. Her nipples could still feel the pressure of his
chest, her loins the delicious warmth of his hips and thighs. Her lips recalled
the taste of his kiss with an uncanny precision.

She emerged guiltily, wearing the new dress, and was shocked to see Jordan
standing tall and handsome before her in a dark pinstriped suit.

"You look terrific, darling," he said in a familiar tone. "I knew the dress
would work out. You're beautiful."

A saleslady, who must have seen Jordan come in and told him where to
find Barbara, smiled from a distance as he took Barbara in his arms and kissed
her lips.

Barbara did not want to make a spectacle of pushing him away, since the
salesgirls were already assuming—with decided envy—that he was Barbara's
beau. All she could do was whisper angrily in his ear, "What are you doing
here? I thought I told you to leave me alone."

He held her at arm's length, admiring her in her new dress.

"You get more beautiful every day," he exclaimed, his eyes sparkling with
admiration. "I've never seen a woman dominate a dress the way you do.
You'll be the belle of the ball tonight, for sure."

And again he hugged her close.

"Aren't we late for lunch?" he said, looking at his watch. "Oh, well, it's
worth it to see you looking so lovely. I'll just wait while they put it in a box
for you. André will hold our table."

Darting him a furious look that the others could not see, Barbara retreated
to the dressing room.

Jordan chatted with the salesgirls while Barbara changed. She could hear
his deep voice charming the other women. He kept interspersing his casual
conversation with admiring remarks about Barbara, how "beautiful" she was,

how "charming," how vivacious. He spoke of her with affectionate possessiveness, as though she were a willful, spirited creature who excited him but baffled him with her mercurial moods.

By the time she emerged she was faced with three salesgirls and a manageress who were all in love with Jordan and green with envy of Barbara. She could hardly dismiss him now. She had to wait until they got outside at least.

"Let me carry that for you," he said, taking the box the dress was wrapped in. "Nice to meet you, ladies," he called back to the salesgirls, who were eyeing him dreamily.

When they were outside he smiled.

"I hope I didn't embarrass you," he said. "I had to see you."

Barbara's car was waiting. She held out her hand for the box.

"Good-bye, Mr. Lazarus," she said, trying her best to sound firm.

"Don't say good-bye," he said, shaking her hand as he gave her the box. "You'll be seeing me tonight."

She began to protest, but already her driver was opening the car door. She got in and looked straight ahead of her.

As the driver pulled into traffic, she glanced out the window despite herself and saw Jordan staring at her through penetrating dark eyes.

Late that afternoon she had herself driven to White Plains, having spent an agonizing day trying to concentrate on work and her preparations for the evening while her thoughts strayed inexorably to the face and body of Jordan Lazarus.

The gathering at the hotel was more numerous than Barbara had expected, and her interviews more difficult. She had to closet herself with three corporation presidents and two board chairmen in succession. She had a specific agenda for each brief discussion, with favors to offer and promises to extract.

In each case she was to report back to her father not only on the explicit answer she was given but also on the executive's demeanor as he answered. For years she had been entrusted, on and off, with this job of being her father's eyes and ears when he needed to be in two places at once. She had distinguished herself by her acute intuition and subtlety of judgment, and on more than one occasion her advice had helped her father through a delicate strategic situation.

She was glad for the busy schedule of interviews. It took her mind off Jordan. But by ten o'clock she was mentally exhausted and unable to go on a minute longer. She took her leave of the meeting's leaders—all of whom treated her with exaggerated respect, for she was Victor Considine's daughter—and went to the special elevator that led from the penthouse ballroom to the lobby. She pushed the button for her own floor gratefully.

When the doors opened, Jordan Lazarus was standing in front of her on the landing, wearing a silk suit that made him look as though he had just stepped off the cover of a fashion magazine.

Before she could protest he had joined her in the elevator and pushed the button for another floor. The doors were already shut.

"What do you think you're doing?" she asked angrily.

He silenced her with a kiss that sent shock waves down her spine and into the very quick of her. His strong arms held her tight, and his tongue explored her with eager urgency.

"Let me go." She tried ineffectually to struggle.

Suddenly he pushed the Stop button and the elevator came to a halt in the middle of the shaft. He pulled her to him and kissed her again. This time he was upon her like a panther, his lithe body moving against hers, his arms pulling her harder onto him. Even as she squirmed in his grasp her hands fluttered at his shoulders, caressed his neck, and buried themselves in his hair. She was beside herself.

"Let me out of here," she moaned.

He released her by a precious inch, decreasing the hot pressure of his limbs against hers. That tiny interval allowed her to breathe.

"Will you come to my room with me for a moment?" he asked. "I don't relish this melodrama any more than you do. I just want to talk to you."

Barbara said nothing. She was thinking hard, or trying to. She leaned backward as though to escape him, but her hands were still curled about his neck. Her senses were confusing her mind, blinding her to everything but him.

"Push the button," she said. There was a note of surrender in her voice, but she tried not to hear it.

Jordan Lazarus reached out slowly and cupped both her breasts in his hands. Then he kissed her again, this time softly, a quiet triumph in his eyes.

When he pushed the button it was for a higher floor. Barbara watched helplessly as the conveyance rose. He was holding both her hands now and looking into her eyes.

The doors opened. There was a landing with a mirror and some antique chairs. Then a hallway. Then a door with a number on it. The key was already in his hand. A warm, inviting room came into view, its shadows lit golden by the reading light over the bed.

She went inside with him. He took her coat and hung it in the closet. Then he came back to her side.

"Your dress looks beautiful," he said.

She smiled to recall that he had seen the dress on her this morning in New York.

"It's too beautiful a dress to get wrinkled," he said. "Let me help you."

Barbara went rigid. She knew what he intended to do with her. His pretense of needing to talk to her was already abandoned.

She wanted to slap him, to cry out her anger at his attempted manipulation of her, to flee this room as fast as her legs could carry her.

But she did not move a muscle.

He unzipped the dress and eased it down her shoulders. She had a slip on. His hands came to rest at her waist, found their way under the elastic band, and pulled the slip down as well. Now she was clad only in her bra and panties.

"You are beautiful," he said. "Just as I knew you would be."

He picked her up and placed her on the bed. He bent to turn off the little lamp, and kissed her as he did so.

Then he stood up, silhouetted by the city lights outside the window. He removed his jacket and tie. She could feel his smile in the shadows as he looked down at her.

He took off his shirt, and she saw the outline of his powerful young body, the straight shoulders, the hard pectorals, the long arms, the strong hands with their surprisingly delicate fingers.

With a smooth motion he slipped out of his pants. For an instant she saw the outline of his sex, impatient and eager under the underpants. Then he took them off, and the penis stood out, hard and strong and proud.

Barbara was beside herself. The sight of him filled her with a longing she could not control. But her body was still rigid. The heat inside her surged wildly against a wall of coldness that would not melt.

He knelt to kiss her. His tongue slipped warmly into her mouth. He crouched above her. Then the whole smooth length of him settled against her flesh, the man's hardness fitting itself quickly and easily to her woman's curves.

"You've avoided me long enough," he whispered.

Barbara could not move to stop him. In a trice he had her panties off and the unresisting bra, and he was tasting her nipples, teasing the warm little buds to eager hardness with his tongue.

The fire in her senses raged hotter than ever. But the frigid cold would not give way. She knew he felt the battle going on inside her, a spinster's struggle against her own bottled-up sensuality. She would have given anything to take leave of herself entirely, to enjoy her surrender to him. But the body she inhabited would not allow that. Nor would the life she had lived all these years.

He was stirring slowly against her, his hands beneath her waist now. His body seemed incredibly wise, giving her more and more pleasure even as, with every delicate movement, he spread her legs a bit more, teased her flesh to greater wanting, positioned her for the thrusts to come.

She was on the edge of the chasm, ready to fall, when the agony inside her exploded.

"No!" she cried. She held him by his shoulders as a flood of tears erupted from her eyes.

He paused, looking into her eyes. The hands on his shoulders were full of supplication. His expression was puzzled.

Then he saw the extremity of her distress. He shifted to a less intimate position and took her in his arms.

"It's all right," he murmured, kissing her tear-stained cheeks. "It's all right, Barbara. Forgive me. I didn't understand."

He petted her gently, cradling her in his embrace.

"They've hurt you more than I realized," he murmured. "I'm sorry. I should have felt it before. I've been a fool."

At these comforting words her sobs redoubled, and she clung to him with all her might.

"That's better," he said. "I want you to feel safe with me. That's more important than anything else. Don't worry, Barbara—you've got a friend."

He held her close, a sweet, lulling warmth emanating from him. Little by little her panic ebbed, and she began to feel as safe as he had promised. His sensitivity and understanding were even more seductive to Barbara than his handsome body.

"Just rest now," he said. "Just go to sleep, and everything will be fine."

She nodded her gratitude against his chest. And indeed, she felt sleep steal over her suddenly. She knew she should get up and return to her own room, but the security she felt in Jordan Lazarus's arms was forcing her deeper into somnolence with every passing second. She made a last feeble effort to call herself back to the old reality, and failed.

Barbara was fast asleep.

Her night was a long one, full of haunting dreams. When she woke up she felt like a changed woman, though she could not say why.

Jordan was beside her, having awakened early to watch her sleep.

"You should have waked me up," she said. "I'll be late."

"You're very beautiful when you're asleep," he smiled. "I didn't have the heart. You seemed so tired last night."

He was wearing a bathrobe. He ordered breakfast while she got up. Somehow she was not ashamed for him to see her emerge naked from the bed. She felt his eyes on her, full of a gentle admiration.

She dressed as he watched. She drank coffee with him before getting up to leave. They said little, but an atmosphere of warm affection and familiarity joined them, almost as though they had made love after all last night.

At the door he took her in his arms and kissed her.

"I hope I did the right thing last night," he said. "Do you hate me for stopping? Or for putting you in a position where you had to make me stop?"

She shook her head. "You did nothing wrong," she said.

Jordan looked at her gravely. "It's important to do the right thing, isn't it?" he asked.

Then he smiled. "I'll miss seeing you wake up in the morning," he said. "It was nice."

"Thank you for that," she said, kissing his cheek.

She went through the door, looking up and down the deserted hallway. His face lingered in her memory as she walked toward the elevators. She could still see him smiling down at her as she awoke. What a paradise life would be, she thought, if every day could begin with that handsome smile warming her and giving her courage!

The thought filled Barbara with longing. By the time she reached her own room her contentment of the morning had turned to sadness.

That night Barbara was back in Manhattan.

It was nearly nine when Barbara got home. Her father was waiting.

"Where in hell have you been all this time?" he asked.

He was in his bathrobe, with a glass of beer in his hand and a newspaper under his arm. He was peering at her over his reading glasses with an irritated look.

"At the Alhambra, of course," she said, trying to seem fatigued and a little irritable. "Mr. Fredericks missed the lunch meeting, and I had to have dinner with him."

The father grunted. "He wouldn't have been late if it was me he was meeting."

Barbara flushed. "Then go yourself next time," she said. "If you don't trust me to get the job done properly . . ."

"Who said I didn't trust you? Don't twist my words, or you'll regret it." Victor Considine was not really threatening her. It was just his manner. She could see in his eyes that he was glad to see her.

She turned away.

"I'm going to take a shower," she said. "I'm exhausted."

"I'll see you when you get out," he said.

Barbara hurried into the shower. She knew what his parting words meant. He wanted her tonight.

She hung the dress in the closet, pulled off her underclothes, and went into the bathroom. She could still smell Jordan all over her. She had not bathed this morning. Had it not been for her father, she would not have bathed for a week, just to keep that fragrance on her skin.

But she had to get the traces of him off. For one thing, she could not risk making her father suspicious. For another, she could not bear to let the precious essence of Jordan Lazarus be tainted by the foul contact of her flesh with that of her father. The two things must remain separate, completely separate, until . . .

Until what?

She was already washing herself when the extremity of her dilemma came to her.

Barbara was a changed woman. What had happened last night and today had ended all resolve on her part to resist Jordan Lazarus. Paradoxically, by sparing her sexually when he had her defenseless, he had sapped her strength to refuse him in any other way.

On the other hand, she could not hide the truth from her father very long. He was too smart for that. Nor could she openly betray him.

There seemed no way out of her predicament.

But Barbara Considine was her father's daughter, in more ways than one. As she felt her fingers reluctantly wash away the traces of Jordan Lazarus's kisses, the secret opportunity behind her dilemma began to reveal itself to her.

When she emerged from the shower she heard her father's barking voice from the other room.

"Come to bed, can't you? Do I have to wait all night?"

As she put on her nightgown, Barbara realized her answer had just been provided her.

18

Detroit, Michigan

ON A BUSY TUESDAY after a heavy Detroit snowfall Jill Fleming left her office in marketing and got on the elevator to go up to the sixth floor.

Just as the doors were closing Harley Schrader darted in beside her.

"How you doing?" Harley smiled in his best executive manner.

"Fine," Jill smiled a bit formally.

"Work going okay?" he asked.

Jill nodded. "Fine."

"How's Roy?" he asked.

Jill said nothing. She looked away, a distant expression in her eyes.

Harley gave her a knowing smile. Then he suddenly reached to touch the Stop button. The elevator stopped between floors. They were alone.

"We shouldn't have secrets, you and I," Harley said, his smile crueler now. "I just want you to know I'm on to you."

Jill raised an eyebrow. "On to what?" she asked in an even voice.

"The big picture," he said. "What you've been up to with Roy. What your plan is. I know him pretty well, you know. We've been friends for twenty years. I know what you're trying to do."

Jill reached for the Start button, but he grabbed her hand.

"You're not going to get away with it," he smiled. "You know why? Because I'm not going to let you get away with it. I may not be much, little lady. But Roy English is my friend. And no gold digger like you is going to twist him around your little finger."

Jill darted him a look of cold hatred that seemed odd on her beautiful face, almost like a mask.

"Let go of my arm," she said. "You and I have nothing to say to each other."

Harley Schrader allowed her to push the Start button. The elevator moved upward again.

"If I were you," he said, "I'd think about finding another job. Before it's too late."

The elevator reached the sixth floor. Jill walked through the open doors without a backward glance, carrying the sheaf of files she had brought with her.

"Be seeing you," she heard him call from behind her.

That night Jill told Roy that his friend Harley Schrader had made a pass at her.

"He stopped the elevator while we were alone together," she said. "Then he tried to . . . Well, I won't go into the details. I was shocked. I thought you said he was a nice person. I thought you said he was your friend."

Roy was looking at her intently. His face was full of confused emotions, rage being the most salient.

"I'll take care of it right away," he said through clenched teeth.

"No, darling," Jill said, taking both his hands as though to restrain him.

She made Roy promise not to do anything about it. She told him this was no time to be making waves within the company. The situation was delicate, with his move for the presidency coming up. She could see he wanted to take out his vengeance on Harley with his bare hands. But she managed to calm him down.

"It doesn't matter," she said. "It was nothing, really. It was more funny than anything else. Perhaps I shouldn't have said anything."

"No," Roy insisted. "You did the right thing."

In the days that followed Roy did nothing. But he could not get Jill's story out of his mind.

He had always taken Harley Schrader for granted as a shallow, back-slapping business friend who was good for an occasional drink, a weekly squash game, and sometimes a round of golf. The two men had remained friends over the years mostly because Roy had introduced Harley to his wife, Jean. Roy trusted Harley as a business ally because Harley was so much less talented and ambitious that he could never constitute a threat to Roy. Harley's very shallowness made him seem an inconsequential and somehow reassuring presence.

But now Roy saw his old friend in a completely new and terrifying light. The idea of Harley trying to put his hands on Jill, daring to trifle with her feminine integrity, made Roy see red. The more so since Harley knew perfectly well that Jill was Roy's girl.

The mental image of the scene in the elevator, with Harley stopping the car to try to gather Jill's small body to his own overweight one, filled Roy with a rage and humiliation he had never thought possible.

Roy had noticed over the last few months that the very idea of other men touching Jill caused him intense pain. Though he did not think consciously of her as a virgin, this was his emotional view of her—an unspoiled little nymph whom he had personally introduced to the joys of love and lovemaking. The idea of her touching other men, much less enjoying their bodies, was so unbearable to him that he dared not allow it to enter his mind.

Thus the notion of Harley, his supposed friend, trying to get fresh with Jill, was intolerable to Roy. From the moment he first heard it he was half out of his mind with jealousy.

But Jill had forbidden him to confront Harley.

So Roy thought of another expedient, based on his long experience in business. He began to take subtle steps to get Harley out of the company.

Roy was now close to a powerful phalanx of executives and board members who were poised to bring him into the presidency while forcing his opponents out. In subtle ways Roy now began letting his friends know that when the time came, Harley might just as well go, too. Harley was dead weight, an unimaginative executive who had peaked a decade ago and was going nowhere.

There was truth in this. More than once in the last few years Roy had used his own influence to protect Harley from those who wanted to oust him because of their own ambition. He had done this out of simple friendship.

Now, out of hatred, he marshaled an even greater influence to have Harley removed.

The weeks passed. On the surface Continental Products was an untroubled company, headed for a strong fiscal year and a solid if uneventful future. But behind the scenes a power struggle was going on, which would soon decide the future of at least a dozen senior executives, and most of all Roy English.

It was during this time of silent ferment that Roy went for his usual squash game with Harley one Friday morning.

Roy had been playing squash with Harley as usual since Jill had had her conversation with him. He wanted to keep an eye on Harley, the better to destroy him when the time was right. During these weeks Roy had been amiable and easy with his old friend.

Harley, though not a very intelligent man, was a cunning one. A lifetime in the trench wars of the corporate world had not been wasted on him. He knew his conversation with Jill must have gotten back to Roy. He was on his guard.

Roy won the squash game handily, as was normal for him. He was in far better shape than Harley and easily outmaneuvered him.

After their game they were in the locker room, chatting about sports, the stock market, and mutual friends.

It was a classic business situation. Each man knew what the other was thinking, but neither alluded to the truth. Harley was aware that Roy was pushing hard for the presidency. He had suspected for some time that Jill Fleming was behind Roy's sudden power play. This could only mean that when the shake-up came, Harley himself would be out.

"Jeannie and I saw you and Jill at the Cumberland last week," he said.

"Oh?" Roy raised an eyebrow. "I didn't see hide or hair of you that night."

Harley let out a low whistle.

"That Jill is a looker," he said. "You were the envy of every man in the joint that night."

Roy said nothing.

Harley turned to him as he closed his locker.

"She's a great girl," Harley said. "I don't know if I told you I dated her once or twice, a long time ago. Not seriously, the way you have—just a few laughs."

Roy had stopped what he was doing and stood staring at his friend.

Harley looked him in the eye.

"A fun girl," he said. "Great in the sack, too. She knows all the tricks."

Roy's hands were fists. He did not believe a word of this, but he was ready to punch Harley in the nose. He remembered Jill's revulsion when she told him about Harley's attempted seduction in the elevator. The notion of Harley actually taking Jill to bed was absurd. The two came from different universes. Harley was a crude, shallow salesman, while Jill was a magical nymph almost too perfect to share the same world with him.

Nevertheless, a nameless tension had seized Roy's body and would not let go. He felt his hands tremble, and clenched his fists tighter.

Harley looked him in the eye for a moment, then turned away and smiled.

"That little beauty mark of hers," he said. "Quite a turn-on. Like Eve with her apple. Right next to her little pussy, that way . . . I've never seen anything like it. I couldn't keep my hands off it."

Roy turned pale at these words. He looked away from Harley. He made a superhuman effort to control his emotions. He could barely get his pants on and loop his belt, so great was the tremor in his hands.

Harley was already dressed and about to leave.

He turned to face Roy. The look in his eyes was serious.

"Don't let a woman make a monkey out of you, Roy," he said with obvious sincerity. "You're too smart for that. As for the rest, well, we're friends. If you become president and I'm out, I'll understand."

He touched Roy's shoulder.

"But don't let a woman make a monkey out of you," he said.

Roy was left alone in the locker room. He sat on the bench before his locker, deep in thought.

The tremor in his limbs had abated. So had the agony inside his mind. He felt as though he were coming back to himself after a long absence, like a drowning man who is plucked from the hungry ocean at the last second.

A lifetime of cold self-interest came to his rescue, slowly peeling the scales from his eyes. The fury inside him, formerly aimed confusedly at Harley, disappeared. In its place was a quiet balance, a steely certainty.

Roy remained alone in the locker room for over an hour, deep in thought. When he got up to leave, he had made up his mind.

The next morning Jill was given her notice of termination by a company security officer sent to marketing for that purpose.

She looked at the notice. It was cold and impersonal.

"The corporation regrets the necessity of terminating your employment as of today. We wish you the best of luck in your future endeavors."

Jill was escorted from her office by the security officer. She was told to turn in her identity card at the security desk, as well as her parking permission.

When she got home Jill called Roy's office. She was told he was out of town. She called his apartment. There was no answer.

She called Harley Schrader's office. She was thinking fast. She would need to talk to Harley immediately, and perhaps promise him certain things she didn't want to promise. But she had no choice.

Harley's secretary told her he was out of town.

Jill knew now what had happened.

She was not surprised at Harley. She knew he realized how much power she had gained over Roy, and he knew that at some point this was going to mean the end of his tenure at the company.

Of course she cursed herself for having slept with Harley during her first week at the company, now nearly a year ago. But there was no turning back the clock. Harley had been a necessary step for her. It was through Harley's bedroom gossip that she had learned about Roy, about Roy's importance to the company, Roy's unmarried status, Roy's stalled ambition.

Thus the key that opened her first big door at Continental Products had ended up being the key that locked her out forever.

Jill was not surprised by what Harley had done. He had simply tried to protect his old friend from a female predator whose charms Harley himself had tasted.

But she was surprised at Roy.

She had been convinced that she had Roy in her pocket. The look in his eyes when they made love proved that she owned not only his balls but his heart. The way he looked at her when he proposed marriage . . . It was obvious he was hers, she could do anything with him she liked.

In another few months he would have been president and Jill his wife. The plan had been proceeding on greased wheels—until Harley stepped in.

Obviously there must have been more to Roy than she thought. A built-in defense against her wiles, which had perhaps been lulled to sleep by her bedroom charms and the personality she had used to snare him with, but which had come back to life when he realized she had fucked Harley.

It was an unforgivable blunder on her part. And it was the only blunder in an otherwise perfect seduction.

She had baited Roy and hooked him like a master. She had used her sixth sense to know what he wanted, from the outset. She had chosen the right clothes, the right demeanor to play to his fantasies about her. She knew he admired performance in his employees, so she had made herself appear brilliant in her work in order to gain his respect. She had played hard to get until Roy had seemed to lose interest, and then gone to his office with that piece of stray interoffice mail to show herself to him and get him back on the hook. She had sat through all those lunches with him, playing his desire like a harp. And when she realized he was following her home, she had hired a friend to play the mugger, just to get Roy into her pants without making herself seem too forward.

It had all worked like a charm. And she had had Roy's proposal in her pocket, and his ascendancy to the presidency in her hand—so close! so close!—when Harley, the necessary evil, had stepped in.

She should have thought of a way to keep Harley quiet. Knowing that the two men were friends, she should have anticipated trouble. But her confidence in her power over Roy had blinded her, and she had almost forgotten Harley's existence. This was her big mistake.

Well, she would never make the same mistake again.

As for Roy English, he was a prey that had gotten away. She had been prepared to become his wife, even to bear his children. Now she could only forget about him and look elsewhere for the right man.

But she would not forget Harley Schrader. He would live to remember Jill Fleming, and to regret this day.

After Jill Fleming's firing Roy English was not seen by his friends or colleagues outside work, and kept very much to himself within the company, becoming an ever more shadowy and inscrutable presence.

Those at the top who had been preparing for the inevitability of his accession to the presidency still saw a lot of Roy, in meetings, over lunch, and in private tête-à-têtes designed to consolidate his power. He seemed as sharp as ever, and as concentrated on the job at hand.

Then he surprised everybody.

Six months after his firing of Jill Fleming, at the very moment when he was expected to succeed Bob Perkins as president, Roy suddenly accepted the presidency of a communications firm in North Carolina. It was a good position, a step up from where he had been at Continental.

Roy never explained his decision to any of his colleagues. He bade them a brisk farewell, gave good-bye gifts to his two lady friends—neither of whom had seen him at all in the last six months—sold his condominium, left the city, and was never seen again.

For a while his friends wondered why Roy had fought so hard for the presidency only to spurn it when it was being offered to him on a silver platter. Then, business memories being short, they stopped thinking about Roy, for they were too busy worrying about their own corporate futures.

No one, not even Harley Schrader—who, ironically, was allowed to remain in the company after Roy's departure, perhaps thanks to Roy's influence—no one dreamed for an instant that cold, ruthless Roy English had left Continental Products because he simply could not bear to be inside the same building in which he had known Jill Fleming. The grief he suffered was simply too great.

Roy was human after all.

19

Chicago, Illinois
February 21, 1972

Dear Tony,

  I love you so much that I can hardly find words to say to you.

  I've missed you so much these past weeks. I didn't think my heart was capable of hurting so deeply.

  I love you, my darling. I love you! I can't stop saying the words. They fill my mind every minute of the day.

  Each night I lie awake wondering about you. Where you are, what you're doing, what you're thinking. The very thought of you makes my heart ache and sing at the same time.

I waited all my life for love to come, and then you came. I didn't think it was possible that my heart could give itself so completely. But now I know it is true. I know I love you. I will love you forever.

Sometimes I feel you inside me almost more than I feel myself. I feel that you own me, and I want you to own me. I've lost myself, and I don't want to find myself. Not without you.

I think of the child we will have someday, and my body feels empty, and so hungry for you. I can't breathe until you come back.

I'll never love anyone but you. I could never feel this way again, never never never.

I can't wait to see you. There's no me without you. All I can do is dream of you. I feel desperate without you.

Please hurry back. I feel you inside me already. Don't make me wait for the real thing.

I love you, I love you, I love you!

Leslie held the letter in her hands. She marveled at the romantic abandon of her own words. They seemed to have been written by a stranger.

She had written the letter a week ago and decided not to send it to Tony. The heat of her passion was shocking even to her. She feared that if she allowed him to see it he would be too alarmed to trust her anymore. It was almost the letter of a madwoman.

But Leslie felt more than a little insane. Tony had been away for three weeks now, on a lengthy job for his company that had kept him from finding time to visit her.

But tomorrow, in the early morning, he would fly in to take her to City Hall for a simple wedding before a judge. By tomorrow night they would be on their honeymoon in northern Wisconsin. She would be Mrs. Anthony Dorrance.

He had called every week to talk with her about their wedding plans. They had agreed to elope. Neither felt that a traditional ceremony was appropriate to their love. They wanted to plight their troth to each other before they informed anyone else of their marriage.

Leslie was not entirely comfortable with this arrangement, for she was very close to her father, and wanted him to feel she had brought her young suitor to him and asked for his blessing before she actually married.

She felt she was betraying Tom Chamberlain by taking a step so important to her without sharing it with him. On the other hand, there was something so secret, so romantic about her love for Tony that only an elopement could do it justice. For the last three months she had joined Tony in a special, magic place out of the ordinary world. She enjoyed the privacy of this adventure, and got a thrill from the idea of consummating it far from the world of her job, her family.

She and Tony had discussed their future plans excitedly. Since they worked in cities hundreds of miles apart, the first question was where they should live. Tony thought they should move to New York, where Leslie could get a job with one of the major advertising agencies.

"With your credentials and your track record," he said, "you won't have any trouble. The headhunters will be falling all over each other to woo you."

As for Tony himself, he assured Leslie that he could find a job in any of a dozen companies. He had been around the corporate track for a dozen years, he said, and he had contacts literally everywhere.

A small-town girl, Leslie was somewhat daunted by the idea of New York. But Tony knew the city well, and had already found a spacious apartment on Central Park West that they could move into any time they liked.

"You'll belong there, babe," he said. "More than you've ever belonged anywhere before. You'll see. Chicago's a nice place, but it's been holding you back. You'll really come into your own in the Big Apple."

Leslie had agreed. She felt that New York would be an appropriate setting for her life with this supremely exciting man. She had already burned her emotional bridges a hundred times over since she fell in love with him. Why not take the last plunge with him?

She took a last look at the love letter she had written and never sent. She blushed to see the reference to a child. It was for this reason above all that she had left the letter unsent, and yet kept it close to her, rereading it almost obsessively.

She and Tony had often talked about their future children. Tony had entertained her with descriptions of the little boy they would have, or the little girl. He had joked about possible names, about personalities, about sibling rivalry and toys and nursery schools and peanut butter and jelly sandwiches.

But a tone of levity had always characterized those conversations. In the letter the reference to their child was so serious, so passionate, that Leslie thought it was too much. She did not want Tony to feel that she was surrounding him with a future full of obligations and responsibilities. She wanted their marriage to be an act of freedom, of liberation, for both.

She realized that she had been separated from Tony too long. She was beginning to lose her grip on herself. Her body craved him as wildly as did her heart. So much of her belonged to him already that it was torture to be separated from him.

She folded the letter and put it in a back page of her photo album. There were other letters to Tony there, also unsent. They all made her blush, but something made her keep them instead of throwing them away.

Then she flipped through the pages of the album from the beginning, seeing the pictures of her father, her late mother, herself, her school friends.

Everyone looked the same except Leslie. The pictures of herself had a new aspect now, colored by her love for Tony and the revolution it had wrought in her ideas about herself.

She had always thought she knew herself so well, from the perky child who had endured her mother's death to the quietly determined teenager who had taken care of her father, to the bright college student who had found her way to Ogilvie, Thorpe and an exciting career.

Now she looked at the pictures of herself and saw a person who did not know herself, a person who was essentially incomplete, living on the surface of her own life without understanding its depths.

At the same time she thought she saw her future love for Tony casting its shadow over her past. She looked at the little girl she had once been and saw a new mystery in her eyes. For the little girl was no longer just the early avatar of a working adult, but the embryo of a woman in love. Inside that child's body waited the grown-up woman who now lived only for her lover—a woman timed by fate to emerge only now, like a stunning, brilliantly colored butterfly from a chrysalis.

How little human surfaces tell us about human beings, Leslie reflected. The self she had taken for granted all her life, so controlled, so deliberate, gave no sign of the real person underneath, a creature of intense and all-encompassing passion. How little she had known her own heart! Until Tony Dorrance came into her life, that is.

But now she had met Tony at last, and belonged to him with her whole soul. Why try to explain it or understand it? Love was its own explanation.

She turned to the back page of her album, where she now kept souvenirs of her trysts with Tony. There were a few little notes bearing the times and places of assignations. There were a some postcards and pieces of stationery taken from hotel rooms to remind her of the ecstatic hours she had spent there. There was a handful of snapshots of herself taken by Tony with his camera, and a few of him as well, taken by her at her insistence.

It seemed appropriate that the thick photo album, documenting her past on her own, led finally to the few precious souvenirs of her time with Tony. For Tony gave her whole past a new color, a new meaning. And Tony was her future.

And if she sensed, in one cautious corner of her heart, that she was being unfaithful to her past in feeling this way, unfaithful to the self she had been and respected and fought for all these years—then this last scruple died away, too, consumed by the flame burning her from the inside out.

So Leslie closed the album, bidding farewell to the pale silhouette that had been her solitary self, and waited for Tony Dorrance to fill in the light and shade that would be the new, the real Leslie Chamberlain.

She had only a few more hours to wait. Then she would be his. And all the banal worries and concerns that had preoccupied her in the past would be as forgotten as that little girl in the photographs, a little girl who had ceased to exist long years ago.

Leslie got up and opened, for the twentieth time, the small suitcase in which she had packed her things for the trip. It included a simple but beautiful wedding dress from one of the finest shops on Michigan Avenue.

Tomorrow she would wear that dress.

Amazingly, Leslie slept through most of the night. She awoke early, made her bed, and cleaned up a last few things in the apartment. Then she waited, pacing back and forth, looking again and again at her watch.

Somehow she survived until seven-thirty. Then she called the airport to make sure Flight 47 was on time. Excited to hear that it was, she could no longer contain her excitement. She locked the apartment behind her, put her suitcase in the trunk of the car, and drove to O'Hare Airport.

On her way there she passed the expressway that led downtown and to Ogilvie, Thorpe. She was not worried about things at the office. All her accounts were in good order. It had taken some doing, for an essential part of a good advertising executive's life is his or her profound distrust of handing over creative responsibilities to others.

Leslie had painstakingly arranged things so that the creative end of the work on her three major accounts was well in hand. For the next two weeks the accounts could be safely caretaken by assistants.

She parked in the airport lot and walked in to the arrivals section. She found the gate number for Flight 47 and walked to the gate.

She was still forty-five minutes early. She bought a magazine and sat in the waiting area, flipping through the pages without really seeing them. She had had nothing to eat this morning, but she was far too excited to be hungry.

Gradually a few people appeared in the waiting area, families or friends of the arriving passengers. Leslie let her eyes stray over them. She saw mothers restraining their restless children, teenagers standing with studied coolness alongside their parents, a young woman looking expectant and embarrassed as she waited no doubt for her husband or fiancé.

Though nearly all those present wore neutral expressions on the surface of their faces, Leslie could see beneath that surface to the profound anticipation with which they awaited those they loved. And she felt joined to them by her own almost painful waiting for her new life to begin.

At last the flight arrived. The plane seemed to take forever to crawl to the gate, and the doors opened with agonizing slowness. The passengers began to trickle out. The faces of the people in the waiting area changed, illuminated by recognition as they rushed to hug those who arrived.

The process was frustratingly slow. Passenger after passenger came through

the gate, each one strikingly individual not only in his or her personal characteristics but because he or she was, above all, not Tony.

Leslie watched as the first trickle became a slow-moving wave of passengers.
The gate was crowded with arrivals carrying hand luggage, briefcases, and
shopping bags. Then, little by little, the wave began to thin. Leslie's heart
was in her mouth. Tony must be only a few steps, a few seconds, from that
open door!

But the stream of arrivals grew thinner and thinner, and the crowd waiting
at the gate became smaller and smaller. Finally two stewardesses appeared,
pulling overnight bags on rolling metal frames. Then, as Leslie watched, the
pilot and copilot emerged and moved away down the aisle.

Leslie was alone in the waiting area.

She spent two painful minutes taking in the fact that Tony had not arrived.
Panic surged inside her for an instant, then abated as her strong personality
began to ask the logical questions. Had Tony missed the flight? Had he been
delayed by business? Had he called her at home, only to miss her because she
had left for the airport so early?

She got up, walked briskly to the airline's information desk, and asked if
there was a message for her. There was none.

She stood uncertainly in the terminal for a few moments, thinking that
perhaps a message might arrive at any moment. At length she decided not to
wait any longer. She went out to the parking lot, got back in her car, and
drove home.

Leaving her overnight bag in the trunk of the car, she reentered the apartment, which looked oddly stale and forlorn despite the fact that she had left
it only two hours ago.

She sat down beside the telephone. She dialed the number of Tony's apartment in Atlanta. There was no answer.

She thought of Tony's company. Only now did she recall that he had never
given her his work number. He had told her it was useless to try to reach
him through the company, since he was never there. At the time she had
accepted this explanation without question. Now, however, she had no choice
but to call Price-Davis.

She got the number through long-distance information. She dialed it carefully, for it was unfamiliar.

A distant-sounding voice answered.

"Price-Davis. May I help you?"

"Yes, please. I'm trying to get through to a Mr. Anthony Dorrance. I
believe he is in your sales division; I'm sorry I can't be more explicit. Could
you look up his name in your directory and put me through to him, please?"

"One moment."

There was a long pause. Leslie sat tapping her foot and drumming her fingers nervously on the table. The rising tide of panic inside her was enveloping all her thoughts, but she fought against it bravely, holding fast to her image of Tony and of their love.

At last the voice came back on the line.

"Hello?"

"Yes, I'm still here," Leslie said with a tense little laugh.

"Well, Miss, I've checked our personnel directory. There's no Anthony Dorrance here. However, it seems that a Mr. Anthony Dorrance worked in sales for about a year and a half, terminating last fall. He's not with the company any more."

There was a stunned pause.

"I—What was his position?" Leslie asked.

"There's no title, Miss. Sales executive, I imagine."

"Well, thank you."

Leslie hung up the phone with shaking fingers. She knew now that something was terribly wrong. A new and harsh light was being thrown on all the mad emotions she had been feeling for the past several months, emotions that flaunted their lack of relation to ordinary reality. She had been in a virtual trance all this time. In one instant the veil was lifting and harsh reality was crashing down on her with all its weight.

She dialed Price-Davis again and asked for the director of personnel, sales division.

"Personnel, how may I help you?"

"Hello," Leslie said, feigning businesslike briskness. "This is Miss Weatherbee, from Ogilvie, Thorpe. We're trying to process a job application from a Mr. Anthony Dorrance, and the records from your office haven't come through."

"Dorrance?" There was a cautious note in the man's voice that did not escape Leslie.

"Yes. Anthony Dorrance. Can you tell me, for instance, why he was terminated?"

"One moment, please."

There was a pause.

"All right, I have the file," came the male voice. "You say you didn't receive a copy? Can you give me your address?"

Leslie gave her own office address. She was curious to see what the file said.

"If you don't mind," she said, "we're in a bit of a rush. We have several applicants for the same position. I just need to know whether this was a routine termination, or whether there was cause. Or perhaps you could read me the job recommendation from your department. It would be a big help."

"Well, to tell the truth, there isn't any recommendation in his file," he said. "Under the circumstances, we felt that the omission was equal to doing Tony a favor. You see, Tony was a talented salesman but totally undependable.

He would return from a sales trip a week late with no explanation. Sometimes he made deals that were fabulous. Other times he made customers so mad that they cut us off completely. And there was—well, he just couldn't be counted on. So we let him go."

From the tone in his voice Leslie gathered there was something else he wasn't saying. But it must be too sensitive for him to reveal over the phone. And thus, no doubt, it was not in the file. Perhaps if Leslie had been a man instead of a woman, the male on the other end of the line might have confided it to her.

"I do appreciate your candor," she said. "You'll send that file along, then."

"I'll put it in this afternoon's mail," he said. "Sorry I couldn't give you better news."

"No problem," Leslie lied. "As long as we have the truth. Thank you again."

She hung up the phone.

Leslie sat on the couch for a long time, staring at nothing. The minutes went by. She did not even think. Her mind was devoured by something beneath its surface, which could neither become conscious nor let any other thought become conscious.

After another hour she began to feel hungry. She had had nothing to eat all day, and it was almost noon.

She went to the kitchen and fixed a sandwich. She brought the sandwich to her mouth and was seized by a wave of nausea that made her dizzy. She put the sandwich in the garbage disposal. Then she made a cup of tea and sat watching it grow cold on the coffee table before her. She looked at the kitchen clock. It was nearly one.

The afternoon lumbered by like an old cripple with a cane. It seemed interminable. The silent apartment was like a crypt.

Leslie sat in the kitchen, then returned to the living room, and finally went to the bedroom and lay on her bed, savoring the pain of each moment, forcing herself to realize what had happened to her.

Part of her was given over to the tormenting hope that any minute now the phone would ring, a knock would come at the door, and this whole nightmare would be over, because Tony would be here, ready to marry her, to take her away from her pain. The clamor of her own hope almost tore her apart.

But the rest of her knew the truth.

She waited all day. At midnight she fell asleep in her clothes, without so much as a comforter over her. She felt absolutely nothing. By now her thoughts were as foreign to her as the moon. The only reality was her solitude.

Outside, in the trunk of the car, her overnight bag remained, containing her clothes, a few cosmetics, her wedding dress, and her hopes.

On Saturday morning she began to think of necessities. She got up, took a shower, and did her hair and makeup carefully. She ate a bowl of cereal, threw it up into the toilet five minutes later, and waited an hour before trying again to eat. This time a cup of bouillon stayed down.

She remained in the apartment all weekend, thinking. With infinite patience she analyzed what had happened to her, and what must happen now. She considered the possibility of going on with her life as though Tony had never been in it. She could simply go back to the office Monday morning, resume work on her major accounts, and try to forget.

But she knew this was impossible. The change inside her would not allow it.

By Monday morning she had made her decision. She called Bud Owens at Ogilvie, Thorpe and told him she was quitting. She would have a friend come in to pick up her things, she said. When Bud expressed his shock and incomprehension, she told him coolly that she had accepted another job elsewhere.

Before noon on Monday she had told her landlord she was moving. She made hurried arrangements to have a neighbor buy her furniture. She packed two suitcases with the most essential of her personal items. The rest of her clothes and possessions she threw out.

Inside one of the suitcases was her photo album. At the back of it nestled the letter she had written to Tony and not sent, along with her few photographs of him and mementos of their affair. In her haste to leave the city she had not thought to throw away this small but eloquent evidence of her greatest love.

At seven o'clock Monday evening she got in her car without so much as a map and left Chicago. She did not know where she was going. But for the first time in months, perhaps in years, she knew where she had been.

And, most important of all, she knew what she had paid for her journey.

Leslie was pregnant.

20

New York City

ON MARCH 15, 1972, the long-delayed meeting of the Lazarus International, Inc. stockholders took place.

Jordan Lazarus was on tenterhooks. He had done everything humanly possible to convince his stockholders not to accept the tempting cash tender offer from Victor Considine. He had sent out mailing after mailing, describing the great future awaiting Lazarus International as an independent corporation, and detailing the disastrous results that must follow upon a takeover by Considine Industries.

During these last frantic weeks he had waited in vain for the one signal meaning that this fateful stockholders' meeting would never have to take place. That signal could come only from Barbara Considine. Her personal influence over her father was the only thing standing between Jordan and the loss of the empire he had spent over a decade building from nothing.

But Barbara had not called. Nor had she answered his many messages. In the wake of their night together in his room at the Alhambra Hotel in White Plains, he had hoped Barbara would take his side against her father. Her silence made it clear she was not going to help him.

The stockholders' meeting took place in the ballroom of the Waldorf-Astoria Hotel in New York. The minutes of the last meeting were read. Several items of current business were dispatched. Then, with an electric charge of anticipation in the air, the main item on the agenda was announced.

"It is proposed," said the chairman, "that the stockholders of Lazarus International accept a cash tender offer for their shares in the amount of seventy-five dollars per share from Considine Industries, Inc. of New York. May we have the vote counted, please?"

The tallying of votes and proxies took nearly half an hour. But the result was clear after only a few minutes. When the votes had been counted the chairman rose to speak. He looked tired and discouraged.

"Mr. President, members of the board of directors, fellow shareholders and employees," he said. "The stockholders of Lazarus International have voted to accept the cash tender offer from Considine Industries. As of this meeting, Considine Industries will hold sixty-nine percent of the stock in Lazarus International, Inc."

There was a sigh of combined defeat and relief in the ballroom. The battle was over. Jordan Lazarus had lost.

Jordan turned to Sam Gaddis, his personal assistant. Sam's eyes were filled with tears.

"It's a bitter pill," Sam said. "I really thought we could pull it out somehow."

Jordan placed a hand on Sam's shoulder and gave it an affectionate squeeze. "We tried," he said. "Don't feel too bad. The future is an open book."

Jordan left Sam and went to join the chairman. They turned to close the meeting and begin the slow process of the destruction of Lazarus International.

It was all over.

Or almost over.

*   *   *

A half hour after the crucial vote, the assembled crowd was still milling about in the ballroom when the chairman rang his bell.

"Ladies and gentlemen," he said in a stifled voice, "I have a sad announcement to make. At nine o'clock this evening, Victor Considine died of an apparent heart attack in his Manhattan home."

A hush fell over the crowd. Everyone was taken completely by surprise.

Jordan Lazarus turned to see Sam looking at him questioningly. Sam was wondering what this event might mean for Jordan, for himself, for Lazarus International.

Jordan looked away. He realized that the death of Victor Considine meant nothing as far as today's meeting and today's vote were concerned. Lazarus International had been acquired by Considine Industries. It did not matter who was at the helm of Considine.

Or did it?

Behind the glare of today's happenings Jordan was already beginning to see a subtle shadow that colored everything in a different way.

He decided to go home and ponder it at his leisure.

Late that night Jordan was sitting quietly in the easy chair he used for private meditation in his apartment.

He was reflecting on what he had lost, and where he was to go now.

He knew he was not finished. Not by a long chalk. His own shares in Lazarus International, when sold to Considine Industries, would bring him a considerable nest egg. He felt himself capable of starting over again and building himself another empire. In fact, he was almost stimulated by the idea. He had complete confidence in his talent and creativity.

On the other hand, he felt tired. Mentally and morally tired, from all the many struggles it had taken to build Lazarus International to what it became. Tired from the battle against Considine Industries. But most of all, tired of having poured so much of his personality, even his soul into a crusade whose real value to his spirit seemed oddly negligible.

Why am I doing this? The question had haunted Jordan for years. There seemed to be a contradiction deep inside him between the relentless upward climb of his business life and the frail but audible call of his real self. He had long since accustomed himself to that contradiction—so compellingly described by his beloved sister Meg—but had never been able to get rid of it. Its constant presence in his life was exhausting and somehow demoralizing.

Tonight, as he sat in his apartment, adding up his gains and losses from today's events, he mused for a moment that this might be his opportunity to get off the treadmill he had created for himself fourteen years ago, and set out in another direction entirely. His personal profits from Lazarus International made him wealthy already. The Considine tender offer for his own stock holdings would make him a multimillionaire.

Why not stop now?

Instead of pursuing the never-ending struggle to force the world to bend to his will, why not try to find out who was the real person behind that will?

There was something peculiar about great wealth. Money did not make a person more worthy, more happy, more at peace with himself. It gave no understanding, no fulfillment. It only created a strange and uncontrollable desire to amass more money. A desire that fed on its own satisfaction, so that no amount of money was enough.

Worldly success was somehow false. It was a golden garment admired by others, but when one looked in the mirror it was like the emperor's new clothes, absolutely nil. This was because success did not come from inside, from who one really was. It came from outside, from one's worldly efforts and their effect on others.

One could go from one success to another, eternally, and never come a step closer to knowing oneself.

These thoughts were very tiring to Jordan. The more so because he had been trying so hard to deny them for so many years. But tonight they seemed to offer him an opportunity.

He wanted to call Meg. She would understand what he was feeling tonight. She, more than anyone else, had always understood why Jordan did what he did, and what he had given up when he became a man of the world, a man of action. She cared more for his soul than anyone else, more than he himself perhaps.

He knew Meg was waiting for news of the results of the stockholders' meeting, as were his brothers, and Mother and Louise. He could call right now. Not to tell Meg he had been defeated, but to tell her that a new door had opened to him tonight, a door he intended to walk through.

He stood up and moved toward the phone.

Before he reached it the doorbell rang. He looked at the silent phone for an instant more, then walked to the door.

His eyes opened wide when he saw who was in the doorway.

It was Barbara Considine.

She was dressed in a magnificent sable coat, which looked inappropriately opulent and also somehow cold and inhuman on her. So did the costly jewelry she wore and the black gown under the coat.

"I'm surprised to see you here," Jordan said. He expected Barbara to be busy making funeral arrangements or dealing with her private grief over her father's death.

She seemed not to have heard his remark.

"May I come in?" she asked.

"Of course." Jordan was oddly relaxed, even languid as he stood back to let her pass.

He helped her off with her coat and hung it in the closet. Her eyes had a faraway, preoccupied look.

"Can I get you something?" Jordan asked with a smile. "Coffee? A drink?"

She shook her head. She seemed different from the young woman he remembered, the sad young woman he had almost made love to. She looked older, more powerful, more determined. Her girlish vulnerability was almost erased by this womanly look of purpose. Yet somehow the overall effect was of a pitiable loneliness.

"I'm sorry about your father," he said.

She stood looking at him. There was grief in her face, certainly. But it seemed twisted somehow. It was not the clean, open grief of a person who has lost a loved one.

"I'm sorry about your company," she responded.

Jordan shrugged. "Easy come, easy go," he said. "Would you like a brandy?"

"Whatever you're having."

He went to the kitchen and poured two snifters of Armagnac. When he returned she was still standing where he had left her. As he handed her a glass she smiled at him appraisingly.

"You're not really upset, are you?" she asked. "What happened today doesn't really bother you, does it?"

Jordan mustered an insouciance he did not entirely feel.

"Life goes on," he said.

"Not for my father."

Her response puzzled him. His eyes narrowed as he looked at her.

"Why don't you sit down?" he asked. "You may be more distressed than you realize."

She sat down. The small evening bag she held in her hands looked extraordinarily expensive.

"Distressed?" she asked, studying Jordan's face. "I'm not distressed. My father was a monster. He ruined my life. I'm glad he's dead."

There was a silence as Jordan listened to the terrible bitterness of these words, and the despair hidden beneath them. He was looking at one of the richest heiresses in the world. She looked like a terrified child trying to masquerade as a world-weary woman. His heart went out to her. One did not need a lot of imagination to picture her life with Victor Considine.

For her part, Barbara was pondering the irony of their situation. Jordan, the defeated one, was cool and self-possessed. She, whose corporation had swallowed his entire family of companies this afternoon, felt as though she had acquired nothing, lost everything.

"Jordan," she said in a tone of brisk decision, as though getting down to business.

"Yes?" he said, reclining in his chair.

There was a long pause, pregnant on both sides. He could see her wrestling with an unspoken dilemma. She seemed to hesitate. Then she sat forward and looked at him, as though screwing up her courage.

"Jordan," she said abruptly, "will you marry me?"

Jordan said nothing. He wondered if she had lost her mind. Perhaps the grief she was trying to deny had skewed her thinking.

Seeing the neutral look in his eyes, Barbara set down her brandy glass.

"Today I inherited fifty-six percent of the shares in Considine Industries," she said. "I am the majority stockholder and chairman of the board. I can do whatever I like with the company. I can sell it tomorrow if I want."

She looked him in the eyes.

"Marry me, Jordan," she said.

"Is that why you came here?" he asked. "I'm sorry about your father, but . . ."

"Marry me, and you'll have all your companies back," she interrupted. "And your new drug research program. And all the money you could ever want to develop it with. You'll have complete freedom to do things your own way. I ask for nothing. Except that you be my husband."

Jordan sat back on the couch and studied her. He could not believe what he was hearing. He would have expected her to be at home tonight, nursing her own grief. Instead she was sitting here coolly offering him a quid pro quo, like a real businessman.

But it was a cruel bargain, cruel for herself. He wondered if she realized this.

Barbara seemed to sense the drift of his thoughts.

"You wouldn't have to love me," she said quite coolly. "You wouldn't have to—give me children. You could even see other women. In fact, I assume you would want to. It would be a sort of—arrangement, between us."

He stared at her. She seemed totally transformed by her own dark purpose, and yet still the same poor bereft young woman she had always been. Her desolation gave her an impressive dignity, even in this humiliating moment.

"I don't think it would be right," he said cautiously. "I think it would be a mistake."

"My whole life has been a mistake," Barbara countered. "This is my chance to do one thing right. You have to look at it from my side, Jordan."

He saw what she meant. From her perspective, colored as it was by her whole miserable past, marriage to him—even a marriage in name only—would be a step forward. But he was not convinced. Pity for her, even empathy, was not enough to justify a marriage without love.

Jordan shook his head. "I can't marry you. It wouldn't be right."

The look in her eyes changed. He saw cold cunning there. It did not become her.

"Then you won't have your companies, or your product," she said. "I'll let Considine keep it all."

Jordan tried to reason with her. "I thought you were a decent, moral person," he said. "I thought you knew how to do the right thing. What you're proposing would be bad for me, but a lot worse for you. Can you really bear to play with people's lives that way?"

His eyes narrowed. "Are you really your father's daughter?" he added.

A look flashed briefly in Barbara's eyes, as though he had hit on the precise truth—and was gone. In years to come Jordan would have plenty of leisure to ponder what that look had meant.

"My father was the worst thing that ever happened to me," she said. "But he taught me one thing. You can't get what you want in this world without leverage." She looked at Jordan. "I've got the leverage now."

"Not if I wash my hands of you and Leo Kaminsky and Lazarus International," Jordan said. "There are other fish in the sea. Other opportunities. I have my whole life ahead of me."

She smiled. "I thought you wanted to make history," she said.

Again Jordan was struck by her cold-blooded business mind. He had not realized she possessed such instincts. She was playing this the way her father would have played it. She knew he had had high hopes for Leo and his research. She was holding it out to him like a carrot on a stick.

"It wouldn't be a marriage," he said. "Nothing can justify that, Barbara."

Sensing the firmness of his resistance, Barbara took another tack. The cold look in her eyes was replaced by a pleading expression.

"I'm not asking you to love me," she said. "I don't ask for your heart. And it doesn't have to be forever. I just—can't go on alone, right now. Surely you can understand that. My father has just died. . . . I need help, to decide who I am and what's happening. When you tried to romance me, you did it for business reasons. But you felt something. I could tell. Pity, perhaps, but it was enough for me. You made me feel wanted. I need that now, Jordan. I need to feel wanted. To feel human. I'm prepared to help you, if you'll help me. It doesn't have to be forever. . . . Don't you understand?"

She paused. Her eyes had misted. "You said you were my friend," she said. "Do you remember that? Were you lying then?"

Her words hit home. He had not been merely lying when he offered her his friendship. He did feel something for her.

And there was logic behind her proposal. Her father had stolen what Jordan had worked so hard for. Now Barbara was offering it back to him. And she was saying the marriage did not have to be forever. Jordan's pride, and his love for the empire he had built from nothing, came to the fore within him.

He decided to remind her of the painful truth.

"I don't love you," he said.

"I know that." Her eyes were averted. In that instant she looked infinitely pitiable. There was a childish pathos and bravery in her that wrung Jordan's heart.

"You want me to pretend I love you?" he asked.

"Oh, no," she said. "You don't have to pretend anything. Just be the man you are. Just get me through this. Just be what you said you wanted to be. Otherwise I—I don't know what will happen."

All at once he understood how desperate she really was. With her father dead, her whole world was collapsing. Her shame and self-hatred were on the point of engulfing her. She saw a chance to bandage herself together until she could heal. And Jordan was the bandage. She could have him at the price of a few hundred million dollars. To a woman who despised wealth as she did, this was a small price to pay. She was literally fighting for her life.

Jordan's musings of earlier tonight about leaving the business world altogether were forgotten now. He felt sorry for Barbara, but he also wanted to get back what was his. Marrying her was not too high a price to pay for the return of all he had worked so hard for.

A curious combination of pity and ambition moved him as he spoke.

"All right," he said. "I'll marry you."

The sadness in her face dissolved into anguished relief. She came to his side and put her arms around him. Tears were flowing from her eyes.

"Oh, thank you, Jordan. Thank you," she wept against his chest. "I know I'm nothing to you. I don't expect to be anything to you. But you won't regret it. I promise you."

"You're not nothing to me," he said, holding her.

And he was telling the truth. He remembered the night at the Alhambra, when he had slept with her in his arms and watched her wake up in the morning. She had looked like a little girl in her slumber. Yet there was so much sadness, so much loneliness behind those closed eyes. It was that loneliness that appealed to him.

He embraced her now. Kissing her cheeks, he tasted her tears. He held her cautiously, not too close. In this moment it seemed to him worthwhile to offer her his tenderness, even his pity, if it would help her out of the hell of her past. But he dared not offer more than he was truly prepared to give. He must not let her misunderstand him.

The warmth of her body felt good in his arms. He pulled her a bit closer and petted her softly. She rested her head on his shoulder. He could not see the look in her eyes as she stared past him at the wall of his apartment.

It was a look of cold determination.

Book Two

THE
STROKE
OF
MIDNIGHT

21

ROSS WHEELER HAD A WEAKNESS for sweets.

At age fifty-one he was overweight and had been warned about it by his doctor. But Ross worked terribly hard all day and found it simply impossible to deny himself a piece of pie after dinner, or a few cookies bought from the bakery at the supermarket, or, most guiltily of all, a couple of scoops of rich French vanilla ice cream with a spoonful of caramel and some chopped pecans.

Ross ran a small advertising agency called Wheeler Advertising, Inc. The business was now a franchise of a national chain called Modern Images. Ross had sold the business to the chain two years ago because he could no longer stand the stress of owning it on his own and watching his income fluctuate wildly with the fortunes of the business. He needed a measure of security now that his daughters were in college.

But it seemed that he worked harder now, and longer hours, since selling the business. Johnsonville was, at 14,000, a small town rapidly being turned into a bedroom community by the relentless suburban expansion throughout Long Island. The village center remained untouched by progress, with its churches, drugstore, department store, and bank looking just as they had thirty-five years ago. But there were new housing subdivisions growing inexorably from the outskirts of town, near the highway, toward those now extending outward from Reedsburg, only ten miles away.

Suburban growth meant new businesses spread out all over the surrounding area. And new businesses meant new advertising clients. In his unfamiliar capacity as salaried president instead of one-man employer, Ross had to take orders from above. And orders were that he expand his operation to keep up with the times. This meant hard work and responsibility.

All the more reason why, at the end of a long day, Ross felt like treating himself to a well-deserved dessert after his solitary dinner.

Dr. Kumel was getting more severe in his warnings now that Ross was over fifty.

"Don't you want to live to see those daughters of yours get married and have children?" he had asked at the end of Ross's last yearly physical. "You can't take four score and ten for granted, Ross. With a cholesterol count like yours, something could go wrong at any moment, and a lot of dreams could fall apart. I'm sure you don't want that."

And Ross did not want that. But the last few years had been so difficult that he simply could not find the strength to adopt the spartan regime the doctor recommended.

It was now ten years since Ross lost his wife. Ruth had died after a shockingly brief illness, leaving Ross alone with two little daughters.

The girls, Dina and Nancy, had been eight and ten at the time. Since then Ross had worked overtime to bring in enough money to put them through college. He had promised each of them that she would not have to attend the state university but could pick out any college she liked.

He had kept his promise. Nancy was now a sophomore at the University of Rochester's Eastman School of Music—she had an academic scholarship, thank God—and Dina had just started at Indiana University. Both girls were happy with the schools they had chosen, and did not suspect how close their father had come to penury in order to send them there.

As things stood, Ross was far from well off. He could barely keep up the mortgage on the house, pay the girls' bills, and keep himself in the suits and ties he wore to work. There was not a dollar left over for frills of any kind. Both girls worked in the summer, Dina at the bank here in town and Nancy at a girls' camp near Southampton.

It was a hard life, and Ross had to work such long hours at the agency that there was precious little time left over for amusements of any sort. He played tennis once a week with an old friend from the neighborhood, and occasionally had a Sunday dinner with relatives or one of the girls from the office. The rest of the time he was alone, worn out by work, by worry about money, and by loneliness.

Was it any wonder, then, that he allowed himself a little bit of oral gratification at the end of a backbreaking day? What was so terrible about a piece of pie, a brownie, or a few cookies? At least he didn't drink. He had given up his martinis the year after Ruth died, realizing that solitary drinking could not be good for a man in his position.

For a man of his age Ross was not unattractive. True, his belt was a notch or two looser than it had been years ago. But with his jacket and tie on, he looked quite presentable. He had graying hair, only a little thin on top, tawny eyes full of humor and gentleness, and a ruddy complexion that gave him a look of male energy. When he went to work in the morning he looked fresh and sharp, and smelled of the cologne Ruth used to like. At the end of the day, of course, he was rumpled, his hair tousled by his habit of running his hand through it, and the smells of tobacco and perspiration had mingled with his cologne. But on the whole Ross Wheeler was a good-looking man, even a desirable one. If he had a little weakness, let the doctor worry about it. Ross himself had more pressing concerns.

It was because of Ross's weakness for sweets that he met Leslie.

The public library had started a policy of providing free doughnuts and coffee every Saturday morning as a means of promoting literacy among the citizens of Johnsonville. The doughnuts were available from nine to eleven, and the librarians gambled that those who ate them would not dare leave the premises without borrowing a book.

Ross had not been to the library in years. Like most working men, he was too busy for books. But now he fell into the somewhat embarrassing habit of coming into the old library building in the village, a brisk and purposeful look on his face, and then raising an eyebrow and saying appreciatively, "Doughnuts? That's nice of you ladies."

Mrs. Babbage, the head librarian, would smile and pass the time of day as Ross ate two doughnuts, one glazed and one chocolate. Then Ross would hurry into the stacks and find something to read, usually a spy novel or a book about World War II. He was rarely able to finish a book within the three-week limit, for he fell asleep early after his hard days at work. But he kept up the pretense, showing up every Saturday morning to return some books, borrow some others, and eat his doughnuts.

One day he noticed a librarian he had not seen before. She was a tall girl, and very pretty, with curly reddish hair and sparkling hazel eyes. She could not be much older than his daughters.

He struck up a conversation with her as he was eating his doughnuts. Her name was Leslie, she said. She was a sometime college student at SUNY Stony Brook who had dropped out "temporarily," and was working here until she made up her mind what to do next.

She was a cheerful, friendly person, and Ross warmed to her instantly. She had milky, freckled skin and an agile, energetic air. But she was too thin, Ross thought. And once, when he saw her face at rest while she thought herself unobserved, he saw a look of sadness and fatigue in her attractive features that was never there when she spoke to the patrons or to the other librarians.

He asked Mrs. Babbage how long Leslie had been at the library.

"Let me see," frowned the middle-aged librarian, who liked precision in all things. "Two years and five months. . . . No. Two and a half years, to the day. I had just lost Janice, my old girl. I had put up a little sign on the bulletin board in the square advertising for an assistant librarian. Leslie walked in, we had a little chat, and she went to work in the stacks five minutes later."

Ross nodded. "She's a pretty girl," he said. "A bit on the thin side, though."

Mrs. Babbage shrugged. "That's exactly what I told her when I hired her. She was even worse then. She looked downright sick. I told her to go to the doctor. She wouldn't listen. She told me she had an overactive metabolism. I've invited her to my house for dinner a dozen times, but she always finds an excuse not to come. To tell you the truth, it was because of her that these doughnuts came to be here. I brought a box of them in every week to try to put some meat on Leslie's bones. It didn't work, but she got the idea of using the doughnuts to attract customers. Leslie is very smart that way. Why, even a week after she started here she was making suggestions about shelving and classification that have improved the library a lot. She's smart as a whip, that girl."

Ross could not help wondering how such an intelligent girl could have dropped out of Stony Brook and gone to work in a small-town public library. He broached the question delicately to Mrs. Babbage, not wanting to wound her pride in her establishment.

"Oh, I've asked myself that question a hundred times," the librarian said. "Asked her, too, if you want to know the truth. But she won't open up about it. Says she likes it here. Says she has plenty of time to make up her mind what to do with her life."

She leaned forward confidentially.

"I'll tell you what I think," she said. "I think she had man trouble. That's why she came to rest in an out-of-the-way place like this. I don't even believe she's a college dropout. She may have dropped out of something, but she's college educated, and as intelligent as they come. She belongs somewhere else. But she's too private to let me figure her out."

This conversation intrigued Ross Wheeler, and he began to look at Leslie differently. No longer merely a friendly girl who was too thin, she became for him a gifted and interesting young woman with a secret.

He tried to penetrate the shell of her personality. He asked her to recommend books for him. She suggested a handful of novels, which she claimed to have read during her aborted college career. Ross borrowed them and read them from cover to cover, staying up past his usual bedtime. Returning to the library on his Saturday mornings—or during the week when he knew Leslie was working—he discussed the novels with her. Her intelligence impressed him, but not as much as something warm and feminine about her personality that reminded him of her secret sadness.

He told her of his doctor's warnings about his weight, and asked her to play tennis with him. When she put him off he persisted, prodding her with little jokes about his failing health and her refusal to help him restore himself. In the end she gave in and joined him for a Saturday game at the tennis courts behind the old high school. He provided both rackets, giving her one that used to belong to Dina when she was on the high school tennis team.

Leslie was a virtual beginner, but she played energetically. It was a pleasure to see her too thin body flushed by good exercise.

It was after the third of these tennis games that he convinced her to have lunch with him at a local café. Not surprisingly, she would eat only a salad. But she did not criticize him for the cheeseburger and french fries he ordered, and seemed to enjoy seeing his pleasure in the food.

"My doctor would say I ought to be eating that salad," Ross said guiltily. "He's always at me about my weight. To be honest, Leslie, I'll bet he'd prescribe this cheeseburger and fries for you. Have you always been this thin?"

She smiled. "Not always," she said ambiguously. "But I don't mind. I really don't have that much of an appetite."

Something about the look in her eyes made Ross drop the subject. He sensed the inner pain that had lurked behind her bright, welcoming personality at the library.

Ross backed off, giving her plenty of distance. But after that day he thought about her more than ever.

Their tennis game became a quasi-regular event, taking place every second Sunday. Ross began to invite Leslie to lunch during the week—either a brown-bag excursion to the park on the square or a quick bite at the café—and she did not refuse him. He had a paternal, protective air that seemed to please her.

Something told him she had no real friends in town, and no boyfriend. He wondered why. She was an enigma—a lovely, bright young woman who had no apparent ambition and kept completely to herself. Ross wondered whether her reclusive personality had made room for him because the solitude she had created for herself was more than even she could bear.

She talked easily about all manner of topics but was very close-mouthed about her past. She would only say that she had a father who lived in the Midwest, and that she visited him twice a year. Her mother, she said, had been dead for many years. She had no siblings.

This was all Ross could learn. But as he conversed with her he became more and more impressed not only with her intelligence but with her level-headedness and her good-humored tolerance toward other people. Decidedly, she was not a bitter person but a naturally happy one. Yet she was so thin, and so solitary. . . .

Ross told her all about his life with Ruth, his bereavement, and showed her pictures of his daughters. She listened attentively to his story and responded with a sympathy so sincere that Ross found himself opening up to her more and more.

As time passed Ross Wheeler began to depend on Leslie as a valued friend and confidante. Though she did not reveal her secret life to him, she learned most of what there was to know about his own dreams and disappointments, and the accommodation he had made to the harsh demands of his life. She handled this delicate personal information with an understanding beyond her years. And Ross knew somehow that she would never repeat a word of it to another living soul.

If Leslie kept a part of herself hidden, she offered Ross a surface that was as honest as it was charming. He told himself he could do without whatever was underneath, because the face she offered him was so kind, so feminine and—why deny it?—so beautiful.

The world was a far more exciting place for him now that he knew she was in it. He did not need to see her every day to renew the spiritual nourishment he got from her. Once or twice a week was enough. But something in him sensed that every day would be better. Better for him, and perhaps better for her as well.

To Ross's surprise, his chance to attain a closer relationship with Leslie was just around the corner.

On a sunny day in early October he met her for lunch on the square. He looked worried.

When she asked him what was the matter, he said his best employee had quit. Leslie knew the woman slightly. She was a spinster who had devoted twenty years of her life to Ross as girl Friday, account executive, and jack-of-all-trades around the office. Her name was Eunice. She had suddenly found the right man and got married. Her new husband was an Atlanta physician who had been on Long Island visiting relatives.

"She's going to live in Atlanta after her honeymoon," Ross said. "It's going to be tough to get along without her. She knew every cranny of the business, and every client."

There was a silence. Ross gave Leslie a long look.

"How are things going at the library?" he asked.

Leslie laughed.

"You could be more subtle about it," she said.

Ross smiled at his own clumsiness.

"Seriously," he said, "will you think about it? You're completely wasted at that library. And just from talking to me, you have a pretty good idea of what makes our business run. I know you and trust you. You're ideal for the job. Why not at least try it out for a few days? Just let me show you around the place. Then the choice will be yours."

Leslie looked at him, a familiar little smile on her face. She had grown to feel very comfortable with Ross over the past months, more comfortable than she had felt in a long time. The prospect of working with him every day was tempting.

"Just for a few days?" she smiled.

"Just for a few days," he agreed.

A week later Leslie had quit her job at the public library and become a full-time employee of Wheeler Advertising, with a modest but competitive salary, a title—assistant accounts manager—and full benefits.

Within an hour of her arrival on the job Ross Wheeler knew he had been right about her. She got along with the other girls, was full of newfound energy, and added a touch of youth and beauty to the place that had been sadly lacking.

She also brought a level of advertising knowhow that she could not conceal from Ross, despite her efforts to seem like a beginner in the office. Almost immediately she began making suggestions that radically improved the agency's performance for its major accounts. There was a professionalism about her work that could hardly come from a college drop-out.

Ross Wheeler had a hunch that Leslie Chamberlain had spent time in the advertising business. On the basis of this hunch, Ross looked for her name in his back volumes of the national directory of advertising executives. There he found out about her tenure at Ogilvie, Thorpe in Chicago.

He called Ogilvie, Thorpe and spoke to none other than Bud Owens, Leslie's former boss. Ross was amazed when Bud told him about her groundbreaking work on the Aurora Lifestyles account and her subsequent brilliant work on a dozen other major national accounts. Bud was full of praise for Leslie's remarkable ability and still puzzled by her sudden resignation.

Ross kept his discovery to himself. He did not want Leslie to think he was spying on her. But the conversation with Bud Owens had filled him with curiosity. Something had happened to end Leslie's budding career at Ogilvie, Thorpe and set her down as an obscure librarian in a city a thousand miles away from her previous home. Her employment record, fascinating though it was to read, gave no clue as to what that something might be.

Whatever the mystery shadowing Leslie's past, Ross felt he had brought off a great coup in bringing her to work for him. Since Leslie's arrival, Wheeler Advertising sparkled with a new energy and originality. The loss of Eunice, formerly so indispensable a presence, was not even felt now that Leslie had brought so much brilliance to her job.

Leslie seemed to blossom a bit more each day in the protective soil of Ross's paternal affection and his confidence in her ability. She became friends with the girls in the office and met Ross's daughters when they came home from college. She began slowly to gain weight. Best of all, Ross discovered, he himself began to lose a few pounds. Perhaps, he mused, something of Leslie's high-speed "metabolism" was rubbing off on him.

Thanks to Leslie, life had become worthwhile again for Ross Wheeler. Not only at work, where her presence seemed to bring new surprises and new opportunities every week. But also in his personal life, which had languished in the monotony of overwork and loneliness as he settled into the existence of a middle-aged widower.

Ross did not stop wondering about the gap in Leslie Chamberlain's personal history. But he decided that it was worth more to have her as a friend and colleague than to know secrets that were none of his business.

The future looked too bright for him to dwell on the past.

22

THE HIGHTOWERS WERE a famous family.

The father, Collier Hightower, had been a railroad and steel magnate who built the family company into one of the Wall Street monsters of the 1920s, and then into one of the nation's premier financial institutions. His wife, the former Andrea Crocker, of the Crocker manufacturing dynasty, brought millions of dollars in cash and millions more in deals to their marriage.

Collier and his wife were both dead now. Their two sons, Ford Hightower and his brother Kegan, were both United States senators. Kegan was a Republican from the family's home state of Pennsylvania, and Ford was a Republican from Delaware, where he had established residency in order to run for the Senate.

Both men were powerful, popular, and intelligent. Both were married to highly visible society women from families with large fortunes. Each could afford to spend millions on his campaigns. Both had degrees from Harvard Law. Both were handsome, with dark hair, flashing blue eyes, and strong jaws.

Both were on the board of directors of the Hightower Corporation, one of the top twenty industrial firms in the nation. They were so rich, and their financial connections went so far, that political opponents had often tried to accuse them of conflicts of interest with their major political contributors.

But none of the accusations had ever stuck, because the financial end of the brothers' political careers had been managed so shrewdly that both were above reproach.

Moreover, these same political careers had been planned with a competitive cunning so ruthless that neither of the brothers' opponents had stood a chance. When Kegan ran for Congress, his opponent was an entrenched incumbent with thirty years' experience and hundreds of thousands of loyal voters. During Kegan's campaign it emerged somehow that this opponent had had a twenty-year affair with his private secretary, and had once accepted a kickback from a financial lending institution owned by his wife's brother.

Kegan had won the election by a narrow margin and gone on, six years later, to win the U.S. Senate seat.

Brother Ford had a similar career behind him. He had defeated powerful opponents for the House and Senate, and was now, thanks to an ingenious and very expensive PR campaign run over eight years, one of the most popular men in the Senate with the voters.

There was talk about both brothers running for the presidency one day. Some observers speculated, only half-jokingly, that if one of the brothers were to switch parties, they could actually run against each other for the White House.

Few politicians in America were as popular as the Hightower brothers. Both were regular visitors to the White House, both were chairmen of important Senate committees, and each had a political influence far exceeding his Senate role. Their pictures were to be found almost monthly on the covers of the major magazines, documenting their high-society lifestyles, their beautiful homes, the achievements of their children, the beauty of their wives, and, of course, their stellar political futures.

No one realized that the strings in the Hightower family were being pulled from behind the scenes by the one member of the family who avoided publicity like the plague.

Her name was Jessica Hightower. She was two years younger than Ford and four years younger than Kegan. She was the head of the Hightower family, and had been since the death of Collier Hightower fifteen years earlier.

Jessica had always been the brains of the family. As a child of six she had been found to have an IQ of 170. She had finished high school at fifteen and college—Columbia—at eighteen, with a major in mathematics. Three years later she had simultaneously completed a Ph.D. in political science and a masters in business, and settled down to work in a high-level post at Hightower.

Collier Hightower, an old-fashioned businessman, did not have a high opinion of women. But he could not deny that Jessica was far superior to both her brothers in all the ways that mattered. Her brothers were mere figureheads, unremarkable men whose achievements would come from their name rather than their character. Jessica was the real future of the Hightowers.

"You're the brains of the family," he told her confidentially. "You have more backbone, more character than Ford or Kegan will ever have. It's up to you to make sure that the family makes as much of itself as it can. It's all in your hands."

Collier Hightower died when Jessica was twenty-five. She was unanimously elected chairman of the board and chief operating officer of Hightower Industries. Every member of the board knew that Jessica was the power at Hightower from now on. No one dared displease her in any way. Those who might have dismissed her because of her sex were quickly brought to heel, either by word of mouth or by the devastating consequences of crossing her.

In her first two years on the job Jessica brutally purged the corporation of any high-level officers who might oppose her in any way, either through their own ambition or through differences in outlook on the corporation's future.

It was Jessica who orchestrated her brothers' rise to political power. Their campaign managers reported directly to her. She handled all the funds and personally planned the campaigns. It was thanks to Jessica's refined sense of strategy and relentless drive toward success that the brothers defeated worthy opponents for high office while avoiding the consequences of their own private peccadilloes.

As the years went by Jessica became more and more reclusive. Her name was rarely mentioned in the press, except in the dryest financial or corporate context. She had many friends in the media, and she used her influence not only to keep her brothers' images spotless but to keep herself as anonymous as possible.

Jessica was a handsome woman, tall, strongly built, with auburn hair and her brothers' icy blue eyes. She kept in fine physical shape by riding, which she did at her stables every morning from five to six-thirty. She ate very little, having no time for food, and she had a trimness of figure that was somehow hard, not at all sensual. Men did not think of seducing her, despite her great fortune, because her personal force was so daunting that they could not imagine her as a lover.

Family and corporate friends saw Jessica as a personality born to rule rather than to love. No one expected her ever to marry, unless she someday conceived a strategic alliance with someone from the business world. But even this latter expedient was generally discounted, because Jessica's pride in the Hightower family was so fierce that she was not likely to share it with an outsider.

She lived quietly, visiting her brothers and their families, working ten-hour days, and pulling the strings of an international business empire that had few equals. Her life had mapped itself out, and would probably not change. Few suspected her of being a happy woman, but all lived in fear of her strong will. She herself had no time to ponder her loneliness, for she was too busy soaring from achievement to achievement, and gaining a kind of power that even her father could not have imagined possible for one individual.

On a crisp October morning at Hightower's New York headquarters Jessica Hightower emerged from a meeting of the board and entered the executive elevator.

She was alone. She had just raked the board members over the coals so viciously that no one had the courage to be at close quarters with her. She had challenged the figures on the key reports and shown their authors to be the incompetents they were.

Jessica loved her work. But she had little patience with the mediocrity and venality of the corporate yes-men around her. She took cruel pleasure in bursting their bubbles just when they thought they had her convinced of the feasibility of a new plan, a new acquisition, a cutback. She liked to wait until the last minute to stick the knife in, showing them she had been a step ahead all along, had done her research much better than they, had known long before they did what was the weakness in their plan and what must be done to overcome it.

She got a thrill out of beating men at their own game, because even behind their fear of her she could feel their contempt for women and for women's brains. To them she was an almost freakish creature, outside her own sex, a creature more intelligent and forceful than they, but only because of her very abnormality.

Jessica liked it that way. No one could understand her, and therefore no one could second-guess her. This added to her power over others.

The elevator doors closed. She stood looking at one of the reports from the meeting as the conveyance, smelling of walnut and cigar smoke, slid down the shaft.

Somewhere on the way down, the elevator stopped and a girl got in. Jessica did not look at her. She was absorbed in her own thoughts.

"It's a beautiful day outside," the girl said. "I wish I were out there instead of in here."

Jessica looked up and saw a candid smile in a remarkably gentle face. She said nothing. She was not in the habit of being addressed by employees. Most of them had long since learned to be too afraid of her to speak, so she moved about the building without being spoken to by anyone.

The girl did not seem to mind not being answered. When the car stopped at her floor she got out. Jessica caught a glimpse of a willowy figure and soft brown hair.

She thought no more of the incident, indeed forgot it completely.

The following weekend she was riding her prize stallion on a bridle path at the Harkness Club when she came upon an accident.

A horse was standing riderless in the middle of the bridle path. At first there was no sign of the rider. As Jessica pulled her stallion to a halt, she heard a low moan of pain. She dismounted and saw a girl lying in the brush beside the path.

"What's the matter?" Jessica asked.

"My horse threw me," the girl said. "I hurt my leg."

She was in obvious pain. Jessica tied up both horses and bent to minister to her. She was familiar with riding accidents, and knew first aid. She looked at the girl's color, which seemed good, and then palpated her injured leg gently.

"It's not broken," she said. The girl let out a little sigh of pain as Jessica felt her knee. "Is that where it hurts?"

"Yes. It got twisted when I fell off. My foot was still in the stirrup."

The girl's leg felt very slim and soft in Jessica's hands. She looked at the girl's face. It looked vaguely familiar.

"Looks like a bad sprain," she said. "Don't move."

The girl was looking at her. "I know who you are," she said. "You're Ms. Hightower. We were in the elevator together, at work."

Jessica, a cold woman by nature, said nothing. She barely remembered the incident. But the girl's candor amused her. And something vulnerable in the young face attracted her interest.

"You wouldn't remember me," the girl said. "But everybody knows who you are."

Jessica frowned ambiguously at this. Though she enjoyed her notoriety within the corporation, the very mention of other people irritated her.

"You work at Hightower, then?" she asked.

The girl nodded. "I've been there for four months," she said. "I'm in product development. I'm a systems engineer."

Jessica looked at her curiously. She seemed too youthful, too girlish and sweet to be an engineer. In her wounded state she seemed vulnerable as a doe.

"Let's see if you can walk," she said. She helped the girl up. The girl winced but said nothing, holding on to Jessica's strong arms.

She was able to limp but could not walk, much less get back on her horse. Her eyes were wet with involuntary tears.

"I'm sorry to be such a bother," she said, her voice distorted by pain.

"Wait here," Jessica said. "I'll bring someone back to help you."

Jessica left her, took both horses back to the stable, and returned with one of the stablemen to pick up the girl. The man drove the girl back to the office in his cart while Jessica followed on horseback.

On an impulse Jessica drove the girl to the hospital herself. It was Saturday, and she had no immediate obligations. She had not been in the odd situation of helping another human being for many years. Because of her remote position at work, she had barely been close enough to someone else to have a conversation in a long time.

While they waited for the X ray to be processed and for the emergency room resident to bandage the girl's knee—the sprain was quite bad, it turned out—Jessica asked the girl about herself. She was unmarried, a college graduate, and a beginner in the business world.

In answer to Jessica's questions the girl said her parents were dead. She was alone in the world. She had finished her education and come to Hightower Industries with no particular ambition in mind except to earn a living.

Jessica was only half listening. Her eyes strayed around the cubicle, partitioned from the other emergency room patients. There were distant groans of pain, sighs of fatigue and boredom from the other patients.

There was a mirror on the wall of the cubicle. In it Jessica could see the girl's unclothed body, only partially hidden by the loose hospital gown the emergency room nurses had made her put on. With her knee raised, the slender shape of her leg was visible. Her arms and hands were as delicate as her legs. Something about her was as fresh as a flower, and as vulnerable. Though her face was still distorted by pain and embarrassment over the fuss being made about her, the remarkable beauty of her features was obvious. It was a quiet, contemplative face, girlish and yet deep. A lovely face.

Jessica found herself fascinated. Something about this whole scene, so unaccustomed, so out of the way, had an odd appeal for her. This girl, like Jessica herself, was essentially alone in the world. Though she lacked Jessica's power and position, she seemed to respect herself. There was no self-pity in her. This only made her present needful circumstance the more touching.

The emergency room procedure took over an hour and a half, including a great deal of waiting. The doctor gave the girl a painkiller that made her a bit woozy.

"Does she have a ride home?" he asked. "She shouldn't be driving. She won't be herself for at least twelve hours."

"I'll take her home," Jessica said.

She and the nurse wheeled the girl to the emergency room entrance where Jessica's limousine was waiting.

"Take us home, Banton," she said to the chauffeur.

"Oh, really, don't do that," the girl complained weakly. "I'll be fine. It's just a sprain. You can drop me back at the stables, and I'll get my car. Or drop me at home."

"Nonsense," Jessica said in an authoritative voice. "You'll come home with me until you get over the medication. Banton will take care of your car. You'll feel better tomorrow. You can go home then."

The girl smiled weakly. "You're awfully nice to do this," she said. "I'm nothing to you. You're going to a lot of trouble."

"You're one of my employees," Jessica smiled. "That's an important relationship, isn't it?"

The girl smiled. Her eyes were half-closed from the pain and the drug.

It occurred to Jessica at that moment, as the woods gave way to busy city streets outside the car windows, that she had not asked the girl her name. She began to speak, but saw that the girl was already drifting off.

Then she noticed the hospital bracelet with its plastic name tag still hanging around the slender wrist of the sleeping girl.

Jill Fleming.

23

IT HAD HAPPENED UNDRAMATICALLY, as most truly important things happen.

Jordan was the head of a rising new conglomerate, intact since his marriage to Barbara Considine. Among the corporation's many subsidiaries was a small chemical and drug firm, now renamed LK Pharmaceutical, Inc. Within this firm Leo Kaminsky continued to toil enthusiastically toward the drug breakthrough he had been working on now for eight years.

Jordan was a board member of Considine Industries. The financial resources of that enormous corporation had been placed unhesitatingly at his disposal by Barbara Considine Lazarus.

Jordan put his capacity for what his sister Meg had called "vision" to work. He saw opportunities for Considine Industries to buy into the mining and shipping industries, which Victor Considine had neglected in his obsession with manufacturing. Barbara Lazarus took her husband's advice and carried out far-reaching mergers in these areas.

Meanwhile, Jordan played faster and looser with his own revived corporation. He bought heavily into the entertainment field, acquiring interests in hotels and casinos, television networks, music and film companies. Jordan understood young people, and he saw the enormous potential in the entertainment field.

He also invested in communications and acquired companies in the budding computer and microprocessor fields. He saw that there had been a delay of over a decade in applying semiconductor technology to computers, and he started a new company that pioneered that interface.

Thus Jordan helped Barbara build Considine Industries through conservative logic, and took greater risks with Lazarus International. He succeeded on both sides.

Then, one windy autumn day, Leo Kaminsky called Jordan to give him the good news he had been waiting for for so long. The long juggling act Leo had done with his chemicals had finally paid off. The drug, perfected now for use in humans and named X-Span, had been approved by the FDA for immediate marketing throughout the United States.

Cardiologists and internists did not need convincing from Jordan's drug company to prescribe the drug for their chronic cardiac patients and for patients with a poor cardiac outlook. Thanks to X-Span, arteriosclerosis as a chronic disorder was far less life-threatening than ever before, and might one day even become an obsolete illness.

Sales of X-Span in the drug's first six months on the market were over $50 million dollars. After that they increased. The eagerly awaited subsequent formulas of the drug, each more powerful than the last, sold even more. Competing drug companies, hastily developing their own versions of the drug, had to pay Jordan for use of his patent.

With the stupendous profits from X-Span Jordan expanded his drug business to Europe. He also expanded Lazarus International's European holdings in finance, construction, and transportation. As a side development, Jordan bought into mining and heavy industry in South America and Europe.

From that point on the growth of Jordan's empire was like a snowball. It gained momentum even without his having to push it. Every day the reports from his financial advisers were more glowing. Good news piled upon good news.

Jordan was busy taking care of one new project after another, and did not have time to step back and assay the entire growth of his fortune.

Thus he did not notice that he was now one of the ten wealthiest men in America. He barely paid attention when he was included in *Who's Who*. He gave interviews to *Fortune, Time, The Wall Street Journal,* and read the articles about himself with a distracted smile on his face.

And when, on April 15, 1975, Jordan Lazarus became officially recognized at age thirty-three as the wealthiest businessman in America, the news came as a complete surprise to him. He had never dreamed that his busy day-to-day activity was leading toward such a spectacular result.

He joked with his closest colleagues about the unexpected news. They gave him a cake in the shape of an enormous dollar sign, and they ate it together, drinking champagne out of paper cups in the office.

He celebrated with Barbara, taking her to Lutèce for dinner and dancing at the Waldorf afterward. He stayed up until 2 A.M., an unusually late hour for him.

The next morning he was at his desk, working as hard as ever.

It had not really dawned on Jordan that he was becoming a living legend.

So absorbed had Jordan been in work over the past few years that he had become virtually oblivious to everything outside the job at hand. This preoccupation was a boon to his concentration, but it made him somewhat remiss as far as certain details of his personal life were concerned. These included the secret feelings of his wife and of other women who crossed his path.

One such woman was a bright but uneducated office worker named Phoebe Grace. Her infatuation with Jordan, and her fate, would become an unchronicled chapter in the legendary story of Jordan Lazarus.

Phoebe Grace was a secretary in a midtown Manhattan office, one of two hundred who worked in the same department of a gigantic insurance company. She spent each day typing up the same forms and drafting the same letters.

She was twenty-five years old, and very good-looking. She had had many boyfriends at school, and many more since she started work. She had had affairs with three of her bosses, and had one of them twisted around her little finger. He paid the rent on her apartment and bought her clothes, especially underwear for their trysts together.

But Phoebe was restless. She was a girl of some cunning, if not of great intelligence, and she had romantic yearnings for something more than what she had. When she looked in the mirror she saw a face hardly less pretty than those of the glamorous women she saw in the movies and on television. She had a fine body, with ripe, hard breasts, a slim waist, and nubile hips. Her legs were very long and elegant. Between them nestled her secret treasure, a warm little weapon she had learned to use to get what she wanted out of men.

Phoebe was sufficiently aware of her own mediocrity as a person to realize that her character and intelligence would not gain her what she wanted in life. She saw that the wiles her body gave her now were her only real chance to make something of herself. So the question of the right man, the man with the right power and the right sensibilities, was always paramount in her mind.

One day the right man came along—or so Phoebe thought.

She met him casually, literally bumping into him on Sixth Avenue in front of the headquarters of what she would later learn was his own corporation. He almost knocked her down, and helped her up with a courtly deference in which there was no personal interest. He was amazingly handsome, lean and youthful as a prince.

He was in the habit of taking a brisk walk every morning at eleven-thirty, she later learned, and she arranged to cross his path again. Eventually they drifted into a nodding-and-smiling relationship, as working people do when they regularly pass each other in the subway or on the street.

She kept her eyes peeled for him and learned that he sometimes brought his lunch in a brown bag to avoid the executive lunchroom. He would sit on a bench in Central Park in warm weather and eat just like the other working people.

She joined him there one day, having brought her own lunch, and they struck up a conversation. He did not tell her his name.

She turned on the charm, being girlish and a little silly. She could see he was amused by her, though she sensed he would never take her seriously.

She met him again, and again, and joked with him on general topics. She knew she lacked the intelligence to impress him, but she combined her rather sexy kittenish ways with a cuddly friendliness, and she could see that he enjoyed her as a break from the more serious women he normally had contact with.

One day she kissed him playfully when he had made a particularly amusing remark.

"You," she had teased him. "You're just a kidder. Here I am a poor, defenseless working girl, and you play with me like a toy."

Her invitation was more than obvious, but he did not take the bait. As a matter of fact he seemed to recoil from her, his eyes becoming distant as he took his leave.

It was only now that she found out who he was.

She saw his picture on the cover of a business magazine at her place of work. The name was familiar, of course. Everyone had heard of Jordan Lazarus. But it seemed incredible that she, Phoebe Grace, was actually on speaking terms with such a great man. She felt like Cinderella.

This made her think more seriously about him.

She bided her time, spending three nights a week as usual with her amorous boss. But she thought about Jordan Lazarus more and more. She thought she had a good chance of enticing him into her bed if she played her cards right. And if by chance he took a real liking to her, the sky was the limit. Lesser girls than she had become the mistresses of famous men, after all.

One day she decided to go for broke. She wore her best outfit, a short skirt with a ruffled blouse that showed off as much of her as could decently be shown on a workday. She managed to meet Lazarus on his park bench. She came to his side looking unaccustomedly serious.

"What's the matter?" he asked. "You look as though you had the weight of the world on your shoulders."

She burst into tears and buried her face in his neck.

"My boyfriend," she sobbed. "He walked out, just like that. We were going to get married. I still can't believe it."

Jordan Lazarus patted her shoulder gently.

"There will be other boyfriends," he murmured consolingly. "You're a lovely girl. You'll be beating them off with a stick."

"No, it's all over. It's all over," she cried. "I don't want to be alone anymore. I hate my job, I hate the people I work with. He was going to take me away from all that. I can't believe it. Where did I go wrong?"

Lazarus was looking at her sympathetically.

"Let me take you to dinner tonight," he said. "You can cry on my shoulder."

She brightened. "Really?" she asked.

"Sure. I'll meet you right here after work. Five-thirty. We'll have an early dinner."

She dried her tears. "You're awfully kind," she said.

"What are friends for?" he asked with a smile.

She took the afternoon off and did her hair and makeup with great care. She put on the sexiest outfit she owned, a cocktail dress in ice blue satin, very low-cut, with spaghetti straps to show off her shoulders. She studied herself in the mirror. She looked as alluring as she was ever going to look.

She wore her raincoat to hide her fancy clothes, and waited in their usual spot. At five-thirty on the dot, Jordan Lazarus walked along the pavement toward her.

"Ah-ha," he said, "you survived the afternoon. Can this be a sign of things to come?"

"Only because of you," she smiled.

He held out a corsage in a small white box.

"For you," he said. "As a sign of your happy future."

"Oh, thank you!" she exclaimed, taking his arm.

He called a cab and gave the driver the name of an intimate and very expensive Greenwich Village restaurant. Phoebe crossed her fingers. She was sure tonight she would have her way with Jordan Lazarus. And even if nothing came of it, she would have a story to tell her girlfriends for the rest of her life.

While Jordan was having his intimate dinner with Phoebe Grace, his wife, Barbara, was pacing their Sutton Place duplex, waiting to hear from him.

He had called from the office to tell her he would be about an hour late. He had a meeting, he said, but he would be sure to cut it short. He would be home before seven-thirty, in time for dinner.

Barbara took a long, hot bath—she herself had worked hard at Considine all day and needed to refresh herself. She lay in the tub listening to the nervous, tiny popping of the bath bubbles as she thought about Jordan.

Since their marriage Jordan had kept his part of the bargain. He had made Barbara happy in a way she had never dreamed of being happy. He had done it without loving her, but done it nonetheless.

She was a different woman today than she had been before her father's death. Not only was she more confident, but she was calmer, happier. She no longer saw each day as a torment to be endured but as an opportunity to be lived. This was because of Jordan. After all, when a woman knows that Jordan Lazarus is going to come home from work and kiss her on the lips, a normal day assumes a far more exciting aura.

In the mirror just now, before getting into the tub, she had studied her body. She looked better, thinner, more feminine than ever before. There was a glow that began in her dark eyes and spread over her naked flesh, down her breasts to her stomach—still the flat stomach of a childless woman, and flatter yet because of the exercises she did—and then to her long legs. She was not a beauty queen by any means. But happiness had made her more nubile, more attractive.

And Jordan seemed really to enjoy her. He kissed her when he came home from work, he sometimes caressed her gently when they sat together, and at bedtime he held her in his arms, letting his warmth spread through her.

Often he would lay his head on her breast almost like a boy, and she would cradle him with maternal protectiveness, bringing him closer to her heart, even though she knew they could never be one.

He did not love her. He had told her that frankly. But if there was no real love in his heart, there was something else almost as good. A kind of empathy, perhaps. It was as though in Barbara he saw a mirror of his own struggles in life, and of his loneliness.

It was at these nocturnal moments of silent communion that she felt closest to him. As she held him on her breast she felt as though he belonged to her, and she to him.

She did not ask more. She would have been afraid to. She had to let him feel unencumbered, so that he could live as a man who enjoyed his closeness with her and was not bound to her by anything but free choice.

They had made their bargain, and she had kept her part of it, giving Jordan total financial control of his own empire and helping it grow with all her own resources. She was his helpmate, his steadfast supporter, and, she felt, his closest confidante.

They talked a great deal. They discussed their respective working lives, the people they knew in common, their families—Barbara had become a great friend to Meg and Louise, and called them every week—and the cornucopia of news, gossip, and politics that is life in Manhattan. They talked about everything, in fact, except their own relationship. That was out of bounds.

Jordan was clearly pleased with the arrangement. He got what he needed from Barbara, and gave what he felt comfortable in giving. Little did he know that his marriage to Barbara was the great passion of her life, the only thing she had ever valued, a thing she would fight to the death to keep as long as she could.

But Barbara knew that it all rested on one condition. She must never let him know her secret—the fact that she loved him.

She had assured him at the time of her proposal that she did not love him, that love was something strange to her, burned out of her, like sex, by her unhappy youth. And Jordan had believed her.

And it was because he believed her that she retained sufficient mystery, in his eyes, to keep him interested.

It was a strange thing, this warmth without passion in the heart of a loveless marriage. They were like two strangers looking at each other through a mirror.

Each saw a reversed image of the other, and of himself, and they related to one another on the basis of this distortion that they could not quite understand, a distortion that suited each for his own purposes. Oddly, their relationship was somehow more interesting for being distorted.

Barbara often wondered how long it could go on. But she told herself, it will go on as long as he never knows. The moment he knows, he will flee in search of his freedom. Then I am lost.

And she kept one more secret from him: her desire to add sexual intimacy to her closeness with him, one day. And after that, to have a child by him.

When the time came, she felt, he would agree to become her lover. Affection and pity would make him agree. As for children, that might be more difficult. She might have to steal a child from him by leaving herself unprotected when he thought it was safe. She would tell him it was a mistake, an accident. She would assure him that the child in no way obligated him to her, that their bargain remained the same.

But she dared to hope that the child, when it came, would change his feelings for her. Jordan was a lonely man, in his own way, a man who had found few things to believe in in his life. Perhaps a child would change that. Perhaps this platonic empathy of their marriage would be consummated by the child, so that Jordan would decide to stay with her forever.

These were Barbara's two secrets, the past and the future. She lived between them as on a tightrope, hanging on to Jordan for her very life while revealing to him nothing of her soul. She lived her days with him as though they were a happy routine that would never change. But privately she cherished her own timetable for a different life with him. And she never let him know.

Barbara was living an enormous lie, and she did not care. The first twenty-eight years of her life had been spent in hell. Then the fates had seen fit to send her Jordan, and to give her the means to capture him. She thanked them for this generosity, and was willing to accept it as a recompense for it her murdered youth. It was a devil's bargain, perhaps, but a bargain she could live with.

The only thing she feared was that he would leave her before she could carry her plan through. That he would get bored with this false arrangement, become restless in it, or find someone new. . . .

So Barbara waited, and loved, and feared.

And she had Jordan watched.

Jordan took Phoebe Grace home in a cab after their dinner. He had seemed genuinely touched by her sadness, but as the wine he had ordered took its effect on her he began to look at her askance, as though sensing the truth behind her tears and her sexy outfit.

He took her to the door of her apartment building. She turned to face him. "Won't you come in for a nightcap?" she asked. "I won't keep you long."

"I'm sorry," he said. "I really have to be someplace. I'm already late."

"I just don't want to be alone," she said. "Not just yet."

"I'll walk you up to your door."

He went upstairs with her and watched her turn the key in the lock. The door swung open to reveal a tacky downtown apartment with hissing radiators, dozens of coats of whitewash on the walls, and a half-hearted effort at a woman's touch in the flouncy decor. There were women's magazines on the coffee table, and no books on the shelves.

"Come in just for a second," she begged.

He stepped inside. No sooner had he closed the door than she was in his arms, her lips pressed to his, her nubile young body fitting its curves to him with a subtlety far beyond anything she ever could have mustered in conversation. All her intelligence was in her flesh, he noted with a mixture of sympathy and contempt.

"Sorry," she said unconvincingly, "I lost control of myself."

But she kissed him again, harder, hungrily, and he felt her loins press themselves to the center of him. Despite himself he began to feel stirrings in his loins, and when she felt his hardness begin to push against her she undulated seductively, a groan stirring in her throat.

"Come on," she said. "Why fight it? I know you like me. . . ."

She buried her fingers in his hair and thrust her breasts against his chest. Her tongue danced expertly inside his mouth. Her hands began to work their way down his back. The whimper in her throat was full of triumph.

Jordan pushed her away, firmly. He looked at her with distaste.

"Isn't it a little soon for you to be open for business?" he asked. "You were crying over your lost boyfriend only twenty minutes ago."

She saw the look in his eyes, and she tried to recapture a semblance of her earlier grief.

"I just . . . I just don't know where to turn," she said. "I'm sorry."

"Don't be sorry," he said. "You're a very pretty girl. When you wake up tomorrow you can start your life all over again. Soon you'll have a new boyfriend. I think I can promise you that."

He turned on his heel.

"Don't leave!" she cried. "Please. You're all I've got."

He shook his head in pity.

"You need more rehearsal, Phoebe," he said. "That line needs a lot of work."

And he left without another word.

Phoebe threw herself on her couch and cried for a long time. She had had the great Jordan Lazarus in her clutches, right here inside the apartment, and she had not been able to hang on to him.

She realized she was simply not subtle enough for him. Her best wiles had come up short. He was out of her league.

"Damn, damn, damn," she cursed as the heat between her legs cooled to a throb of frustration. "Damn, damn, damn."

Two hours later Jordan was in Barbara's arms.

He had arrived home a little later than he had planned, and had only picked at his dinner. But he had had a pleasant conversation with Barbara. And when they moved to the living room he had stood behind her and curled his arms around her shoulders.

"I'm lonely," he said, touching his cheek to hers. "This day turned out to be longer than I expected. I missed you."

They sat down together on the couch. He ran his hands slowly up and down her back, massaging away the tension of the day. She purred her satisfaction. A glimmer of sexual interest made itself felt in his stroking fingers, and then was banished by his own control and her palpable discomfort. But these latter forces were not as strong as they had once been. Jordan and Barbara both felt this, though they did not acknowledge it openly to each other.

As he held his wife closer Jordan wondered why he had resisted Phoebe Grace so easily early this evening. She was, after all, more good-looking than Barbara. Sexier, certainly.

Or was she? Barbara's depth, her intelligence, and even her unhappiness, made her much more interesting than Phoebe.

Maturity had taught Jordan this lesson about women. Phoebe was as common as dirt. Barbara was a subtle woman, a complex woman.

This was why Jordan had been faithful to Barbara all this time. He did not love Barbara. But he could not betray her with a woman he did not love. Part of him belonged to Barbara, in a way he did not quite understand. But it was all the more powerful for being incomprehensible.

Barbara drew his face to her breast.

"You're such a good boy," she said.

He lay his head gratefully on her breast. Languor deepened within him. He felt words come to his lips. But he did not trust them to be the words he wanted to say, so he stopped them before they could come out. He closed his eyes and felt the beating of her heart. It was like an anthem bringing him precious rest after his busy day.

He was happy.

Later, in the bedroom, a phone call interrupted her while she was lying in his arms. It was her private line, on her side of the bed.

"Hello?" she asked.

She listened in silence for a moment, her hand in Jordan's.

"Fine," she said at length. "You go ahead then. And thanks."

Jordan was looking at her.

"Anything important?" he asked.

"Nothing important," Barbara said, putting her arms around him. "Nothing important at all."

At the other end of the line the phone was hung up by a hard-looking man in a dark suit. He was standing in the bedroom of Phoebe Grace's apartment. Two other men were holding the struggling Phoebe on the bed. Her nose had been broken, and her jaw.

The man reached into his pocket and brought out a small glass bottle. Using his handkerchief to protect his hand, he opened the bottle carefully.

"Okay, watch yourselves," he said to his confederates.

"Are you sure you want to do this?" one of them said. "She's already got a broken nose, for Christ's sake. She'll never be the same. Give her a break."

"Orders are orders," the dark man said, remembering Barbara's instructions. "Shut your mouth, if you know what's good for you."

He saw the terror in Phoebe Grace's eyes as she looked up at him.

He lowered the bottle to the bloody surface of her face.

"Don't worry, honey," he smiled cruelly. "This won't hurt a bit."

He poured the acid in one quick motion. The girl's scream shattered the air like a fire alarm.

They had to put a pillow over her face until she passed out, just to keep her quiet.

24

FROM THE FALL ONWARD Jessica Hightower was seen with a new companion.

Jill Fleming recuperated from her sprained knee in Jessica Hightower's Park Avenue house. While she was recovering, her things were brought from her small downtown apartment. A room was prepared for her in the mansion, adjoining the upstairs bedroom of Jessica herself.

Jill was removed from product development and given a new title: executive assistant to the president. She became Jessica's closest adviser, as well as her eyes and ears within the corporation.

By winter the executives at Hightower Industries had learned to fear and respect Jill. Jill showed an extraordinary intelligence and acumen in keeping her finger on the pulse of the various corporate divisions. Wherever she went, it seemed, Jessica Hightower's brains and ruthless ambition went with her. No department head seemed able to hide waste, slackness, or lack of productivity from Jill. Her murmured reports to Jessica brought swift and cruel action wherever it was necessary. Executives at all levels were subjected to disciplinary action, transferred, or even fired based on Jill's reports to Jessica and the two women's discussions of the company.

Jill became a familiar figure at Hightower, endowed with a halo of power. This was ironic, for she moved through the corridors of the enormous corporate headquarters in an almost diffident manner, dressed in modest, nonthreatening clothes. She was a curious figure, soft and ladylike, quiet in her manners, friendly to all. But the more simple and unaffected she was in her behavior, the more people feared her, because they knew she had the ear and the trust of Jessica Hightower at all times and on the most sensitive issues.

Such was the professional relationship of Jill Fleming to her new employer. Their private relationship was far more complex.

They were very close. They had breakfast together at home, sometimes still dressed in their nightgowns or pajamas. They met for an informal lunch at work when possible. They dined together without fail, often cooking together rather than letting Jessica's cook do the work.

In the late afternoons they sometimes met at the basement pool at Hightower headquarters for a swim. They went riding together every weekend. Jill, a beginner when she met Jessica, quickly became a first-rate horsewoman.

After dinner Jessica had telephoning and reading to do. But nowadays she entrusted some of the research to Jill, whose intelligence and thoroughness, combined with her trustworthy nature, made her an ideal surrogate. Jessica had learned that she could act based on Jill's recommendations, for Jill was never wrong. As time went on Jill even began to mirror some of Jessica's intellectual qualities, such as her instinctive lack of trust for those beneath her and her sharp eye for the future of a given marketplace. It was as though Jill were taking on some of Jessica's essence, becoming a sort of intellectual alter ego.

At ten o'clock or so, the women would emerge from their bedrooms, compare a few notes on their evening's work, and then sit down in Jessica's den. Jill would turn on some quiet music, or perhaps the television with the volume very low, and give Jessica a back rub. The feel of the soft hands on her back and shoulders gave Jessica a sense of physical release she had not felt in many years.

Jill's knee sprain had healed in good order, but as Jessica got to know her better she learned that Jill suffered from a chronic anemia that sometimes caused weakness and required medication and even occasional transfusions.

Jill was, however, full of energy whenever it was necessary and was hardly a malingerer. It was just that there was a delicacy, a fragility about her that was never far from Jessica's mind.

Sometimes Jill's condition would cause terrible, crippling headaches. No medication could lessen their severity. Jill was very brave in enduring them, and joked at her own expense when she had to take to her bed for an afternoon or evening to "sleep it off." At these times Jessica would rub her temples gently for forty-five minutes or an hour at a time. She realized Jill was suffering more than she let on. And it gave her a wonderful feeling of being needed to soothe her friend's pain.

There was a quiet pride about Jill that made her downplay her orphaned childhood, her emotional scars, and her physical sufferings. Jessica identified with Jill's loneliness, for she herself had been alone in her illustrious family. Her mother had been a distant figure, and her brothers, older, had never warmed to her. Even the father who admired her so much did not really love her. It was her ability he cherished rather than Jessica herself.

Jessica felt an overwhelming need to mother Jill, to care for her and nurture her. It had begun when she rescued her on the bridle path at the Harkness Club and continued now that Jill was, in a manner of speaking, under her protection.

As time passed Jill, though candid and open with Jessica, began to efface herself more, and it was Jessica who did most of the talking. Jessica revealed more and more of her private feelings in these conversations. A deeper dimension of her personality wanted to share itself with Jill. And Jill was a perfect listener, tactful and full of sympathy.

Soon their initial roles seemed reversed. Jessica, the maternal protectress, became the grateful recipient of Jill's understanding. And Jill, the protected one, became Jessica's confidante, her supporter and caretaker.

The two women's physical closeness assumed an almost spiritual dimension. Their intimacy grew deeper and deeper. They seemed to understand each other, to fit each other perfectly as friends and companions. In every way Jill's softness, her pliant, yielding essence, became the foil for Jessica's hard-boiled, self-sufficient personality. And under Jill's influence, Jessica herself began to soften, and learned to show more of her feminine vulnerability. Jessica began to let down her hair. For the first time in her lonely life, she felt like a woman.

So intense was this closeness that when, at evening's end, it came time to go to bed and rest up for tomorrow's hard day of work, Jessica would find herself lulled by a longing and a delight she had never felt before. Her whole past life, devoted to impersonal achievement, seemed irrelevant compared to this delicious proximity of another soul to her own, a heart joined by invisible threads to hers.

She stood looking at Jill in the night-darkened living room, warmed by a complex ache of loneliness and relief as the city hummed and throbbed beneath them. Then Jill would come a pace closer, and the two women's hands would meet as the lights went out and they turned toward the bedrooms.

It was in the midst of one of their quiet evenings together that Jill told Jessica a sad story about herself.

She had worked for a corporation called Continental Products in Detroit. Jessica already knew this.

"What decided you to leave them?" Jessica asked casually.

Jill looked uncomfortable. "Are you sure you want to know?" she asked. "It's not a pleasant subject."

"Of course I want to know," Jessica smiled. "We don't have secrets from each other, do we?"

Reluctantly Jill told Jessica her story.

She had been taken out on a date by an executive at Continental Products named Harley Schrader. He had couched his invitation in terms of discussing something important about work. She had gone with him despite her second thoughts, for he had promised her more responsibility if she let him fill her in on some important corporate problems. Jill was ambitious for herself, and bored with her current job, so she took the chance.

Schrader had plied her with liquor and tried to get fresh with her in the most crude and violent way. Unfortunately for Jill, because of her delicate physical condition she had passed out on his living room couch.

The next morning she had awakened with the distressing conviction that she had been violated. She had left Schrader's apartment without saying good-bye, and hurried home. Frantically she had taken a hot shower, cleansing herself as thoroughly as she could. She had tried to forget the episode. Schrader had asked her out again, a lascivious look in his eyes, and she had refused.

For a week she went about her business within the company as though nothing had happened. Then, to her horror, she found out that Schrader had bragged about his conquest to others within the company, claiming that Jill was his willing victim. At the time she had been dating a nice young man in the company, and he had dumped her after he heard of Schrader's bragging.

Jill had quit her job on the spot, unable to bear the humiliation. But before she left she protested to the director of personnel about what had happened. The fellow, a friend of Schrader, had contemptuously told her that if she could not handle her private life, that was her own problem. He seemed full of scorn for her female concerns.

Despondent and confused, Jill had drifted for nearly a year, taking jobs as a secretary, a baby-sitter, a counselor in a children's camp. She tried her best to forget what had happened.

"Then I decided to pull myself together," she told Jessica. "I wasn't going to let what happened ruin my life. So I went back to school, got my MBA, and applied for the job at Hightower." She smiled at her friend. "You know the rest," she concluded.

Jessica was looking at her with a mixture of pity and righteous anger.

"What did you say this fellow's name was?" she asked.

"Schrader," Jill said absently. "Harley Schrader. It's a name I'll never forget as long as I live."

Nor will I, Jessica mused. *Nor will I, Jill.*

One week after Jessica Hightower's nocturnal conversation with Jill Fleming, Harley Schrader was summarily fired from his executive position at Continental Products.

Harley's friends wondered what had prompted the firing. Only the board chairman and the CEO knew the reason, and they would not tell anyone.

Harley was not sorely missed, for he had never been a creative force at the company anyway. For the first two weeks his duties were divided among several other executives, and soon one of the junior department heads was kicked upstairs to take over Harley's position.

Harley, at age fifty-three, was in a tough spot. It was always hard for executives over forty-five to find new jobs. Like anyone else in his position, Harley wrote hundreds of letters applying for positions. He called every contact he had ever made in the business world, and he waited.

When nothing came he got his attorney to demand a copy of the recommendation written by his superiors after his firing. To his astonishment the recommendation was entirely positive, stating that his work for the corporation had been exemplary, and that he had been let go simply because of organization problems and a financial squeeze within the company.

Harley went on applying for jobs and coming up empty. For two long years he struggled. During this period he began to drink more. He cheated on his wife with a variety of rather cheap girls, for he had always been a womanizer. He began to gamble away what little remained of his savings. His wife divorced him and married a tax attorney from a neighboring city.

At the end of those two years Harley found himself working as a salesman in a furniture store, dressed in the threadbare relics of his executive suits, holes in the soles of his shoes, bowing and scraping before ignorant blue-collar customers with their pregnant wives and squalling children in tow. He wondered what had become of his life, where he had gone wrong.

Harley never knew that all his misfortunes began the day he underestimated young Jill Fleming, with her lovely body, her provocative beauty mark, and her subtle bedroom seductions. In separating her forever from Roy English, he had thought he was doing Roy a favor and scoring one on Jill in the process. Instead he had sealed his own doom, thanks to Jill's eventual meeting with Jessica Hightower.

Thus the unforeseeable future, always a coy handmaiden just out of sight, joins the forgotten past in undoing the best-laid plans of men.

25

Johnsonville, Long Island

THE MONTHS FOLLOWED one another in an orderly procession. An unusually snowy Long Island winter deepened, barely noticed by the employees of Wheeler Advertising, whose lives went on at a brisk and happy pace.

Thanks to Leslie the agency was doing better and better, distinguishing itself among its competitors in the Long Island marketplace as well as its counterparts within the Modern Images family of agencies. It was Leslie who provided the brilliant ideas that revolutionized Wheeler Advertising's old accounts. And it was Leslie whose charm and intelligence attracted new clients. Most of all, it was Leslie's youthful energy, and her seemingly limitless capacity for hard work and long hours, that kept the office humming.

Things had never been better at Wheeler Advertising. There was nothing to do but let events run their course from here. More and more successes could only follow.

Yet Ross Wheeler did not feel entirely comfortable with the way things were going. For underneath the general contentment at Wheeler Advertising, his own emotions were undergoing a profound and unsettling change.

Ross admired Leslie as he had never admired a woman before. And he was proud of the contribution he had made to her own life. She no longer resembled the too-thin, preoccupied librarian he had first met eight months ago. She had blossomed into a young woman who knew what she was doing and was happy with her life.

Ross knew that his many displays of confidence in Leslie had played a large part in this transformation. In a quiet way he had acted as a sort of father to her, bringing her out of her shell and helping to restore her balance as a person. Whatever the private chagrin that had caused her three-year tailspin, it was Ross, his friendship, and his little agency that had rescued her from it.

This paternal metaphor had been in Ross's mind for many months now. He was alone since his daughters had left home, and he was glad for the chance to be as indispensable as possible to this lovely girl who had seemed so troubled when he first met her.

But Leslie was more than a daughter to him. His memory of the sadness

190

he had seen in her eyes when he first met her left no doubt that she had been through the mill—not only professionally but personally. She was an adult, a woman through and through—though she might be only a few years older than Ross's daughters.

This mature femininity mingled with girlish charm gave Leslie a new halo in Ross's eyes. It did more than command respect. It also filled him with strange longings, disturbing fantasies.

Ross fought against these feelings with all his strength. Leslie was young enough to be his daughter. In no time she would be meeting young men, perhaps getting engaged. She had her own life to live.

Yet Ross could not deny what he felt. The more he reflected that Leslie was off-limits to him, that his impulses were guilty and out of line, the more powerful they became. It was as though Leslie had turned back the clock for him by coming into his life, and was offering him a second chance at finding his ideal woman, at being happy in love.

After a long day at work he would lie in bed at night and try to forget her. But exhausted sleep, his steadfast companion every night at eleven o'clock for the last fifteen years, would not come.

He could not get her image out of his mind. He saw Leslie in her fresh dress or suit, her hands filled with layouts or invoices; Leslie fixing the broken water cooler, her fingers working at the mechanism while a paper clip was held between her lips; Leslie insisting on fixing his car the day the distributor wire came loose and he was about to take it to a repair shop; Leslie breezing into the office on a snowy morning with rosy cheeks and jokes about the inclement weather.

It was all too much, this kaleidoscope of youth and beauty and creativity that was Leslie, a girl who had come into his life by chance and somehow turned it upside down. Ross was lost, and he knew it.

"My God, I'm in love with her," he thought, lying alone in his bed, alone in his house.

The next question was what he was going to do about it.

He would do nothing, he decided. Even if his own feelings were out of control, he was lucid enough to see that he must never allow Leslie to find out about them.

When he saw her at the office, he noticed her happy demeanor, and told himself the only reason she felt so at home there was because she trusted him as the gentle, fatherly figure who had rescued her from her private doldrums—no more.

Her very confidence, her blithe humor and daughterly protectiveness toward him—all these things showed that she was secure in her friendship for him but not at all aware of him as a man, not at all attracted to him. This was natural. This was the way it should be.

But little things gnawed at Ross's certainty of his position toward Leslie, and attenuated his resolve to maintain that position.

One day they were alone together at the lunch hour, eating their sandwiches in the back room. There was a moment's silence. They were both lost in thought. Then he caught Leslie's eye, and she smiled at him, a slightly embarrassed, girlish smile that put him completely off guard.

Another time they were closing up, and he helped her on with her coat. There was a sudden, charged instant as his hands rested on her shoulders. She was not looking at him, but he caught a glimpse of them both in the large mirror at the front of the office. With his hands on her shoulders, he looked more like a lover than a father. And in her posture he thought he saw something he could not name, something that gave him hope.

Another time he was helping her out of the car and she took his hand, looking up at him with a peculiar, warm little glimmer in her eye. He tried to tell himself it meant nothing, but the memory of that look kept him awake most of the night.

Finally the flood Ross was trying to hold in became too much for him.

On a Friday he went to her desk in the middle of the day. She smiled up at him. He was just about to speak when the phone rang. It was one of their important clients, and she had to take the call. Ross made a sign that he would return, and went back to his office. He sat at his desk, looking helplessly at the framed pictures of Nancy and Dina, and hearing the lovely, musical voice echoing from the other room. Leslie's conversation seemed to go on forever. When she finally hung up he hurried to her side.

"It was Dunlop again," she said. "They're all excited, and they want us to—But never mind that. What did you want?"

"Will you have dinner with me tonight?" he asked.

She raised an eyebrow, surprised more by his nervous manner than by the invitation. They often had dinner together.

Then an easy smile lit her face.

"I can't say no to a handsome man," she said.

"Seven-thirty?"

"It's a date. What's the occasion, by the way?" she asked, a curious look in her eyes.

He smiled. "Declaration of love. Proposal of marriage."

"In that case, I'll wear my best dress," she joked.

Ross walked away, cursing himself for tipping his hand so clumsily. Now she would never take him seriously when the real moment came.

They had dinner at the best restaurant in town. Without planning it, Ross turned the conversation to serious, personal topics. He talked about his divorce, his daughters, his loneliness. He tried to draw Leslie out about her life. She told him about her dead mother, her closeness with her father.

But, as always, her confidences dipped only a bit under the surface of her private life.

"You're a mystery to me," Ross said, twisting his glass of wine a bit nervously. "You're so much a lady, Leslie. So womanly, and yet so very young. I admire you, but I'm not sure I understand you."

"Why should you, if I don't understand myself?" she smiled. "Maybe I'm not old enough to know who I am. Sometimes I think there's no sense in trying to figure things out. Let them figure themselves out in their own time."

This was not what Ross wanted to hear, but he managed a smile.

They lingered a long time over coffee and brandy. Ross thought she shared his reluctance to leave. But their conversation drifted into small talk, which put him more off balance than ever.

At last, miserably, he had to get the check and take her home.

In the car he was subdued, uncomfortable. Half of him dared to think that there was an unspoken understanding between them, that she knew what was in his mind and was waiting for him to say something. The other half cruelly assured him that she thought they had just passed a pleasant evening together, no more, and she would be shocked and unbelieving were he to tell her of his feelings.

Halfway to her apartment he dared to say, "What would you say to a nightcap at my place?"

"Won't the neighbors talk?" she smiled.

Again he had that agonizing feeling that she understood him, combined with the certainty that he was barking up the wrong tree.

But he took advantage of her assent and drove to his house. It was dark. He opened the door and she preceded him. She had seen the place before. Once he had invited the employees to help him cook a spaghetti dinner for them all. Another time he had invited Leslie to meet Nancy and Dina when they were home from college. Both girls had taken an instant liking to her, of course.

She was looking at their pictures on the mantel.

"You're a lucky fellow, Ross," she said. "Your girls are beautiful."

He said nothing. He was noticing how much more beautiful Leslie was than either of his girls.

He wondered how they would feel about having Leslie as a stepmother. The thought made him furrow his brow in consternation. Oh, this was crazy, he thought. Crazy!

He had taken Leslie's coat and hung it in the hall closet. To his chagrin he noticed that the living room had not been dusted. His cleaning woman, Mrs. Merritt, was getting nearsighted, and didn't take him very seriously anyway.

"The place is going to seed," he said.

"It needs a woman's touch," Leslie smiled, her back still to him as she looked at the pictures.

He brought her drink and placed it on the mantel before her. She stood with her back to him. The fire inside him was burning out of control. If he did not let it out he would explode.

"Leslie," he said.

She turned to him. He was still in his suit and tie.

"Don't you look handsome! I'm not sure I can trust myself with you."

"Leslie, I—"

His hands had taken hers before he could frame another word. He was pulling her closer. The lips he had so admired all this time were approaching. The scent of her suffused him, natural and healthy and irresistible.

But her hands were on his chest, applying a subtle pressure that was enough to make him back off.

"My God," he said, retreating from her. "I don't know what's got into me. You must think I'm crazy."

He went and sat down on the sofa. She came to his side.

"Want to tell me what's on your mind?" she asked. Her eyes were fixed on him inquisitively.

He looked away. He could not find the words he had been planning for so long.

"I'm old enough to be your father," he said miserably.

She said nothing. But she reached to squeeze his hand.

He allowed himself to think that this was a gesture of encouragement.

"Leslie," he said, "will you marry me?"

For an instant he did not look at her. When he did, he saw, with a sinking feeling, the expression of surprise he had been afraid of. She was taken aback. She had never expected such a suggestion.

But her hand was still around his, holding him gently.

"I know how foolish it seems," Ross said. "But I love you. I'm crazy about you. Ever since you came, I've—I've been . . ."

He trailed off miserably. The look in her eyes had taken away all his courage. He felt like a pathetic old man making an outlandish proposal to a girl who could not possibly be interested in him.

"I'm so sorry," he said. "I tried to hide it as long as I could. Just say no, and I'll understand. I'm head over heels in love with you, Leslie. I've never felt this way about anyone. Never."

She put a hand on his shoulder and patted him gently. Then she kissed his cheek.

"Ross, you're a very fine man," she said. "You've been a lifesaver to me. You gave me a whole new life when the old one had given out on me."

Ross smiled sadly.

"You're saying no," he said. "You don't have to sugarcoat it. I shouldn't have asked."

She was pensive.

"This is something I'll have to think about," she said.

He brightened.

"Do you mean that?" he asked.

"Can you be patient?" she asked. "My life has made some unexpected turns in the last few years. I'm still trying to get my bearings."

He took both her hands. "Take as long as you like," he said. "It's enough for me to know it was worth your thinking about."

He saw that she was very deep in thought. She was taking his proposal seriously. Yet there were many forces in her mind, forces he could not see. He knew there was affection for him inside her, but he suspected it was not the same sort of love he felt for her.

Yet it was enough to promise a happiness he had never dreamed possible for himself.

So he held her hands, and began the long process of learning to take what he could of her, and to trust to heaven for the rest.

And somehow in this moment, separated from her by so much and joined to her by so frail a link of hope, he loved her more than ever.

26

IN THE SPRING OF 1976 something happened that was to bring an abrupt change to the orderly existence of Jordan Lazarus.

A European conglomerate named AMZ Ltd., which had spent the past decade acquiring enormous financial and corporate holdings inside the United States, suddenly found itself the target of a hostile takeover attempt by an even larger multinational corporation based in South Africa.

As part of its defense against the takeover, AMZ Ltd. went in search of a "white knight," or friendly corporation which would acquire it on better financial terms than those promised by the "raider" from South Africa.

That white knight turned out to be none other than Lazarus International, Inc. Jordan Lazarus's mergers and acquisitions specialists had advised him that

AMZ Ltd., with its profitable American holdings, would be an ideal acquisition for Lazarus International, which at the moment possessed plenty of liquid capital and could easily accommodate a major purchase.

On March 1, AMZ Ltd. became a part of the Lazarus family of corporations. The AMZ stockholders, aware of the humane and forward-looking management practices of the Lazarus people, were happy. Jordan Lazarus's own stockholders were happy, for the acquisition caused the price of their own stock to go up. Everybody was happy, in fact, except the South African raider, which lost its chance at acquiring AMZ and was forced to look for a new victim elsewhere.

Jordan and his investment bankers were far too busy dealing with the big picture to see that, buried somewhere in the crazy quilt of American companies acquired by AMZ Ltd. in the last ten years, was a nationwide chain of small advertising agencies known as Modern Images.

And one of those agencies, now a minuscule cog in the multinational machine of Lazarus International, was Wheeler Advertising of Johnsonville, Long Island.

On March 25 a meeting was held at the Hilton Hotel in Boston to welcome representatives of the many franchises of Modern Images to the Lazarus family of companies, and to outline management policies and procedures that had been developed by Lazarus specialists for the newly acquired corporation.

Jordan Lazarus put in a personal appearance on the opening night of this meeting. It was Jordan's hard-and-fast rule to meet with the employees of every corporation he acquired, so as to reassure them about the intentions of their new management and about the safety of their own jobs. No one knew better than Jordan how demoralizing financially motivated takeovers were for the employees of acquired companies. He felt that this demoralization was destructive to productivity, and did everything in his power to make the employees of newly acquired companies feel that they had a home at Lazarus, and that their hard work would be recognized and rewarded by the parent corporation.

Jordan's afternoon speech before the Modern Images representatives gathered in the hotel ballroom had been enthusiastically received. He was on his way to the airport for a quick flight back to New York in his private jet. He had important meetings at Lazarus headquarters early in the morning, and had some long-overdue phone calls to make tonight.

He was driving the Alfa Romeo he kept in Boston. It was a custom-built model with high torque and a specially designed suspension. He had picked it up this morning, and would leave it with an aide at the airport in an hour's time. He found it relaxing to drive himself rather than to be chauffeured wherever he went—even if the traffic, as in Boston, was awful. Jordan did not like being insulated from real life by his enormous power and wealth. He did his own driving, his own shopping, helped Barbara with the cooking whenever they could both spare the time, and even built furniture in a workshop he kept in the Manhattan penthouse.

Jordan was steering the tiny Alfa between the rows of vehicles in the hotel parking lot when an accident happened.

Someone backed out of a parking space and rammed the passenger door of Jordan's little car, quite hard.

"Damn," Jordan cursed under his breath, slamming on the brakes. He would probably be delayed by an hour or more, thanks to this accident. He pulled the car a few feet ahead and got out, slamming the door hard behind him. The other driver was already getting out of the car. He saw that it was a woman.

He was about to ask her where the fire was, or something to that effect, when his eyes opened wider, and the angry words died on his lips.

The other driver was the most beautiful woman he had ever seen.

She looked confused and upset. There was fatigue in her features. Jordan guessed that she had had a long day at the meetings.

"Why don't you look where you're going?" he asked, not without a hint of sympathy.

She was looking at his car. The passenger's door was badly dented.

"I thought I *was* looking," she said. "I guess your car was too low for me to see in the rearview mirror. Or perhaps," she sighed, "I was in too much of a hurry."

Jordan looked at her. She was rather tall, with a willowy figure. Shapely, aristocratic legs emerged from her business skirt, and the outline of small, rounded breasts was visible under her silk blouse. She had evidently taken off her jacket, for it was warm in the sun.

She had lovely hair. It was very curly, almost frizzy, and with its strawberry blond color it seemed alive and vibrant in a uniquely feminine way. It made a perfect harmony with her milky, freckled cheeks and the complex green eyes under her long lashes. There was something contained and perhaps a bit shy in her personality that was charmingly contradicted by the brilliant hair and sparkling eyes.

She was very young, and intelligent. He could see that at a glance.

Though he was thrown seriously off balance by her attractiveness, Jordan managed to affect a banteringly reproachful tone.

"Do you know how long it will take to get that door from Italy?" he asked.

She raised an eyebrow, looking at him. "What kind of car is this?"

"An Alfa Romeo," he said. "Nice model, too," he added with a rueful look at the little car.

"Aren't there dealers you can take it to?" she asked worriedly.

He shook his head. "It was custom made," he said. "Imported from Rome. It won't be easy to fix."

She sighed. She looked very tired and irritated, but more beautiful than ever.

"I suppose we'd better exchange insurance cards," she said. "It's my fault, obviously. I'm very sorry. I really didn't see you."

She was mad at herself more than anything else. The sight of her distress made his heart go out to her. Her car was an older model. She was probably not well off financially. There was something very young underneath her competent exterior. He liked her; it was impossible not to.

She fumbled in her purse, found her wallet, and gave him her insurance card. Jordan looked at it, noticing her name. He made no move to get out his own card. He was thinking fast.

"I wonder if you'd consider doing me a favor," he said, moving to look at the rear bumper of her car. "The damage to your bumper is slight. I just remembered that my insurance lapsed three weeks ago, and I didn't get around to having it renewed. I tend to be forgetful that way. It would be— awkward, if this accident were to be reported. I could get a big fine for driving without insurance."

He looked at her.

"Why don't we just forget about this?" he asked. "I'll take care of my car myself. I don't want the insurance companies involved, or the law. What do you say? You'll be doing me a favor."

The girl seemed worried by his suggestion.

"Well," she said, "if that's the way you feel about it. . . . But I feel funny about not reporting the accident."

"No one will know," he said. "It will be our secret."

He studied her, savoring her obvious honesty. The accident had really been as much his fault as hers, but she had been prepared to take the blame and see her insurance premiums rise as a result. Even now she was having difficulty accepting a solution that went outside the law.

"Well, I guess it's all right," she said, glancing at his car again. "I'm sorry about your door."

"Oh, don't mention it," he said. "I never liked that door anyway."

His attempt at humor seemed pitiful to him. The girl gave him a pained smile.

There was a pause. Jordan could not stop admiring her. She was more beautiful than ever now that he had heard her speak. Her honesty and candor were like an open door to something deeper in her personality, a shrouded charm against which Jordan found he had no resistance. He wondered if she knew who he was. So far she had given no sign of it.

"Listen," he said, "would you have dinner with me? Just to prove that there are no hard feelings. You've been a sport about this. Me being practically a felon and all, driving without insurance."

A boyish smile lit up his face, alloyed with a look of hopeful expectancy.

She blushed, but seemed sure of herself. "No, thank you," she said. "I'm afraid I'm busy. But thank you very much for being so nice."

"Not at all," he said. "And thank *you*."

She stood looking at him for an instant. She seemed to be waiting for something.

"May I have my card back, please?" she asked.

Jordan laughed. He had forgotten he still had her card. He handed it back to her now. Their fingers did not touch as the card changed hands.

She stepped back and got into her car. Jordan wanted to pursue the dinner invitation, but an almost adolescent embarrassment had come over him so suddenly that he lacked the courage.

He moved his car out of the way and watched as she pulled her car out of the space and drove out of the parking lot. He noticed the small dent in her bumper as the car receded. He made a note of her license number.

And he remembered the name on her insurance card.

Leslie Chamberlain.

Jordan did not fly back to New York that afternoon.

He sat in his damaged Alfa Romeo in the parking lot, thinking, for forty-five minutes. Then he parked the car, walked back into the hotel, and called his pilot at the airport to tell him the flight to New York was cancelled.

Jordan ordered a drink at the hotel bar. After sipping distractedly at it for a moment he went to the nearest phone and called Lazarus headquarters in New York. He told his executive secretary he would be delayed in Boston at least for tonight, and that his New York appointments would have to be rescheduled.

After this call he finished his drink, returned to the telephone, and called Barbara to tell her he would not be home tonight. He gave her the excuse that there were problems with the management of Modern Images, and that he did not want to offend the company's executives by flying away after giving his little speech and leaving them to do the dirty work at the meeting.

Barbara was affectionate and sympathetic.

"I'll miss you," she said. "Hurry home."

"I'll miss you, too," Jordan said. "I'll call you first thing tomorrow."

After hanging up he breathed a sigh of relief and ordered another drink.

But neither the liquor nor his successful change of plans calmed the crazy tingling in his senses.

He sent for one of his aides and had him bring a copy of the directory of those who were attending the meetings. He flipped through the pages with trembling fingers.

Chamberlain, Leslie, he read. Asst. Accounts Mgr., Wheeler Advertising, Johnsonville, L.I.

The directory gave no further information about the young woman. Jordan would have to find out her room number from the hotel registration desk. Jordan closed his eyes. His second drink sat almost untouched before him. A delightful confusion made him almost unable to decide what to do next.

Then he remembered the license number on Leslie Chamberlain's car.

He went back to the telephone for a third time and made another call. When he returned to finish his drink he felt refreshed and full of purpose.

He had started the ball rolling.

The next morning Leslie was up early.

She was staying in an inexpensive motel two miles from the hotel where the meetings were taking place. She was in the tiny bathroom putting on her makeup when the phone rang. She padded to the phone in her slip and answered it.

"Hello?"

"Miss Chamberlain? Something at the front desk for you, miss."

After she was dressed Leslie went down the rather dingy corridor to the desk.

"Morning, miss," said the manager. "These came for you."

He showed her two dozen roses in a tasteful and obviously very expensive arrangement. While Leslie was trying to take in this unexpected arrival, a man in black livery stood up and approached her.

"I beg your pardon, miss," he said. "I've been sent to take you to the meetings. Your car's bumper will be repaired this morning while you're at the hotel. I'll bring you home tonight."

Leslie looked at him in surprise. Then it occurred to her to read the note that had come with the roses.

"I apologize for the inconvenience I caused you yesterday afternoon," it read. "I hope you enjoy the rest of the meetings."

It was signed "Jordan Lazarus."

Leslie studied the card for a moment, and then looked at the chauffeur.

"Who sent you?" she asked.

"Mr. Lazarus sent me, miss," he replied.

Leslie pondered her situation for a moment. Then she took the roses back to her room. A few minutes later she returned with her briefcase. The chauffeur drove her to the hotel, leaving her at the main lobby and promising to meet her there at the end of the day.

After thanking him politely, Leslie went in to the meetings.

The morning was a busy one. Leslie went to a financial meeting and two seminars for advertising executives. When lunchtime came, she was on her way to one of the banquet rooms where some new advertising acquaintances had promised to meet her. She stopped in her tracks when a now-familiar figure crossed her path. It was Jordan Lazarus.

"Hello," he said. "How are the meetings going?"

"Fine," Leslie said. "I'm learning a lot. It's a good conference."

"Did you get the flowers?" he asked.

She nodded. "Thank you. It wasn't really necessary."

"Was the chauffeur there to drive you here?" he asked a little anxiously.

Again she nodded. "Yes, he was very nice."

"Good," he said. "So often when you try to make an arrangement, it gets fouled up in one way or another."

She said nothing. The look in her eyes was friendly but decidedly cautious.

"Would you like to have lunch?" he asked.

A pained looked came into her eyes.

"I can't," she said. "I'm busy, I'm afraid."

He did not hide his disappointment.

"I still feel bad about that accident," he said. "It must have been rough on your nerves, after such a hard day, with so many meetings. Are you free for dinner tonight?"

She smiled again, but shook her head.

"I'm sorry," she said. "I have a dinner meeting."

With any other woman Jordan would have pushed harder. He knew she knew who he was. No dinner meeting could be as important to her as dinner with Jordan Lazarus himself. But with this woman, the very fact of his importance seemed a clumsy bludgeon to use to try to influence her. He could not bring himself to do it.

"Well, maybe another time," he said. "By the way, I haven't properly introduced myself. Jordan Lazarus."

She shook his hand firmly. "I know who you are," she said.

He sensed that she had misunderstood his introduction as an attempt to use the leverage of his fame over her. This made him beat a hasty retreat.

"I'm glad you're enjoying the meetings," he said. "Let me know if you have any more problems with your car."

She simply smiled.

"Good-bye," she said. "And thanks again for the flowers. That was nice of you."

Jordan now embarked upon twenty-four of the most difficult hours of his life.

It was now noon on Saturday. The conference would not be over until this time tomorrow. Jordan had a dozen important appointments to keep in New York today. His wife, he knew, was waiting eagerly for him to return home tonight.

He returned to his room, called his top aide in New York, and told him he could not come home yet. There were problems to be wrapped up here in Boston. There was a chance he might return late this afternoon. He would keep the aide informed of his decision.

He asked the aide to call Barbara immediately and inform her of the additional delay. Jordan himself would call her later in the day. Jordan bit his lip nervously as he hung up the phone. Later, he knew, he would have to speak to Barbara. That would be difficult.

Jordan wandered the corridors and meeting rooms of the hotel, shaking hands with conferees and executives who were all in awe of him. In their eyes he was a bigger-than-life figure, a prince of the business world. But Jordan felt like a lovesick adolescent following in the wake of the pretty cheerleader upon whom he has conceived a hopeless crush, a girl who does not know he exists.

The trail he followed led inexorably to the banquet and conference rooms where Leslie Chamberlain was attending meetings. He had found out her personal schedule from the secretary in charge of registration, and could not keep himself away from the places he knew she was to be found.

Meanwhile, he pondered the unforgettable mental images he had retained from his two encounters with Leslie. Every detail of her seemed to be burned into his memory. The cotton suit she had had on in the parking lot yesterday afternoon, and the pastel skirt and blouse she had worn this morning. The frizzy look of her hair in the parking lot, and the more careful, controlled wave she had put into it the next morning. The look of surprise and worry in her eyes just after the accident, and the look of thanks, combined with deliberate caution, he had seen when he met her again.

And he remembered all her smiles and the gentle, poised way she held her beautiful body as she spoke to him. Even her reserve had a quality so fine and feminine that it only increased his fascination with her.

He crossed her path three times in the course of the afternoon. The first two times he was able to restrain himself sufficiently to salute her from a distance and continue on his way.

The third time he could feel time running out, and approached her.

"How are things going?" he asked. "Still enjoying the meetings?"

"Things are going fine," she said, brushing a wisp of hair from her eyes as she smiled at him.

"I don't suppose," he began weakly, "you would have time to join me for a late drink tonight. After the meetings are over . . ."

"Thanks, but I have to get to bed early," she said. "I'm leaving right after the morning meetings tomorrow, and I have a long drive."

"Where are you headed?" he asked.

"Long Island," she said. "A little town called Johnsonville. It's near Southampton."

"That is a long way," Jordan said. "I see what you mean."

He searched madly for something else to say but found himself utterly tongue-tied. She murmured something tactful by way of leave-taking, and melted into the bustle of people in the corridor. Jordan felt crushed.

He lingered miserably for the rest of the afternoon, knowing that his aides back in New York were shuffling madly to reschedule the meetings he was missing now. But he could not tear himself away. Even if Leslie Chamberlain would not agree to have dinner or a drink with him, he simply had to see her again. He could not bear the idea of losing her so soon.

At four o'clock his sense of corporate responsibility finally won out over the storm in his emotions. It was time to give up, time to go home.

He called New York from his room and told them he was leaving for the airport in twenty minutes. He would conduct his business from the telephone on his jet and from home later tonight.

Feeling forlorn and defeated, he went down to the lobby with his overnight case in his hand. He stood uncertainly in the corridor for a moment, trying to gather his courage. Then he decided to call Barbara from one of the public phones. He needed to hear her voice, and to tell her he would be home with her in a few hours.

The receiver was in his hand, and he had begun to dial, when he saw Leslie Chamberlain walking by in the corridor. She was alone.

Jordan hung up the phone and hurried to join her.

"So," he said. "Meetings all finished?"

"Yes," she said. "It's been a long day."

He looked at his watch. "I guess you have to get ready for your dinner," he said.

She shrugged ambiguously. The question was too ridiculous to answer. She had already put him off.

"Do you have time for a quick drink?" he asked. The note of supplication in his own voice disgusted him.

She shook her head. "I have to meet some people for cocktails," she said. "You're nice to ask, though."

Jordan was defeated. He had no strength left for subterfuge.

"Aren't I going to see you any more?" he asked miserably.

There was a pause.

"Well, I don't see why you should want to," she said.

"Miss Chamberlain . . . May I call you Leslie?"

"Of course, if you like."

"Leslie, please be nice and say you'll spend a couple of minutes with me before you go." He sounded as though he was on his knees to her. The feeling was unbearable, and yet fascinating. He could not recall feeling this way since he was a boy.

Again there was a pause. She looked at him through narrowed eyes. Then she sighed.

"I have to leave by ten tomorrow morning," she said. "If you'd like to have a cup of coffee before I go, we could meet in the coffee shop."

"Can we make that breakfast in the executive dining room?" he asked.

"I don't eat breakfast," she replied. "Besides, I'm going to be pressed for time. As I told you, it's a long drive."

"All right," Jordan surrendered. "Coffee at nine o'clock?"

"Can we make that nine-thirty?" she asked. "I really do have a lot to do."

Jordan sighed.

"Nine-thirty," he said.

Jordan called New York to tell his aides he would not be home until tomorrow afternoon. He called Barbara and told her the same thing. Barbara accepted his excuses with good grace. If she suspected something untoward behind them, she gave no hint of it.

Exhausted, Jordan went to bed early. An hour later he was tossing and turning in his bed. He turned on the light and tried to read himself to sleep. It was no use. In the end he turned off the lamp and lay in the dark, thinking of Leslie Chamberlain as the wee hours of the morning crept by.

Her face floated before his mind's eye, a clearer image now because of his repeated encounters with her, and yet confused by his own emotional disarray. He could hardly wait to see her again. He needed to fix that fugitive image in his mind once and for all, so that, whatever happened in the future, he would never lose it.

When Leslie arrived at the coffee shop punctually at nine-thirty, Jordan was waiting for her. She carried a briefcase and raincoat.

"Good morning," Jordan said, getting up to extend a hand. "You're looking very lovely this morning."

He had planned the compliment in advance—not too familiar but as affectionate as possible—and yet it sounded clumsy and presumptuous on his lips.

It was an understatement. She was dressed comfortably for her drive, in dark blue slacks and a cotton blouse that hugged her delicate breasts. She wore flats instead of high heels, and her hair was pulled back in a ponytail for the drive. She wore no earrings. Her informality only made her the more beautiful.

They sat in a booth by the window. The restaurant was sparsely occupied, for most of the guests were leaving, and those who weren't were busy in meetings.

"So," Jordan said. "You're going back home."

"Yes," she said.

"Glad this circus is over?" he smiled.

"Oh, I wouldn't call it that," she said. "It was hectic, but I learned a lot. That was what I was sent here to do."

"What do you think of Lazarus International?" he asked.

Leslie shrugged and smiled. "It's big," she said.

"Yes, it is," Jordan said.

Leslie's eyes widened imperceptibly as she noticed the sadness in his voice. There was a silence, embarrassed on both sides.

"It must be quite a responsibility for you," she said.

Jordan nodded, not taking his eyes off her. He was torn between his fascination with her and his awareness that her resistance to him was strong. He sensed the firm backbone behind that gentle exterior of hers. If he were to ask her to see him again, and she refused, she would stick to her refusal.

"It tends to take over," he said. "You work to build up a business because you think you're protecting something. But the work gets so hard, so consuming, that you begin to forget what it's all for. It's a sort of snowball."

"What were you protecting?" Leslie asked.

"My family, originally," he said. "We were very poor, and we got kicked around a lot. I wanted to make my fortune, so that that could never happen to us again."

"I guess you succeeded pretty well," Leslie said.

He nodded ambiguously. He seemed to want to change the subject.

"What about you?" he asked.

"Just a working girl," she said.

"But a dedicated one," he offered.

"Well, our business is small," she said. "I do a little bit of everything. Soliciting clients, slogans, layouts, taking people to lunch. I haven't had to clean the bathrooms out so far, but I may get to that yet."

"Sounds like a nice situation," he said.

There was a pause. Jordan felt atrociously uncomfortable, and he thought she did, too. But he could not tell whether this was because she liked him better now that they were at close quarters, or because she liked him less.

At last he could not stand it any longer.

"What do you know about me?" he asked.

"Not a lot. You're very rich, very famous. You're married. You run a big corporation." She smiled. "And your car has a dent in the door."

"You see, you're already part of my life," he joked. But again he felt that his humor was weak.

And he had heard her say that he was married. The importance of this remark was not lost on him.

"How about you?" he asked.

"You mean, am I rich?" she asked.

"No. Are you married?" he asked.

She shook her head. "No, I'm not married."

With these words she reached to brush an errant lock of hair from her eye. There was something brisk and a trifle nervous about the gesture, but at the same time very feminine. Jordan thought he remembered having noticed it earlier. It filled him with admiration for her natural grace.

I'm not married. Jordan tried to hide the emotion her response had brought to his eyes, but he did not succeed, and he knew it.

The words danced crazily inside his mind, obscuring all the small talk he tried to make with her. He could not take his eyes off her as she sipped her coffee, toyed absently with the cup in her hands, and glanced shyly at him. Those last ten minutes were perhaps the most delicious form of torture Jordan Lazarus had ever experienced. He could hardly hear her words, so entranced was he by the melody of her voice. He did not know what he was saying. He felt like an actor who has been forced out onto the stage without having learned any of his lines. He was faking everything he said, trying to sound natural and falling all over himself.

At last she looked at her watch.

"Well, I have to go," she said. "It was nice of you to take such good care of me. My car, I mean. And I enjoyed the meetings. I really did."

"That's good," he said.

He walked her to her car.

"Bumper looks good," he smiled.

She threw her briefcase into the back seat, folded the raincoat on top of it, and got in behind the wheel.

He bent down to say good-bye. He could smell her fragrance, natural as a meadow in spring.

"Well, now we're part of the same family, so to speak," he said. "I hope I'll see you again."

"It was nice to meet you," she said noncommittally. "I hope you get a new door all right."

"Oh"—he shrugged—"that doesn't matter."

He wanted desperately to say something else, but she smiled and turned to look through her windshield. Her car began to pull away. He stepped back and stood watching her recede from him. He could not recall the last time he had felt so lonely.

He knew he had a long way to go today. All the way back to New York, and to Barbara, with a dozen important phone conferences in between. For an instant he hoped it would all take Leslie Chamberlain off his mind. Then he gave up. He knew nothing would take her off his mind.

I'm not married.

She was not married. But he was. And he knew everything she had said to him had been because of that fact.

He stood watching her car recede, his heart going out painfully to her. She already had her signal on to turn the corner.

Jordan sighed. In a way this moment seemed like death to him.

He could not know that as Leslie drove away from him she was looking at his image in her rearview mirror. Her hands were trembling on the wheel as she struggled to concentrate on the road ahead of her.

A moment later Jordan had turned and gone back into the hotel.

But Leslie's hands did not stop trembling on the wheel all the way out of town. And the deeper tremor inside her was still with her when she reached home, four hours later.

27

He WAS PLAYING WITH TOY SOLDIERS and blocks on the carpeted floor of his room.

It was a braided rug, and it was hard to pile the blocks high without their falling down, unless he put them on top of one of his picture books.

He had built them into a castle. Inside the castle was the leader of the good guys, a handsome prince with a sword. He was a small figure on a horse, part of a set that had come with a box of cereal.

But now the chief of the bad guys came on his horse—he had been in prison but had escaped—and attacked the castle. He shot his arrow at the highest rampart—Pssshhh!—and the prince came out to fight him.

The bad guy shot another arrow, and this time the prince was wounded. But the prince sat up bravely and took out his sword. He would fight to the death to save his kingdom.

The two figures came closer, held in the boy's hands.

All at once the blocks fell down, covering the boy's hands and the two combatants.

This was not the way it was supposed to have turned out. The boy thought of rearranging the blocks and starting over. The prince was still in his hand, his sword drawn. The bad guy remained on his horse, immobile on the carpet.

A soft breeze came in at the window, making the curtains stir. A bird sang somewhere outside. The languor of spring overtook the boy. He stared at the prince, lost in fascination. It was astonishing to think that the prince, so alive, needed the boy's hand in order to move. If one wished hard enough, perhaps he would move on his own.

A voice interrupted the game.

"Terry? Guess who's here."

Mom's face was in the doorway, her big, dark eyes smiling down on him.

He left his game and trailed unhurriedly out to the living room.

There was a lady there, sitting on the big chair by the couch. When she saw him she leaned forward with a mischievous look in her eyes and said, "Remember me?"

He did remember her—and yet he did not. It had been a long time since she was here. His three-and-a-half-year-old mind had difficulty combining distant visits with a single face.

He went to his mother and touched her skirt defensively. The beautiful lady was still smiling.

"He'll get used to you in a few minutes," he heard Mom's voice from above.

"Sure he will," the lady said. "When is Cliff coming home, Georgia?"

"Six, probably. If they let him out. Can you stay for dinner?"

"No, I'm sorry, I have to run," the lady said. "I just thought I'd look in since I was in the neighborhood."

The women chatted. As they did so the boy looked at the lady's face. It was framed by curly hair of a reddish blond. She had a rosy, freckled complexion and strange greenish eyes that seemed to change color as she talked. She was beautiful because of those eyes—which were more mysterious than even the best of his cat's-eye marbles—but most of all because of her smile.

Now he was beginning to remember her. He moved across the carpet slowly. She kept talking to his mother. But when he reached her side she extended a hand and gently drew him to her.

Now he could smell her—a fresh, sweet aroma—and feel her thigh against his hip. It was a different feeling from Mom; this lady was much thinner. The hand on his shoulder was as gentle as Mom's, but there was an odd energy in the fingers that he now recalled from before. This lady was more like a girl.

Now she leaned down to whisper in his ear.

"I'll bet you remember my name," she said.

He shrank away in childish embarrassment, but said the name at the same time.

"Auntie Leslie."

"That's right," she said.

And now that the ice was broken he felt at home in her embrace. The interval since her last visit had been blotted out, and it was as though she had never been gone. She was herself again, his Auntie Leslie, the woman he loved almost as much as Mom.

A few minutes later, after the women had had their tea, Leslie took the boy out for a walk. They walked around the block, then headed down the street to the little park that was used by the local children. There was a jungle gym, a merry-go-round, and three swings with heavy rubber seats. There was a slide, a sandbox, and benches for the mothers to sit on.

Aunt Leslie watched him go down the slide several times. It was fun to see her face zoom closer as he went down. She was squatting with her hands on her knees, and when he shot off the slide she caught him and hugged him.

Then she said, "Let's try the merry-go-round."

He ran ahead of her and jumped on the seat. She came up behind and touched both his hands to make sure they were tight around the handles, and then began to push the seat around, slowly at first, then faster and faster.

This was his favorite ride. He saw her face go by again and again, each time a flash of color. She was somehow more beautiful somehow for the fact that her appearance was fugitive, an image glimpsed over and over again instead of a constant thing one could touch and hold.

She was very different from Mom, for many reasons. In the first place Mom was dark and warm and heavy, while Leslie was tall and slim and light. He had called her "the light lady" when he was younger.

Also, there was a different quality to the gentleness of the two women. Mom was spicier, deeper. It was nice to lie in her lap and almost fall into her. Aunt Leslie was trim and lithe. When she held you, it was her hands you felt most of all, and her smile.

Most important of all, Mom was there all the time. Aunt Leslie only came once in a long while. And every time she came she was different. There was something different about her hair, her clothes, and something different about the light in her face and in her eyes.

And, of course, the boy himself was different. He was older, his mind was filled with the great flow of new thoughts and feelings that had borne him along like a river since her last appearance. He had forgotten her.

But when she appeared she changed all that. Like the kaleidoscope he played with in his room, she gave the world a mighty spin and it came to rest with all its colors in new places, with her at the center. The world made room for her suddenly, joyously, and the colors shone with a new brilliance because she was here.

Leslie was different. Instead of the reassuring sameness of the passing days, she brought with her the sparkly difference of occasional days, days separated by spaces of time that seemed to rub out her image like a pencil eraser when she was gone but were canceled out by her in their turn when her smile caressed him, as now.

They walked slowly around the park. Her strangeness was forgotten. He held her hand. At length they stopped at a raised knoll of grass under a tall oak tree.

"Shall we lie down and look at Mr. Oak Tree's branches?" she said.

They lay down side by side and looked up. The branches were enormous, groaning softly above them in the fresh breeze.

"I think this tree is very old," Leslie said. "That's why his branches are so thick."

The boy said nothing.

"I'll bet he's older than us put together," she said, turning on her side to look at the boy. "I guess he's seen a lot in his time. Don't you think?"

"Yes."

"Do you think he's sad or happy about what he's seen?"

"I don't know."

"Well, I don't think he laughs much," she said. "He's too old for that. But I think he smiles. When he's not sleeping, that is. I'll bet he sleeps a lot. Do you think he's sleeping now, or watching us?"

"I don't know."

"You don't?"

The boy smiled. "Watching," he said.

There was a quality of thought that separated Leslie from his mother, just like the quality of smell, of smile, of hands. Mom was soft and reassuring, and called things by their proper names. Mom explained things. Leslie did that, too, but she also told stories about things, like with the tree just now. She made them come alive, gave them feelings. She made them strange, but then she made them nice.

It was almost like having two mothers. Mom was the mother of home, of familiar things and of the gently passing days. Aunt Leslie was the mother of the faraway, the mother of changes, and of live things that had their own feelings.

"Do you see any monkeys today?" she asked.

He looked into the branches. One time she had spoken to him of monkeys chattering in the tree and leaping from one branch to another, her voice so eloquent that he had actually thought he saw the animals. Since then the monkeys had been a sort of private joke they repeated whenever they looked at the tree.

"I don't know," he said.

"Oh, I see lots of monkeys," she said. "Look at that silly one, peeling his banana. He's going to throw the peel down on us, because he thinks we're silly."

She smiled.

"We went to the animal fair," she sang. "The birds and the beasts were there."

"The big baboon, by the light of the moon . . ." Terry sang slowly, falling silent as he searched for the last words.

"Was combing his auburn hair," she finished for him, laughing.

She hugged him. "You remembered," she said.

He turned on his side to look into her eyes. They were sparkling deeper than ever now, as they looked at him.

"Aunt Leslie," he said.

"Yes?"

"When I grow up, will you marry me?"

She laughed.

"Well, that's a long time away," she said. "Maybe you won't want to marry me when you grow up."

"Oh, I will."

She smiled, reaching to caress his cheek.

"Well, then," she said, "I'll be the proudest lady on my street. Because I'll be married to the handsomest fellow."

He lay back. They both fell silent. But their conversation continued.

That was another of her secrets: she could talk when she was silent. He had found that out about her a long time ago. She could sit by him on a couch, or walk alongside him on the sidewalk, when he was jumping over the cracks or balancing on the curbstone, and all the while she talked to him without saying a word out loud.

The things that came from her were not words, but more like kisses, kisses with meanings to them. Kisses about the weather, about the curb he was balancing on, kisses about the street, kisses about himself.

It was during these silences that he felt he knew her best. They were wonderful, but after she left they were the first things about her to disappear. And when she came back, weeks or months later, they were the last things to reappear, a thing he always recognized with an inner sigh of happiness. She was the time lady, the different lady—and the lady with the silent words.

Yes, he thought. When I'm grown up I'll marry her.

Leslie had Terry back home within an hour, as she had promised. It was getting later, and he needed his quiet time in his room. Leslie hated to upset his routine in any way. She wanted to be a part of that routine, if a small and very occasional one.

When he was in his room she talked to Georgia, who showed her the latest pictures of him and kindly gave her some copies. Georgia was an extraordinarily thoughtful and understanding woman. Leslie had always felt that her chance to know Terry came from Georgia—for Cliff would have gone along with anything his wife had wished. Georgia was willing to share her son with Leslie, and trusted Leslie with this great gift.

When it was time to go Leslie hugged Georgia. "See you in a month or so," she said.

Then she got into her car and drove away along the calm suburban street.

Her eyes were so full of tears that she had to stop as soon as she had got around the corner and wipe them so as to see through the windshield.

But the pause was too much. She began to sob, and she cried for a long time, her car stopped next to the curb. She was afraid passersby would see her, a strange woman weeping uncontrollably in a parked car. But she could not help herself.

When she finally got control of herself she pulled away very slowly and drove toward the highway.

As she did so she thought about Georgia Beyer and her kind husband,

Cliff, the young married couple who had adopted Terry when Leslie gave him up, six hours after his birth in a New York City hospital.

Leslie had driven straight to New York after her abrupt departure from Ogilvie, Thorpe in Chicago. She had picked her direction by whim, as her car, loaded with her clothes and a handful of possessions, was speeding along the Eisenhower Expressway and two overhead signs offered her the choice, INDIANA AND EAST or MILWAUKEE AND WEST.

She had lived in a furnished room in Brooklyn Heights while bringing her baby to term. During those forgotten months she had seen a lot of Manhattan, wandering aimlessly from Central Park to Greenwich Village and back again. The city did not become more familiar to her as time went by. Instead it became more alien. By the time she entered the hospital she knew she would leave the area as soon as her baby was born.

But when she found out, almost by accident, that her baby had been adopted by a young couple on Long Island, she changed her plans. She left her furnished room, took the Long Island Expressway and found her way by pure chance to Johnsonville, and stopped for lunch. An hour later she had found her job at the public library and been directed to a reputable apartment house by Mrs. Babbage.

She had a new home.

At that time nothing in her life had meaning. Desolation and loss had cut her off from her profession and her hopes. She had followed her son because he alone offered her a remnant of the reality she had once taken for granted, and a ray of hope for herself.

She had been terrified the first time she went to see the Beyers. Georgia was a quiet young woman with long, dark hair, expressive eyes, and a kind face. When Leslie had explained her situation, Georgia had said she had to talk to her husband.

Cliff, a good-looking young man who worked as an accountant in the area, thought the matter over very seriously, and had a long talk with Leslie.

The Beyers were sympathetic to Leslie's plight but concerned most of all for the welfare of their adopted son. It was decided to try an experiment. Leslie would visit, being introduced to the boy as "Auntie Leslie," a sort of vague cousin of Georgia's. Leslie would be allowed to visit the boy every couple of months, and be as close to him as a distant aunt might be to a boy.

Leslie could see that Georgia and Cliff loved Terry very much. She assured them that she wanted no more than the opportunity to see her boy, to know something of his life. They were convinced by her sincerity.

The first few visits were painful for Leslie. The boy clearly did not recognize her, did not need or wish to know her. She was just a friend of his parents.

But then he began to warm to her. Perhaps because he somehow felt the depth of her love for him, he began to feel closer to her. She played with him in his room, took him for walks, told him stories. With an almost superhuman tact and subtlety, she managed to forge a link between herself and his little personality without invading his privacy or in any way coming between him and his parents.

By the time he was three the boy called her Auntie. She sent him presents on his birthday and Christmas, and his mother sent her his fingerpaintings, which Leslie kept on her kitchen walls and refrigerator.

When Ross Wheeler saw these fingerpaintings on a casual visit to Leslie's apartment, she explained that they were by her "nephew once removed," the son of her only close cousin.

The visits were still painful, though Leslie would not have traded them for anything in the world. Georgia's letters, which contained photographs as well as news of the boy's development, painted a continuous, reassuring picture of a little person who always looked the same in Leslie's mind. But when Leslie came to see the boy his growth shocked her. He looked so different, and she had missed so much. And he was shy, finding her strange and sometimes barely remembering her.

Yet only an hour later the frail thread of their private relationship had grown so strong that they seemed to understand each other perfectly, as though they had never been apart.

Then she had to leave, and that precious thread was cut off once again. It seemed as though her very heart was being torn out of her when she left him. She hurried home, as today, to put herself back together, to survive the first few hours away from her son, and to begin waiting for Georgia's next letter.

Had it not been for Terry and his parents, Leslie would never have come to Long Island. Her destiny would long since have carried her far from here. And she would never have known her son.

But now that she had a relationship with the boy—however tenuous, however intermittent—she could not bear the thought of giving it up. It was Terry, ironically, who gave her the strength to carry on her life far from him, to face her own future, and to feel that the past was a foundation on which she could stand, instead of merely a broken heart and a dislocated life.

She would thank Georgia and Cliff Beyer as long as she lived for this precious gift they had given her, the gift of knowing her son. And she would never reveal her secret to anyone.

With this thought in mind she turned onto the highway and drove faster. Though the drive from Johnsonville and Ross Wheeler to Farmington and the Beyers was only an hour or so, Leslie felt she had come a very long way.

And the road back was even longer.

28

JORDAN HELD OFF as long as he could.

A month was all he could manage. But it was not really a month. The day after his breakfast with Leslie he ordered one of his research assistants to find out all about Wheeler Advertising and her role there. He also asked for a copy of her employment history.

He was surprised to learn that she had come to Wheeler from Ogilvie, Thorpe, where she had been a fast-rising young executive. He raised an eyebrow when he learned that she had conceived the Aurora Lifestyles campaign and several other million-dollar campaigns like it. He could not understand why she would have dropped so brilliant a career to surface in a remote Long Island town, working for two and a half years as a librarian before returning to advertising in a very small agency.

But he stopped wondering about her past. All he cared about was her future, and when he could see her again.

No, I'm not married. The words echoed in his mind crazily, temptingly, keeping him awake nights. She was unattached. This was the most important piece of information about her, the crucial piece of the puzzle. He hardly cared about the rest.

He began to think of ways of approaching her. He thought of calling her, writing to her. But every strategy seemed impossible. She had made it clear that she was unavailable to him. She knew he was married, and she was obviously not the kind of girl who would play around with a married man. She respected herself. There was something healthy and firm about her, mingled though it was with her soft beauty. Something upright and immovable.

This quality reminded Jordan of the crushes he had had on girls when he was an adolescent. That was a time when he had coveted the clean suburban girls at school from afar, and spun elaborate fantasies about them in his mind. It was not so much their sexual secrets that fascinated him during that early idealistic period as a fantasy of their prettiness, their uprightness, which he had elevated into a kind of romantic ideal.

That ideal had been long since tarnished and worn away by his adult relations with women. But Leslie Chamberlain brought it back to life. Even now, as he struggled to recall the details about her image that last morning at the meetings in Boston, it was not so much her face he recalled as her self-respect and honesty.

Unfortunately, it was precisely this old-fashioned respect for propriety that seduced Jordan the most, even as it made his hopes wither.

She seemed farther than ever beyond his reach, while closer and closer to his heart. The temptation to see her was all the harder to resist because she lived so nearby. The little town of Johnsonville was scarcely an hour from Jordan's Manhattan penthouse. The very words *Long Island* resonated in his emotions like an exotic music he had never heard before.

At the end of a month Jordan's defenses were exhausted.

He had to see her.

On a cool Saturday morning in April he drove to Long Island, arriving late in the morning. He did not call first, for he feared she would refuse to let him come. He wanted surprise to be on his side, though he was afraid surprise itself would irritate her and prejudice her against him.

It was hard to locate the address given in her file. It was an ordinary-looking apartment building, rather attractive, with a small lawn in front, a crabapple tree, and a white-painted wrought-iron bench. It was located about a mile from the picturesque center of this old Long Island town, with its square and its village hall and small businesses.

Jordan stood in the foyer like a schoolboy, shifting his weight from one foot to the other. He knew she might not even be at home. He did not care. He had not been able to delay a day longer. If she wasn't here, he would drive back to New York and begin working up his courage to try again.

At last he rang the buzzer.

There was a long delay. Then an almost unrecognizable voice squawked through the little speaker.

"Yes?"

"This is Jordan Lazarus."

He thought he should say something more, but words would not come. The next five seconds were an eternity.

Then the door lock buzzed. Jordan almost jumped. He managed to open the door before the buzzer stopped.

He stood in the unfamiliar hallway, wondering where her apartment was.

Suddenly a door right in front of him opened, and Leslie appeared.

She was dressed in jeans and an old painting smock. Her hair was pinned back under a scarf. The old sneakers on her feet were spattered with white paint. She was holding a paint roller in her hand. There were two or three drops of paint on her cheeks.

Her eyes were open wide. Though he could not see it in the dim light of the hallway, she turned a shade paler before recovering herself and smiling at him.

"Well, fancy meeting you here," she said.

"Uh-oh," Jordan smiled. "I think I picked the wrong time."

"What brings you here?" she asked. "Are you in town on business?"

"Not exactly," he said. "It's more a case of being in your neck of the woods, and deciding to drop in. I guess I should have called first."

There was a pause, very painful for Jordan. He could see he had caught her at a bad time. She was probably very annoyed by his unannounced visit.

She smiled. "Well, you're here now. Come on in. I'm afraid the place isn't in shape for visitors at the moment, but you're welcome anyway."

She stood back in the doorway to let him pass. He saw drop cloths thrown over the furniture and spread across the floor. It was probably a cozy little apartment when it was not under this paint-spattered shroud.

She closed the door behind him. She was looking at him curiously. Though it did not occur to him, she was noticing that his slacks, shoes, shirt, and jacket were from the finest designers in the world. The casual clothes he was wearing were probably worth a month's salary for her.

But her appraising smile faded when their eyes met. She looked away uncomfortably.

"Maybe I should go," he said.

Then she regained her composure.

"Not at all," she said, "I'd ask you to make yourself comfortable, but it's not the right day for that."

Jordan had to suppress a sigh of frustration. She was obviously very busy, and not prepared to see him. On the other hand, the sight of her in those dirty old clothes, with that paint roller held in her delicate fingers, took his breath away.

Desperately he searched for a solution, and found one.

"Why don't I help you?" he asked. "We can get done in half the time."

He looked at the living room, which had only just been started, and the dining room, which was also full of drop cloths. "What do you say?" he asked.

"That's not necessary, really," she said. "I can't ask you to do that."

"Really," he said. "I insist. It will be fun."

He looked for words he could use to convince her, but none would come. His proposal seemed absurd, and he was sure she would not accept it.

But she surprised him.

"Well, as long as you know what you're getting yourself into," she said with a laugh. Then she noticed his clothes again. "But I can't let you get paint all over those beautiful clothes," she said.

He had completely forgotten what he was wearing. He had eyes only for her.

"Don't you have an old shirt or something that I could wear?" he asked.

"Hmm," she murmured, frowning. "Let me think."

She put the roller in its pan and moved quickly into another room. He heard her opening a closet and rummaging inside it.

A few moments later she emerged with an old pair of overalls.

"They're my father's," she said, handing them to Jordan. "I used to use them when I worked on the car. They'll be too short for you, but I think they'll do the job."

Jordan had removed his jacket and begun putting on the overalls. "You worked on the car?" he asked.

"Daddy isn't good with mechanical things," she said, watching him. "And we were always too poor to have routine work done at the station. So I did all the oil changes and tune-ups and filter changes. Things like that. I got to know carburetors pretty well in my time. . . . I always wanted to work on a transmission, but I suppose it's probably best that I never did."

He had the overalls on now. They were indeed too short for him, and the cuffs of his expensive slacks stuck out from under the legs. It made an absurd impression.

"What's the matter?" he asked, seeing her smile. "Don't I look the part?"

"Not exactly," she said.

"I don't want you to think I'm a stranger to hard work," he said in a joking tone. "I'll bet we were poorer than you were. After all, you didn't have three brothers and two sisters, and the odd cousin or aunt or uncle sleeping in the back room. I've done quite a bit of whitewashing in my time."

He came forward to pick up the roller.

"Here," he said. "Watch this, young lady."

As she looked on he began to paint the living room wall in long, practiced strokes, the roller moving against the wall with firm sucking sounds. His limbs moved this way and that, the arms stretching toward the ceiling, the legs extending ridiculously from the overalls as he worked. She watched in fascination as his body moved unseen under the ugly old overalls.

"There," he said, still painting. "See what I mean?"

Jordan could not see the look on her face as she watched him. If he had, it might have gone a long way toward easing his suffering.

She found another roller and joined him. Soon the living room wall was finished, and they were opening a second can of paint. The job went very fast with both of them working.

When the living room was finished Leslie put down her roller.

"I'm thirsty," she said. "Would you like a glass of iced tea?"

As he turned to her she saw a spot of paint on his cheek, and a couple of drops on his shoes.

"Oh, look at your beautiful shoes!" she cried. "Here, let me get the paint remover. I should have found you something else to wear."

"Never mind that," he said. "I'll get it off later."

They drank a refreshing glass of iced tea, both sitting on the drop cloth–covered sofa. It was a good moment for small talk, but their conversation was stilted. Neither seemed to be able to find the right words. Jordan stole as many glances at Leslie's face as he dared. There were more spots of paint on her, and they made a strange and somehow lovely counterpoint to the freckles on her cheeks. Under her scarf, he knew, was that magnificent, wild hair. As she sat with her legs crossed, he saw the outline of the beautiful long legs under her jeans.

He looked away, feeling a pain in his heart.

"Well," he said, "I think we're on a roll. If we work hard, we can finish the dining room in an hour. What about the rest of the place?"

"I did it last week," she said. "This is all that's left."

"Shall we?" he smiled, standing up.

They worked in virtual silence the rest of the way. Jordan was torn between satisfaction and dread as they covered the walls of the dining room. It was a job well done, and she had accepted his presence and his help so far. But what now? What was he to say to her?

He grew more and more tense as they put the finishing touches on the walls. When the dining room was done he put the roller down and returned to the living room with her. Their glasses of iced tea were still sitting on the covered coffee table, the liquid turned a pale orange color in the bottom of the glasses.

He tried to find something to say.

"Looks like we're finished," was all he could manage.

She herself seemed a little sad. There was something touchingly pensive in her expression.

Feeling the pain his heart grow deeper, he looked away from her. He began to remove the overalls.

She noticed his shoes again. There were more spots of paint on them now.

"Let me get that paint remover," she said.

She went to the kitchen and returned with a can of paint remover and a rag. She knelt down in front of him and began to dab at the spots.

Jordan's last defenses collapsed at the sight of her long, beautiful body crouched before him like that of a shoeshine boy, her hands dabbing at the spots of paint on his shoes.

His own hand, moving with a will of its own, reached out to untie the scarf over her hair. The paint-spattered fabric came away softly, and the curly hair shone like a rainbow in the afternoon light.

She looked up at him. The expression on her face made it clear that their long shared subterfuge had reached its end. There was no avoiding the truth any longer.

Jordan had thought of this situation a thousand times in the last month, but now the words he had planned to say failed him. She was looking at him with something between reproach and supplication.

"I held off as long as I could," he said. "The days were not so bad, but the nights . . ."

She said nothing. Her eyes seemed to deepen, as though to make room for him.

He let his fingers move from her hair to her cheek. His pain was unbearable now. Something surrendered deep inside him.

"I love you," he said.

He looked away shamefacedly, like a boy. When he looked back he saw that there were tears in her eyes. She looked frightened, as frightened as he, but also resigned.

She nodded quietly, and he drew her face to his.

29

Six Weeks Later

THE OCEAN WAS THEIR ACCOMPLICE.

It rocked the boat gently, soothing it above long, slow swells, as Jordan came deeper and deeper. Leslie held him in her arms, opening more and more of herself to him with each soft roll of the movement that joined them.

In a very short time his groans came to join the sigh of the great ocean beneath them. Her little cries of ecstasy harmonized with the calls of the gulls in the distance.

He was crouched over her, the perfect image of the beautiful young man whose wiry limbs were made for love. She held his face in her hands, gazing into his eyes with a look of passionate delight. Her legs were wrapped around him, pulling him deeper into the warm sweet place at the center of her.

"Oh, Jordan . . ."

Their intimacy grew more and more intense, swelled by the great rocking of sea and sky, until at last, with a spasm that shook the deepest part of her, she was his. She felt the surge and stream of him, male and triumphant, yet gentle somehow, gentle and liquid as the infinite water on which they floated.

When it was over she held him against her breast. Her thighs brushed his hips. Her body still trembled with little spasms as she cradled him with her hands.

They said nothing. More and more, in these passion-stunned weeks, they had found that there was nothing left to say.

Jordan was thinking of her body, of the remarkable way she used it in making love. Her flesh was lovely, yes, and irresistible in its silken temptations. But she made love with her heart, giving herself so completely that he almost felt as though there were something too absolute about their intimacy, something dangerous about knowing another person so intimately.

But this feeling of unease was eclipsed by his admiration for her. Her honesty was as beguiling as her magnificent body. The unique style of her, so clean and unpretentious when she walked or talked or laughed, became an indescribable seduction when she was naked in his arms.

He had once read in a book of speculative philosophy that the secret of the sirens' song that lured sailors to their deaths was their innocence. This secret could certainly be said to apply to Leslie. She was so unspoiled in her essence that each tryst seemed like the first time for her. She made love like a virgin, surprised and vulnerable and delighted.

He looked into her eyes now. He searched for words that could do justice to what had just passed between them. As usual, there were none.

"I love you," he said.

She smiled, pulling him closer and caressing his neck with both her hands, an odd little gesture of affection she always bestowed at this languid moment.

"I love you, too," she said.

Her eyes were dazed by love, her body numbed by pleasure. But she was beginning to come back to herself. He felt her youthful energy begin to stir in his embrace. Soon her bright, happy personality would come out from behind the mask of her passion. In this little moment of eclipse, between the fire of desire and the contentment of companionship, he loved her almost more than he could bear.

He looked from her to the boat around them. It was called *Meg*, after his sister. It was a beautiful little craft, just small enough to be handled by two sailors, and beautifully decorated inside. Lying amid the tumbled sheets that way, Leslie looked indeed like a siren, a sea creature brought in here by some sort of dark magic to belong to him.

They had been lovers for six weeks. They had met as often as possible, first in the city and then here on the boat. Jordan was an avid sailor, and Barbara hated sailing, so this was the ideal place for them. They found that being away from dry land, being joined spiritually by the water and the sky, added to their sense of intimacy and isolation.

When he first asked Leslie to come sailing with him, he was thinking of the privacy and the convenience afforded by the little boat. He never dreamed that the ocean would become something so symbolic, so deeply personal in his view of her.

She had never sailed before. When she first came on the boat, a little nervous, she looked so sensational in her jeans and sneakers and the white cotton tank top she had worn, that he had had trouble keeping his hands off her long enough to explain the basics of sailing to her.

She had learned quickly. Soon she was handling many of the simpler functions, for her acute intelligence, combined with her cheerful willingness to get her hands dirty, armed her to learn new things quickly. She learned to judge the wind, to rig the sails, to handle herself and the boat when tacking and sailing across the wind. He understood why she had been a mechanic for her father, and why she painted her apartment and fixed things. This was part of her naturalness, her easy accommodation to the real world.

Later, when he had bought her deck shoes and a little jacket for the brisk breezes of the Sound, she was such a vision of youthful energy and soft loveliness that Ben, the irascible custodian at the marina, had taken a liking to her, and always greeted her with a smile and a few friendly words.

"A lovely day for a sail, miss," Ben would say, helping her into the boat or just standing watching them. "Take care, now," he would warn Jordan. "It's a little bit rough out there."

Ben displayed an avuncular protectiveness toward Leslie, and had grown to consider himself a sort of watcher over their love. For he could not fail to see what was between them from the way they looked at each other.

Ben had never met Barbara, for she had never been to the marina. But even if he had known her, he would never have betrayed the secret that joined Jordan to Leslie. He had learned a lot in his time, and he knew the kind of love that deserves to flower, whatever the rules against it or the obstacles it faces. Seeing Leslie was like seeing the vision of what he himself had never had but only dreamed of. Being an accomplice to such a love, even in a small way, was for Ben a sort of dream come true.

Each time they went out was the same. They made sail, working together in silence, and sometimes laughed as they scudded quickly across the bay. Then, far out upon the water, they stopped, and Jordan lowered the sails and dropped the anchor. And when he went below she was waiting for him, her tank top already coming off to reveal the small bra, then her jeans slipping down her long legs so that only the silken panties remained like a delicate flower covering the magic of her sex.

Her eyes would sparkle as she saw his reaction to her nudity, the darkening of his irises, the tensing of his hands, the subtle outline of desire between his legs.

"Come here, Prince Charming," she would say, slipping the bra off as he came to her side.

The nickname had begun as a gentle joke, but had persisted. He had come to enjoy it, for he knew it signaled her respect for him as well as her humor. And now it had taken on the deep erotic heat that he saw in her lithe, soft body, and most of all in her eyes.

He possessed a favorite photograph of her, which he kept locked in the desk at his office and looked at whenever he had a free moment during his busy workday. He had taken it on her birthday, just before taking her to a bucolic Long Island restaurant for dinner. She had worn a flowered summer dress and a wide-brimmed hat that set off her natural beauty to perfection.

He had given her an emerald necklace, which she had immediately put on, discarding the one she had been wearing when he picked her up. She was smiling brightly in the photo, showing off the necklace. But in her eyes was that glimmer of love that told him she wanted to thank him for his gift in a more intimate way.

The photo captured both her innocence and her sensuality so eloquently that sometimes his eyes misted just to look at it. He considered it his most treasured possession, not only for the memory it evoked but for the truth it bespoke, the truth of his love.

These thoughts were in Jordan's mind as he looked at her now. The lovely eyes, their depths green as the ocean, were fixed on him, and the naked skin beckoned to him. He kissed her, and buried his face in her breast.

"You're a witch," he said. "I can't get enough of you."

"Mmm," she murmured, running her hands through his hair. The purr in her throat charmed him, and the scent of her body, mingled with his own, was so intimate that he wanted to drown in it.

But he managed to sit up again, and drew the sheet over her lovely breasts so he could speak to her sanely. The look in his eyes was serious.

"I spoke to Barbara about us," he said.

She looked at him through beautiful eyes in which he could read nothing. He knew how she felt about this love. She had surrendered to it, as had he, but she was not the kind of girl to accept it as a way of life. Without a commitment from him she would not allow it to continue.

"She took it well," he said. "She's a woman of honor. You'd have to know her as I do, to understand what I mean. Her childhood was a hell on earth. Her life with her father did some terrible things to her. But it never hurt her honesty. That's what has kept her going. I've always respected that in her, and I always will."

He looked down at Leslie, comparing her glorious, sunny beauty to the sad, dark image of Barbara he carried in his mind.

"She always knew this day was coming," he said. "She told me that last night. The deal we made was beneficial to both sides. But there was no love in it. It couldn't last very long. She understands that. And she's happy for me."

Leslie seemed pensive.

"Jordan, tell me one thing," she said.

He smiled. "Anything."

"Did you ever love her?" Leslie asked. "Even in some little way? I want you to be honest with me."

He pondered for a moment.

"Love . . ." he said. "That would be too strong a word. Much too strong. But, yes, I felt something for her. I still do. I understand her sadness, her loneliness. I feel that in my heart. And it makes me want to not hurt her."

He looked at Leslie. "Does that answer your question?"

She nodded.

"It's what I wanted to hear you say," she said. "You're human, you're a man. I wouldn't want to believe you could have married a woman for whom you felt nothing at all."

Jordan felt a shiver of relief inside him. It was as though he had passed a test.

Now he looked down at the thoughtful face beneath him. Concern made Leslie more beautiful. Slowly he pulled back the sheet and saw her long body, tanned by the summer sun, and still warm from his caresses.

Almost at once he knew they were not going to get up and go on deck. He had to have her again. And he saw in her eyes that she knew it, too. He bent to kiss her. The sensual body grazed his own nudity, and he was hard again, erect and hungry for her.

This time, as he covered her with himself, the shadow of Barbara's sadness lingered before him, coloring this particular chapter of his love with a mixture of melancholy and pity.

Ironically, as pleasure overtook Leslie, plunging her far from dry land into this watery element where she and Jordan were alone together, it seemed to her that the last shadow over her love for Jordan Lazarus had now been lifted.

30

ON JUNE 10 Meg Lazarus collapsed while paying a visit to a neighbor lady in Webster, Pennsylvania.

Meg was rushed to the local hospital. By the time she reached there her breathing was labored, her skin pale, she was almost too weak to move, and she had a high fever.

Jordan was notified immediately. It was decided that Meg was too weak to be moved to the university hospital in Philadelphia where Jordan had had her treated a year ago for a similar, though less severe, attack. So Jordan brought the chief cardiologist from Philadelphia, Dr. Jaffe, to Webster.

Jordan took his leave of Barbara, who was familiar with Meg's problems and understood that he might be gone for several days or even a week. He also called Leslie to tell her what had happened. Then he flew straight to Webster, arriving only four and a half hours after Meg's attack.

Dr. Jaffe was there already, waiting for Jordan at the nurse's station down the hall from Meg's room.

The two men shook hands.

"How is she?" Jordan asked, not without trepidation.

The doctor frowned.

"Well," he said, "it looks like she's got a new attack of subacute bacterial endocarditis. Worse this time than last, I'm afraid. The damaged valve has become infected again, and the heart isn't pumping enough blood. You'll find her symptoms similar to last year."

"What have you done for her so far?" Jordan asked. "Antibiotics?"

The doctor smiled sadly at Jordan's familiarity with the treatment for Meg's condition.

He nodded. "Massive doses this time. And we're taking blood cultures at regular intervals. I've added cortisone to try to get things under control. Believe me, Jordan, we're doing our best."

When Jordan entered Meg's room he had to hide his shock. She looked worse than he had ever seen her. She was pale and was receiving oxygen through a tube. Her eyes seemed enormous. He noticed a couple of small skin hemorrhages on her arms and neck; the doctor had told him these were symptoms of her heart failure.

"How are you, sis?" Jordan asked, coming to her side and taking her hand.

She gave him a weak smile. "Fair to middling, as Uncle Sid used to say," she whispered.

Jordan sat on the edge of her bed. A great wave of emotion rose up within him, combining rage at his own impotence and an almost childlike terror that this most beloved of women would leave him.

How ironic, he mused, that Jordan Lazarus, the man whose face had been on the cover of every medical magazine as the savior of heart patients, had discovered nothing that might help his sister—when the only real reason he had ever become interested in heart therapy was Meg!

X-Span, so effective against arteriosclerosis, was irrelevant to infectious valve problems such as Meg's. Jordan had realized this long ago, when he had educated himself about heart disease in conjunction with Leo Kaminsky's research. Even then he had understood that nothing he was doing would help Meg. But he had fooled himself emotionally into feeling that his work was somehow related to her illness, and therefore might somehow be helpful.

Now he saw that Meg was slowly dying. She was so much weaker and paler than last year. The ugly transformation of her body from that of a lovely if frail young woman to that of a terminal patient was speeding up. A year from now she would probably be gone.

He bent to kiss her cheek. He took her hand. Her eyes glistened in her emaciated face as she looked at him.

With a great effort he put his own chagrin out of his mind and spoke to her blithely.

"How are they treating you?"

"Everything first-class as always," she said, letting her hand rest in his. "This is almost better than home."

He knew she was lying. She hated nothing more than hospitals. He squeezed her hand.

"Well," he said, "Dr. Jaffe says we'll be able to get you out of here soon. I spoke to Louise. She says things at home are a mess already. They need you."

She smiled, acknowledging his feeble joke.

But then her eyes narrowed. He could feel her studying him, probing beneath the signs of his obvious grief and anxiety to something else.

"What about you?" she asked. "You look different."

Jordan sat back a bit, almost defensively.

"Different how?" he asked.

Meg took a deep breath of oxygen. Her eyes seemed glazed for an instant. Then she focused on him again. The light of her old love shone through her pain as her gaze caressed him.

"You look," she said, "as though somebody just told you what you were going to get for Christmas."

Jordan smiled. He recalled their youth, when he and Meg had waited for Christmas together. Even then she had understood him so intimately that she always knew what he wanted most.

And that old insight of hers had allowed her to see the change that had taken place in him these past weeks. It was impossible to hide from her intuition.

"Well, I made a few million dollars today," he said. "Maybe that perked me up."

This reference to their old conflict was intended to distract her. But it did not work.

"Don't kid me," she said. "I know my brother."

Jordan sighed. This was par for the course—he had not been in the room for two minutes, and already she had seen through him. He admired her for knowing him so well. And he was grateful that there was a person on earth who knew him this well. For an instant he looked at Meg's face and saw a resemblance to himself in it. He could feel his own blood running through her veins, giving her almost cosmic insights into his own heart.

But he could not tell her the truth about Leslie. Not yet. Not here. It would not be right, with Barbara waiting for him only a hundred and fifty miles away.

A smile curled his lips briefly as Leslie's name sang through his consciousness like a melody of love. He squeezed Meg's hand. He felt like a schoolboy.

Meg was watching him closely through her haunted eyes.

"It's something new, isn't it?" she asked.

He looked away. Grief and joy rose together within him as he held the hand of his dying sister and thought of Leslie, the first woman he had ever really loved. The spiritual link between these two women was so strong that he could almost see Leslie reflected in Meg's eyes.

Meg could feel his emotion. She smiled up at him.

"I'm happy for you," she said. "You deserve something new. Something good."

Jordan sighed. He was frustrated by his inability to tell her the truth. Meg knew Barbara and liked her. She had always made a pretense of believing that his marriage to Barbara was happy. He could not proudly announce to Meg, here in the hospital, that he had met another woman and was going to leave Barbara. He simply couldn't.

Nor could he hide from her the exultation in his heart. It mingled crazily, painfully with his grief over Meg's condition.

They talked for half an hour, skirting the obvious issue between them as though it were a wall they had to shout across to speak to each other. It was tiring for each, but more so for Meg. Soon she began to look drained and sleepy.

"I have to go, Meg," he said. "You've had enough conversation for one night. I'll be back in the morning."

He tried to stand up, but she grasped his hand and held him down on the bed.

"Jordan," she said. The given name shocked him. She only used it when she was very serious.

"Yes, Meg," he said. "What is it?"

"Happiness doesn't come often," she said, looking intently at him. "Sometimes one chance is all we're given. It's worth fighting for. Worth a sacrifice."

"I know," he said.

She held him tighter, as though he had misunderstood her, perhaps was trying to misunderstand her.

"You've already sacrificed enough for other people's happiness," she said. "It's time to think about your own. Will you do that? For me?"

Jordan felt his eyes mist. His sister knew she was near death. She had spent a lifetime vainly trying to steer him away from his dogged crusade for success, and seeing him resist her. Now she sensed he had discovered a way out of his self-imposed prison. She wanted to give him the courage to take the crucial step. But her own strength was draining away fast. She looked at him with pleading eyes. Her grip on his hand weakened. Her head fell back against the pillow.

"Yes," he whispered, his lips close to her ear. "I won't let you down. Do you believe that?"

But Meg had lapsed into unconsciousness. She could not hear him.

When Jordan emerged from the room his eyes were full of tears. Thankfully there were no nurses or patients in the corridor to see his emotion.

He spent another half hour with Dr. Jaffe and then drove to his parents' home in silence. He greeted Mother and Louise, who tried vainly to force him to eat something. He went to bed early.

He could not seem to think straight. His mind was too numbed by thoughts of Meg and Leslie. Their two faces hung before his mind's eye as he waited three long hours for sleep to come. Meg's face was growing dimmer but calling out to him with a greater eloquence and beauty than ever before. The face of Leslie came closer and closer, calling him forward dizzyingly into life. Part of him feared he was being unfaithful to his past and to his grief in adoring Leslie this way, in throwing everything away for her. But Meg, lovely, delicate Meg, was summoning him precisely to this new life, even as she herself drifted slowly away from him. He had never felt so torn, so happy, so desperate.

At last, filled with anticipation of seeing his sister tomorrow morning and the woman he loved in a few days, Jordan slept.

* * *

When Leslie heard that Jordan was to be away for several days, she seized the occasion for a brief trip home to see her father.

Tom Chamberlain had not seen his daughter in nearly six months, and he was thrilled. He picked Leslie up at the airport in his old sedan—a car on which she had done numerous repairs in her time—and drove her home along straight, endless country roads turned purple by early dusk.

"The car feels good," she smiled. "I think it could use a tune-up, though."

"Like me," her father joked. "We're pretty similar. Not as young as we once were, but we keep rolling along."

Leslie smiled. Dad looked just the same as always, if a bit grayer and a bit more bald. His eyes were bright with his joy at seeing his daughter again. He seemed full of energy. Leslie felt reassured to be in his company. Her world had been turned so completely upside down by recent events that her father's familiar face and steadfast affection were like a drug that soothed and excited her at the same time.

But the visit was not as easy for Leslie as she had hoped. During that first evening Leslie talked about Wheeler Advertising, and repeated what she had already told her father in a dozen letters: that she enjoyed the small agency much more than the big, competitive Ogilvie, Thorpe, that Ross Wheeler was a lovely man to work for, that the girls in the office were nice, that it was fun to get her hands dirty knowing every nut and bolt of a small organization rather than to be lost in the impersonal bustle of a huge agency.

Tom Chamberlain listened to all this with a smile. He could see that Leslie was happy. There was a sparkling, excited look in her eyes that intrigued him. He knew that in the past she had shielded him from some painful facts about her life. Tonight he suspected she was hiding something very positive, something happy. He wondered when she would reveal it to him.

The next night they went to dinner at the Hilltop, a popular restaurant specializing in steaks and seafood, located in the country twenty miles from Ellicott. Tom Chamberlain dressed in his best slacks and shirt, with a string tie. Leslie wore a long cotton skirt with a silk blouse and the emerald pendant Jordan had given her. There was a feeling of celebration about the evening, but she could not get up her courage to tell her father the real reason for her happiness. Instead she kept repeating the old lies about her change of jobs and the pleasure of her new, quieter life.

The depth of her deception created a sort of screen between them, which prevented her from contacting him as she had once done. The little girl inside her wanted to take refuge from her tumultuous, stressful life in the Daddy of the past, the Daddy who had watched over her so tenderly during her youth. But that was impossible now. She was a woman, she had a woman's hurts and a woman's secrets. And those secrets cut her off forever from the past.

Worst of all, the skein of lies was more tenuous now, because Leslie's life had taken a dizzying new turn, one that threw all her ideas about herself into question. Her advertising career, past and present, was completely eclipsed by her love for Jordan Lazarus, as was everything else in her heart. This final secret she was keeping from her father was literally burning to get out.

On the way home from the restaurant, it found its way to her lips at last.

They were driving home along the dark county road, the headlights sending their brilliant beam over the road ahead and the cornfields on either side. Occasionally a rabbit or other small animal showed its alert eyes to the powerful beams before disappearing into the undergrowth.

Tom glanced at his daughter. She was smiling to herself.

"Penny for your thoughts," he said.

"I was just looking at the headlights," she said. "When I was a little girl, and we went to visit Aunt Alice or Chet and Carol, and we came home after dark, I used to think those headlights were magic. The way they reached out into the darkness . . . I thought they could light up the whole world if they wanted to. It was as though nothing could hide from them."

Her father nodded. He was not used to abstract thinking, but he admired Leslie's tendency toward wistful poetic impressions. It had been with her since she was a little girl, and marked her personality as strongly as did her great intelligence.

"Adult things often seem magical to little kids," he said. "You had more imagination than most, so I'll bet the whole world was magic to you."

She leaned back in her seat, warmed by his sympathy. All at once it did not matter to her if there was a gulf of circumstance between them. He was still her father, he still knew her, in a sense, better than anyone else. As long as Tom Chamberlain was on this earth, she would never be alone.

With this thought she spoke to him now.

"Daddy," she said.

He turned to her. "Yes, dear," he said. "What is it?" He seemed expectant.

"Daddy, I've got a fellow," she said.

Tom Chamberlain hesitated. In that split second Leslie could feel his intuition of all that had happened to her these past years, perhaps of the real reason for her leaving Ogilvie, Thorpe. She could feel the quiet probing of his mind over the ground of her secrets, just as the headlights, once magical in their power, had thrown their triumphant light over the night-dark countryside, laying bare everything they touched, and perhaps capable of seeing more, seeing everything.

Home was within view now. He pulled into the gravel driveway, stopped the car, and took Leslie in his arms.

"I'm so happy for you," he said. "So happy, sweetie." There was relief in his voice, as though he knew she suffered great unhappiness in love in the past, and was now getting her second chance.

She nodded against his chest. "Me, too," she murmured.

229

He petted her shoulder affectionately.

"Does he—work with you?" he asked.

She shook her head.

"I met him through work. He has his own—he has his own business," she said.

Her father smiled. "How long have you known him?" he asked.

"Oh, I—not too long," she replied. "A few months."

She began to feel the wall of lies rearing up again between her and her father. He was beginning to ask the logical questions every father asks when his daughter tells him she is in love. Who is the young man? What does he do? What is his name?

She could not tell him any more of the truth than she already had. She was in love with a famous man. A married man.

"When do I get to meet this young man?" he asked.

"Oh, not yet," she said, sitting back. "We haven't quite reached—reached that point. But I hope it will be soon. I really do. I know you're going to like him, Daddy. He's a fine person, a wonderful man. And he . . ."

He loves me. These words came quickly to Leslie's lips, and died there. She simply could not say them right now.

"I'm sure he is," her father said. "I'll look forward to meeting him. But there's no hurry. I can be patient. As long as you're happy, honey."

"Oh, I am!" she cried. "I really am. Happier than I've ever been."

He hugged her again. "I can see that without glasses," he said. "You haven't looked this way in a long time, Leslie."

She nodded, pensive. "Yes, I know," she said.

He looked at her for a long moment, measuring the distance between them and perhaps the secrets behind her words. Then he took her hand and squeezed it. She was grateful. The wall was still between them, but his love could still find her and warm her in spite of it.

He got out of the car. She followed him into the house, the night sounds of the country calling out to her from the darkness like so many voices welcoming her home.

While Leslie and her father were entering their quiet house in Illinois, and Jordan was sitting in the chair watching his sister sleep in the hospital room in Pennsylvania, Barbara Lazarus was sitting on the large couch in her Manhattan penthouse.

Spread out on the coffee table before her were a dozen pictures. The envelope they had come in was on the floor.

Barbara was not looking at the pictures. She sat back on the sofa, thoughtful. Deliberately she closed her eyes. She allowed her mind to focus for a moment on the city sounds far below her—the rumble of a truck moving through an alley, the abrupt bark of a horn, a muted call from one pedestrian to another. And, of course, the dissonant song of various sirens echoing across the busy, dangerous island in the dark.

Barbara felt remarkably calm. She savored her solitude. Though it was a condition she had found herself less and less able to bear in recent years, she could still draw lucidity and concentration from it, as in the old days when she had hidden from her father in her bedroom and tried to insulate herself from her life with him.

She took a deep breath, then another. She opened her eyes. She sat forward. The city's murmur disappeared, eclipsed by her attention to the photographs on the table before her.

Some of them showed her husband.

Some showed a little boy.

But all of them, as though celebrating one theme, showed the face of Leslie Chamberlain.

31

A WEEK AND A HALF AFTER Jordan's return from Pennsylvania, Jordan sat with his wife in the solarium of their Sutton Place penthouse, having a nightcap.

It was ten o'clock at night. Jordan and Barbara had formed the habit several years ago of adjourning here after their dinner together. Jordan would drink Armagnac, and Barbara an aged amontillado sherry. The lights were kept low, and outside the window they could see the East River and the dark outline of Roosevelt Island.

This was their hour for languid conversation as the stress of the day ebbed slowly toward the somnolence of bedtime. They avoided serious topics, preferring to chat about friends, relatives, or the surprisingly provincial day-to-day news of Manhattan, as they sat together.

Tonight, of course, things were different. Since Jordan had told Barbara about Leslie, no amount of small talk could distract either of them from the final truth facing their marriage.

There was no violence between them, no conflict. Instead, a strange climate of resignation prevailed. Jordan and Barbara did their best to act normally.

And this meant a thousand little gestures of support, of affection, which had made their marriage what it was. But now there was a new coefficient to all that tenderness, and to all the familiar little domestic habits that joined them. For it was all doomed now, their long adventure together. Doomed by Jordan's love for Leslie Chamberlain.

Jordan had not exaggerated in telling Leslie how well Barbara had taken the news, and how understanding she had been.

"I'm glad to have had you for as long as I have," Barbara had said. "But I have no claim on you. I've always known that. You were free to go anytime you wanted to." She had been brave in holding back her tears when she spoke. Jordan had admired her for this, and felt his heart go out to her.

Tonight this odd atmosphere of dying intimacy reigned between them as they sat in the darkened solarium, gazing in silence at the city that was their home.

Jordan cleared his throat.

"I saw your cousin today," he said.

Barbara raised an eyebrow. He was referring to her second cousin, Renée Archer, a mindless socialite whose obligatory visits to Barbara on holidays and family occasions were a constant source of irritation and amusement to Barbara and to Jordan.

"Where?" she asked.

"The Plaza," he said. "Where else? She introduced me to Count Somebody-or-other, and to a bunch of other people. She and the count seemed very thick. It looks as though marriage number five may be in the works."

Barbara nodded. "She'll never stop," she said. "She chews them up like candy and spits them out. I know the count. He's really a nice fellow. Too bad for him. I thought he had more sense than that."

There was a silence. Barbara raised her glass of sherry to her lips but did not sip it. Her hand fell back in her lap. She looked at her husband.

"Jordan," she said. "Will she make you happy?"

Jordan sighed. The image of Leslie appeared instantly before his mind's eyes, smiling, irresistible. He felt uncomfortable sitting in the darkness and hearing Barbara ask about the woman he loved. His pity for Barbara tore at his insides. Yet his love for Leslie was more powerful than anything else.

"She will," he said. "She loves me. And she's a fine person. You would like her."

You'd be proud of her. Jordan did not say these words, but they expressed his feelings perfectly. If Barbara knew Leslie, really knew her as he did, she would be proud of Leslie, as he himself was. His love for Leslie went far beyond mere physical passion. He loved her for qualities that anyone would have to admire—courage, honesty, humanity. There was something so brave about the way Leslie experienced her life and shared herself with other people.

Jordan had never seen this quality before, and remained in awe of it whenever he was with her.

Part of him wished he could extol these virtues to Barbara. He wanted to sing Leslie's praises to her, to confide his admiration for Leslie much as a youth would excitedly describe his new girlfriend to a confidant. But he knew this would be unbearably painful for Barbara. He could only reassure her that he had chosen a woman who would make him happy. For he knew that his happiness was what Barbara wanted. It was for his happiness that Barbara was willing to give him up.

Again there was a silence. The darkness joined Jordan to his wife, but the deepening chasm of time and impending separation sundered them. With each passing day it was becoming more difficult for them to be together. Yet he did not want to lose Barbara yet. She had been his companion and confidante for four years. He was going to miss her.

"I'd better go to bed," she said. "It's been a long day."

She kissed his cheek and left the room. He sat for a moment, lost in thought, still torn by the seductive image of Leslie and the memory of Barbara's sad, understanding face.

He finished his brandy and drifted into the bedroom, intending to take a shower. Barbara was sitting on the bed in her nightgown, holding the book she had been reading lately. It was a selection of Somerset Maugham's short stories. He had given it to her for her birthday last summer.

She seemed undecided, not yet getting under the covers, holding the book somewhat nervously. She looked up at Jordan. He was standing in the doorway, unbuttoning his shirt.

Her eyes filled with tears.

"Oh, Jordan," she cried.

He went to her side and hugged her close. He covered her face with kisses. The taste of her tears on his lips filled him with a terrible sadness.

"I'm going to miss you so much," she said. Her grief was so intense that Jordan felt his own eyes grow misty.

Seeing his emotion, she gathered his face to her breast, as she had so often done in the past. She petted him gently, as though to comfort him. He felt the old maternal flame of Barbara's tenderness. It was as though she were a mother arming her child with her love to go out into the world on his own.

And somehow this warmth of her breast, this sweetness of her petting, became a kiss. He was holding her in his arms now, kissing her lips, pulling her closer. Her body melted into his. Her breasts, naked under the nightgown, pressed against his chest. Her tongue slid shyly into his mouth. A strange passion took possession of him, born of his affection for her, his love for Leslie, and the change overtaking his life.

For an instant he wondered if she could bear this, or indeed if he himself could bear it. But she was holding him closer, and her body seemed terribly warm and soft.

"Just this once," she moaned, hugging him tighter. "Just this once, Jordan. Give me this to remember. . . ."

An almost painful heat leaped through his loins. He saw the irony of possessing his wife's body only now, at the end of their marriage. He was afraid of hurting Barbara in some way by breaking the lock of her last secret. The more so because Leslie owned his passion now, and forever.

But Barbara's kiss had deepened, and her hands were beneath his waist, pulling him gently onto her.

"Only once, my darling," she murmured.

He reached to turn out the light.

At the moment that Jordan's bedroom lamp was being extinguished, Leslie Chamberlain was being dropped off from work by Ross Wheeler.

They had spent a long evening at the office going over the books with Ross's accountant, a yearly undertaking that Ross always dreaded, for he lacked a head for figures.

Not long after Leslie went to work for him he had asked her if she would be willing to help with the books. By that time he was already beginning to depend on her for just about everything. She had cheerfully agreed, and soon became far more familiar with the agency's accounts and overhead than he was. Her presence tonight had been a virtual necessity.

"Thanks a million, sweetie," he said, turning to her. "You saved my life. I don't know how I got along before you came."

"Oh, you're not as bad as all that," she said. "You just don't trust yourself enough. A little column of figures can't hurt a big strong man like you. You just need me to remind you of that."

Ross's eyes were resting on her in the darkened car.

"I need you for a lot more than that," he said.

There was a silence. He was talking about his heart as well as his business, and she knew it. He was waiting for her answer to his proposal. Ross was a patient man, but he knew what he was up against in asking a girl like Leslie to marry him.

He had played his hand, and could only wait to see whether she, for whatever reasons, could find it in her heart to accept marriage to an older man. He lived in fear that she would meet someone younger. A more appropriate match.

Leslie could not help wondering whether he suspected that she had fallen in love with someone else. She could not hide the glow that lit up her eyes these days as she went about her business. Everyone in the office had noticed it and remarked on it. Leslie had done her best to laugh it off.

On one hand, she wanted Ross to think it was her happiness in her work with him that had released her from her former sadness and made her a new person. On the other hand, she feared that he would misunderstand it as a reaction to his proposal—for this could only increase his pain when she had to turn him down.

With all this in her mind, Leslie was keeping a new distance from Ross, using an armor of levity to hide herself from the question in his eyes and from her own power to hurt him by refusing him. She could not bear to think about it more than absolutely necessary. Her heart was too busy soaring over her love for Jordan Lazarus to linger over the life she would sacrifice for him.

"I don't know about you, but I'm out on my feet," she said. "I have to sleep all those numbers off."

"Me, too," Ross said, a slight trace of discomfort in his voice. "Get a good eight hours, now. Don't come in until you're rested. We can get along without you for one extra hour."

"Sure thing."

He knew she was lying. She would be there bright and early, probably opening the office herself. She was a workhorse, as he had learned a long time ago. No one worked harder, or cared more about the business, than Leslie.

He watched her get out of the car and move with brisk strides to the apartment building. Knowing she could not see the look in his eyes, he allowed his gaze to feast on the long, shapely legs moving under her skirt, the slender back under her light jacket, the beautiful curly hair over her milky skin. An ache stirred suddenly inside him as he realized how much he wanted her, how much of his heart had now committed itself to the idea that he loved her, must have her.

Reluctantly he watched her disappear into the building. Then he started the car and drove away.

Leslie stood in the foyer opening her mailbox. As usual, there was not much mail for her. A flyer from an insurance company, a renewal letter for an advertising journal she subscribed to, and a phone bill. No letter from her father, whom she had just seen. She would not hear from him for another week or two.

She entered the building and walked up the stairs to her apartment. She felt a chill in the hallway. This was odd, for the day had been quite warm.

Her apartment was silent. She had to fumble for the wall switch to turn on the lamp. The living room came into view, poor but homey with its used couch and chairs, its chipped old tables and cheap framed landscapes. Leslie had bought it all at garage sales when she first moved here. She had been too depressed to consider replacing any of it while she was working at the library, and was too busy to think about it now that Ross and his business kept her so busy.

She would have to get rid of it all soon and find something more presentable. But for the moment she took a strange pleasure in coming home to it every night. The battered furniture reminded her of her own dislocated life. Like herself, it had been through a lot and survived.

Now that she had met Jordan, the old furniture seemed even more eclipsed by the changes in her heart. Like Mole in *The Wind in the Willows,* one of Leslie's favorite books, she felt drawn by this poor little place that she had already left behind but that was still, in spite of everything, her only home.

She went quickly into the bedroom and stripped off her clothes. She felt sweaty and ink-stained after her hours with the account books. She threw the clothes in the hamper and padded naked into the bathroom.

She was closing the door when she thought she heard a noise. An involuntary shiver went through her limbs, and goose bumps stood out on her skin. She stood listening for a moment, but heard nothing. She decided the noise had come from another apartment, or perhaps from the building settling.

On an impulse she locked the bathroom door. She took her shower quickly, enjoying the hot water coursing over her body, and washed her hair. When she emerged from the shower the mirror was frosted over with condensation. She toweled herself off, put on her terry cloth robe, and opened the door. Suppressing the tiny edge of anxiety inside her, she saw the living room come into view, silent and empty as always.

She dried her hair quickly, went to the bedroom to turn on the bedside lamp, and returned to the living room to turn out the light. She felt spooky for some reason she could not name. She checked the latch on the apartment door. It was hooked, of course. She had locked it upon entering.

Smiling at her own attack of nerves, she got into bed and opened the book she was reading. It was a library book, checked out by Mrs. Babbage, her old employer, only last weekend. Leslie began to read, but quickly realized her long hours with the account books had made her eyes too tired to read. She sighed and closed the book.

She lay in bed for a long moment, looking at the bedroom, with its little desk and the dresser with its pictures of her mother and father. She reflected that in a very short time this bedroom, this apartment, even this town would be just memories for her. This was her launching pad to a new life.

She reached to turn out the light. As she did so another brief surge of anxiety went through her. She pulled back her hand and left the light on. Listening intently, she looked around the bedroom. She felt an impulse to get up and check the living room again, but was torn between contempt for her own nerves and a pang of fear that made her hesitate to go into the other room.

Finally, exasperated with herself, she turned out the light.

"Settle down," she said to herself. "You've been working too hard."

She wondered whether the profound division in her emotions of late had caused this mood of anxiety and dread. Perhaps it was because her familiar life was threatened by her new love that her own home seemed a place of menace tonight.

She lingered over the question for a moment as the warm walls of her room hovered over her. But almost immediately the veils of sleep began to confuse her reflections, and the question before her mind's eye was eclipsed by the face of Jordon Lazarus, which drew her deliciously toward the world of her dreams.

A moment later she was fast asleep.

Her sleep was not as restful as she had hoped. She dreamed she was on the *Meg* with Jordan. They were struggling to sail downwind, but repeated bursts of spray from the Sound were splashing their faces and preventing them from doing their work. Jordan was shouting some sort of instruction to her, but the spray kept banging into her face, drowning his words.

She tried to fight her way across the deck to him, but he was waving her urgently back to her own side as though she were making a mistake in leaving her post. He shouted the same words over and over again. But, maddeningly, the blasts of spray obscured his warning every time he made it.

Suddenly she came awake. The crashing of the spray had become an urgent ringing in her ears. She reached for the alarm clock, assuming it was already morning. But the ringing continued.

Already on her feet, she staggered sleep-dulled into the living room, where the phone was ringing insistently. She did not notice the clock on the book-case, which said 2 A.M.

"Hello?" she asked sleepily.

"Leslie? Is that you?"

"Yes, this is me." At first she did not recognize the voice on the line. Anxiety had distorted its timbre.

"Leslie, this is Georgia Beyer. We've got trouble."

Instantly Leslie came fully awake. The news could only be about Terry.

"What's the matter?" she asked. "Is it Terry? Is he all right?"

There was a silence, filled with anxiety on both sides. Somehow Leslie knew already that something was terribly wrong.

"Oh, Leslie," Georgia said, a sob drowning her voice. "He's gone. Some-body took him. Terry is gone."

32

FROM THE MOMENT Georgia told Leslie what had happened, everything seemed confused.

Leslie could barely make out Georgia's half-hysterical words. Cliff had to come on the line to explain to her that Terry had been put to bed as usual tonight at eight-thirty, and had been sleeping peacefully when Georgia looked in on him at ten. But Cliff himself, awakening at one in the morning, had checked on the boy and found his bed empty.

The Beyers had called the police immediately, and a sheriff's car had arrived at their house within five minutes of Cliff's call.

Leslie was still standing in the living room with the phone in her hand, listening to Cliff's account of these events, when the buzzer sounded. She put the phone down long enough to listen through the intercom. It was the police.

Leslie let the officers in—two detectives and two uniformed officers—and picked up the phone. As she listened to Cliff the detectives stood looking at her with inscrutable policemen's expressions on their faces, waiting for her to finish. She was so frantic about Terry that she did not even think to be embarrassed about the four officers staring at her in her pajamas.

"Cliff, there are policemen here," she said.

"I know. They said they'd go right over to let you know," Cliff said.

Leslie nodded, not yet drawing the logical conclusion from the presence of the police in her home. She asked to speak to Georgia again, and tried to assure her that things would turn out all right. But her hand was shaking uncontrollably on the receiver. And when she finally hung up the phone she realized that tears had been streaming down her cheeks almost since she picked it up.

One of the two detectives had moved a pace closer to her. He was apparently the authority here.

"Miss Chamberlain? My name is Detective Hirth. This is Detective Stokes, and Officers Valentine and McCann. I take it Mrs. and Mrs. Beyer have filled you in on what happened?"

"Yes," Leslie said, the tears still running down her cheeks. She looked at the detective's face. He was a tired-looking man in his forties, a bit overweight, with hair cut very short. But the watchful look in his eyes blinded her to everything else about him.

"Do you know anything about this?" he asked.

"About . . . ?" Leslie stammered, wiping at the tears on her cheeks. "Just what Georgia told me. Have you—I mean, do you know—I mean . . ." Her words trailed off miserably.

"Perhaps you'd like to come with us," the detective said. "I know how concerned you must be."

Leslie nodded. She hurried back into the bedroom to put some clothes on. As she did so she crossed paths with one of the uniformed officers, who was coming out of the bedroom. She caught a glimpse of the other officers moving purposefully around the apartment.

Still she did not see what was going on. It was not until she emerged and found herself faced with four policemen who were all looking at her with cautious scrutiny in their eyes, that she realized they had come here to find out whether she herself had kidnapped Terry.

"Oh!" she said, her hand going to her mouth. "I didn't think . . . Did Georgia tell you about me?"

"Yes, Miss Chamberlain," Detective Hirth said. "Now why don't you come with us?"

Wiping at her tears with embarrassment now, Leslie left with the officers.

An hour and a half later Leslie was at Georgia's house in Farmington.

She had spent a brief half hour at the police station being interrogated by Detectives Hirth and Stokes. Apparently her frantic worry had satisfied them that she had had nothing to do with the disappearance of Terry Beyer. She was so beside herself that a female officer was produced from somewhere, and offered her a shoulder to cry on.

After questioning her briefly about the birth of Terry, the Beyers' adoption of him, and her relationship with the family, the detectives drove her to Georgia's house. There were half a dozen more officers there, both in plain-clothes and in uniform. A sort of low-key pandemonium reigned in the house as the officers came in and went out, talked on the phone, and gave each other orders.

Georgia had regained sufficient control of herself to fill Leslie in on the details and to speak rationally to the officers. But as she sat beside Cliff on the living room couch, she seemed a mirror image of Leslie's own emotions. Her words were reasonable, but her hands shook, and a steady stream of tears kept coming from her eyes.

Leslie sat on the couch with the Beyers, and the three of them faced the police, answering question after question and going over the same ground again and again. They explained their lives with Terry, Leslie's continuing relationship with the boy, and repeated over and over that they could think of no one, no one in the world, who might have a motive to kidnap Terry.

The question-and-answer session went on for the rest of the night. No one seemed tired. Leslie herself felt comforted by the officers' questions, for they distracted her from the dread eating away at her insides.

When dawn lit the windows with a depressing gray glow, Georgia got up to make coffee. More officers had arrived, male and female. One of them had brought several boxes of doughnuts for the crowd now occupying the house.

It was not until nine in the morning that Leslie even thought to call Ross. He did not seem surprised to hear from her, for he had suggested that she sleep in. But when she told him that a family emergency would keep her away from work for the rest of the day, he seemed concerned.

"What is it, honey?" he asked.

"Just my cousin," Leslie lied. "Her little boy is sick. I have to help take care of things. I should be back by tomorrow. If not, I'll call. Sorry to leave you in the lurch."

"No problem. We'll be fine. But call to let me know what is happening."

As she listened to him Leslie found herself wondering whether the police had been in touch with him about her. Perhaps, given the urgency of Georgia's situation and their suspicions of Leslie herself, they had thought to question her employer. She did not have the courage to ask Ross about this, and his reassuringly normal voice seemed to indicate that no one had contacted him.

She hung up as quickly as she could and spent the rest of the morning sitting on the couch with Georgia and watching the police move about the house. It was not until Cliff whispered in Leslie's ear that she realized the police were waiting for a ransom call. This thought sent new waves of panic through Leslie, and she had to cling to Cliff for support. As she looked into his eyes she could see the hope draining slowly out of him.

Now it was her turn to make a show of strength. "It's going to be all right, Cliff," she said firmly. "I know it." But her own words had a hollow ring to her.

Thus the day went on, with courage ebbing and flowing from Leslie to Georgia to Cliff and back again, as the police stood around in increasingly languid postures. The phone rang often, but never with news. Dread filled the house like a poison gas.

Leslie had slept very little, and by the end of the afternoon she was drained. She had barely touched the soup Georgia had made for lunch, and she could not get down more than a bite of the sandwich a policewoman made for supper.

At Georgia's insistence Leslie agreed to go home and wait for news there. She could see that despite Georgia's affection for her, her presence was making

Georgia even more nervous than she would be on her own. Georgia and Cliff needed to be alone to face their dread. Leslie was in the way.

Two of the officers drove her home on the expressway. She felt like a criminal, sitting in the back of the squad car behind the iron grillwork. Sleeplessness was making her jittery. Irrationality seemed to color her every thought.

The policeman took her to her door.

"Try to get some sleep," he said. "We'll call you the minute we hear anything."

Leslie gave them the phone number at the office, though she doubted she would be in shape to go to work tomorrow. She stood in the foyer watching the squad car crawl away down the street. She felt atrociously alone. Only now did she realize that Georgia and Cliff, despite their own nightmare, were condemning her to an agony of solitude by asking her to go home.

As she slipped her key into the front door lock she was thinking seriously of calling Ross and telling him the whole truth about Terry and her past, simply in order to feel the sympathy of another human being, and not to be alone tonight.

And she would have made the call, had not something stopped her at the threshold of her home.

In the vestibule she opened her mailbox. A magazine and two flyers were in the mailbox, along with a white envelope with her name scrawled on it in block letters. Leslie opened it almost without thinking.

The message inside made her blink.

"Go to the pay phone at the corner of Main and Walnut," it read. "Make sure you're not followed. Bring pen and paper. Do it now."

Leslie's breath caught in her throat. The message fluttered in her trembling fingers like the leaves in the breeze outside.

She hesitated for a long moment, staring at the message. She thought of going inside to call the police. They should know about this immediately. But something told her she was perhaps being watched even at this moment. She could not take a chance where Terry's safety was concerned.

She went back out through the door she had just come in and walked hurriedly the three blocks to the phone booth. She glanced behind her at the quiet village streets. It was obvious she was not being followed.

The night wind was blowing angrily when she arrived. She went inside the phone booth for shelter. Her eyes squinted in the sudden light. She had opened her purse and found her pen and notebook when the phone rang, making her jump. She waited, unbelieving, until the second ring jarred her into action. She picked up the receiver.

"Hello?"

"Leslie Chamberlain?" The voice was male. It sounded raspy and perhaps disguised.

"Yes. Yes, this is me. Who are you?"

"Do you want to see that little boy again? Do you want him to come home alive?"

"Yes! Yes! Who are you?" she almost shouted in the phone. "What do you want?"

"Got the pen and paper?"

"Yes, it's right here. Tell me what you want. Please!"

"Get out the pen. Write down what I say. Every word exactly as I say it. When I'm finished I want you to read it back to me. Got it?"

"Yes. Yes, I'm ready." Leslie's breathing was shallow, hurried. The voice sounded evil and full of purpose.

She wrote down the first words as they were dictated. Her hand trembled. At first the words made no sense. They seemed as alien as a foreign language.

Then the anxiety inside her turned to despair as she saw what her hand was writing on the paper.

The voice continued dictating. Tears came to her eyes as she went on writing. The dictation took no more than three minutes, but it seemed like an eternity of suffering to her. She felt as though the world were ending, destroyed by her own hand at the command of the disembodied voice in her ear.

When she had finished she read the message back word for word. The voice stopped her several times to make her repeat what she had written. Only when she had repeated the complete message three times did the caller seem satisfied.

"Go home and write it on your own stationery," the voice said. "Send it special delivery. When it's been received, the boy goes home. Any funny stuff and the boy dies. If you show that message to the cops, or tell them about this call, the boy dies. Understand?"

Leslie looked at the message she had written. A deep chill had settled in her hands, even in her eyes. Nothing looked very real any more. Except what she had written, that is.

"Yes, I understand," she said dully.

"Send it right away."

The phone went dead.

The letter Leslie sent was delivered only a few hours after she put it in the mailbox at the Johnsonville post office. It did not have far to travel.

Less than six hours after that, Terry Beyer was found by the Farmington Police on a bench at a town bus stop only two blocks from the police station. He was unharmed.

Terry was returned to his frantic mother, who kissed him several hundred times, gave him a special dinner with his favorite ice cream, gave him a bath, and put him to bed before subsiding into hysterics and being put to bed herself by the family doctor with a powerful sedative.

Leslie Chamberlain was called by Cliff Beyer within minutes of the call from the police.

"Terry is safe," Cliff said, trying to control his own tears. "They're bringing him over now. Do you want me to have someone come and get you?"

There was a long pause. Cliff wondered if Leslie had fainted.

"Leslie? Are you there?"

"Yes, Cliff," Leslie said in a surprisingly controlled voice. "Don't send anyone over. You and Georgia need to be alone with him. I'll come tomorrow night, if that's all right."

Cliff told her the sketchy details of the boy's return, and hung up after suggesting that she get some sleep.

Leslie did that. She had not slept more than three hours in the last forty-eight. Exhausted, hopeless, she went to bed and fell into a deep but troubled sleep.

She had done her part. Terry was safe.

But the future she had saved for her son was forever cut off for Leslie herself.

Jordan Lazarus did not come home from work until very late that night.

He sat at his desk, high above Manhattan, reading and rereading the note he had received by special delivery this afternoon. For a while he looked at the phone, and his hand actually reached out toward it. But he did not pick it up.

He destroyed the note before going home to Barbara. He looked at it for a last time as it burned to ashes in his ashtray.

It read:

Dear Jordan,

This is a painful letter for me to write, not only because I should have sent it a long time ago, but because it will hurt me as much as it hurts you.

I am involved in a long-standing relationship that means a great deal to me. As a matter of fact, I am getting married soon.

I made a mistake when I became involved with you, and a bigger mistake when I let you think our relationship could become something permanent. I was running away from myself, I now realize, and running away from the truth. I took advantage of you, and I can't go on doing that.

In asking you to give me up. I am asking you to do what is best for you as well as for me. Go back to your own life, Jordan. Love the people you were meant to love, and forget me. For my own part I will try to forget, too. It is the only way for both of us.

Please, please don't call or write. If you do I will not be able to answer—and that will hurt us both even more.

Good luck, and good-bye.
Leslie

Jordan did not feel the tears in his eyes as he watched the crumpled note burn, a skeleton crawled over by little red worms of flame that devoured it like the emptiness that was devouring his own heart.

He had never thought this moment possible. For the first time in his adult life he had forgotten the cautious defenses that had seen him through so many adventures, and gone out on a limb heedlessly, ignoring everything but his love, believing only in the future.

And now, as that future flew mockingly from him, a voice came from the past to echo in his ear like an anthem, as bitter as it was mortally sad.

Never trust a woman.

33

WEEKS PASSED, THEN MONTHS. Ross Wheeler worked side by side with Leslie during the day but saw less and less of her outside the office.

He knew something terrible had happened to her. She looked like a person who had just lost a loved one. Her face was a mask of grief. At work she was the same as always, alert, dependable, sometimes even jocular. But there was a distanced, controlled air about her. And underneath it was that mask of sorrow, standing out on her beautiful face like the shadow of some unspeakable wound.

It reminded him of the look on his mother's face when she was still a young woman, right after his father's death. And it reminded him of his own face and his daughters' faces after his wife's death, now eleven years ago. It was the mask of grief in its cruelest form.

He did not ask Leslie what was wrong. He knew by instinct that this was a private agony upon which he must not intrude. He worked by her side and waited for her to recover. He knew how proud and resilient a person she was. When she felt the time was right—if ever—she would tell him.

In the meantime he tried to be a friend to her, and to give her plenty of breathing space. He gave her lots of work to do, and saw her rise to the challenge with her strong, bright personality.

Ross's own feelings for Leslie became more ambiguous and more painful during this period. On one hand, he had to back off, to keep his distance, for she obviously could not share her chagrin with him. Frankly, he suspected that she was suffering from a love affair that had not worked out. On the other hand, he could not help recalling that he had asked her to marry him not long before the disaster—whatever it was—occurred. This made him feel embarrassed and unsure of himself.

So Ross reverted to the fatherly role he had affected toward Leslie when he first met her. It hurt him to take this backward step when Leslie had come to mean so much to him, but he had no choice.

The sight of her courage and determination as she fought her way through the long workdays made Ross's heart go out to her. He had never known a person of such strength and integrity. His admiration for her grew in proportion as his love was forced to hide itself.

But her mask of grief did not fade. As the months went by she seemed to become more inward, more enigmatic. Ross realized that the wound she had suffered, whatever it was, would not heal in a matter of months. It might take years, or scar her forever.

Then, one blustery autumn day, an unexpected event came to interrupt this uneasy status quo.

Leslie's father died.

The news came by telephone at the office. Leslie took the call, listened in silence, spoke a few confirming words to her unseen interlocutor, and came to Ross's side.

"My father died," she said. "I have to go home and see to the funeral arrangements. I'll need a few days."

Ross put his arms around her.

"Of course, honey," he said. "Take all the time you need. Shall I come with you? Maybe I can be of some help."

He knew Leslie had no one in the world except her father. He could imagine how lonely the next few days were going to be for her.

She shook her head.

"I'll be fine," she said. "Besides, you're needed here."

He knew it was true. Between the two of them, Ross and Leslie carried the entire business on their shoulders. It would be tough enough to get along without her for several days. He himself would have to work overtime.

"Are you sure?" he asked, thinking of the pain he had seen in her face these past months.

"Positive." The tightly controlled look on her face seemed to have clamped down even harder to hide her emotions. There was no sign of overt grief over her father's death. She seemed blank and efficient.

"Well, then," he said, still holding her by her shoulders. "But call me every night. Will you promise me that, anyway?"

She smiled and patted his cheek. "Okay, boss," she joked.

But there was no humor in her smile.

Tom Chamberlain had died of a ruptured aneurysm that took everybody, including his internist, by surprise. He died instantly and almost painlessly.

At first the loss of her father afforded Leslie a measure of relief from the agony that had been twisting slowly inside her for months. The image of Jordan Lazarus retreated into the shadows of her mind, eclipsed by her immediate grief over her father's death. She felt cleansed by her own sadness, and even calmed, as though this overriding sorrow had a painkilling side effect.

She was calm and orderly as she flew home to Ellicott and was met by a distant aunt at the airport. She watched the old streets of town go by the windows of the car, looking alien and forlorn, buried under the weight of the years that had passed since they had any genuine reality for her.

Some Chamberlain relatives were gathered at Tom Chamberlain's house to greet Leslie. They all looked much older, and they seemed to share the faded, not quite real look of the old street and the neighboring houses.

They were all proud of Leslie's courage and friendliness as she greeted them with kisses and hugs and questions about their children and their provincial concerns. She immediately took charge of the funeral arrangements, visiting Mr. Norvell, the funeral director, that first evening.

It was Mr. Norvell, twenty years before, who had said the last words over Leslie's mother. Somehow his presence on this occasion lent a particularly macabre note to the proceedings. Leslie had traveled far and wide, seen many things, and been through crises that had changed her forever. Yet Mr. Norvell, his old funeral home, his sympathetic manner had not changed a bit. His hair was a bit thinner, his chin drooping with advancing age, but everything else was the same.

That faded sameness, reflected in the faces of those she knew and in the sights of the town, was the drug that kept Leslie from feeling anything. She was a perfect hostess to the friends and relatives who came to commiserate. Most of them spoke a kind word about Tom, his hard life, his dead wife, before proceeding to irritating small talk about their own petty problems. Leslie smiled inwardly to witness the eternal egoism of the living in the face of death. Even the shallowness of this display, and its pitiable aspect, helped her to get through it all without feeling anything.

She feared that the eulogy would break down her defenses at last, but it did not. Pastor Reynolds had never been a very articulate man, and his attempts to evoke the personality and value of Tom Chamberlain were completely futile. He spoke in the tired clichés of his profession, praising Tom as a churchgoing family man, a good friend, a credit to his family and his community. There was no trace in his sermon of the real Tom Chamberlain—a quiet man whose dry humor and intuitive, generous personality had made up for his humdrum life and lack of education. And this also comforted Leslie. At least her father was safe in her own memory, where she could keep him as he really had been.

Leslie almost made it through the entire weekend unscathed.

But on her last night at home, as she was gathering up the few Chamberlain possessions that she did not want to be sold with the rest, she came upon the family photo album. It contained all the old black-and-white pictures of Leslie as a child, the pictures of her mother from before Leslie's conscious memory, and the pictures of Tom himself that Leslie had taken with her Brownie and later with her Pentax.

Leslie contemplated the snapshots of her mother. They showed a pretty woman, slender, with careworn eyes in which a quick intelligence glimmered. Tom had always claimed that Leslie got her brains from her mother.

Leslie compared the pictures of her mother and father, and tried to discern the hereditary traits that had modeled her own face, her own character. They were there, to be sure, in her mother's eyes, her father's nose and chin—and in something about their expressions. For a moment she was interested and almost amused to see how heredity spanned the years as it patiently modeled the human face.

She recalled her father looking at this very album when Leslie was a college student, and pointing out that she was beginning to resemble her mother now that she was growing up. And had not Aunt May suggested this very thing at the funeral service yesterday, with tears in her eyes?

Leslie wondered what the significance of this could be. If she was growing to resemble someone whom she never really knew, someone who was lost too long ago even to remember, did that mean that fate was allowing her in some strange way to become closer to Mother after all? Or did it mean that the distance in her heart, the loss, was only working itself deeper into her flesh with each passing year? So that resemblance was the sign of a permanent wound, an incurable grief?

She turned to the back of the album and found a letter she had written to her father only ten days ago. The handwriting on the envelope looked like that of a stranger. She did not need to open the letter to know that it was full of lies, like all the letters she had sent since she met Tony and left Ogilvie, Thorpe, since she had her baby and moved to Long Island, since she met, loved, and lost Jordan Lazarus. All lies, accepted quietly by her father in his tactful way, never challenged by him, but always part of the image he must have carried of her in his heart.

Somehow the maze of her own lies joined the distance of time and space and death to make her realize only now, this minute, that Tom Chamberlain was lost to her forever, and would never come back to hold her in his arms or warm her with his smile.

With this thought Leslie found silent tears beginning to flow down her cheeks. She lay down on the old battered couch with its afghan and over-stuffed cushions, and began to cry in earnest. The tears she had held back for so many days came to her now. The pain was unbearable. She knew how much her father had counted on her to be strong, to be happy. He had always worried that the death of her mother, and his limited qualities as a caretaker, had scarred Leslie. He had hung on every word, every letter that assured him she was happy and doing well.

And he had waited, in vain, for her to bring home a young man and tell him she was in love, she was to be married.

Leslie wept for a long time. But her tears did not bring the relief she sought, for each one seemed to symbolize an opportunity missed, and a lie invented to cover over that lost chance to give her father what he had so longed for.

At last she closed the album. She could not bear to contemplate the past any longer. It only reminded her that she was totally alone in the world now.

No one ever knew about those private tears. The next day Leslie finished packing her small cache of family memorabilia and left the sale of the house and its furnishings to her father's attorney, a friendly man whom Leslie recalled from her youth, and who was himself suffering now from what would probably be his final illness.

Leslie was taken to the airport by the same Aunt May who had met her four days ago.

"Be happy, honey," Aunt May said. "You know that's what Tom would have wanted. Your happiness was all that ever mattered to him."

She could not know the effect her words had on Leslie, who had never been able to find the happiness her father wanted for her. Leslie hid her emotion behind a gentle smile—another lie, she mused exhaustedly—and hugged her aunt.

"Come back and see us, now," Aunt May said. "We miss you, honey."

Leslie nodded, knowing she would never go back to that little town again.

Her many lies wrapped invisibly around her, she got on the airplane and was borne into the cold, gray sky toward home. But as the surge of the engines flung her headlong into her own future, it seemed that home was receding forever into the past, and would never again offer her a safe haven.

Ross Wheeler was waiting for her at LaGuardia. She was surprised to see him, for she had not called to say she was coming back. She had wanted to be alone with the emotions inside her for a while longer before going back to work.

"How did you know?" she asked as his arms curled around her.

"I called your aunt," he said. "She gave me the flight number. Did I do wrong to come here? I don't want to intrude, honey."

Leslie said nothing, but shook her head against his chest. The feel of his arms around her was so lulling that she never wanted him to let her go.

"Can I drive you home?" he asked.

She smiled. "I'd go anywhere with you."

He was very kind on the long drive to Long Island, asking few questions about the funeral. He wanted to give her plenty of room. Her clipped responses made it obvious that she was not ready to talk about what had happened.

When they reached her apartment dusk was just falling. Ross stopped the car at the curb, but did not turn off the engine.

"You don't really want to go in there, do you?" he asked.

She shook her head, looking straight in front of her like a little girl.

Ross drove her to his house. The lights were on inside, making the place look homey and warm. He took her inside and helped her off with her coat. She stood in the hallway, gazing at nothing.

"You haven't been eating," he said. "I can tell. I'll make you some supper. How about a drink?"

He took her into the living room, leading her like a child, and sat her on the couch. As he went to get her a drink she looked at the pictures of his daughters on the mantel. They smiled out from the frames with fresh faces full of youth and strength, a strength that had finally been burned out of Leslie herself.

Ross returned with a glass of whiskey. The golden liquid burned pleasantly inside Leslie's frozen body when she drank.

"I have some spaghetti sauce all made out there," he said, sitting down beside her. "We can put some noodles on to boil and make a salad. You'll feel better. . . ."

He could see she was not hearing him. Yet when his voice trailed off she looked up at him so pathetically that he came to her side and put his arm around her.

"That bad, eh?" he asked.

She did not answer. She seemed tense and cold in his arms, strung tight as a wire.

"I know," he murmured. "I know all about it, Leslie."

He petted her gently, almost like the father she had just lost. She felt like a girl in his arms, herself so thin, while he was middle-aged and heavy, his dry hands holding her protectively. Something began to weaken inside her, a first rampart.

"You don't have to hide from me," he said. "Just let it go, sweetie."

Her tears came so suddenly that they welled up in her expressionless eyes and rolled down her cheeks like a flood. The whiskey glass shook in her hand, and Ross took it away and put it on the table. Then he held her close, rocking her like a little girl while the tears came in endless torrents. He could not know what was going on in her mind, but his affection gave him a direct line to her pain and told him how to soothe it.

She wept for a long time, quietly, violently. He did not let her go. After a while she sat drained against him, shaken by little sobs like those of a child.

When it was over he brought her some tissues and made her drink the rest of the whiskey. He watched her wipe her red eyes and blow her nose, and thought to himself that she had never been more beautiful than tonight.

She managed a smile. She felt better now. It seemed she was in the right place, with the one person who would never let her down, whose warm arms and sympathetic heart could be counted on absolutely. She thanked heaven for Ross Wheeler.

Now he looked at her with a serious, almost stern expression in his eyes.

"Leslie, my dear," he said with a little twinkle of humor in his voice, "you're a very beautiful girl, and a strong one. But you're only human, you know. I don't see how I can allow you to run around on your own any more. You're getting hurt too much."

She looked at him with an uncomprehending smile.

He took out a small ring and placed it on her finger.

"Let's end that loneliness," he said.

Leslie looked down at the ring in surprise. In the tumult of the past few months she had actually forgotten that Ross had proposed to her. She was about to blush at this unforgivable oversight when it suddenly occurred to her that she needed him now more than ever before. And he had not forgotten his promise. He was giving her a second chance.

"No one will ever, ever love you like I do, Leslie," he said. "I don't know what's gone on in that heart of yours these past years, and I don't need to know. But I do know that a love like I feel for you doesn't come along every day. Will you accept it? If you do, you'll be making me the happiest man in the world. And I'll move heaven and earth to make you the happiest woman you can be."

Leslie looked into his eyes. She knew that the web of lies she had spun around herself these past years now stood between her and Ross, just as it had stood between her and everyone else, including her father. She had made herself a cocoon of lies in which she was entirely alone.

Yet Ross Wheeler's gentle, intelligent eyes did not need to see through her lies, for love made them see her heart, and how to heal it.

The light in those eyes was not the same light that had illuminated her soul so briefly, only months ago, when she had looked into the face of Jordan

Lazarus and felt sure that her destiny as a woman was revealed to her. But it was a light that would never go out.

And in this moment that seemed the only thing that mattered. Not even her lies could ruin it.

He was holding her hand. The ring fit perfectly.

"I know those fingers pretty well," he said. "They've helped to put my life back together. Let me do the same for you."

Leslie searched quickly, vainly for a reason to say no to him. But she had hit bottom tonight. There was no courage inside herself to refuse his love. Why go on holding the world at arm's length behind a screen of lies, when love was offering itself to her at last with no traps, no thorns, no lies of its own?

The words came with a will of their own from deep inside her, almost like the flood of her tears. In that one instant she felt simultaneously that she was making the biggest mistake of her life, committing the greatest sin, and doing the one decent thing she had ever done for herself.

"Yes, Ross," she said with a marvelous sense of relief. "I will marry you."

34

New York City
December 21, 1976

IT HAD BEEN a very long day.

Jill Fleming was sitting in her pajamas, rubbing Jessica Hightower's tense shoulders as the eleven o'clock news murmured on the television in the study of the Park Avenue house.

Both women were exhausted. There had been a board meeting at Hightower today for which Jessica had been preparing for several weeks, with Jill working overtime to help her with the research.

There had been fireworks at the meeting, as Jessica had expected, because a majority of the board members were committed to a multimillion-dollar manufacturing project that Jessica had been against from the beginning. Even her brothers wanted the deal, and Ford was not speaking to her because two of his most powerful industrial constituents from Delaware stood to gain thousands of jobs because of it.

But Jessica had stood firm. And, with Jill's help, she had proved beyond the shadow of a doubt that the short-term gain offered by the deal for Hightower Industries would be offset by huge losses down the road. In ten years, she was able to show, the deal would cost the corporation $100 million in lost profits.

After nearly two hours of arm-twisting on both sides, the project was voted down by a narrow margin. Jessica had won.

By day's end both women were drained. They had a quiet dinner of cold lobster salad and caviar at home, and drank a glass of champagne to celebrate their victory. During their meal they were almost too tired to talk.

Jessica had developed a splitting headache from the bitter conflicts of the day, and after their showers the two women met in the little study with its gas fireplace. The flames were leaping silently behind the grate as they sat together on the deep leather couch.

Jill was rubbing gently at Jessica's shoulders. The rhythm of her fingers was nearly putting her to sleep, but she managed to keep going. She could feel Jessica's muscles beginning to relax. She knew Jessica's tension as well as she knew her own.

Suddenly Jessica said, "Do you know him?"

Jill opened her half-closed eyes. "Who?"

"Lazarus."

Jill looked blearily at the TV screen. The eleven o'clock news was doing a story on a new building being erected in midtown by Lazarus International. Jordan Lazarus and his wife had been present for the laying of the cornerstone. Reporters were interviewing them together after the ceremony.

"No," Jill said. "No, I don't."

There was a pause. Jordan Lazarus was holding his wife's hand and chatting with the reporters. He was an astonishingly handsome man. Jill could not recall ever seeing his face before. This was odd, for he was internationally famous as the wealthiest man in America, and Jill had heard his name many times.

The wife, Barbara Lazarus, was a dark, handsome woman, almost as tall as her husband. They made a strange couple. They complemented each other in an unexpected way, like the jarring combination of two previously incompatible colors in an expressionist painting. He seemed too young for her. As for Barbara, she seemed to have gone to great lengths both in diet and in wardrobe so as to minimize this very fact.

Their affection for each other was obvious, but one had the feeling that each had been meant for a different partner, one who would have suited him or her more naturally.

"I know him," Jessica was saying. "We've dealt with him a few times at Hightower. He's a nice fellow. Something of a dreamer. Almost like a boy, really. Very sweet. To talk to him you'd never know he's so ambitious."

She sighed, lulled by Jill's gentle fingers.

"But his wife is another story," she added. "She's her father's daughter. Hard as nails. I wouldn't trust her as far as I could throw her."

There was a pause. Jill went on rubbing.

"I never could understand what he saw in her," Jessica added. "Except money, of course."

Jill said nothing. Her eyes rested on the handsome face of Jordan Lazarus. She was only half listening, only half seeing.

Book Three

A
VISION

35

Tony DORRANCE'S LIFE HAD CHANGED. He was no longer the man he had been.

He could not put his finger on the change, or on when it had started. It might have been three years ago, or perhaps more. One morning he had awakened to find he was not the same man. That was a long time ago now, and he had been drifting imperceptibly ever since.

All through his adult life Tony had thought he knew himself rather well. He understood his own needs and made sure they were met. This often did not endear him to others, but he cared little for others anyway.

Now, however, he was not sure who he was anymore, or what it was he was seeking in life.

The routine of his life remained the same. He went to work, used his charm and ability to achieve a measure of success, and spent his leisure time drinking, gambling, and seducing women. But the pleasure that had seen him through his days was no longer there. He felt an emptiness in everything he did. Even his successes, both at work and with women, left him cold. There was an unfulfilled longing in him that made him feel lonely and useless.

Occasionally he would take a night off from his normal prowling and sit home in his apartment, staring at the walls and wondering what had gone wrong.

Once, out of boredom, he opened the envelope in which he kept a handful of photos from his childhood and glanced through them. It was a painful experience. He had not looked at these pictures in years, and had practically stopped remembering his childhood.

He had grown up in Philadelphia, in one of the toughest parts of the city. His father was a metalworker and jack-of-all-trades and, unfortunately for the family, a drunk and a womanizer.

Tony had two younger sisters whom he tolerated, and a mother he adored. Her name was Theresa, and she came from an Irish family that lived not far from their own poor neighborhood. Though tired and worn out by the time she was thirty, she still possessed a faded beauty, and her image dominated his dreams and fantasies throughout his youth.

His father abandoned the family after a series of particularly brutal quarrels with Theresa over another woman. Tony became his mother's helper and protector, cleaning the house, watching over the girls, and bringing in money, nearly all of which he made on the street in various extralegal ways.

Tony enjoyed this somewhat piratical lifestyle. He was a natural rebel and would probably have been in trouble anyway. But since his father's departure he was allowed to express his rebellion toward the world while dutifully passing along his ill-gotten gain to his mother. He was a good son and a misfit at the same time. This life suited him.

Then the great tragedy of Tony's boyhood struck. His mother abandoned the family, running off with a handsome traveling salesman she had met in a tavern not far from home.

After a hearing from the local Child Welfare Board, Tony and his sisters were separated, each sent to a different foster home. Tony never saw his sisters again.

The loss of his mother was a devastating blow to Tony. He had always idealized her and tried to protect her from the cruelty and betrayals of his father. After the father's departure Tony felt he was his mother's man. When she left him, without so much as a note or a word of good-bye, Tony's world literally fell apart.

Within a few months of his placement in a foster home he was in trouble with the law. He became a rising member of a street gang, and made his money by stealing, fencing stolen goods, and dealing in drugs.

There was something wild about him, a secret desire to tempt fate, perhaps even a desire to get caught. He was reckless in the course of burglaries, taking unnecessary chances. He could be inexcusably brutal when involved in an armed robbery. There was a self-destructive streak in him that alarmed even his felon friends.

He was arrested twice. The first time he was let off with a warning. The second time he was sent to a tough reform school where he remained until age eighteen. He was a hardened miscreant by then, a danger to himself and others.

Then fate took a friendly hand in his life. Upon his release from reform school, Tony and some friends were caught in the act of a robbery by a tough street cop named Cody Sheehan. The officer had dealt with many street punks before and saw possibilities in young Tony that others had failed to see.

He had a long talk with Tony before his arraignment. The conversation had a great effect on Tony. This was the first man who had ever taken the trouble to really talk to him. His father had certainly never done so, and neither had any of the other male authority figures who had drifted through his young life.

"With a college degree in your hand you can make more in five years than these punk pals of yours will make in a lifetime," Cody Sheehan said. "And you'll be on the street to enjoy your money. Your pals will have to spend at least half their life behind bars for the sake of a few thousand dollars in stolen goods. Does that seem worthwhile to you?"

Tony had listened, pensive.

"You've got brains," Officer Sheehan said. "And you've got style. Put that together with a little education, and you could make something of yourself. Of course, it's your decision. You can spend the rest of your life as a cheap hustler if you like. It's no skin off my nose. I just hate to see you turn into a chump like your buddies."

By the end of an hour Tony had opened his mind enough to see the possibility of a life on the right side of the law, and to see the inevitable failure and degradation that would result from continued activity as a felon.

Officer Sheehan used his personal influence with the judge in the case to get Tony's sentence reduced. Tony spent one year in prison. During that year he was visited regularly by Officer Sheehan. He also began a course of study to get a high school equivalency degree.

Tony had learned his lesson. Upon his release from prison he enrolled in a college correspondence program and finished a degree in business while working as a bartender, waiter, and bouncer in a Philadelphia tavern. No one worked harder than Tony, or with a greater sense of purpose. He got good grades in his college courses, and in the process transformed himself from a shaggy street punk into a smooth, convincing man.

It took five years for him to earn the college degree but only two to make himself into a man few women could resist. He had many girlfriends during those years, girls who were dazzled by his dash and confidence. He played as hard as he worked. And he enjoyed the life he had chosen for himself. He looked back on his old street pals as a bunch of brainless suckers too limited to see what life was really about.

What his correspondence degree and his lack of connections cost him was made up by his assurance and charm. For eight tumultuous years he advanced in the business world, first with a manufacturing firm in Philadelphia, then with a hotel chain in New Jersey, and finally with the Price-Davis Company of Atlanta.

Unfortunately, his career as a businessman did not advance as quickly as he had hoped. There was something lacking in Tony. Not ambition—he had that to spare—but focus. He could not seem to harness the great energy of his personality in one endeavor and stick with it until he achieved something important. His vision was limited somehow. He could be brilliant in using his charm and cleverness to solve an immediate problem, but too often he could not see the larger picture, and was not prepared when real opportunity knocked.

And the chip on his shoulder, inherited from his youth and the loss of his family, had not entirely disappeared. Often his quick temper got the best of him where members of the same sex were concerned. Somehow he always managed to run afoul of one boss or another, just as he was about to "hit the big time." His upward climb was bedeviled by repeated slides into mediocre positions from which he had to work his way back up.

Because of his frustration Tony drank more than he should have. He also gambled, and lost. He was always short of money and in hock to a dozen friends, tavern owners, and girls. He was always working on a "deal" of some sort, with one of many business associates, always planning to buy into a restaurant, a new hotel, a chain of drugstores. Always full of big plans, none of which ever worked out.

The many women he romanced were taken in for a while by his charm, his reports of his many prospects and deals. But sooner or later they found him out for what he was. Most often he abandoned them before that moment could come, usually still owing them money.

The cities he had lived in were filled with disappointed women who looked back on his lies with anger, but on his bedroom charms with retrospective longing, and on his overall undependable personality with a sort of tender contempt. He was a charmer, nice to look at and fun in the sack, but not worth much inside. Every woman knows the type.

Leslie had been one of his many conquests. He had romanced her, seduced her, and abandoned her just as he had done to many women before. During their brief affair he had not been unaware of her special depth, her honesty and integrity. She was more beautiful than the other women he had known—almost too beautiful. And loving, too, in a way that made him want to love her back. But rather than endear her to him these qualities had made him nervous, for they symbolized a life of commitment and stability, and a kind of intimacy that he thought impossible for himself. Leslie herself was so honest that when he was with her he felt he had no place to hide.

He was almost relieved when he got rid of her.

Or so he thought.

Now, however, things had gotten worse for Tony.

The women he seduced no longer stimulated him. His work bored him. He sensed the go-nowhere pattern of his life, and it filled him with frustration. Looking in the mirror, he saw that he was not as young as he once had been. He was thirty-four years old, an age at which many of his business peers were vice presidents of large companies. Life was catching up with him.

But it was not just the face in the mirror or the date on his birth certificate that alarmed him. The change went deeper. Where previously he had struggled through life on solid ground, now he seemed to be fighting against a sort of quicksand dragging him down.

Something was missing in his life. The irony was that it had never been there in the first place, at least as far as he could tell. But it was missing now. He felt the lack like a hole in his gut.

This was the second great identity crisis in Tony's life, the first having been his unexpected loss of his mother. He was no better prepared now than then to cope with it.

So his response to it was to seduce more women, to drink more, to gamble more, to court danger in subtly self-destructive ways.

He found himself screwing married women more. And often he tried to bed them in compromising circumstances, only minutes before their husbands were to return from work. He could not seem to find sexual excitement without danger.

It was this pattern of sexual deviltry that now got him into trouble.

Tony was now working for a real estate firm in New Jersey. He sold business properties as well as expensive homes. His charm and good looks made him a natural for the real estate business. He was doing better and making more than he had in the last few years. Real estate seemed the perfect profession for him. He was hoping to become a partner in the business before long.

His current boss, a portly, irascible individual named Roscoe Greve, had worked his way up from poverty and had a humorless, dictatorial attitude about running a business. Tony had had to go out of his way to charm him into amicable relations, and had had to work hard at his job to avoid the boss's wrath.

It so happened that Roscoe Greve had a nubile daughter named Wendy. She was seventeen years old, not terribly bright, ran with a fast group of friends, and in a bathing suit looked good enough to eat. She had strawberry blond hair, creamy skin, a slim rib cage, and breasts like lush fruit.

Tony first saw her at a dinner at his boss's house, and had trouble forgetting her. He fought against his inclination for a few futile weeks, then arranged to run into her at the local hangout where she partied with her friends. He did not hide who he was or what he wanted from her. He knew that his charm, combined with her own sense of forbidden adventure in seducing a man who worked for her father, would be all that was needed, provided she was "that type of girl." Which she was, as Tony found out on their first secret date, which began at the movies and ended in a motel on the outskirts of town.

Wendy made love in a rather callow but eager way, and her body felt and tasted as good as Tony had hoped it would. He made love to her roughly, something dangerous in him coming to the fore. She seemed turned on by his violence, for it made contact with her own inner wildness.

It should have been obvious to Tony that the girl had serious problems with her father and wanted to hurt him as much as possible. This was why she took particular pleasure in sleeping with a handsome man who was Roscoe Greve's employee.

But Tony was not perceptive enough to see this. He was too wrapped up in himself and in his own need to court danger. Had he thought things through more carefully, he might have avoided the fate lying in wait for him.

The lovers met in secret for several weeks. At first the arrangement ran smoothly. Then, to Tony's surprise, Wendy Greve began to show signs of jealous possessiveness toward him. She found out somehow about one of the older women he was sleeping with, and insisted that he stop seeing her. Absurd though her claim on him might be, she demanded fidelity.

This attitude resulted in quarrels between the lovers. Shouts were exchanged, vases were thrown, complaints were lodged by neighboring guests in the motels where they stayed. Brief reconciliations gave way to angrier quarrels, for Wendy's character was every bit as hot-tempered a character as Tony.

Finally they had a knock-down, drag-out battle that led to blows. Wendy threw everything she could find at Tony, and he hit her hard enough to split her lip and black her eye before storming out of the motel room they had rented, leaving her nude and furious in the double bed.

The result of this incautious move on Tony's part was that the offended girl told her father everything. Tony was summarily fired, his office cleared out, and his things sent to him before he was even informed of his termination.

Tony was out in the cold in more ways than one. Without a good recommendation from Roscoe Greve he would have great difficulty finding work in a major real estate firm, at least in New Jersey. He would have to pound the pavement looking for a new job.

Tony asked himself what had gotten into him. The Greve girl had meant nothing to him, less than nothing. Yet, through his own foolishness, he had cost himself the best job he had had in the last five years. Why had he done such a needlessly self-destructive thing?

Unfortunately for Tony, while he possessed cunning and charm, he was completely without introspection. Thus he never realized that what had happened to him with Wendy Greve and her father was no accident. His foolish affair was the symptom of his problem rather than the cause. He had gone into it with his eyes firmly closed, oblivious to the secret conflicts behind his behavior, and had suffered the consequences.

Tony began looking for a new job. He did so, however, without his usual energy and panache. Though he went through the motions of applying for new positions, of charming prospective employers, his heart was not entirely in it. The prospective employers sensed this, and did not hire him.

He floundered through his days and nights, drinking and gambling away what remained of his money, and bedding all manner of women. He picked them up in bars and restaurants, he met them in shops, he even stopped them on the street and endeared himself to them with a few well-chosen words and his patented smile.

Somehow it was the women, more than anything else, that depressed him. They were bland and interchangeable, like cardboard figures without depth. Their seductions, their jealousy, their tantrums were entirely predictable. Nubile little Wendy Greve had just been a seventeen-year-old version of this race of creatures who always gave their bodies with strings attached, who possessed no real souls behind the attractions of their flesh.

During this period Tony sometimes became so discouraged that he stayed home at night, too spiritually drained even to drink, to gamble, or to chase a new woman. It was on one of these nights that he opened the envelope of photos from his youth, gazed at the yellowed images for a few uncomfortable moments, and put them away again. He could not bear to look at his past.

For three months Tony drifted in the worst depression of his whole life. He seemed to have burned his bridges behind him, and ahead there was nothing but blackness. Try as he might to commit himself forcefully to the future, somehow he had lost heart.

On the rare occasions when he looked inside himself and asked what had gone wrong, he found himself cursing the female sex with a black hatred and loathing. Women, he decided, were the cause of all his problems. They had been put on earth, as the Bible said, to tempt men to destruction.

36

New York City

TIME HEALS ALL WOUNDS, it is said.

When Jordan Lazarus got up each day and went to work, the old maxim had little reality for him.

His heart did not feel healed. It never had, since the terrible moment when he had lost Leslie.

He had never really recovered from that shock. Perhaps this was because he had been so sure that Leslie was the one woman for him, the woman he had waited a lifetime for.

Grieving for Leslie was therefore not a simple matter. It required the closing of a door deep inside Jordan's psyche, and a constant, exhausting mental effort to keep that door closed.

Another man would have chased pathetically after Leslie, or cursed her, or written her angry letters, or even tried to kill her. But Jordan's pride, and his firm belief in his own control over his emotions, would not allow such vulgar displays of need. He had always kept his disappointments private and shown the world only his strengths. This strategy had seen him through long years in the hard business world, and he did not intend to change it now.

So Jordan kept the hurt inside. And he never opened that mental door to his own heart, because behind it lay a ruined hope he could no longer bear to contemplate.

Jordan went back to living.

The world was not the same as it had been before. It was painted in grayer colors. Its sunshine looked bleak and strident to Jordan, and its shadows had a funereal depth that made him grimace every time he greeted it. He no longer trusted it as he once had.

But he still trusted himself. So he went about his business, working perhaps harder than ever before. He was a strong man, and he bore this burden bravely and well. He went through the motions of living, taking the days one at a time, and waiting for something to come along and release him from the demon inside him. In his long business life he had learned patience and flexibility. He used those qualities now to help heal himself.

And he never thought about Leslie Chamberlain, not once. He would not or could not allow himself that torture.

Jordan's work had a different quality now. Those around him noticed a new daring in his ideas, an almost cruel incisiveness in finding new solutions to long-standing problems. They could not see the void behind this brilliant surface activity. But they were impressed and even awed by his amazing bursts of creativity.

And a new interest came from nowhere to give direction to Jordan's business career. He was touring the South Bronx one day with the mayor and a group of businessmen and local politicians—one of those cosmetic electioneering junkets that mean nothing—when all at once he noticed the monstrous urban ghetto that fulminated on the outskirts of the gleaming financial capital.

It was a thing Jordan had never really noticed before, because it offered him no opportunity for financial gain. All at once he saw it for what it was— a blighted landscape coiled around the glittering financial center of the great city like a disease.

In that instant Jordan saw the misery of the ghetto, the hopelessness of its idle inhabitants, the families broken by abandonment, crime, and drugs—in a new light. This hellish vision was not just a sad by-product of a larger wealth or prosperity. This was a malignancy capable of engulfing the entire land. The wealth of the nation could not long endure if the people and resources of its cities were allowed to continue deteriorating at its very core.

These ruined urban people were not merely the victims of progress; they were the future that awaited everyone, if progress were allowed to continue creating such misery as its price.

Jordan paid no attention to the prattle of his companions and their guides as they deplored the urban blight around them. He knew their pious words concealed the firm intention to do nothing about the problem.

Instead he pondered his own thoughts about what he was seeing. And soon his initial shock began to give way to the analytical intelligence for which he was so famous.

As he looked at the urban ghetto with the instincts of an experienced business-man and financier, he suddenly thought he saw a solution to the problem.

It was a revolutionary notion, so eccentric on its face that Jordan could not even put it into words at first. But he saw its importance, so he made time to ponder it more closely.

Turning his hardheaded realism in a visionary direction, he began to work on his new idea at home in the evenings. He devoted more and more time to it. He began to study economics and taxation and finance in a new way. He read books about local government, about the sociology and economics of the ghetto. He looked for traces of his own idea in the best books on the subject.

There were none. No one had ever looked at the problem of urban decay as Jordan was looking at it now. Scholars and specialists had always viewed it as a by-product of progress. Jordan saw it as an opportunity for growth. He saw a way for the major corporations, through their own self-interest as well as their financial relationship to the cities and states, not only to rebuild and reclaim the ghetto but to turn it over to its own inhabitants, to give them true self-determination for the first time in their history.

The idea was extremely simple. It used basic business concepts, combined with a new notion of tax incentives, to view the ghetto as a genuine opportu-nity for new wealth, based on the inherent productivity of its inhabitants as well as the corporate and tax base of the inner city.

Jordan spent more and more time working on his idea. After the first few months he started sharing it privately with a few trusted associates in the business world. All were impressed by its originality, but they were unanimous in their belief that it was absurd and could not work.

But Jordan was undaunted. He knew that every original idea is pronounced unworkable by those who first hear of it. This is because their vision is equipped only with hindsight, not foresight. But the full force of Jordan's powerful intellect told him that his plan could work.

He realized that two things would be necessary to make it a reality. The first was enormous lobbying clout with government, both at the state and national level, to pass a few crucial fiscal laws. The second was a lot of arm-twisting of the major corporations to get them to work together on this plan and to believe in its feasibility. An enormous, unprecedented coalition of powerful business forces would be required to make the plan work.

This would not be easy. Major corporations worked against each other, not with each other. Competition and rivalry were their very nature. But there was one man in America who possessed not only the personal force and financial clout but also the high public profile to create a corporate coalition: Jordan Lazarus.

So Jordan took this work on his own shoulders. More and more he came to see it as a crusade. It gave his days new meaning. He worked harder than ever before. And as he pushed at the stubborn edges of the business world to make it bend to his wishes, he felt it begin to yield. Its openness to change was slight, of course, almost imperceptible. But it was there, and Jordan resolved to keep pushing until he got what he wanted. He could actually feel history calling to him to help bring about a change that could prevent economic disaster and bring about a new and healthier America.

He worked so hard that he never stopped to reflect that perhaps his demanding new plan was drowning his sorrows as well as filling his days; that the love for his fellow man implicit in his new plan was concealing another love, covering it with a scar that could free him from its unbearable pain so he could find some reason to go on living.

With a view to solidifying his influence with the major American corporations and gaining as much financial power as possible in a short period of time, Jordan made some clever and complex deals, calling in some old favors and granting new ones at the same time.

One of the most important of these deals was made with Hightower Industries.

In recent years, thanks to Jessica Hightower's aggressive stewardship, her corporation had acquired subsidiaries in Latin America, Canada, and Western Europe, subsidiaries whose common goal was the development of computer technology.

This was part of a master plan on which Jessica had been working with her closest advisers for nearly a decade. Hightower was to transform itself slowly from a heavy-industry conglomerate to a high-technology innovator. Jessica had long believed that heavy industry in America was destined for decline, but that high technology, if properly managed, was the wave of the future. But she correctly foresaw that high labor costs in America would require that key electronic components be manufactured elsewhere.

Hence her acquisition and retooling of the companies in Latin America, Canada, and Europe.

It was at this point that Jordan Lazarus intervened. Lazarus International possessed important electronics and computer subsidiaries in South America

266

and Western Europe. Jordan proposed a complex deal with Hightower that would involve the acquisition and exchange of several subsidiaries on both sides, as well as a mutually beneficial stock deal with huge tax benefits to both corporations.

When Jordan sent out feelers to Jessica Hightower, she was immediately interested. A shrewd judge of the international business scene, she saw that this deal with Lazarus International could be just what her company had been looking for in the last decade. She had her lieutenants hammer out the details with Jordan's legal and financial advisers, and in a few months the deal was made. The papers were drawn up and were to be signed with great ceremony at a combined meeting-reception to be held at the Waldorf-Astoria on January 21, 1978.

There were about twenty people present, all of them high executives, attorneys, or board members of the two companies. The discussion was less than an hour long, for the deal had long since been finalized by the two corporations' legal departments. Jordan Lazarus gave a gracious speech in praise of Jessica Hightower's open-mindedness and initiative, and Jessica, in her polished and regal way, paid tribute to the originality Jordan had shown in conceiving the deal.

Hands were shaken around the room, and both guests and hosts repaired to the banquet room, where a meal prepared by one of the finest chefs in the country was served. It was a happy occasion, and a lot of champagne was consumed. Nearly all those present realized that their individual careers would be vastly advanced, and indeed assured, if the deal was a success.

Jordan Lazarus enjoyed himself thoroughly but did not stay late. He took Jessica Hightower aside for a quiet half-hour while the rest of the guests were drinking their champagne, and congratulated her again on her farsightedness and intelligent attention to detail in working out the deal.

Jordan had known Jessica casually for years, and had always respected her as the brains of Hightower Industries and as the force behind the Senate campaigns of both her brothers. She was the ideal executive: brilliant, thorough, dedicated not only to the wealth of her own company but to the well-being of American business as a whole.

But Jordan had never warmed to her personally. There was a coldness about her, a steely quality, that put him off. He had always been happy in his dealings with her—never more so than tonight—but happy also not to know her better than absolutely necessary.

When he and Jessica emerged from the quiet anteroom in which they had had their private conversation, he gestured to his lieutenant Sam Gaddis, who stood up to join him. As he did so he noticed Jessica giving a similar gesture to a young woman who got up from the table and came to her side. She was a remarkably pretty young woman in her twenties, with sandy hair, a willowy figure, and liquid blue eyes. She came smiling to Jessica's side and was introduced to Jordan, who did not get her name. A moment later the two women had disappeared from sight.

Sam was looking at his watch. It was time to go. The deal was made, and Jordan had important meetings tomorrow morning.

Jordan left in a pleasant state of mind. The deal he had made with Jessica was going to be good for Lazarus International, perhaps even better than he himself had hoped.

By the time he got home he was very tired, and fell quickly into a dreamless sleep. He had forgotten the very existence of the pretty young woman who had gotten up from the table to come to Jessica Hightower's side.

A week and a half later Jordan was entering the Four Seasons restaurant for lunch with three of his board members, and encountered a face that attracted his attention.

At first memory did not come to his aid, and his only interest in her was as a pretty girl. She was indeed very attractive as she walked from the dining room toward the exit. She was wearing a silk dress that showed off something very feminine and delicate about her body. Her hair, more blond now than he remembered, flowed over her shoulders, and her legs moved with a subtlety that Jordan's sharp eye for female attractions did not miss.

Her eyes were fixed on her destination. But as Jordan watched, they darted in his direction, looked away again, and then focused on him in a look of recognition. Amazingly, at that instant the irises actually seemed to change color. A violet tinge sprang from the blue depths and glowed perceptibly as she smiled at him.

Driven by a force that overmatched his usual aloofness, Jordan moved toward her and held out a hand.

"Haven't we met?" he asked.

She smiled.

"You have a good memory for faces," she said. "Yes, we have."

There was a silence as he looked at her. Her hand was still in his. It felt very soft and pliant. He struggled to place her.

"I'm sorry," he said. "I can't seem to recall where we met."

A gentle laugh stirred in her throat.

"That's not surprising," she said. "I would be amazed if you did remember. It was at Jessica Hightower's meeting with you. I'm one of her assistants."

Jordan released her hand.

"Jordan Lazarus," he said.

"You don't need any introduction," she smiled. "My name is Jill Fleming. Ms. Hightower introduced us briefly, but you were very busy that night."

Again there was a pause. The girl's eyes darted to the exit. Jordan could see it was time for her to leave. But he did not want to let her go. Something about the softness of her presence attracted him.

"Have you been with Jessica long?" he asked. "I've probably crossed paths with you before. I'm sorry for the memory lapse. Normally I have a good memory for names."

"About three years," she said. "No, you haven't met me before, Mr. Lazarus. But even if you had, I don't stand out much."

"Call me Jordan," he said on an impulse. Only now, listening to the melodious lilt of her voice, did he realize how attractive this girl really was. To say that she didn't stand out was absurd.

She nodded. "Jordan," she said.

As he held her hand her smile changed. It was brighter, more energetic. The delicacy of her demeanor, bordering on fragility, was not completely erased, but was now eclipsed by a brisk, healthy quality that he had not noticed before. She looked very young, very happy, and straightforward.

"Call me Jill," she said.

Jordan was thrown off balance in that instant. The change in her demeanor seemed to respond to a need inside him, and he felt a great reluctance to leave her and return to his board members. Something long dormant inside him came to life almost painfully at the sight of her.

"Well," he said, "I'm afraid I have some people waiting for me. It was nice seeing you again."

"Me, too," she said. "I have people waiting, too, I mean. But I'm also glad to have seen you. Yes to both things," she concluded with a little laugh.

He held out his hand again. This time her hand disappeared into his palm in a quite different way. Her handshake was firm, honest. There was femininity in it, but of a warm, straightforward style.

Yet the look in her eyes was complex. He saw regret at leaving him, and something else he could not name.

"Well," he said. "Be seeing you."

"Yes," she said. "Bye-bye."

And she turned on her heel and walked away with smooth, natural strides. There was something fascinating about her receding figure that made him hesitate for a long moment before returning to his table.

As he sat down with his board members he was struggling not to forget her name.

Jill Fleming.

He need not have worried. Though his mind was filled with a million details and plans that had all been marshaled to conceal his grief, the face and figure of Jill Fleming had penetrated that painstakingly constructed wall, and now occupied a place that had been perhaps prepared for her a long time ago by forces he did not recognize in himself.

He would not forget her name.

37

*I*T TOOK JORDAN A WEEK to call Jill Fleming.

During much of that week he was overworking and had almost no time to think about her. But when he did think about her, he found himself intrigued.

The attraction she had exerted on him was powerful. Simply remembering it sent a twinge through his senses. Yet he could not put his finger on what the attraction had been. It was so fugitive, in fact, that he found himself having difficulty recalling just what Jill's face had looked like.

When he finally did call her, it was to refresh his memory as much as to recapture the odd charm he had felt in her company.

Her voice sounded strange over the telephone. She seemed very distant, almost like a voice over a buzzer in an apartment building. Jordan wondered if he was making a mistake.

But she accepted him. He picked her up that Friday night—he told Barbara he had an unexpected appointment and would not be home until late—and took her to dinner at an intimate and very expensive uptown restaurant.

Over dinner their conversation was unremarkable, almost stereotyped. She told him about her work with Jessica and, in a sketchy way, about her past experience in the business world. Jordan found himself confiding perhaps more than he should about his own life, and the long road from his impoverished family to his enormous success. Something about Jill Fleming kept him off balance, and he talked to fill up the gap.

He realized from the moment he saw her that he had not been mistaken the first time, at the Four Seasons. She was astonishingly attractive. With her nubile, slender body, her sandy blond hair, her delicate features, and those bottomless crystalline eyes, she was a beautiful girl.

But it was not her physical beauty that exerted this strange attraction on him. Her charm was too complex to characterize. It seemed to come from a place inside her that responded to invisible signals from within him, or that created those signals somehow.

He understood now why he had had difficulty remembering her during the week before he called her. When he was with her his mind's eye was fixed so obsessively on this invisible center of her charm that he barely heard what she said, and did not pay close attention to her body or her features. Thus, when he was away from her, he could not recall her physical appearance.

She was like a drug, or a dream. When one is under its influence, the whole outside world is forgotten, and one lives only for its intoxication. But once one has awakened, one cannot quite remember what the drugged state was like.

Two hours of this perplexity created an almost painful storm in Jordan's senses. He looked into Jill Fleming's eyes. She was contemplating him calmly.

"Shall we go?" he asked with clumsy significance.

She gave him a soft smile.

"Yes, let's go."

A half hour later Jordan was naked with Jill Fleming in the penthouse suite at a small and discreet Manhattan hotel.

As he held her small body in his arms, savoring the fine, delicate taste of her on his lips, he recalled the way she had put on her coat as they left the restaurant. There was something brisk and honest about her movements that harmonized oddly with the soft, languorous body under her dress.

She had worn a very faint perfume, preferring to allow her own natural scent dominance. She had worn a simple dress with spaghetti straps to show off her slim shoulders, and a bodice that neither hid her shapely breasts nor displayed them too crudely. Around her neck was a thin gold chain with a pendant in the shape of a peacock. Her hair, a bit more fluffy tonight, seemed richer, more beautiful to look at.

She said nothing after they entered the hotel room. He helped her off with her clothes, kissing her and caressing her as he did so. Her body emerged naturally, almost vulnerably, like that of a child. She did not pose before him with the studied narcissism of most beautiful women, but stood naturally and innocently as her dress came off, then her bra, and finally the panties.

He picked her up in his arms, astonished by her lightness, and held her that way for a long time, kissing her and savoring the odd insubstantiality of her. It was as though something were missing from her, something whose absence made her lighter, more fugitive. And it was precisely this absence, this lack of something, that made her so attractive.

He placed her on the bed and lay down beside her. He felt her tongue slip into his mouth shyly, and almost at the same instant his sex, hot and throbbing, found its way inside her. A few frantic moments brought them both to almost painful orgasm, and he lay with her in his arms, pondering the sudden surge of wanting that had overtaken him.

For a long time they said nothing, but merely lay naked, touching each other, letting their eyes and hands do the talking. He found Jill's silence amazingly restful. It seemed to demand nothing of him. It joined with the pale glow of her naked body to create an impression of remarkable naturalness and composure. She was comfortably within herself. Her remoteness calmed and reassured him.

But her body was deliciously soft in his arms. And before long the silence, the touching, the quiet eyes were too much for him, and he was hard again. A shy smile touched her lips at the sight of his alert organ, which strained and throbbed as she looked at it, almost as though she was caressing it at a distance.

Softly her hand reached out to touch it. She cradled the balls underneath it, and they stirred and swelled in her hand.

A deep groan sounded in his throat, and he shuddered at her caress. He touched her shoulders, her slender rib cage. In that instant he felt almost afraid of his own desire. It seemed to spring from something unacknowledged within him that she had tapped while bypassing his free will.

Now he knew that the first time had been only an overture, that their silent interval of intimacy had been the preparation for the real storm, which was exploding in him now. He knelt above her, his penis held in both her hands. He throbbed and jerked madly in her grasp. Then he reached beneath her waist to pull her up, and she guided him quickly inside her.

He began to pump, to strain. A great coldness seemed to melt inside him, a coldness that had been sustaining him for two long years. The smooth, pretty loins of the woman in his arms encouraged him, and the hungry penis worked and plunged and stormed with all its might inside her.

He heard a little gasp escape her lips. Her legs were wrapped around him now, helping him to come deeper inside her. The slippery flesh inside her was hot and willing, excited by his thrusts, trembling nearer and nearer to orgasm.

Suddenly her hands left his hips, where they had been resting lovingly, and came to cup his cheeks. The tenderness of the gesture struck a chord in him. He looked down into her eyes. They were open, gazing at him with a look of sweet acceptance that was already dissolving into the unseeing stare of ecstasy.

A huge tremor shook him. A groan scalded his throat. His body strained forward, pushing the penis deeper into the secret place inside her, where it spent its delight in a long series of spasms. She shuddered in his arms, and then was still, letting the hard shaft nestle within her, and feeling it strain occasionally as aftershocks coursed through it.

She cradled his head in her hands and brought his lips to her breast. He kissed the warm flesh, grateful for its sweetness as for a gift. She petted his neck softly. In her warm arms there was a protectiveness that added a final grace note to the tempest she had stirred in him.

As he lay in her embrace Jordan pondered her mystery. He knew nothing more about her from possessing her physically than he had known from shaking her hand the first time he met her. Not that she withheld herself. She was quite natural as a lover. But her mystery somehow increased in proportion as her body surrendered itself.

It was as though Jill Fleming were a puzzle with one piece missing, or a chemical compound lacking the one crucial catalytic ingredient that would cause it to crystallize. But this lack was not really a lack, for Jordan's desire, springing from some unseen source within him, came to fill in the empty place.

The more she gave of her body, the more Jordan wanted her. In possessing her he only wanted to possess more of her. The paradox went on infinitely, because the tiny gap, the tiny void inside her, was itself infinite. And the very thought of this emptiness sparked once again the surging heat that sought to fill that emptiness. Jordan was getting hard again.

They made love twice more. Their bodies were so intimate that later he wondered if the long, hot shower he took would suffice to erase her scent from him. He felt her in his every pore.

Each time they made love there was on Jordan's part a curious sense of detached observation, of whimsical clarity as he studied her body, felt her smooth skin. But this detachment was combined immediately with a rising desire so terrible that even orgasm could not assuage it.

It was only the third time that he saw the birthmark. It nestled vulnerably beneath her navel, close to her sex, like a talisman indicating the treasure waiting nearby. And, paradoxically, it was this little something extra, this fresh, pink emblem, that seemed to symbolize the lack, the one missing piece that made her so attractive. He bent to kiss it, and smelled the mingled aromas of her own body and his.

Beside himself, he spread her thighs and came to her again, knowing that the sweet little mark was rubbing against his own loins with every thrust. She lay with her eyes half-closed, holding his arms. Her lush hair was splayed over the pillow. She seemed so innocent, and yet so coyly tainted by the mystical little mark on her flesh, that he spent himself inside her almost immediately.

By the time they separated Jordan was completely drained. Yet the excitement inside him was only beginning to grow stronger, as though tonight had been the overture to something truly enormous. The coldness that had sustained Jordan for so long was melting, and in its place a rising, infinite heat was expanding.

He took Jill home in a cab, walking with her to the door of her apartment building and kissing her lips as she got out her key.

"Thank you," she said quietly. "I've had a lovely evening."

There was something so spontaneous in her words that Jordan's heart went out to her.

She saw the look in his eyes, and her smile had an element of amused pity in it.

"When am I going to see you again?" he asked.

"Anytime you like," she replied.

He nodded, and took her hand in his. He wanted to feel the enigma of her flesh this one last time. She stood looking at him through inscrutable eyes which darted from the hand holding hers to the handsome face contemplating her. She seemed to know what was going on inside him, and not to be surprised by it at all. She felt his obsession and welcomed it, just as naturally as she had seen his desire earlier tonight and generously allowed him to possess her.

Then he released her, and she was gone.

Jordan took the cab home, leaving his own car for tomorrow. When he arrived the apartment was dark. Barbara was in bed asleep. He got in beside her and lay with his hands behind his head, staring at the ceiling. He heard Barbara's soft breathing.

He felt wonderful, more alive than he had felt in two years. The old pain inside him, so long eased by the thick wall around his heart, was now out in the open again, but somehow lessened by the exultation in his senses.

The mystery of Jill Fleming, the missing piece of the puzzle, was the secret of his happiness as well as his desire. Perhaps to find that missing ingredient, or to explore more deeply the peculiar charm of its absence, Jordan knew he would see her again.

Alone in her apartment, Jill Fleming was wide awake.

She had found this place, and convinced Jessica Hightower to let her live on her own some of the time, because she knew this night was coming. Nothing had been left to chance. She could not allow her closeness with Jessica to stand between her and Jordan Lazarus.

She thought over the events of the evening, one by one, reconstructing the complex language that had joined her to Jordan Lazarus. Her mind focused on tiny details that would have escaped even the most alert observer of the dinner or the tryst afterward. She studied them in memory, and concentrated her entire intellect on the subtle strands that wove themselves into a single fabric.

Most of what she recalled she felt she understood.

But one thing she did not understand. It was this thing that kept Jill awake all night long, gazing at the shadows on her bedroom ceiling with a pensive expression in her silver eyes.

38

"COME ON, SLOWPOKE. Can't you run faster than that?"

Ross Wheeler held his tennis racket as he watched Leslie chase the ball he had hit. With a little thrill of pleasure he watched her body move. The long, beautiful legs, the slim arms emerging from her tank top, the delicate hands holding the racket were poetry in motion. Her tennis skirt showed a flash of her panties as she ran, and he smiled.

She was not able to reach the ball. Though she was twenty-five years younger than he and in better physical shape, her tennis still lagged behind his. He had been an ambitious, aggressive player in his youth, playing on the varsity squad in high school and keeping up the hobby in later years. Leslie had only dabbled in the sport, and was not yet a match for him.

Nevertheless, her natural athletic ability, combined with her instinct to master new challenges, made her a rapidly improving player. More than once she surprised him by catching up with balls he thought out of her reach, and sometimes by hitting winners when he thought she could not even return the ball.

But not this time. She chased the ball in vain, picked it up, and hit it back to him in an easy arc.

"Show-off," she called mockingly. "You don't give a girl a chance."

"Forty-fifteen," he said, preparing to serve for the game. "You ready, honey?"

"Ready as I'll ever be," she smiled. She looked a bit flushed, so he waited a moment to give her time to catch her breath.

Then he served the ball, giving it plenty of pace. She had to dash to her right to reach it, but she did, and lobbed it high in the air. He ran backward, his legs working smoothly from long experience, and hit it back at her sharply. The ball would have hit her right in the face had her quick reflexes not allowed her to get her racket up quickly. She hit it back, and he tapped another one into the center of her end. He came to the net as she returned it.

275

The winner was easy, bouncing toward the baseline. Nevertheless she chased it lamely, bent almost double and laughing.

"You win, you stinker," she laughed. She came forward, flushed, and kissed him.

The headache he had had since this morning—or was it since yesterday?—sent a brief wave of pain through his temple. The sun made it seem worse. Ross was not used to having headaches, and the aspirin he had taken this morning was the first he had needed in years. It did not seem to help, but he had shrugged the whole thing off, telling himself that no headache was going to spoil his precious Saturday with his wife.

He forgot the pain as he felt Leslie's lips on his own. The flush in her cheeks and the fine mist of perspiration on her arms and legs made her almost unbearably attractive.

"Mmm," he murmured. "I can hardly wait to get you home."

"I'm more of a match for you that way," she said. "I can't keep up with you on the tennis court."

"You'll learn," he said. "You're still a growing girl, and I'm an old man. By next summer I won't be able to win a single point from you."

"Nonsense," she said. "Unless I get better soon, you'll have to get a new partner. I can be the ball girl."

This was already an old argument, though their marriage was nearly two years old. Ross often drew attention to the difference between their ages and expressed his doubts about his ability to keep up with Leslie. She pooh-poohed his complaints, telling him he was athletic as a boy and virile as a billy goat, and would live to be a hundred.

Privately she worried about Ross's excessive concern with physical fitness. During their monthlong engagement, during which Leslie had met all Ross's far-flung relatives and become very close to his two daughters, it had almost seemed as though things were out of control.

Soon after their engagement Ross had started working out at a local gym and running in the evenings. At first Leslie was not aware of this, but when she found out she asked him why he was doing it.

"You don't want to be married to an old man, do you?" he had asked. "Besides, my doctor has been telling me for years that I need to be in better shape."

He would not listen to Leslie's remonstrances that she was marrying him for himself, not for his muscle tone.

"Don't you worry about me," he said. "I'll be a new man by the time you're Mrs. Ross Wheeler. You'll thank me then."

Leslie began to understand that from the beginning of their courtship Ross had been conscious of the May–December aspect of their match, and painfully aware that Leslie was almost the same age as his daughters.

Ross apparently considered it a matter of personal pride to be in good condition, strong and healthy, when he married Leslie. He did not want her marrying a flaccid, out-of-shape middle-aged man old enough to be her father.

Perhaps he suspected that Leslie had recently had an unsuccessful and quite serious relationship with a much younger man. Perhaps Ross could not tolerate the idea of her comparing his aging physical attributes with the virile charms of someone closer to her own age.

Whatever the case, and though it seemed out of character for the man Leslie had now known for three years, Ross doggedly continued his workouts. He ran three miles a day, cut out his weekend bottles of beer, stopped smoking except for an occasional furtive cigarette in the bathroom, and lost fifteen pounds.

Leslie expressed reluctant acceptance of this spartan regime, but tried to remind her future husband why she was marrying him.

"I want *you*, Ross," she said. "Just the way you are. For heaven's sake, you don't have to turn into Charles Atlas to impress me. I'm already impressed."

"That's nice to hear," he said. "But I don't want to get a hernia when I carry you across the threshold. So, with all due respect, we'll do it my way." And he had given her his best boss's scowl, with tongue in cheek of course, to remind her who was giving the orders.

And she had smiled and let him go on. She was amused and a little saddened by his compulsive exercise. She found it absurd that he denied his age so fiercely and tried to do everything a younger man could do. She herself considered his age, his maturity, to be precisely the attractive thing about him. It made her feel protected, safe, and happy.

She assumed he would get over this silliness after they got married.

But he had not gotten over it. They had played tennis every day on their honeymoon, gone swimming, played golf. Leslie found the tennis exhausting, but she enjoyed the swimming, as she always had. And the golf, though she was a terrible duffer, was fun. She enjoyed walking the course with her husband, teeing off together, seeing him go his own way to find his ball, and coming together with him on the green. There was something curiously romantic about the game itself, when a husband and wife played it together.

And they had made love.

They made love in the morning before breakfast, at noon after tennis, in the late afternoon before cocktails, and of course always at bedtime.

Ross Wheeler was a wonderful lover: considerate, inventive, and affectionate. Leslie never failed to feel the special charm of his devotion when they made love. She had learned a lot about his body—now so tanned, so much harder than it had been when she first knew him—and about how to give him pleasure.

In his understanding and his paternal warmth there was a peculiar sexiness. She welcomed it and enjoyed it.

And every time she made love to him she thought of his child, their child. She wanted it more than anything in the world. And as soon as possible.

Thus Leslie was particularly disappointed when, during the first six months of her marriage, she failed to get pregnant.

Perhaps pushing the panic button too soon, she told her gynecologist about her worries. He shrugged them off.

"I'm afraid you've got some romantic ideas about childbearing, my dear," he said. "Conception doesn't come by pushing a button. You have to be patient. There's not a darned thing wrong with you inside that I can see. Just let things take their course. Worrying will do more harm than anything else."

As for Ross, he continued with his physical fitness craze, perhaps because he feared that in some symbolic way Leslie's failure to get pregnant had to do with his age and his physical inadequacy. He had himself examined and was pronounced completely fertile, but the nagging feeling stayed with him.

So he continued to work out. And Leslie, more to express her sympathy for his feelings than for any other reason, went along with him. But she tried to make him take it easy at swimming.

"All I really want from that body of yours is what happens at night," she told him. "When are you going to learn that?"

"Well, I have to keep in shape to give you a good time," he joked. But she suspected he felt he had to improve his manhood in order to be potent enough to get her pregnant. He felt he was failing her in some way, that he had lured her—perhaps on the rebound—into a marriage that should never have been. And the only way to prove the legitimacy of his love, of their love, was to make her pregnant.

On this balmy Saturday night they were to have a romantic dinner after a long day of play together. Their morning's tennis was followed by a picnic lunch at Enfield Park, Ross's favorite place in the countryside. There they had a leisurely meal from a basket prepared by Leslie, and sat watching the afternoon progress. They enjoyed a languid, slow conversation, learning more about each other. Ross was a wonderful listener. His curiosity about Leslie seemed as boundless as his understanding. She loved to talk about herself to him, loved to feel him taking her in and accepting her. Though she could not tell him the entire truth about herself, she had learned to bask gratefully in the gentle rhythm of their talks.

At three they went to the country club and joined a couple Ross had known for twenty years, for a round of golf. By the time they had finished it was after five, and both were famished. They were looking forward to the dinner they would cook together, and to the evening ahead. Ross played hard, but he also knew how to relax.

This weekend dinner was not so special. They also had romantic evenings during the week. Leslie enjoyed this perhaps more than any other aspect of her married life. They worked side by side all day, concentrating on the business at hand, but at home they changed gears completely. Leslie felt a bit like the young woman in her old Aurora Lifestyles commercial, who changes from a brisk businesswoman to a wife and lover, and really enjoys it.

Ross helped her make a Caesar salad and marinated lamb roast, and they lingered over coffee and brandy for a long time. The dining room window looked out on a particularly lush back lawn, with a lovely flower garden and a wisteria plant climbing over the white planks of an arbor. The place had gone to seed while Ross was alone, but Leslie had restored it to its former glory. It was a delightful setting. In the summer Leslie loved sitting in the back lawn reading and listening to the songs of the blackbirds and whippoorwills.

They did the dishes together, Ross insisting on helping, and met in the bedroom as Leslie was coming out of the shower.

She had nothing on but a towel wrapped around her, and Ross, already in his pajamas, stopped her in the doorway of the bathroom.

"If you could only see yourself through my eyes . . ." he murmured. Then he stepped forward and kissed her lips, loosening the towel and seeing it fall to the floor.

She stood naked before him, droplets of water still in her hair and on her shoulders. He held her gently by her arms and kissed one of the droplets. The sight of her pink skin, firm breasts, and long, slender limbs took his breath away.

He hugged her close.

"Leslie, I love you so much," he said. "When I see you like this, I feel it's just too good to be true. Can you really love an old man like me?"

She looked at him through reproachful eyes.

"How can you say that?" she asked. "You're not an old man. I love you for what you are, Ross."

"Just checking." He smiled.

And he led her to the bed.

For some reason he was more passionate than ever tonight, though their day had been a long one, and his tennis and golf ought to have tired him out. The sight of Leslie's nudity seemed to inflame him more than ever. They made love twice, the silent darkness of the house seeming to enfold them. Ross's excitement infected Leslie, and she found herself responding to him with a passion that left her limp.

When they were finished at last Ross kissed her and fell back exhausted onto his pillow. It was nearly midnight, and he would be tired tomorrow. He felt a new throb of the headache that had been bothering him all day, and excused himself to go to the bathroom, where he took three aspirins.

When he returned he was more tired than he had realized. He slipped between the sheets, and Leslie leaned over to kiss him good night. He murmured an indistinct endearment, for sleep was overtaking him quickly. She lay beside him, listening to his regular breathing and contemplating her happiness.

She had a lot of heartache to forget in her young life, heartache she had never expected to experience, and scars she would bear forever. But beside her was a man who loved her, who would never let her down or abandon her, a man whose children she would soon have. She told herself that it was perhaps impossible to get through life unscathed, and perhaps every other young woman had her tale of personal agony. Leslie counted herself luckier than most, because she had Ross. She could forget the past, or at least put it behind her where it belonged.

She snuggled a bit closer to her husband and fell into a deep restful sleep.

Toward morning troubling dreams began to disturb her, and she was so lost in them that the ringing of the alarm clock seemed to come from a great distance away. She had to reach across Ross to turn it off.

"Come on, sleepyhead," she said, giving him a playful nudge in the ribs. "Up and at 'em. We can't run a business on good intentions, you know." The latter remark was his favorite imprecation at the office, when things were not running smoothly enough to suit him.

Ross did not move.

Leslie sat up in bed beside him. She looked down at him. His face seemed different somehow. There was a stern expression on it, as though he were firmly anchored in sleep and resistant to the idea of waking up.

"Ross?" she said. "Ross, wake up. Are you all right?"

There was no response.

Leslie shook him again, harder this time. A faint moan stirred in his throat, but he did not wake up.

"Ross!"

Leslie was deeply worried now. She got out of bed, went around to Ross's side, and took hold of his shoulders. He did not stir. When she opened one of his eyes with a tentative finger she realized it was time to call an ambulance.

She made the call from the bedside phone, holding Ross's inert hand in hers. A half hour later, when the ambulance arrived, she was still sitting in the same position, dressed only in her pajamas. She threw on a pair of jeans and rode with Ross in the back of the ambulance.

The wait in the emergency room seemed to last an eternity. In reality it was ten minutes.

The emergency room resident had little difficulty in diagnosing Ross's condition.

"Your husband has had a stroke, Mrs. Wheeler," he told Leslie. "I can't tell how massive it is until we've done some tests. The admitting nurse will want to get some information from you. We'll move him to intensive care for a few days. Just take it easy, now. There's nothing to worry about."

His manner was reassuring, but the look in his eyes told Leslie volumes about what had happened to her husband, and to her new life.

39

JORDAN SAW JILL FLEMING as often as he could manage during the weeks after their first date.

The intimacy of their relationship deepened quickly. They made love in nearly every way possible. The varieties of their passion were inexhaustible. They seemed to come together with two minds that never met directly but touched only through their bodies. This absence of inner contact only made the surface of their loving all the hotter.

Jordan Lazarus did not know whether he loved Jill Fleming. But he did know he was rapidly finding it impossible to live without her. His days were spent in silent anticipation of the next time he would see her. Often he would find his concentration on work interrupted by a taunting recollection of her body in one of its many poses. The coy curve of her thigh, the shape of her upraised knee, the sweet movement of her buttocks as she crossed a room, the shy surprise in her eyes as she noticed his excitement—these and many other images would float up from somewhere in his consciousness, making him hard under his pants even as he was busy at his desk or on the phone.

He knew her no better now than the first night he had taken her to bed. But he needed her a thousand times more. And that need had brought him back to life somehow.

Jordan's days were full of adventurous new work on his inner cities project. Each day he fleshed out his idea and sold it to one or more major business or government leaders. Jordan continually surprised himself as well as others with the originality of his ideas.

And somehow his relationship with Jill Fleming mirrored and complemented this newness of things, this feeling that he, Jordan, was capable of ideas, actions, and emotions he had never been capable of before.

As for Jill, she was more than satisfied with the way things were going.

In approaching Jordan Lazarus, Jill had used her time-honored, proven technique. She looked into his eyes and tried to become what she saw there.

A master chameleon, she changed her colors to suit his needs, even if those needs were not consciously known to him.

Her old talent did not leave her in the lurch. On the contrary, it was sharper and more efficient than ever before.

In the first place she had altered the fragile, sickly persona that had seduced Jessica Hightower, and in its place put an image of youthful freshness and good health—a decided, firm way of walking, talking, smiling. Yet she had left a remnant of the fragility behind, as a sort of grace note.

Then, improvising quickly, she had added a veneer of honesty, of feminine integrity to this image of springy, youthful health. And she had made this honesty of a peculiarly girlish sort—the vibrant straightforwardness of a nice girl who has yet to be corrupted by life.

Jordan's response had been so immediate that she knew she was on the right track.

Jill had spent a lifetime sharpening her natural talent at being what men and women wanted her to be. Though not a psychologist intellectually—she had never read a word of Freud, she had never heard of Piaget—she was a great natural psychologist, a psychologist with her body.

Years ago she had known almost instantly that what Roy English wanted in a girl was youth, adolescence. It was a nymph Roy wanted, a virgin. And so Jill had made herself a nymph. She had selected clothes to make her look schoolgirlish, and sculpted her manner in order to incarnate everything that was nubile, innocent, and freshly seductive.

It had almost worked. Harley Schrader had ruined the final effect, but that had been her only mistake. She had bungled the practical side of things through inexperience. But her seduction of Roy had been flawless.

With Jessica Hightower she had been far smarter. She had researched the ground carefully. She knew and understood Jessica's contempt for the opposite sex. She realized in advance how desperately lonely Jessica must be.

Jessica needed a woman. But more specifically, Jessica needed a woman to take care of. That was why Jill had created the horseback riding accident. She had wanted to show herself as someone in need. That was also why, when she got to know Jessica better, she created the fiction of her anemia, so that Jessica could always perceive her as weak, needing comfort and support.

Jessica, a powerful woman, had eagerly stepped into the role of protector. It was Jill's fragility that she came to need, to love. And it was thanks to this need that Jill had risen to a position of great power within Hightower.

But Jill's power was informal, dispensed by the fiat of Jessica Hightower. Jill knew it would never lead to the kind of power she really wanted.

That was where Jordan Lazarus came in.

Jill's careful research, begun when she first heard of a projected financial deal between Lazarus International and Hightower Industries, had alerted her to the fact that Jordan Lazarus was a potential catch of the highest order. He was powerful, he was incalculably rich, he was attractive, and he was, in an odd way, unattached.

Jill understood that Jordan's marriage to Barbara Considine was a business arrangement. Having lost his growing corporate empire to her father, Jordan had gotten it back through Barbara. Once he had done so he had used her financial and corporate resources to help make himself the richest man in the nation.

In return he had played the role of husband to her. There must have been as much pity as self-interest in this agreement on his part.

Jill did not know how intimate their marriage was. But she did know that whatever Jordan might feel for Barbara, it did not stand in the way of Jill's seduction of him. The last few weeks had proved that.

She soon realized she was playing her role for Jordan with a perfection of detail that she had never achieved before. Why this was she did not know. It was almost automatic, this jelling of the persona that grew inside her every time she was with Jordan, every time she spoke to him on the phone. There were dozens of little gestures, tics of body language, modulations of her laugh or her smile, that came out with a will of their own. A way of adjusting her collar, of stretching out her arms to yawn, a way of walking, a contemplative way of pushing a lock of her hair away from her eye—it went on and on. Not one of them was calculated consciously. They all sprang from something unseen inside her that knew Jordan Lazarus perhaps better than he knew himself.

The proof that her seduction was working efficiently was Jordan's bedroom behavior. He was like a man possessed—which was precisely what she wanted him to be.

Very soon Jill began to feel subtle new cues coming from Jordan, cues that allowed her to give him more pleasure, to increase his obsession with her.

She found that he particularly enjoyed her in informal clothes. He liked her in shorts and sandals, or in jeans and sneakers or loafers. He loved the sight of her in a simple T-shirt or tank top with a band to hold back her hair, or a ponytail.

He also liked to see her in down-to-earth situations, such as cleaning up her apartment, washing windows, scrubbing the sink, fiddling with a mechanical object. These were things Jill did not normally do. She hated to dirty her hands on housework. She considered her body a machine made for seduction, and she did not relish using it to do a maid's work. But when she saw that this posture attracted Jordan, she quickly adjusted her persona to give the impression of the healthy, down-to-earth girl who has a hands-on approach to everyday living.

Along with this went a tendency to easygoing, unaffected language. She sensed that Jordan was charmed by unpretentious, simple manners of speech. She would call him "my fellow," and say she was "tickled" by something amusing. She never said anything in any way crude; she made sure that her personality seemed naturally elegant and feminine. It was precisely the combination of this delicacy and refinement with a down-to-earth turn of phrase that touched Jordan.

And she learned one day, to her surprise, that a gentle irony in matters of sex was a virtual aphrodisiac with him. He had just finished making love to her with tremendous power, and she was lying back naked, feeling the lingering throb in her loins as he sat up to look down at her.

"Mmm," she purred. "My hero."

And another day, on an impulse, she had called him "my Prince Charming."

The phrase seemed to strike a chord in him. The look in his eyes deepened from affection to something like obsession.

Jill made sure she repeated the phrase later.

So things continued through the spring. Though Jill and Jordan did not grow closer as one human being to another, the hot ember of desire that bound Jordan to her grew more and more powerful.

If there was one thing in all this that troubled Jill, it was that everything seemed too easy. It was as though she possessed an inner talent or gift that made her the perfect seductress of Jordan Lazarus, but she didn't know precisely what characteristic of her it was that made her so irresistible to him. And the thing that came forward in him to covet her was also not as easily readable as in other men. It was a mystery too.

It was almost as though another person, unsuspected by Jill all these years, had existed inside her like a genie, and was now springing forth as though in response to a magic word, perfect in all its details, made for Jordan Lazarus and only for him. Moreover, it was as though Jordan Lazarus was primed, somehow, to love her, long before she even crossed his path. This thought was the most puzzling of all.

All her life Jill had lived on the surface of herself and of her relationships with others, because this was where advantages were to be gained, this was where power was to be found. She had transformed herself for the purpose at hand, conveniently ignoring her own long-forgotten depths.

But the mythic creature that was emerging from her to charm Jordan Lazarus was so complete, so perfect that she suspected something deeper inside her was involved than ever before—though she could not put her finger on what this something was. She tried to watch calmly from outside herself as she did the magic dance that brought Jordan further under her spell. But she was not completely outside this process, not completely free. It was as though the very fact of being the object of a desire so enormous was working a metamorphosis upon her. The feeling was unsettling.

But the prize, she told herself, was worth a little discomfort. This masterly improvisation she had embarked upon was no doubt her greatest achievement as a woman. She intended to see it through. She might not be quite so sure of who she was anymore, but she knew more than ever where she was going.

One day Jordan gave her an additional clue to what he wanted of her.

He pointed out a picture of a model in a fashion magazine. The girl had reddish hair with glints of blond in it.

"That's my favorite hair color," he said.

"Really?" she asked. "Why didn't you tell me? I'll have my hair done in that color."

"No," he shrugged. "You're perfect as you are."

But she insisted. She went to the beauty parlor, taking him with her, and had him discuss the color and perm with the beautician before sending him back to the office while she had her hair done.

It turned out that what he really admired was a sort of frizzy look, combined with the reddish strawberry blond. A look which pulled the hair up to reveal more of the neck.

When it was finished Jill was surprised by the change in herself. This new perm made her quite different. She looked a bit less controlled, less inward. There was a playfulness in it, a wildness, that was not characteristic of her.

She felt off balance at first, as though she didn't know herself. But the minute Jordan returned to pick her up, she could see that this new hair was the final piece of the puzzle. He could hardly wait to get her home to bed. He made love like a stallion, his strokes reaching a level of passion she had never seen in any man before. It was like having touched off an explosion, an earthquake.

She was sure he belonged to her now. But even in this certainty she felt a twinge of fear at the intensity of his obsession. She resolved to proceed with more caution than ever.

A few days after this final transformation Jordan invited Jill to go sailing with him.

"Sailing?" she asked. "I've never been sailing before. I don't know . . ."

"Come on," he said. "It will be fun. And I'm a good sailor. You won't drown, I assure you."

She gave him a playful smile.

"You wouldn't kid a girl, would you?" she asked. "I'm not a strong swimmer, you know."

She was lying naked in his bed with his head in her lap. He was gazing up at her, still suffused by the scent and taste of their lovemaking.

"No," he said, obviously charmed by her down-to-earth language. "I wouldn't kid you."

That Sunday he took her to the marina. She had to smile when she saw his boat. It was a magnificent little craft, obviously the work of master boatbuilders.

Actually, Jill was a good sailor. She had sailed with Roy English and with other lovers in the past. But she saw that the idea of her inexperience charmed Jordan.

They walked down the dock to the boat. Jill was wearing shorts, a tank top, and deck shoes that Jordan had helped her shop for. He had admired her attire when he picked her up this morning.

Jordan was just helping her on deck when a gravelly voice rang out behind them.

"Good morning, miss. Long time, no see!"

Jill turned to see a wrinkled old boat steward coming toward them. His face fell when he looked into her eyes.

"Oh, I'm sorry, miss," he said. "I thought you were someone else."

He looked at Jordan. They both realized it was too late to undo his gaffe. "Morning, Mr. Lazarus," the boatman added miserably.

"Good morning, Ben," Jordan smiled, making the best of the embarrassing moment. "Looks like good sailing weather."

"Yes, sir." The boatman was already shuffling away, tipping his cap embarrassedly to Jill.

She was smiling at Jordan.

"So," she said. "You have a past."

Jordan smiled. "Don't we all?"

She kissed him on his cheek as he came aboard.

"It doesn't matter," she said, affecting the direct, playful tone she knew he liked. "I've got you this week."

There was a look of real pain in Jordan's eyes. She could not tell whether this was chagrin over the embarrassment the boatman had caused, or a deeper sadness coming from some hurt inside him.

They made love on the boat as soon as he had dropped anchor in the Sound. A trace of Jordan's melancholy remained in his eyes as he gazed at her in her sailing clothes. As he stripped them from her, there was an odd whimsy in his touch. He sat on the edge of the bed, gazing down at her nudity. The salt air filled the boat.

Jordan studied Jill lovingly. The new look of her hair, wilder, curlier, seemed to hypnotize him. She was more than ever aware of being part of a puzzle that was coming together as though by magic.

He covered her whole body with kisses. He seemed to be drinking her in as though for the first time. To her surprise she enjoyed these kisses. When he spread her legs to touch her, she felt an answering ember deep inside her. She buried her fingers in his hair and pulled him closer.

An odd urgency possessed them both, born of the balmy sea air, the coolness of the cabin, and perhaps the boatman's embarrassing remark with its allusion to a past from before their romance. Jordan poised himself above her, and with a long, slow sigh buried himself inside her. A gasp sounded in her throat. Somehow he had never been this deep before.

The rocking of the boat added its magic to his slow strokes. Her hands were all over him, moving with a will of their own. A crazy excitement she had never felt before spread quickly through all her senses. He felt it, and moved faster.

Her legs were wrapped around him now, pulling him deeper. Something began to stir dangerously inside Jill, a kind of hunger she had never felt before. She wanted more of him, and more and more. Each stroke increased her desire. The idea that he might ever stop filling her this way made her feel empty and abandoned. This terror became an integral part of the frantic ecstasy she was feeling.

She began to moan, to whimper. He probed deeper, deeper, his hands on her shoulders. Her fingers drew long scratches along his back, and dug into his straining buttocks to encourage him in his thrusts.

Then an invisible wall crumbled inside Jill.

"Oh!" she cried. And all at once her whole body gave itself to him in a single paroxysm. She realized she had just had the first orgasm of her life.

She trembled in his arms for what seemed a very long time. She came back to herself slowly. Her own abandon had unnerved her.

But Jordan seemed delighted with her. The look in his eyes was exhausted and satisfied. It mirrored the peculiar fulfillment she felt, but not her concern over the passion that had bypassed her will.

When he sat up she saw the scratches on his back.

"Uh-oh," she said. "I've scratched you. You'd better not let your wife see that."

He simply smiled.

"Don't worry about that," he said. And there was an odd confidence in him. He seemed tranquil, almost beatified, as though he had everything in the world he wanted and was afraid of nothing.

Jill wondered what was making him so sure, so calm. And at that moment she felt, oddly, that the control she had thought was hers was passing to him. That some crucial element of mastery had slipped through her fingers, or was doing so even now.

She watched his beautiful body as he moved to put on his jeans. The scratches were on his back, not hers. And yet it felt as though the real wounds, the telltale scars, were on her own soul already, and might not heal as quickly as she liked. They had been put there by Jordan Lazarus.

40

"OH," THE GIRL MOANED. "Oh, baby. You feel so good. Come on . . . Just a little bit more . . ."

Tony Dorrance was astride the naked girl, buried to his hilt inside her. She was lying on her stomach amid the tumbled sheets of his bed. He looked down into the shadows, tinted pink by the neon sign outside the window. The sign blinked on and off, its rhythm joining that of the girl's pelvis, which jerked spasmodically as she approached her orgasm.

"Baby . . . Oh! More . . ."

He smiled as he ground into her. She was really excited, really turned on by him.

They were both quite drunk, but this was not slowing either of them down. Tony had long ago found that drunkenness did not make him lackluster or impotent as it did other men. On the contrary, it gave him a sort of distance from his own excitement, and even from his own hard-on, which he felt as an impersonal tool he could use expertly.

He was using it now, sliding it in and out of the girl without hurry, feeling her shudder around the shaft.

"That's right, honey," he murmured, forgetting her name. "That feels good, doesn't it?"

Now he pushed into her an extra inch and held himself there, straight and hard as a lead pipe. A harsh moan escaped her lips.

"Oh, my god. Oh, baby . . ."

Her orgasm came suddenly, the sinews inside her gripping him with hot little spasms. A tremor went through his whole body, shaking the stiff penis like a lightning rod in a storm. He felt his back begin to arch, his hips strain. His hands strayed over her buttocks, which glowed pink under the artificial light. How lovely girls were when they were naked, and had their backs turned to him! So vulnerable . . .

Almost without his realizing it he had begun to come. He gripped her shoulders and pushed harder into her. The sperm shot out in a hot little stream that drew a gasp from her. For a long time, abetted by his drunkenness, he stayed inside her, his sex not ebbing in the slightest but encouraged to endure hardness by the aftershocks of her delight.

At last he withdrew and lay beside her, stroking her shoulders. She smelled nice, though her perfume was cheap and her hair scented by a low-quality spray. The aroma of a woman always pleased Tony.

Then she turned to face him. She seemed to come back to reality.

"Can I have a drink?" she asked.

"Sure, hon. Scotch all right?"

"Sounds good."

He got up and padded naked to the kitchen, whose counters were piled high with his dirty dishes. He found two glasses, rinsed them hastily, and filled them with scotch from the bottle he had brought in just now with the girl.

He had picked her up in a tavern a half-mile from his apartment. It was a sleazy place, patronized by local regulars in the afternoon and a rougher, more transient clientele in the evenings. Tony was part of both groups. He went in the afternoons for a beer when he wasn't looking for work. In the evenings, having spent the day job hunting or, if he lacked the courage, betting on the horses, he came back to get drunk on bar whiskey and look for women.

He had struck up a conversation with her at the bar tonight. She had immediately sent the right signals. She found him attractive and would gladly share his bed for the price of a few drinks, provided he was not too rough with her.

She had told him her name at the beginning of their conversation. He had forgotten it instantly, calling her Honey all evening.

On their way out he had called to Bruno, the bartender, for a bottle. It was cheap bar booze, the same unlabeled swill the patrons drank, and this was not the first time Tony had bought it to take home with a girl. It had been years since Tony could afford good liquor; and even if he could, this girl would not be worth it.

He went back into the living room, where the girl lay on the Murphy bed, smoking a cigarette. He handed her the glass and she took a sip. She showed no sign of noticing the cheap quality of the liquor. It was about her speed, after all. She looked up at Tony.

"You're a tiger, honey," she said.

Tony noticed her sagging breasts and flabby stomach. She was not as young as she had looked at the bar.

"You bring out the beast in me, kid," he smiled.

He watched her light a cigarette. She inhaled hungrily. They sat in silence, sipping at their scotch. After a while he saw her eyes stray around the room. She was noticing the cheap furnishings, the threadbare rug, the tables and dresser piled high with scattered personal items and empty glasses. All of it was bathed in an unnatural, almost macabre glow by the pink neon light that flashed on and off, on and off.

It was the seedy pad of a bachelor who was down on his luck.

"Hey," she said at length, her voice remarkably sober. "Let's go out."

"Out?" Tony said thickly.

"I feel cooped up," she said. "It's kind of close in here. You know what I mean? Let's go out."

Tony looked at her. "Out where?"

She took a long swig from her glass. Decidedly, this girl and cheap liquor were on familiar terms.

"Out to get something to eat," she said. "I'm famished. Aren't you?"

Tony thought for a moment. He was hungry, too. Liquor and sex, at this hour of the night, always made him hungry for a snack. A hamburger, perhaps, or a hero sandwich.

"Where did you have in mind?" he asked.

"Jimmy's," she said. "They have the most divine late snacks there."

Tony frowned. Jimmy's was a well-known restaurant a few miles away. The girl was right, it was a perfect place for a snack. But, truth to tell, Tony was simply too low on cash to afford Jimmy's or anyplace like it just now.

"It's too far," he said. "I'm too tired to go all the way over there. Why don't we order a pizza?"

The girl looked at him, raising an eyebrow. Her face was momentarily obscured by the smoke she blew from her nose.

"Pizza?" she said. "I don't like pizza."

Tony was rapidly coming to dislike this girl. He had already forgotten his conversation with her at the bar. It was as though he were waking up at this moment, greeting her as a stranger, seeing her swathed in smoke tinted pink by the neon light, an irritable frown on her face.

"How about a hamburger?" he asked. "We can go right down the block here."

She did not hide her disappointment. She looked around the seedy apartment, and at Tony.

"I don't like hamburgers, either," she said. There was a note of challenge in her voice.

Tony smiled. "What do you like, then?"

She looked at him. "A soufflé is always nice," she said. "Not too heavy, not too light."

Now he could feel the contempt in her voice.

"Well, babe," he said, taking a puff of his cigarette, "if it's a soufflé you want, you'll have to go down to Chez Paul or Gerard's alone. I'll call you a limo. Or better yet," he joked, "I'll wake up my chauffeur and have him take you."

"Don't bother," she said. "I can add two and two. You're not exactly well-heeled, are you, champ?"

Tony absorbed this blow in silence, watching her through the haze of smoke between them. He saw her eyes dart to the clothes she had thrown on the chair. She wished she were out of here already. She had had her fun with him, and now she was bored and restless, and contemptuous of her surroundings.

She was a bitch. That was what he had failed to realize in his conversation with her at the bar and during their brief walk here. He must have been too drunk or too horny to notice. Or perhaps she had hidden it deliberately as part of her own barstool act.

In any case, he was close to hating her now.

"I guess we understand each other, anyway," he said.

"Yeah," she said, putting out her cigarette and standing up. "I guess we understand each other."

He studied her body. The stomach hung down like a small spare tire. The buttocks were flaccid, the breasts sagging. Her blond hair was dark at the roots. Her makeup, smeared by their lovemaking, looked grotesque.

She was hardly the one to be looking down on him, Tony thought.

He watched her slip on her dress and stoop to put on the high-heeled shoes she had been wearing at the bar. She looked like a cheap drifter.

"What did you say your name was, honey?" he asked, a note of scorn in his voice.

"What's it to you?" she sneered. "You won't remember it tomorrow, anyway, stud."

She had picked up her coat and purse. She looked around the cheap furnished room.

"I wish I didn't have to remember this," she said. "But I probably will. That's life, I guess."

She paused at the door. Tony was still sitting naked, his drink in his hand.

"You're quite a tiger in the sack," she said. "Too bad you don't have as much on the ball as I thought. Just my luck. I always pick the losers."

Her lips curled in contempt. "So long, big spender," she said.

Tony got up and came to her side. "Let me get that for you," he said.

In that split second she admired his body, which was still hard and manly despite the obvious dissipation of his life and the cheap liquor he consumed.

This momentary inattention was her undoing.

His arm reached to the doorknob but suddenly swung back in a vicious arc. He hit her flush on the mouth with the back of his hand. She was flung backward by the blow and struggled to keep her balance.

But his other hand had already come from nowhere to strike her across her temple, even harder, and she slumped to the floor in a daze.

With a catlike quickness that belied his inebriation, Tony dropped to his knees astride her. He hit her with his open hand, watching her head jerk this way and that under his blows. How many times he struck her he did not know. His hands worked automatically, as though outside his own will. A moan of complaint came from her lips, but her eyes were rolling back in her head. She was half unconscious.

He was about to hit her harder when he regained control of himself. For a long moment he sat on top of her with his eyes closed, listening to his own breathing scald his throat. His hands were trembling.

Then he looked down at the girl. Her inert body made him nervous. He pulled up her eyelid and examined her eye. When he heard a few more stifled moans in her throat, he decided she was all right.

He threw on his clothes and took her down to the parking space in the alley where he kept his car. He held one arm under her shoulder as though she were drunk. No one saw him, for it was two o'clock in the morning.

He drove her along the silent streets until he came to a small park. He deposited her on a bench. She was still too woozy to speak or stand.

Gently he let her slump to a fetal position on the bench. Then he looked at her face. It was badly swollen, but she would probably not need medical attention. She would be black and blue for a few days, that was all. For an instant Tony contemplated the results of his own violence with surprise. He had not known he had this in him before tonight.

Then he shrugged. The bitch had deserved it, he decided.

He drove away, leaving her lying there. He found his way home after a dazed odyssey through half-familiar neighborhoods, went upstairs, and fell into the bed where he had had sex with the girl. In five seconds he was sound asleep.

The next morning Tony awoke to find he recalled everything very clearly.

He was worried about the girl. He wondered if she would come back to Bruno's to look for him, perhaps with the police, perhaps with a boyfriend. She might even remember the way to this furnished room. She was a real bitch. There was no telling what she might do.

But beyond his worry about the girl Tony was shocked by what he had done. He had never struck a woman before. Somehow he had lost his grip last night.

He looked around the apartment, and he realized what had happened. Last night, seeing her lying in that bed, her lip curled contemptuously as the smoke from her cigarette drifted up through the pink neon light, he had seen his own apartment through her eyes. A cheap fleabag.

What was worse, he had seen his own life through her eyes as he listened to her insults.

I always pick the losers. . . .

So long, big spender. . . .

Tony was filled with loathing for himself and for the life he had sunk into. The descent had been slow; he had not really realized how low he was sinking, until the girl's sneering derision had made him realize it.

He got up and looked at himself in the mirror. Mercifully, his face still looked young and handsome. His body was trim and hard. The liquor had not had its effect on his flesh yet.

He still had a chance. If he could pull himself together . . .

Tony shaved carefully, went out for a razor cut for his hair, put on his best suit, and began to look for a job. This time he was serious.

The hunt was not an easy one. It took three weeks of telephone calls to old friends, former business colleagues, every contact, in fact, that Tony had made in his long career.

Nearly all of them brushed him off, of course. Business friendships mean little at the best of times, but Tony's record was a spotty one, full of sudden terminations and lacking in glowing recommendations. He was the very portrait of the loser. Asking old acquaintances for help was asking a lot.

But Tony stuck with it, not scrupling to humble himself before men he had once worked alongside or had business dealings with. When they protested that they could not help him find a position worthy of him, he told them he would take anything, anything at all.

His break finally came from an old pal and drinking partner named Tip Kimmons, who was now working as a sales manager for an insurance company on Long Island.

"I can give you something in sales," Tip said, the joviality in his voice hiding a note of concern as he realized how desperate Tony was. "You'll have to go on the road, though. Can you handle that?"

"Of course I can handle it," Tony said. "When do I start?"

"Come in Monday for our sales course," Tip said. "We should have you out in your territory by a week from then."

"Thanks, Tip," Tony said. "You won't regret it."

"Don't thank me," said Tip. "The fact is we just got taken over. There's some new money from the parent firm, and I'm dipping into that to hire you. If it weren't for that, I wouldn't have a thing to give you."

It was not until Tony reported for work the next week, and began his career as a lowly insurance salesman doing telephone soliciting and road sales, that he realized what had happened.

Tip Kimmons's company was called The Stone Life Assurance Company, after its long-deceased founder, Taylor Stone. The Stone Life Assurance Company had been on the edge of bankruptcy four years ago when it was acquired by the national life insurance corporation called Benefit Life, Inc.

Benefit Life, Inc. was a subsidiary of a conglomerate called Griffin-Ellis Inc., which owned two other large insurance carriers as well as dozens of other companies in fields ranging from manufacturing to building supplies to steel mills.

Griffin-Ellis had run into trouble in the recent bear market, and had nearly fallen victim to a hostile takeover by a multinational conglomerate based in Italy. Had the corporation been taken over, it was clear it would have been broken up and sold piecemeal to balance the Italian group's accounts.

But at the last minute, by a decision of Griffin-Ellis's stockholders, with the help of a dozen friendly investment bankers, the hostile takeover was prevented, and an American conglomerate came to the rescue, acquiring Griffin-Ellis for $41.57 per share and committing itself to keeping Griffin-Ellis alive under its own name.

It was only because of this merger that Tony Dorrance had his new job. His immediate superior would be Tip Kimmons. Above Tip there were the directors of Benefit Life. Above them were the Griffin-Ellis managers who were responsible for the financial performance of the company.

Continuing up the corporate ladder were the board members at Griffin-Ellis. Above them were the top-level managers of the new parent company.

And above them all, at the head of the parent company, was its founder, chief operating officer, and chairman of the board, Jordan Lazarus.

So it was Jordan Lazarus, in a way, who had resurrected Tony Dorrance's disintegrating career as a salesman, and as a man.

41

New York City

CALVIN WEATHERS WAS A TALL MAN, very tall for his profession.

Private detectives were supposed to be unobtrusive men who slipped around corners without being noticed, who didn't attract attention.

Calvin Weathers was the opposite. At six feet four inches and two hundred twenty pounds, he was an imposing figure. He wore suits and sport jackets that showed off a powerful athletic frame now grown just slightly soft as he entered his forties. His dark hair, sprinkled with gray at the temples, was impeccably cut, giving him the look of a successful businessman, or perhaps an aggressive salesman. He affected a rather loud manner to suit this persona. He flirted with waitresses and bar girls, and cultivated the irritating habit of addressing everyone he met by his or her first name, just as a salesman might do.

When he wanted to make a different impression he often carried an athletic bag with a tennis racket sticking out of it. This, combined with jeans and a sweater or T-shirt, made him look like an amateur athlete. He was very convincing.

Wherever he went, people noticed him immediately.

But they did not notice him as a detective.

In reality Cal was a soft-spoken man, very private and very intelligent. His discretion, combined with his thoroughness, had earned him a job as one of the highest-paid operatives at Anspach & Cates, one of the finest detective agencies in the country and the agency preferred by the rich and powerful.

He had spent seven years as a detective on the New York City police force, first in Vice and then in Homicide, and had seen every variety of venality that the city could offer. A conflict with his superiors over a controversial investigation ended his career, but his abilities were so great that he had no difficulty finding work at a reputable local agency, and five years later he had worked his way up to a well-paid position at the prestigious Anspach & Cates.

He was a strong, agile man who could handle himself in dangerous situations. But because of his careful research and preparation he almost never had to use physical force. He hung back, did his work from a distance, and stayed with it until he had found all the answers. For this reason his superiors earmarked many of the most sensitive assignments for Cal. He was a top professional, one of the very best in his field.

On this rainy April day Calvin Weathers met Jill Fleming in a small midtown hotel only a few blocks from Hightower Industries.

Jill had hired Cal through Anspach & Cates. She had specifically requested him for this assignment, and had paid extra for the privilege, for the agency did not like to be told which operative to assign to a given case.

Jill had been impressed by the detective from the very first. His brains, his attention to detail, and, in a sense, his personal vision, had shown her he was the man she needed.

And Cal Weathers had been impressed by Jill.

She opened the door for him without a word. She was dressed in a leather skirt and a tight sweater. The jacket she had worn, hanging on a hook on the wall, was in Italian leather as well. The detective noted her attire with an appreciative eye before sitting down at the table by the window.

"What do you have for me?" Jill asked.

"What you've been waiting for, I think," Calvin Weathers said.

He opened a file folder and turned the pages as he spoke

"Barbara Considine was an only child," he said. "Her mother died when she was seven. She was brought up by her father. She had a nanny for a few years, but the woman was let go when Barbara was eleven. After that she and the father were alone, except for a handful of family visits. Considine didn't allow the cook or servants to come into the house until he had left for work each day, and had them leave before he got home. He hated having servants underfoot. He demanded complete privacy."

Jill was listening quietly.

"Victor Considine had suffered from chronic heart failure from around age forty," the detective said. "Arteriosclerosis. He had been tried on every type of therapy available at the time, and had had a number of heart attacks and hospitalizations. I won't go into the physical details. Anyway, the outlook for him was not good. His life expectancy was perhaps sixty, perhaps sixty-five if he was lucky. He didn't like those odds, especially since he was accustomed to exercising a lot of power as head of his conglomerate. Men that rich don't like being outwitted by Mother Nature."

He glanced at Jill, who nodded, crossing her legs. A small leather purse sat on the floor beside her.

He turned a page, then another.

"Now, Jordan Lazarus owned a company that was developing a new drug that might have helped Considine. Might have saved his life."

Jill nodded. Most of this she already knew.

"Considine tried to take over Lazarus's company," he said, "just to get at the drug research facilities. It was a pure power play. In the end, he succeeded. He made a cash tender offer that the stockholders couldn't resist, and took over Lazarus's whole conglomerate. But just at that moment he died. His daughter married Lazarus, gave him almost complete financial control of the Considine empire, and it was from that merger that Lazarus International became one of the biggest companies in the world."

Merger, Jill thought. The perfect word for Jordan's marriage.

"It's plain enough," Calvin Weathers said, "that the death of the father and the marriage were beneficial both to Barbara and to Lazarus. Lazarus got his empire back and much more. As for Barbara, she got a husband, and she got rid of her father."

Jill looked at him. "Why would she want to get rid of her father?" she asked.

The detective smiled. "I'm coming to that," he said

He turned a page in the file.

"Barbara Considine was a very quiet girl," he said. "Except for her debutante ball she was almost never seen in society. She went to college, got an MBA from Harvard, and went to work for Considine. She never married, until Jordan Lazarus came along. In all those early years there's not a single indication of anything strange about her life—except this."

He turned the file so that it faced Jill. She looked at the page he had marked for her attention. Her eyes narrowed.

"Age sixteen," she said.

The detective nodded. "Mexico City. It was very expensive. I talked to the doctor involved. The amount of money he was offered made him suspicious, so he kept careful notes on the case. It was a simple abortion."

Jill nodded. This fact seemed to satisfy her.

"But there's more," the detective added, pointing to the bottom of the page. "As you see."

Jill studied the page. Her eyes narrowed as she saw the part of the report indicated by the detective. She was obviously intrigued.

"Yes, I see," she said.

The detective took back the file and turned the pages.

"Now," he went on, "Considine's serious heart condition was well known. The final heart failure didn't surprise anyone, so he was buried without an autopsy. Since Barbara was handling his routine medication at the time, she explained to the medical examiner the dosage and so on. No one questioned her word. Why should they?"

He turned another page. "But I managed to catch up with the special nurse who took care of Considine after his second hospitalization. Her specialty is cardiac patients. She knew what medication he was receiving, and what his condition was. And while she was living in his house, she got some strange impressions as to the sort of life he was living. She didn't feel like talking about it, but I managed to persuade her."

"What do you mean, the sort of life he was living?" Jill asked.

The detective hesitated for a moment.

"Let me come back to that in a minute," he said. "At the time of his death, Considine was receiving digitalis. Now, digitalis leaves very clear traces in the body. If Considine died the way the coroner thinks he did, there would be clear evidence of it in his tissues."

He turned the page of the report. "I had a little theory about this, and I took it to some medical friends of mine. A pathologist, a heart specialist, and a pharmacologist. All three confirmed that the report of death doesn't make sense on its face. Considine couldn't have died of a spontaneous coronary. Something caused him to go into heart failure. An autopsy would prove it."

Jill was eyeing the detective closely.

"How did he die, then?" she asked.

The detective smiled. "We come back to the life Considine was leading with his daughter," he said. "She was his only confidante. She gave him his medication. She fed him. She took care of all his needs. No servants were ever allowed in the house when they were home. They were always alone. That's a pretty odd situation, isn't it?"

Jill looked skeptical. "You're giving me inference," she said. "I need more than that."

He nodded. "I know you do. Now, picture the situation. Here's a girl whose father has been her only world since she was a small child. He dominates her completely. She can't refuse him anything. She idolizes him. And, beneath the surface, she probably hates him just as much. Now, all of a sudden, Jordan Lazarus enters her life. He tries to enlist her help in preventing her father's hostile takeover of his conglomerate. She refuses him. But in the process he manages to get under her skin. She falls in love with him. What is the result of all this? The takeover goes through, but suddenly old man Considine is dead, out of the picture, and the daughter offers Considine Industries to Jordan Lazarus on a silver platter. Seven years later Lazarus is one of the five richest men on the planet."

Jill nodded thoughtfully.

"I still need more than inference," she said.

"I found that nanny who took care of Barbara until she was eleven," the detective said. "It turns out she wasn't let go because of general principles. She was getting suspicious. Based on what she told me, I spoke to the maids who did the work at Considine's house. One of them was smarter than Considine or his daughter gave her credit for. In the confusion after Considine's death, this maid took the bedsheet he had slept on the night he died. She still has it. Or rather, I have it."

He turned the file to Jill once more and let her look at it. She read slowly, her finger touching the file folder.

He watched her take in the information. Her face had become more beautiful in its concentration. A slight smile curled her lips. This was what she had hoped for, and more.

At length she closed the file and looked up at him.

"You've done your work well," she said. "They told me you were good."

He was looking at her intently. "I'm a sucker for a pretty face," he said.

She closed the folder. "Is this for me?" she asked.

"It's all for you," he said, an ambiguous note in his voice.

She picked up the folder and put it in the briefcase she had brought with her.

Then she turned and stood in front of the detective.

"Well," Jill said. "You're a man who works hard. You deserve a bonus, I think."

The detective said nothing. His eyes had deepened as she posed before him.

Slowly she reached for the zipper of her leather skirt and undid it. She stepped out of the skirt and softly put it in his lap.

He was staring at her naked crotch. Underneath the skirt she had worn nothing. She took off her blouse. Only a tiny bra remained.

"Be a good boy," she said, taking a step toward him, "and help me with this."

42

Barbara Lazarus was in her office at Considine Industries, waiting for an important message.

She was to meet Jordan for dinner at "21" tonight, where a few important corporate guests would join them. It would be a stiff and boring gathering, but Jordan had a suave way of getting these things over with quickly. The two of them would be home in their Sutton Place penthouse by nine-thirty.

Barbara had scarcely seen Jordan in the last two weeks. During that time Jordan had been rushing from conference to conference all over the country, making stops in Chicago, Denver, Cleveland, Phoenix, and San Francisco. He was doing the corporate groundwork on his new plan for the cities, and he had to grease a lot of palms to get the cooperation he needed.

Jordan was truly a man possessed. He had explained the essentials of the plan to Barbara. It was a visionary plan, one that might change the face of the nation. If it worked—and Jordan seemed convinced it could not fail—the American inner city would be transformed into a vibrant economic base, its real estate values high, its citizens happy and productive. The urban blight that had been strangling the cities since before the turn of the century would be ended. The urban neighborhoods would become economic showplaces with suburblike living conditions. The underclass of today would become the prosperous middle class of tomorrow.

If this plan worked, Jordan would become to the nation's economy what Martin Luther King, Jr., had been to racial morality, what Abraham Lincoln had been to the Union, what Roosevelt had been to the poor during the Depression.

But Jordan was not doing it for personal glory. He was doing it to fulfill some private dream whose existence Barbara had not suspected in him before, and did not really understand.

Barbara would have resented being neglected so much by her handsome husband recently, if the whole thing were not making Jordan so happy, so excited. She herself felt infected by his enthusiasm, and proud of him.

Nevertheless, she was concerned by his long absences. And there was something about his newfound contentment that Barbara, knowing him so well, could not ascribe merely to business.

Barbara sensed that something was wrong.

That was why she was expecting something important today.

Her detective agency had reported to her that Jordan was seeing a young woman named Jill Fleming, an administrative assistant to Jessica Hightower. Barbara knew Jessica, as everyone in the business world did, but had never heard of or seen this Fleming girl. Her detective had informed her that Jordan had met the girl at the big Lazarus-Hightower financial meeting. That must have been where they struck up their relationship.

Barbara had ordered her detective to find out everything there was to know about Jill Fleming, her position at Hightower, her relationship to Jessica, her past. She also wanted to know how serious Jordan's involvement with this young woman was.

The detective, one of the best in the business, had sent her two reports indicating that the deep background check on the girl was still in progress. As to whether or not Jordan had been intimate with her, he promised a report one way or the other this afternoon.

Barbara needed that report badly. The delicate balance she maintained as Jordan's wife was always painful, and more so when she knew he was seeing someone.

She held on to Jordan by making him feel completely free in his marriage. She knew how deeply indebted he was to her for her role in the rise of his corporation. She kept her promise as his wife. She gave him his freedom, she assured him that she did not ask him to love her.

And she destroyed any woman who attempted to lure him away from her.

So far her task had been relatively easy. Most of the young women who set their sights on him were mere gold diggers, after his money and his power. Jordan was too sensitive a person to be taken in by them. On a few occasions she had had to intervene to get rid of them. Jordan had not seemed to notice.

Once, of course, the danger had been far more serious. The girl had been a small-time advertising executive from Long Island, an apparent nonentity unlikely to attract the interest of a man as important as Jordan. But the reports of Barbara's detectives, combined with her own observations of Jordan at the time, had left no doubt that he was in love.

Barbara had needed all her wiles to find a way to separate Jordan from that girl for good. The process had taken two months, and had been torture for Barbara. She had hardly slept a single night in all that time. So drained was she by the battle that it took her a week in bed to recover herself after she finally won.

But she had won. That was the important thing.

Since that day Jordan had seemed different, sadder. He was more inward, as though at once fighting and cherishing a great inner wound. Like a man carrying a torch.

But Barbara had comforted him. And gradually he had recovered. Nowadays he was almost himself again, cheerful and full of energy. But she dreaded the day when he would fall in love again. So she kept a close watch on him.

From the photographs she had received, the Fleming girl was very pretty. Beautiful, perhaps, to Jordan. There was an odd quality to her, a chameleonlike look, so that she seemed different from one photo to the next. Perhaps that was part of her charm, that ambiguous, camouflaged look.

Was it a charm that Jordan could not resist? That was the question.

Jill Fleming had a powerful protectress in Jessica Hightower. It might not be easy to scare her off.

But Barbara would do it. Even if she had to destroy the girl. Even if she had to go up against Jessica Hightower.

After all, Barbara Considine herself was a powerful woman.

And a determined one.

It was four o'clock when Barbara's executive secretary knocked timidly at the door.

"Yes?" Barbara called.

"A messenger brought this envelope," the secretary said. "It's completely unmarked. Shall I accept it?"

"I'll take it." Barbara took the envelope and closed the door on her secretary.

The envelope was heavily sealed, and she had to use a knife and a staple remover to get it open. She assumed it was from her detective. No doubt this was the information she had been waiting for.

A small sheaf of papers fell out onto her desk top.

Barbara's breath caught in her throat. This was not the dossier on Jill Fleming that she had expected. It was a dossier on herself.

There were three sheets. The first was a confidential deposition from the Mexico City physician who had performed her abortion when she was sixteen. The physician, made suspicious by the enormous fee he had been paid, had typed the blood of Barbara's dead fetus.

Appended to the physician's report was a hospital record of Victor Considine's blood type—which had, of course, been exhaustively analyzed more than once in view of his heart problems.

Barbara quickly saw the thrust of these documents. It could be proved that Victor Considine had been the father of her aborted child.

Her hands shaking, she turned the page.

This time the medical documentation was even more damning. An analysis of the medication Victor Considine had been taking at the time of his death was compared to the coroner's report on the cause of death. Inconsistencies

ELIZABETH GAGE

were noted and analyzed. The participation of a talented but anonymous pathologist was obvious.

Barbara had turned pale. With a deep breath she turned to the last page.

Analysis of bedsheet slept on by Victor Considine the night of his death. The heading was enough to make Barbara's blood run cold. Once again the remarks were detailed and absolutely convincing.

A typed note was appended to the three reports.

Dear Mrs. Lazarus,

You killed your father on March 15, 1972. You killed him by cutting off his required medication at least 48 hours prior to his death and substituting, the night of his decease, a massive dose of adrenaline, which caused him to die of heart failure as he was having sex with you.

The cause of your father's death can be proved by an exhumation of his remains. The fact that he had sex with you the night of his death can be proved by analysis of the bodily fluids found on his bedsheet.

Your lifelong sexual relationship with your father was no secret, Mrs. Lazarus. His precautions were not as effective as he thought. We are ready and able to produce those who knew what was going on. We are also prepared to make public an exhaustive analysis of the blood type of the fetus you aborted on September 3, 1959, in Mexico City, when you were sixteen years old. The results will not be flattering to you or to the memory of Victor Considine.

Your motive for the murder of your father can be easily shown in a court of law. Having been asked by Jordan Lazarus for help in fighting off your father's takeover of his corporation, and having fallen in love with Jordan Lazarus, your future husband, you murdered your father and offered Lazarus control of his corporation and the benefit of your own corporate assets. Thus you killed two birds with one stone, gaining a husband and burying the evidence of your long life of incest.

Do not force us to reveal all these facts in court, Mrs. Lazarus. They would surely be your undoing. Instead, follow our instructions to the letter. You will be avoiding a very long prison term.

Barbara closed her eyes. Her frozen hands rested on top of the pile of papers. She knew someone had gone to a great deal of trouble to find the weak spot in her past. Someone intelligent and determined, someone who already knew and understood the twisted life that had made Barbara into the person she was.

Barbara tried to think. Did she have weapons against the people behind this package? Could she fight them?

But not even Barbara's ruthless instincts as a fighter, inherited from her father, could help her now. She realized the enemy behind this damning

302

evidence had found her Achilles' heel. And that enemy possessed weapons that could be used against her publicly, in a court of law.

Her situation was hopeless. For, even if she tried to fight back with the army of lawyers at her disposal, even if she survived the scandal that was sure to follow, Jordan would know the truth about her. About her relationship with Victor Considine, about her sordid past—and about her marriage to Jordan himself.

And, knowing what he knew, Jordan would no longer feel the same way about her. The respect, the tenderness and pity that had bound him to her these last few precious years would vanish. He would demand his freedom, and she would have to give it.

Now Barbara looked to the bottom of the page where the blackmailers' demand was written. At first it surprised her, for it seemed so simple, such a small sacrifice compared to the enormity of her guilt.

Then she smiled sadly as she realized that in this way, too, the blackmailer had been way ahead of her.

It was over.

Barbara was still sitting at her desk, her eyes closed, when the secretary rang again.

"What is it?" Barbara asked, pushing the intercom button.

"Another package for you," the secretary said.

Barbara remembered the detective's report she had been expecting.

"Bring it in."

The secretary brought in a manila envelope, saw the look in her employer's eyes, and left the office quickly after putting the envelope on the desk.

Idly Barbara opened the envelope. There was a single page inside it, under the letterhead of her detective agency.

Dear Mrs. Lazarus,

To date we find no evidence of any intimate involvement between Mr. Lazarus and Miss Fleming. Their social contacts have been limited to a few lunches and one sailing afternoon. Miss Fleming is very close to Jessica Hightower. We strongly suspect a homosexual involvement of the two women, and will try to document this if so ordered. Our conclusion is that there are no grounds as of the present to suspect a romance between your husband and Miss Fleming.

The report was signed, "Anspach & Cates Investigations. Calvin Weathers, Operative in Charge."

43

LESLIE WAS DREAMING.

In her dream she was alone in a dark place. She had come here with her father, but had lost him somehow. She kept calling his name—*Daddy! Daddy!*—but he did not answer.

Oddly, though, she could see him right in front of her. The darkness did not seem to obscure him. And she was sure he saw her, too. But he did not respond. He just stared at her, listening to her frantic cries in silence, as though he heard them but could not or would not answer. She reached out her hand to him, but he did not take it.

She felt herself sinking into the earth as into quicksand. Now her father was above her, looking down indifferently, not making a move to save her. She cried out his name, but he receded, a sad and exhausted look in his eyes.

"Daddy!" she cried out. "Daddy!" He was almost out of sight now, and turning away listlessly as the earth engulfed her.

Daddy! Daddy! Daddy! . . .

Leslie woke up with a start. The sound of her own moans was still in her ear. She was covered with cold sweat. The dream still surrounded her with its unbearable sense of abandonment, like a cold liquid settling in all her limbs.

For a long moment she lay staring up at the ceiling, frightened as a child. Then she began to realize who and where she was.

She smiled, trying to shrug off her dream. She was herself, after all. The world was still the world. And she was not alone.

Only now did she realize why she had woken up. There was a faint tugging at her hand. She turned on her side. Ross was there, gazing at her with a helpless but concerned look in his eye.

He was trying to say something. She could see how much the effort cost him.

"Mm—bad dream?" he managed at last.

She hugged and kissed him.

"Yes," she murmured. "I had a bad dream. But I'm okay now."

For a moment she huddled against him, feeling the warmth of his body as he patted her with his uncertain hand.

She patted him back, and kissed his cheek.

"I'm fine now," she said. "Did you sleep?"

He nodded and managed a mischievous smile. "Mm—mmmlike . . . like a top," he said.

He pulled her hands to his lips with limp fingers and kissed them. She saw from his eyes that he wanted to say something to her, an endearment of some sort. But the words would not cooperate. So he simply sent his love through his eyes. It was a new form of communication for them, necessary since his stroke.

Leslie smiled back. Then a familiar smell reached her, and she realized he had wetted himself during the night.

"Be right back," she said.

She went and got the diapering towelettes to wipe him. She removed the plastic cover and the diaper. He had not fouled himself during the night. She could feel his relief. He could bear the humiliation of wetting his pants, but not of defecating like a helpless infant.

"Do you want to go now?" she asked.

He looked embarrassed. His mouth, still sagging a bit on the right side, moved spasmodically as he searched for words.

"Guess so," he said.

She helped him out of bed and into the bathroom. He moved on uncertain legs and had to hold her arm for support, but got where he was going on his own power. This was the pattern he had managed to establish through hard work with his physical therapists and through his own great courage. He did a lot on his own now. He did it very slowly, but he did it.

As Leslie left him at the door he smiled again. But she could see the look of deep pain and preoccupation that had been in his eyes since the first day after the stroke. It had never entirely left him. She wondered if it ever would. She told herself that the day he was really well, that look of inner pain would disappear.

She left him in the bathroom and put the coffee on to perk. She started breakfast and was back in the bedroom to help him dress when he came out of the bathroom.

They had an intricate routine, born of six months of practice. Ross did everything of which he was capable—removing his clothes from the drawers and closet, getting his shirt on, sitting down to slip his clean underpants over his ankles—and Leslie intervened only where he could not finish the job. She pulled up the underpants as he stood up, helped him on with his pants, helped him button his shirt. He could handle the zipper himself now. She rarely had to help him open doors. She had to drive for him, of course, but that could not be helped.

Ross wore house slippers, or loafers when they went out, so there were no laces to tie.

Leslie walked alongside him as he made his slow progress to the kitchen, watched from a foot away as he pulled out his chair to sit down, and left him to turn the pages of the newspaper himself, which he did slowly but efficiently.

She poured his coffee and watched out of the corner of her eye as he laboriously added cream and sugar with uncertain fingers, stirring the coffee carefully.

While the eggs were boiling she returned to the table and saw a familiar quirk of his eyebrow. He was pointing at a word in the newspaper.

She touched his shoulder as she leaned over him. She looked at the word.

"Butting up against each other," she said.

She watched him furrow his brow. Then his eyes lit up.

"Confrontation," he said.

"You got it," she smiled.

"Mmm—mmnn—knew it all the time."

Leslie had given him a clue rather than the word that had stumped him. This was a game she had worked out in concert with Ross's doctor. She kept Ross's brain active, challenging him to do as much thinking as possible rather than merely bailing him out.

The strategy worked. Ross's intellect was as lively as ever, despite the damage done to his cognitive faculties by the stroke. So was his humor. He almost never asked for help or accepted it without making a little joke to poke fun at his own infirmity and put Leslie at her ease.

Leslie had come to love and respect Ross more than ever during this painful and difficult time. The Ross she married had been an ordinary man, if a loving and kind and protective one. The man who had emerged from the ordeal of Ross's serious stroke was an indomitable one, an extraordinary one.

In the beginning, right after the stroke, there had only been pain and confusion and anger in his eyes. But he had quickly rebounded and thrown himself enthusiastically into the task of rehabilitating himself as fast as possible. He worked as hard as his demanding physical therapist asked, and even harder. He often surprised both Leslie and himself by doing, saying, and comprehending things that had seemed out of the question only days before.

Because of his considerable intelligence, combined with his pride and resourcefulness, Ross was able to express many delicate shades of emotion in his eyes, even when the word he wanted to say would not come, or the action he tried to accomplish was beyond his capabilities. His frustration was balanced by a brave humor and a tenderness that melted Leslie's heart. He had achieved a dignity in his time of need that made her love him all the more, and truly made her indifferent to the little embarrassments caused by his condition.

Of course, she could never entirely convince Ross of this. He was ashamed of his weakness. A man brought up in the old school, he was sensitive about his own virility. His helplessness exasperated him. He had married Leslie in order to take care of her, to protect her.

Instead, he seemed to have become a sort of child she had to take care of. When she helped him dress, diapered him, explained an unfamiliar word to him, or drove him somewhere in the car, she seemed more like a mother than a wife. This did not sit well with Ross at all, for he saw himself as a husband and provider. He wanted to give Leslie a safe and happy home, a family, a child of her own.

His impotence, of course, was the worst of all his agonies.

After breakfast she helped him on with his coat and got out the car. She drove him into town to the hospital and let him off at the door to the Physical Therapy Center, where his therapist, a friendly girl named Bette, was waiting.

Until recently Ross had insisted on walking from the hospital parking lot himself, but as the weather got colder he decided it was better to be let off at the door than to make Leslie take that long walk with him, a walk that was agonizingly slow for them both.

Leslie kissed him good-bye.

"Have a good time," she said with a trace of irony.

"You, mmm, sure know how to hurt a guy," he said, alluding to the agonies he experienced every day in physical therapy.

"I'll be here at three," Leslie said.

She watched him close the door on his own power and walk in alongside Bette. For an instant she saw what the stroke had done to him. He looked like an old man shuffling pathetically beside the robust young therapist, a girl of twenty. Quickly Leslie put the image out of her mind and replaced it with her familiar view of Ross as a strong, attractive man who was merely very ill at the moment.

With that image in her mind she drove out of the parking lot, bound for Wheeler Advertising, two miles away from the hospital. She had a long day ahead of her.

Since Ross's illness she had become the true boss at work. Though she made a pretense of discussing the day-to-day problems of the business with Ross, and of relaying his wishes when she gave the staff orders, the leadership was all coming from her.

Ironically, though she had found no time to think of herself in these six exhausting months, she had found mental energy to think about the business and to improve it. She had devised new strategies for existing clients and ways to find more clients. She had upgraded the office, hired two new assistants, and taken out a series of ads for the agency in the local newspapers.

Her mind was in a sort of overdrive, full of creative thoughts and ideas necessary to help Ross and his business, on condition that she never thought about herself. She had become an involuntary expert on expressive aphasia, receptive aphasia, verbal apraxia, dysarthria, and all the complexities of stroke symptoms and their treatment. But she had not bought herself a new blouse or a pair of shoes since before Ross's stroke. She was badly in need of underwear, makeup, even new stockings. But she was too absorbed in helping Ross get stronger to think about her own appearance.

Thanks to Leslie's efforts, business was better than ever. She tried to hide this fact or at least downplay it with Ross, for she did not want him to feel as though he had been put out to pasture. But he was too intelligent not to see evidence of the changes on his visits to the office. If he felt jealous he did not show it. Instead he covered Leslie with compliments and expressions of his pride in her.

Leslie still enjoyed the challenge of work. Nevertheless, the dual task of taking on so much responsibility at the office and dealing with the enormous burden of Ross's convalescence was so mentally and emotionally draining that she was completely exhausted at the end of the day. She had lost nearly fifteen pounds in the last six months, and most of her dresses were a size too large. She could not weigh more than a hundred and five pounds. She felt cold even on balmy evenings, and wore sweaters around the house when a blouse would have sufficed a year ago.

Perhaps it was due to this constant anxiety that she sometimes forgot little things. Right now, for instance, when she stopped the car outside the office, she realized she had left her briefcase at home. She had been too preoccupied with getting Ross into the car to remember it.

She threw the car into reverse, backed out of the diagonal space, and drove quickly home. It was nearly ten-thirty now. She would be behind schedule for the rest of the day.

She left the car in the driveway and hurried into the kitchen. The briefcase was on the counter where she had forgotten it earlier. As she picked it up she caught a glimpse of herself in the kitchen mirror. She looked pale as a ghost, and her hair was awry.

Sighing, she went upstairs to the bathroom and brushed out her hair. She needed a cut badly. The hair had always been frizzy, and now that it was overlong it was almost uncontrollable.

She ended up pulling it back with a band and resolved to call the beauty shop later today. She applied a touch of color to her cheeks, turned out the bathroom light, and started downstairs.

She had reached the foyer and was turning toward the kitchen when the doorbell rang.

Leslie almost jumped at the sound. She was never home at this time of the day. The house seemed like a tomb to her, and she could not imagine anyone coming to call.

She moved somewhat hesitantly toward the door. Turning the latch, she opened it an inch to look through.

Her eyes opened wide.

Standing in the doorway, not looking a day older than when she had known him, was Tony Dorrance.

44

TONY LOOKED EVERY BIT as surprised as Leslie was. In fact, he looked as though he had seen a ghost.

"Mrs.—Mrs. Wheeler?" he asked in a stilted voice.

There was a silence. Leslie's eyes had opened wide.

"Leslie?" he asked incredulously.

In that instant she realized he had not come here to find her but had been brought to her doorstep by some bizarre accident.

"Tony," she said, struggling to recover her composure.

"I—my God, this is incredible," he said.

She had the presence of mind not to invite him in. She stood her ground, keeping the door half closed between them. But she was shaken by the sight of him. On one hand, he was ancient history, a relic of her heedless youth, a man she never should have been involved with. He was her greatest mistake, her greatest chagrin.

On the other hand, he was the father of her child. As such he had an extreme, an almost tremendous reality to her. And as he stood before her, amazingly unchanged by time, looking at her through those handsome, dark eyes, she felt shaken to the core. She was seeing her own life's history, and that of her body, standing before her in flesh and blood.

"What brings you here?" she managed.

"I work for Benefit Life Insurance. I'm a salesman. You have a policy with us. I was sent here to see if you were interested in some additional coverage."

A flush came over his features as he explained himself. Leslie was far from being able to interpret it. So devouring were her own preoccupations that she did not notice that Tony was embarrassed to admit he was a traveling insurance salesman. Seeing her comfortable suburban house, he was comparing her life to his own, and felt ashamed. He had come a long way down in the world since he knew Leslie.

She was looking at him, irritation mingling with her surprise.

"Benefit Life?" she asked.

"Yes," he repeated a bit sheepishly.

Leslie shook her head in confusion. This was all too much to take in.

"We received our benefits from you," she said. "Considering the situation, I think the last thing in the world Benefit Life would want to do would be to sell us more insurance."

"I can explain that. I—do you mind if I come in for a moment?" he asked.

At that instant Leslie finally understood his embarrassment. This question-and-answer session, with him as the insurance salesman standing on her stoop, was humiliating for him.

"Of course," she said. "But I'm on my way out to work. It will have to be for only a moment."

She let him in. He looked at the living room. In it were pictures of Ross's daughters, of Leslie herself, and of Leslie and Ross. Also in it was Ross's orthopedic chair and the walker he still occasionally used.

"How is your husband doing?" he asked.

Leslie looked at him. "Fine," she said uncomfortably.

Tony smiled. He seemed to be recovering his composure. A trace of the insurance salesman's patented decorousness showed in his handsome face.

"Let me explain why I'm here," he said. "We have a special offer for existing policy holders who have had major health problems. It's a promotion, in a way. We're offering high-risk whole-life insurance at a special low rate, for a limited time only. They sent me here because of your husband's stroke. It's an excellent offer."

His expression clouded as he looked into her eyes.

"I'm sorry about your husband," he said.

Leslie stood staring at him. She could not believe that, with the past that joined her to this man, they were standing here speaking of something as absurd as insurance. Fate had acted with an almost slapstick whimsy in bringing them together this way. Insanely, it was Ross's stroke that had caused Tony's path and hers to cross again.

"Thank you," she said. "That's nice of you."

"And I'm sorry we had to meet again under these circumstances," he said.

He was looking at her closely. She wondered what he saw. She knew she was thinner, and older. She also knew that tragedy had etched its shadow into her features, just as it had done with Ross. She could see that in the mirror every morning.

Suddenly she was shocked by these narcissistic thoughts. The last thing in the world she cared about was looking good for Tony Dorrance. Tony no longer existed for her.

"I have to go to work now," she said briskly. "Why don't you send us your offer in the mail? I'll discuss it with my husband, and we'll see." There was an involuntary trace of condescension in her tone, the brush-off of an impatient and unwilling customer.

"Of course," he said. "I'm sorry to have disturbed you."

But his eyes did not express apology. He seemed to be appraising her. A strange energy glowed at the back of his irises.

Leslie preceded him to the door and opened it.

"Well," she said without warmth, "good-bye."

He extended a hand. Reluctantly she shook it. At the touch of their flesh she knew he was the same Tony. She blushed.

"It's really absurd, isn't it?" he smiled in an almost comradely way. "Us meeting this way."

She gave him a tight little smile. She thought his words presumptuous.

"I never thought I'd see you again in this world," he said.

She said nothing.

"Well," he said, turning on his heel with an odd jauntiness, "I'll get that paperwork off to you right away. It's a good offer. I'm sure your husband will be pleased."

She thought this last was a provocation as well, and did not smile.

He started to walk away. Then he stopped. She knew what was going through his mind.

He turned back to her, a pained look on his face.

"Listen," he said. "I know this isn't the time or place, but, what happened between us, Leslie . . ."

His discomfort was obvious. But Leslie thought she could see a sidelong glimmer of triumph in it. He knew what he had once meant to her.

"You're right," she said. "Besides, that's ancient history, Tony. You needn't trouble yourself about it." Her tone was firm and more than a little contemptuous.

Still torn between his professional role as a polite salesman and the intimate knowledge that bound him to her, he simply shrugged and walked away to the street, where his car was parked. She saw a trace of his old cockiness as he threw his briefcase onto the seat and slammed the door.

She watched him drive away, remaining inside the house until he was gone. Then she locked the house carefully and got into her car. It was not until she touched the shift lever that she realized her hands were shaking uncontrollably.

With a gasp of irritation at herself, she flung the car into reverse. But the gasp came out as a sob. And when she paused to look at her face in the rearview mirror, she saw to her surprise that tears were streaming down her cheeks.

*   *   *

That afternoon Leslie picked Ross up at the hospital as she had promised and took him to the office for one of his many visits. He chatted with the staff, looked at the work being done—a pro forma exercise, as everyone knew—and then Leslie took him home.

They had a quiet dinner during which she tried her best to hide her frayed emotions. But Ross, always alert to her state of mind, saw that she was upset.

"Is anything wrong, honey?" he asked.

She could see the concern in his eyes. He was always worrying that the burden his condition placed upon her was wearing her down, sapping her strength.

"Nothing you can't fix," she said, reaching to take his hand.

He squeezed her hand. He let the subject drop. A massive stroke had not made Ross Wheeler any less tactful or considerate than before.

After dinner he said, "Come with me."

He took her to the bedroom, had her help him lie down, and held out his arms. She lay down beside him, and he put his arms around her.

"My girl," he murmured.

Leslie felt tears come to her eyes as he cuddled her to him. She buried her face against his chest.

"I've put you through a lot," Ross said.

She shook her head.

"No, Ross. Illness has put us both through a lot."

"My girl," he repeated.

He caressed her gently. And now, why she did not know, she let the tears come. Her body was shaken by silent sobs. Ross held her tenderly, squeezing her close to him.

"I know," he said.

She nodded and hugged him back. He could not know what was going through her mind. He thought it was the accumulated stress of six months of coping with terrible illness. He could not know it was a visit from her former life, this very afternoon, that had dislocated her existence and made her realize how far she had come in her young life, and how much she had endured.

No, Ross could not know what she was thinking, what battles she was fighting for herself and for him at this very moment.

But that did not seem to matter. His embrace was no less tender, his love no less complete. And, in an odd sense, his understanding was no less effective for his failure to know her heart.

45

IN A CHEAP MOTEL ROOM near Great Neck, Long Island, Tony Dorrance paced back and forth like a caged animal.

He could not believe what had happened to him. Leslie! Leslie, after all this time!

He felt a weird energy thrilling through his body, forcing his restless movement around the room. It filled him with an almost painful exultation, on the edge of anxiety.

She had never been more beautiful, he mused. Indeed, she had never been half so beautiful as the day he had seen her at her Johnsonville house.

In that first moment, as she stood in her doorway still not recognizing him, and he not yet recognizing her, he had been overwhelmed by her. Even had she not been Leslie, *his* Leslie, he would have fallen for her in that instant and done anything in his power to get her to see him.

Or so it seemed to Tony.

In any case, he had seen her now. And it must have been fate that brought them together after all this time. Nothing else could explain it.

Tony's meeting with Leslie seemed to have awakened him from a long sleep. The sight of her forced him to confront the emptiness of his whole life. And the reason for that emptiness. It was not by mere accident or ill luck that he had sunk so low these past six years, both in his professional life and in his personal life. It was because he had lost Leslie.

In that first instant, seeing her beautiful face so serious as she looked out her door at him, he had realized what he given up so long ago in letting her go. She had been so special, so extraordinary even then—but Tony himself had been too young, too immature to realize what a diamond he had possessed in her.

Now Leslie's magic had come back to him—but transformed into something indescribable by the changes the years had wrought in her face. There

313

was a dignity about her now, born of experience, responsibility, and misfortune. A maturity, a womanliness that left him breathless.

Only now did Tony realize that he loved her, had loved her all along, and had languished without her as though without his own heart.

And only now Tony understood why he had wasted himself with so many women, and found himself completely unable to take them seriously. He understood why they had bored him so much that he had to court danger in his affairs with them, often to his own undoing.

It was all because of Leslie. It was all because she had been the one, *the* one, all along, and he had known it with his heart but not with his mind. In being untrue to Leslie—what an awful crime it seemed now!—he had been untrue to his own destiny.

Tony now recalled something he had conveniently forgotten all these years—the fact that he had deflowered Leslie before abandoning her. A rush of guilt accompanied this recollection. But an equally powerful emotion told Tony that he had been Leslie's first lover for a reason. Fate had wanted him to love her, to be her man, right from the start. Why else would she have given him the treasure she must have denied to many others before he came along?

But another emotion, no less powerful than his exultation, possessed him as well. It was frustration. Not only at his own stupidity in so foolishly letting her slip through his fingers, but at the fact that she had gone on with her life, that she was married, that she had forgotten him—or tried to.

He recalled the look in her eyes, a look of indifference mixed with displeasure at the memory he represented. It was, after all, a memory of being seduced and abandoned.

He could see she was preoccupied with her present life and had little time or mental energy to think of him. And the little attention she had given him had been tinged with contempt.

And why not? He had come a long way down in the world. Today he was in no position even to approach Leslie, much less to ask her to see him. Time had changed all that. She was a married woman with a sick husband to take care of. And she looked upon Tony with scorn and indifference.

Or did she?

Tony thought back on the obvious disarray his presence had produced in her when she let him come into the house. The look on her face as she listened to his description of the insurance policy had been eloquent. It was a look of shock, of astonishment—and of something else.

The disarray in her eyes had betrayed the effect his presence had upon her heart, and her senses.

Yes! thought Tony. That was it! Even after all these years she was not over him. That had been the secret message throbbing in her eyes despite her pretense of coldness.

He was sure of it.

Now Tony began to pace more quickly about the motel room, actually talking to himself in his excitement.

If Leslie still cared for him—as either the facts or his pride told him—that could only mean fate had sent him here for a reason. She was as unhappy without him as he had been without her. It had been a sort of sin for them to separate. Misfortune had resulted for both. Fate had brought them back together in order to undo this sin.

On the other hand, not even Tony's pride could blind him to the truth he was trying so hard to deny. He had dumped Leslie years ago. And now she had a new life without him. She had a husband.

Yes, these were obstacles. Serious obstacles. It would not be easy to get her to talk to him, to get to know him again.

But had not fate already accomplished a miracle in bringing them together this way? Had not fate woven the tangled threads of his own life together with her far-flung existence to make this crucial meeting possible? Was this not a miracle? And did it not justify some effort on his part to recapture his destiny?

After all, it was not just a woman he had found today. It was his own heart. It was his salvation.

With this thought in his mind, Tony downed the glass of bourbon he had poured from the pint bottle he had brought on this trip with him. He decided to go out and look for a woman. The storm in his senses could not be quelled by anything less than sexual intercourse with a passionate woman, a woman he would make passionate by his own seduction.

But as he looked at himself in the mirror, he changed his mind. No cheap bar women for him tonight. No more. He had cheated on Leslie, and cheated himself, enough. The opportunity fate had placed in his path today was too exalted to be tainted by sleazy sexual encounters in motel rooms. There could be no more dallying with women who meant nothing to him.

Those days were over.

With that thought Tony threw off his clothes, took a hot, cleansing shower, and went to bed.

The next morning, when Leslie took Ross to the hospital and drove on into town for work, she was doing everything in her power to forget her encounter with Tony Dorrance. Seeing Tony on her own doorstep in the pathetic but not unexpected guise of an insurance salesman had added a note of painful absurdity to her already difficult existence. It had reminded her of terrible things in her past, things too intimate to forget, but simply impossible to think about nowadays. Tony's face was like an image from a black comedy, thrown over her private life in the most outrageous way.

From the moment she closed her door on him she had resolved not to waste a moment's thought on him. He was not worth it. His new and lower station in life, combined with the shallow and presumptuous look in his eyes, had made that abundantly clear.

Tony was out of her life. And good riddance, Leslie mused.

It never occurred to her that as she was thinking these thoughts, Tony was following her from half a block back.

46

New York City

IT ALL HAPPENED ACCORDING to plan.

Jordan Lazarus and Barbara got a divorce, after a series of brief conversations in which very little truth was told. Their arrangement had served its purpose, Barbara insisted, and it was time to move on. Jordan agreed, not without a feeling of pity for his wife and an equally strong sense of guilt over the secret thoughts motivating him.

Two months after the divorce Jordan married Jill Fleming. Their wedding was heralded by the business and gossip press not only in America, but all over the world. After all, Jordan Lazarus was the wealthiest man in America, a heartthrob to millions of women and a hero to as many men. He was the very image of the self-made man, and the architect of the most revolutionary plan ever devised for reclamation of America's inner cities.

Jordan Lazarus was a man of the future. And now Jill Fleming, after a whirlwind romance, was his wife.

Things could not have gone more smoothly if they were choreographed by the fates. All the pieces of the puzzle had fallen into the proper places.

In fact, it all would have seemed too perfect, too inevitable, had it not been for one unforeseen event—an accident, really—that occurred in the midst of all the hoopla, and added a new and sinister halo to things. At least in the mind of Jill Fleming.

It happened on her honeymoon.

They spent those two weeks on a beautiful little island on the Aegean Sea where Jordan kept a house overlooking the harbor. They made love day and night. They took long walks. They looked at the sunset. They existed in a silence made of contentment on both sides, and complete sensual satisfaction.

Jill felt like the cat that had eaten the canary. She had accomplished the greatest coup of her life. She had successfully separated one of the world's richest and most powerful men from a determined, possessive wife.

During those first days in Greece, Jill felt wonderful, invigorated. Furthermore, she experienced a repose, a serenity that she had never known before.

This, she realized, came from Jordan. There was something relaxed and soothing about Jordan's attentiveness as a new husband. He seemed contented, even relieved to be with her.

True, there was a faint, barely perceptible distance between them, even when he held her in his arms. As they gazed out at the Aegean or took long walks in the village and the surrounding hills, an intimate silence joined them, but Jill felt she did not quite know him. He was more like a suitor than a husband. His tenderness was without deep knowledge of her.

But this distance was necessary. The last thing on earth Jill would have wanted was for him to know her as she really was. The mask she wore was the only possible means to possessing him. It was her only link to his heart.

During her long, subtle seduction of Jordan, she had concentrated on reacting with her body and her personality to the imperceptible signs that came from an unseen place within him. It had not mattered to Jill that the sources of his desire were invisible to her, or that the mask she used to tempt him was false. The point was not to know him but to capture him. Her great talent was her ability to follow by improvisation a script whose cues are only being given from moment to moment, with no advance warning.

This she had accomplished. She had taken Jordan from his wife as a fox snaps a baby chick from its mother's nest. She had been ruthless, efficient, and inspired at every step of the way.

And if there was a certain lack of intimacy in her new marriage, a failure of husband and wife to know all there was to know about each other, Jill saw no reason why she could not make Jordan happy in spite of this. After all, she reasoned, did not all women hide a few little secrets, little personal weaknesses or past peccadilloes from the men they marry? Was she really so different from any other woman in showing her best face and hiding her faults in order to catch Jordan?

Besides, her most dominant impression of him on their honeymoon was that he seemed so satisfied, so content, almost as though he wanted no more of her than this surface she had given him.

And their sex together, so hot, so intense for both, was proof that something must be working right between them.

There was no yearning in Jordan's demeanor. There was only this repose, as though a long painful struggle were over and now he was at peace with himself.

At first this situation did not alarm Jill. It merely left her a bit bemused.

But then something happened.

*   *   *

One night they made love in the wee hours, after a midnight supper and a swim in the warm pool beside the house. The occasion was almost too romantic. The moon was full, and its reflection illuminated the ocean almost as brightly as a sort of nocturnal sun.

After their swim they both felt excited by the moonlight and their nudity, and they made love on the silk sheets of their bed. Jordan had never seemed more passionate. He took her with long, knowing strokes, and she was shaken by spasms of ecstasy that left her limp. Ever since the fateful day of their first sailing expedition back home, Jill had never failed to have an orgasm when making love to Jordan. It was a kind of pleasure she had never had before and never really imagined. Now she was coming to need it, and to be grateful to him for giving it to her.

As she lay in his arms she reflected complacently upon her conquest. Jordan was hers now. Her grip on him was secure. Had he not proved over and over again that her body was a sort of obsession with him?

With this thought Jill fell asleep.

An hour later she woke up. She lay gazing at the moonlight bathing the room. Then she got up to look out the window. The moon was lower now, unbelievably intense and powerful as it sent a shimmering cataract of light across the ocean.

Jill felt a contentment she had never felt before in her life. The moon seemed to caress her across the warm surface of the sea, and to bless her marriage to Jordan.

She went back to the bed.

He was lying naked in the sheets; he had that boyish look of innocence on his face that had always charmed her. He seemed candid and vulnerable as a child.

And suddenly he murmured, "I love you."

The words were indistinct, coming from his sleep, and muffled by his pillow. But it was the look on his face that caught Jill's eye.

It was not a look of happiness or contentment. It was a look of infinite longing and pain, as though something were escaping him and he was trying to call it back.

"I love you," he repeated. The words were plaintive, a groan in his throat. Then he turned on his side, facing away from Jill, and was silent.

She lay there looking at his back, listening to his quiet breathing. And when she tried to get back to sleep, she could not.

She kept thinking of the pain in his voice, the distress that furrowed his brow in his sleep. She knew that that pain had nothing to do with her, nothing at all.

And she compared that deep, private longing to the look of quiet satisfaction, the happy but slightly impersonal serenity he showed when he was with her during the day.

Jordan was a good, attentive husband. But there was no longing, no hunger in his behavior toward Jill. Even when they talked, and she told him new things about herself—most of which were, of course, lies—she could see that he felt only idle curiosity about her. She knew he was pleased with her now that they were married, and he would have been just as pleased had she not told him the things she did about herself.

All he cared was that he had her now, that she belonged to him and with him. He possessed the vessel; he did not care about the contents.

Jill's great intuitive intelligence, lulled by a false sense of conquest until now, began to warn her that she was in deeper water than she had thought. Her husband had just murmured "I love you" to a faceless fantasy inside his mind.

And Jordan Lazarus had never said the words "I love you" to Jill Fleming.

From that night on Jill felt different about Jordan.

She was no longer so complacent in her triumph. It seemed to her that Jordan was holding back something essential of himself that she had not captured after all.

She possessed him as a seductress who had found his weak spot and imprisoned him with her charms. But she did not really know him as a man. In capturing his desire, she had fallen short of capturing the rest of him.

This tiny lack became the grain of sand around which a pearl of jealousy began to form inside Jill.

She sensed the presence of another woman in Jordan's heart, not only from his anguished "I love you," spoken in the innocence of sleep, but also in his placid, rather remote contentment when he was with Jill herself. It was as though Jill were a sort of drug that he needed to excite his senses and to soothe his hurt over the unseen woman he had lost.

This notion made Jill feel like a pawn, rather than the mistress of her fate. She did not like the feeling.

She returned from Greece with her mixed emotions well hidden inside her. She put on a pleasant, ladylike face for the reporters who besieged her and Jordan for interviews. She became the darling of the press, which had long been frustrated by Jordan's unexciting marriage to Barbara Considine and wanted to celebrate his romantic, bigger-than-life union with a beautiful young woman.

Jill gave many interviews on what it was like to be the wife of the great Jordan Lazarus. She saw her own face on the covers of the women's magazines, and that of Jordan on all the business journals. Mr. and Mrs. Jordan Lazarus were America's darlings. No couple since Jack and Jackie Kennedy had captured the public imagination so compellingly.

For a while Jill basked in all this attention, hiding behind the mask of her public image, and almost forgot the nagging worry at the back of her mind.

Then another chance event came along to crack the mirror of her happiness.

* * *

Jill was finding it harder to sleep nowadays.

Her continual meetings with the press made her nervous. It was difficult to keep playing the role the reporters demanded of her for hours at a time. And she found it painful to be separated from Jordan, whose days were very busy as he pulled the strings at Lazarus International and worked on his inner cities plan.

At night the newlyweds never failed to share an intimate supper, though it was often a late one, and to make love. Nothing had changed in their private relationship since their return from Greece. The same physical passion joined them, but Jill felt separated from Jordan by that stubborn diaphanous screen that allowed her to see his face but not his heart.

She found herself clinging to him a bit more possessively, begging him to spend more time at home, reproaching him gently for his long hours at the office and on the telephone. Charmed by her affection, he tried to make more time for her. But during those long hours together she still felt him slipping through her fingers somehow. Thus their intimacy served to aggravate her longing rather than to assuage it.

She began to fall prey to insomnia, a complaint she had never suffered from before. She lay in Jordan's king-sized bed, watching him sleep, and she could not drift off. She got up, took a sleeping pill, and went into another room to pass the time while the drug took effect. Sometimes she sat in the large living room with its overstuffed couch and Abstract Expressionist paintings. Sometimes she went to the solarium, with its magnificent view of the East River and Roosevelt Island.

Sometimes she went to the library to read herself to drowsiness. Only when she was somnolent, the words of her book dancing crazily before her eyes, did she return to bed and fall asleep beside her husband.

During this time she got to know Jordan's collection of books. He was an avid reader of the classics as well as modern literature, and had accumulated a priceless collection of rare books and first editions. Jill liked to curl up in the big leather armchair in the library and feel herself surrounded by the old volumes, which smelled of leather bindings and old paper. These volumes had known hundreds of forgotten readers in their time, and had all felt the hands of Jordan Lazarus and the caress of his eye.

The combination of Jill's insomnia and her fascination with the library was to lead to her undoing.

One night Jordan was out of town on an unavoidable business trip, and Jill was home alone. She tried to go to bed early, eager for tomorrow and Jordan's return. But she could not sleep, so she got up and padded into the library to look for a book.

She noticed the beautiful three-volume set of Shakespeare that Jordan had acquired at auction several years ago and often read in his hours of leisure. Jordan adored Shakespeare, and sometimes quoted lines from his plays or sonnets in speeches he gave to business people or political leaders.

She pulled out one of the volumes, feeling a warm tingle in her fingers as she touched the book she knew to be so dear to Jordan. She flipped through the pages distractedly, and saw them come to rest somewhere in the middle of *Macbeth*.

Her eye was caught by a speech given by Lady Macbeth.

Nought's had, all's spent,
Where our desire is got without content.
'Twere better to be those we destroy,
Than by destruction dwell in doubtful joy.

Jill allowed her eyes to linger on the lines for a moment. She was struck by their peculiar poetry. But something made her lose interest, and she let the volume fall open on her lap. Shakespeare was far too deep for her, particularly in her exhausted condition.

Suddenly she heard a rustle of paper, and looked down into her lap. Something had fallen out of the back pages of the volume, where the love sonnets were located.

Jill picked up the paper and turned it over.

It was a photograph.

The photograph was of a young woman, about Jill's own age. She was dressed in a soft summer dress in a flowered pattern, with delicate off-the-shoulder sleeves and a low-cut bodice that showed off rounded breasts and healthy skin with a summery dusting of freckles. She was standing, so one could see the billowing cut of the skirt and her long, very aristocratic legs. She had on high-heeled shoes, but looked as though she was not used to wearing them.

She wore a jeweled necklace in emeralds. Her neck was long and delicate. It was particularly visible because her hair was pulled back from her shoulders. In her hand was a wide-brimmed summer hat with a pink ribbon. She had sparkling green eyes that seemed to match the necklace. She was apparently dressed for some special purpose. She was smiling, a touch of laughter in her eyes at being photographed. Again Jill got the impression she was not used to being so dressed up, and found humor in the occasion.

Her hair was strawberry blond in color, and rather wild, with energetic natural curls tending toward the frizzy. No wonder it was pulled back for this rather formal pose. The hair seemed to contradict the quiet control one felt in her body, but to harmonize with the impish energy of her green eyes. It was her most striking and endearing feature.

Upon closer examination, the look of amusement in her sparkling eyes was mingled with a core of tenderness directed at the photographer. There could be no doubt he was the man she loved. Her eyes caressed him gently, and seemed full of secrets that bound her to him in ways the photograph could not show.

She was a beautiful young woman. But her love made her more than beautiful.

Jill's hands had turned cold around the photograph. She stood up and moved to the library mirror. She looked from the photograph to her own image. The hair in both was the same.

Jill felt a slight tremor inside her. She remembered the day Jordan had so casually shown her the strawberry blond hair on the model in the magazine. It had been Jill herself who had insisted she have her hair done in that color. But Jordan, at the hairdresser's, had given the more detailed instructions, making sure the hair came out precisely the way he wanted it.

Precisely the way it looked in this photo.

Jordan had seemed far more attracted to Jill with her new hair. It was after this change, this makeover, that he had suggested, as though out of the blue, that they go sailing together.

And it was at the marina that the old boatmaster had greeted Jill with such affection, mistaking her for someone else. She still remembered his embarrassment when he discovered he was wrong.

Someone else . . .

Jill went back to her chair and held the photo under the library lamp. She studied it, trying to fix the girl's features in her mind.

But it was not so much the features that struck her as the overall impression. It was an impression of youthful directness and honesty, of fresh good health and robust humor, combined with something delicate and fine. This was a girl who would hold nothing back, who would be an honest and passionate partner in sex or in love—but whose very vulnerability would command a man's respect.

Jill tried to clarify her view of the strange girl, but the image kept moving this way and that, blurring her vision. She looked down and realized that the tremor in her own hands was making it impossible for her to hold the picture steady.

Only now did Jill realize why her hands shook. She was looking at the woman of whom she had made herself, with Jordan's help, such a convincing model.

There could be no doubt about it, none at all. What Jill saw in the photo, not so much on the girl's face as underneath it—the delicacy, the candor, the strength of character, the pride, the youthful vulnerability—a whole skein of qualities that fitted together as inevitably as the threads of a great tapestry—was precisely the face she herself had been creating instinctively to attract Jordan all this time.

I love you.

The words rang suddenly inside her mind with a mellifluous poetry that quickly became nightmarish. For only now Jill was realizing with her heart that Jordan had sought her out, courted her, and finally married her, because she reminded him of this girl.

Somehow this simple notion, which had never bothered Jill in all her past seductions, never really occurred to her in fact, now had a tremendous destructive power, a power to scald and savage the very inside of her mind.

With trembling hands she picked up the volume of Shakespeare. She turned to the love sonnets at the back of the volume. Cursing herself for losing the place where the photograph had been hidden, she slipped it in among the pages. The lines of one of the sonnets flashed before her eyes, eerie in their tenderness.

I may not evermore acknowledge thee,
Lest my bewailed guilt should do thee shame,
Nor thou with public kindness honor me,
Unless thou take that honor from thy name.

Jill slipped the photo between the poems, closed the volume of Shakespeare, and put it back on the shelf. She went to her bathroom, found the bottle of sleeping pills, took one capsule, then a second.

She got into bed and closed her eyes. Within seconds she realized she would not sleep tonight. The presence of the damning photograph under her roof was like a poison inside her heart.

Ten minutes after going to bed she was back in the library, riffling hurriedly through the pages of the Shakespeare volume until the smiling image sprang into view once more.

Averting her eyes so as not to look directly at the girl in the picture, Jill reflected that Jordan would not be home until tomorrow afternoon. That would give her time to have the photo copied at a developing store in the morning, and replace the original before he got home.

Somehow this plan of copying the image gave Jill a measure of control over her emotions. Though the idea of multiplying the photo seemed to her a dangerous increase of its power, she could not resist her need to possess a copy of it for her own, so she could study it, learn its secrets, and perhaps find a way to defend herself against it.

She went back to her bedroom. She propped up two pillows behind her back, turned on the light, and got between the sheets with the photo still in her hand. She looked calmly and steadily at it. Her plan of action seemed to have eased the tremor in her fingers.

She stayed that way all night. The two sleeping pills had as little effect on her as two sips of weak tea. When dawn was an amber glow outside the windows, and the sounds of the city's awakening thrummed under the building, Jill got out of bed, showered and dressed quickly, and left the penthouse.

The photo was in her purse.

47

FOR A COUPLE OF WEEKS Jill felt almost like herself again.

She had a guilty secret, of course. The copy of the photo she had found in Jordan's volume of Shakespeare was carefully put away among her private things. It seemed to exert an influence on her from its hiding place, like a magnet that pulled at her wherever she was. But this effect was certainly not visible to Jordan, who seemed his usual contented self.

Life went on as before. The famous newlyweds were invited to countless receptions and parties, and received visits from government and business leaders, celebrities of all kinds, and even foreign heads of state who either had dealings with Jordan's international business empire or who wanted to learn more about the Lazarus Plan for future reclamation of their own cities.

It was a busy, hectic life, the sort of life that makes it all the easier to bury one's problems under the weight of a thousand activities and obligations. And if Jill had one extra secret to hide, this was not really anything new to her. She had been keeping her very soul a secret throughout her life. She was an old hand at this, a past master.

Then something went wrong.

One night, after a particularly hard day of work followed by a business dinner at the Plaza, Jordan went to bed early. Jill slipped in beside him at eleven-thirty, but soon realized she was not going to get to sleep without medication.

She got up and padded to the bathroom naked. She found the bottle of powerful sleeping pills and optimistically took only one.

Then, realizing the pill would need at least a half hour to take effect, she put on her slip and moved through the dark rooms of the penthouse. After standing for a long moment before the picture windows, staring out at the East River and Roosevelt Island, she went idly into Jordan's library and turned on the table lamp.

She scanned the bookshelves looking for something to read. Most of Jordan's books were a bit over her head, for she had no taste for the classics.

But he had modern novels as well, and even some mystery stories she had enjoyed one rainy afternoon.

The three-volume set of Shakespeare caught her eye as she was looking over the shelves. She saw the volume that contained the love sonnets, and could not resist the temptation of taking it out. She knew the snapshot of the beautiful girl was in its back pages, replaced there by Jill herself only two weeks ago.

She sat down in the leather easy chair and opened the volume. She found the sonnets and riffled through the pages, at first idly, then more urgently.

Her breath caught in her throat as she realized the photo was no longer in its place.

Perplexed, Jill closed the book and sat for a moment trying to collect herself. What did this mean?

She opened the book again and turned the pages very deliberately, one by one. There was no doubt about it. The picture had been removed.

Somehow this disappearance was as disturbing to Jill as the finding of the photograph itself two weeks ago. She thought of Jordan coming in here and prudently removing it, to hide it somewhere else.

Had he perhaps come in to look at it while she was having it copied, and noticed that it had been removed? Had she failed to put it back on the right page? Perhaps it was kept intentionally alongside a favorite love sonnet . . .

Perhaps, on the other hand, Jordan had simply removed the photo as a precaution, without having any notion that it had been discovered.

Or perhaps some sixth sense had told him his wife was suspicious—perhaps he had sensed it in her nervous demeanor of late—and thus had removed the photo to keep it out of harm's way.

Whatever the case, Jill had the odd feeling that the removal of the photo indicated that she herself was found out. It indicated a secret understanding between Jordan and herself about his past, an understanding without words, without trust.

This thought gave Jill a sinking feeling somewhere between despair and disgust. It made her marriage seem more false, more a travesty than ever. With trembling hands she closed the book and replaced it on the shelf.

She returned to the bedroom, pausing in the bathroom to take another sleeping pill. She saw that the bottle was getting empty; she would have to call her internist to renew the prescription, or to prescribe something more powerful.

She lay down next to Jordan and watched him sleep. The sight of his handsome face was a drug more powerful than the sleeping pill. She could feel him dreaming, and she knew she could never find out what he was dreaming about.

I love you.

She turned her back to him. The thought of his secret life, his private heart, made her feel she was losing her mind. Only a few weeks ago that unseen core of him had been a matter of indifference to her, like the inner workings of a radio, or the bowels of this building. What did she care for the innards of things or people, as long as they gave her what she wanted?

But now the inside of Jordan was an obsession with her, a poison that had found its way into her own veins. Though she could not see it or fathom it, it was part of her now. And he must have sensed this. Had he not prudently removed the picture that had been secreted among his love poems?

The tremor that had tormented Jill two weeks ago was starting inside her body again now. She got up from the bed and sat naked in the chair by the window, staring at her sleeping husband. She felt so far away from him, and so lonely. His separate, unknowable existence was like a curse. It was unbearable to sit across a room from him this way, alone in her nakedness. But what would it profit her to go closer to him, when she could not share his heart?

A sudden thought came to bring her relief from the pain twisting inside her. She was not helpless, she mused. She could still take action.

With the aid of this thought and the drug, she returned to the bed and eked out four hours of troubled sleep.

The next morning, as soon as Jordan had left for work, Jill called the Anspach & Cates Detective Agency and asked for Calvin Weathers.

48

MERCIFULLY FOR JILL, she only had to wait four days—four of the hardest days of her life—for Cal Weathers' report on the mysterious girl in the photograph.

Cal met Jill at the same midtown hotel where they had met several times before, when the job he had done for her seemed far less dangerous than the one he was doing now.

He was dressed in corduroy slacks and a sweater, his large body hidden by the rather shapeless clothes. Another one of his clever disguises, Jill mused. He always looked like anything but a detective.

He stood over the double bed and took out a large envelope. He opened it and began to spread the contents on the bed.

"You were right," he said. "The girl in the photograph is someone your husband had an affair with."

Jill suppressed the gasp in her throat.

"Her name is Leslie Wheeler," he said. "Maiden name Leslie Chamberlain. She works for a small advertising firm in a town called Johnsonville, on Long Island. She's married to the firm's head, a man named Wheeler."

Jill's ears pricked up at the mention of marriage. Somehow this notion had not occurred to her. A ray of desperate hope entered her mind as she watched Cal spread more photographs over the hotel bed. He was brisk and rather ceremonious, almost like a salesman arraying his product before her.

"She had an affair with your husband three years ago," Cal said bluntly. "Back in 1976. As close as I can figure it, the affair lasted about three months."

She looked at the photographs. They showed the young woman from the snapshot in Jordan's volume of Shakespeare. She was caught in a variety of poses at a variety of times and places. She looked different from picture to picture. But the impression of naturalness, good humor, and feminine dignity united all the images. And, to Jill's chagrin, the same haunting attractiveness shone in each of them . . . Leslie Wheeler was a beautiful woman.

Jill noticed a photograph of a little boy inserted among the others.

"Who is the boy?" she asked, perplexed.

"Her son," Cal replied. "Born before she ever met your husband. He is now about six and a half years old. I haven't been able to determine who his natural father is. In any case it's not your husband. The blood types rule that out."

Jill was struggling to take in this new information. She was not sure whether she should be encouraged by it or not. There was no time to sort it out.

"I probably shouldn't be telling you this," Cal said, "but everything I've just given you comes from an old investigation we did for Barbara Considine at the time of his affair with this girl. It was our agency that dug up the dirt on the girl—what there was of it. We kept an eye on your husband—your future husband—after that, and we determined that he never saw the girl again."

He looked at Jill. "When you gave me that photograph last week, I thought it looked familiar, so I started by checking the file of the investigation we did for Barbara. It didn't take me five minutes to find out about Miss Chamberlain."

There was a pause. Jill glanced at Cal. He was still wearing the brisk, businesslike expression behind which she could not see his real thoughts. She wondered whether he saw the irony of her position. She had taken over Barbara's place as Jordan's jealous wife. The same information that had been bought by Barbara from Cal's agency was now being given to Jill, warmed over after nearly three years in the Anspach & Cates files.

She cleared her throat nervously.

"Did Jordan find out about her child?" Jill asked slowly.

"I don't know," the detective said. "We gathered the information for his wife. Whether she shared any or all of it with him, I don't know. In any case, he stopped seeing the girl."

He gestured to the photos on the bed.

"Except for the child," he said, "there's nothing on her. She's led an exemplary life. She's a clean girl, as clean as they come." This remark could not fail to sting Jill, whose life had been anything but clean. She wondered if Cal had intended this, or whether he was simply stating a fact about Leslie.

He sat down in the chair by the window and looked at the file he had brought with him. Jill remained standing, her eyes on the photographs spread across the bed.

"Let me start from the beginning," he said. "She's a small-town girl from Illinois. Her mother died when she was a child. Her father brought her up. He was an uneducated factory worker. The daughter went through school at Cornell on a full scholarship and graduated with honors. She went to work at Ogilvie, Thorpe in June of 1971. She distinguished herself by some fine work on the Aurora Lifestyles account—she's single-handedly responsible for their new image, I might add—and some other big accounts. She was on her way to a great career. Then she suddenly quit her job. She had the baby eight months later. Here in New York."

He sat forward to turn a page of the file.

"She put the baby up for adoption," he said, "and then settled on Long Island. She got a job as a librarian, giving up her advertising career. There's one wrinkle here: I believe she moved to Long Island to be near the adoptive parents of the baby. They're a young couple; the husband is a real estate salesman. Apparently she got them to agree to let her visit the boy regularly, under the guise of an aunt. To this day she visits him at least once a month."

Jill moved closer to the bed to look at the photograph of the little boy. It was easy to see that the boy was Leslie's son. He had her features, her bone structure, and even something of her personality. He seemed intelligent and vulnerable, like his mother.

"After two and a half years at the library," Cal went on, "she went to work for this Wheeler fellow, at his small advertising agency. What changed her mind about the librarian career, I don't know. She became an important part of Wheeler's agency, which makes sense, given her talent." He looked at Jill. "Whether there was a romance with Wheeler at the time, I don't know," he added.

He turned a page of the file.

"It was after she went to work for Wheeler that she met your husband.

328

Lazarus International had acquired the parent company of which Wheeler Advertising was a part. There was a conference for new Lazarus companies, and she was sent as her boss's envoy. She must have met your husband there. They had an affair that lasted about three months. Barbara Considine hired us to find out what we could about her. All we got, of course, were the pictures of the little boy and the information about Wheeler. Barbara must have used that to confront her husband—your husband—and the affair ended just like that. Very soon afterward, Leslie married Wheeler."

Jill took this in.

"And she hasn't seen Jordan in all this time?" she asked.

He shook his head. "If they had made contact, we'd know about it."

He produced a second sheaf of photographs from his file and handed it to Jill. These were photographs of Leslie with Ross Wheeler.

"She's led a quiet life with him," Cal said. "For the first year and a half they worked together at the agency and played house. Then he had a stroke. A bad one. Since then she's been dividing her time between nursing him and handling the bulk of the work at the agency."

Jill looked through the photographs. The earlier ones showed an apparently happy young woman. There were shots of her walking with a firm, healthy stride; shots of her using her hands, which had long, elegant fingers; shots of her in informal outfits as well as business dresses. She wore both with equal ease and naturalness.

The more recent photos showed a different Leslie, and a different Ross Wheeler. Leslie looked pale and preoccupied. She had lost weight. Her husband, withered by his illness, looked like an old man. He was bent and obviously frail.

Leslie Wheeler was obviously in a state of exhaustion caused by the burden of caring for her husband while running his business. Jill also thought she saw signs of premature grief in the beautiful young face. Leslie suspected her husband was going to die, and was no doubt fighting hard to deny her own knowledge.

One of the pictures showed Leslie helping Ross out of their car. The look on her face was eloquent. It was brisk, concerned, as though this was something she had been through many times, a daily task. Yet it was full of tender solicitude and a sort of brave resignation.

But there was one thing missing from Leslie's face in all the photos taken after her marriage to Ross Wheeler. That was passion. Jill, a shrewd judge of human nature, easily saw through Leslie's loyal, supportive demeanor toward her husband. Leslie cared deeply for him, perhaps, and had committed herself to him with all her strong will. But she did not love him. Not the way a woman loves the one man her heart belongs to.

This fact only made the agonized anticipation inside Jill the more terrible.

Nothing she had heard about Leslie's little son or Ross Wheeler served to lessen the worry inside Jill's mind. She sensed that the worst was coming.

"Did Jordan know anything about this Wheeler fellow?" she asked.

"He might have," Cal said. "Wheeler was her boss at the time. Whether there was a conflict, I don't know. Maybe she already had an understanding with Wheeler. Maybe that was part of the problem with your husband. We couldn't find that out."

Jill knew somehow that this reasoning was empty. She looked at the pictures of Ross Wheeler.

"What's the prognosis for him?" she asked.

"Guarded," Cal said. "He's fighting his way back from the stroke. In a case like his, another one could come any day."

Jill reacted thoughtfully to this news. Leslie Wheeler was a caring and solicitous wife. But if and when her much older husband died, she would be free again. Free and available.

"Is there anything more for you to find?" she asked.

Cal shrugged.

"There may be a last piece of the puzzle that we don't know about. But that last piece may not be something a detective can lay his hands on. If it's inside her mind, or inside your husband's, we can't see it. That's always the limitation on what we can know."

Jill moved forward a bit unsteadily and bent to pick up the photographs, taken three years ago, which showed Leslie with Jordan.

There were a lot of pictures. There were shots of the couple going into hotels together, getting into cars, walking together on the street hand in hand.

And sure enough, there were compromising photographs of Jordan touching Leslie, kissing her. Mercifully for Jill, there were no nude photographs.

"They were too discreet," Cal said, reading her thoughts. "We couldn't get a shot of them in bed. But there was no doubt they were intimate. We got all the usual dirt on that." If his words were intended to hurt, they could not have wounded Jill more.

But the coldness settling deeper in Jill's veins as she held the pictures came from two things—her knowledge that Leslie was deeply in love with Jordan, as she had never been with the Wheeler fellow. And, more frighteningly, the obvious, undeniable fact that Jordan loved Leslie.

In the pictures there was a look in Jordan's eyes that wrung Jill's heart. A look of impassioned exultation and of delight, as though he were experiencing something that made his soul literally overflow toward Leslie.

Jill could not deny that she had never seen this look on Jordan's face. At the same time, she realized, she had seen a sort of pale facsimile of that look, a sort of ersatz expression that held more sadness than passion, more bemusement than delight. A pale, faded travesty of real love . . .

That was the look Jordan had had for Jill, both during their courtship and after their marriage.

With this thought Jill turned to a picture that showed Jordan with Leslie on the deck of the sailboat Jordan kept in Oyster Bay Harbor for use on Long Island Sound.

Cal was watching her.

"We used a telephoto lens," he said. "We couldn't get closer than fifty or sixty yards, and even then my operative was afraid he'd be noticed."

The photograph showed the boat with sails furled. Leslie was sitting on the deck holding both Jordan's hands. The close-up was grainy, but it eloquently caught the look on her face. She was telling him with her eyes that she wanted to make love.

The look on Jordan's face was a revelation to Jill. Passion transformed his features so dramatically that he seemed like a different person. His usual expression of adult competence was stripped away. He looked almost like a little boy. His desire was absolute, all-encompassing, and because of this very fact, somehow sanctified. One did not have to see what went on below the deck of that boat to know that it was love, the realest of love.

The old tremor had returned to Jill's hands, making the photo move in slow waves, almost like the waves of the ocean that rocked the boat in the picture. She recalled the boat steward's smile the day she went sailing with Jordan, when the old man mistook her for someone else.

It had been the sly look of a matchmaker, of someone who facilitates a beautiful love between two people.

Jill had laughed the embarrassing episode off that day, now so long ago. Or had she? Perhaps it had gotten under her skin even then. Was it not only a few minutes after the boatman's remark that Jill, inside the boat with Jordan on the Sound, had had the first orgasm of her life? An explosion of passion that had sounded the final knell for her carefree career on the surface of herself and opened a sort of trap door into murky depths in which she had been flailing desperately ever since . . .

Cal Weathers was sitting in his chair, saying nothing. Jill wondered whether the look on her face was betraying all her secrets to him. But she was beyond hiding things now. The truth was coiled around her like a serpent hungry to squeeze the life out of her.

A long time later, when she had lost Jordan and seen her own life approach its finish line, Jill would look back and remember this moment as the beginning of it all, or indeed the end: Cal calmly watching from his chair as the truth pierced all her masks, letting the air out of her carefully constructed life as out of a child's balloon.

And it was a double truth, a truth that began in the outside world and ended inside Jill herself. On one hand, the pictures showed that her fears about the nameless girl hidden in the volume of Shakespeare were true. Leslie Chamberlain had owned Jordan's heart.

On the other hand, and even more terrible, was the fact that the unseen model Jill had imitated from the moment she met Jordan—the model she had come to resemble more and more uncannily, even changing her hair to fit it, in a disguise that had fooled the poor boatman at the marina, just as it had fooled Jordan himself—that model was Leslie Chamberlain.

The irony was not lost on Jill. She herself was proof in flesh and blood that Jordan had not gotten over Leslie, and never would.

Cal was saying something, but Jill did not hear him. She stood with the photographs in her hands, no longer looking at them, but staring at the wall above the bed through unseeing eyes. She had lost contact with herself as well as her surroundings.

At length Cal took his leave, no doubt promising to keep in touch. She did not hear his words. His voice was lost in the inhuman murmur inside her, a seismic rumble that shook her to her foundations.

A few minutes after he had gone she found herself in the bathroom, staring at herself in the mirror. The sheaf of pictures of Jordan with Leslie Chamberlain were still in her hand.

She no longer recognized the face in the mirror. It was as strange to her as an image in a nightmare. Obscurely she realized that the enemy she had been fleeing all her life, since she was a tiny girl, was face to face with her now, having waited patiently through all her adventures, all her triumphs, for the moment of this final confrontation. That enemy was herself.

There was nowhere to flee. Jill stood mesmerized for a long time, staring wide-eyed into the mirror. The strong will inside her began to dissolve.

The monster in the glass beckoned again, and came forward. Jill cried out and cringed away, dropping the pictures at her feet. Too late. The change was made.

When she left the hotel a few minutes later, no one saw the difference in her.

49

LESLIE WAS AT THE HOSPITAL, waiting for Ross to come out of his latest battery of neurological tests. These tests, which had seemed rather innocent when Leslie had first been familiarized with them by the hospital technicians, had now assumed an increasingly ominous significance in her mind. Along with Ross's skull X-rays, electroencephalograms, and CAT scans, they were like a judgment from a high court. The doctors studied them long and hard to determine the blood supply to Ross's brain and the state of his cognitive function. A bad score on the neurological tests could indicate that Ross had suffered additional strokes, and that the overall trend of his brain function was downward.

When and if this was found to be the case, there would be no treatment. Medical science had no weapons against the death of brain cells due to insufficient blood supply. Leslie had questioned Ross's specialists closely, and although their language was abstruse and their bedside manner full of deliberate reassurance, she knew they were watching and waiting for signs that Ross's condition was crossing over into the incurable. In the meantime the hard work of rehabilitation went on, but with no certainty of long-term improvement.

So today Leslie was on tenterhooks as usual. She had already tried and failed to concentrate on the magazine she was reading. The words blurred before her eyes. The TV in the waiting room was turned up too loud, and the game show that was on made it even harder for Leslie to think.

Suddenly a voice said, "Would you mind if I turned that down?"

Leslie looked up to see a young woman in jeans and a knit blouse smiling uncertainly at her. The young woman was pointing at the blaring TV.

"Be my guest," Leslie said. "It's driving me crazy, if you want to know the truth."

"Me, too," the girl said, rising to turn the volume down to a murmur.

When she sat back down the girl looked at Leslie.

"Are you new here?" she asked.

Leslie shook her head. "My husband has been coming for six months," she said.

The girl nodded. "It's been two years for us. My father had a coronary. I'm surprised I haven't seen you before."

Leslie put down her magazine.

"My husband had a stroke," she said.

The girl nodded. "Most of the people are here for stroke. My dad's the oddball."

Leslie instinctively liked the young woman. She seemed a bit common, uneducated. She wore an obvious wig, too dark and not of the highest quality, and she wore too much makeup. She might be a waitress, a cashier. But she was very pretty. And her worry was as palpable as Leslie's own.

"I never thought waiting could be such a terrible thing," the girl said.

"I know what you mean," Leslie smiled.

The girl moved a seat closer and held out her hand.

"My name's Shielah," she said. "Shielah Fahey. Pleased to meet you."

"Leslie Wheeler. It's nice to meet you, Shielah."

"I hate this place more than anything," the girl said. "I've always hated hospitals. My mother died in a hospital five years ago. Now Daddy . . . It's hell."

There was something thoughtful about her that caught Leslie's eye. It was obvious she was intelligent despite her lack of education.

"Is your husband in rehab?" she asked.

Leslie nodded. "He has physical therapy every afternoon," she said. "He's here for some neurological tests today."

"You're lucky in a way," the girl said. "At least you get to fight back. With my dad we can't do anything but wait. When he gets out of here I'm taking him back to the nursing home. He's in too bad shape to do anything right now."

The two young women fell into conversation about the headaches of hospital life. Shielah Fahey knew something about strokes, having had two grandparents who had suffered them. One of them, the grandfather, was still alive, though living in a nursing home.

"I never thought anything could cost so much," she complained. "Social Security and Medicare are just a drop in the bucket. My grandfather had a pension from his company, but that doesn't amount to a hill of beans. With Dad it's the same way. We're going to have to bring him home next fall even if things don't get better."

She looked at Leslie. "How about you?" she asked.

"Well, Ross—that's my husband—can pretty much take care of himself at home," Leslie said. "But he can't drive, so I bring him here and pick him up. We run a little ad agency in town, and I work there. He tries to help, but it's not very easy." She sighed. "You just have to do the best you can, I guess."

"Wheeler Advertising?" the girl exclaimed. "On Church Street? Sure, I know it. My dad used to do business there. So your husband's Mr. Wheeler."

Leslie nodded.

"I guess you're pretty squeezed, financially, yourself," Shielah said.

Leslie grimaced. "Pretty much," she said.

The girl opened the magazine in her lap.

"Now, if we had this guy's money," she said, gesturing to a photograph on the cover of the magazine, "we wouldn't have to worry so much."

Leslie leaned over to look. It was a copy of *Time* magazine with a picture of Jordan Lazarus on the cover. The headline read, SAVIOR OF THE INNER CITIES? The subhead, no doubt about Jordan Lazarus's lobbying efforts in Congress on behalf of his urban reclamation plan, was too small for Leslie to read from where she sat.

She turned a shade paler than before but fought back her emotion. Jordan Lazarus seemed a million miles away from this drab waiting room with its molded plastic chairs, its dog-eared magazines, and old TV set.

"Yes," she sighed. "I'm sure you're right about that."

The girl jiggled her foot nervously—she was wearing jogging shoes—as she looked at the magazine. "I've always wondered what it's like to be rich," she said. "All my life I've been so busy trying to make ends meet, I haven't had time to think about much else. What do you think it's like to be loaded, really loaded?"

Leslie was looking straight ahead of her now. She seemed a long way off. She was making an effort not to look at the photograph of Jordan.

"I don't know," she said. "I guess I can't imagine it, either."

"Well, I suppose they have their problems, too," Shielah Fahey said. "My dad used to say that money only makes big problems cost less. It doesn't make them go away."

Leslie smiled wanly. "I'm sure he was right," she said. "Anyway, I'll never know." She was painfully aware of how much Ross's treatment was costing them. It was quickly reducing Ross's comfortably suburban lifestyle to something on the edge of poverty.

She felt oddly calm, here in the company of this sympathetic stranger, with the cold, indifferent world at arm's length outside this little room. Even their shared unhappiness seemed to help.

They chatted for a few more moments, and then fell silent. The girl sat with crossed legs, bouncing her foot nervously as she read her magazine. She smelled faintly of cigarette smoke, but had not lit up since Leslie had been in the room.

Leslie had taken an instinctive liking to Shielah, and was on the point of asking her to have coffee with her next time their hospital visits brought them together. Before she could say anything, Shielah stood up.

"Excuse me," she said. "Do you know where the nearest ladies' room is?"

"Just down the hall to the right," Leslie said.

Shielah got up and left the room, throwing the copy of *Time* on the table top.

Leslie sat staring at the television screen. The game show was still on, but she did not see it. She could feel the magazine pulling her eyes like a magnet. After a moment she leaned forward and picked it up. Her fingers trembled as the image of Jordan smiled up at her. He looked older than when she had known him, and a bit thinner. It seemed that great success had taken something out of him.

But the old Jordan was still there. Leslie saw the gentleness in his eyes, the humor, and that touch of adolescent sweetness that had stolen her heart so long ago.

She closed her eyes and held the magazine to her breast for one painful instant. Then, thinking of Ross undergoing his frightening tests just down the corridor, she let the magazine drop and held it in her lap.

As she did so a single tear fell from her eye and dropped on the magazine cover, staining the cheek of Jordan Lazarus.

A little gasp escaped Leslie's lips as she hurriedly reached to rub the tear into the glossy paper. She watched the tear become a moist wrinkle in the magazine cover. She could not hear the moan of sorrow that stirred in her throat as she tried to erase the trace of her emotion.

She threw the magazine on the table and sat back to watch the murmuring television and try to regain control of herself. The distant busy sounds of nurses and doctors down the corridor helped her to recall where she was.

It never occurred to her that for the last sixty seconds—the duration of her eloquent little pantomime with the magazine—she had been watched.

Leslie did not see Shielah Fahey again. Ross came out a few minutes later and Leslie took him home. On the way she mentioned she had met a nice girl in the waiting room, a girl whose father had had a heart attack. Ross could not remember having met anyone named Fahey. On the other hand, there were so many patients coming in and out of the testing area that it would have been easy to miss one.

Leslie did not think any more about pretty Shielah Fahey that day. She was too busy taking care of Ross.

Thus she never thought to wonder why a young woman who had ostensibly been coming to the hospital for two years would not know where the nearest ladies' room was.

Leslie had far too much on her mind to think about such things.

* * *

336

As for Jill Lazarus, she sat behind the wheel of her car, watching Leslie's station wagon inch its way out of the parking lot.

The last question in Jill's mind had been answered this morning. Not only had she confirmed what she already suspected in coming here, but she had gathered a hundred little observations from her few minutes with Leslie Wheeler, observations that would be invaluable to her in what she now had to do.

She started the engine. She glanced at the rearview mirror. She knew that if she were to turn it toward her she would see what she had seen in the bathroom the day Cal Weathers had brought her the truth about Jordan and Leslie. She shuddered at the thought. She knew that if she ever looked at that face again she would have to kill herself.

Her greatest enemy now was the mirror. If she let it see her as she really was, she was finished.

Her only hope, her last chance, lay in one final camouflage.

50

New York City
February 10, 1979

IT HAD BEEN A DIFFICULT DAY for Jordan Lazarus.

He had had morning and afternoon meetings with senators and representatives from Illinois, New York, California, Ohio, Georgia, and Michigan—the states with the biggest cities in the nation—and a long lunch with the president's closest adviser on domestic policy.

Jordan had expended an almost inhuman amount of energy and persuasiveness in lobbying these powerful men for support of the Lazarus bill in Congress. He had offered them favors that, in other circumstances, they would have jumped at the chance of accepting.

But their reaction had not been what he had hoped for. To a man they were friendly, supportive, and impressed by Jordan's logic as well as his power. And, as representatives of states whose economies depended on the well-being and vitality of large cities, they were genuinely in favor of the Lazarus bill. Their states' futures depended on it.

But they also knew that the majority leader of the Senate, a ranking member of the Senate committees on finance and appropriations and a close personal friend of the president since their days as Yale undergraduates, was dead set against the Lazarus bill, and was using all his influence in both houses of Congress to stop the bill's passage.

The majority leader hailed from Wyoming, a state with no major cities. He feared that passage of the Lazarus bill would take precious federal funds away from his own state and make him look bad in the eyes of his constituents. His political stock at home had been slipping in recent years, thanks to his own rather lackluster election campaigns and to the emergence of some aggressive young opponents within his own party. This was hardly the time for him to assent to the passage of a bill that might greatly anger his grass roots supporters.

However, his influence inside Congress was as strong as ever. And not even those most enthusiastic about the Lazarus bill dared to vote for it until the majority leader had been won over.

So far Jordan, despite his personal charm, fiscal power, and popularity with the public, had failed to accomplish this. The majority leader was a stubborn man.

In another year, with a different Congress, Jordan's bill would have passed easily. But at this moment in history, with the majority leader standing squarely in the way, the Lazarus bill had no realistic chance of passage.

Jordan came home from work exhausted. Never had his work seemed so difficult or so frustrating. Even though it was this very plan that had saved him from his grief after he lost Leslie, it now seemed he had bitten off more than he could chew. His heart was heavy. His vision for the cities was clearer than ever in his mind, but the struggle to sell it to self-interested politicians and business leaders was making it seem more improbable and unrealistic than ever.

Tonight Jordan wanted a hot shower and a strong drink. And he wanted to see his wife, to hold her in his arms and try to forget the dirty business of the day.

He turned his key in the lock. The foyer was dark.

"I'm home, dear," he called out in his joking way, putting down his briefcase and taking off his coat.

He hung the coat in the closet and looked at the dark living room. There was no sign of Jill. He walked down the hall toward the kitchen. There was not a sound in the apartment. He wondered if she was asleep. That would be unusual. She never slept at such an early hour. Perhaps she was out.

He glanced into the bedroom. It was dark. He went to the living room and poured himself a glass of bourbon. He stood in the silence, thinking. Where could Jill be? Was she out somewhere?

338

Jordan began to worry. Jill had not been herself lately. For the last few weeks she had been nervous, edgy, and secretive. He had tried to draw her out about her feelings, but she had retreated within herself. His own hard work and exhaustion had prevented him from finding the time to discuss things with her, and he felt remiss as a husband.

He started down the hall, checking the guest bedrooms. All were dark. The silence in the apartment was oppressive. The muted sounds of the city outside only served to accentuate the dark and somewhat foreboding atmosphere within.

At last Jordan came to the solarium. It was dark. This was the last room he would expect Jill to be in at this hour. She rarely came here after dark.

Jordan opened the door. The enormous window on the East River loomed before him, dimly illuminated by the glow of the city outside. In the instant before he turned on the light he thought he saw a shape before the window. But he did not wonder what it might be until it was too late.

He flipped the wall switch. All at once the entire room was bathed in bright light.

Jordan's breath caught in his throat.

Standing before him, wearing the flowery summer dress he had loved so well, was Leslie Chamberlain.

For a long moment he stood staring at her. It was as though a ghost had appeared before him.

"Leslie."

He did not know whether he actually spoke the word. It came to his lips like a foreign body that had been hiding deep inside him.

His knees felt weak. Had there been a wall or a piece of furniture next to him he would have grasped it for support. He stood trembling, his eyes riveted to the figure before him. He could not see his own expression, which was worth a thousand words.

Jordan was caught between terror and longing. The sight of Leslie, after all this time, stripped away the many defenses he had so cautiously constructed against her, and left him helpless as a child.

But there was something macabre about the figure before him. It seemed calculated to create this response in him, this floundering helplessness. It looked more like a symbol than a real person. A symbol of his love and of his loss. The apparition cast a spell so powerful that Jordan felt he would drown in it if he did not fight to hang on to himself.

And it was in that struggle to return to his own identity that he recognized Jill.

The resemblance to Leslie was uncanny. Jill had managed to find the same dress, the same hat, the same shoes, and to make herself up in a virtual mask of Leslie as he had loved her most.

But the illusion was more than physical. It included Leslie's posture, her bearing, the look in her eyes, the smile on her lips. This was a spiritual resemblance. The very essence of Leslie seemed stamped on the face of Jill for some awful reason.

The look of love that had spread over Jordan's features upon first seeing her was gone now, replaced by shock.

"I—what do you think you're doing?" Jordan asked, his voice shaking.

She was silent. She did not move a muscle. She simply posed for him, flaunting her ability to copy the object of his desire down to its finest subtlety. And perhaps it was this hint of triumph in her posing that showed up the falseness of what Jordan saw before him. This was not Leslie at all. This was Jill, her entire being focused with insane intensity on dissolving herself into the image of another woman.

He took a pace forward. His approach did not seem to shatter the illusion she had created. She became more real, and yet more unreal, as he came nearer.

"I asked you a question," Jordan hissed, his blood rising within him. "What do you think you're doing?"

Her eyebrow raised slightly. Her eyes sparkled as she looked at him.

"I'm doing what you want," she said. "You know that."

He moved slowly toward her. The sight of her made him sick at heart, and yet stirred something uncontrollable within him.

"Jill," he said. "Have you lost your mind? What put this idea into your head?"

Jordan looked as though he were going to explode. Jill, behind her mask, was calm, brought to a strange stillness by months of desperation.

"Welcome home," she said in a voice uncannily similar to Leslie's. "I've missed you, Jordan."

He stared at her in consternation.

"You're crazy," he said. "Stop this."

She lifted her hand from her hip and brushed it across her forehead to remove a lock of hair from her eyes. It was Leslie's gesture, performed as simply and naturally as Leslie would have done it herself. There was a look of trusting affection in her eyes. It was a look he had seen in Leslie's eyes a thousand times.

"I love you, Jordan," she said in a whisper that sent a chill down his spine. "I want you to have what you want."

Jordan ran a hand through his hair. His jaw was clenched tight. He almost rubbed his eyes to try to erase what he was seeing.

"You're insane," he said. "You're out of your mind, Jill."

She smiled. "You can call me Leslie if you want to," she said. "I won't mind. It's what we've both been waiting for."

He stepped back a pace as though to defend himself against her. But distance was no more helpful to him than nearness. The power of the illusion she had created was too great.

"I know what you want," she said. "You don't have to lie anymore, Jordan. Just come to me, and it will be like it always was."

She held out her arms. "My Prince Charming," she said.

Jordan felt his world tilt crazily toward her. Her madness was infectious, spreading through his limbs. He could not take his eyes off her.

"Come on," she said. "I love you. Don't make me wait . . ."

Jordan took another step backward.

"Jill," he said. "I'm worried about you. Let me get you some help. You're not . . ."

You're not yourself. Comically the words were on the tip of his tongue.

She began to walk toward him. It was Leslie's walk, her hands curled gently at her sides. Her eyes glimmered with Leslie's humor and kindness.

"Do you remember the day I wore this dress?" she said. "We were so full of love that day, so full of hope. Do you remember, Jordan?"

She was close to him now. The scent of her was Leslie's scent. Jordan felt his last defenses begin to crumble. It was not only the perfection of the illusion that seduced him but its perversity.

"Come on," she said. "Just like old times. Just like on the Sound. Help me off with this."

She guided his hand to her dress. His eyes closed as her lips brushed his own. Then his hands were behind her back, loosening the dress, finding the hook of her bra. The fabric tumbled to the floor with a muted sigh, and he felt the skin of her back under his fingertips.

"Oh, I've missed you so much," she sighed, kissing him again.

He knew she was acting. There was not an ounce of truth in her whole performance. Yet the words she had spoken struck straight to his heart. They were the things he had longed to hear for three terrible years, without daring to admit it to himself. And the voice that had spoken them was Leslie's voice, full of tenderness and understanding.

Jordan was atrociously hard under his pants. He was on the brink of losing himself. She was sucking him down the same chasm into which she herself had fallen.

He tried to recover his balance, his identity, but she was nearly naked now, clad only in her panties. She moved closer, fitting her body to his. The small, firm breasts were against his chest, and his own fingers, guided by her hands, were pulling the panties down her thighs.

"Oh, Jordie," she purred. "I've missed you so." Her tongue touched his own in light, subtle strokes. Even the taste of her on his lips was full of Leslie's freshness.

She gazed into his eyes with a look of triumph from which anguish was not absent.

He wanted to strangle her. His hands encircled her neck. But she only smiled. Even his violence seemed to confirm her power over him.

"So this is what's been in your mind all along," he said.

"In *your* mind," she corrected. "Don't fight it, Jordan. You know you don't want to."

There was something witchlike about her as she nestled in his arms. And now she was naked. He kissed her. He felt her limbs stir against him. She knew that, in her disguise, she was irresistible to him.

"Yes," she murmured. "Yes, Jordan . . ."

He swept her into his arms. She was light as a feather, lighter than air. She seemed less than real, and yet more attractive, more powerful than a merely real object.

He placed her on the bed and took off his clothes. She watched in silence, a look of satisfaction on her beautiful face.

When he was naked, his desire visible between his legs, she lay back and smiled up at him.

"Come on," she said. "What are you afraid of? I want you so, Jordan. I'm waiting for you."

Jordan covered her with himself. Her flesh caressed him from head to toe. He felt her hands press at the small of his back. Her legs curled about him with shy intimacy.

The waiting door at the center of her opened for the tip of him, sweet and moist, and in a trice he was inside her. Their bodies began to move, the music of their arousal almost inhuman. She glowed and fluttered in his arms, tantalizing and unreal as a will-o'-the-wisp.

A hand stole between his legs to find him and encourage him. The tongue inside his mouth moved catlike, licking him to greater excitement. Female sinews clever as fingers worked up and down his sex, tickling and urging and teasing. Sweet undulations of female hips pulled him deeper, deeper.

Something began to come forward within him, and he strained harder inside her. But his wanting was so inseparable from the horror he felt that it grew and grew, ever more painful, without spending himself. He thought that soon he must burst.

He was teetering on the edge of this abyss when he looked into her eyes again. Their falseness was bottomless, like a mirror in which a thousand images of his own need were reflected. He saw her victory. He knew he was found out. Through her disguise she was touching something far deeper in him than what he had ever showed her before. He felt naked and exposed. And his body throbbed with a ghastly, perverse pleasure born of her own falseness and his.

"I love you," she said.

The wave inside Jordan was crashing higher and higher, and he could barely catch his breath. Leslie's murmur was still in his ears, Leslie's hands still caressing him to surrender.

"I love you," he groaned.

"Yes," she whispered. "Yes . . ."

Aghast at his fall and at her victory, Jordan gave himself.

The next morning Jill woke up alone.

Dazed, she looked at the alarm clock on her bedside table. It was nearly ten o'clock. Jordan must have long since left for work.

Jill felt confused but well rested. She reflected that this was the first time in months she had slept so well.

In a sense it was no wonder. The passion that had joined her to Jordan last night had been like an earthquake. It had left them both so drained that they fell asleep like children, side by side in the large bed.

Jill would remember that endless, exhausting tryst as long as she lived. It had been a sort of phantasmagoria, a ghastly coupling fired by desire and shame, devouring them both. Jordan had been like an animal, a crazed madman, in his possession of her.

As she lay numbed by pleasure, she knew that her gambit had worked. The illusion she had forced on him had indeed been irresistible. He had not been able to fight it. He had given in. She had found out the truth about him, and with his body and his moans of love he had given her that truth. They had been naked together, naked as never before, their masks pulled off once and for all.

Jill was frightened by what she herself had achieved. Yet there was satisfaction in her soul as well as her body this morning. Her lifetime of falseness had reached its pinnacle last night. And that falseness, ironically, had at last given her a hold on truth. The truth about Jordan.

The next question was what she was going to do about it. What they were both going to do. She lay in bed musing over this for another half hour. Then she got up and moved on unsteady legs to the closet.

When she opened the closet door she saw that several of Jordan's suits were gone. So were some of his shirts, his slacks, his underwear.

Jill felt a coldness spread inside her. So she had pushed him too far. Intimidated by what she had made him do, he had fled. But he would come back. She was convinced of that. He could not resist her now. Last night she had unveiled a weapon against which he had no defenses.

She went back to bed. She stayed there a long time, pondering her choices. Then she called Jordan at the office. He was in a meeting, she was told, and would call her back.

She put some coffee on to perk and took a shower. She dressed and drank her coffee, waiting for the phone to ring. She waited all morning, then into the afternoon. The call did not come.

At four o'clock a message was brought to her by a Lazarus employee who picked up some more of Jordan's clothes and toilet articles before he left.

The message was in Jordan's hand.

"You're on your own now," it read. "We have nothing more to say to each other. My attorneys will be in touch with you."

Written below this, as on an afterthought, were the words "Take care of yourself."

The note was not signed.

Jill watched the messenger leave with another suitcase full of Jordan's things. The scribbled words, *You're on your own now,* throbbed inside her breast like a knell of doom. Jordan must know that solitude was the worst punishment he could inflict upon her. His choice of words had been intentionally eloquent, cruel.

When she was alone she went to the bedroom where her husband had made love to her last night. She stood before the full-length mirror, looking at herself.

The image was still colored by last night's obsession. The hair was Leslie's. Traces of the makeup she had used to complete the illusion remained. Even her posture, the look in her eyes recalled the perfection of her performance.

But this was not Leslie. This was Jill. The mirror winked back at her, canceling all her illusions and reminding her of the one reality she could bear least of all.

She was alone.

51

SIX WEEKS WENT BY. Jordan did not see Jill, nor did he allow himself to think about her.

Not for the first time in his life, Jordan Lazarus threw himself into his work.

He worked eighteen-hour days at his office, most of the time on the telephone, calling in favors, making contacts, making arrangements for meetings. The rest of the time he spent in silent meditation, the telephone turned off, his secretary forbidden to ring or knock.

He thought only about the Lazarus bill and the weapons he could improvise to get it passed. This was the final battle of Jordan Lazarus against the world. And Jordan was determined to win.

During that time Jill barely glimmered for a second before his preoccupied mind. He told himself that a plan capable of changing the face of a whole nation was more important than the petty emotional life of one married couple—a couple soon to be divorced in any case.

But this pretense at objectivity was merely a screen covering the truth. Jill was never really out of Jordan's mind for a single moment. Her shadow lingered behind all his preoccupations and actions. And because of her there was an edge of desperation in everything Jordan felt during this period.

A great, angry coldness settled inside him now, giving him an icy sense of control in all his dealings with other men. Perhaps because he had buried his own feelings so deep inside him, he saw the chessboard of his professional life with an almost inhuman clarity.

The challenge before him was the most important he had ever faced, and the stakes were higher than anything he had seen in his business career. This time history itself hung in the balance. Jordan's own self-interest played no part in his plans. The welfare of his country was his only concern.

At last Jordan Lazarus had become a visionary, just as Meg had always predicted. Through the circuitous route of action and worldly ambition, he had finally succeeded in painting his picture, writing his poem. That picture was the Lazarus Plan.

Yet the final brush stroke could never be applied until the key obstacle in Jordan's path was removed. And that obstacle was the majority leader of the United States Senate.

Perhaps because of the historic significance of the challenge before him, or because of the deep personal crisis he was trying so hard to evade, Jordan now found the solution to the puzzle.

He conceived an ingenious quid pro quo that would weaken the majority leader's opposition to the Lazarus bill. It included a plan to move one of Lazarus International's biggest and most wealthy corporations into Wyoming. This move alone would bring the state twenty thousand jobs and millions of dollars in revenues.

The plan also called for the opening of major new branches of one of Jordan's richest banks throughout Wyoming. Another deal included the acquisition of one of the biggest Wyoming television stations by a Lazarus communications subsidiary and the syndication of some of the station's programming on the new cable network Jordan had formed in the previous year.

This was only the beginning. Jordan proposed a stunning array of financial plans that would do wonders for Wyoming's economy and contribute importantly to modernizing the state's antiquated industrial and financial base. It would be the most important single advance taken by the state since before the Depression.

But the deal Jordan offered was more complex than its surface indicated. Underneath, the advantages to the majority leader himself were enormous.

Nearly every element of Jordan's multifaceted offer bore hidden links to companies in which the majority leader held stock or was a board member, or to banks with which he did business. Jordan's offer was a patchwork quilt of apparently innocent business incentives, good for Wyoming, but also bringing millions of dollars indirectly into the pocket of the majority leader, increasing his personal fortune by nearly half.

Tempting though it was, this package might not have swayed the majority leader had it been proposed by Jordan himself. But it was precisely on this point that Jordan chose to apply his master stroke.

The package was outlined not by Jordan but by the president himself, in the Oval Office, after a cordial hour spent reminiscing with the majority leader about the two men's undergraduate days at Yale.

What Jordan himself had begun, the president finished. And he did so with great conviction and few scruples, because the passage of the Lazarus bill was crucial to the future of the nation he led—not to mention his chances for victory in next year's election.

Within twenty-four hours after that private meeting, the majority leader revealed to his Senate colleagues that he was throwing all his support and influence behind the Lazarus Inner Cities Reclamation Act. He would twist every arm he could, and call in three decades of favors, in order to get the plan passed in Congress and approved by the White House.

The congressional log jam surrounding the controversial bill collapsed overnight. Opposition to the plan in the Senate withered. Eloquent speeches were made on its behalf, and the committee vote was 27 to 2 in favor of passage of the Lazarus bill.

Within days it was a foregone conclusion that the bill would be passed by both houses of Congress. The president let it be known that he would not veto the bill if and when it passed. Insiders close to the Supreme Court assured the bill's supporters that there was no danger of a constitutional barrier to implementation.

City planning experts as well as specialists in taxation and economics were buzzing with speculation about the eventual effects of the revolutionary bill. Articles about Jordan Lazarus and his visionary plan for the cities appeared in political and economic journals as well as popular magazines. The whole nation began to awaken to the notion that something epoch-making was afoot in Congress.

Jordan Lazarus's dream was about to become a reality.

On a breezy Thursday at the end of March Jordan finished a day spent answering congratulatory phone calls from all over the country, and prepared to leave his office.

When he stood up from his desk Jordan suddenly realized how exhausted he was. He actually felt lightheaded. He had been too busy to eat lunch today. He would have to start taking better care of himself. There was a real reason to start living again now. The obsessed overwork of the past few weeks would have to give way to steady, cautious forward progress without undue stress. Up until now he had been trying to outrun his own demons. In the future he would pursue a dream that gave new meaning to his whole life.

It was with this thought in mind that Jordan left his inner office.

He stopped in his tracks when he saw he had an unexpected visitor.

It was Jill.

Jordan's eyes opened wide. He had not seen his wife in over six weeks. He had expected never to see her again. His attorneys had written to hers but had not yet received an answer.

Jill looked pale and drawn. He had not seen her since the night she had presented herself to him in her insane disguise, a night he would spend the rest of his life trying to forget.

"Fancy meeting you here," he said.

"Hello, Jordan."

"To what do I owe the pleasure?" He could feel a great coldness arming him to reject her.

She got up and took a small step toward him. There was a strange look in her eyes, somewhere between challenge and supplication.

"I have some news," she said. "I'd like to talk to you for a moment."

He raised an eyebrow with studied arrogance.

"That's funny," he said. "I thought we had pretty much exhausted our news, Jill. Can there be more surprises left?"

She looked truly wounded by his sarcasm.

"Maybe I should go, then," she said.

He had never seen her look so pathetic. She seemed shrunken and defenseless, like a shadow of her former self. In that instant his heart went out to her.

But he would not allow himself to soften toward her. No person in his life had hurt him as this woman had. She had married him under false pretenses. She had penetrated his emotional defenses when he most needed to keep them strong, and then laid bare his own obsession in a way that destroyed his heart. He did not hate her, but he could not bear to see her face or hear her voice again. He just wanted her out of his life.

"All right," he said coldly. "If you must."

He moved toward her. Even the act of decreasing the physical distance between them filled him with revulsion. He would always regard her as a sort of witch who had entered his life by a gigantic stroke of ill luck and come close to destroying it.

He picked up her coat and held it out to her. She took it with a trembling hand and tried to put it on. Forgetting himself as a host, he watched her without offering to help. She struggled with the sleeve; he came to himself and reached to help her.

As she stood with her back to him he heard her say something. The words, spoken very softly, were obscured by the rustle of the fabric on her shoulders.

"What did you say?" Jordan asked.

She was turning. She looked up at him.

"I said I'm pregnant." Her eyes were on him, clear and unblinking.

Jordan actually backed up a pace, as though struck in the face by her words. Then he forced himself to stand his ground.

Pregnant. Somehow that word had never occurred to him in connection with Jill. She was a siren, yes. A seductress. But a mother? The notion was impossible.

Hoping to defend himself against it, he looked for the cruelest words he could find.

"How do you know it's mine?" he asked.

She smiled sadly.

"It's yours, Jordan."

He stepped back another pace, staring hard at her.

"Why should I believe you?" he said. "You've never told me the truth about anything before. Why change now?"

He was speaking quickly, as though to silence the words he knew were coming to her lips. She waited patiently for him to finish.

Then, without looking at him, she spoke.

"That night," she said. "It was that night."

Anger hot as molten steel flared inside Jordan's mind. He wanted to kill this woman for what she had done to him. But somehow he knew she was telling the truth. This made him hate her the more, but destroyed the armor he had so carefully built against her.

"You're a liar," he said unconvincingly.

Jill simply shook her head. She looked very small and weak, but armed with a weapon he could not fight.

"And even if you were telling the truth," he said, "it wouldn't make any difference between us."

His lie sounded hollow on his lips. He realized that her news meant everything, changed everything. Except for his aversion for her, that is, which would never die.

There was a long silence. They stood only two feet from each other. He wished he could put a world between himself and her. The sight of her sickened him.

"What do you want to do?" she asked at last.

The sound of her words made him want to strangle her. But his own child was inside her. Killing her now would do no good.

"Get rid of it," he said, his voice shaking.

She looked up at him. "Do you mean that?"

She had seen through him, of course. He knew her baby was his. He also knew when it had been conceived. He would remember that night as long as he lived.

He gazed darkly at her. She had already torn him apart with her lies, her clever masks, and the perverse ray of intuition that had allowed her to see beneath his own surface. She was falseness incarnate, and she had made him false. Nothing that might join them in the future could change that.

But she had his child.

"No," he said, defeated. "I didn't mean it."

He looked at her in consternation. The crystalline depths of her eyes were opening wider, as if to drink him in. In that instant she looked more beautiful, more horrible than ever before.

Conflicting forces impelled Jordan toward his wife and pulled him away with unbearable power. What strength he had was exhausted in simply standing his ground.

As for Jill, she remained staring at him, her raincoat hiding the slender body, which had hypnotized him with its charm, contaminated him with its deceit, and which now bore the embryo of his child.

"All right," Jordan said. "All right."

Neither moved. Husband and wife stood gazing into each other's eyes, separated by a gulf as infinite as the living flesh that bound them together now, for all time.

52

Johnsonville, Long Island

ON MARCH 30, 1979, Ross Wheeler suffered a minor stroke.

He lost some of the motor function he had regained in the left side of his body after months of physical therapy, and "flunked" some questions on his cognitive tests that had been easy for him before.

The doctors were encouraging to Leslie, telling her that episodes like this were common among stroke patients, and were a "setback" that patients and families had to live with. Leslie was not convinced by this version of things, but lacked both the financial resources to seek a second opinion and the courage to listen to such an opinion. She clung to the doctors' optimism with childlike dependency, even as she sensed inwardly the ominous truth they were trying to hide from her.

Ross had to spend two weeks in the hospital for observation and further tests. The cost of this latest hospitalization would force Leslie to take out a second mortgage on the house, and perhaps even to seek loans from some of Ross's far-flung relatives and her own. The embarrassment of asking for money did not distress her half so much as the progress of her husband's illness. She dreaded seeing the end of her life with him come close. She spent half her time frantically trying to deny it, and the other half struggling to prepare herself somehow for whatever was coming.

On this day she left Ross's room in the late morning and told him she would not be back until evening visiting hours. She had a lot to do at the office, she said. Recent events had put her behind schedule on a number of accounts.

Ross was sympathetic, and urged her to get her work done, even if it meant not seeing him again that day.

"And make sure those girls take some of the weight off your shoulders," he said. "Tell them the boss said so."

He squeezed her hand. They were both afraid, but Ross was the braver of the two. Though he looked weaker, and his face was distorted by that look of inner pain that so disturbed Leslie, he kept the armor of his levity around them both, and helped keep her despair at a distance.

Leslie hugged him hard. "I love you so much," she murmured in an anxious little whisper.

"Love you too, kid," he said.

There were tears in her eyes as she waved good-bye from the doorway. He had noticed this about her ever since the first stroke, this touching inability to control her tears every time they were separated.

Leslie did not go to the office. She drove straight from the hospital to the Long Island Expressway, and managed the trip to Farmington in less than an hour, driving too fast all the way.

When she arrived Cliff Beyer was at work, but Georgia was at home with Terry.

Leslie could hardly contain her surprise at the sight of the little boy. His legs were longer, his face narrower, and something about his eyes was more mature than she remembered. It had been almost six months since she had seen him. Ross's illness had taken up so much of her time and attention that she hadn't even called the Beyers in weeks.

Georgia knew about Leslie's troubles, and greeted her with a warm, understanding hug.

"How is Ross?" she asked in a low voice.

"As well as can be expected, I guess," Leslie answered, whispering so as not to let the little boy hear the worry in her voice.

Terry, now six and a half, was shy with Leslie as usual. But he showed his shyness by speaking to her in remote, polite tones, instead of hanging back in his mother's skirts the way he used to do. Leslie felt a pang in her heart to think of the months of growth she had missed in him. She felt as though she had betrayed him, and herself.

At first she was off balance and clumsy as she tried to make conversation with him. For a long time she could not bridge the distance between them. Her preoccupation with Ross seemed to have sapped her talent at communicating with the little boy.

But then their old intimacy began to assert itself. Terry showed her some toys and games he had received for his last birthday. Among them was a story book she had sent. His mastery in handling the toys and in explaining their uses filled her with pride.

"You've grown," Leslie said, feeling her heart beat harder as she contemplated his little face. "You're more handsome now, Terry. Soon the girls will be running after you wherever you go."

He smiled. "Oh, I don't know," he said in a diffident and very mature little voice.

Leslie tried to hide the anguish in her eyes. He was so much bigger now, and changing so fast! Six months was a short interval for adults but an enormous space of time for children, who went through huge metamorphoses during it.

"You're thinner," Terry said, showing off his own memory and surprising her by his perception.

Now Leslie reflected that the last year had been a revolution for her as well. In that time her married life had changed completely, as had all her expectations for herself. She had been forced to adjust to a new sort of life, and it had left its mark on her.

"Why don't we help Leslie make a snack?" Georgia said.

They made a sort of afternoon tea, with coffee for the adults and milk and fresh-baked cookies for Terry. The old spirit of conspiratorial fun joined them once again, and by the time they had eaten they felt at ease with each other again.

Then Terry showed Leslie his papers and drawings from first grade. The sight of his childish printing of the capital and small letters brought tears to her eyes, and she had to hide them. He sat on her lap as she looked through the papers, his little body nestling close to hers as it always had. The feel of him sent thrills of happiness and longing through Leslie.

More than once she caught Georgia's eye, and saw her familiar look of sympathy and cooperation. Georgia was not at all afraid of being upstaged by Leslie in Terry's eyes. Leslie was a shadowy figure in his life, an aunt whom he felt close to and looked forward to seeing, but whose role in his memory and in his heart would always be occasional, fragmentary, like a series of snapshots. But Georgia was permanent, the very soil and air of his existence, and nothing could move her from her place in his heart.

Because Georgia knew this so well she could afford to encourage her son's relationship with Leslie. It could hardly hurt Terry, and it meant so very much to Leslie.

At three Leslie took Terry out for their ritual walk. They went along the suburban sidewalk, passing small houses with bicycles standing in the driveways and occasional basketball hoops.

"Do you remember the way to our secret place?" she asked.

"Let me show you," he said.

He took her hand and led her down the two blocks to the park. She was pleased to see that he recalled exactly where their special place was, on the little rise of grass beneath the oak trees.

"You remembered," she said.

He nodded, smiling.

"Do you want to play?" she asked. "Shall I push you on the merry-go-round? Do you want to slide down the slide?"

"Not yet."

He lay down on the grass and looked up into the branches of the tree. After a moment she lay down beside him.

"So you remembered this, too," she said.

"Yes." There was something grave and almost manly about him that made her feel very new in their old place.

"See any monkeys today?" Leslie asked.

"Monkeys?" he asked.

Leslie's heart turned within her as she realized he had outgrown their old game, forgotten it.

"Don't you remember how we used to make believe we saw monkeys in the trees?" she asked. "Remember how they chattered away? And the song we sang?"

He was silent for a moment.

"We went to the animal fair," she sang.

He smiled faintly.

"The birds and the beasts were there," she added.

"The big baboon, by the light of the moon . . ." He spoke it rather than sang it, as though embarrassed to sing like a little child.

"Was combing his auburn hair." She hugged him to her. "So you did remember," she said.

"Not at first," he said. "But I remember now."

Leslie felt secretly desperate. She knew that Ross was in the hospital, being treated by doctors who feared he might have another massive stroke. Such a stroke would kill him, there was no doubt about that.

And this little boy who liked her, perhaps loved her in a small way, was outgrowing himself at every step of his life, changing so fast that it was impossible to expect him to have a clear memory of their times together or their little rituals. He was leaving her behind as he plunged forward into his own world.

Leslie felt as though, in hugging this tender little packet of male flesh, she was clinging weakly to something that was being inevitably torn from her by time. Time was her great enemy, not only with Ross, who was being driven by disease closer to the end of his life, but with this little boy, who was being changed every day into someone new, into a person who could only forget her as his heart made room for new experiences and new people.

But she would hang on to what she had left. This last year had taught her to stop complaining about what the world took away, and be grateful for what it still gave. Misfortune had turned Leslie into a soldier. She was becoming an expert at making the best of bad situations.

"Tell me about your teacher," she said.

"Well," he said dreamily, playing with the fingers of her left hand and noticing the wedding ring, "her name is Miss Coopersmith."

"Is she nice?" Leslie asked, her eyes half-closing in pleasure as the little fingers touched her own.

"Oh," he said, "she's nice. She bought a new car last summer. She says she's going to take me for a ride in it some day."

"That will be fun," Leslie said.

She listened as he went on, and asked questions to draw him out. He began to talk about his friends in school, the things they did together, where they were going on vacation next summer, and where he and his parents would go. And every word he spoke was like a blessing to Leslie, a precious elixir that brought her closer to him for this brief moment.

"Now that you're old enough to write, I'll bet you'll write me a letter some day," she said.

"Yes," he said. "And you'll write me back."

"Could we be pen pals?" she asked.

"What are pen pals?"

She explained. As she did so she held his little hand in hers, and clung despite herself to this one frail arrow into the future, this contact that might continue to join him to her.

"But we won't have to write," he said suddenly.

"Why?" she asked.

"Because," he explained, "when you grow up you'll marry me. So we won't have to write."

"Ah, that's right," she nodded, thanking him for his fantasy.

And somehow this bittersweet moment, in which she held on to him and let him go at the same time, was the more beautiful for being so fleeting. In her arms she held a fugitive, changing creature, made of the quicksilver of time and of her love.

It seemed to Leslie in that instant that only fleeting things were real. The important things in life were, alas, the ones that eluded one's grasp. The things one could possess as one's own were the unimportant things. At least this was her own truth, for all the people she had loved had slipped through her fingers, just as this beautiful boy in this tender moment was slipping away even as he promised to belong to her forever, to grow up and marry her.

And so Leslie sat with her boy's head in her lap, looking up into the branches of the old oak, which hovered over them like a protector. She was a grown woman now and had had her education in the impermanence of life. She was learning the hard way that one must be quick and clever with the people one loves, seizing one's moments with them like precious shooting stars before they disappeared. The art of love consisted in holding these golden flares in one's heart forever, though their reality might be long gone, vanished, and forgotten by all others.

To a child like Terry the future was unlimited, a place marked out for his initiative and his curiosity, a place where he could do anything he wanted. For Leslie the future was an enemy, all too quick to devour the things and people she loved. The past was assuming greater and greater importance with her, for it was the past she could hold and explore at her leisure.

She was too absorbed in this hard lesson, and in learning the special skill of loving from a great distance in time as well as space, to notice anything in the world beside the little boy in her lap.

Thus she never thought to glance behind her to the bushes at the back of the park, where Tony Dorrance was watching her.

And thus she could not see the look on Tony's face as he watched them.

But Tony, this time, was not looking at Leslie at all.

He had eyes only for the little boy.

As surely as Leslie recognized her own heart in Terry Beyer, Tony Dorrance recognized in that little face his son, and Leslie's son.

Book Four

THE
FAIREST
ONE
OF
ALL

53

As IT TURNED OUT, Ross's condition was not as bad as feared.

He seemed to rebound during the course of the spring. His memory for words and names improved slightly, and his intellectual capacity regained the level it had been before Christmas. Thanks to his strong will as well as his backbreaking physical therapy, he had better control of his movements and could accomplish a number of tasks that had been impossible since his last stroke.

Leslie willed herself to look on the bright side. The doctors were her eager accomplices in this.

"The brain is such a complicated organ that we can't predict what it will do," Dr. Gaeth told her. "I've seen patients bounce back from problems worse than your husband's. Just remember: hard work and love are the most important things. Keep believing in Ross, and he'll keep believing in himself. Anything is possible."

On this sunny Wednesday the streets of Johnsonville bore a premonitory glow of the hot summer to come. Leslie had been at work all morning, and returned home to take Ross to the hospital for his physical therapy. She was on her way back to the office now to finish up some important work she had been neglecting too long. This day would end like so many others, with her picking Ross up at three, returning to work for another couple of hours, and going home for a brief evening before falling into bed at nine or nine-thirty for a night of exhausted sleep.

So far today she had eaten nothing but a bowl of dry cereal at the office. She had weighed a hundred and three pounds the last time she dared to weigh herself. Even when she remembered to eat, she had no appetite. The idea of food was both irrelevant and disgusting to her. She was losing weight steadily. Ross's nurse, a kindly woman named Connie, had raised an eyebrow and suggested that Leslie see her family doctor. Leslie had listened politely and forgotten the suggestion within minutes. She had just enough strength and concentration to do her work at the office and spend the rest of her

357

time on Ross. There was no mental energy left for thoughts of herself or her health.

She inched the car out of its space with a careful glance at the rearview mirror, then drove to the parking lot's gate. She stuck her ticket into the little slot and watched the barrier lurch upward.

At that moment the passenger's door opened suddenly and someone got into the car.

A little cry of alarm escaped Leslie's lips. She thought she was about to be robbed.

Then she turned pale as she saw who it was.

Tony Dorrance was not smiling. He had a stern, purposeful look on his handsome face.

"Let's go," he said.

Leslie was too shocked to move. She sat staring at him, a look somewhere between alarm and irritation in her eyes.

"What are you . . . ?" she stammered.

"Just drive," he said. "I want to talk to you."

Leslie recovered herself quickly.

"Get out of this car," she said. "Get out or I'll—"

"Before you make a stink," Tony interrupted, "I know who my son is. His name is Terry Beyer. He lives in Farmington, on Long Island. I've seen him. I've seen you with him."

Leslie was gazing at him open-mouthed. His words had canceled all thought from her mind as completely as an eraser empties a chalkboard of all that went before it.

Tony was looking at her coldly. His dark eyes seemed inhuman, like raisins or black pebbles.

She had to struggle to regain the use of speech.

"What do you want?" she asked. "Why are you here?" The note of irritation had left her voice now. She was frightened and off balance.

The sound of a car horn made her jump. She glanced in the rearview mirror. There was a car behind her, waiting to go through the gate.

"Let's move it," Tony said.

She stepped on the gas and drove through the gate, turning in to one of the small residential streets adjacent to the hospital. She had no idea what was to happen next. The sound of Terry's name on Tony's lips had obliterated the familiar world around her.

"Turn right at the next corner," Tony said.

She followed his instructions. He took her through several residential streets to a large graveyard she often passed on her way to the hospital.

"Go on in," he said. "We can have some privacy here."

She drove into the graveyard. She had never been in it before. The sight of the graves made her shiver. The names on the tombstones looked uncanny, as though there were people watching from behind them or beneath them. This was a macabre place to be trapped with Tony, this man who had done her so much harm in her life, and who had now so insanely returned.

She drove slowly along one of the lanes until Tony told her to stop.

"Turn off the engine," he said.

Leslie did as she was told.

She turned to look at Tony. She felt a massive sense of dislocation, of absurdity.

"What is it you want?" she asked.

There was a pause. Tony gave her a long slow smile.

"You," he said.

Leslie laughed. It was a contemptuous laugh, and he saw this instantly. He grabbed her wrist, hard.

"Don't laugh at me, babe," he said. "That is a big mistake. You won't be laughing when this is over."

She saw the look in his eyes. He was serious in a way she had never seen him before. Somehow he did not look like himself. Not like the Tony she had known in the old days, and not even like himself from six months ago, when he had appeared so unexpectedly on her doorstep. There was something different about him now, something hard and concentrated.

"I don't know what you think you're doing," she said. "You're out of my life, Tony. You have been for many years. Long before I met Ross Wheeler and fell in love with him, I had already forgotten you. If you've got some crazy idea that you can turn back the clock after all these years . . ."

"I saw the boy," he said. "I saw our son, Leslie."

A brief strangled light of acknowledgment shone in her beautiful eyes, and then was extinguished.

"We have no son," she said. "What are you talking about?"

"No stupid lies, Leslie," he said. "We don't have time for that. When I saw you at your house I knew something about that setup was wrong. I could feel it in my bones. So I kept an eye on you. When you drove out to Farmington to see the boy, I was right behind you. I even followed you to the park. I was only a few feet from you when you were lying under that oak tree with him." He laughed. "I'll bet you thought you were free as the birds. You thought you had been so careful. . . ."

He looked out the front window, and back at Leslie.

"Of course I knew he was mine, right from the start," he said. "And I knew he was yours. Nothing was ever so obvious. He's got your eyes, your smile—but everything else is mine. The nose, the chin—everything. He's my son, Leslie."

Leslie said nothing. She knew she could not deny what he was saying. But she wanted to find out where he was leading.

"I checked out the Beyers," he said. "I found out about the adoption. It was easy; I'm good at that sort of thing. You delivered the boy nine months after we were together. You had already made your arrangement with the Beyers. They took him home from the hospital. They've got the adoption papers, but the original birth certificate still shows you as the mother. I have a copy of it."

He shrugged. "Not that I needed any of this information," he said. "I know my son when I see him."

Leslie's eyes narrowed.

"You have no right," she said, "to discuss the Beyers or their son. No right at all. It's none of your business."

Tony shook his head with a knowing smile. "I'm the boy's father," he said.

Leslie thought carefully. She could see from Tony's face that he thought he had some sort of hold over her. But she remembered him as a man who was not insensible to logic.

"All right," she said. "Let's say you were the natural father of the Beyers' boy. That doesn't change anything. You abandoned the mother long before the boy's birth. I had the child and gave him up for adoption. His parents were kind enough to let me visit him every once in a while. That's a normal enough occurrence in this world. You have no legal rights as far as he's concerned. None at all. You'd be laughed out of court if you tried to claim otherwise."

Tony shook his head in bitter amusement.

"You think you're pretty clever, don't you?" he said. "You think you've got it all figured out."

Leslie looked at him contemptuously. "What is there to figure out, Tony? You have your life. You walked out on me a long time ago. Don't you remember? It was the day we were to be married. I waited for you to come, and you didn't. You dropped me as though I were nothing to you. You didn't even look back. Do you remember, Tony? Do you?"

A sudden intensity had colored her words. They were like hard fingers pulling at him, fingers full of anger. She had to make an effort to bring her voice back to normal.

"I went on with my life," she said. "I have a husband, a marriage. The baby I had six years ago has an adoptive home. He's a happy, normal child— no thanks to you. Now why don't you go on about your business and leave me to go about mine?"

Tony shook his head again.

"You really don't understand, do you?" he said. "It was no accident that I crossed your path after all these years. That was fate, Leslie. Something was wrong with my life all this time. I felt it, but I never understood it. I thought it was just a run of bad luck, the wrong choices, whatever. But something was missing deep down. Then I saw you again, and I realized what it was. It was you. It was you all along. Do you think fate would have led me to your doorstep after all that time if it wasn't trying to tell me something?"

Leslie was looking at him, puzzled.

"That was coincidence, Tony. Nothing more."

He shook his head. Now a look of tenderness came over his face.

"No," he said. "When I saw you I thought I was going to faint dead away. You were what was missing all along from my life. If I told you how hard it was for me to stand there in your house and talk about insurance, when my heart was breaking . . . You'll never know how I felt. I love you, Leslie. I've loved you all along. It took that stroke of luck to make me realize it."

Leslie's eyes widened. She saw that he was sincere.

"You're crazy," she said. The words slipped out, cruel and angry, before she could stop them.

Now the look of dark purpose came back into his eyes. There was something feral about him, as though his masculinity had been crystallized and concentrated by his own obsession. It made Leslie nervous and a little disgusted to be at close quarters with him.

"And I knew that first day," he went on, "that something was wrong with that little suburban house of yours, and your sick husband. It didn't ring true. That's not where you belong. Not my Leslie. It was just a front."

He looked out the window. There was a rapt expression on his face that she had never seen before.

"I knew that if I kept my eye on you, I'd find out the truth," he said. "And sure enough, it was easy. You led me right to the boy, Leslie. Right back to our love—where you started. Where we left off."

Once again the inner feeling of painful dislocation shook Leslie. In a sense Tony was right about her. But not in the way he thought. He had found her out, sure enough. There was more to her present life than met the eye. She had long since admitted this to herself and come to terms with it. But Tony could not see the missing links between her long-lost relationship with him and her current existence. That was why he could believe she still loved him.

But it would be hard to convince him he was wrong. She could see how logic played into the hands of his obsession.

"Yes," he repeated. "I followed you. And I found out your secret."

He looked back at her. There was triumph in his eyes, but also something more.

"And your secret was me," he said. "Me, and my son."

Leslie was exasperated. He was talking pure nonsense. But he was embroidering that nonsense into something tight and suffocating that included himself, her, and innocent little Terry Beyer.

"Tony, you're crazy," she said.

He leaned forward quickly. He grabbed both her hands before she could stop him.

"I knew you'd say that," he said. "I knew it all along. You'd try to say it was nothing, you'd try to say it was ancient history. But you're wrong, Leslie. You've always been wrong about me. True, I walked out on you. That was my big mistake, the biggest mistake of my whole life. Because I loved you then, and I love you now. And you loved me. Don't try to deny it. It was only too obvious then, in the way you looked at me, the way you made love . . ."

He sighed at the memory. She blushed, for she could not deny that he was her first lover, the man who had taken her girlhood from her and made her a woman.

He saw her blush. He nodded slightly, an understanding glimmer in his eyes.

"You were the only woman who ever meant anything to me," he concluded. "And the baby, the little boy, is the proof, you see. Not even you can deny that. Proof that you loved me. Proof that we were made for each other. I wasted my life for seven years trying to hide from that fact. But then fate made me find you again. Now I know who I am. Now I know where I belong. And where you belong."

There was a pause. She did not meet his eyes, but she could feel the pressure of their gaze on her face.

"I love you," he said. "You're all I've ever loved in this world. And you love me, too, Leslie. I already know it. I just want to hear you say it. Please. You owe me that, at least."

Leslie shook her head as though to clear cobwebs from her mind. His fantasy was not based on absolute nothingness; it had a certain twisted relationship to reality. To her it was simply insane, but to him it must have a compelling logic.

Tony must have sensed these thoughts, for he touched her hand gently.

"You see," he said, "I'm not crazy, Leslie. I've been wrong. Very wrong. I've done the wrong things, taken the wrong path. A path that led away from you. But now I've found you. And whatever else may have happened, it can't change that. I belong to you, and you belong to me."

Leslie flushed with anger.

"I've heard enough of this," she said. "If you want to build castles in the air, that's your business. I'm sorry if your life hasn't gone the way you would have liked. But don't try to hang that on me. You see, Tony, you haven't really changed a bit. You don't have the courage to take responsibility for your own life, so you drag me into it after all these years, as if that could save you. After you seduced me and dropped me, and left me to go on alone as best I could . . ."

An involuntary tear welled in her eyes at the memory of what this man had been to her, and of the anguish she had endured on his account.

She did not look up. Had she done so she would have seen the genuinely stricken look in his eyes.

"And now," she continued in a halting voice, "now you think you can waltz back into my life as though your place was laid for you. Well, it isn't. There is no place for you in my life. I don't need you, I don't want you."

"I know how much I hurt you," he said softly. "And you'll never know how terrible that feels for me. But you have to understand, Leslie, we've been given another chance. Fate has given us another chance."

Again anger flashed in her eyes.

"You're wrong about that," she said. "Fate has given you a chance to see what a muck you've made of your life. That's what it meant, Tony, when you came to my doorstep as an insurance salesman. That's what it meant!"

He looked away. Her slashing words had hurt. He had not stopped thinking about that humiliation since he first saw the look on her face when she answered her door and found him there on her stoop. It was a look of impersonal disinterest and ill-concealed contempt. The look every housewife reserves for an unwanted salesman.

"If you're worried about money," he began, "that's no problem. Once I have you back I'll be the man I could have been all along. I'll get a better job. You'll live in a house just as good as the one you have now . . ."

His words trailed off as he saw the look in her eyes. It was a look of scorn for the absurdity of his fantasies. In a way she seemed to look down on him not only for his unimpressive fortunes in the business world but also for his desperate obsession with herself.

A hot flush of shame covered Tony's face. He felt that she had humiliated him deliberately. He almost hated her now.

He opened the door and got out. He came around to the driver's side and leaned down to speak to her.

"Think things over," he said. "Take your time." His tone was cold and businesslike.

"I don't need time," she said. "And I don't need to think about you. Good-bye, Tony."

She reached to turn on the ignition, but his hand seized the key and pulled it out. He dangled it in front of her musingly.

"Does your husband know you have a kid?" he asked.

Leslie's hands shook on the steering wheel. She stared straight ahead.

"Yes, he knows," she said. Her voice shook. She prayed the lie sounded convincing.

Tony continued to dangle the keys, studying her intently.

"Well, we'll see about that," he said.

Gritting her teeth, Leslie said nothing and kept her eyes fixed on the windshield.

"You haven't had any kids with him, have you?" he asked. "And I'll bet you've tried. You see, babe, that just proves my point. He's not the man for you. He's an invalid. A loser. I made my mistakes, and he's your mistake. Some day you'll have lots of kids. But they'll be my kids."

Leslie felt as though a cord was tied tight around her chest, squeezing her for all it was worth. Mustering all the strength in her trembling body, she took a deep breath, as though to break that cord.

"You're very sad, Tony," she said. "Go away and try to live your life. I wish you luck."

She took the keys from his hand. He did not try to stop her. She managed to get the key into the ignition and start the car. He started to say something as she threw it into gear, but she did not hear him, for she was pulling away with a great roar of the engine, her foot pressed hard to the accelerator.

As she drove away along the unfamiliar cemetery lane she could see him in the rearview mirror, standing tall in his business suit, framed by the leafy trees and the gravestones. It was a macabre sight, the image of a ghost from her past rising among those graves to confront her in flesh and blood.

Fighting back the tremors inside her, Leslie fixed her eyes to the road ahead and told herself she would look back no longer.

54

People, September 9, 1979

BEAUTIFUL PEOPLE AWAIT BIRTH

Billionaire visionary Jordan Lazarus and his beautiful wife, Jill, are thinking about more than the famous and controversial Lazarus Plan for reclamation of urban America these days.

While husband Jordan works long days with government and business leaders on implementation of the epoch-making Lazarus Plan, wife Jill is busy feathering an elegant nest in the couple's Sutton Place penthouse for the baby she will have in November.

Asked how the process is going, the beaming Mrs. Lazarus spoke with eloquent brevity to reporters. "I'm in heaven," she said. "Ever since I first met Jordan I've dreamed of having his baby. And now it's happening. It's too good to be true."

As for Lazarus himself, he was unavailable for comment, being closeted twelve hours a day with the hand-picked force of urban and financial experts who are at work to make his inner city plan a reality. But sources close to the billionaire say he has never been happier or more at peace with himself.

"Jordan has always been a man who lives for the future," says close aide Sam Gaddis. "He's a visionary. That's why the Lazarus Plan means so much to him. He wants to leave his mark on the future. He feels the same way about his child. The child will be his future, too—his connection to generations still to come. To put it mildly, Jordan is a very happy man."

The Lazaruses are reportedly inundated with congratulatory mail, most of which includes speculation on whether the child will be male or female. Lazarus himself smilingly refuses to answer questions about whether he wants a male heir.

Whatever the outcome, we add our own best wishes to those of a grateful nation. To Jill and to Jordan—enjoy!

It was the worst year of Jill's life.

As the months passed she was forced to put on a smiling face for the press while her private world was in shambles. The ordeal was taking a lot out of her—perhaps too much, she feared, to allow her to be a real mother to her baby when it was born.

The news of her pregnancy had effectively thwarted Jordan's plan to leave her. He had dropped divorce proceedings immediately and begun thinking about his new life as a father.

Jordan's response to this change in their plans had been uncanny. He seemed totally concentrated on preparations for the baby's arrival, almost possessed, in fact. Contrary to the press's reports, it was Jordan, not Jill, who oversaw the building of a magnificent nursery in the south room of the penthouse, with the best view in the entire apartment. He saw to every detail, leaving only the final trim to be added after they knew whether the child was a boy or girl.

To Jill he was coldly attentive during this time, making sure she took care of herself and avoided overexertion. He took her to the doctor himself, and learned everything he could about pregnancy and childbirth.

But there was no love in his protectiveness. Jill felt like the mere vessel of his dawning love for his unborn child, and not a human being in herself.

In the early days of her pregnancy she hoped they would make love. She thought the baby might open a new avenue of tenderness between her and Jordan, and repair some of the damage that had been done to their marriage.

Jordan did not touch her. Once or twice she dared to approach him. He recoiled from her with a look of loathing on his face. She was not sure whether he simply hated her, or whether the memory of the last time they had made love, when she had intentionally disguised herself in order to challenge and torment him, was too painful for him. In any case, his coldness effectively put her off. She did not ask him again.

He continued to sleep in the same bed with her, but it was no longer a marital bed. He was simply keeping an eye on her for the sake of her unborn child. He wanted to be at hand should some sort of medical problem arise that might threaten the fetus. He slept with his back turned to Jill.

Jill had never felt so alone in her life, or so out of control. Her obstetrician had forbidden her to take any medication, and she tried hard to obey his instructions. But the daily emotional pressure she lived under was so unbearable that she could not sleep a wink without tranquilizers.

She hid her bottle of pills at the bottom of her vanity. One night Jordan found it and confronted her with it. The flashing anger in his eyes frightened her.

"If I catch you with any of these again," he warned, "I'll have you locked in a hospital under observation until the baby is born."

His cold stare expressed a mixture of fierce concern for his child and hatred for his wife. Jill turned her eyes away.

"It's an old bottle," she said. "It was there from months ago. I haven't been taking anything. And I won't. I promise."

Jordan put the bottle in his pocket.

"See that you don't," he said, and left the room.

After that night Jill felt like a prisoner. She managed to get her hands on some more pills through a friend, and hid them cleverly, changing her hiding place several times a week. She took them as seldom as possible, for she could feel Jordan scrutinizing her when they were together, alert to any sign that she might have tranquilized herself.

As her pregnancy entered the later months she found that the pills were not so necessary. Though her nerves still felt frayed, sleep came of its own accord, ending her troubled days and bearing her through the long, empty nights like a magic carpet. She realized that a process deep in nature, beyond her own plans or worries, was following its course, something primordial and irresistible that was ensuring the health of her unborn child by forcing her own body to sleep.

During these months the distance between Jordan and his wife increased. Yet his loving concern for the baby growing inside Jill became stronger as she got bigger, and he was almost ecstatic when the baby began to kick.

Jordan would sit beside Jill in the evenings, his hand rubbing her swollen abdomen with gentle care. When the baby kicked he would remark on it— "There! Did you feel that?"—and smile with boyish excitement. At these moments there were echoes of the contented, beatific happiness Jordan had manifested on their honeymoon a year and a half ago. It was as though he had what he wanted at last, was satisfied and even delighted with his life.

But this budding happiness had nothing to do with his feelings for Jill herself. He made no secret of his alienation from her. When he touched her stomach, it was his baby he sought and wanted, not his wife.

How strange, how terrible it became for Jill to feel his proud hand on her abdomen as he felt the baby kick! To see his affection grow and flower as his gentle fingertips caressed the skin only an inch from his baby's body. He was separated from this beloved child only by this veil, this fleshly surface without importance, without substance—Jill herself.

Jill thought she would go mad feeling his love bypass her that way, directed toward an unseen being inside her. She wanted those gentle fingertips to linger on her own flesh, to cherish her own self. But Jordan bore her no love. The faceless baby was a perverse link that bound him to her against his own will.

Thus it was that Jill began to feel, in her distressed state, that she was carrying a foreign body inside her. And, in proportion as Jordan's delighted love for this invisible stranger increased with the passing months, Jill found herself feeling something like hatred for the creature inside her. Her own emotion shocked her, and she tried to fight it. After all, this was her baby, too. She should love it, look forward to its birth.

But all her emotions had become twisted and uncontrollable things since she fell in love with Jordan Lazarus. She felt like a helpless pawn in a crazy game that used love to destroy those who played it rather than to bring them happiness.

How could she feel a natural mother's love for this unborn child when the child had been conceived in a perverse, tormented masquerade of love based on Jill's devouring jealousy of another woman? And how could she claim Jordan's love for herself, when she had seduced and won him in the first place under the guise of that other woman?

It was as though the child had really come from another mother, and Jill was merely the surrogate being used to bring it into the world. How else to explain Jordan's passionate love for the unborn infant, and his complete indifference to the living woman who was bearing this child for him?

Jill stood before her bathroom mirror naked and watched her stomach grow bigger each day, each week. Her fascination with the strange beauty of pregnancy was mingled with her horror at the travesty she and Jordan were making of this joyous natural process.

Jill was not the happy, expectant mother the world thought her to be. The baby was not the cherished growing being she herself wanted it to be. Jordan was not the loving husband the press described him as. It was all a huge lie.

And all because there was a fourth member of this nuclear family, a forbidden member whose presence haunted all the others and made them into what they were not. And this dreaded extra member, owning a place in Jordan's heart, now cast her shadow over Jill's very existence. She could feel her inside her belly, where her baby had been conceived. And she could see her in her own face, like a mask that could not be taken off once it had been put on, an ineradicable taint.

Or were these thoughts insane? Were they twisted mental meanderings born of the stress Jill had lived under all these months, born of her jealousy and her terrible thwarted passion? She did not know. She only knew she could not shake loose of them. They tightened their grip on her every day, slowly, brutally, as her child grew bigger inside her.

As for Jordan, he did not doubt that his child had been conceived the night of Jill's perverse masquerade. And he, too, could not look at Jill without seeing the mask she had worn that fateful night. The haunting image Jill had brought to life so perfectly could no longer be erased. He could not look at Jill without seeing that image and remembering that night. And this fact, more compelling than any reproach, was what kept him away from Jill now.

He realized with hindsight that when he first met Jill and fell under her sexual spell, during his mourning period for Leslie, it had already been Jill's odd resemblance to Leslie, that odd commonality of charm, that had attracted him to her. At the time he had not seen it; he had been too wrapped up in the moment to notice it. But now he saw that it had been there from the outset, a strange aura that Jill seemed to bear, like a talisman adding some part of Leslie's essence to her own.

No wonder that Ben, the boat steward, had mistaken Jill for Leslie. Jordan should have seen the significance of that event at the time, but he had not. Desire had blinded him to the truth.

Jordan saw that he had taken Jill to his heart under false pretenses from the beginning. Today her face was like a mirror that threw a cruel light on his own falseness and hers, the bottomless, infinite falseness of their marriage.

In spite of everything Jordan felt a deep, primordial bond with Jill as the mother of his child. But he could not bring himself to forgive her for what she had done. Nor could he bring himself to touch her, for the deception at the heart of their intimacy was too horrible to behold. If he were to touch her today, to open his heart to her even by an inch, it would not be Jill herself he coveted. And thus he would be revealed in all his nakedness, as he had been the night of her masquerade. This he could not bear.

So Jordan turned his back on his lonely wife. He spent his days working on the Lazarus Plan, and spent his nights trying to see through Jill's body to the innocent child inside it. The baby was in a sense his future. Once it was born he could be rescued from his tainted past and begin living again.

He knew this was an unhealthy way to bring a child into the world, but he could not help it. He wanted this baby more than he had ever wanted anything in his life. It seemed to be his only chance for happiness.

He would endure a few more months for its sake. Then he would start life over again. Or so he thought.

Such was the painful standoff between Jordan and Jill, a standoff invisible to the outside world, when a sudden turn of events threw a new light on their agony.

Meg Lazarus died.

Jordan got the news of Meg's final heart failure in the middle of a warm September night, and flew by private jet to Pennsylvania immediately. By the time he arrived Meg was in the intensive care unit of St. Joseph's Hospital. A priest had already been called to administer the last rites.

Jordan felt nothing but an almost businesslike haste as he sat in the plane and then drove to the hospital. The emotions inside him had been so painful for so long that it seemed tonight there was no room for anything but pure movement, pure will.

His brothers and sister were gathered in the waiting room when he arrived. Gerald, Clay, and Ryan sat weakly in the steel-and-plastic chairs, looking drained and ineffectual. Mother was in the room with Meg. Louise threw herself into Jordan's arms.

"Jordan," she said. "Thank God you're here."

The entire family seemed helpless, leaning pathetically on Jordan for support. Meg was their spiritual leader, and losing her was like losing the ground under their feet.

"Is she . . . How is she?" Jordan asked.

Louise looked away, tears welling in her eyes. "She's asking for you," she said. "I think she's been holding out . . ." A sob stopped her from saying more.

The nurse took Jordan in to Meg. Mother got up from the chair beside the bed, kissed Jordan silently, and left the room. Jordan looked down at Meg's face. The mask of death was already beginning to obliterate the features he loved so much. Meg looked like a rag doll, her eyes staring emptily at the ceiling.

"Meg," he whispered, taking her hand. "It's Jordan."

She lay for a long moment without responding. But her hand stirred in his, and her chest moved as she struggled to find breath to speak.

He leaned over her so she would not have to turn her eyes to see him.

"Meg, it's me. It's Jordan."

"Jordie?" Her voice was a mere echo, so faraway and distorted by impending death that it almost seemed unrecognizable.

"I'm here, dear," he said. "It's all right."

Her eyes were fixed on him, but without focusing. He saw tears on her cheeks, and realized to his surprise that they were his own. Though he felt nothing but a nameless urgency, a terrible attention to her, tears were pouring quickly from his eyes.

"Jordie," she said again. And now she saw him. Her hand squeezed his weakly. "You came."

"Yes, I came. Did you think I'd let you down at a time like this? Not me, kid."

She lacked the strength to return his smile. Death was pulling her away from him quickly.

"Jordie," she said again. Then there was a terrible pause. He could feel her struggling for a last moment of lucidity, when the holocaust going on inside her body left no strength for thought.

"Yes, love, I'm right here," he said. If she lacked the breath to talk, he would at least comfort her with his presence until the end. "I'm right here," he said. "I won't leave you again, Meg. Never."

He lowered his face to hers, and kissed her lips. Her skin was cool, already withdrawing into the frigidity of death.

"I love you," he said. "I love you, Meg. I'm here with you . . ."

"Jordie." With a superhuman effort she managed to make her voice work, and to make her eyes focus on him. "Listen."

"Yes, dear," he said, holding both her hands in his. "I hear you."

"I want you to be happy," she said.

There was a silence. Though she was at the brink of extinction, he could feel the power of her vision seeing through him as it always had, sure and true.

"I am happy, Meg," he said. The shallowness of his lie shocked him, and he looked away.

"No," she said. "There's no time. . . . Listen."

"Yes." The word came out as a sob. "Yes, I hear you, Meg."

"You've worked so hard," she said. "Too hard. You gave yourself up. You left yourself behind, all along. Find yourself now—for me. No more running away . . ."

"Yes, Meg," he said, holding the frozen hands. "Yes, darling. Whatever you say."

He tried to hide the pain she was causing him. She saw what he had done with his life. Now, too late, she was summoning him to turn back the clock and become the man he had never been, the man he should have been from the beginning.

"You can't live without love," she said. "Don't try. No more."

A spasm shook her. She looked deeper into his eyes.

"Be good to Jill," she said. "She loves you."

"Yes," Jordan lied. "Yes, I know, Meg. I know. And I will. I promise." The words tumbled meaninglessly from his lips. He was talking too much, he knew, in an attempt to cover up the emptiness of his speech.

His tears dripped on her face like cold rain, futile as his lies. He knew from the frail grip of her hands that she was using the last of her strength to try to hold him to his promise.

Something invisible seemed to fall upon her, crushing her. Her hands went limp in his. There were words on her lips. He bent to try to hear them.

"... still time ..."

The light in her eyes went out. The color left her cheeks. She was gone.

Jordan sat up, holding her hands. He glanced down at the dead face, which already looked unrecognizable.

Then he got up and opened the door. His brothers and sister looked up at him with desperate, insane hope. He told them with his eyes that it was over.

Mother cried out and hid her face in her hands. Louise dashed into the room, as though her haste could make a difference. The brothers stood up helplessly. Ryan held out his arms to Jordan.

The doctor came, and the priest. It was a long night. Jordan made all the arrangements, took charge of everything. Though he looked as if something had drained all the blood out of him, he was cool and efficient with the strangers, tender and supportive with his family.

He called Jill just before dawn to tell her the news. He would be home in a few days, he said. Jill seemed stricken, but her voice was so far away that he barely noticed her emotion.

He asked her about her condition before hanging up.

"I'm fine," she said. "Don't worry about me. Take care of your family. Take care of yourself."

In her words he heard the echo of Meg's final plea. *Be happy. You can't live without love.* As he began the draining process of burying his sister, he gave her words a new meaning, as though deliberately. He would be a good father to the baby Jill was carrying. He would find in fatherhood what he had lacked as a man, what he had not found in love.

Was this what Meg had meant? He did not know. Nor had he ever completely known Meg, or himself.

But he would make his child safe and happy. Or die trying.

With this private thought Jordan turned his back on Meg, and on a great part of himself, in order to face the future once again.

55

THE BABY WAS BORN on November 10. It was a girl.

They gave her the name Margaret, in memory of Meg.

When the infant was brought in to Jill, she took it in her arms with mixed feelings. For nine months she had dreaded this moment as much as she had looked forward to it.

The baby was incredibly beautiful, with fresh, pink skin, eyes the gray of infancy, and adorable little hands that curled and uncurled as she cooed. She cried very little, but nestled comfortably on Jill's breast. Her innocence, her sweetness, her hunger for life, were entrancing to behold.

"She's got her father's eyes, all right," said one nurse.

"And her father's hair," said another.

The child did look a great deal like Jordan. She had his clean, honest features, his inner calm, and that strange, visionary look in the eyes.

The nurses all admired Jordan Lazarus for his great fortune and fame as well as his renowned good looks, so it was natural that they saw resemblances between the infant girl and her father.

But Jill could not help noticing that no one spoke of a resemblance of the child to Jill herself.

For the first few days Jill tried to tell herself that this meant nothing. In time the baby would exhibit a typical amalgam of its mother's and father's features.

But Jill could not resist holding the baby close to her and examining its face with an almost obsessive attention, as though in search of some obvious trace of herself in the child's physiognomy.

Whether that trace was there or not, Jill could not seem to find it.

Jordan was passionate in his love for the baby. And he was clearly thrilled that it was a girl.

From the first time he saw Meg, his face lit up in a way Jill had never seen before.

He carried the baby, he held her, he talked to her as few men ever did with babies, girl babies especially. There was an odd, unsettling intimacy between them, as though they belonged together, had belonged together all along, and had only needed Jill as the intermediary required by nature to bring them together.

Jordan glowed. He behaved as though he had endured a long period of loneliness with Jill in order to deserve this reward. In Meg he had at last found someone of his own blood, someone he understood and trusted by instinct. And now he was giving of himself delightedly and unstintingly to her, as though in meeting her he had found himself.

Watching this, Jill felt left out. She sat in her hospital bed, and later on the couch at home, watching Jordan enjoy a closeness with the baby that Jill herself did not feel. And when Jordan, after playing with Meg, would hand her back to Jill—with visible reluctance—Jill felt unwanted. It was as though the child's affections were already being alienated from her by the seductive attentions of its doting, charming, wonderful father.

More and more, despite her daily intimacy with little Meg, Jill sensed a disturbing foreignness in the child. Though she admired Meg and felt an undeniable affection for her, she could not feel the oneness, the inner bond she knew every mother should feel with her daughter. Jordan seemed to feel enough of a bond for both parents. His euphoria, encompassing Meg like a warm cloak, shut Jill out.

Perhaps for this reason Jill found herself more and more struck by the baby's lack of resemblance to her. Meg reflected so much of Jordan, but nothing at all, it seemed, of Jill.

For all she knew, the baby in her arms could have been born of some other woman, with Jordan as the father. Had Jill not seen the child emerge from her loins with her own eyes, she might have wondered if it was hers at all.

This thought tore Jill from the initial contentment of new motherhood, and plunged her into a haunted state of mind as painful as the one that had dogged her throughout her pregnancy.

In this state of mind, it seemed to her that the baby's lack of obvious resemblance to her made a crazy sort of sense.

After all, she mused, the seed of this child had been planted in Jill by a man who loved another woman, at the very moment when Jill had poised the essence of her will in an effort to imitate the other woman, even to become her.

It was Jordan's child, true enough. But was it Jill's child, in any important sense?

Little Meg was not the result of a love that joined Jordan to Jill, but of a chasm between them, an unbridgeable distance. And that distance, in flesh and blood, was symbolized by another woman.

Jill told herself she was crazy. This was a defenseless, innocent, beautiful baby. *Her* baby. Jordan had planted this seed in Jill's body, and there it had grown into a human being.

But was Jill's mere body a match for the other terrible forces that had torn apart her marriage to Jordan? That was the question. Jill's womb was a physical reality. But was it a match for her husband's heart?

These thoughts tormented Jill when she was alone with Meg. As she breast-fed the baby, she had the uncanny feeling that her own essence was being sucked from her by something foreign, something that did not belong to her. She fought the feeling with all her strength.

Perhaps she would have been able to keep her fears at bay and regain some personal balance, had Jordan treated her with the tenderness a new father feels naturally for the mother of his child.

But the birth of Meg had not melted Jordan's coldness toward Jill.

He was not obvious in his rejection of her. He joined her in smiling at the baby, he offered her a gentle caress from time to time, was solicitous of her health, and kissed her good night as a good husband should. But his few gestures of affection toward her were so blatantly outweighed by his passionate devotion to Meg that it soon became obvious the brick wall between himself and Jill had grown thicker rather than thinner since the baby's birth.

Jordan had eyes only for his daughter. And when he paused in his adoration of her long enough to glance at his wife, the old grudge shone in his dark irises. He could not express it openly, for it would ruin the atmosphere of familial well-being his new daughter had brought to the house. But he did not try to pretend it was not there. And he knew Jill saw it.

Nothing had changed. The birth of Meg had merely confirmed the fatal flaw in Jill's marriage to Jordan, deepened the chasm between herself and him. Jill was more alone now than ever.

And it was in the depth of this solitude that a new and terrible idea came into Jill's mind.

One day about three weeks after Meg's birth Jordan came home from work at lunch as usual to see the baby. He held her in his arms, talked to her, diapered her, and only made up his mind to tear himself away when his secretary called to remind him of a pressing meeting.

He handed the baby to Jill. As he leaned down to her she smelled his fresh male aroma mingling with the new baby's powdery fragrance.

"Call me if anything cute happens," he joked. With a last loving glance at Meg he left the room.

Jill held the child in her arms. It was feeding time. In a moment she would open her blouse and offer the baby her breast. But she stopped, holding the infant before her and looking into its face as Jordan disappeared behind it. Jill's hands trembled. She turned pale. The baby felt her distress and began to whimper.

Jill was looking at the child's eyes, its nose, its brow, the shape of its face. As usual, she could see no resemblance to herself in Meg. But now, to her horror, she saw in those pretty features an undeniable resemblance to some-one else.

She closed her eyes tightly, as though to shut out a nightmare. When she opened them again, it was only little Meg she saw, beautiful as ever, her eyes screwed up in a frown, for she was hungry, and alarmed by her mother's emotion.

Yet the face of Leslie Chamberlain, having winked at Jill in the features of her daughter like the secret behind the pieces of a puzzle, lingered in her mind's eye still. And even as it faded, the image hung between her and Meg, projecting itself over the infant's face like a magic lantern of beauty and desirability.

I'm going crazy, Jill thought, fighting to push the uncanny vision out of her mind.

And she held the baby to her breast, as though only the child itself could save her.

56

Johnsonville, Long Island
November 15, 1979

IT WAS A BUSY FRIDAY. Leslie left the office at 11 A.M. and drove quickly home to get some paperwork she had forgotten when she left for work in the morning.

She left Ross in charge of things at the office. Since the summer he had once again begun taking an active part in work. He spent as much of each day at the office as his limited strength would allow, kept himself familiar with all the major accounts, and worked on ideas and layouts when he was not chatting with the staff.

Of course, it was all a charade. Ross had neither the strength to handle an executive's responsibilities nor the lucidity required for the quick, hard deci-sions the advertising business demands of its practitioners.

Leslie did all the real work. It was she who made the key decisions, dealt directly with the clients, and made sure the office ran at peak efficiency. She made a place for Ross at work in order to help him feel useful and alive. His presence at the office was almost purely ceremonial. But it was therapeutic for him and, in a way, morally helpful to the staff and to Leslie.

Despite the doctors' optimism, Leslie had come to realize in the past few months that Ross would never again be the man he once was. Not that he had lost his warm, intelligent personality, or that he was less of a husband to her. But illness had forever stripped him of the mental and physical strength to handle his old job.

Leslie and Ross had entered a new phase of their marriage, and perhaps the final one. They could no longer hope to reverse the damage done by Ross's strokes. But with love and commitment and hard work they could become closer in the time remaining to them. Their love was the only weapon they had left to fight the disease inside Ross.

Perhaps because they both knew where they stood, and had made their final commitment as husband and wife, some of the pressure had lifted in their daily life together. Life was less hectic now, more restful somehow.

Today, for instance, Leslie felt good. The weather was pleasantly brisk, and she had worn a wool skirt and the sweater Ross had given her for her birthday. Her body, albeit weakened by stress and weight loss, seemed firm and even energetic. As the suburban streets passed by her windshield she felt an inner echo of the physical well-being she had once enjoyed, when youth and freedom were the only problems she had to deal with in life.

She looked forward to the rest of today. She and her staff had just completed the new campaign for a major New York bank that had branches all over Long Island. It was an account that would normally have gone to a major Manhattan agency. But Wheeler Advertising's recent string of successes had attracted the attention of the bank's executives, and Leslie's personal charm had done the rest.

There would be a small celebration tonight at the office, followed by a quiet dinner at home with Ross. Leslie would lie in his arms on the couch, as she always did in the evenings. Then they would go upstairs and, if Ross was strong enough, make love.

They were once again trying hard to make a baby. The idea of a child had assumed a new significance for both. Ross no longer saw it as a confirmation of his manhood, as he had in earlier, simpler times. Nor did either of them see it as a justification of their May-December marriage, or as proof of Leslie's love for Ross. That love had long since proved itself in a thousand sacrifices.

No. The hoped-for child now signified the final rebellion of their love against inevitable death, Ross's death. Leslie knew her marriage could not last much longer. She wanted a child to incarnate her love for Ross, and to carry on for him in the future.

Making love was always a touch-and-go proposition for a man in Ross's delicate condition. But he approached the challenge with his usual combination of courage and good humor. And always with great tenderness and love for Leslie. In an odd way, she had never enjoyed being with him sexually as much as now. She held him in her arms and used her body in inventive ways to help him to the pleasure that had once come so easily and naturally. Her very creativity and initiative as a lover made her feel more committed to Ross, more a wife to him. Their successful trysts were like little victories of love over illness.

This thought was in Leslie's mind as she drove into the driveway. She left the car outside, opened the garage door, and entered the house through the kitchen.

The paperwork she wanted was in the study, but she stood for a long moment in the kitchen, listening to the silence of the empty house. Then she walked cautiously into the living room, glancing this way and that, and again stood listening.

There was no sound, not even the muted crack of the house settling or the tap of a branch against one of the windows. It was an empty house in the middle of the day—nothing more.

She did not consciously admit to herself that she was worried about Tony as she stood in the silence. She had not told Ross about her encounter with Tony outside the hospital. Nor had it occurred to her to call the police or to confide in anyone about the incident.

For one thing, she was firm in her belief that Tony was a remote and insignificant part of her past. She simply would not accept the notion of his daring to intrude upon her life now. It was absurd. She had told him as much in the graveyard that day, and she knew he had seen how determined she was.

For another thing, she was simply too drained by her commitment to Ross at this difficult time to take Tony very seriously. Seeing Tony again had made Leslie realize how little moral weight he possessed as a man. Though he was tall and handsome and strong, he was so lacking in depth, so bereft of the seriousness she had come to expect from a real man, that he did not impress her either with his protestations of love or his threats.

In retrospect she found it hard to believe she had ever been naive enough to think she was in love with such a person. All the more reason, she felt, to keep a thick wall between her youthful indiscretion with Tony and her present life, which was in all respects deadly serious. It would be as absurd for Ross to know about Tony as it would be for him to know about a puppy love his wife had had when she was twelve.

Nevertheless, when she came home from work, especially when Ross was not at home, she found herself standing with her ears cocked, listening to the silence with a new vigilance. She remembered the manic look in Tony's eyes in the graveyard, his crazy certainty that he was right. That look worried her sufficiently to put her on her guard.

After a long moment of solitary vigilance Leslie left the kitchen and walked into the study. She found the papers she had left there this morning and put them into her briefcase.

On her way back to the kitchen she glanced at herself in the hall mirror and saw that the busy morning at work had marred her makeup. Her face looked shiny, and her mascara had been smeared.

She hurried upstairs to the bathroom to powder her face and fix the mascara.

She had to pass through the bedroom to get to the bathroom. She saw the bed on which she would lie tonight with Ross, when the party was finished and a weekend of rest spread before them. A half-smile touched her lips as she applied powder to her nose and touched up her mascara.

She was still thinking about Ross and the weekend as she passed quickly through the bedroom on her way downstairs.

A strong arm came from nowhere and locked itself around her neck before she could cry out.

Tony pulled her roughly down onto the bed beside him. She did not need to see his face to know it was he. Her body's ancient memory of his touch sufficed to inform her who was holding her. She wondered for a split second how he had hidden so effectively in her own bedroom.

She tried to struggle, but the arm holding her was very strong, and in her weakened physical condition she was no match for it. Her cheek was pushed into the pillow. She saw the glass on the bedside table and the little bottle of medication for Ross. A terrible anger burst within her. She felt outrageously trapped.

"What do you think you're doing?" she hissed against the spread. "Get out of here."

"I love you."

The words were a whisper in her ear, almost confidential. Somehow they took her by surprise, though she had heard them on his lips during their conversation in the graveyard. She had not taken him seriously then. But the anguished, almost plaintive note in his voice made her take him seriously now.

She stopped thrashing, but her body remained tense, refusing his touch by its very rigidity. She thought quickly, searching for the quickest way to get him out of here.

"No, you don't," she said.

The arm pushed her down again, more violently this time. She felt a knee curl over her thighs. Now she realized that Tony's tender words masked a huge anger.

"You love me, too," he murmured, his lips touching her ear. "Admit it. Say it."

"Never." She could only mumble her reply, for her mouth was pushed into the pillow. But the distortion of her voice only made her response sound more angry.

There was a moment's pause. She could feel him taking in what she had said, measuring her resistance to him. There was a suspended feeling, as though both of them were on the edge of something.

Then Tony's knee inserted itself between Leslie's thighs. Exasperated, she began to thrash again with all her might. He forced her face deeper into the pillow.

"Scream if you want," he said. "The neighbors are all out at work. Yeah, I cased the neighborhood, Leslie. I know all about you. But just in case anybody hears you, that's all right with me. I don't care if they all know about me. Your husband, too. I'm not afraid to tell the world who I am and what I am to you."

Leslie said nothing. She could barely breath, much less cry out. The pressure of his body was suffocating.

"Now, listen," he said. "All I want from you is something very simple, very basic. Just tell me the truth. Admit to me that you love me, and that you've never stopped loving me. Admit to me that you don't love that broken-down old husband of yours. That you've never loved him—not the way you loved me. Just stop lying, Leslie, and everything will work out. I promise you that."

She shook her head. She would not give in to him, no matter how much force he applied to her. Her own will was stronger than his. Even motivated by love, Tony was not the person she was. He lacked the force to dominate her.

But this thought flew from her mind when his hand pulled up her skirt and found the elastic band of her panties.

An instant later she felt the light touch of his finger between her legs.

Something went crazy inside her. She trembled and shook and flung herself this way and that. She cried out protestations that were drowned by the pillow against her mouth. Every sinew of her body tensed in desperation.

But the finger still rested between her legs, rubbing softly at the quick of her.

"That's where you wanted me before," Tony murmured. "Don't you see, Leslie? You were made for me."

He pulled the panties down her legs.

A long slow sigh escaped his lips as he saw her nudity.

"You're so beautiful," he said.

The creamy round globes of her buttocks, the long, beautiful thighs, the slim waist made slimmer by anguish and overwork and worry, all touched his heart.

"My God, I love you," he said. "You'll never know how much. The years I wasted . . . I've ruined my life for you."

Craziness mingled chaotically with logic in his voice, which now sounded hoarse with passion.

"Say you love me," he said. "Just say it, and you'll save both me and yourself. It's so simple, babe."

"I hate you."

The words had come out with a will of their own. She hoped he had not heard them, but he had. She felt him tense.

He grabbed her hair and yanked her head this way and that.

"So you hate me, do you?" he asked, a furious mocking tone in his voice. "You hate me?"

The panties were halfway down her legs. With a mighty wrench he tore them away. His arm pressed hard into the small of her back.

"So you hate me," he said. "We'll see who hates who."

She felt his body move, and heard a menacing rustle of clothing being removed. She knew what was about to happen. Rage exploded within her, and she fought madly against him.

"Damn you," she cried. "Get out of here. Don't you dare . . ."

But she was no match for him. Very soon he had his pants down, and she felt his naked legs against hers.

"I was your first love," he said, crouching over her. "I popped your cherry, and you thanked me for it. You begged me for more. Remember? You couldn't get enough of me. I gave you your little boy. And now you say you hate me."

Her whole body was trembling like a leaf. She felt the hardness of him come to her loins. He pressed himself warmly there, and began to move. He was moist already, poised to enter her.

"Tony, if you do this . . ." She tried to warn him, but the words would not come. Her voice became a cry of rage and helplessness.

Slowly he entered her. The feeling of him inside her was the worst thing she had ever experienced. It was like a monster inside her, a horrid, hateful thing taking up residence in the moist intimate and vulnerable part of her.

He began to move in and out, holding her down with his powerful hands, the thing inside her grinding and working, driven by his obsession with her and by his own rage.

"Ahhh," he breathed. "I'll bet you haven't had that in a long time, have you, babe?"

He worked smoothly, rhythmically. It was a grotesque parody of tenderness.

"I'll bet that husband of yours can't do this for you," he sighed. "I'll bet he can't get it up for you this way, can he? Not even before he was sick, I'll bet. He's an old man. Did you think he could be a man for you like I am? Did you think he could give you babies like I can?"

There was triumph and challenge in his voice.

"I'll bet you've tried," he said. "Haven't you? Sure you have. You've tried, but he couldn't give you a kid."

Leslie stopped struggling all at once. She lay still now, pulling herself in deep beneath her flesh where he could not touch her. She left her body to him as a dead thing. Let him have it, then. He would never have her freedom, her soul. That belonged to Ross, and to herself.

Tony felt this withdrawal instantly. Her coldness enraged him.

"You goddamned bitch," he hissed. "You leave me hanging out to dry. That's been your game all along. You throw me to the wolves and go on with your life, playing house. . . . You goddamned bitch."

He slapped her head, hard. Seeing the beautiful hair splay out over the pillow, he slapped her again. Her scalp burned from the blows.

"Come on, pussy," he said through gritted teeth. "You can't hold out on me. . . . Come on! Come on!"

He pumped into her harder, and harder still. He slapped her head again, then buried his fingers in her hair, pulling it roughly, playing with her head like a cruel child with a toy.

But she felt nothing now. She had found a hiding place from him deep inside her heart, and it was much stronger than she thought. In that hiding place she kept her love for Ross and her faith in the piece of life she had saved for herself and him. Tony could not penetrate it with his body or his anger.

"Fucking bitch . . ."

She could hear his curses and insults as he jerked and pumped inside her, but she felt nothing at all. This was her victory over him. He had no place in her heart, and she was proving it to him.

But somewhere behind his rage she did hear and feel his desperation. She understood that something in him had snapped when he saw her again after all these years—years that must have been terrible for him, years of defeat and humiliation and dissipation. She saw that he had reached for her as for a life preserver, a final buoy to keep him from being devoured by the quicksand of his own life. And by her rejection, justified though it might be, she was letting him drown.

So there was more than rage in his punishing thrusts. There was a limitless frustration and a despair that she could observe almost calmly from this great distance she had created between them.

And when at last his fury erupted inside her, and she heard his gasps and his hoarse moans, she understood that they were the moans of a desperate child, and not of a powerful, strong man. There was no strength in Tony. Not anymore. Perhaps there never had been. Not when she first knew him, not even long before that. In any case, now he was finished, defeated by life and by his own inadequacy. And he had pathetically tried to take out his failure on her body. Absently she reflected that this was perhaps the essence of rape—the impotent rage of the male who takes out his weakness on a woman's body. An act of hate, certainly, but also an act of anguished, frustrated longing.

She did not move as he ebbed from her. She felt the mattress bounce under her as he got up from the bed. She heard him putting on his pants.

"You made me do it," he said, still short of breath. "I didn't want to hurt you. I wanted to love you. But you threw me to the wolves. You've got your little setup here, playing house with your old man. You don't care about me. You don't care what happens to me. You're the only woman I ever loved, and you don't give a shit about me. Do you?"

She heard the abjection in these last words. But she did not move. She lay on her stomach, listening to the beating of her heart and to her breathing against the pillow. She allowed her immobility and her silence to stand as her final refusal to be moved by him.

Yet she realized he had spoken sincerely when he said she was the only woman he had ever loved. The spectacle of his despair and his loneliness hurt her almost as much as his violation of her. In this way, and only in this way, Tony had touched her after all.

Now he seemed to pull himself together.

"Think about what's happened here today," he said. "You're coming back to me. You'd better prepare yourself. Nothing is going to stand in my way, Leslie. Nothing is going to stop me."

The sound of his insanity, resuming its prattle after all that had just happened, maddened her. She wanted to cry out her contempt for him, to burst his childish bubble with the cruelest words she could find. But she knew that would be a mistake. Things had gone too far. She had to get him out of here, and find time later to plan a strategy for how to deal with him.

She did not look up. He gazed down at her. In her silence she seemed at once defeated and secretive, helpless and mysterious.

"And don't call the police," he said. "Because if you do, I'll kill Ross."

The sound of Ross's first name on Tony's lips was unbearable to her. But she said nothing.

"He's the obstacle, anyway. Isn't he?" Tony said. "He's not doing you any good—he's too sick and too old for that—but he's in the way. That's the bottom line, isn't it?"

Leslie felt her body turn cold. So that was his game. He was threatening Ross, not her. He saw Ross as the key to her resistance to him. And in a sense he was not wrong.

"You never loved him," Tony said. "I could feel that all along. And I felt it just now. He's just a shield you've put up between yourself and your own past. But you can't get away with that, Leslie. You're going to have to let him go, and come back with me, where you belong—or it will be him who gets hurt. Mark my words, Leslie, I'm not kidding." He paused. "He's half-dead already," he added.

Tony's obsession had given him cunning. He knew what would frighten her the most. Not a threat to kidnap her, to hurt her, even to kill her. Instead, a threat to kill Ross, a defenseless invalid, her last lifeline to happiness.

He stood for a moment measuring the effect of his words on her. Then he squared his shoulders and prepared to leave.

"I wasn't here today," he said. "I have a good alibi. Yeah, I thought of that, too. I thought of everything, Leslie. You can't keep me out of where I belong."

He looked at her, a sneer curling his lips. "But you won't call the cops, will you? Not if you want your husband to go on living."

He stood looking down at her. She seemed pathetic, and yet incredibly beautiful, with her skirt pulled up over her waist, her slender legs spread on the bed, and his seed inside her. In this instant, somehow, he felt he had regained his power over her. And he loved her more than ever.

"Pull yourself together and go to work," he said. "And remember: you'll be seeing me."

Then he walked out of the room.

57

New York City
January 10, 1980

IT WAS JILL'S FIRST SESSION with the press.

At the insistence of both the media and his own advisers Jordan had at last asked his wife to allow herself to be interviewed with the baby. The worldwide press was devoured with curiosity about the first child of the richest man in America. Jordan's marriage to Jill had made so many headlines in itself, coming on the heels of his divorce from Barbara, that the fruit of that marriage was big news.

But there was a more important reason why Jordan asked his wife to give in to the media's importunings. Jordan needed all the good press he could get at this crucial moment of the initial implementation of the Lazarus Plan. He had found that getting his bill through Congress was only the beginning. The cooperation of any number of very powerful people, in and outside of government, was required at every stage of the process. Many of those people were already beginning to drag their feet, withholding their cooperation and influence until Jordan either twisted their arms or offered them favors.

It was crucial that Jordan maintain not only his behind-the-scenes influence, but also his high and positive public profile at this moment. The future of his plan could depend on it. As the youngest and most dashing of America's rich men, Jordan already had a glamour that his financial peers lacked. His beautiful wife and new baby added to that glamour and made him an admired public figure. He needed to use that advantage for all it was worth.

Therefore he needed the press on his side. And the press wanted Jill and Meg.

"It will only take an hour," he had said to Jill. "I'll have my press secretary choreograph the whole thing."

He was holding Meg in his arms as he spoke to Jill. He smiled at the baby and held her up.

"You want to meet the press, don't you, honey?" he asked, chucking her under the chin and kissing her cheek. Meg, two months old, smiled and giggled at her father's attentions.

Jill was sitting quietly by the window, regarding them. She was tranquilized, as she had been ever since the baby's birth. Reality had assumed a different face for her during these last months. There was something unreal about Meg, about her growth, her smiles, and about Jordan's doting attentions to her. It was all behind a sort of screen, confusing, menacing even, though it was an image of joy and contentment.

"I suppose I have no choice," Jill said without warmth. In recent times she had slipped into the habit of speaking to her husband in a rather chilly voice. An instinctive defense mechanism made her hold him at arm's length.

Since the baby's birth Jordan had shown no interest in making love to Jill. For a while Jill had hoped that her recovery of her slim figure would attract him. She had exercised diligently and taken special care with her makeup and wardrobe in order to make herself attractive. To no avail. Jordan's old passion for Jill's body was clearly gone.

His passion nowadays was Meg.

He held the baby as he cajoled Jill.

"Do it for me," he said, "and for the Plan. If the press decides it likes you and the baby, it could put us ahead by months, or even a year. I know it won't be fun, but please do it."

He was sincere in his request. And yet there was an impersonality in his manner toward her, a sort of formality, that had been there since before the baby's birth, and that made Jill feel painfully alone in the heart of her own family.

Hearing that cool note now, she dared to defy him.

"And if I refuse?" she asked.

He looked at her, holding the baby in his arms. A spark of anger glimmered in his eyes, and was replaced by a look of disappointment.

"If you refuse, we'll have to try to work out something else," he said. She could feel him withdrawing even further from her.

She decided to surrender, hoping that in giving him what he wanted she could slash one tiny hole through this thickening veil separating them, make one small step toward getting her husband back.

"All right," she said.

The relieved smile on Jordan's face was her reward. He kissed the baby. Then, on an apparent afterthought, he came to Jill and kissed her cheek.

"You're going to be on television," he cooed to Meg with a happy smile. "Won't that be fun?"

The reception was held in the beautiful playroom Jordan had designed for Meg. The baby was in her crib, lying quietly among stuffed animals, as the reporters asked their questions.

"Tell me, Mrs. Lazarus," asked a New York television interviewer whose report would be passed up to the network. "What's it like to be the mother of Jordan Lazarus's little girl?"

Doing her best to ignore the unintentional irony in the reporter's words, Jill managed a smile. In her long life of deception she had never felt herself so completely at a loss. The tranquilizers, effective though they were at giving her a measure of relief from mental pain when she was alone, made her feel jittery and confused in situations where quick decisions or actions were required of her. She struggled to find words that would hide her real emotions while sounding sincere and reflecting well on Jordan and Meg.

"I've never been so happy in my life," Jill said. "Ever since I was a little girl I dreamed of happiness like this, but I never thought it could become a reality."

Her own falseness shocked her. She felt the tranquilizer surge upward, almost slurring her words. She wondered if she could continue to lie convincingly in her debilitated condition.

"Do you think the baby takes after you, or after her father?" another reported asked.

"Well"—Jill smiled—"she's got her father's temper. That's for sure. But I think she has my—"

It was difficult for her to find a word. In two months she had failed to find a single characteristic of herself that had been passed down to her daughter.

"—my sense of humor," she lied at last, not even really knowing what she was saying.

"How does Mr. Lazarus feel about having a daughter?" asked another reporter. "Do you think he wanted a son?"

Jill laughed out loud.

"To say that he was pleased to have a little girl," she said, "would be the understatement of the year. *This* little girl, anyway. He's absolutely crazy about her."

"And I assume the feeling is mutual?" the reporter smiled.

Jill nodded. "They get along beautifully," she said. "They're very close, and I think they're very alike."

"What do you mean?" the reporter asked.

Again the tranquilizer sapped Jill's ability to think on her feet. What had she meant, she wondered? How were Jordan and Meg alike? What was she talking about? What was she doing here with these strange cold-eyed reporters, who didn't like her or care about her, who only wanted their stories?

"Well," she said, "they both have a remarkable ability to enjoy themselves. Meg can lie for hours just staring at the mobile in her crib. And Jordan can sit for hours just looking at a painting, or even watching people go by in the street. Or staring at Meg, for that matter. They're both so at home in the world, it amazes me. While I myself—well, I'm more the busy type, I suppose. Always running this way and that way, always doing things. I don't have that contemplative knack. . . ."

Her words trailed off. She didn't know what she was saying. With every sentence she seemed to fall deeper into a hole that had no bottom, no meaning.

The questions went on for another hour, merciless, intrusive, sometimes tactless. Nearly all of them were the sort of fluff questions the press asks the wives of famous men. And yet so many of them seemed to jab at the wounds in Jill's psyche that had been caused by her estrangement from Jordan and his intimacy with the baby. And the closer they struck at her pain, the more inventive she had to be in making up lies to answer them with. She had never experienced anything so draining in her life.

Why do you think Mr. Lazarus loves his daughter so much?

Do you feel closer to your husband now that you have a child?

What's it like being three instead of two?

Do you feel that your marriage has become more intimate since you've had a baby?

What's it like being the wife and lover of one of America's most admired sex symbols?

And on and on and on, pitilessly. Jill lied more and more, digging her hole deeper and deeper, all the while feeling the cruel truth about her marriage coming closer and closer to the surface of her lies. She was in agony.

After ninety difficult minutes it was over. Jordan's press secretary began steering the reporters toward the buffet that was provided in the living room. Jill could hardly wait until they were gone. She would leave Meg with the nanny, go upstairs, take another tranquilizer, and have a long bath. She could feel the perspiration running down her underarms from the television lights and her own emotional disarray.

She was on her way to say good-bye to the reporters when something astonishing happened.

A figure detached itself from the group and came toward her. As it did so several reporters turned to look. Resplendent in a magnificent Chanel suit that made her look at once dressy and casual, her hair a new, lighter color, wearing a bright and happy hat with matching purse, Barbara Considine moved toward Jill.

"Jill!" she called out. "I'm so glad to see you!"

Jill tried to compose her face, for she could already see the photographers turning to snap the picture of Jordan Lazarus's two wives meeting in public. She wondered how in the world Barbara had got in here. She stepped forward and extended her hand.

Taking hold of it, Barbara pulled Jill to her and gave her a warm hug.

"It's so nice to see you after all this time!" Barbara exclaimed.

To Jill's horror several of the reporters rushed back to them, their notebooks open, and the television cameraman turned his lights back on. Barbara was smiling invitingly at the journalists.

"It's certainly heartening to see you two together," said a reporter for a well-known gossip magazine. "In this world that's an unusual thing."

Barbara turned confidently to the reporter.

"Not at all," she said. "Jill and I have been friends for a long time. There have never been any hard feelings between us. Jordan and I had a good marriage, but then we grew apart. I was happy for him when he married Jill. She's a beautiful girl and a wonderful person."

She turned to Meg, in the nanny's arms.

"But *this* is the one I came to see today!" Barbara exclaimed, taking Meg from the nanny. "How are you, darling?" she asked the baby. "Are those silly reporters tiring you out?"

The reporters were looking on, smiling.

"You look like you're one of the family," one of them observed. "Is that what you hope to be for Meg?"

"Of course!" Barbara said. "I'm her good old Aunt Barbara, and that's what I intend to be. And no child will ever be spoiled the way I'm going to spoil this one, if I can ever get Jordan and Jill to let me take her overnight. So far you can't pry her loose from her father with a pair of pliers."

Barbara was in astonishing form, joking with the reporters, holding the baby, speaking of her affection for Jill, her enduring friendship with Jordan. There was no trace of the shyness that had always made her subdued in public. She behaved for all the world like a celebrity who thrived on the attention of the media.

At one point she grew serious with the reporters, speaking gravely of her love for Jordan, of their marriage and separation.

"In a way," she said, "I have a special feeling for Meg, and for Jill. You see, I could never give Jordan the baby I wanted to give him. We tried everything, but it just wasn't to be. That was not the reason why we separated, but I always felt it as a great loss. When Jordan married Jill, I was rooting for a baby from the outset. And now that Meg has come along, I really feel like a godmother. No one wanted her to come into this world more than I did. And no one loves her more—except her parents, of course."

Jill watched this in amazement. Barbara was lying like a master. The reporters were genuinely touched by Barbara's devotion to the child. Little did they know that Barbara had never been here before today, never sent a congratulatory card when Jill became pregnant or when Meg was born, and had never shown a shred of warmth toward Jill.

This was a great performance, a performance worthy of Jill herself at her best. But Jill did not realize where it was all leading.

After fifteen minutes of chatting with the reporters, Barbara said she had to leave. Jill could hardly wait to get her out and retreat to her bedroom.

The photographers insisted on a picture of the two women with the baby. Meg was getting sleepy, but Jill picked her up gently and held her to her breast. Barbara came to Jill's side. Pictures were taken of Meg being held by Jill, then by Barbara, then by both. Thankfully for Jill, the baby put up with this without complaining.

Then the nanny took Meg, and Jill was left alone with Barbara as the reporters packed up their things for a second time. Jill glanced at Barbara, whose eyes were resting on little Meg in her nanny's arms.

"How did you get in here?" she asked in a low voice, knowing she could not be overheard by the reporters.

"One of them is a friend of mine," said Barbara. "She told me about this little gathering, so I came over. I wanted to see the baby."

Her eyes narrowed as she looked at Meg.

"She's beautiful, isn't she?" she asked.

Jill nodded. "Yes, she is."

There was a tiny pause, just long enough for Jill's raw nerves to sense a weapon being sharpened inside Barbara's mind for use against her.

"But she doesn't look like you, does she?" Barbara added. Her voice was hard, intimate, inaudible to the others.

Jill tried to hide her reaction to these words. She had to keep smiling, for one or two of the photographers were still snapping pictures.

"I don't know what you mean," Jill said.

"You know exactly what I mean," Barbara said, taking Jill's hand possessively as she smiled for the reporters. "She doesn't look like you. She looks like *her*. That's why Jordan is so crazy about her."

"Like who?" Jill asked, turning pale.

Barbara turned to look into Jill's eyes.

"If you don't know that by now," she said, "I feel sorry for you."

Jill experienced a wave of dizziness. The room literally swayed before her eyes. Barbara's words were so outrageous, and yet so close to the wound inside her, that they burned in her mind like a poison.

Events rushed by like pictures on a distorted screen. The baby was being handed back to Barbara for a good-bye kiss. Then Barbara hugged Jill before taking her leave amid the applause and well-wishes of the reporters.

Jill managed somehow to bid Barbara good-bye and then to help get rid of the journalists. The veil between her and the world had grown thicker in these past few moments. She felt as though she was fighting her way through quicksand.

She doesn't look like you. She looks like her.

The words were a sinister anthem, tolling darkly inside Jill's soul. And they rang true, horribly true, because they echoed the irrational fears that had been haunting her since the baby's birth, fears that sundered her from both Meg and Jordan and left her in a miasma of loneliness and despair.

She looks like her.

Jill dragged herself upstairs, leaving Meg to the nanny. She took two tranquilizers instead of one, and managed to finish a hot shower before collapsing on her bed. The reporters were gone and Meg was taking her nap. Jill was alone. But she did not sleep. Nor did the tranquilizers bring her anything resembling rest. The words were inside her now, impossible and yet true, insane and yet cruelly logical.

She looks like her.

Jill lay on her bed, watching the shadows of afternoon creep across the ceiling with malignant stealth. She wondered if she would ever sleep again. The words in her mind would not let her, for they had opened the door to something unthinkable.

In the other room, far away, she heard the sweet murmur of her daughter dreaming.

58

Johnsonville, Long Island

LESLIE WHEELER WAS LOOKING into the eyes of her husband.

"I love you," she said.

Ross smiled through his pain. Though that curiously preoccupied, almost stern look still haunted his face, the light of love outshone it, and warmed Leslie deliciously.

"I love you too, kid," he said, his humor come to stand as an armor around them and their love.

She was still naked, though she had helped him into his pajamas. They had just made love. They had performed sex in the subtle, complicated, and difficult way they had been forced by illness to learn. And they had been successful tonight. Ross's seed was inside Leslie, and she was happy.

He lay admiring her. Though worry and overwork had made her thinner, she was as beautiful as ever. There was a luminous quality about her that made her irresistible.

He touched his hands to her breasts. He savored her physical existence, nourishing himself from her love for him. His eyes glowed with fascination and gratitude.

Then, gradually, weakness began to show in his face.

"Don't stay up too late," he said.

"I won't," she said.

Ever since his first stroke he had gone to bed an hour or two before her. The enormous effort of rehabilitation left him so drained that he had to retire in the early evening. Leslie stayed up, finishing work from the office, sometimes cleaning the house, or just reading or thinking.

He watched her nightgown slip over the silhouette of her naked body.

"What a woman," he smiled. "I don't know what I did to deserve you."

She came to his side.

"Good night, Ross," she whispered, kissing his lips. "I love you."

"That goes double," he murmured, already half asleep.

She turned out the light. She heard his regular breathing as she left the room.

She went down to the kitchen and stood looking down at her list for tomorrow. It would be a long day at the office, including lunch with a client. She would have to shop for groceries on the way home. A typical exhausting day, like the many she had gotten used to over the past year.

She left the kitchen and went into the basement, checking doors and windows. Then she returned to the living room, the garage, the back porch, the side door of the kitchen. Finally she tiptoed upstairs and checked all the windows.

When she was finished she returned to the living room, where a single light burned beside the piano. She read for half an hour, turning the pages of her library book slowly. It was a novel. She smiled as she recalled checking the same book out and reshelving it many times when she worked with Mrs. Babbage at the library.

At ten-thirty she turned out the light and sat in one of the armchairs, listening to the routine sounds of nighttime. An owl hooted in the woods outside. A car turned the corner at the end of the street with a low murmur of tires on pavement. She heard the familiar scurry of a squirrel that often ran across the roof.

In her hand was the longest, sharpest carving knife she owned. She would not let it go as long as she sat here. She knew she might fall asleep in this chair tonight, as she had numerous times in the past few weeks. Ross would never know about this, for she always came to bed during the night and woke up with him in the morning.

Leslie was guarding her house.

She had decided to do so after a long and unsatisfying interview with a local police lieutenant named Greg Clements.

She had described her situation clearly and unemotionally to the lieutenant, telling him about her past association with Tony Dorrance, her marriage to Ross, Ross's stroke, and Tony's return. She had hid nothing, including, at great cost to her own emotions, what had happened the last time Tony was in her house.

The lieutenant had been kind and understanding, but not helpful.

"Had you brought rape charges against him immediately, we might have done something," he said. "The circumstances are difficult. . . ."

Leslie's sad smile had told him why she had not pressed charges against Tony. She knew how slim were her chances of putting Tony behind bars for rape. It would be his word against hers. Besides, Tony had said that he had a good alibi. And he had probably not lied about that. His obsession with Leslie seemed to have given him a ruthless cunning that she must not underestimate.

She had another reason for not wanting to fight her battle with Tony in a public arena. She wanted to keep the two halves of her life separate. She did not want Ross, an already sick and deeply preoccupied man, a man literally fighting for his life, to have to know about Tony. The thought repelled her. She wanted to shield Ross at all costs.

"What can I do now?" she asked. "Tony will come back. I know that. I think he'll try to hurt Ross. He sees Ross as the obstacle between himself and me."

The detective had nodded thoughtfully. "Well," he said, "I can find out where he lives through the insurance company he works for. We'll check him out and see if there are any outstanding charges or warrants against him. But beyond that, there's nothing we can really do until he tries something again. You can't arrest somebody for something he might do. I can have a squad car drive by your house every night, just to check up on you. But that's about it. I sympathize with your problem, but we just don't have the resources or the manpower to handle situations like this, ma'am."

Seeing the fear and the worry in Leslie's eyes, he leaned forward.

"I know the names of some reliable private detectives," he said. "You can hire a man to watch your house. It will cost money, though."

And it wouldn't stop Tony, Leslie mused. If Tony had been clever enough to get into her house before, he would be clever enough to find another opportunity.

Besides, she had no money to spare for private detectives. Illness had taken away what savings she and Ross had managed to collect.

Leslie had thanked the lieutenant and gone home to think the situation over.

Her conclusion had been simple: she must herself assume the responsibility of standing guard over her own house, her own life, until Tony was no longer a threat to her.

From that day on she had sat in this living room, her weapon in her hand, waiting for Tony to make his move.

Leslie sat in the armchair, feeling sleep begin to steal over her in seductive waves. The afterglow of her lovemaking with Ross, combined with twelve hours of work at the office and at home, had left her drained. She could not keep her eyes open much longer.

She looked quietly into the darkness. As a child she had been afraid of the dark. She still had vague memories of her father coming into her bedroom to hold her hand and comfort her when she felt afraid at night.

But now the darkness had become her accomplice. She almost felt herself part of it now, as though she were invisible. She would use it to help her protect her life and her husband.

Leslie felt a new strength within her, a cold resolve. In violating her physically, Tony had in a sense exhausted his weapons against her. He had penetrated to her most vulnerable place with the superior power of his body, but found that in that very place she had constructed a brick wall against him. He had left her bedroom in rage and frustration, because he knew that in raping her he had not won her over.

He might still want her, might still be stalking her, but now she was morally armed to fight him. She was not afraid.

With this thought she sat alone in the armchair, listening to the house. It seemed more friendly and solid than ever, hovering around her in the darkness, for it was her home. Its old walls joined with her in silence to wait out the dark hours until daylight could bring her together with Ross again.

Her head lolled against the armchair. All was still and restful. She closed her eyes again, dream images surging forward like swelling waves to bear her into delicious slumber.

A low voice suddenly brought her awake.

"It won't work, Leslie."

Leslie sat up with a start. Her hand closed tightly around the knife. She felt her body turn cold.

It was Tony.

She fought for control of herself. She had waited for this moment, and now it was here. She was ready.

"Get out of here," she said to the darkness. "Leave now, or I'll kill you." She heard a low laugh.

"You're not going to kill anybody," the voice said. "You're a lover, remember? You're not a fighter."

There was a silence. Leslie was shaking in every limb. If she could see him, find him, she would kill him with her bare hands. He had haunted her life long enough.

His next words made her jump, for he had moved nearer without her hearing him.

"Listen, now," he said. "You're going to come with me tonight. There's no need to pack a bag. I'll give you everything you need. You're going to come quietly and reasonably. When your husband wakes up tomorrow morning, you won't be here."

Again he fell silent, blending uncannily into the darkness. She looked this way and that, trying to sense where he was.

"But if you try to fight me any longer," he said, "if you refuse to come with me quietly, then your husband won't wake up tomorrow at all. Because he'll be dead."

He paused to let her measure his words.

"If you care enough about him to save his life, get up from that chair and come with me," Tony said. "I know you don't really love him. Not the way a woman loves a man. You've just fastened yourself to him in order to forget the past, to forget us. You've used him as a shield between yourself and reality. That can't go on any longer. Either come with me now or I'll eliminate him myself. I don't want to hurt him, Leslie, but I will if I have to."

He gave a low laugh.

"I heard you upstairs tonight," he said contemptuously. "You call that making love? You're living a lie, Leslie. You're not a wife. You're a nursemaid."

She could feel him moving closer as he spoke. In another moment he would be close enough for her to strike. She held the knife tightly in both her hands. If she could slash him once she would have the initiative. The distance to the stairs, to the phone, was very short, and she knew this darkness well.

And no one would blame her. She was defending her house, after all. . . .

Before she could finish framing this thought, something hard struck her in both wrists, making her cry out in pain. The knife fell to the carpet. Her hands went numb. Then a wave of pain shot through her fingers and up her arms.

Tony must have hit her with all his strength. Even now he was at her feet, searching the carpet for the knife. Using her instinct Leslie aimed a kick into the darkness. She heard him cry out as her foot struck him somewhere about the neck or face. She tried to get up, but a powerful arm curled about her shoulders.

"Don't try that again," he growled in her ear. "Do you want to save your husband's life, or don't you?"

He had pulled her close to his face. She smelled his breath. There was something sour, feral about the scent of him. Obsession had taken the man out of him and left only the beast.

He had outwitted her again. And upstairs, oblivious to her battle and her defeat, slept her husband.

Leslie went limp in Tony's arms.

"All right," she said. "I'll come with you."

She could feel Tony's reaction in his embrace. He relaxed, holding her more tenderly now. Her wrists and fingers were still numb. She seemed weak as a kitten.

"Well, that's more like it," he began. "I knew you'd come to your senses—"

He was still talking as she broke his grip with one mighty spasm, leaped from the chair and ran for the stairs.

Surprise gave her an instant's advantage over him. And she was right: she did know the darkness better than he did. She heard a table being knocked over behind her as she reached the stairs. She began to charge upward, taking the stairs two at a time.

She heard a hard thump behind her, and a purposeful grunt. A hand caught her leg as she was reaching the top step.

She turned and kicked at Tony frantically with her free foot. She heard him curse as her heel smashed painfully into his nose. Her hand had curled around the newel post at the top of the banister, and she was holding on for dear life, her legs flailing and kicking.

Neither of them said anything. Their battle needed no words now.

Leslie fought furiously, but Tony's hands were strong. He hung on to her ankle, got a grip on her other leg, and began methodically climbing up her body. She fought harder, scratching at his face with her free hand. She wanted to kill him.

"Bitch," she heard him say. "Little bitch."

She could feel the pent-up violence under his obsession with her. She knew there was no real love in his pursuit of her. Only hate. Hate for his own inadequacy, for his wasted life, and for her independence. He was a tragic figure as he clutched at her feet from the staircase, trying to gain some sort of hold on the life he had lost.

But now her own strength was ebbing away. She was no match for him. She had fought too long, waited too many nights, worked too hard for months on end without adequate food or sleep or peace of mind. She could not fight anymore tonight.

Tony felt her capitulation. He climbed on top of her, his body covering her almost as it had the day he raped her in her bed. Her hand still clung to the banister, but she was exhausted now. He curled an arm around her waist with triumphant languor, enjoying his power over her. He breathed in the scent of her hair, mingled with the aroma of fear. In a moment he would take her away from here. Then he could do as he liked with her.

Tony was lingering over this thought when, all at once, the hall light was turned on.

Blinded by the sudden light, Tony looked to the top of the stairs. Ross Wheeler was standing on the landing in his pajamas and bathrobe, looking down at him.

It was a strange moment, the handsome young man staring into the eyes of the older one, the healthy young man face to face with his sick rival.

A bellow of rage sounded in Tony's throat. He began to push Leslie aside so he could attack Ross.

It was not until that instant that he saw the gun in Ross's hand. Too late. The gun went off.

Ross Wheeler was a severely disabled man. But he had wielded many guns in his time, and he knew their mechanisms well.

Tony had flung himself backward when he saw the gun. He cried out as the bullet struck him, and fell down the stairs. The darkness of the living room engulfed him. There was a sound of crashing furniture, then the bang of the kitchen door as Tony fled the house.

Leslie lay at her husband's feet, still clinging pathetically to the banister. Ross knelt slowly to help her. The gun slipped from his hand to the rug.

Leslie pulled herself painfully to the top of the stairs. Her body ached from her struggle with Tony. She put her arms around Ross's neck.

"Oh, my God," she said. "Oh, Ross . . ."

He held her gently, patting her shoulder. He felt her beautiful body through her nightgown, and smiled.

She looked at him.

"What did you . . . ?" she stammered. "How did you . . . ?"

"I knew something was wrong," Ross said. "It didn't take too much figuring. And I have lots of time on my hands for thinking, Leslie. I can still put two and two together if I have to."

"Where did you—get the gun?" she asked, looking at the revolver on the floor.

"Had it," he said. "This is the Wild West. Didn't you know that? I've got to protect my women."

Amazed by his blithe humor, Leslie smiled and kissed him. Then, surprising herself, she erupted in sobs.

He held her for a long time, kneeling at the top of the stairs with her head against his chest. He stroked her hair and petted her shoulder.

"You should have told me about it," he said. "I could have helped you earlier."

She nodded.

"I wanted to keep it separate from you," she said. "It was all such a long time ago, you see. It was crazy, him coming back this way. I just thought I had to handle it, to . . . I don't know what I thought."

Ross sat down beside her on the top step, not without difficulty. She realized he was an invalid, a man who could not do many simple things. Yet he had just saved her life, perhaps. He had just defended their house. She was torn between her bursting pride in him and her shame at what she had brought on them both.

His next words took her completely by surprise.

"Have you told the Beyers about all this?" he asked.

She shook her head. "I didn't think of that," she said. "It was me he wanted. He only mentioned Terry to try to convince me . . ."

"You should call them," he said. "And the police. As a precaution."

"Yes, you're right."

Suddenly she turned pale. She stared at Ross incredulously.

"You mean," she asked, "you knew about . . . ?"

"For a long time," he said. "I found out even before we were married. But I didn't want to tell you. It was your own private business. I figured you'd tell me in your own good time."

"And you never—blamed me?" she asked.

"Blame you for what?" he asked. "For being human? For having a past behind you? I loved you more, if anything. I'm only sorry that you've had to endure so much of this alone. It should have been me protecting you, instead of the reverse."

She hugged him close.

"You did protect me," she said.

And she was right. In that moment, for the first time in many months, Leslie felt safe.

Two nights after Tony Dorrance's invasion of Leslie's home, a man knocked at the door of Cliff Beyer's house in Farmington, Long Island. When Georgia Beyer answered the door the man pointed a gun at her and demanded that she hand over her little boy.

Georgia backed slowly into the house. The man followed her.

As the door closed behind him, six uniformed policemen greeted him with drawn guns. Within seconds he had been disarmed, handcuffed, and read his rights.

Tony Dorrance—wearing a bandage on his left hand from the bullet wound he had suffered two nights before—was taken in the back of a squad car to local police headquarters and ordered held without bond by a local magistrate. A month later he was tried for attempted kidnapping, home invasion, assault, battery, illegal possession of an unregistered gun, carrying a concealed weapon, and sundry other charges related to his terrorizing of Leslie Wheeler and his attempted abduction of Terry Beyer.

A jury brought in a unanimous guilty verdict, and Tony Dorrance was sentenced to forty years in prison. After sentencing he was transported to Attica Prison, where he began his new life as a convict.

59

New York City
February 20, 1980

THE EYES OF THE WORLD were on Jill Lazarus.

Her picture, with that of little Meg, was on the cover of all the gossip magazines as well as many of the news and fashion magazines. The national media had taken her to their heart, not only because of her beauty and her celebrity as the wife of Jordan Lazarus and the mother of his first child, but also, ironically, because of the newsworthy display of "class" and nobility with which Barbara Considine had drawn attention to them both.

Somehow the episode with Barbara had ignited a firestorm of press interest. The public was beguiled by the notion of an amicable relationship, even a close friendship, between Jordan Lazarus's two wives. Jill was besieged by interviewers who wanted to ask her not only about Jordan and Meg, but about her friendship with Barbara. There were even interviewers who wanted lengthy interviews with the two women together, but Barbara tactfully refused, claiming her work kept her too busy. In fact, Jill had not seen Barbara since the day of her surprise appearance at the press reception for Meg.

The siege of requests for interviews with Jill was unremitting. Jordan had to hire a new secretary simply to field them. And Jill could not refuse them all, for her newfound public profile was turning out to be a great boon to Jordan and his plan. Each week the major wire services buzzed with news of bold new changes taking place in the inner cities thanks to Jordan's army of engineers, business leaders, and financial planners. The Lazarus Plan was big news. And Jill Lazarus was part of it.

When she was not giving interviews Jill took pills and more pills, mixing them in potent combinations in a vain attempt to quell the volcano inside her. But the more pills she took, the less effective they seemed. With each passing day the ground slipped further from under her feet.

She stayed at home as much as possible, searching for a sense of refuge against the prying outside world. But home had become an inhospitable place to her, full of ominous reminders of her own lonely disintegration.

She saw less and less of Jordan, for her own public responsibilities kept her away from him now. And when they were together his armor of politeness shut her out. It was almost more painful to see him than to think about him when he was out of sight.

Meanwhile, being with Meg was an agony. The more Jill studied Meg's face, watched her little smiles as she played in her crib or playpen, the more strange the child looked. Far from being a much-loved extension of Jill's own flesh, Meg seemed like an alien creature whose very existence was part of the prison walling Jill off from the world.

Jill had already reached the point at which she no longer entirely trusted herself around the baby. She was afraid not only of the effects of her constant drugged state, but more profoundly of the raging welter of feelings inside her. The harder she tried to shake free of her own obsessions, the more stubbornly they stole back into her consciousness, blurring lucidity and filling her with terrifying and incomprehensible thoughts. She no longer knew herself, so she could not know what she might be capable of.

Sometimes she looked at Jordan when he was holding the baby in his arms, telling her how much he had missed her during his workday, taking her to look out the window at the East River, pointing out the barges to her and oohing and aahing at the wonders of the world. At those moments Jill found herself staring at her little daughter with jealous hatred. She had to look away before Jordan caught the expression on her face. And when he had handed Meg back to her she cuddled the child nervously, struggling to show a mother's easy warmth even as the frightening, hateful impulse lingered inside her.

And she had to endure this agony entirely alone. Meg was only an infant, and could hardly support her. And Jordan could no longer be bothered to notice Jill either as a wife or as a human being. He had eyes only for his daughter.

After a month of this ordeal Jill was at the end of her tether.

On a cold Thursday afternoon she left the penthouse and had her driver take her to midtown. She had him let her off on Fifth Avenue and told him she would call when she needed him. She had shopping to do, she said.

In reality she just wanted to get out on the streets, away from home. Out among normal people, and away from her own life.

As she walked, unrecognizable behind her sunglasses, she studied the preoccupied, indifferent faces of the New Yorkers streaming past her on the sidewalk. She was grateful for them. They were human, ordinary people, living humdrum lives of struggle and aggravation. Whatever their imperfections, even their evils, they were worlds apart from the rarefied, unbreathable air of her home, a home in which she had no place.

She window-shopped disinterestedly, pausing at a jewelry store where she saw a pair of cufflinks that might be nice for Jordan. She did not buy them. She was far too weak for such a conciliatory gesture. Then she passed a toy store where she saw a magnificent stuffed kitten, something Meg would adore. With the last of her strength she went in and bought it. It cost a hundred dollars, but it was worth it, incredibly lifelike, with beautiful tiger fur.

She walked toward Sixth Avenue and paused at Rockefeller Plaza, watching the skaters.

Then she looked up and saw a familiar sight.

On the right, just beyond the RCA Building, were the headquarters of Lazarus International.

Jill craned her neck to see to the top of the skyscraper. She felt dizzy. Her husband seemed to tower over her, his will and his passion dwarfing her, smashing her.

On the opposite side of Sixth Avenue stood the Manhattan headquarters of Considine Industries. In that building, at this moment, Barbara Considine was in her office. The woman Jordan had married, the woman he had never loved. The woman who had exhausted her wiles trying to hold on to him and finally lost him to an opponent of superior skill and viciousness, Jill herself.

Yet Barbara had seemed so happy, so full of life when she burst into the reception for the press in Jill's penthouse. Almost like the cat that had swallowed the canary. While Jill, the victor in their battle for Jordan, now held an empty prize, and was suffering a torture as deep as the lies she had lived with all her life. How ironic, Jill thought, that the loser should be so vibrant and complacent, while the victor, haunted by her own spoils, was slowly going crazy.

Jill looked for a long moment at the skyscraper, thinking of Barbara and what Barbara had said to her last month as the photographers snapped their pictures.

She doesn't look like you. . . .

On an impulse Jill started across the street, holding her stuffed kitten in its plastic bag.

She heard the cry of a horn and a screeching of brakes. She had not only crossed against the light, she was not even in a crosswalk.

Chagrined, she jumped back onto the sidewalk, went to the nearest corner and waited for the Walk sign, listening to the palpitating of her heart. When the sign came on she crossed the street and entered the headquarters of Considine Industries.

There was a security gate in front of the elevators.

"Can you phone a message to Ms. Considine's office for me?" she asked one of the two security men.

He looked at her suspiciously. No one visited the powerful Barbara Considine in this manner.

"Who shall I say is calling, Miss?" he asked.

"Jill Lazarus," she said. "Mrs. Jordan Lazarus."

He raised an eyebrow. "One moment, please," he said.

There was a pause. Jill stood gazing around the opulent marble lobby. Everything she saw seemed heavy, almost lethal in its power, from the shining rock walls to the polished banks of elevators.

After an astonishingly brief pause the phone rang, and the guard told Jill to go up to the 56th floor. She took the elevator. When she reached the unfamiliar floor she saw a clearly marked office with the name on the glass doors:

BARBARA S. CONSIDINE

CHIEF OPERATING OFFICER

Jill walked in. The secretary smiled and buzzed the inner office. Almost immediately Barbara appeared. She was wearing a crisp business suit with a foulard and a beautiful emerald bracelet. She still had that vibrant, healthy look that had struck Jill a month ago. She looked slim and trim. As she came forward she seemed very tall, towering over Jill.

"What a surprise," she said, ushering Jill into her private office. "Have a seat. Can I get you something? Coffee? A drink perhaps?" In the last remark Jill thought she heard a probing allusion to the secret drinking she had been doing lately, but she could not be sure. Her emotional disarray was causing her mind to play tricks on her.

"Nothing, thanks."

"Well," Barbara said. "To what do I owe the honor?"

Jill looked into Barbara's eyes. The cottony veil that had hung between Jill and reality these last months made Barbara look distant and a little sinister. Jill cursed her own weakness. In the old days she had seen other people, their petty concerns and their weaknesses, with a pitiless clarity that had allowed her to manipulate them as she liked. Now that clarity was gone, and with it her power over herself as well as others. But she mustered what was left of her own strong will and spoke out.

"What did you mean," she asked, "when you spoke to me while the photographers were snapping their pictures?"

Barbara raised an eyebrow in apparent puzzlement, but quickly dropped the feint and looked at Jill with a penetrating expression in her eyes.

"What do you mean, what did I mean?" Barbara asked.

Confused by this turn of phrase, Jill blinked.

"You know what I'm asking," she said. "About Meg. You said she didn't look like me."

Barbara came around the executive desk and sat down in the armchair beside Jill's. Jill could smell her perfume.

"You really want to know?" Barbara asked.

Jill nodded.

"Sometimes," Barbara said thoughtfully, "Nature can speak through the flesh of a child. You see, I knew all about Jordan and Leslie. I watched them carefully. I saw the way he looked at her. I saw the shape of their love. I understood her character. Even her heart, in a way. I came to know what Jordan loved in her, what he saw and prized in her."

She hesitated for a moment, as though motivated by pity. Then she spoke coldly.

"It's not you he loves in that child," she said. "It's Leslie."

Jill closed her eyes briefly as these terrible words registered in her soul. Then she opened them and saw the other woman gazing hard at her.

"That child doesn't belong to you," Barbara said. "She belongs to Jordan and to Leslie. That's why she makes Jordan so happy. That's why he dotes on her the way he does."

There was a pause. Barbara seemed to choose her words carefully.

"I couldn't give him children," she said. "You know the why of that. But even if it had been possible for us, he wouldn't have wanted a child from me. It was Leslie he wanted. And now, through you, he has her child. You were just the surrogate mother, just the vessel."

She smiled. "That's why she doesn't look like you," she said. "It's only natural."

Barbara might have been grandstanding, encouraged by Jill's obvious deterioration. But she could not know how monstrous was the effect of her words. No one knew better than Jill how she had masqueraded as Leslie, brought Leslie's soul to life from the depths of her own empty heart, in order to capture Jordan. Now she was taken in her own trap. The baby, Meg, was the living proof of her success and her failure, her crime and her punishment.

Surrogate mother. The words were awful in their truth.

Jill steeled herself to fight back against Barbara.

"You're wrong," she said. "Meg looks like me. A lot of people have said so."

Barbara gave her a long, skeptical look.

"I think you're lying," she said. "But even if you're not, or think you're not, I know what *he* sees when he looks at her."

These words struck Jill a hammer blow. Barbara was watching her carefully, and saw her weapon hit home.

"You can see how happy he is, can't you?" Barbara said. *"You* never made him happy that way. Did you? He's happy now because you've given him Leslie's child. He doesn't need you anymore. He has what he wants."

Jill forced herself to return Barbara's stare. From deep inside her came a last glimmer of her old clear vision. She fought to see into Barbara's soul. What did Barbara want? Why was she going out on a limb this way, saying these insane things as though they were true, announcing these lies with such an air of confidence and power?

The answer seemed to glimmer for a split second in Barbara's eyes. There was a motive there, a comprehensible human motive that Jill could feel, could almost touch. If only her vision were clearer, just one small degree clearer . . .

But now Barbara was vague again, her perfume and her lipstick and her perfectly manicured nails all part of a picture that floated before Jill's eyes like a hallucination. And somehow Barbara was rising, looming higher than before, while Jill shrank into a tiny thing, like Alice in Wonderland after ingesting the fateful cookie. Smaller, smaller, smaller . . .

Then Barbara was not there at all. Jill had slumped to the floor, unconscious.

When she awoke she was lying on the deep leather couch at the far end of Barbara's office. One of the secretaries, looking very worried, was fanning her with a magazine while another rubbed her palms.

Barbara was standing behind them, saying nothing.

"Are you all right, Mrs. Lazarus? Shall I call a doctor?" asked the secretary.

Jill came back to consciousness very slowly. The combined effect of drugs and emotional fatigue on her body had been long in accumulating, and could not be erased in a minute.

"A glass of water," she asked. "Please . . ."

The secretary brought her a glass of ice water. Jill drank weakly from it.

"Shall I call a doctor?" asked the secretary. "There's one right in the building. He's helped us before."

"No . . . no. Just my driver. If you'll call my driver, I'll be fine. I'll wait for him," Jill said.

"Nonsense," said Barbara, taking control. "My own driver will take you home. Veronica, you go with her, to make sure she gets up to her penthouse all right."

"Yes, Ms. Considine," said the obedient secretary.

"Now leave us alone for a moment," Barbara commanded. "Buzz me as soon as the car is ready."

The secretaries left. Barbara and Jill were alone. Barbara sat in the chair beside the couch and took Jill's hand.

"Are you all right?" she asked.

Jill said nothing. She measured the solicitude of this false friend, this executioner with a smiling face.

There was a long pause. The two women looked into each other's eyes. Clearly the tables were turned. Barbara was the strong one now. Though she was only a flesh-and-blood woman, she was armed with the truth; while Jill, whose lack of ordinary human frailty had once made her inhumanly strong, lay limp as a rag at the feet of her triumphant rival.

Barbara sighed.

"I'm sorry if I upset you," she said. "Sometimes the truth hurts. No one knows that better than I."

She was referring to the way Jill had gotten Jordan away from her. She was thinking of her own tragic past, and the way Jill had exploited it to steal her husband from her.

Jill had seen through Barbara then. She had found Barbara's weak points and attacked without mercy. Just as Barbara was attacking now.

And with this thought Jill recalled her fleeting impression of a few moments ago, before she fainted, when she thought she saw a glimmer of what was going on behind Barbara's display of power and cruelty. It was as though she saw the game Barbara was playing. A waiting game . . .

Jill pulled herself together and spoke bravely to Barbara.

"You're crazy," she said. "You're talking this way because he threw you out. He never wanted you. He wanted me."

Barbara laughed, a low, sinister laugh.

"It takes a woman to see through a woman," she said. "You might have beaten me, but I saw through you then, and I see through you now. You were playing a role from the beginning. I know about you. You're an expert at that. You twist men around your little finger by being what you think they want you to be. But your gambit backfired on you. It was never you he wanted. It was the woman you were imitating. You never knew that until it was too late. Until your little masquerade became a child, a living human being. Now it's too late for you. Do you see? Because now that he has the child, he doesn't need you anymore."

Barbara's eyes were locked on Jill in a stare of hatred and triumph. Jill met them with difficulty, retreating even as she tried to return the stare. She cursed her own weakness. If she had her old strength back, she could fight off this woman, no matter how aroused Barbara was.

But Jill was too weak to fight back now. Her old weapons had left her in the lurch.

The secretary knocked at the door.

"The driver is ready, ma'am," she said. "Shall I help you?"

"In a moment."

The door closed. Barbara helped Jill up from the couch. Jill seemed a wraith, emaciated to the point of death, while Barbara was tall and full of fine strength.

Barbara walked Jill to the door. Jill was leaning on her like a child.

Suddenly Jill stopped, just before the door.

"What do I do now?" she asked in a supplicating tone.

Barbara smiled.

"That's simple," she said. "Kill her."

Jill looked at her through wide eyes.

"Leslie?"

Barbara shook her head.

"You still don't understand," she observed. "I gave you credit for more intelligence than that."

Jill turned pale as she realized what Barbara meant.

"Meg," she whispered.

For an answer Barbara gave her a long, penetrating gaze, full of knowledge and purpose.

60

New York City
March 1, 1980

JILL WAS LYING IN HER BED.

The evening was still young. Meg was fussy, and it was Jordan who had given her her bottle. His patience and warmth were amazing. Few men, least of all busy corporate executives, were capable of such tender solicitude for a baby.

Jordan was a perfect father. He always seemed to have the secret to calming Meg down when she was irritable or putting her to sleep when she was restless. He knew her moods very well, and she seemed to trust him utterly with her tiny body and her outsized emotions. Their intimacy was a wonder to behold.

Meg was too young to lie to him, too young to have learned a woman's wiles. He seemed to savor her childish candor. Her little rages and fussing spells endeared her to him as much as her affectionate smiling and cooing. She hid nothing, and that was why he could accept every beloved facet of her. Or so it seemed to Jill.

Meanwhile, Meg was not the same with Jill as with Jordan. Meg did not nestle and coo with Jill as she did with Jordan. Instead she lay passively in her mother's arms, as though living on the warmth of Jill's presence while not, in some deep way, feeling at home in her embrace.

Jill sensed this and was devastated. She realized that her inner turmoil had managed to communicate itself to this helpless child. And the process of alienation was completed by Jordan's delighted, almost passionate displays of affection for Meg.

After the baby's bottle tonight Jill had bathed her and dressed her for bed. She did this with jealous possessiveness, knowing that Jordan would have been eager to do it himself had she let him.

As she soaped and rinsed Meg's sweet little body, she was troubled by the child's mute passivity. Perhaps because her tranquilizers made her hands feel numb, Jill was afraid she would somehow blunder and harm Meg, perhaps by letting her little head bang against the side of the tub, or even by letting her slip under the water. More and more nowadays Jill was tormented by fears that she would accidentally injure Meg.

After the bath she took Meg into the nursery and stayed with her for a few minutes before turning out the light. Jill stood biting her nails as she watched the child's innocent face. Meg looked so beautiful, so foreign.

Before long Jordan came into the room. He swept Meg up in his arms and cuddled her. Jill could hear his murmured talk from the next room as he said a lengthy good night to the baby.

Many was the time these past months that Jill had seen him talk to Meg. The baby would lie on her back on the floor and Jordan would lean over her, taking both her hands in his as he talked to her. She answered him with smiles, little gurgling noises, and eloquent facial expressions that showed she trusted him completely, understood his love perfectly. They were one.

Jill had never had such communication with Meg.

This only confirmed her in her inner belief that in some way, even in the womb, the baby had been alienated from her. Alienated by Jordan's passion for another woman. Brought closer to Jordan by this passion—but sundered even in the womb from Jill herself.

Each day Jill tried to fight this crazy theory of hers. But now that she had heard it articulated by Barbara, had seen its twisted logic confirmed by an outside observer, she could no longer fight it. It was part of her behavior toward Meg, toward Jordan, part of the face she saw in the mirror each day.

When Jordan emerged from the nursery Jill herself went in again. Meg's eyes were already closed, and she barely noticed as her mother bent to kiss her.

Then Jill went to bed.

She paused in the bathroom to take another tranquilizer, brushed her hair out quickly, added a touch of color to her cheeks, and lay down in bed to wait for Jordan.

This was a moment she had been thinking about all day, and for weeks before.

She was wearing a new slip, which she had bought for the occasion on a bleary but effective shopping trip earlier this week. It was not an overtly seductive slip, but sensual in its silken fabric and design. It showed off her rounded young breasts and her supple thighs to advantage. It made her look less like a siren than an attractive young wife and mother whose body retains its charms for her loving husband, the father of her child.

Jill had prepared herself emotionally for this night with all the strength remaining to her. She needed to forge a new link to her husband. If she failed, she was lost.

She no longer blamed anyone but herself for everything that had happened. She had set her cap for Jordan out of ambition, without love. She had been caught in her own trap when she discovered that he had had a great love, a love that could not be so easily removed from his heart as the wife whom Jill had removed so surgically from his life.

Jill had begun to need him, to want him, only when she knew his heart was spoken for. Thus she had gotten the punishment she deserved. She had made her bed, and, because of Meg's birth, was forced to sleep in it.

But the torment she was enduring nowadays, from morning to night, was inhuman, unbearable. Her soul was literally coming apart. She had to try to contact Jordan somehow, before it was too late.

Jordan came into the room. A smile still played across his lips from his time with the baby.

He glanced at his wife as he took off his shirt.

"She's so adorable," he said. "She has a good head on her shoulders. I can feel it already. And I think she really understands some of what I'm saying to her."

He was beaming with happiness. He did not notice the look on Jill's face. He was preparing to go back to the living room and do some of his nightly paperwork and reading.

She had to interrupt him.

"Jordan," she said.

He turned to her. The familiar politeness, superimposed over a look of cold appraisal, was in his eyes.

"Yes?" he asked.

"Jordan, I . . ."

For a second she could not find words. She had been preparing this moment for weeks. She dared not lose her courage now.

"What is it?" he asked. "Are you all right?"

She managed a smile.

"Don't you like my new slip?" she asked.

His eyes darted to the garment, noticing the subtle curves of her breasts and hips underneath it. She was thin, but still very beautiful, with her long blond hair flowing to her shoulders and the fine slender limbs stirring under the flimsy garment.

"Very nice," he said. His voice was peremptory, but he had gotten her message.

"Jordan," she said, "I miss you."

He turned from the mirror, his shirt half unbuttoned. He stood looking down at her, his black eyes inscrutable.

"Jordan," she whispered. "Please."

He seemed to hesitate, as though he was of two minds.

Then he moved forward. She helped him by turning out the bedside lamp quickly.

The room was thrown into shadow, the dim nightlight from the bathroom the only illumination.

Jordan sat on the bed beside her. Slowly he touched a hand to her cheek, then her shoulder, and down to her breast. Her eyes half closed at the feel of his flesh on hers.

Then he kissed her. She put her arms around him and pulled him to her. His kiss tasted foreign, unfamiliar. It had been so many months. . . . Over a year, in fact.

A moan stirred in her throat, more a sound of pain than of excitement.

He cradled her body in his strong arms. She was like a doll, for she had grown smaller, while he was tall and powerful and in fine condition.

He pulled her closer. She tried to make herself pliant and willing, but in that instant a small spasm, born of her months of anguished solitude, made her tense in his arms. Instantly he let her go. She could tell he thought she was rejecting him after all. He was preparing to leave her. She grasped him by both arms and managed a soft smile.

"Give a girl a chance, can't you?" she asked, mustering an echo of the gentle levity that had seduced him when they first met.

He took her in his arms again. They kissed, and she felt his hands close around her cheeks, the fingers in her hair. It was a gesture he had often repeated in the past, gazing into her eyes as the blond hair framed her face.

He was getting excited; she could feel it in his touch. Her own senses were throbbing with something between terrible heat and tense, arctic cold. She ran a hesitant hand along his thigh, closer and closer to the sex that was already hard under his pants, waiting for her.

"Oh, I've wanted you so much," she whispered.

He said nothing. She helped his hands to push the slip up over her uncovered pelvis and breasts, over her head. Now she was naked, slim and lovely as ever, perhaps more beautiful to him for the fact that her body bore the traces of motherhood. She was the mother of his adored child, and she wanted him inside her again.

His hands had come to rest on her breasts. The nipples stood up eagerly under his thumbs. She could see him gazing down at her, fascinated, perhaps as he once had been when he first met her and she was a mystery to him. His breath was coming short, as it always had in those early days when he looked at her nudity.

And now her old persona, the one with which she had originally seduced him, came to her rescue. She lay back with a smile and pulled his head down to her breasts. Her hands curled around his neck as he kissed her. She was, or seemed, natural and willing as her nipple offered itself to him.

"I want you so much," she said.

With girlish boldness she turned him on his side. She unbuttoned his shirt, then unzipped his fly. She unclothed him quickly, seeing the tense penis burst forward as the underpants came off. His body was so beautiful, so lean and hard. . . . She wondered how she had survived without being touched by him for a whole year.

I love you.

The words were on the tip of her tongue, but she did not dare say them. She was afraid they were the last words he wanted to hear from her now, the last words he would believe from her lips. So she pulled him back on top of her, her hands coming to rest at the small of his back.

"Mmm," she murmured, "you feel good."

These were words she had said to him long ago when their bodies were ready for intimacy. She prayed they would strike the right chord in him, as of old.

He was silent, but the urgency in the naked flesh against hers left no doubt as to what he was feeling. His hands were on her shoulders, savoring the softness of her. His eyes were wide open, contemplating her in the shadows.

Her legs spread to invite him. Her thighs grazed his hips. She buried her hands in his hair.

"It's been so long," she whimpered. "I've missed you so much."

Now the long, hard sex between his legs was poised to enter her. A single delicate touch told her they were both moist and ready for love. His body tensed, long arms holding her tighter, pelvis ready for the thrusts to come. And he probed deeper, an inch, and an inch more, caressing her with the tip of himself before coming to her with his whole hard length as he had always done.

An immense relief came over Jill, as though the worst were over, as though the chasm between herself and her husband were at last to be bridged tonight. The agonies she had suffered, the solitude, the suspicions, the desperate impulses, were all to be banished now. Things would be as they once had been, when she was the girl she knew Jordan wanted, when his desire and his passion were things she could be sure of.

"My hero," she gasped as he came deeper, deeper toward the very core of her. "My Prince Charming . . ."

At these words he stopped. His hands tightened around her shoulders. He looked down at her through narrowed eyes.

"Still playing a part, eh?" he said. There was anger in his voice, and a terrible coldness. "Is that the best you can do after all this time?"

She gazed up at him in terror. She held on to his arms, as though to prevent him from escaping her.

"Jordan, no. I was excited. I didn't know what I was saying. Please, Jordan."

But it was too late. He withdrew from her quickly, his strong back tensing to help him get away from her. He disengaged himself from her embrace and stood up, naked.

"I thought you might have learned something in all this time," he said. "But I see I was wrong. You're still the same phony you always were. Well, you'll have to sleep alone tonight, my dear. My tolerance for fakes hasn't increased in the last thirteen months."

"Jordan, no!" she cried. "You don't understand. I wanted you so much. . . . I just lost control of myself. Please, Jordan. Come back. I love you. . . ."

"Love?" he asked with bitter sarcasm. "What would you know about love?"

He threw on his slacks and shirt and left the room. She lay alone in her bed, the covers pulled up over her breasts, the center of her body hot with wanting for him, her heart ready to break. Quiet sobs shook her. She wanted to get up and run after him, to cling to him and beg him to come back. But she knew it would be no use. He had made up his mind. The hatred in his eyes had left no doubt of that. She had had her last chance and bungled it.

She heard Jordan leave the penthouse. The closet opened, the hangers clanged softly as he grabbed a jacket. Then the front door opened and closed. She did not know how long he would be gone.

Alone in her bed, Jill wept openly. The grief tearing her apart was as genuine, as natural as that of any normal woman who has loved with all her heart and been rejected. The old Jill Fleming would have considered such an emotion an impossibility for herself, a thing reserved for lesser creatures.

Now Jill had been initiated into the human race with a vengeance. And the tools with which normal people learn to withstand the horrors of grief, the panic of spurned love, were not in her, for she had never needed them until now, when it was too late.

So Jill lay in her bed, as cut off from the human race as she was from her own soul.

How long she slept she did not know. Somehow the tranquilizer joined with her emotional exhaustion to free her from consciousness. Uncanny dreams taunted her, full of images of Jordan with other women, Jordan with Meg, Jordan cursing Jill and turning his back and leaving her forever.

She was awakened by the ringing of her bedside phone. She was so woozy that she could not pick it up until it had already stopped ringing.

She looked at the clock on the bedside table. Twelve-thirty. Jordan must still be out.

Dazed, she got up and went down the hall to Meg's room. She padded into the room and looked at the sleeping baby. Meg was lying on her stomach, with her little fanny pushed up in the air. Her breathing was soft, inaudible. Her little hands curled once, and then were at rest.

Softly Jill petted her on the back, then grazed her cheek with her fingers. The child gave no sign of having noticed.

Then Jill went back to her room. She sat on her bed wondering where Jordan was. She was too tired to decide whether to take another pill.

The phone rang again, jolting her into wakefulness. She picked it up eagerly.

"Jordan?" she asked.

There was a brief silence.

"Jill?" It was a woman's voice.

"Yes, this is Jill. Who is this?"

"So he's out, is he?" There was amusement in the voice. "You're all alone."

Now the voice had a note of cruel triumph in it. Jill knew who it was.

"Barbara," she said weakly.

"Have you thought of a way yet?" the voice asked.

Jill sat up straight. Her hand trembled around the receiver.

"I—what?" she asked.

"You'll want to make it painless," the voice said, "because you're a good mother. But remember: it has to be done."

There was a click. The line was dead.

Jill sat alone on the edge of her bed, holding the receiver in both hands like a live thing that might be dangerous if she did not immobilize it.

After a while the phone began to whine noisily, to tell her it should be hung up.

But Jill did not hear it. The slow keening cry in her own throat drowned it out.

61

IT WAS SATURDAY.

The day was unusually warm. Leslie and Ross had a long way to walk. Ross carried the smaller bag with the potato chips and napkins, and Leslie carried the picnic basket itself. Ross used his cane. They both walked slowly. There was no embarrassment on the part of either. They had long since gotten used to Ross's infirmity as a fact of life.

They were both in a good mood. The weather was balmy. Pastures and an orchard were on either side of the farm road leading to their picnic site, a knoll under an ancient elm tree where, many years ago, Ross had often brought his daughters and his wife.

It was a beautiful spot, rustic and peaceful. A handful of cows stood in the pasture across the road. Two or three of them were lying down languidly, warmed by the sun. A tractor stood motionless in the field. A crow came from somewhere and flew across the bright blue sky, its large wings spread wide. As it wheeled out of sight, the sunlit scene was left behind it like a painting, silent and eternal.

"It's so quiet!" Leslie observed.

"It always was," Ross said, watching her spread the blanket under the tree. "That's why the girls and I used to love it. There's never a soul here. Dina used to say it was *our* place."

"It does feel that way," Leslie smiled. "As though it was never here for anybody else before we came, and will never be here after we go. A sort of bewitched feeling."

"You've got it, kid," he said.

She had knelt to open the basket, and she looked up at him. He was framed by the brilliant blue sky, the heavy branches above, and the deep woods at the end of the pasture. His hair was white now, and he was very thin. He had never looked more feeble. But in his eyes was a light of love as warm as this sunlit scene.

Leslie came to his arms.

"I love you," she said.

He petted her softly, as though he were as strong and old as this tree, and she could nestle securely in his shadow.

"Love you too, babe," he said.

They stood that way for a long time, swaying in the dappled sunlight, loath to let each other go.

It was Ross who broke the spell.

"Let's eat," he said. "I'm famished."

Their lunch was a happy one, though neither ate very much after all. They had brought a bottle of wine, which Leslie opened while Ross watched. They talked about their future plans. Plans for tomorrow's Sunday dinner with Nancy, who was flying down from Rochester. Plans for the coming week, which would be a busy one at the office. Plans for the summer, which would include a two-week vacation at the cottage in Southwest Harbor, Maine, where Ross had taken his family when the girls were little, but which he had not visited for several summers now and wanted Leslie to see.

And there were plans for next year and the year after, which included an elaborate expansion of Wheeler Advertising's client list, the hiring of at least three new people, and taking over the storefront next door on Church Street. These were bold, innovative plans that Ross would never have made on his own, but he approved them without question when Leslie showed him the financial benefits they were sure to bring. Her thinking, as always, was ambitious and imaginative but not rash. She was, Ross often reflected, a natural-born businesswoman. She could have been the president of her own corporation had she wanted to.

And she might still make it, he thought.

Now their lunch was over and the picnic things put away. Leslie sat back against the trunk of the old tree with Ross's head in her lap.

"I can hardly wait to see the cottage," she said. "I've never been to Maine. I was landlocked all through my youth. I didn't even see Lake Michigan until I was thirteen. We never really took vacations, except for a camping trip or two in Wisconsin."

She smiled. "Summer for me meant no school, and running around town in my shorts and T-shirts with Cathy Erwin or Heidi Everhardt. Buying junk food at the drugstore, going to see the same movie over and over again, sitting on the Everhardts' front porch and playing gin rummy . . ."

"Mmmm," Ross murmured. "Tell me more."

"There's so little to tell," Leslie said. "It was such a quiet childhood. Nothing ever happened. That's the way I remember it. Perhaps because so much has happened since. It seems like there hasn't been a dull moment since I got out of college."

Ross was silent. She squeezed his hand.

In her mind she saw the hectic pageant of her adult life. There was Ogilvie, Thorpe, with dour, suspicious Bud Owens and her desperate gambit on the Aurora Lifestyles account. She would never forget how frantically she had researched the life of Barton Hatcher and decided on the crazy plan of making herself look like his beloved late wife in order to get him on her side. She had been shocked when the plan worked, and even more shocked when the Aurora Lifestyles campaign made the company millions of dollars and Leslie a celebrity.

After that initial victory her life had been a rushed succession of challenges, each more ambitious than the last. She had watched her talent increase with experience, and had begun to think of herself as a real woman, an adult who was in control of her own destiny.

How vain that self-image had been! Emotionally she had been a babe in the woods, light-years away from really knowing herself. And it had been at that moment, when she was so full of false ideas about who she was, that Tony Dorrance had come along.

Tony had dislocated her life completely and set it on a new course, the course that led eventually to the man she now held in her arms. What strange tricks life plays on us, she thought. The worst disaster that befalls us can have silver linings we don't begin to see until years after the fact. And perhaps never . . .

In a crazy way she had Tony to thank for Ross himself. She would never have met Ross had she not desperately and hopelessly followed the trail of her child to Long Island. From Tony through Terry to the Beyers, her fate had led to Ross Wheeler.

For a brief moment she reflected on Tony's unexpected return to her life in the past year. She still had trouble believing it was all real. Everything about it seemed so wrong, so twisted. It made no sense for her life to come full circle and to cross the path of Tony again. There was no poetic justice, no proportion or rightness in it. Even now she looked upon this twist of her fate as something insane, something wrong. It was a sort of blunder on the part of the gods, a wrinkle in the fabric of fate.

She looked down at Ross and caressed his thinning white hair. He looked more than ever like an old man. But he was her old man. She smiled at the aptness of the familiar expression. Yes, fate had given her a new foothold on life when she met Ross. Not the life she would have dreamed of for herself, perhaps, but a good life nonetheless. A life of being loved for herself by someone she trusted and respected. A life worth sacrificing a lot for.

In this instant another face came into Leslie's mind, and she had to make an effort to force it away. She realized that, had things gone a bit differently, she would not be sitting here under this tree with Ross Wheeler. She would be far away, married to Jordan Lazarus, and she might be reflecting joyfully that the sinuous path she had followed since her girlhood had led to Jordan, the great love of her life, the man who had owned her heart from the moment she met him and who would always own it. How contented, how amazed that reflection would be! Like Cinderella in the arms of her Prince Charming at last, she would still be haunted by the idea that it was all too good to be true.

But she could not think of this, she could not think of Jordan. Not if she wanted to be a happy woman and to walk the real earth. Jordan had come from another world and had transported her there with his love. He had literally swept her off her feet. Her time with him had had a mythic aspect, filled with a happiness too good to be true.

But the forces that had taken him from her had also come from that other world, a world too big for her, too violent, too dangerous.

Jordan would always be kept in a private, locked place inside her, a place she would never visit willingly. Even today, when she saw the constant items in the media about Jordan, his wife and baby, his dedication to the cities, and his ever-increasing fame, she always averted her eyes as from a thing either too painful to behold or too foreign to concern her.

Yet Jordan was in her dreams almost every night. He assumed a dozen guises—strange men, most often, or her father, or Ross, or even herself sometimes—but it was always him. Upon awakening she would recall her dream and recognize him behind his disguises. Then she would put him firmly out of her mind and face the day ahead.

Such was life, she mused. One must put one's Prince Charming out of one's mind if one hoped to live in the world and not be broken by it. Let him live on in one's dreams, if he must. Perhaps that was where he belonged from the beginning.

With this thought she smiled down at her husband's face.

Ross looked up at Leslie, and saw the gentle, caring look in her eyes.

He knew she was thinking about something hidden. Many was the time, in the course of his illness and even before, that he had seen that look. It was as though she were far away and had to bring herself back to him by a brave effort of her heart and her will.

Ross had never felt jealous about this. Though he knew he had never possessed all of her, this only made his love for her the more poignant. The part of her that was devoted to him was more than anything he had ever hoped or dreamed for himself. His cup ran over at the very sight of her beautiful, mysterious face.

He understood now that their efforts to make a child together had been doomed from the start. Not because he was older, and not because he had become ill. The cause was deeper. Leslie had given him all she could of herself, but the rest was not hers to give. And only in that invisible inner place could she have made a child for him.

He accepted this. It was his place to be thankful that she had sacrificed so much for him, and to admire her for pulling stubbornly back from whatever ghost was inside her heart, to give herself to Ross—for better or worse, for richer or poorer, until . . .

As Ross was lingering over this thought the world suddenly lurched beneath him. He opened his eyes wide to find Leslie, but she was not there. The tree had disappeared, and the pasture. He was standing in his mother's kitchen as a little boy. Something was cooking on the stove.

His mother stirred the pot quickly and muttered, "For Heaven's sake, I asked him fifty times to fix this thing." She turned to Ross. "Honey, get me a pot holder, quick."

He turned, but the kitchen was gone now, too. He was on a train. They were walking between cars, and he looked down at the crack in the metal floor. He could see the ground whizzing by underneath the cars. He was dizzy and terrified. He struggled to cry out his alarm, but his voice was gone. An intense smell of burning oil filled his nostrils.

Then the smell was gone, replaced by a pungent aroma of saltwater. He heard the cry of sea birds. The ocean was all around him. The wave under him pushed higher and higher.

A huge pain crashed inside his head. He knew the wave was carrying him out of himself to nowhere. The pain was unbearable.

The earth was turning wildly now. And he would have given in to this crazy whirling, just to get rid of the pain, were it not for the fact that if he let himself go he would never see Leslie again.

So he made a mighty effort, pulling with the last of his strength against the world itself, against the wave. A groan came from deep inside him and rushed forward as he struggled.

His strength was failing, and he was about to give up when, for one precious instant the world gave in, spun backward on its axis, and brought him back to his starting point. Leslie was there, looking down at him.

I love you.

The words sounded in his heart, but his lips were already cold.

Her face was the last thing he saw.

62

Washington, D.C.
April 1, 1980

THE ROSE GARDEN AT THE WHITE HOUSE was packed with reporters.

They were there to see the official reception of all the major staff and leadership of the Lazarus Plan by the president.

It was a large group. The administrative and executive staff alone numbered nearly two hundred people. They came from cities all over the country. In the last year they had been organized into a tight-running team, as efficient in its operations as the best task force in either government or business.

Many of them were young, but by no means all. Jordan Lazarus had chosen his team for experience as well as energy. A lot of his people had been working as urban specialists all their professional lives, and knew the problems of the inner city as well as they knew themselves. Of these, nearly all had long since grown weary and resigned as they saw the cities decay further and further despite their best efforts, and watched the urban inhabitants sink deeper into poverty and despair.

Jordan Lazarus had given them a new vision, and with it new optimism.

Today they sat listening with happy smiles as the president of the United States spoke to them.

"We are here today," the president said, "to welcome you and to thank you. No team of professionals has ever been more talented or dedicated than you, and no single task force has ever been more important to this country."

The president's eyes scanned the large group. He was in a contended frame of mind, and it showed. The Lazarus Plan's success had increased his popularity with both parties by at least a hundred percent, and almost ensured his reelection.

"As I speak to you today," he said, "the Lazarus Plan, after only eight months of implementation, has already made significant changes in the face of our inner cities. To cite only a few examples: in Chicago, the notorious West Side has been partially rebuilt by its own inhabitants with advice and funds provided by government and business in a new partnership. In Harlem, a similar but even more exciting development has taken place. In Los Angeles, the Watts and Inglewood sections have been revitalized.

"All across the country the results are similarly encouraging. Not only have jobs been created for the unemployed of the ghetto. These people are becoming owners of the very buildings they have seen rot around them for the last five generations. Gang activity is dropping every day. And, most amazing of all, the entire process is bringing financial profit not only to the corporations and financial institutions who have invested in it but also to the local, state, and federal governments cooperating with those institutions."

The president paused to glance at Jordan Lazarus, who was seated with three of his most trusted aides near the podium.

"One might say that the Lazarus Plan is decades ahead of its time," the president went on. "Or one might say that we as a nation have been decades behind our time for as long as we can remember, and the Lazarus Plan has finally brought us up to date. Either way, I feel safe in saying that the plan is a work of socioeconomic genius. Thanks to all of you, the blight and the horror of the inner cities, so long considered a sad but necessary by-product of economic progress, is today being wiped away. And as it is wiped away, not only the inhabitants of that urban ghetto but we as a nation are being given a second chance to live in harmony, in progress, and in opportunity."

The president smiled. "The whole world is watching us this year, as the Lazarus Plan moves forward faster and faster toward its goal. And I am proud to be able to say that for once the world is not looking at our cities with pity but with admiration."

His eyes scanned the crowd.

"I want to thank you all for your energy, your creativity, and what can only be called your patriotism. But I think no one here will disagree with me if I say that all our collective efforts would have accomplished very little were it not for the vision and the dedication of one man, the man who started all this, and who will forever be known as the creator and initiator of perhaps the most important single social initiative of our century—Jordan Lazarus."

The audience of staff, onlookers, dignitaries, and press was instantly on its feet. Nearly a thousand people cheered Jordan Lazarus, who stood up to acknowledge the applause with a wave, and who gave a thumbs-up sign of encouragement and pride to the Lazarus workers gathered before him.

The press was in ecstasies. Never had there been a more newsworthy occasion or a better photo opportunity, as Jordan Lazarus flashed his famous smile to the assembled press.

The photographers' only regret was that Jill Lazarus was not there to stand beside her husband. According to the Lazaruses' press secretary, little Meg was suffering from a severe ear infection, and Jill was home taking care of her. Mother and daughter, it was said, would be watching coverage of this great event on tonight's news.

Jill was alone at home, reading the morning paper.

The reports about Meg's health were untrue, planted by Jordan's press secretary. Meg was in perfect health, except for a slight case of the sniffles.

The real reason Jill had not gone to the White House reception was that she was simply too emotionally prostrated to drag herself there.

The atmosphere between Jill and Jordan had become so unbearable since their failed tryst of the month before that Jill had bluntly refused to go to the reception when Jordan mentioned it.

Jordan had seemed of two minds about her refusal. For the past year he had forced her to use her public image to help him and the Lazarus Plan. And she had gone along with his wishes, at great and obvious cost to herself, given the circumstances of their marriage.

But today the plan no longer really needed her. And he could see that she was truly in bad shape. Her pallor and emaciation were beginning to show up in press photos of her.

"All right," he had said. "Take care of yourself. I'll see you tomorrow night."

That was last night. Jill had woken up alone this morning. It was now nearly eleven. Her pills had made her miss the early morning, but at least she had eked out six hours of sleep.

After checking on Meg, who was with her nanny, she had retreated to her bed and drunk two strong cups of coffee in an effort to gather strength for the day ahead. It was not easy.

Now she scanned the newspaper indifferently, taking in the news. The eruption of Mount Saint Helens volcano was in the headlines. The economy remained as bad as ever. A state of siege existed in El Salvador. America had decided to boycott the Moscow Olympics because of Russia's intervention in Afghanistan. Ronald Reagan had won the New Hampshire primary by a landslide. U.S. embassy personnel remained hostages in Iran.

Some of these things might have an impact on Jordan and the Lazarus Plan in one way or another. Jill had long since learned to pay close attention to international and economic developments, for they affected the fortunes of Jordan's plan, and thus his mood. But today the headlines blurred before her eyes. It was only eleven o'clock in the morning, but Jill felt like it was midnight. She just wanted to turn her back on this day and sleep.

Then she saw something in the newspaper that made her sit up.

Though Jordan was in a happy frame of mind, he gave his short speech to the guests and press in the Rose Garden as though in a dream, his real thoughts elsewhere. He had awakened this morning in a strange mood. He felt as though something had changed somewhere in his life, something terribly important, though he could not see what it was.

Last night he had felt a twinge of nameless anxiety when he kissed Meg good night as she lay sleeping in her crib and took his leave of Jill, who was lying in her bed looking at him through exhausted eyes. Jordan had felt as though his little world were endangered somehow, and this filled him with anxiety. At the same time he had the peculiar feeling that fate was about to take a hand in his life, perhaps in a good and liberating way. He could not get to the bottom of his contradictory emotions, and chalked them off to his own nervous anticipation of the White House reception.

When his speech was over he shook hands with the president and the other dignitaries present, and looked forward to leaving as soon as possible. He realized that today was a great moment for himself and for the Lazarus Plan, but he still felt uneasy, and anxious to get out of here.

He could not leave yet. He had to take part in the president's luncheon for the Lazarus staff, and meet with some White House advisers in the afternoon before heading to the airport. Jill was expecting him home for a late dinner.

He thought of calling her now, but realized he had nothing to say to her. With a sigh he moved toward the president, holding out a hand.

Jill was looking at the front page of her newspaper. She noticed a penciled note in neat, hard handwriting in the margin of the paper. It read, "Obituaries. Page 112."

Jill looked at the note for a long moment. She took a sip of her strong coffee. A small chill went through her.

Then she turned the heavy newspaper to the obituary section.

There was a small check mark in pencil beside one of the obituaries.

WHEELER, A. ROSS

Aaron Ross Wheeler, of Johnsonville, Long Island, died Saturday of a stroke. Mr. Wheeler, the founder and longtime president of Wheeler Advertising, a successful Long Island agency, leaves his wife, Leslie, and daughters Nancy and Dina, by a previous marriage.

Visiting hours are from 11 to 3 at Mr. Wheeler's home. Services will be held at the First Congregational Church, Johnsonville, Tuesday at 10 A.M.

Alongside the small obituary was an additional note in pencil. When Jill saw it she turned pale.

"She's free," the note read.

Jill's hands were frozen around the newspaper. For a long time her mind was a blank. Then she began to think. Her thoughts were not rational, but her logic grew out of everything that had happened to her in the past two years.

She closed her eyes. She saw Jordan with Leslie. She knew they would find their way back to each other now. No force on earth could keep them apart. Jill herself, in trying to come between them, had only made of herself a sort of cosmic conduit linking them, her very flesh facilitating their intimacy, producing a child that belonged more to them than to her.

The obituary, and the cruel pencil message with it, made painfully clear that Jill's ill-starred idyll with Jordan Lazarus was at an end. Soon he would ask for his freedom. She would have to give it to him.

And when he left he would take Meg with him. This only made sense. He adored Meg, he lived for her. And Meg, after all, had never really been Jill's child.

Yes, it all made perfect sense. Jill was about to become an irrelevancy, a fifth wheel in the way of Jordan's new, happy family.

Jill had begun to twitch like a mental patient as she sat thinking. The newspaper trembled in her hands. She no longer saw the room around her.

Yes, she thought. It was all over. This was the end. There was no point in trying to stand between Jordan and Leslie. Even if she were to murder Leslie, Leslie would still own his heart. Jill herself would always be a mere ersatz version of Leslie, a sort of pathetic mask whose existence only made Leslie's place in his heart the more secure.

There was nothing she could do. Nothing except to quietly disappear.

But with this thought something snapped inside Jill's mind. It occurred to her that there was, after all, one thing she could do. Even if she herself was lost, there was one mistake she could rectify.

She looked down at the newspaper. She recognized the handwriting in the margin now. She smiled sadly, folded up the newspaper, and put it in the wastebasket.

She got up, wobbled for a minute in her disarray, and steadied herself.

She walked into Meg's bedroom. The nanny was reading a magazine while Meg played quietly in her crib.

"Mrs. Kirkwood," Jill said, "you can leave early today. I'm taking Meg to Washington. We're going to meet Mr. Lazarus there."

Mrs. Kirkwood looked up in puzzlement. "But Mr. Lazarus told me he would be home this evening," she said.

"There's been a change of plans," Jill lied. "We have to have some pictures taken with Meg this afternoon. We won't be home until very late. We won't need you until tomorrow. Would you pack a small bag for her? I'll be ready in a few minutes."

"I worry about her sniffles, ma'am," the nanny said.

"Don't worry about that," Jill smiled. "We'll take her medicine with us."

Jill went back into the bedroom, removed her slip, and took a very hot shower. She caught a glimpse of her emaciated body in the full-length mirror. Somehow the sight of herself, of the long agony Jordan had put her through, gave her a new lucidity. She knew what she had to do. She had never felt so sure of anything in her life.

She began to pack her things. The tremor in her hands had stopped.

It was a long afternoon for Jordan Lazarus. His meeting with the president and his aides went on for more than three hours. This should not have come as a surprise, for the Lazarus Plan was an extremely complex topic, but Jordan had not expected it. He was well behind schedule when he left the White House.

The weather had turned foggy during the long afternoon, and flights were delayed at Washington National Airport until after five. By the time Jordan reached LaGuardia it was six-thirty. He did not enter his Sutton Place apartment house until seven-thirty. He had called Jill to tell her he would be late, but there had been no answer. He had assumed she was asleep or out on a walk with Meg and Mrs. Kirkwood.

He drummed his fingers nervously in anticipation as the elevator went upstairs. The key shook in his hand when he opened the lock. He felt almost desperate to see his family.

The door opened to reveal the empty penthouse. It seemed completely silent.

"Jill? Mrs. Kirkwood?" Jordan called.

He hurried through the rooms, turning on lights as he went. There was no one in the nursery, no one in Jill's bedroom. Mrs. Kirkwood was nowhere in sight, nor was the cook.

Jordan stood in the living room, thinking. Where could they all be? Even if Jill had taken Meg for a walk, Mrs. Kirkwood or the cook would be here.

Jordan looked in the foyer, then in the kitchen for a note from Jill. There was none.

By now he was worried. He searched all the rooms again. Nothing seemed to have been disturbed. The sheer normality of the place was uncanny. Not a cushion or ashtray was out of place.

In the master bedroom he saw a folded copy of *The New York Times* in the wastebasket. This was normal. Jill often read the newspaper in bed. It was today's paper, as the headlines about the volcano confirmed.

At last he returned to Meg's room, the room he knew the best. He stood looking at Meg's things, his eyes darting nervously from the bed to the playpen. Within a few seconds he realized something was wrong. Meg's teddy bear was gone, and her baby blanket. He moved to her closet and threw open the door. Her little suitcase was missing from its shelf.

Jordan stood musing for a few moments. Then he went back to the kitchen and picked up the phone. For a long moment he wondered whom to call.

He recalled his uncanny feelings of this morning at the White House, his sense that something was to happen to his life today, some sort of eclipse or turning point. A great change, for good or ill. The receiver shook slightly in his hand as he dialed a number at his New York headquarters.

"Is Sam Gaddis there?" he asked.

"No, Mr. Lazarus. He's still in Washington. Is there a message?"

"Beep him, will you, and have him call me right away," Jordan said. "I'm at home. Tell him it's urgent."

He hung up the phone and stood alone in the kitchen. He was afraid to walk through the penthouse again. He knew he would find no trace of his family there. And the meaning of that terrible emptiness was coiling inside his gut more painfully with each passing instant.

Mercifully, the phone rang within two minutes.

"Sam," Jordan said. "We may have a problem here, with Jill and Meg. I want you to get on a helicopter to New York right away. Meet me at the penthouse."

He looked at the empty kitchen.

"And, Sam, you'd better call your friends at the NYPD. I think we're going to need the police today."

63

New York City
April 2, 1980

WITHIN HOURS OF JILL LAZARUS'S DISAPPEARANCE, an army of law enforcement professionals and private detectives had been mobilized to search for her.

Though the FBI had refused to become involved because Jill had committed no federal crime, the local and state law enforcement agencies were willing to help Jordan Lazarus because of the enormous benefit his inner cities plan had brought to police departments around the nation. The routine missing persons procedures were bypassed, and an all-points bulletin was put out on Jill and Meg. The police were joined in their search by hundreds of private detectives assembled by Jordan from a dozen agencies in as many states. Until further notice Jill was to be treated—unofficially, of course—as a fugitive, and a top priority case.

But the operation was difficult, because the search for Jill and little Meg had to be kept secret. At this critical juncture in the Lazarus Plan, and given Jordan's high public profile, it would be disastrous for the public to learn that his wife had run off and kidnapped their baby. The Lazarus Plan was a sober, realistic endeavor, covered with prestige by no less an authority than the president of the United States. A lurid news story arising from Jordan's private life might set the plan back many months, even years.

Jordan could not help suspecting that Jill had had precisely this in mind in running off. She wanted her famous husband to feel embarrassed by her. She wanted him to have to cover up her disappearance even as he frantically searched for her. In her emotional disarray Jill felt useless, worthless. And Jordan, to his own shame, had allowed her to feel that way. Now she was using her own low self-image to hurt him. She had picked the perfect moment. If she could not make him happy as a wife, if she could not be a mother to his child and hers, then she could hurt him with her very misery. She could turn his own hatred of her against him. In this entirely unexpected way Jill was getting her revenge for over a year of emotional punishment at the hands of her husband.

Police everywhere were to be on the lookout for a young, attractive woman traveling alone with a baby. Jill's photograph was circulated, but officers everywhere were ordered not to display the photos or allow them to be seen by the general public.

Never in the history of police work had so massive an investigation been pursued so secretively. Every airport, train station, bus station was covered. Every hotel or motel was visited, and Jill's photograph discreetly shown to the proprietor.

The dilemma was that every time a member of the public was shown the beautiful face of Jill Lazarus, there was the danger that this member of the public would share his personal curiosity with others. The police did their best to tell the motel owners and railway clerks that this woman was not Jill Lazarus, that the investigation had nothing to do with Jordan Lazarus or his wife. But their denials had a hollow ring. It was only a matter of time before the public knew all about what had happened, and before Jordan became the focus of a million eager reporters.

The news media, always hungry for the opportunity to report a scandal, were sniffing around the edges of the investigation already. Soon one or another savvy reporter would figure out what was going on. Then there would be a firestorm of inquiry. Jordan and his press secretary had prepared a story to that effect that Jill and Meg were out of the country for a rest. This would hold off the press for a few days, perhaps. But not longer.

Meanwhile, Jordan had far deeper worries than the mere embarrassment that might be caused by his wife's disappearance. And for the first few hours he could not even bring himself to confide these worries to the police and private detectives closest to him.

He did not trust Jill with Meg.

Jill was a desperate woman. Her behavior over the past few months had become increasingly unstable. Worse yet, Jordan knew that her feelings for her daughter were not those of a normal, happy mother. She viewed Meg as an alien creature who stood between herself and her own husband, a rival who had played a great role in destroying her marriage.

This was a crazy point of view, but Jordan could not chalk it up to mere mental illness on the part of his troubled wife. For he himself had done a great deal to foster it.

This he did not admit to the police.

Now that the law enforcement agencies were at work with a vengeance on the investigation, an even more menacing hurdle facing them revealed itself.

The head of the New York State Police contingent assigned to the case had asked Jordan for routine personal information about Jill, including her medical history, parents, education, and employment history. Jordan had told him what he knew—that Jill had been born in Maryland, that her parents had died when she was a child, that she had been raised by her maternal grandparents before going to college at the University of Maryland, and finally that she had completed an MBA at Ohio State. Jordan did not know where Jill had worked before she became Jessica Hightower's executive assistant. He had not had the curiosity to ask.

Detective Lanier, a cold-looking man in his fifties whose face bore a cynical expression imprinted by many years of police work, sat Jordan down the morning after his men had gone to work on Jill's disappearance.

"You wife lied to you," he said without ceremony. "We've checked with Maryland. None of the hospitals show a record of her birth. There's no trace of her in the public schools or at either of the universities you mentioned. Her Social Security number is a fake. The grandparents she told you about never existed. Personally, I doubt that she ever set foot in Maryland. Not long enough to leave a trace, that is."

The detective's hard face was not without its hint of pity. Jordan Lazarus, the nation's richest man and one of the most respected men in the world, did not know who his own wife was.

Jordan had turned pale when he heard this shocking news.

"What about the name she used on our marriage license?" he asked.

The detective shook his head.

"Fake," he said. "We've put it through our computers. I don't know who your wife is, Mr. Lazarus. But I know she isn't who she says she is. Because that person doesn't exist."

Jordan took a deep breath.

"Well," he said. "That makes our job a little harder, doesn't it?"

Detective Lanier smiled coldly. "You could say that."

From that moment on the enigma of Jill herself became as much a focus of the investigation as her current whereabouts.

And as the hours crawled by, filled with waiting and dread, Jordan was forced to measure the fact that now, when he needed a personal knowledge of Jill more than ever before—her past, her character, what she would be likely to do under stress—his hands were empty. He knew his wife scarcely at all.

And because of this failure on his part, his daughter might be in danger.

Since everything Jill had told Jordan about her past was false, and since he had learned almost nothing about her since their marriage, he was forced to think back to the time when he first met her.

He referred the detectives to Hightower Industries, where Jill had worked before he met her. The results of this inquiry were not helpful. The employment history Jill had written on her Hightower personnel file proved to be completely false. Jill listed work at two companies, a marketing consulting firm in Delaware and a computer firm in California. Neither firm existed. The recommendations in Jill's file, signed by putative personnel officers in the firms, were fakes.

The personnel director at Hightower who had hired Jill was no longer with the company. A retiree who now lived on a houseboat in Florida, he was located within a few hours by the police. He remembered Jill, he said, because of her subsequent fame first as Jessica Hightower's right-hand woman, then her marriage to Jordan. But he claimed not to recall the circumstances of her hiring. She had been a low-level employee, he said, and it was a long time ago. It was not routine procedure, he said, to check the references of each and every prospective employee. And Jill's performance on the standard intelligence tests had been so outstanding—her IQ was 160—that he had simply hired her without question.

The police thanked this man and went on their way. His story made sense. He had not told them the whole truth, however. He had slept with Jill Fleming the day of her hiring, at three o'clock in the afternoon in a downtown hotel. The ability shown on her intelligence tests was nothing compared to her expertise as a lover. He had never forgotten that afternoon, and would take the memory to his grave.

He saw no reason to tell it to the police. It would not help them find her now. And it would not do him any good, certainly. Not if Jessica Hightower found out about it. She was a willful woman, and her arm was long indeed.

On the Hightower personnel form Jill had listed her parents as Grant and

Martha Fleming of Meriden, Connecticut. She had been born in Holy Family Hospital in Bangor, Maine, on February 22, 1950. She had attended public schools in Maine until second grade, finished her public education in Connecticut, and attended the University of Rochester, where she completed her B.S. in business. She had never been married. She had two siblings, both older sisters, both married. Their names were Jocelyn and Alissa.

All these statements were false. Grant and Martha Fleming did not exist. Nor did Jill's putative sisters. There was no record of her public school education in Maine or Connecticut. The University of Rochester had never heard of her.

Jill was a nonperson, a walking fake. Though she was now known all over the world as Jordan Lazarus's wife, and she had given interviews to a hundred publications—though she was a "household name" in every sense of the word—she did not exist. She was a pure profile, a surface without depth, unknowable despite her celebrity.

Jordan cursed himself for not having been more curious about Jill when he first met her and fell under her spell. It would have been so simple to have her checked out by his own people. How he could have used that information now!

But he realized with a bitter smile that it had been precisely her spell that had rendered him incurious about her past, and even about her character. And that spell did not come only from Jill herself. It came from his incurable, desperate love for another woman, the real face behind Jill's mask, the real secret behind her charm. It was his own obsession with Leslie, reflected by Jill, that had blinded him to Jill's reality. And Jill herself had not only acquiesced in this deception, she had willfully engineered it.

So the secret of Jordan's false marriage, which had already done so much harm, was now coming back to haunt him in this final ironic way. He could not help the law enforcement agencies to find his wife, because he knew nothing about her, had never been curious enough to find out anything about her.

He could almost see Jill smiling to herself about this helplessness of her husband as she ran further and further away toward her secret destination. She knew Jordan had no trail to follow. His indifference to the real person underneath her surface was making him helpless to pursue her.

The only trail leading past this apparent dead end came from Jessica Hightower herself. Jessica met privately with Jordan and the head of his task force of detectives. After being told enough about the present situation to understand why Jordan was so desperately worried, she agreed to share what she knew about Jill and to keep Jordan's secret.

Jessica was shown the personnel file Jill had filled out at Hightower a few months before the two women met. It was the first time she had ever seen it. As she studied the file Jessica's face showed more than a trace of the embarrassment Jordan himself was feeling. Her own obsession with Jill, dating from the horseback riding accident that had begun their relationship, had also made her incurious about her young friend's past. She knew nothing about it except that Jill was—she claimed—alone in the world, with no living relatives.

But Jessica did find one discrepancy in the file that gave the detectives a new thread to follow.

"Jill told me she had worked for a company called Continental Products, in Detroit," she said. "It's not listed here in her employment record, but I know it was genuine, because I had it checked out. She held a low-level position in the company. A man named Harley Schrader did her a bad turn, and she was fired."

Jessica cleared her throat a bit nervously.

"I know where Mr. Schrader can be found," Jessica said. "I worried when Jill told me her story, so I kept track of him."

She gave the detectives an address. Jordan thanked her warmly for her cooperation. If he wondered why and how she knew the whereabouts of an obscure business executive named Harley Schrader, he was tactful enough not to ask. He knew that Jill Fleming, before her marriage, had meant a lot to Jessica. Perhaps too much.

On the basis of Jessica's information, detectives visited Continental Products that very afternoon.

The personnel files at Continental Products indeed revealed the hiring of Jill Fleming some nine years earlier. These files were sent by fax to Jordan and his aides in New York.

They were interesting files. Like the ones at Hightower Industries, they listed an employment record that was absolutely false. It included education at two universities and stints at two nonexistent companies, and recommendations from two former bosses who also did not exist.

The personal life story told by Jill on her job application flatly contradicted that told by her later application to Hightower Industries. Yet there were strange, telling similarities.

Jill named different parents. Her mother's name was Jocelyn, the application said. The father's name was Charles. This time there was a brother and a sister, David and Bethany. Jill's birthplace was listed as Homestead, Florida.

The detectives noticed the repetition of the name Jocelyn in both applications. But they could draw no conclusion from this apparent coincidence.

With this the trail of Jill Fleming dried up.

As for former business executive Harley Schrader, his business career since he left Continental Products was a one-way street to nowhere.

He had been summarily fired from Continental in 1975. Since that time he had worked in half a dozen companies, in positions of ever lower responsibility, and been let go by each of these companies in turn.

The detectives saw the profile of a man disintegrating in middle age. What they did not see was the fine hand of Jessica Hightower pursuing Harley Schrader from job to job, using her power and influence to get him fired from one position after another. They did see evidence of his descent into alcoholism, and of his sexual adventures with women of a lower and lower stripe.

Acting on Jessica's information, the detectives found Harley Schrader working as a salesman in an automobile dealership in Denver. The suit he wore had seen better days. His collar was frayed, and his shoes had obviously come from a discount house.

Harley expressed surprise when they asked about him and Jill Lazarus. Yes, he had known Jill briefly, he said, when they were both working at Continental Products. But their acquaintanceship had been slight.

"She was just a girl in the office downstairs," he said. "I wasn't on real speaking terms with her."

He looked at the detectives, and saw the concern in their faces.

"But a colleague of mine knew her much better," he said, not without a hint of suggestiveness in his voice. "You might look him up. He's no longer with the company, but he shouldn't be hard to find. His name is Roy English. He and Jill were pretty thick there for a while. He ought to be able to give you a personal detail or two about her."

Harley of course did not reveal the truth about his brief physical relationship with Jill, or the bad turn he had done Jill in denouncing her to Roy as his lover. The very fact that law enforcement officials were looking for her, combined with her great fame, sufficed to shut Harley's mouth. It would not do for the great Jordan Lazarus to find out that his beautiful wife had once had a lover and an enemy named Harley Schrader. The reprisal for such a piece of information could be far worse than the misfortunes Harley had already suffered since being terminated by Continental Products.

So Harley put the detectives off, giving them the name of Roy English in the process.

That same evening Jordan Lazarus flew to Miami, where Roy English was now the president and chief operating officer of a large and successful shipping and manufacturing firm called ADF, Inc.

Roy English occupied a spacious office with a view of the ocean. He greeted Jordan warmly and offered him a drink, which Jordan refused.

Roy was in his fifties now, his hair turning gray, his hard face tanned dark by the Florida sun. He looked fit and strong, though there was a tired look in his eyes. On his teak desk was a photograph of his wife, a beautiful and much younger woman, and two small children.

"You have a lovely family," Jordan said.

"Thank you," Roy said. "They keep me interested, so to speak. I got married relatively late in life, and it has made me a happy man."

Jordan quickly got the impression that Roy English viewed his work with cynical detachment, caring little for the company he stewarded so efficiently.

He seemed to have lost interest in the corporate wars, and lived only for his family.

"Family is why I'm here," Jordan said, looking the older man in the eye. "I need a favor from you. And I need your promise to keep our conversation a secret. If you cooperate, I'm sure I can find a way to return the favor. But I'd like to think you'll help me simply from man to man."

"Of course," Roy said. "Name it."

"You knew my wife once, at a company called Continental Products," Jordan said. "She was known as Jill Fleming then, according to the personnel records at Continental. She knew a fellow named Harley Schrader, whom we've already talked to. And she knew you. What I need is any information she might have given you about her past. Where she came from, where her family was located, and so on. I won't pry into your own relationship with her. That's your business. The fact is, I'm looking for her. I need to know where she might have gone."

Roy English's face clouded. He lit a cigarette and regarded his visitor.

"That was a long time ago," he said.

Jordan let these words sink in.

"I know," he said. "That's why I hope you can help me."

Jordan could feel the canny businessman, an old pro, wondering whether he could come to grief by admitting to the richest man in America that he had once been the lover of his now famous wife. Jordan could also feel Roy weighing the possibility that he was already on thin ice because of this, and could perhaps help himself by telling Jordan the truth.

It was one businessman sizing up the other, and worrying, as always, about his own ass.

"As I say," Jordan repeated. "No hard feelings, either way. You help me, and I can help you."

Roy English took a deep breath and stubbed out his cigarette.

"I was in love with her," he said. "We had a relationship for six, maybe seven months. It ended when I found out from Harley—from Harley Schrader—that she had slept with him, too."

He looked Jordan in the eye. "I've always been a man who prided myself on my self-control," he said. "You need all the control you can get to survive at this level. Well, I lost it with Jill. She had me—well, she had me wrapped around her little finger. I had proposed to her. We were going to be married. But she wanted me to take over the presidency of Continental at the time. I didn't see the connection—I was too crazy about her—but my assuming the presidency was the precondition of her agreeing to marry me. Then Harley told me he had slept with her. I realized she had used Harley to get to me, and only wanted the power and money I could give her."

He sighed and leaned back in her chair.

"I fired her," he said. "Summarily. I never saw her again after that." A look of pain came into his eyes as he remembered. "It was the most difficult thing I ever did," he added, "before or since."

He looked at Jordan. "I don't suppose you would understand that," he said.

Jordan said nothing. He was thinking of a similar struggle that had gone on inside his own emotions, long ago. It had concerned a woman named Rebecca Jarman.

"That's the way I remember it," Roy English was saying. "But I never really knew her. I realize that now. She's your wife. You'd know her better than I would."

He saw the look in Jordan's eyes, and avoided it. He knew his story must have hurt Jordan. But he felt an instinctive respect for Jordan, and wanted to help him in any way he could.

"That's all there is," Roy said. "I wish I knew more—but I've told you the truth."

"Thank you." Jordan regarded his host. It was obvious from the look in Roy English's eyes that it had cost him something to dredge up his own memory of Jill.

"How did you know," Jordan asked suddenly, "that Schrader was telling the truth when he told you he had slept with my—with Jill?"

This was a logical question. Roy expected it. As a businessman Jordan would assume Harley was bluffing, just as Roy himself had—until there was proof.

"There was a—" Roy English hesitated. He thought of Jill's seductive birthmark. But he saw the look in Jordan's eyes, and decided to take pity on him. "Let's just say I knew Harley well enough to know he was on the level." He looked at Jordan. "I'm sorry," he said.

Jordan let out the breath he had been holding.

"What's past is past," he said. "I'm looking for my wife, Mr. English. Did she ever tell you anything—anything at all—that would give me a clue as to where to look for her?"

Roy English frowned.

"Did you check the personnel files at Continental?" he asked.

"Yes, we did," Jordan said. "They're a dead end. Everything in the file is false. Her personal data, her employment record. There's not a word of truth in it. What I need is something she might have let slip with you, or something you might have noticed about her, that would give me a clue. No matter how small."

Roy English smiled to hear of Jill's skill at deception. Then he sat back and half closed his eyes. Jordan watched him concentrate. A full minute went by, then two.

"She was a good sailor," Roy English said.

Jordan had to suppress the pang this remark caused inside him.

Then Roy English sighed.

"I wish I could help you more," he said. "But somehow there's nothing to remember. She didn't share the ordinary sort of things about herself. And

I was too crazy about her to check her out. I had no curiosity about her past. Do you understand? When you're that deep under a woman's spell, you become blind. You only see the surface."

Jordan frowned. "I understand," he said.

The two men stood up and shook hands.

"If you remember anything—anything at all that might help," Jordan said, "call me at this number. Day or night." He handed Roy a card bearing his private number.

Roy looked at the business card and raised an eyebrow. "It's that urgent?" he asked.

Jordan nodded. "I don't believe there's much time," he said.

"Good luck to you," Roy said.

There was a silence between the two men, a silence of understanding. Both men had been too hypnotized by this mystery woman to ask the logical, simple questions about her background, the reality of her life. That incuriosity had cost Roy English a lot during his relationship with her. Now it was costing Jordan Lazarus a lot more.

With a sad smile of sympathy, Roy ushered Jordan out of his office.

As Jordan was leaving he glanced again at the portrait photograph of Roy English's young family.

He could not help noticing that the young wife in the photograph bore a subtle but unmistakable resemblance to Jill Fleming.

64

The New York State Thruway
April 3, 1980

LIONEL CRUZ HAD BEEN A TROOPER with the New York State Highway Patrol for six and a half years. He was a career cop, having finished college at SUNY with a degree in criminology and passed the patrolmen's course with highest honors.

His father had been a beat cop in Albany, and one of his three brother, Rodney, was also a state trooper working out of Rochester.

Lionel was the youngest in the family, and the smartest. Already his father was pressuring him to put in for lieutenant at the end of next year. It was hard for Lionel to explain to the old man that he enjoyed being a trooper. He loved cruising the roads and highways alone in his squad car, loved first-hand contact with people, especially when he could help them. Even the speeders who gave him dirty looks as he wrote out their citations filled him with ironic affection.

Lionel Cruz was uncomfortable with authority, and always had been. Perhaps this had something to do with his father's dominating personality, or with the family's expectations for its sons. In any case, Lionel was in no hurry to move up in the police hierarchy. At present he was walking a career tightrope, doing his work well and garnering his share of honors, but avoiding the natural step of putting in for a promotion.

His superiors could not quite make him out. But many of his beat colleagues understood him perfectly. They knew that a certain kind of man becomes a cop in order to feel the street under his feet, to collar the criminal one-on-one, to offer the victim a helping hand in the flesh, and thus to feel his manhood, his pride, in a physical and immediate way. These young cops understood that honors were not the name of the game. That, in a sense, the absence of professional ambition was what made a real cop.

It was with them that Lionel Cruz felt most comfortable. Frankly, he wished his retired father would tend his garden and get off his sons' backs. But that was perhaps too much to hope for. The father, after all, wanted his children to have advantages he himself had never had. And a trooper's salary was nothing to write home about.

Lionel was a tall, handsome man of twenty-seven, with gentle blue eyes that belied his chiseled features and thickly muscled frame. He had a pretty young wife and two beautiful children, a four-year-old boy and a girl still in diapers. He did his job well, was happy at home, and felt nothing but confidence in the future.

He just wished his father could understand that.

On this Tuesday evening Lionel was cruising the thruway near the Pennsylvania line. His morning briefing had included the usual roster of wants and warrants, hot plates, and fugitive profiles.

Today something had been different. Sergeant Terwilliger had given all the men copies of a photograph. It was the photo of a beautiful woman.

"I want every man to be on the lookout for this face," the sergeant said. "Keep your eye on possible fugitives. Watch your rental cars, your buses, and especially your hot vehicles. Just make sure it isn't her when you make your collar. Careful pulling over women drivers. She may be dangerous, but we're not sure."

He had hitched up his belt importantly.

"She'll probably have a child with her," he said. "A little girl, about five months old. Be careful. We don't want either of them injured. No high-speed chases."

He scanned the assembled troopers.

"We're doing a favor for someone here," he said, not without a hint of resentment. "Someone important, who has helped this department in the past. As a courtesy to this party, we're keeping this quiet. Just keep your eyes open. If you see her, tail her and report in immediately. And most important of all, don't get curious about who this is. Our business is to find her if she comes through our neck of the woods. The public is not to know about this. Absolutely."

Lionel Cruz had recognized Jill Lazarus immediately. He was an avid reader of the newspapers and had an eye for faces. He prided himself on this, and had often impressed his superiors by picking the faces of obscure felons out of mug files when none of his peers had a clue.

Lionel wondered why the police were looking for the famous Jill Lazarus, wife of the nation's richest and most admired man. If there had been a kidnapping, the sergeant would have said so, and told them to have their weapons ready. Instead, it was just find her and keep an eye on her.

What had she done?

There was nothing in the papers about her. As a matter of fact, Lionel had read this morning that she was on vacation with her daughter in Europe. So why were the New York State police looking for her?

Lionel put the photograph on the inside visor of his passenger window, where he could see it. More than once in the course of the day he glanced at it. Jill Lazarus was an incredibly beautiful woman. Lionel loved his own wife for her fresh looks and the natural sensuality of youth. But there was something preternaturally fine and elegant about Mrs. Lazarus that ordinary women did not have. A sort of composite, crystalline quality—as though in studying her face one were looking into a kaleidoscope of images rather than a simple human visage. It was a face with many values, many secrets perhaps.

Its presence on the visor made the day more interesting for Lionel.

But it was a boring day of work, spent cruising the highway, stopping speeders, most of whom were interstate travelers in a hurry or locals who thought they had outwitted him. He came to the aid of a half dozen stalled cars, and received the thanks of the distressed drivers, which did something to counterbalance the obvious dislike of those he ticketed.

Not a single hot plate crossed his path all day, though he heard on his radio that two of his colleagues had made a collar near Jamestown, a stolen station wagon with two bank robbers inside. Guns drawn, suspects resisting arrest—the whole thing. Lionel wished he had been there.

At six-thirty it was already getting dark. Lionel was cruising languidly toward a little town near the state line where there was a truckers' diner that served an apple pie he was fond of. He would not get off work until eight, and would not arrive home until nearly nine. He was sick of this day. He missed his wife.

Hunger was just beginning to groan painfully in Lionel's stomach when he came to an accident scene.

A semi trailer had rear-ended a broken-down flatbed truck filled with farm equipment and bags of feed. The highway was littered with feed. There were several people standing here and there, and a couple of cars stopped, apparently gawkers.

It took Lionel a few minutes to send the gawkers on their way and to report the accident on his radio. Neither vehicle seemed to have sustained serious damage, but the semi driver was furious at being delayed in his route.

"I gotta get to Harrisburg tonight," he said, buttonholing Lionel as though he could somehow help him, "or they'll dock me half a day's pay. Christ . . .''

Lionel only nodded and took down the driver's name, looking at his registration and license.

"How did this happen?" he asked.

"He didn't have no brake lights," the semi driver said, pointing at an overweight farmhand who was standing glumly by the flatbed truck. "It was getting dark. I was doin' the speed limit, and just about to pass this guy when he hits the brakes. Before I knew it I had popped him."

Lionel took the license and registration of the flatbed driver. The truck was duly registered, all right, though it lacked a recent inspection sticker.

"Let me see your insurance card," Lionel asked the driver.

"Well, sir, that would be at home," the farmer said. "I generally don't keep it in the truck, because . . .''

Lionel was listening to the fellow lie when he noticed three people standing by the side of the flatbed. There was a young man in a sailor's uniform and pea coat, and a pregnant woman who bore a child in a backpack. They looked very poor, and road dirty.

"Who are they?" Lionel asked the flatbed driver.

"Hitchhikers," the man said. "Picked them up outside of Elmira. They're going to Erie. The sailor has to get back to his duty. I thought I'd give them a lift."

"You know it's against the law to pick up hitchhikers, don't you?" Lionel asked somewhat wearily.

"Sure, officer," the farmer said. "But his wife is pregnant, see? And they have the baby and all. I figured, have a heart. Know what I mean?"

Lionel was not distracted from the business at hand by this conversation. He cited the farmer for traveling without evidence of insurance, for failure to have his vehicle inspected, and for traveling without working brake lights. He gave him a ticket with a court date. Then he turned to the semi driver, examined his own insurance card, and pointed to the hitchhikers.

"Were they in the back of the truck when you hit it?" he asked.

"I guess so," the trucker said. "I didn't see them, though. Christ, I hope they're not gonna take it into their heads to sue my company. That would fuck me up royally."

Lionel left the trucker waiting for the tow truck and approached the sailor and his wife.

"Are either of you hurt?" he asked.

They shook their heads. The sailor, a blond fellow with a Navy crew cut, seemed eager to speak to Lionel. His wife, a common-looking creature with stringy dark hair, a bad complexion, and a stare of undisguised hatred for the police, hung back. She was very pregnant, at least seven or eight months. But the dark look in her eyes made it hard to feel much sympathy for her.

"Where are you headed, sailor?" Lionel asked.

"Presque Isle Navy Base in Erie," the sailor said. "My orders are to get there tomorrow by six A.M."

"Why are you hitchhiking?" Lionel asked, with a glance at the young wife. "Isn't that a little hard on your wife?"

"We were going to take the train," the sailor said. "But our money ran out back in Syracuse. I was out of time, so we decided to go this way."

"May I see your identification?" Lionel asked.

The sailor held out his Navy ID. The picture was not a good one, and the gathering darkness made it hard to recognize him. But Lionel could see he was on the level.

"Why are your wife and child with you?" he asked. "They don't have to be with you when you report, do they?"

"Marcie has a job near there," the sailor said. "We were visiting my uncle back in Vermont."

Lionel looked from the man to the woman. The baby on her back was fast asleep. The woman looked tired and dirty. She smelled strongly of sweat, of road dirt, and of something that might have been garlic. She was shifting her weight slowly from one foot to the other as a means of rocking the baby.

"Are you feeling all right, ma'am?" he asked. "Not hurt in any way?"

She answered him with a silence so hostile that he turned back to the husband.

He thought of asking for her ID, but saw there was no point. These were impoverished, ignorant people, down on their luck, without education or prospects.

"You sure no one was hurt in the accident?" Lionel asked.

"We hardly felt it," the sailor said. "Marcie and the baby were asleep. They didn't even wake up."

"I'll give you a lift to the next town," Lionel said. "But you'll have to call your uncle and get him to wire you some money. Hitchhiking is illegal."

"Yes, sir. I'll do that, sir."

Lionel sent the farmer on his way with his three citations, wished the trucker luck, and drove the sailor and his wife to the nearest town with a telegraph office. On the way the sailor talked volubly in a country accent about his duty and his prospects. The wife spoke only to her husband, in a small, whiny voice. The baby was dead to the world, never making a sound.

The back of the cruiser began to smell from the moment they got in, and got worse and worse as they went toward town. It was a smell of old body odor and garlic, almost sickening in its intensity. Lionel was glad to be rid of them. The sailor shook his hand, but the wife gave him a last suspicious look, the look poor people so often reserve for the police, as they entered the telegraph office. Only as he saw her in the light did Lionel notice a black-and-blue mark on her cheek, and a swelling on her nose.

So the friendly sailor was a wife beater, Lionel thought. Well, he could not get involved in that this late at night. Let the woman complain to the police in Pennsylvania about it, if she ever took it into her head to do so. Lionel Cruz was not the world's policeman.

Lionel got home a few minutes after nine. His wife had missed him. He made love to her—the children were always asleep by this hour—and lay by her side in their bed before getting up to drink a beer.

He enjoyed his wife's fresh body and her candid, gentle lovemaking. Once or twice during their quiet tryst the unsavory image of the sailor's filthy wife crossed his mind. He thanked his lucky stars for the fact that his own wife did not look like that.

At ten-thirty they had a snack together, and he sat talking to her about a brother-in-law who was giving the family problems. Lionel gave his advice thoughtfully, seriously, and his wife was grateful.

An hour later they were in bed together, in each other's arms. There was nothing Lionel liked more than to sleep with his wife curled up in his embrace. He loved the warmth of her body, the feel of her trust.

He drifted off to pleasant sleep before midnight.

It was not until three o'clock in the morning that an image from his dreams joined the always wakeful portion of his mind to jerk him to a sitting position in his bed.

"What is it, Lionel?" asked his sleepy wife, rubbing her eyes.

"Never mind, babe," he said. "Just a call I have to make."

Lionel Cruz's legs carried him faster than he expected on his way into the kitchen. His fingers were surprisingly tense as he dialed the phone.

The night sergeant at the station answered after two rings.

"This is Cruz," Lionel said. "Get me Terwilliger right away. I think I saw the woman from the all-points tonight."

"What time?" the sergeant asked.

"Six-thirty or so. I didn't put it together until now. She was well disguised. Made up to look pregnant. Different hair. Goddamn it."

"Ten-four. Call you right back."

Lionel sat in the kitchen, cursing his slowness to recognize the Lazarus woman. Now that he thought back on the brief encounter by the roadside, he realized there had been something strange about the young woman all along. A trick of demeanor, a grace note in her posture that did not quite fit with the identity she was doing such a brilliant job of putting across.

When the phone rang Lionel told Sergeant Terwilliger about the hitch-hiking couple and the young sailor's destination. An all-points bulletin was put out on them immediately. As a precaution, troopers and local police were put on the alert in the vicinity of all the Navy bases within a thousand miles.

Lionel Cruz left his sleeping wife and joined the search. He was not on the scene when the sailor was stopped early that morning, but arrived within an hour. It was the same young man, all right. Lionel accompanied the sergeant into a squad room with him.

"Sailor, you may be in a lot of trouble," the sergeant said. "I'd advise you to tell us the whole truth right now, unless you want to end up in the brig."

The sailor looked frightened.

"She gave me a hundred dollars," he said. "Said she was running away from her husband. She looked as though she was in trouble. I figured, why not? A hundred dollars is a lot of money."

"Did she look the same when you picked her up as she did when I found you by the roadside?" Lionel asked.

The sailor nodded. "She looked pretty bad off. Pregnant and all. Smelled bad, too. But I guess you know that."

"How long were you together?" the sergeant asked.

"A day and a night," the sailor said. "We slept in a motel in Watertown last night."

"What did you talk about?" Lionel asked.

"We didn't talk," the sailor said. "She hardly said two words the whole time. I tried to strike up a conversation once or twice, but she froze me. She had a sort of ugly look in her eyes. I wasn't sorry to get rid of her, if you know what I mean. And the smell . . ."

"All right, sailor," the sergeant said. "We're not going to get you in trouble for this. But I want you to look at some pictures."

The sailor had some difficulty in picking out the photograph of Jill Lazarus from the group shown him. Even thirty-six hours spent with her had left him unsure, so fine was her disguise.

But Lionel Cruz was confirmed in his own opinion when he saw the photographs. It had been Jill Lazarus, all right. Not the phony bruises on her face, nor the changed hair color, nor the false pregnancy could fool him.

But it was only now that Lionel realized why he had recognized her with such ease, albeit seven hours after the fact, and why he was so sure. Though the sailor's filthy wife with her hateful eyes had put Lionel off at the roadside accident scene, it had been that same face, with its camouflaged beauty, its secret charm, that had hung before his mind's eye while he was making love to his wife—still disguised, still fooling him, but there nonetheless, and undeniably seductive behind its mask.

His three hours of troubled sleep must have been spent making the difficult connection between the two faces, until the truth had finally awakened him. In time to pursue her, but not to catch her.

Lionel Cruz could still congratulate himself on his knack for spotting faces. And, like many a civilian before him, he could say that he had seen the famous Jill Lazarus in the flesh.

But he had not caught her. She had slipped through his fingers, cheating him of the greatest coup he would have achieved in his still-young career. He could only bow to her superior cleverness, and ponder the fact that despite her filthy face and her hateful stare she had haunted his mind's eyes as he made love to his young wife.

The all-points bulletin on the traveling sailor and his pregnant wife was changed to a bulletin on the wife alone. Police everywhere were on the lookout for a pregnant woman traveling with a young child.

But the unkempt young woman with the baby in her backpack was seen no more.

By the time the state police caught the young sailor, Jill Lazarus was three hundred miles away, dressed in a tight skirt and tank top that had been packed in her backpack the night before. Her hair was cut off and dyed red. She wore red shoes and net stockings, and carried a tiny red purse. She did not look a day over fifteen.

She was chewing gum and walking languidly through a shopping mall in southern Kentucky. The baby was in a stroller. Any observer would have identified her as a baby-sitter or big sister.

No one recognized her. But she was careful, noting the look in people's eyes as she passed them in the mall, and paying close attention to the clerks who sold her some additional clothes and a bottle of hair dye.

Just as she had been careful when she showed her disguise to Lionel Cruz twenty-four hours ago and spotted in his eyes the capability of seeing through her. He had recognized her, just as she feared. But Jill had been, luckily for her, a large step ahead of him.

65

ON APRIL 4, some seventy-two hours after the disappearance of Jill Lazarus, Calvin Weathers found out what had happened.

Cal's contacts in the law enforcement and detective communities went deep. He had heard twenty-four hours ago that something major was afoot, something that was being hushed up. By calling in a favor Cal managed to learn from a friend in one of the detective agencies working on the case that Jill Lazarus and her baby were missing persons. A nationwide manhunt was in full swing, although top secret. From the moment he heard this news Cal Weathers had not stopped thinking about Jill.

In one way Cal was far behind the army of investigators searching for Jill Lazarus. In another way he was far ahead—though he did not realize it yet.

He was behind because he had not seen Jill since before the birth of her baby, and was not clear about what had been going on in her life since his last investigation for her. He had not even spoken to her in over a year.

But Cal was ahead because, in an odd way, he knew Jill Lazarus even better than her husband did. And during the last year, while Jordan Lazarus had been studiously ignoring his wife, Cal had made it his business to think a great deal about her.

Since Cal's last meeting with Jill she cut the public figure of the happiest, luckiest woman on earth. She was the wife of America's richest and most admired man, a man who was using his wealth and influence to remake the map of urban America. She was on the covers of all the best magazines, she was considered a model of elegance and poise. She had a beautiful little daughter. But Jill Lazarus was an unhappy woman, even a desperate one, behind her mask of marital contentment. Cal had known this a year ago.

And now she had disappeared.

Cal thought back to his last investigation for Jill. That investigation had revealed that her husband had once had an affair with another woman, an affair that had lasted only a few months. But the other woman and Jordan Lazarus had married after their affair ended. It would appear their relationship was a closed book.

One would have thought this piece of news would come as a great relief to Jill, who at the time of the investigation was already Jordan Lazarus's wife. But Cal would never forget the look on Jill's face when he showed her the pictures of Leslie Chamberlain. Jill was a troubled woman indeed, a woman in great pain.

It was this clue that led Cal Weathers like Ariadne's thread through the maze of lies on which Jill had based her marriage and her life, toward a truth she kept hidden from all the world.

Cal knew Jill Lazarus in the flesh, so to speak. Not only had she given him her body as a way of binding him to her and ensuring his loyalty. She had, as it were, revealed to him her technique as a seductress. The secret of her success . . .

In seducing Cal, Jill had penetrated intuitively to needs, to fantasies he had never communicated to a living soul. Her power of attraction was based on this ability to find the secret images inside a man's senses, inside his heart even, and to make herself a reflection of them. An irresistible reflection.

Cal could still see, as clearly as though it were yesterday, the look in her eyes as that leather skirt had slipped to her knees the first time he had slept with her. It was a look of calm emptiness, probing for his own desire and finding it quickly. A look that measured his surprise, his excitement, and finally his surrender. She was like a surface without depth, an image graven on the mirror of his own need. Her very unreality had made it impossible for him to keep his hands off her.

Cal suspected that Jill conquered all her men this way. Thus he concluded it was in this manner, with these tools, that she had snared Jordan Lazarus.

Jill's attraction had nothing to do with love. She must have targeted Lazarus, baited him and hooked him, with all the cold skills of her huntress's heart. And she won him, she took him away from his wife. With Cal Weathers's help.

The task had not been terribly difficult, despite Barbara Considine's willful character, because Jordan had never loved Barbara. His marriage to her was one of convenience. But suppose Jill found out, after marrying Lazarus herself, that his heart was not as empty as her own. That he had had, in the past, a great love, a love he had not gotten over and would never get over.

And suppose that his marriage to Jill was, in its own subtle way, a marriage of convenience. After all, not even a woman with Jill's talent for engendering desire could provoke love in a man like Jordan. Not if his heart was already spoken for.

If Jill became aware of these facts, or was brought to see her marriage in this manner, one could easily imagine her frustration. She had conquered Jordan Lazarus, true, but only in the flesh. His heart still belonged to someone else.

And from this frustration, love might grow. Even in a woman as empty as Jill. Her emptiness, indeed, might make her love more difficult to control. In

a sense, her long life of loveless adventures must have left her heart as untouched as that of a virgin. And, like a virgin, she would fall hard when she
fell. She would become obsessed with the man she loved. And obsessively
jealous of any other woman who might have a claim on his heart.

On its face it was an improbable theory, thought Cal, almost gothic in its
dark logic. Women like Jill Fleming do not fall in love. They do not know
the meaning of the word.

Cal would have rejected the theory out of hand were it not for two things.
The first was Jill's haunted, almost desperate reaction to the photos of Jordan
with Leslie Chamberlain that he had assembled for her. Jill had never displayed
any human emotion before that day. In retrospect her disarray was that of a
woman in love, a woman scorned. And Leslie Chamberlain was the source of
her torment.

The second proof was now in Cal's hand.

It was a copy of *The New York Times,* opened to the obituary page on
which the death of Ross Wheeler was announced. Jill Lazarus had disappeared
six hours after the newspaper appeared.

Cal Weathers had long since learned that coincidence plays a far smaller role
in human affairs than necessity. At least where detective work is concerned. It
was no coincidence that Jill Lazarus had disappeared with her baby only hours
after the death of Ross Wheeler was announced. Cal would lay heavy odds
on this proposition.

But where was she headed?

Thanks to a friend at the FBI who owed him a rather large favor, Cal
Weathers had this evening come into possession of the two job applications
that had given the law enforcement agencies their only clues as to Jill Lazarus's
background. Both applications were open on the coffee table before him now.
He sat smoking a miniature cigar and studying them, his glass of beer sitting
untouched on the table.

Each application was as full of lies as the other. Cal's friend had made that
clear in handing them over. Cal had to smile at the maze of lies that Jill had
patiently woven to hide her past, to hide the real face of her character. Jill's
life's work had been this maze, this surface without substance. It was the
secret of her domination of other people—but also perhaps the source of
her undoing.

For Jordan Lazarus had penetrated that emptiness and inserted his own
handsome image inside her heart. That must have felt like an incurable wound
to Jill, a monumental breach of her most basic defenses. And this, combined
with finding out about the other woman in Jordan's life, had set her off like
a time bomb.

It was after midnight. Cal was tired. It was time for sleep. But he could
not stop looking from one job application to the other. Something about the
parallel series of lies, at a distance of four and a half years, would not let him

rest. The false job references, the imaginary brothers and sisters, the parents with made-up names—there was something hidden here, something he sensed without seeing it clearly.

He was about to give up and go to bed when a small detail caught his eye.

He looked at the blanks on the Hightower Industries application: Siblings: *Jocelyn, Alissa.* These were phonies, of course, as were the parents named on the application and the Meriden, Connecticut, birthplace.

But now Cal looked at the Continental Products application, now nine years old: Mother's name: *Jocelyn.*

Cal's eyes narrowed. The repetition of the name Jocelyn struck a chord in him. He studied the two applications. There were no other repeated names. The name Jocelyn must mean something to Jill.

Cal got up with a sigh, went to the small kitchen, and dialed a number on the wall phone. He had to wait a long time for an answer.

"Jimmy," he said, "Cal. Yeah, I know. It's late all over. Listen. Have you people cross-checked all the names on these two job applications?"

He listened as the FBI agent wearily explained that every name on the applications had been run through the agency's computers.

"Did you notice that she repeated the name Jocelyn?" Cal asked.

Not without sarcasm the agent said the repetition had been noticed from the outset. But the computer search had revealed no connection between Jill and the five thousand or so felons, crime victims, and suspects whose given name was Jocelyn.

"It's a dead end," the agent said. "Believe me, we ran it into the ground. It's probably somebody she knew someplace. Maybe she thought of it because it's the same initial as her own first name. Anyway, it leads nowhere. Forget about it, Cal."

"Okay," Cal said. "Just checking. Thanks for the tip."

Cal hung up the phone. He was turning back to the living room when he closed his eyes and saw Jill's face. As he did so he heard her voice in his memory. The unique lilt of it stopped him in his tracks. He stood in the silence of the apartment, his ears cocked, as though listening to nothing.

It was a voice that had been around, its complex accent marked by lengthy stints in far-flung parts of the nation. One could hear the South in it, at least as far south as Maryland. And the Pacific Northwest, perhaps southern Oregon. A year's worth of California, perhaps. There was a strong strain from the Eastern Seaboard, Connecticut probably. And underneath all these shifting currents, as though covered over by the rest, was the Midwest. Missouri or Illinois. Cal could not mistake it, because he himself grew up in Chicago.

Jocelyn.

Jocelyn . . .

Suddenly Cal Weathers had an inspiration.

He took the atlas from his bookshelf and began flipping through the index, state by state. His eye ran quickly down the alphabetical lists of cities and towns. Within two minutes he had found what he was looking for.

Excited, he got up, left the apartment, and drove to the office. It was one o'clock in the morning by the time he got there. He used his key to let himself in, greeted the night watchman in the corridor, and took the elevator to the reference room on the fourth floor.

He sat down at a computer terminal and opened the main research file. He had not turned on the overhead lights, and the green display looked eerie in the darkened room.

Child welfare, Cal typed in. *Orphanages.*

View by? the computer asked.

State, Cal typed.

The states came up in alphabetical order. He began to move from state to state, concentrating on those areas of the country where he suspected Jill had lived. In each state he simply read down the list of orphanages or shelters for homeless children.

He found his answer in Illinois.

Jocelyn. It was the name of a small town south of Springfield, where the largest state shelter for homeless and abandoned girls had been located until ten years ago, when the facility was torn down, replaced by a new one near the southern border of the state.

Cal tapped his pen nervously on the desk.

"Great," he murmured. "So where are the records?"

He would not be able to call the Illinois authorities until morning.

He looked at his watch. One-thirty. What could a detective accomplish at one-thirty in the morning? The whole nation was asleep.

But Chicago was only two and a quarter hours away by plane.

Why wait for the night to pass? Here was something to look for. And time might be of the essence now.

Cal quit the file, turned off the computer, and called the airport. As luck would have it, there was a red-eye flight to Chicago leaving in forty-five minutes, with connections to Springfield at dawn.

He could be at his destination by the opening of business hours.

Cal did not go home to pack a suitcase. He hurried downstairs to his car and drove straight to the airport.

It did not occur to him until he got there to call his detective friend and suggest that Leslie Chamberlain be put under protective surveillance as soon as possible. His fascination with Jill had made him forget this side of the question.

He made the call. But, as it turned out, his warning was unnecessary.

66

JORDAN SAT ALONE IN THE LIBRARY of his Sutton Place penthouse, staring at nothing.

Through the silence of the small book-lined room he could hear the distant sounds of the detectives making and answering phone calls. His eyes were closed. He had not slept in nearly seventy-two hours. But the dread inside him was more powerful than fatigue. He felt as though an invisible power source made of the purest cold, colder than any ice, was driving him. He would not sleep until this was over.

Wearily Jordan opened his eyes. He scanned the shelves of books. Nearly all of them were old favorites—Shakespeare, Sophocles, Mark Twain, O'Neill—which he had learned to love long ago and later sought out in rare first editions as a hobby. He got an odd thrill from reading a copy of a book that had been printed during the lifetime of the author. It made him feel as though he were journeying through time to the lost world in which the author actually talked and breathed.

The folio edition of the Shakespeare was, of course, the most dramatic of these finds. Jordan had paid nearly a million dollars for it five years ago. The print was bad, the lines uneven, some of the spelling was wrong—but the book had been printed and sold when Shakespeare was alive. Reading about Othello and Lady Macbeth and Hamlet in this volume was an uncanny, almost metaphysical experience.

Jordan's eye moved from the shelves of books to the large mahogany secretary by the window. It bore a Federal lamp, an antique pen set, and photographs of his family. Nothing else. He made it a rule never to do business at this desk. It was used only for quiet reflection. He liked to sit in the large swivel chair and gaze out at the East River, watching the barges pass and letting his thoughts wander.

But tonight there was no leisure for wandering thoughts. Tonight every aspect of the world Jordan had built for himself was threatened.

Jordan looked at the photographs on the desk. There was a photographer's studio portrait of himself with Jill and Meg, another of mother and daughter, and a third photo, taken by a news photographer, of Jordan with the baby.

The photos were eloquent in their disparity, and that was why Jordan had put them here together. The studio portrait looked posed and stagy. Jordan would not have displayed it were it not for certain old memories he had of people who lived in quiet, workaday homes with pictures of their families on their mantels, pictures that had this stiff but domestic look. For Jordan the picture was a gesture toward his own past, and toward his youthful longings.

The picture of himself with Meg was the dearest. It showed Meg in his arms, a child of three and a half months, leaning back from him and pawing playfully at his face. Her youth made him look older, and the flailing movement of her body made him look solid and almost stern. She was all motion, a blur almost, and her hungry joy in living, her security in his arms, made the picture tug at his heart. Many was the night he had sat here looking at this photo and smiling, even when he felt depressed about other aspects of his life. Meg's happiness, created out of his own veins, seemed to make his whole life worthwhile.

The third picture was the most beautiful, but also the most troubling. He had taken it himself with his newly bought Nikon on a sunny day when he and Jill had taken Meg down to Battery Park. It showed mother and daughter together, with the chilly Atlantic in the background. The Statue of Liberty was a small but eloquent grace note toward the top of the picture.

Jill had urged Jordan to hurry up and take the picture because the breeze was cold. Her own cheeks were rosy from the wind, as were Meg's. They had both been laughing an instant before, but now, as they waited for Jordan to adjust the focus, their faces fell into momentarily reflective poses. Their extraordinary beauty was captured all the more eloquently for this.

The resemblance between them was obvious, at least to Jordan. Though Meg would have Jordan's dark hair when she grew older, there was something airy and blond about her. Her features owed a lot to Jordan, as many observers had pointed out; but her fineness and delicacy made it obvious she was Jill's daughter.

On the other hand, there was an indefatigable energy about Meg, a hungry, almost angry delight in living, that cast her own shadow over her parents' features, and made her her own woman. She was a true individual, and had been from the moment she came into the world.

It was this eager happiness that had stolen Jordan's heart from the time Meg was the tiniest infant. She seemed to know how to live, right from the start. And since Jordan's marriage was so troubled, it seemed that Meg was born to transcend all this, to be a normal, happy girl and woman. Jordan had resolved from the start to make this possible for her, no matter what the cost to himself.

But now this vitality, this unspoiled innocence and joy in living, was perhaps in the gravest possible danger.

This thought brought Jordan cruelly back to reality. He closed his eyes, his dread making it unbearable for him to look at the photo any longer. The idea of harm coming to Meg at Jill's hands was more than he could stand. The last seventy-two hours had been spent in trying to fight off that fear. But it had been growing inside him with each passing moment, each negative report from the police and detectives. Though Jordan retained his calm exterior, he was literally being eaten alive by the terror inside him.

If only he had been kinder to Jill! If only he had done more to support her during this difficult past year. He might perhaps have avoided this crisis. But he had not been able to forgive her for what she had done to him. Her falseness had gone to the very heart of their marriage, had even begun their relationship. Jordan could not bear the thought that he had been made a fool of, not in his head but in his heart.

And somehow Meg's birth, opening the door to something beyond his false marriage to Jill, had thickened the wall between him and Jill. He had found it impossible to reach out to her. He had closed himself off with Meg, had eyes only for Meg, and had left his wife to her own devices.

If he had it to do over again, he would give anything to do it differently, he thought now. He had behaved like a monster. He owed it to Meg, if not to Jill, to make something of this marriage. How could he hope to make a daughter happy if the mother was miserable, and by his own fault?

Jill had tried to reach out to him, he recalled now. And it must have cost her a great deal to do so. But he had rejected her every time.

It was all the more agonizing to think back on this because, deep in his heart, Jordan felt something important for Jill.

Not like his old obsession with her, the surface obsession that had filled him with an almost hypnotic hunger when he first knew her. Not like the false feeling of contentment he had felt right after their marriage, when she was like a precious drug that eased his pain and calmed him. No, his feeling for her had grown beyond all that.

As time passed, and her own misery and loneliness began to play a greater and greater role in their marriage, his mindless passion for her body and her face began to deepen to something more. For in her desperation and her solitude he saw something of himself. A mirror of his own loneliness, perhaps. The happy Jill of their courtship had never really touched his heart. But the unhappy Jill of their troubled marriage had, ironically, touched him in a way he could never forget.

So that, on the terrible night when she used her cruel masquerade to unmask his own obsession, when she taunted him with her uncanny incarnation of Leslie, it was more than just Jill's falseness that seduced him. It was Jill herself he had embraced, Jill's agonized loneliness and emptiness, when he made love to her.

And it had been from that commingling of two troubled souls that Meg had emerged—sunny, eager, blessedly normal Meg, planted by the gods in a sick soil but armed by them to outgrow it, to transcend it.

Yes, Jordan was closer to Jill than he had ever let on, even to himself. And Meg was the proof. But he had never told Jill this. His resentment at her falseness, his humiliation at being caught out by her was too great. He could not forgive her.

He had had his chance to repair the damage, to make a new start for Meg's sake. And he had not taken it. Now he was paying the price.

He was thinking this thought, his eyes closed so as not to have to look at the photograph of Jill with Meg, when a quiet knock sounded at the door of the library.

"Come in," he called.

He swiveled in the chair to see Craig Salek, the chief of his detective task force, standing in the doorway.

"I have news," Craig said.

Jordan sat forward eagerly. "What is it?"

"They've been seen," Craig said. "A New York State highway patrolman made the identification after an accident involving two trucks. She was masquerading as a sailor's wife. She had made herself look pregnant. The baby was in a backpack."

"Where are they now?" Jordan asked, standing up.

Craig Salek shook his head. "They slipped through our fingers. It was a brilliant disguise. This young cop is a crackerjack with faces, but it took him four hours to tumble to who it was. By the time we caught up with the sailor who had helped her, she was long gone. She was very sharp. I'd bet anything that she looks as different from that pregnant young mother as night from day by now."

Jordan sank back in his chair. "Do you have any clue as to where she might be headed now?"

The detective shook his head. "None at all. I'm sorry. We're keeping up the all-points, and watching all the roads in that area. But obviously I can't promise anything."

Jordan sighed. He realized that Jill was marshaling all her powers as an actress in order to elude the police. And she would probably succeed. After all, had she not married him under false colors? Had she not fooled Jessica Hightower and Roy English and who knows how many others before seducing him? There was no limit to her powers of deception. And now she was using them with an unprecedented sense of purpose.

But to what purpose? Where was she going? What was her plan? Jordan cursed himself for knowing her so little that he had not the slightest clue.

He was so devoured by these hopeless thoughts that he had completely forgotten the detective's presence in the room. He started when he heard his voice.

"There's one more thing," Craig Salek said, holding up a folded newspaper. "One of my men found this in your bedroom wastebasket. I wondered if you had seen it."

Jordan held out his hand dully. It was *The New York Times* from three days ago, the day of Jill's disappearance. The headlines were about Mount Saint Helens, the economy, the primaries, and, of course, the Lazarus Plan. They seemed ancient and irrelevant now.

But the detective was pointing out a penciled note on the front page of the newspaper.

Obituaries. Page 112.

Jordan furrowed his brow in puzzlement.

"What's this?" he asked.

"That's what I was going to ask you," the detective said. "Have you seen it before?"

Jordan shook his head. "I didn't see the *Times* that day. I read *The Washington Post* on the plane. I never saw this paper."

"That's not your wife's handwriting, is it?" asked Craig Salek.

Jordan shook his head, looking at the penciled note. As he did so he turned a shade paler.

"Now look at the obituaries," said the detective.

Jordan turned to page 112. He saw the obituary for Ross Wheeler. Beside it was the penciled notation, "She's free."

Craig Salek was watching Jordan closely. "So you never saw this?" he asked.

"Not until this moment," Jordan said.

"But *she* must have," said the detective.

There was a silence. Jordan recognized the handwriting in the newspaper. He knew it very well.

He also realized that he had been taking advantage of his own detectives, and perhaps tying their hands for the last seventy-two hours, by not telling them the whole truth about his married life and the real conflict between himself and Jill.

He took a deep breath.

"Do you think she left because of this?" Craig Salek asked.

Jordan nodded.

"You'd better sit down, Craig," he said. "I have a story to tell you."

As the detective came forward Jordan took a last look at the notation beside the obituary.

She's free.

67

THE HOUSE WAS EMPTY, and had been for six years.

Its last occupants, seven or eight weeks ago, had been intruders: two pairs of teenagers drinking beer and petting on an old mattress in the smaller of the two bedrooms. Five bottles of beer remained from that evening, along with certain stains more representative of embarrassment than of pleasure, and a handful of cigarette stubs.

Similar groups had penetrated the house over the last few years, less frequently at first. The evidence of their brief sojourns in the empty rooms was sprinkled over that of the last real inhabitants of the place, a welfare family that had moved in seven years ago and stayed eighteen months. This family included a father who spent most days looking for work, a mother who sometimes took in laundry, and two little girls.

Both parents drank heavily, as the house could still attest through a scattering of vodka and gin bottles, a few of the beer bottles that did not belong to the later teenage visitors, and, more important, the broken mirror in the little upstairs bathroom, two doors downstairs that had been kicked in—the father's foot easily penetrating the cheap wood—and, of course, the springs of both beds.

If the kitchen counters echoed still with the distant sounds of prickly, slurred conversation always on the edge of violence, the old chairs still felt the nervous warmth of bodies living close to despair. The walls, occupied now by cobwebs and spots of grease, could still hear voices raised in menace, arguments that went around in circles.

And the beds still bore the imprint of illicit love, not only the innocent coupling of adolescent bodies in recent times, but the adult male atop his own child, grunting in the darkness years ago, careful not to wake the sleeping mother, grunts full of caution and warning, "You'll get in trouble if anyone finds out." And, years before that, in the same room, the voice of another father atop another child.

In its forty-five years of life the little house had heard those sounds many times. Sounds of furtive pleasure and of guilt. It had also heard sounds of punishment, the scurry of little feet trying to get away, the frightened yelp of little voices when caught by the hand of the punisher.

And always, these silent walls knew, alcohol was part of the equation. Alcohol was the potion that turned love into violence, loneliness into incest, frustration into abuse and torture. The rooms had seen countless bottles, drained by eager lips and then discarded. Bottles of cheap gin, of vodka, bottles of cheap rye and bourbon and, less often, scotch. Hundreds of bottles of beer, of crude malt liquor, of cheap California wine . . . All bore mute witness to the secret well into which humans sink their anger and from which they draw their courage.

The other traces left by adults in the house spoke of routine and of quiet desperation: the magazines read through by distracted eyes, telling always the same stories; the newspaper, studied quickly for bargains in the ad pages or jobs in the want ads, and then used to carry coffee grounds to the trash, or placed under the dog's water bowl.

But the traces of children, blamed as signs of messiness at the time, now had a iconlike, ceremonial elegance as they remained on walls and in corners, bespeaking inchoate dreams, fantasies, and hopes of a good future, a friendly world. Crayon drawings on the inside walls of closets, little carvings on a banister, pages fallen from a long-forgotten school notebook, a scrap of paper from an easel on which watercolor paintings had once crystallized a child's vision of safety and bliss.

The house was a privileged eavesdropper on the most intimate of human affairs. Had it been a thinking being, it would long ago have concluded that the human world was divided between two sets of creatures as different as night from day: the children, strong and adaptable in their gift for fantasy, fearful where fear was justified; and the adults, driven to an agony of frustration by the loss of their own innocence, and fearful of everything, including most of all themselves.

The house was old and would soon be torn down. Its only inhabitants were spiders, ants, a scattering of moths, the mildew in the basement and bathrooms, and the bacteria growing in forgotten cans of food. The only decor consisted of old armchairs with broken springs, two or three mildewed books on a shelf, an old burst cushion with a silk screen of Niagara Falls, and a faded painting of a smiling hobo on a wall.

But the house, if lacking in intelligence, was gifted with its own sort of memory. Everything in it had been preserved, at a price of decay. The adults had left behind the smells of their cooking, their drinking, their lovemaking; the sounds of their conversations and their bitter conflict. The children had left traces of their hopes, their play, their pain. The house kept it all, an archaeology in dust and crayon, like rings inside the trunk of a very old tree, invisible to the eye that sees only the bark.

And the house was gifted with patience. Helpless to intervene in the suffering that had groaned inside it for so many years, it endured. It watched in silence, taking everything in, missing nothing.

Now the house was in its old age. Its own decay was part of its very structure. Shingles dropped like autumn leaves from time to time. The breezes flowing through its cracks whistled more loudly now, just as, once, the laughter of children had been part of its own youth.

Tonight the house slept in the balm of a warm April evening, particularly fecund for the mildew growing in its corners, particularly inimical to the timbers crumbling under the eaves.

Then something happened.

A sound echoed suddenly through the rooms, like the falling of a twig in an uninhabited forest. It was a hollow groan of old wood, followed by a sharp thump, then the creak of a floorboard. The old screen door at the side entrance, hanging from one stubborn hinge, had been pulled loose, and the inside door forced open.

There were sounds of entry, little scufflings of fabric against wood, of shoes on the dirty floor. Then the sound of a child being put down.

Then a woman's voice.

"Stay right there a minute, honey."

A coat was removed with a soft rustle and flung on the counter that, eight weeks earlier, had held the body of a girl kissing her boyfriend in the darkness of a Saturday night.

Now a sigh. And, again, the woman's voice.

"We made it, Meg. We're home."

68

Springfield, Illinois

CAL WEATHERS STOOD in the basement Hall of Records at the Illinois State Welfare Department. It was ten o'clock in the morning.

He had been directed here by a series of clerks and supervisors. The records of state shelters and orphanages were kept here in endless tiers full of boxed papers and ledgers. Computerization of the vast material had been begun two years ago but was far from complete. This was the only place where records of defunct institutions were kept.

The clerk, an elderly lady with a droopy right eye and pronounced Parkinsonism in the hands, had peered long and hard at the card he had shown her, holding it at an angle as though to facilitate her poor vision. Then she had laboriously written down the call number of the volume Cal wanted.

"To your right, and about twenty rows down," she said in a crusty voice.

He wandered along the ranks of oversized shelves, craning his neck sideways to study the titles embossed on the volumes.

At last he found what he wanted. *Jocelyn, Illinois,* said a series of volumes. *State Shelter for Homeless Girls.* Each volume bore a date. Cal thought a moment about Jill's age, and picked out the volume whose spine read 1955–65.

He sat down at the nearest table and began turning the yellowed pages of the volume.

Immediately he frowned. The volume bore only a list of names and personal data. No pictures. Idly he looked up the name Fleming. There were no girls at the Jocelyn home with the last name Fleming. He smiled at the faint hope that had been dashed by the records.

Cal left the volume open on the desk and walked along the row of books to the desk where the old lady sat.

"Excuse me," he said with a practiced smile. "Were photographs taken of inmates in the state shelters for orphans?"

The old lady looked up with a frown.

"Certainly," she said, her quick reply belying her frail exterior.

Cal thought for a moment.

"Would I be able to find these photographs here?" he asked.

"Simply look in the last volume of each series," she said. "Did you try that?'

"I will now," Cal smiled. "Thank you very much."

He went back to his row of volumes, trying to control his hastening steps. He opened the volumes one by one until he saw one with photographs.

He pursed his lips. There were photos, all right, but not individual ones. These were group photos of the inmates by class and building.

"Damn," he said, moving slowly back to the table with the volume open in his hands.

He sat down and began perusing the pages. The pictures showed groups of forty or fifty girls, sometimes more. Indistinct faces bearing indifferent expressions, from twenty-five years ago. It was hard to tell them apart somehow. Institutional life seemed to erase the humanity from them, leaving blank stares that puzzled the eye and tired the mind.

Cal looked through the photos one by one, forcing his eye to scan each row of girls, missing nothing. He looked for the shapes of noses, the chins, the brows—anything that might strike a chord.

Thirty minutes passed, then forty-five. The fatigue of his sleepless night was beginning to catch up with Cal. His eyes were burning. He suspected he was wasting his time. He had come all this way because of a word that seemed a clue—Jocelyn—but that might mean nothing. Perhaps Jocelyn was simply the name of a girl Jill once knew, as his FBI friend had suggested. Or a girl she had read about in a story. Or simply a name she liked, for no reason at all. . . .

Then Cal's breath caught in his throat. He pulled the volume closer. It was the 1955 file of new girls. The third row, fifth girl from the right . . .

It was Jill.

She could not have been more than six or seven years old. But Cal recognized her instantly. How could one mistake those eyes, with their eloquent look of caution and defiant loneliness? They were the same eyes that had looked into his with triumphant sensuality after twenty years of living had formed Jill into a dangerous, predatory adult. But in the picture they shone with childish vulnerability. She was a new girl; she was afraid and unsure of herself in her new surroundings.

Cal almost let out a whoop of excitement. Controlling himself, he took out his pen, noted the year, the class group, the volume number, and page number.

He looked at the list at the bottom of the photograph.

Third row: Fanning, K., Eiden, B., Cline, K., Holzman, J., Fellows, K., Isaacson, S.

Cal rubbed his eyes. Since the name Fleming was nowhere to be seen, he had to count the names carefully from the beginning of the row.

Gable, J., Heuser, S., Hemphill, M., Rogge, D., Orlando, K., Sundberg, J.

Sundberg, J.

Cal's hand was trembling with excitement. The nondescript name seemed uncanny when applied to the haunting face before him, a face now known all over the world.

Putting a finger on the page where the photograph was located, Cal began to search the volume for additional photos of the same girl, whether in the same group or others. The photos were in chronological order. He was able to find a second photo of Jill, a year older, in a different group. Moving on to the next year, he found her in a larger group, this time as an eight-year-old.

With each picture her face became more inscrutable, more blank. The emptiness of institutional life was erasing the expression she had originally worn. This made sense. Orphans were not happy young people. One did not expect them to reveal their emotions in photographs.

But she was beautiful in all three pictures. Cal felt his heart go out to her in her youthful avatar. A frail blond nymph, blossoming perversely in the arid gray soil of the orphanage.

After the third year he could find no more pictures of her. Keeping the page numbers for reference, he consulted the alphabetical listing of inmates. The name Sundberg had only one reference.

Sundberg, Jill, he read. Intake 10/15/55. Age 6. Y Section, Briscoe House, Jocelyn. Mother S. Sundberg, whereabouts unknown. Father unknown.

The file told a few basic details about Jill's physical characteristics, including blood type. Some childhood illnesses were listed. The results of an IQ test were given. Cal's eyes opened wide when he saw that the girl had an IQ of 160.

There was an enigmatic notation in a sort of bureaucratic shorthand that caught Cal's eye: TRV 145, 146.

He thought of the old lady at the desk, who seemed to know these files well. He took the volume with him and approached her.

"There's a notation here regarding an inmate of a state shelter," he said. "I can't make it out."

"What does it say?" the old lady asked.

"It says TRV one forty-five, one forty-six."

The old woman nodded.

"That means physical and sexual abuse," she said. "One forty-five is physical, one forty-six is sexual." She smiled. "They didn't like to call things by their names in those days. Nowadays they just write it in."

Cal thanked her and returned to his table.

After a few more insignificant remarks, the file on Jill Sundberg came to an abrupt end.

Inmate escaped custody 4/60, read the note. Whereabouts unknown.

Cal Weathers sat back, letting out the breath he had been holding. So Jill had escaped. It was no wonder. Even as a girl she was not the type to waste her life in an institution.

For a moment Cal felt torn between elation and discouragement. His hunch had proved correct. He had found Jill, even seen her image in the heart of her own prehistory. But he had lost her again. The years after her stint in the state shelter were like the Dark Ages. Her whereabouts from the time of her escape to her job application at Continental Products, eleven years later, were a mystery. There was no time to try to follow her trail through that dark decade.

But perhaps those missing interim years did not contain the key to Jill's personality after all. Perhaps that key was to be found here, in her earliest youth. In the orphanage, or more specifically the reason why she came here.

It was the only lead Cal had left. Without it he was back where he started.

He turned back to the beginning of her file.

Caseworker: H. Fleming, he read.

Cal smiled. So this was where she had gotten her name.

He got up, returned to the feeble old woman at the desk, and asked, "Do you have a chronological directory of caseworkers? Names, addresses?"

The old lady smiled.

"You mean the employees' directory," she said. "That's not here."

Cal frowned. "Where do I look for it?" he asked.

"In the computer, upstairs," she said. "I'll show you. I programmed that file myself."

Cal Weathers grinned as he helped her pull back her chair. This day was full of surprises.

69

New York City

JORDAN LAZARUS SLAPPED Barbara Considine across the face.

The blow was so well timed that Barbara was knocked off her feet. She fell backward against the sofa in the living room of her Park Avenue duplex. Blood came from the corner of her mouth. Her cheek glowed an angry red in the subdued light.

She looked up at him, her eyes open wide.

"Where is she?" he asked, taking a step forward. "Where is she?"

Barbara said nothing. A composite look of fear and rigid stubbornness was in her eyes.

"What was your part in all this?" he asked, holding out the newspaper that bore her handwriting in the margin. "Have you been tormenting her? Have you been trying to goad her into something like this? Don't try to deny it. I can see it in your face."

He looked down at her, contempt vying with the anguish in his own eyes. He had never hated Barbara before, but tonight he saw her as a pure enemy. And the look on her face, obsessed, defiant, confirmed him in his hatred.

"That's why you showed up at the press conference, wasn't it?" he asked. "That's why you stuck your nose back into our life. You were trying to get under her skin, weren't you? Trying to put ideas in her head. I see through you now. Don't try to deny it."

Barbara shook her head. The big, dark eyes still stared up at Jordan, fearful but unmoving.

He pointed to the newspaper.

"I didn't tell the police who wrote this," he said. "I'm the only one who knows. But the important thing is that *I* know, Barbara. You haven't fooled me. If anything happens to my wife or my child, I'll know who to hold responsible."

He came forward and grasped her hard by both shoulders.

"If I don't find her in time," he said, "I'll kill you."

Their faces were close together. He could smell her familiar scent, and feel her flesh. This was the woman he had held in his arms countless times, the woman he had trusted and pitied and even counted on for his happiness. But tonight her physical reality seemed eclipsed by her falseness.

Jordan's hands trembled. It seemed as though the falseness that had destroyed his marriage to Jill was spreading through all the corners of his life. He was seeing a new Barbara, a woman he had not known existed. A phrase he had once told himself, *Never trust a woman,* came back to his mind now. He should have heeded it a long time ago, he told himself. Now it was too late.

"What were you doing?" he asked. "Watching Leslie and her husband all along? Waiting for him to die so you could spring this on Jill? Was that it? Tell me."

Barbara said nothing.

"Where is she?" he asked. "Tell me what you know, or I'll show this newspaper to the police."

Barbara shrank back an inch more against the cushions of the sofa. Though alarmed by his threat, she was still defiant.

"Tell me what you know!" he said, raising a hand to strike her again.

"I don't know anything," she said in a small voice.

He held up the newspaper. "But you wrote this."

Barbara nodded imperceptibly, an unwilling admission of guilt.

"Tell me, then," Jordan said.

"Unless she's gone to Leslie . . ." she said. "If it isn't that, then I don't know. I never knew anything about her, you see. About her past . . ."

Jordan was watching her closely. She was no longer the sad young woman he had married, no longer the strong, even subtle woman he had lived with for six years. She was a child, a frightened child who had been caught in a guilty act and was shamefacedly admitting her guilt. He believed her words.

"All right," he said.

He was not worried about Leslie Wheeler's safety. From the moment he had found out about the cryptic note in the margin of *The New York Times* he had dispatched a team of detectives and police to keep Leslie under close surveillance. No harm would come to Leslie. She was as heavily guarded as a head of state, though she did not know it and, he hoped, never would.

He looked at Barbara now.

"Maybe you're telling the truth," he said. "I'll find out eventually. But at least tell me why. Why did you do this?"

Again she shrank away from him.

"I love you," she said in the same little-girl voice.

The defiance came back into her eyes. She looked up at him, trembling slightly.

"You love me," he said.

The words sounded odd on her lips. And he realized why. In six years of marriage she had never told him those words. The two of them had skirted the subject of love as delicately as if it were a fatal disease, a skeleton in the family closet. But she had loved him all along.

"Well, at least you've told me," he said.

But now Jordan saw something else in Barbara's face, something that might have fooled him five minutes ago but was clear to him now that he had seen his mistake in ever trusting her. The scales were being peeled from his eyes, and the world shone clean and cold now. He felt as though no woman could ever keep a secret from him again.

"Now I understand," he said. "You've been playing a waiting game all along. Haven't you?"

She said nothing.

"Sure you have," he said, his lip curling in contempt as he looked at her. "You saw that our marriage wasn't a happy one. You thought that if you could make it worse, make Jill jealous, get under her skin, you could tip the scales and break us up. Then you'd be waiting. Waiting to pick up all the marbles."

Barbara said nothing.

"You really are your father's daughter, aren't you?" Jordan said. "I should have known it all along."

Barbara had turned pale. She was looking away now. It was the first time since he came in that she had not met his eyes.

In that instant it occurred to Jordan that Barbara's machinations may have started far earlier than he realized. The fine hand of Barbara might have been behind his loss of Leslie herself, two years before he met Jill Fleming.

And perhaps even behind the death of Victor Considine . . .

These thoughts were too terrible to pursue now. Jordan had urgent business to attend to.

"Well, I'll let you in on something," he said. "Whatever happens to Jill, you're finished. You'll never see me again."

He tapped the folded newspaper against his arm, giving her a cruel smile. Then he threw it on the couch beside her.

"Good-bye, Barbara," he said.

He turned on his heel and left the apartment.

Barbara sat alone on the couch beside the newspaper that had been her final gambit and her undoing. She knew Jordan had been telling the truth. The look in his eyes had left no doubt of it. She had lost him forever.

In a moment the tears would come. Many tears, more than she had ever shed before.

But before they could come she reflected that she had not told Jordan the whole truth tonight. Not even his damning newspaper or his threats could get it out of her.

She had not told Jordan about the child.

No doubt he was rushing to protect Leslie with all his powers.

But it was too late to save his daughter.

70

Chicago, Illinois

JILL STOOD LOOKING at Meg.

The child was sitting on the dirty floor of the upstairs bedroom. Though there were no curtains on the window, the interior of the room was not visible from the neighboring houses, even supposing any of them were occupied.

"I guess we fooled them all, didn't we?" Jill asked.

Meg was dressed in a jogging suit with a large Chicago Bears insignia emblazoned on the sweatshirt. She wore tiny jogging shoes and white socks. Her hair had been cut off, only a short fuzz remaining. She looked like a boy.

Jill herself was wearing jogging clothes. They were somewhat too big for her. She had padding under her shirt to make her look at least thirty pounds heavier than she really was.

Her own hair had been dyed black. She wore cheap earrings, a jingling collection of bracelets on her right wrist, and a blatantly false beauty mark on her cheek. She looked like an attractive but rather crude housewife. On the last stage of their journey she had adopted a brusque, blue-collar demeanor with the few people she had spoken to. She had introduced Meg as her little boy, Mike. Two people, a bus driver and a storekeeper, had chucked Meg under the chin and smiled at her. "Hello, Mike. Whaddaya say?" the storekeeper had joked.

Meg made a beautiful boy.

And Jill made a perfect mother.

After their arrival she had given Meg some fruit juice from the athletic bag she had brought with her. Jill had added a one-quarter dose of one of her own tranquilizers to the juice. The child had slept most of the time since then. Jill had brought an air mattress for her, and blew it up in the darkness after their arrival.

Meg was sitting quietly now. But despite the effect of the tranquilizer she looked frightened. The filthy, decaying old house was worlds away from her normal surroundings. She gazed around her bemusedly, and glanced at her mother every few seconds.

"I know what you need," Jill said suddenly. "Just wait here a second, honey, while I get my bag."

Jill went downstairs to get the athletic bag and returned quickly. But when she reached the landing she stood for a long moment without moving, gazing from one bedroom to the other. A profound indecision seemed to overtake her. Her breathing was labored. Her hands shook slightly.

After a time she came to herself. She took the bag into the room and set it on the floor. She reached inside it and produced a tiny stuffed giraffe, still bearing the price tag from the truckstop where she had bought it.

"Here you go," she said, handing the giraffe to Meg. "Here's a special friend who came along on our trip. What do you think we should name him?"

The child accepted the animal in silence. Her eyes were on her mother.

Jill managed a happy smile.

"Shall we name him Bobby?" she asked. "Would you like that?"

Meg looked from her mother to the giraffe, which she was holding with both hands.

"Well, we'll think of a name together, won't we?" Jill smiled. "We'll try out all sorts of names, until we find the right one."

As she spoke she began removing things from the athletic bag. There was a pad of sketching paper, a bag of cookies, a book of nursery rhymes, and a small set of paints. There were also some cosmetic supplies Jill had bought at a drugstore, and a bottle of hair dye.

She gave Meg her baby blanket and teddy bear.

"Are you hungry, darling?" Jill asked.

With her back to Meg Jill took out the gun and placed it on the floor behind the athletic bag.

Then she reached for the package of cookies. She had not eaten a bite in over thirty hours.

She ate in silence for a moment, staring out the window. She looked like a child herself, her mouth working quietly, her eyes emptied of adult preoccupations. A few minutes passed without her realizing it. Then she turned around. Meg was lying down with her little giraffe under her cheek. She was fast asleep.

Jill took out another cookie and munched it thoughtfully as she watched her daughter sleep.

71

Mrs. CHRISTENSEN WAS IN THE GARDEN at the side of the house, planting tulip bulbs.

Last year had been a terrible year for flowers. Half her plants had not even come up, and those that did were frail and withered, needing just the right amount of sunlight and water, and dying quickly if they did not get it. She hoped this year would be different. Her garden was her only real recreation, and she tended to invest exaggerated hopes in her flowers.

She paused a moment, spade in hand, thinking of her late husband. Charlie Christensen had brought her a kind of happiness she had never expected to find in this life. Charlie had been her sunshine. Without him it seemed no wonder that the world lacked enough sun to bring up a poor little flower.

It was strange even now to think that so carefree a man could have been so serious in his work.

Charlie was a philosopher. He held a chair in philosophy at Johns Hopkins, had published several major works, including a definitive study of Hegel's early years, and was considered the foremost expert on phenomenology in the United States.

Yet Charlie, renowned as he was and so in demand for lectures and visiting professorships, thought of his job no differently than a plumber or carpenter might have viewed his work. It was just a living to him. Charlie closed up his books every Friday afternoon at four and spent the weekend watching baseball games, barbecuing bratwurst, or taking Sunday drives in the Maryland countryside. He rarely missed an Orioles game, walking the half mile to Memorial Stadium and sitting in the upper deck behind third base.

His manner was unpretentious, his speech colloquial, his humor down-to-earth and sometimes a bit corny. He was a plump little man, florid and bald, with a tiny mustache that was the first thing that attracted her to him. They met in an elevator in St. Louis, where they were attending separate conventions in the same hotel. They noticed each other's name tags, and Charlie made bold to speak to her, joking about the bitter St. Louis cold and his beloved Baltimore weather.

Two weeks later they were married.

They were both in their forties at the time. Charlie had lost his first wife to multiple sclerosis years before, and had reconciled himself to the musty life of a solitary professor. He bloomed like a rose, right in that elevator, and the smile never left his face after that first night at the convention.

They lived together for fourteen years, Charlie working at Hopkins and taking every opportunity to travel with his new wife to the Grand Canyon, the Painted Desert, Niagara Falls, the Smoky Mountains. Their marriage was one long lark. The intimacy behind their smiles was bottomless, and their happiness seemed undeserved.

Then Charlie died suddenly of a heart attack, and Mrs. Christensen became the widow lady in the old house in Roland Park, beloved of her many friends and of the neighborhood children, who interrupted her in her gardening to pass the time of day, and were given cookies and lemonade and occasionally a word or two of free advice as a reward.

On this day two of those children—Della Snow and her younger brother, Ray, the children of the agricultural chemist down the street—crossed the lawn languidly to pass the time of day with Mrs. Christensen. The unseasonable heat made their movements seem slightly unreal. They bore the waiting, curious expressions of children everywhere. Mrs. Christensen knew children like a book.

"Good afternoon, Della," she said. "You're looking mighty fresh and pretty, considering this heat. Raymond, are taking good care of your sister?"

The little boy said nothing, being of shy temperament.

"Now, what do you think of my garden?" Mrs. Christensen sighed, taking off her wide-brimmed hat to wipe her brow with a handkerchief. "All that beautiful sun, and not a single flower to enjoy it. Why can't Mother Nature send us the sun when we really need it? Last year this whole garden was nothing but a cemetery for flowers."

"My teacher would say it was a sign for us to repent of our sins," said the little girl with a serious look in her eyes.

Mrs. Christensen looked at the child. Della was an intelligent girl, and not unkind, despite her habitual severity toward her weaker brother.

"Is that what you believe too, honey?" the widow asked.

"Oh, no," said the child. "I repented only last night. So did Ray. We always repent when we say our prayers. I'm quite sure we repented all last year. And, as you know, it didn't do a thing for your flowers."

Mrs. Christensen smiled. She did not wish to encourage Della's agnosticism, for her Sunday school teacher lived only a block away and would this very Saturday be at a picnic to which Mrs. Christensen was invited. It would not

461

do to alienate that woman, who was a notorious gossip with many friends and had a nasty turn of mind.

"Well, if you two don't get a spot of lemonade, you're going to wilt just like my poor zinnias," she said. "Ray, help an old lady to her feet and we'll go inside where it's cool."

The boy, only seven years old, extended a hand, and Mrs. Christensen made a pretense of using his strength to help her get up. She noticed a twinge in her hip that used to be there only in cold weather. Time was catching up with her. She thought of Charlie, and smiled. Wherever he was, she would join him before many more years passed.

The children were following her toward the house when a large car pulled up and a stranger got out. She paused, watching him move up the sidewalk toward the front porch. He was a tall man, dressed in slacks and a sport shirt. He carried a briefcase and a large book of some sort, like a ledger or a volume from a hall of records.

He was smiling at her. She paused, the children standing beside her.

"Mrs. Christensen?" he asked, shading his eyes from the hot sun.

She nodded inconclusively, wondering what his business was. Were it not for that sport shirt she would have pegged him already for an insurance man.

"Mrs. Holly Christensen?" he added, holding out a hand.

She shook it, her eyes meeting his.

"Formerly Ms. Holly Fleming," he added.

She raised an eyebrow. "That's a long time ago," she said.

"It wasn't easy finding you," he said. "My name is Calvin Weathers. I have some questions to ask you. It concerns someone from a long time ago. Someone from Jocelyn, Illinois."

He glanced at Della. "A little girl, as it happens," he said.

Holly gave him a long, slow look that went over the children's heads. Then she invited him into the house.

Ten minutes later the children had gone, and Cal Weathers was sitting on the living room couch where for fourteen years Holly Fleming had sat in the evenings with Charlie Christensen. A glass of untouched lemonade was on the coffee table before him. The look in his eyes was serious.

In Holly's lap was the volume of pictures from the Illinois Department of Child Welfare, opened to the page on which Jill Sundberg's class photo was displayed. Holly had put on her reading glasses to look at the photo, but had already removed them. Recognizing Jill had been easy.

"I never thought I'd see that face again," she said.

"You've probably seen it a hundred times since without knowing it," Cal Weathers said. "She grew up to be someone important."

Holly looked up from the book. "Is that why you want something with her now?" she asked.

"It's best that you don't know about that," he said. "Let's just say she's in some trouble. I may be able to help her. But her adult life can't give me the clues I need now. I'm hoping you can remember something about her childhood that will help me."

Holly Christensen put her glasses on to study the photograph again. Then she looked up at Cal.

"I was the caseworker who took her in," she said. "I was working with a fellow that day—I can't remember his name. We were sent to a house on the South Side because the little girl hadn't been in school. We found her in the house alone. Her mother and the boyfriend had skipped town some time before. Weeks, in fact. The little girl had been alone in the house. What amazed me is that she had fooled everyone for a long time, feeding herself, dressing herself, going to school as though nothing was wrong, even though her mother had left her and she was completely alone in the world. Another little girl would have toddled over to the neighbors to say her mother had gone. But this one put on an act of complete normality."

She sighed. "Then, of course, she got discouraged. She stopped going to school. In a child's way she probably went a little crazy. When we found her she was cowering in the basement. I'll never forget the look in those little eyes. She was like a trapped animal. So innocent, so tormented . . ."

Holly's eyes misted at the memory. Her hands moved nervously over the surface of the photograph in the record book.

"She had been severely abused," she said. "Physically and sexually. Even the doctor was upset. We couldn't find the mother, so we never found out the details. The child did not speak for about eight months after intake. I used to visit her every week. Couldn't get a word out of her. It was a terrible thing to see. She was hidden so deep inside herself. There was nothing on the surface but a mask. A beautiful blond little mask without a soul."

Cal said nothing. He could see that Jill Sundberg had made a great impression on Holly Fleming. He was thinking that the reverse must also have been true, since Jill had taken Holly's last name for her own.

"Then," Holly sighed, "she came out of her shell. Or seemed to, anyway. She started to talk. She took part in all the usual activities. She survived in the institutional setting. Her schoolwork was normal. Her intelligence tests showed something astronomical—that I remember. But her psychological tests showed the results of the abuse, and perhaps of some constitutional or congenital problems. She was far from normal. Far from normal."

Holly shook her head, looking at the picture.

"I was transferred a year after I met Jill," she said. "I couldn't get over to Jocelyn see her very much any more. Once a month, or every six weeks. I watched her grow. The bigger she got, the prettier she got. But every time I saw her she was hidden deeper inside her shell. The fear was gone, the terror—but what had replaced it was worse. I've seen a lot of kids affected that way by prolonged abuse. But with her it was harder to bear, because she was so beautiful. You see, she just wasn't there. And I knew she would have been such a good person, had she been there at all. . . ."

Tears were in Holly's eyes.

"Were you still in touch when she ran away?" Cal asked.

She nodded. "I found out about it when I made one of my visits," she said. "I had brought a set of books with me. Novels for children. I had read them when I was a little girl. She was gone when I got there. I thought we'd find her, but we didn't. I never heard another word about her, until you came here today."

There was a long silence. Holly Fleming dried her tears. Cal Weathers was looking at her, apparently lost in thought. Then he cleared his throat.

"I won't burden you with the story of her later life," he said. "Most of that is as much a mystery as her childhood. But I will tell you this. Something happened recently to put her under extreme stress. She disappeared from her home. She's on the run. I need to find her. For her own safety, and for—for other reasons."

Holly said nothing.

"She's in the sort of situation," Cal went on, "where people look to last resorts. She's running away. But if I understand her as well as I think I do, she has nowhere to run to. Do you see what I mean?"

Holly nodded. Her eyes had narrowed.

"She feels abandoned," Cal said. "She's out of control—but that doesn't mean she isn't clever. She's too smart to let us catch up with her in the normal way. Not in time, that is."

He looked at Holly's face, whose natural warmth shone through the tears on her cheeks.

"I have reason to believe that you meant a lot to her," he said. "At one time in her life, she used your last name as her own. Fleming. I think her meeting with you left a lasting impression on her. In fact, I'm sure of it."

Holly seemed thoughtful.

"Can you help me?" Cal asked.

Again there was a silence. Holly looked from her visitor to the book on the coffee table.

"Excuse me a moment," she said.

She got up and left the living room. He heard her going up the stairs. There was a long pause. He heard distant sounds in the house, a door being opened, a rustle inside a closet.

After several minutes Holly Fleming returned. In her hand was a rolled-up piece of drawing or sketching paper. She handed it to Cal and went to sit down on the couch.

"When we found her," she said, "there was a whole easel full of these watercolor paintings. Nearly all of them were of this same woman. A sort of fairy godmother, I figured. You see, her mother must have been such a monster, and then the little girl was alone—she must have painted this imaginary lady to keep her company. To watch over her. I kept one of the pictures to remember her by. The idea of a little girl being so forsaken, so lonely . . . I felt I had to keep it, to remind me of her courage and her inventiveness. But the picture was so distressing that I have never looked at it until this day. She was living in hell, you see, and this was her only way out."

Cal studied the picture. It was a childish painting, of course, full of bright colors and crude forms. But he sensed the terrible anxiety behind the brush strokes.

The woman in the picture bore a warm smile. She was tall, with red hair and green eyes.

He rolled up the picture.

"In the state records," he said, "there is no mention of the address of the house where you found her. Would you have it in your own records?"

Holly's eyes opened in surprise.

"Goodness, no," she said. "That's so long ago. . . . I cleaned out most of my records after I married Charlie and moved here. Whatever was left I probably threw away sometime in the last twenty years. When Charlie died I did a thorough housecleaning."

Cal pursed his lips in frustration.

"There's a chance she might have gone back there," he said. "An outside chance—but I would sure like to check it out. It might make all the difference."

Holly Fleming stared off into space. Her eyes were half-closed, her emotion unreadable.

Then, all at once, she sat up.

"I can take you there," she said.

Cal Weathers raised an eyebrow.

"Of course I can," she said, excited now. "I worked in that neighborhood for fifteen years. I knew that end of town like a book. I'm sure I would recognize the house if it's still there." She smiled. "That place has haunted me all these years because of Jill. Maybe the memory can do some good after all."

A long silence joined them. The face and life of Jill Fleming Lazarus filled that silence, signifying separate things to the two people, just as she had meant disparate things to all the people whose paths she had crossed.

"What are we waiting for?" Cal Weathers said.

Holly Fleming stood up.

"Let me pack an overnight bag," she said. "It's a long way to Chicago from here."

72

IT WAS LATE AFTERNOON. The shadows were just beginning to fall, giving the dust and litter in the bedroom a particularly sinister air.

Meg had slept away most of the day, knocked out by the pill Jill had given her this noon. Jill had spent some of the time watching her. Jill was not sleepy, though she had not closed her eyes for four days.

Occasionally Jill had got up to wander about the house, moving on tiptoe so as not to disturb the sleeping child. She had stood in the other bedroom for a long time, her head cocked as though listening for something. She had gone downstairs to the kitchen, where she ran her hands slowly along the counter tops. She turned the kitchen tap; there was no water.

For a while she stood in the living room like a somnambulist, absolutely motionless, listening to the house creak and settle around her. She could feel its decay. A smile played over her lips.

In the middle of the afternoon she went down to the basement, treading carefully on the old stairs. She did not notice the old beer bottles or the mattress that had been brought down here by someone years ago. The foul smells reached her nostrils, but did not penetrate to her mind.

She sat down on the floor, her legs crossed, and breathed in the ancient, closed-in air of the basement. A cockroach moved unhurriedly along a wall. Cobwebs were everywhere. The timbers of the ceiling looked rotted and unsafe.

An old Popsicle stick caught her eye. She picked it up and played with it for a while. Then she moved behind the furnace and curled up on the floor. She stayed there a long time, her thumb in her mouth. The feeling was so delicious that she almost fell asleep. But then she remembered Meg and went back upstairs.

She pushed gently at Meg's shoulder. When the child did not stir, she pushed harder.

"Wake up, sleepyhead. We have work to do. We have to make our surprise for Daddy."

Meg seemed dazed, but a sleepy smile curled her heart-shaped lips. She seemed to expect a kiss, but Jill was already turning to gather the things she had brought in the athletic bag.

She opened the drawing pad and spread it out on the floor. Then she broke open the plastic cover of the paint set and took out the little bottles, one by one.

"We're going to paint a picture," she said. "It's a present for Daddy."

When the bottles were all open she realized she had no glass or bowl for rinsing the brush. She got up and left the bedroom without saying anything to Meg.

She searched the kitchen, opening the drawers and cupboards one by one. They were all empty, except for an old can of cat food, bloated by time and bacteria, which sat on one of the upper shelves.

Jill stood biting her lip. Then she remembered something she had noticed in the basement. She hurried down the stairs, excited as a child, and found an old plastic water bowl beneath the basement stairs. It had probably been used by a cat, to judge by the strong smell of kitty litter in the basement.

Jill picked up the bowl and went up the stairs. When she got to the bedroom she found Meg crouched over the little jars of paint. Paint was spilled over the bedroom floor. The bottles of blue and green were half empty, having been partially overturned by the child. Some of the other bottles had only been slightly jarred, spattering the floor with a few drops of color.

Jill came forward quickly and struck Meg a hard blow to the face. The little girl tumbled on her back and lay staring open-mouthed at her mother. Then she began to scream.

Jill paid no attention to her daughter's cries. She righted the paint bottles, one by one, and lined them up in a neat row. She took out the two brushes and put them on the floor, humming quietly to herself as she worked.

Then she noticed the empty water bowl and remembered that the water taps in the bathroom and kitchen did not work. The water to the house must have been turned off years ago.

Jill thought for a moment. Then she reached into the athletic bag and found a can of apple juice she had bought on the road two days ago. She opened it and began pouring it into the water bowl.

She thought of Meg, and stopped pouring the juice before the can was half empty.

"Would you like a drink, honey?" she asked.

Only now did she realize that Meg had not stopped weeping since she had been struck in the face. Her cheek had turned bright red. Tears were running down her face in a steady stream, and her cries echoed loudly through the empty house.

Jill put down the can and crawled to her daughter's side.

"Stop that," she said.

Meg was sitting up, her little legs in front of her, rubbing at her tear-stained face with both hands. She hiccuped, looking into her mother's eyes and resumed crying.

"I said stop it," Jill said, grabbing both the child's hands and giving them a hard shake. This only made Meg cry louder.

Jill looked out the window. She was afraid someone would hear Meg. She looked at the frantic little face. Something about it enraged her.

I'll give you something to cry about.

I'll teach you to behave.

The words came from somewhere behind her memory. No sooner had they entered her mind than they were on her lips.

"I'll give you something to cry about," she said.

She raised a fist to strike Meg. The child cried harder at the sight of the hand that had already hit her once. A sort of pantomime began to play itself out inside Jill's mind. She saw a second blow to Meg's head, then a third and a fourth, each one harder than the last.

I'll give you something to cry about.

She saw the blows raining down upon the little cheeks, saw blood begin to mix with the tears. The blood did nothing to mute the cries, which sounded like taunts of rebellion. The child scurried and fought and flailed, but already she was being tied down. Things were being used to cut her, other things to penetrate her. Jill thought of the paint brushes, and of the Popsicle stick in the basement. Weapons ready to hand.

I'll teach you to behave.

The punishment had its own choreography. It was all in place inside Jill's mind, forgotten for twenty-five years, but waiting for this day like a genie waiting to get out of a bottle. Jill's hands and arms were ready for what they had to do. The screams and tears were like musical notations telling the instrumentalist where to strike, where to hold, what new sound of pain to produce before the ultimate silence came.

But the sight of Meg lying helplessly on her back stopped the explosion inside Jill. There was trust in the little girl's eyes along with her terror.

Jill paused, staring into space. With an effort she managed to silence the screaming inside her. The image of the tied-up little body, its guilty holes filled by instruments of punishment, moved back a pace in her mind. She took a deep breath. She tasted blood. At first she thought it was part of the memory. Then she realized she had bitten the inside of her own cheek, hard.

She released the child and crawled back to the paint set.

"Let's get to work, honey," she said. "We don't have much time." The afternoon light was waning fast. Jill picked up one of the brushes, dipped it into the jar of black paint, and began outlining a figure.

She worked quickly. She admired her own skill. The figure took shape quickly. Jill found the red paint, then the green, and filled in all the details with loving care.

A peculiar buzzing had overtaken Jill's nerves. Her body seemed like an electric wire sparked by high voltage. She realized she did not have much more time. The end was near.

But Jill kept calm. Soon the picture was finished.

"There," she said. "What do you think of that, honey?"

Meg was silent, still rubbing the tears from her eyes. But she looked at the painting with interest.

"Now," Jill said. "I have to go to the bathroom for a minute. I'll be right back. Don't be scared, honey. I'll talk to you from the bathroom. All right?"

Jill took her purse and went into the bathroom. She began taking off her makeup, including the false beauty mark she had worn on the road. The face in the mirror seemed as formless and empty as the coloring paper upon which she had painted the figure a few moments before. This offered Jill some comfort. She had a clean canvas to work on, after all.

There was a humming as she worked. At first she thought it came from Meg in the bedroom. Then she realized it came from the past, and was using her own lips to sing itself with. It was a familiar song, though she could not recall the name. The notes followed upon each other naturally, without doubt or fumbling.

She did not notice how sloppily the mask was being applied to her face. The lines were smudged, hectic. But to Jill they seemed perfect in every way, matching the image in her mind down to the finest detail.

When she was finished, the only false note was the short black hair from her last disguise. She reached into her purse and got out the wig. She put it on quickly. There was no time to lose. Only this final mask could save her, and only if she hurried.

She looked in the mirror. She was perfect, except for the tears streaming from her eyes. She wiped some of them away.

She rushed into the next room. Meg, sitting on the floor, looked up at her in surprise.

"Don't I look wonderful, honey?" Jill asked.

Meg looked from her mother to the painting, and back again.

"That's right, honey," Jill said. "I look just like the lady, don't I?"

Jill knelt beside the athletic bag and picked up the gun. She looked out the window for a last time. Night was coming.

With a nervous, almost embarrassed little laugh, Jill turned to her daughter.

73

IN THE OFFICE of his Manhattan headquarters Jordan Lazarus fainted.

The room was full of police officers, FBI men, and private detectives manning banks of phones. Jordan himself had been on the telephone with the regional FBI director in Pennsylvania when a sudden blackness came over his vision and he slumped to the floor.

Sam Gaddis was at Jordan's side within seconds.

"Somebody get some water, quick," he shouted.

There was a brief hubbub among the detectives. Jordan's private secretary, a hard and efficient woman named Arlene Caceres, burst into tears when she came to the door. She thrust aside the nearest policemen and brought a water-soaked washcloth as well as a pitcher of ice water.

"What have you done to him?" she asked, looking from one detective to another. Their impassive faces angered her. "The man is only human, for God's sake. Step back, will you? Let him breathe."

She knelt by Jordan's side and began rubbing his palms energetically. Sam put the cold compress on Jordan's forehead.

"How could you, Mr. Gaddis?" Arlene said reproachfully. "You're supposed to be watching out for him."

Sam Gaddis was stung by her words. In fact, he had not thought of Jordan's physical condition for four days. Jordan had not slept a single minute since this ordeal started, and had eaten practically nothing, maintaining himself on innumerable cups of black coffee. It was no wonder the strain had finally got to him. Sam felt personally responsible. He should have insisted that Jordan eat something, and get at least a couple of hours' sleep out of every twenty-four.

Sam could not know that physical exhaustion had nothing to do with Jordan's seizure.

While Sam and Arlene hovered over him, Jordan was lost in a dream. He was thinking of his sister Meg, and her dying words.

470

There's still time . . .

The words had been echoing at the back of Jordan's mind for four days, beneath the surface of his frantic thoughts about Jill and the baby. He had clung to them without realizing it, as though they were a sort of prayer that might keep his wife and daughter alive, wherever they were.

But only now was he really hearing them. Because now he knew that it was too late.

He had been talking to the FBI man quite coolly over the phone, hearing as usual that there was no good news to report, that everything possible was being done—when Meg's dying face had suddenly reared before him and her words had exploded inside his brain. He could feel Jill and the baby at that instant, somewhere in the world. And he knew that the disaster he had been trying to prevent was taking place after all.

That was when he had passed out.

As Sam and Arlene struggled to bring him back to consciousness while one of the detectives called a doctor, Jordan heard none of the commotion around him. A black shroud had descended over his mind, and the knife twisting in his heart for four days was at last withdrawn, letting the blood flow freely from his hopes.

Too late.

Too late . . .

The words would be on his lips when, ten minutes later, he at last began to revive.

74

Chicago, Illinois
Midnight

THE CITY HAD CHANGED.

A tangle of expressways now crossed through the poor neighborhoods where Holly had worked twenty-five years before. Urban renewal had scorched the landscape, tearing out whole blocks of houses and apartment buildings. Low-cost housing projects loomed twenty stories high, and small groups of young people, black and Hispanic, watched through baleful eyes as the car threaded its way past the littered streets that were their turf.

The darkness did not help to make things more recognizable. Holly Fleming peered uncertainly through the windshield.

"It's all changed so much," she said. "It didn't look at all like this when I was here."

Cal Weathers said nothing. He kept driving slowly, hoping a landmark would come into view that would help to jog Holly's memory. His high hopes were already deflated by the urban landscape before him. Perhaps the house had long since been torn down.

Once again he questioned his judgment in being here at all. It was a slim hope at best. Why would a woman with Jill's tormented past come to the very location of her worst agony at a moment like this? It seemed insane.

But it had to be checked out. And it was the only clue he had.

"Wait," Holly said, looking out the passenger's window.

She was looking at a large junction of railroad tracks, at least seven tracks wide, that went between two aged factory buildings with transom windows.

"These buildings were here," she said. "And the tracks. I remember driving over them every time I came down here. If only . . ."

Cal had slowed almost to a crawl. Across a littered vacant lot that occupied the next corner there was a small tavern with a pool hall. The whole block of apartments had somehow survived the ravages of urban renewal. Perhaps someone in there would know something.

But Holly's voice stopped him.

"Turn left at the next corner," she said. "This is the way. I'm sure of it!"

He turned left into an ancient street lined with inner-city houses that had been home to factory workers fifty years ago. They seemed literally blasted by age. Their roofs were decaying. Grass grew luxuriantly between the slabs of sidewalk. Vehicles with flat tires lined the street. Half the houses had boarded-up windows.

"Yes," Holly said. "Yes, it was in this neighborhood. Keep going."

Cal drove slowly along the block. Then, at Holly's direction, he turned a corner. The houses were worse here. Most bore fake brick or shingle exteriors. There were fewer vehicles. Broken glass was everywhere. It was hard to believe the city had not gotten around to razing this area as well. It was an eyesore.

"If only I could remember . . ." Holly was saying. "There was something female about it."

"Female?" Cal asked.

"Oh, I don't know anymore," Holly said, shaking her head. "It's so long ago. If only I weren't old. My memory is gone."

Cal inched the car through the gauntlet of broken glass and abandoned vehicles as though it were a minefield. There were no people now. The houses and sidewalks were covered with graffiti. The final destiny of the neighborhood was as gang turf. Shootings probably took place here regularly. Drug deals and perhaps rapes were the only likely movement inside these houses.

"There!" Holly suddenly cried. "There, look! I knew it was female."

Cal turned to look at the street sign on the corner in front of them. Rosa Street, it read.

"Turn left," Holly said, excitement in her voice.

Cal turned the wheel. This street was perhaps a bit less decayed than the one they had just come down. There were a few windows that had not been broken. But it was obvious no one lived here except vagrants. This entire area could not possibly escape the city bulldozers for more than another year.

Cal was truly losing heart now. How could Jill have even found her way here, even supposing she wanted to? The street seemed to be off the end of the earth.

"Stop the car," Holly said suddenly.

Cal stopped in the middle of the street. He didn't have to worry about traffic; there were no other moving cars anywhere in sight.

"Over there," Holly said. "The white front with the tall upstairs windows."

Cal followed the direction of her gaze. He saw a tumble-down little house with a white wood front and a driveway overgrown with weeds. The windows were boarded up. There was no sign of life.

Cal parked the car gingerly, avoiding as much of the broken glass as possible. He looked up and down the street warily, alert for signs of muggers or gang members. This was not a safe place to be.

He took his flashlight from the glove compartment and left the car. Holly was moving quickly ahead of him toward the house. In her soft body he saw an echo of the intrepid social worker's forward stride, intent on her job regardless of the neighborhood.

The house came closer. As it did so a slight chill went down Cal's spine. He thought of Jill Lazarus, a woman known the world over for her wealth, her beauty, her legendary husband, her adored daughter. Was it possible she could be inside that horrible old house at this moment? The notion had something dark and almost mythic about it.

Holly reached the front door first, but it was Cal who knocked on it. He knocked very hard, several times. There was no answer.

"I doubt it's locked," he said, turning the handle.

Amazingly, the door was locked. With Holly behind him Cal moved to the side door. The cement driveway had buckled in a hundred places, and footing was not easy. The concrete stoop leading to the kitchen door had pulled away from the house, leaving a six-inch-wide chasm at the top of the steps.

A screen door without a screen protected the side door, whose wood had long since lost its paint. Cal tried the handle. It gave way rustily and the door swung open on one hinge.

The beam of the flashlight illuminated the kitchen garishly. It looked like any kitchen that had been used only by intruders for a decade or more. There were beer cans, old condoms, marijuana joints, bottles of cheap wine, and an acrid smell of urine mixed with rotting wood.

Cal stood in the silence. He looked at Holly. She seemed frightened.

"Are you all right?" he asked.

"It's as though it was yesterday," she said. "The house wasn't as decayed, of course. But it felt like this. Spooky. Haunted."

He watched her take a deep breath.

"Do you want to wait here while I look around?" he asked.

She said nothing. She seemed truly unnerved.

"Where did you find her the first time?" he asked.

"The bedroom . . . No, wait. The basement," she said.

"I'll look there. Wait for me."

Cal took out his gun and moved away from her. She could hear the crunch of his shoes on the litter in the living room. She stood in the kitchen, feeling the past coil around her. She had come so far in life, such a long way, only to find herself back here. . . . The face of the little Sundberg girl hung before her memory, beautiful, silent, empty.

She thought of the upstairs room where she had found the little girl's easel and watercolors, and the neat bedclothes she had used during her monthlong solitude.

Drawn by a nameless force, she forgot Cal and headed for the staircase. There was just enough light from the streetlamps outside for her to see her way through the shadows.

"Jill?" she called quietly. There was no answer.

She found the stairs and mounted them gingerly. The stairs creaked loudly under her feet.

When she reached the landing she cleared her throat.

"Jill?"

The silence enveloped her like a shroud. She shivered. She looked to the left and right. The child's bedroom had been the one to the right. That long-ago day was coming back now. She could almost hear her male colleague—what was his name?—searching alongside her.

The door to the bedroom was open. She moved toward it.

She stopped in her tracks.

Inside the room, standing against the wall, was a painting.

Holly rushed forward, picked up the picture, and held it up to the window. As the dim light illuminated it her breath came short.

It was the same picture she had seen here twenty-five years ago, the picture she had shown Cal Weathers this afternoon in Baltimore. The picture she had not dared to look at for a quarter of a century.

Holly felt faint. Now she knew Cal had been right. Jill was here, or had been here.

The picture showed a woman, tall, beautiful, with red hair and green eyes. A fairy godmother. She was smiling and holding out her hand.

The picture trembled in Holly's hands, as though her own fear gave it life. She turned from the window to look into the room.

On an inflatable mattress under a blanket she saw the child.

"Oh, my God," she murmured.

She came forward, knelt beside the baby, and touched her hand. There was no response.

"Oh, my God, my God," Holly cried.

She turned to the door. "Cal!" she cried. "Up here, quick! The little girl! The little girl!"

But Cal Weathers did not hear her. He was in the basement behind the furnace, holding the dead body of Jill Lazarus in his arms. The blood from the bullet wound in her head had almost completely dried. Her clothes were covered with dust, and the wig she had worn, blown askew by the force of the bullet, was half off her head.

But she looked, for the first time in Cal's memory, at peace.

75

One Year Later

Farmington, Long Island

LESLIE WAS ALONE in the park, sitting under the oak tree where, only a half hour ago, she had sat with Terry Beyer.

Terry was back home now, and Leslie would get in her car for the drive back to Johnsonville in a couple of minutes. There was a lot of work to do at the office, as usual. And since Ross's death, Leslie alone was responsible. She had taken over as president of Wheeler Advertising. The little company was her private link between the past and the future, and she was grateful for it.

But for the moment she could not tear herself away from the park. She lingered, glancing down beside her at the soft little bed of grass between two of the oak's large roots. This was where Terry had sat with her only a short while ago. It was his familiar place.

But Terry was gone now, and the claims of his own growth would soon bring an end to the current era of her closeness with him. His body was already too large to lie down in that little space of grass. And he was already too old for fantasies about talking trees. Soon he would be too old even for outings to the park. He was eight and a half years old now; in no time he would be a teenager. Where would he find space in his life for Leslie then?

Leslie put the thought out of her mind. She leaned back against the tree and looked at the children playing in the park. All were small. Each had a mother or big sister or baby-sitter watching from a bench.

None belonged to Leslie. Perhaps no child ever would.

The clouds shifted momentarily, and a bright shaft of dewy sunshine bathed the entire scene. There was something unreal about it, something anointed and mystical. Leslie reflected that all these children were caught in a brief moment of time that could not last. All were growing so fast that this quiet moment of careless play in a neighborhood park would soon be left behind by the dizzy pace of their lives. The games they played today, the friends whose names they shouted, their pleas to stay longer when it was time to go home—all this would be as forgotten as this fugitive ray of sunshine dancing across the park. Not even a memory . . .

Two little girls were playing with a smaller boy on the whirligig. They ran around it as fast as they could, calling out as they pushed, and then jumped on when they could not get it going any faster. The boy, thrilled to be the beneficiary of their effort, leaned back and gazed up at the sky, enjoying his ride. The look on his little face was rapt, almost beatified. He gave himself up to the pure movement with a heedless innocence that made Leslie smile.

It occurred to her that the whirligig was something like the earth itself, a whirling thing whose ceaseless movement made it impossible for the human being ever to keep his feet entirely on the ground. Its spinning orbit through space made the sun come up and go down. But its movement through time made all of its creatures subject to a deeper change that tore away everything they were, everything they took for granted, and plunged them willy-nilly into a future they could not predict.

Children had the beautiful, fleeting ability to lean back on that whirligig, open their eyes to the tilting sky, and let the swirling eddy of time flow right through them. They feared nothing. The daily change inside their little bodies was so enormous that they lived in the sheer fascination of it, confident that it could not hurt them, could never dash their hopes.

Adults had forever lost that sunlit moment of belief. Adults lived in rigid fear of what accidents the morrow might bring, and clung desperately to what they had. Yet they, too, must change. Like it or not, they must make room for the new in their lives and in themselves. Such was the price of survival.

Leslie was no exception. She had already journeyed a very long way in life, and seen the dreams she took for granted shattered by events. But she had also seen new dreams take their place, and new challenges, and new talents rise up in her to meet those challenges. Like the ability to love Ross, to care for him and learn from him.

Yes, she was alone now. Terry was back home, three blocks away, doing his third-grade homework, no doubt. And soon he would be two years away from this day, then five years, then ten years. Time must carry him into his own future.

Leslie lay back on the grass and looked up into the branches of the huge swaying oak. Her childhood seemed to take form around her, echoing in the distant shouts of the children. She remembered a time long ago, when she was still a little girl whose mother was alive. She had played on the swing set at the side of her house, just as these children played now, with the protective voice of a loving mother always nearby.

And in their cries she heard her own tender youth, her vulnerability, her sunlit days filled with mistakes and false starts and disasters—but above all her strength, and her ability to pick herself up again when she had fallen. That's what these children were doing right now, in this park—making mistakes, learning from those mistakes, falling down again and again and picking themselves up with an indefatigable strength that would see them through to their own future.

Hearing those happy shouts, Leslie knew that somehow she would be all right, she would go on. She was more than a little afraid of the world, now that she had seen its power to take away the people and things she held most dear. But an ancient confidence come from before her memory told her that the world would not let her down. Though one's balance on its spinning surface might never be certain, with a little courage and willingness to risk oneself, one could be carried by this world to wonderful, unexpected places— the future of one's own self. It was a harsh challenge but worth the effort.

In a moment she would get up to leave. But for now she allowed the mingling of past and future in this quiet place to lull her, to give her courage for the journey.

Her reverie was interrupted by a small shadow that fell across her face.

There was a little girl standing beside her. She was dressed in a pretty little coat in tartan wool, with corduroy pants underneath. She had sandy hair with splashes of blond in it that shone like a halo in the bright sunshine. Her face was in shadow, so Leslie could not see her eyes.

"Hi," Leslie said, still lying on her back. "What's your name?"

"Meg," the child said.

"Well, Meg, my name is Leslie. I'm pleased to meet you."

Leslie shaded her eyes with her hand. Now she could see the little girl's eyes. They were blue-green, and full of mischief. Her milky skin was touched by a sprinkling of freckles.

"Would you like to sit with me, Meg? I was feeling kind of lonesome, so I was talking to this tree," Leslie said.

The little girl giggled. "Talk to a tree?" she asked.

"It's easy," Leslie said. "You just lie back and close your eyes and wait until the tree says something to you. Then you talk back—in a low voice, of course, so no one will hear you. Trees don't like being overheard."

The child seemed intrigued. Though she was very small, she seemed to have understood most of what Leslie had said. Intelligence sparkled in her little eyes.

"Do you want to try?" Leslie asked.

"I don't know," the child responded shyly.

Leslie sat up, leaning on her elbow.

"Are you here all alone, Meg?" she asked. "Where's your mom?"

The girl shook her head and looked away.

Leslie said nothing. She felt a sadness inside the child. She wished she could reach out and hug her, but she knew she could not. She was someone else's child.

"My Daddy's here," the little girl offered. "Over there."

The girl pointed to the bench near the back of the park. Leslie turned to see a man sitting on it. He smiled.

Leslie turned pale. She looked from the distant man to the little girl's face, and then back to the man.

Jordan was already on his feet. Leslie took the child's hand in a reflexive gesture and held it while Jordan approached.

When he arrived he smiled.

"So you two have already introduced yourselves, have you?"

Meg smiled. "She's Leslie," the girl said proudly. "She can talk to a tree."

"She can?" Jordan raised an eyebrow. "Good thing I sent you over here, Meg. I could never talk to a tree. Do you suppose Leslie would teach us how?"

The little girl laughed, and nodded happily.

Jordan looked down at the two of them, their faces dappled by the sun shining through the branches of the oak.

"You two make quite a picture," he said.

Then he noticed that Meg's shoelace was untied.

"Would you mind?" he asked, looking at Leslie.

She turned to tie the lace.

"She needs a woman's touch," he said. "I do the best I can, but I'm not a mother."

The child was looking from Leslie to Jordan as the tree branches groaned high overhead. Leslie reached to pull a strand of hair from the little face.

Then she looked at Jordan. His eyes were serious now, full of urgent inquiry.

"Can we at least talk about it?" he asked.

Leslie's eyes had filled with tears. They shone with a passion she had not felt since the last time she looked into that face.

"Not yet," she said. "We're talking to trees now."

"Later, then," he said, very gently.

"Later," Leslie agreed, putting her hand around the little girl's waist.

76

The New York Times, May 12, 1981

JORDAN LAZARUS TO WED

Jordan Lazarus, America's richest entrepreneur and the architect of the world-famous Lazarus Plan to reclaim America's inner cities, has announced his engagement to Ms. Leslie Chamberlain of Johnsonville, New York.

The couple plans a civil ceremony, with a reception to be held at the Waldorf-Astoria on June 5.

This will be the third marriage for Lazarus and the second for Ms. Chamberlain. Ms. Chamberlain was widowed last year when her husband, advertising executive Ross Wheeler of Long Island, suffered a fatal stroke. Mr. Lazarus lost his second wife, Mrs. Jill Lazarus, when she committed suicide a year ago.

Mr. Lazarus declined comment on his new marriage, except to say that he and Ms. Chamberlain "are old friends," having met for the first time when Ms. Chamberlain was working as an advertising executive under the Lazarus corporate umbrella in 1976, and that they plan an extended honeymoon in the Greek Islands, at a villa owned by Mr. Lazarus.

Calvin Weathers stood over the grave of Jill Lazarus.

He was standing in the center of Woodlawn Cemetery. Here the famous dead of New York history—the Vanderbilts, the Belmonts, Ralph Bunche, and even Fiorello LaGuardia—were buried in elaborate vaults with extravagant monuments to celebrate their fame.

Amid all this splendor Jill Lazarus, a lonely woman who had come from nowhere and ended up where she started, lay under a small stone deliberately placed off the beaten track where no passerby would notice it.

The folded-up *New York Times* with Jordan Lazarus's engagement announcement was in Cal's pocket. He smiled to think of Lazarus marrying Leslie Chamberlain at last. So Jill had been right all along: it had been Leslie who occupied the permanent place in Jordan's heart for which Jill fought so long and in the end lost everything.

Yes, Jill had been right. If not in her actions, or in her tragically twisted life, then at least in her intuition. Jill had won many small battles in her life, but lost the big one, the only one that mattered.

At least she had known the name of her rival. That, to a woman like Jill, must have been worth something. A warrior by nature, she would not have wanted to face defeat without knowing who and what was destroying her.

Now Jordan Lazarus would go on with his life, and perhaps enjoy a love he had deserved long ago and been unfairly denied. To all accounts, Lazarus was a good man. He had helped millions of people who had lived entirely without hope until he came along. He should have his share of happiness.

As for Jill, she was finished. She was just a memory, and even less than a memory—for those who had been closest to her never really knew her. The blight on her soul, planted there when she was still a tiny child, had put a wall between her and the real world. She had passed through life like an unhappy ghost, first glorying in her power to haunt others, and finally suffering the agony of not being able to touch them as a real human being, to give her love and to receive theirs in the simple human way.

In the end, maddened to distraction by her own lonely fate, she had fled the man she had fought so hard to conquer, and had returned to the scene of her earliest and greatest horror. And there, facing her demons at last, she had given her own life in order to spare that of her daughter.

This was her final gift to Jordan Lazarus. Cal was sure of that. Perhaps the knowledge that she was giving it had brought her a semblance of peace at the end, even as she killed herself in the very place where Holly Fleming had found her twenty-five years before, a terrified waif cowering behind a furnace in the house where the world had abandoned her, while her innocent daughter, drugged to long sleep by Jill's own pills, dreamed innocent dreams.

Now Jill was gone. Perhaps she had always been gone. Never quite human, never quite real, she had played her desperate game in the world of human beings, and finally lost.

Rest in peace, Cal thought.

He turned and left the cemetery. He would never come back.

As the detective got into his car and drove off along the lane, Jessica Hightower watched him recede.

She was in her limousine. She had taken an hour off from work to come here. It had been pure chance that she saw the visitor at the graveside. He was the first she had seen.

Jessica came here at least twice a week, sometimes more. She could not seem to tear herself away. She put flowers on the grave, and watched for the flowers put there by others.

Once she saw a man in a black town car arrive here on a Sunday morning, deposit a large wreath of flowers, and drive away. She came back on other Sundays and saw him return. Finally she realized that he was one of Jordan Lazarus's employees, given the job of coming here alone to bring flowers.

She never saw Jordan Lazarus himself. Perhaps he was too preoccupied with his new life to bother. Or perhaps, for some unknown reason, Lazarus simply could not bear to look at the grave.

In any case, Jessica could bear it. Indeed, she was not able to stay away. And so she was here today, as usual, taking time off from her busy work schedule to see Jill.

She got out of the car, carrying her flowers. She approached the grave. She could hear the murmur of the limousine's engine behind her. And behind that, the huge, quiet murmur of the city.

She stood before the stone. A little bouquet of flowers, left by the man who had just departed, lay on the grass.

JILL FLEMING LAZARUS

Died April 5, 1980

Wife of Jordan   Mother of Meg

There was no birthdate. The precise date of Jill's birth was not known. Nor was there any family except for Jordan and the little girl. Ironically, the epitaph said all that could decently be said. Everything else was too secret to be put on a tombstone. Including Jessica.

Poor Jill! Her memory would be as circumscribed as her life. No one could properly mourn her, because no one had really known her.

But to Jessica Hightower, Jill had been a real woman, a flesh-and-blood proof that life is worth living, that no sacrifice is too great to make for love. Jessica had lost her but had not forgotten her. And nothing else in her celebrated lifetime had ever been as real as Jill.

Sleep well, she murmured. *I love you.*

While Jessica Hightower stood before the grave of Jill Lazarus, Barbara Considine sat in her office at Considine Industries, *The New York Times* open on her desk.

The item about Jordan's engagement was modestly placed on the society page with other similar items, but a secretary had judiciously put a pencil mark on the front page of the paper to direct Barbara's attention to the section. Just as Barbara herself had once put a pencil note on the front page of *The New York Times,* to direct another eye to a crucial item buried in the paper.

And that pencil mark had perhaps been Barbara's undoing. For if she had had enough self-control to sit back and bide her time, instead of trying to force the hand of fate, she might once again be Mrs. Jordan Lazarus.

But her love had made her desperate, and she had courted danger when she should have been patient.

As a result she had lost everything. And Jordan would now have what he had wanted all along. Jordan would have his happiness at last.

There was no picture of Leslie accompanying the item. Barbara was thankful for that. The sight of that pretty face, so honest and clear, would have been more than she could bear.

Despite everything she felt happy for Jordan. Fate had kept him dangling for a long time before giving him what he had earned and deserved. Fate had used Barbara herself, and Jill of course, to keep Leslie from him. And that long separation had brought only harm to the women who stood in his way— Barbara, who tried so hard to love him without letting him know, to keep him without letting him see the bars of his prison; and Jill, who awakened to love only when she saw she could not possess Jordan, and who bore him a child out of her desperate longing to be for him what she could never be.

As for Leslie, she must have shown the greatest courage of her life in hiding from her sick husband the great love that lived unseen in her heart. And to Jordan, of course, every day far from the woman he loved must have been an intolerable punishment, an exile from his very self.

Well, it was over now.

Barbara closed the newspaper. She folded it up and threw it in the wastebasket beside her desk. But the front page was still visible to her, and on it the pencil mark directing her to the wedding announcements. A sad smile, not without irony, curled her lips. She pressed the intercom button.

"Yes, ma'am?" came the secretary's voice.

"Cheryl, come in here and empty my wastebasket, will you?"

A moment later the secretary entered and moved to the wastebasket. Seeing that there was only one item in it, she hesitated for a brief second before picking it up. Then, without a word, she left the room, holding the folded-up newspaper in her hand.

Barbara prepared to go back to work. She had deals to make, battles to be won, competitors to outwit. Hers was a busy life.

But as she glanced for a last time at the empty wastebasket she could not help reflecting that this was not the last time she would hear news of Jordan Lazarus. The Lazarus Plan was now revolutionizing the face of urban America, and was being hailed the world over as the most visionary cure for the problem of urban decay since the beginning of the Industrial Revolution.

Stories about Jordan, his fame and his vision, his happy marriage and his future children, would be part of Barbara's life from now on. Perhaps as long as she lived.

That was her punishment.

And Barbara was clearheaded enough even at this lonely moment to realize that the punishment was well deserved.

Mr. Lazarus declined comment on his new marriage, except to say that he and Ms. Chamberlain "are old friends," having met for the first time when Ms. Chamberlain was working as an advertising executive under the Lazarus corporate umbrella in 1976, and that they plan an extended honeymoon in the Greek Islands, at a villa owned by Mr. Lazarus.

In the library of the temporary minimum-security facility at Cheningo, New York, Tony Dorrance sat reading *The New York Times* article over and over.

His brow was knitted in concentration. He was thinking faster and harder than he had ever thought in his life.

"Lazarus," he thought.

Old friends . . .

Met for the first time in 1976 . . .

Tony's hands clenched around the newspaper. Everything was changing perspective inside his mind, like the fragments of glass inside a kaleidoscope, to paint a picture of the truth he had lived in ignorance of all these years.

It had been Lazarus Leslie loved. He was her great love. She had met him years ago, before she married the Wheeler fellow. Years ago. She must have carried a torch for him all along, and waited for him.

And now that they were both free, with Wheeler and Lazarus's wife out of the way, they had come straight back to each other.

Tony saw everything now. And with the advantage of hindsight he could paint a picture of Leslie in the right colors. Leslie's marriage to Ross Wheeler, who was far too old for her, had always seemed inappropriate to Tony. Leslie was not the type of girl to marry a man so much older. It was not in character for her.

But she might have married such a fellow on the rebound from Lazarus. That would make sense. She must have met Lazarus, fallen for him, and lost him somehow. She was lonely, desperate. And so she allowed Wheeler to take her in.

1976 . . .

Tony recalled the way she had fought him when he came back into her life and told her he loved her. At the time he had been puzzled by her fierce loyalty to Wheeler. It had seemed guilty, as though she were hiding something.

But it was not guilt over her physical passion for Tony himself, as he had self-servingly believed at the time. It was guilt over the fact that she still wanted Lazarus, and had only come to rest on Wheeler out of pity, on the rebound.

This also explained why she was so contemptuous of Tony when he came back to her. And why his protestations about the baby had so little effect on her. She didn't love Tony. She had forgotten him completely. She had set her sights much higher now.

She wanted Lazarus.

Jordan Lazarus. The man at the top of the corporate pyramid within whose giant wheels Tony had labored as a tiny cog, a lowly salesman. The man who had it all. The richest man in America. That was Leslie's great love.

Tony burned with hatred to think of his own humiliation, and of Leslie's ingratitude and perfidy. He had given her a child. More important, he had given her his heart. And she had never cared about him. She had worked her way patiently upward in life, while he, Tony, had fallen lower and lower.

While putting on her great act of loyalty and honesty, she had only been thinking of herself. And as soon as Wheeler was dead and Lazarus was free, she had run to him again. Because he was the one she wanted, the one she had had in her mind all along.

Tony thought all these things, and many more. But all his thoughts came down to the same proposition: he himself had never been anything to Leslie but an early mistake, a false step in the life of an ambitious, privileged young woman who forgot all about him as she worked her way relentlessly toward success and accomplishment.

A mistake that had produced a child.

She had cared about the child, all right. She had moved halfway across the country to be near it. But she had not cared about the father who sired him. She had put Tony out of her mind with ease. After all, how much money was he worth? What was he the president of? Who had ever heard of him?

And now, after a few detours, she had reached her goal at last. In a month she would be Mrs. Jordan Lazarus. And now her children would be conceived with him, and bear his name.

While Tony, whose love for her was far greater than any that ever could have been felt by a sick old man like Wheeler or a spoiled, pampered philanthropist like Lazarus—Tony languished in prison. A prison whose concrete walls were only symbols of the wall she had erected against him in her heart.

Tony closed the newspaper and sat deep in thought.

He had been sure of few things in his life. But today he knew what everything meant. He saw the injustice that had been done. It was a crime against love, a crime against nature.

And all because of the perfidy, the self-interest, the evil, of one woman.

Tony put the newspaper back carefully. He asked permission before leaving the library. He had been on his best behavior ever since entering prison. That was why, when overcrowding caused three hundred convicts to be moved from Attica to this temporary minimum-security facility three months ago, Tony had been among them. He had freedom of the grounds and could go almost anywhere he wished. Security here was a joke compared to Attica. A man could walk out the gate in broad daylight and barely be noticed.

Now Tony understood everything. Fate had taken a hand in his life once more in moving him to this lax institution.

And now fate was giving him his final marching orders.

77

June 25, 1981

LESLIE WAS WITH JORDAN in his island house on the Aegean Sea.

United at last, Leslie and Jordan could not believe their good fortune. They had long since given up clinging to the secret dream of a life together. Thus they felt at once ecstatic and a little nervous in each other's company.

They were not the same people who had fallen in love five years ago, when life seemed very different. Leslie had since married a man she cared deeply for, and fought with all her strength to preserve that marriage in the face of the pitiless onslaught of disease. She had so fought against her love for Jordan, since that love could only interfere with her commitment to Ross. Thus Jordan was now like a temptation she could give in to deliciously, after years of resisting it.

As for Jordan, he had lived through two difficult and complex marriages since he first gave his heart to Leslie. He had been a victim of deceit and unhappiness. A visionary in the business world, he was only a human man in her personal life. He had floundered in his marriages without ever knowing quite where he was going. Thanks to his own weaknesses, and those of his wives, he had almost seen himself and his beloved daughter destroyed.

And in all this Leslie had played a part without knowing it. For both Jordan's wives had had to contend with the presence of Leslie in his heart, and had broken themselves in the effort. During those painful years of exile from Leslie, Jordan never knew how close at hand she really was.

Jordan and Leslie had come a long way on their separate journeys. And now that they were together at last, their happiness seemed completely new.

It was only fitting that this exotic foreign place, far from the scenes of their old lives, should be the setting for the renewal of their love.

A great part of that renewal took place through sailing. Jordan took Leslie out nearly every day on his yacht. They sailed along the coast again and again, and to neighboring islands, one of which was the home of some old friends of Jordan's who welcomed Leslie with open arms.

They made love in the solitude of the boat, as of old. But now the boat was different. And the Aegean air smelled different, felt different from the sea air on Long Island Sound that had once been their accomplice.

This difference only made them love each other more. For they realized how improbable was their rediscovery of each other, how capricious fate was in allowing them to come together after so many things had separated them.

During these long, restful days on the water, and their nights in the house overlooking the bay, they talked. They talked at great length, obsessively, as though determined to cut through the murky haze of misunderstandings and obstacles that had separated them in the past. Their love had been lost for so long that they were almost desperate to make it safe, to lock it in with every precaution now that it had been returned.

These conversations were difficult, often wrenching. But gradually, as their nights of love alternated with their long days of talk, the air between them began to clear, and their love to shine over the past like the bright Aegean sun over the sea. They had rediscovered each other as new people, older people who had fought for happiness when they were far from each other. And this only made their love the stronger.

As the third week of their honeymoon began, a new calm had settled over them. They felt like a couple that has been married a long time already, with many memories to look back on together, and an ember of passion between them that has already been tempered by time and shone its strength and permanence.

They had found each other at last. And this time for life.

It was Friday. On Monday they would return home to a busy life. Jordan had his work on the Lazarus Plan, while Leslie had to return to Johnsonville, sell Ross's house, and set about finding a new president for Wheeler Advertising. She felt that her time with Ross must now end. She would move all her things to Jordan's penthouse—including, as with every second marriage, mementos of her time with Ross—and there she would live from now on.

Little Meg was staying with Jordan's family in Pennsylvania, and would return home Tuesday. Jordan was visibly anxious to see her. Being separated from her for three whole weeks was painful for him. But Leslie was not jealous of his devotion to his daughter. She was in a hurry to be a mother to Meg and, as soon as possible, to give her a little brother or sister.

Meg had taken to Leslie with a naturalness and spontaneity that almost made one think she suspected the uncanny spiritual link between Leslie and her real mother, Jill. This made Leslie feel both joyful and sad. She understood that Jill, with her great love and her tragic destiny, would forever be a presence in Leslie's own relationship with Meg.

After Jill's death Meg was rushed to meet her father at the Chicago FBI headquarters. It was ascertained that Jill had given Meg enough of one of her tranquilizers to keep her asleep for many hours, and then had retreated to the basement to kill herself. In the end Jill had sacrificed herself for Meg.

Leslie knew Meg would one day want to know the whole truth about her mother's death. When the time came, Leslie and Jordan would try to tell her in such a way as not to cause her distress. Jill's marriage to Jordan was a tragic story. Meg should not have to deal with it until she was much older.

There was work to be done. The fates had not been tractable in allowing Leslie and Jordan to consummate their love. Many obstacles had been put in their path, and Meg had been touched by those obstacles. They now had a life to build together. And their love made them eager to get home and get to work. It would be a joyful burden.

On this Friday night they were tired but happy. They had spent a long day on the water. Tonight they would make a special dinner together. On the way in they had stopped and bought a magnificent sea bass from one of the fishermen in the village. They would cook it together.

But first they made love. It was five o'clock in the afternoon. The unaccustomed hour only added to their passion. Losing themselves in each other, they seemed to step off the edge of the world.

Jordan's body no longer felt physically unfamiliar to Leslie, because they had been together again now for several weeks. But a deeper difference, the difference made by the years, by the fact that he had believed he had lost Leslie forever—this difference remained, made him feel new, and gave a mysterious, deep luster to their love. Leslie had never dreamed that sex could be so intimate.

The sun was setting. They got up to watch it together. They were wearing the silk bathrobes Jordan had had waiting for them when they arrived here three weeks ago.

They stood on the parapet, their arms around each other, and watched the sun dip languidly into the waiting sea. The village looked sweetly domestic against its gigantic ocean backdrop. The fishing boats shone in the sunset like little grace notes to this symphony of crimson and blue. It was an amazing sight.

"I hate to think of it," Jordan said.

"What?" she asked gently.

"How easy it was to lose you," he replied. "And how hard it was to find you again. I'd give anything to have those years back."

"Darling," she said, taking his hand. "Maybe they weren't wasted years at all. Maybe they were necessary in their way."

She was thinking of her own odyssey through life, and how much more natural it seemed now that she knew it had been leading her back to Jordan all along.

"Maybe," she added, "we were never really separated at all."

He turned to look at her. She saw the dying sunlight reflected in his eyes. It seemed to her at that moment that neither her solitude nor her struggles had ever been real, not the way Jordan was real to her now. Her painful wanderings had only been another way of belonging to him.

"I love you," she said, raising her lips to his.

He moved suddenly in her arms. A spasm shook his body as she heard a shot ring out somewhere behind her.

Jordan went limp and slumped against her.

"Jordan, no."

A gasp escaped her lips. She struggled to support him. Together they sank slowly toward the stone floor of the parapet.

"No, Jordan, no . . ."

Something flashed inside her mind. She placed his head gently on the ground and rushed into the bedroom. She cursed herself for not having been on her guard every minute, for daring to believe in the future.

She returned with a pillow and the blanket that had been on the bed. She knelt beside him and placed the pillow under his head. His eyes were open, but unseeing.

"Oh, my God. Jordan, Jordan . . ." Panic made her tremble. She struggled with the blanket. There was a great deal of blood. She did not know where Jordan was hit, but she could tell it was serious. Perhaps those unseeing eyes meant he was dead already.

"Darling," she said. "Look at me. Speak to me. Please!"

A deep voice rang out behind her.

"Well, that's over."

She looked up to see Tony staring down at her. A gun was in his hand. The look in his eyes was excited, feverish. He had shot down the great Jordan Lazarus, and he knew it.

"You," she said.

He nodded. "You can't run away from the past," he said. "I thought you had learned that by now."

He looked at Leslie and gestured to Jordan's body.

"You did this," he said. "You thought you could have it all. Now you see where it's gotten you."

Leslie had pulled the blanket over Jordan and crouched with his head in her lap.

"Get back," said Tony. "Get back or I'll kill you too."

She looked up at him. The fear in her eyes was real, but there was something else as well, something that told him his victory was not as complete as he wanted it to be.

He looked at her with undisguised hatred.

"All right," he said. "Stay where you are, then. You've asked for this. Now you're going to see the bullet go in. Then you'll know."

He pointed the gun at Jordan.

"No!" she cried.

He looked down at her and smiled.

"What's the matter?" came the voice. "You brought this on. You did it to me. Now I'm going to do it to him. You thought you could hide from the truth forever. But everything has to be paid for. Are you afraid of a little justice?"

He aimed the gun carefully at Jordan's head.

"Justice," he said.

The explosion took him by surprise. His eyes turned to Leslie, wide and amazed.

She had shot from under the blanket. The gun was Ross Wheeler's, the same gun that had shot Tony in Leslie's Long Island house, a year and a half ago.

Tony held his ground, though he had been hit in his midsection. The amazement in his eyes turned to bitter humor, then to hate.

"Do you think you can stop me?" he asked. "I've got fate on my side. Your man is finished, babe."

Gritting his teeth, he took aim at Jordan.

Leslie pulled the gun out from under the blanket and shot Tony again. He had not thought to defend himself against her, so intent was he on killing Jordan. Only now did he begin to swing in her direction.

"Justice," he said softly.

She stood up and shot him again, moving forward to attack. This time the bullet hit him in the chest, pushing him back on his heels. Again she pulled the trigger. He toppled to the ground.

Leslie was standing silent, motionless, watching him. His gun was still in his hand. He pulled himself to his knees with a great effort. Blood was coming from his mouth. He pointed the barrel at Jordan, but his eyes were on Leslie. There was a plaintive look on his face, almost childlike. As he struggled for control of the gun Leslie understood that his love for her was the force holding him up. Tony's last weapon . . .

He trained the gun on Jordan and started to pull the trigger. She moved a pace closer and shot him again. A groan of unwilling surrender escaped his lips, and he fell on his back.

He lay with his eyes open to the foreign sky, oblivious to Leslie at last.

Epilogue

Twelve Years Later

New York City

IT WAS THREE O'CLOCK in the afternoon.

Mary had come home from school twenty minutes ago and was bickering more or less amicably with little Joe, who, though two years younger than she and not as strong, was more than a match for her in stubbornness.

They were lying on their stomachs on the floor of the living room, looking at the pictures in the book Joe had received from Aunt Louise for his fifth birthday last November. It was a book about a little duckling who was afraid he was not going to be allowed to go to a picnic. The story was far too immature for a streetwise second grader like Mary, but the pictures were attractive, and she had missed this particular book during her own preschool years.

"Turn the page," she was saying. "I want to see the locomotive."

The boy was lingering over the picture of the duckling in the meadow. A dreamer by temperament, like his father before him, he usually did things slowly. This never failed to irritate Mary, who had her mother's impatience to get things done, and who could be mercurial and even explosive when she did not get her way.

"Come *on*," she urged. "You always take all night to read a page."

After another ten seconds she had had all she could stand, and was ready to provoke an incident. She reached to turn the page, and the little boy clamped both his palms on the open book to stop her.

"No!"

A brief, silent struggle ensued, with the girl crouched over the smaller boy, grasping angrily at the book.

Shouting would have followed in short order had a warning not come from their father, who was sitting in his easy chair by the window.

"Children," he said in a low but authoritative voice. "Play nice."

Mary, who never gave up easily, turned to him with a scowl.

"Dad, he takes forever," she said. "Why do I have to wait all night?"

"Whose book is that, sweetheart?" The father's innocent question carried

493

its weight of instruction as well as warning. Mary turned away, acknowledging the rebuke by kicking her legs peevishly behind her.

"Well, he still takes forever," she muttered.

At that moment Mother, alerted to the skirmish by her own radar, emerged from the kitchen.

"Are you children fighting again?"

Mary, with a glance at her father, opted for a diplomatic course.

"No, Mom," she said. "Just reading Joey's book."

A skeptical smile curled the mother's lips.

"Good for you," she said. "Try to keep it that way. Meg will be home soon."

At that moment the phone rang. Dad answered it as the children looked up curiously.

"Lazarus," he said.

There was a long pause. The children went back to their book. The father watched them as he listened. He did not seem very interested in what the caller had to say.

"I'll be in tomorrow morning," he said into the phone. "Can't it wait until then?" And after another pause, "Handle it yourself, then. Use your own judgment."

He hung up the phone and looked down at his children with a little smile. They were turning the pages of the book quietly now, though he suspected that their show of cooperation was being put on for his benefit.

Before he could return to his own book the front door opened and closed with a slam, and Meg was in the room. Her cheeks were rosy from the cold outside air, and her wool coat and a scarf bore a few flakes of the snow that was falling over the park.

"Well, I like that," she observed, glancing at the torpid scene in the room. "Is this the welcome I get?"

As though on cue the two younger children leaped to their feet and ran to embrace her. Meg had stolen her reproachful homecoming speech from her father a couple of years ago and made it her own. Since then it had become a private joke and family ritual. Now that she was in junior high she was often away at rehearsals or concerts—she sang soprano in the Manhattan Children's Chorus, which met three times a week—and returned at odd hours. She took her accomplishments very seriously, and expected the family to render homage to her hardworking lifestyle.

She need not have worried. The younger children looked up to her as to a goddess. Her wit and intelligence, combined with a sort of daring feminine vitality and adventurousness, made her their heroine. They were always quick to abandon their own play in favor of games in which she was the leader, and they never failed to feel the crackle of electricity that entered the house when she came home.

"Well, now what?" she said, throwing her coat and scarf on the chair and kneeling to look over Joe's shoulder at the book. "Is Ducky going to get to go to the picnic, or not? I've got to know."

She gave a gentle tug to one of Mary's pigtails. She had a touchingly maternal attitude toward the younger children. Her father, who was watching now, felt a private lump in his throat at the sight of her protectiveness toward them. As often as not it was Meg who made the gingerbread or popcorn or peanut butter cookies, Meg who took them skating in the park in winter or to the zoo in summer. Meg seemed to take a special and very deliberate pleasure in knowing their childish concerns, as though they might slip through her fingers if she remained wrapped up in herself and did not make the effort to know them.

Her father and mother often reflected that this was because Meg was only their half sister. Had she been completely of the same blood as they, she would probably have paid them no attention. Somehow Meg's difference, even as it made her seem exotic to the whole family, acted as a glue that drew them all closer together.

But now Mother was standing at the door to the kitchen, looking at the three children and their father.

"Sweetie," she said to Meg. "You've got two choices."

"Uh-oh," sighed Meg, looking up from the floor. "I know what's coming."

"You can either help these two make their gingerbread," Mother said, "or you can go in and clean your room."

"Gingerbread," Meg said quickly.

"I thought so." Mother's smile was close to the borderline of real irritation. Meg's sloppiness was a source of conflict between the two. Ever since she was a little girl she had been too preoccupied with her future plans to pay attention to the piles of toys, books, and dolls she left strewn behind her. Impending adolescence and school responsibilities had worsened the problem, and now bottles of makeup, school notebooks, clothes, and teen magazines had added themselves to the litter. Her room looked like the nest of a strange bird, feathered with a chaotic detritus of teenage female artifacts.

"That's fine," her mother said. "But you're only off the hook until five. I want to see all clothes put away, and nothing on that floor of yours before you come to dinner."

"Mom, I've got homework!" Meg protested.

"We've all got work," her mother said. "But that doesn't mean we can't live like humans."

Meg stood up and went to her father.

"Dad, she's on me again," she began.

But before she could say another word the other two children rushed forward and literally fell into their father's lap. This was another family ritual, the "ganging up" of the children as a group whenever a single one decided to go to their father's embrace.

"Ouch!" he complained with a mock grimace. "Don't you three have any respect for a man's wounds? I'm a veteran of combat, you know."

He had long since learned to joke about the wound to his abdomen, for he could not completely ignore it. The wound had caused damage to several internal organs, and had nearly killed him. The doctors had given him up at first, and even gone as far as to telephone his family to come to his deathbed. He had been in the hospital for two months and had undergone several operations.

Nowadays he was recovered, of course, and kept up an athletic lifestyle. But he used the old wound as an excuse to stay home from the office whenever he wanted to be with the children, as today. In the inevitable conflict between family and work he had made his choice before the younger children were even born. He let the office take care of itself as much as possible. His personal fame had suffered, but he liked it that way.

He only referred to the old wound when he wanted to use it to his own advantage in routine family banter. The children had been told it was the result of a hunting accident around the time of his marriage to their mother. Sometimes, when he wanted to tease Mother, he would claim that she had shot him in the stomach after a lovers' quarrel, and that he had never trusted her around guns since.

Now the smaller children, satisfied with the hugs they had received, went back to their book. Meg remained sitting on her father's knee, enjoying the unfamiliar perch. She had been too distracted by her busy life to notice that she had given up sitting on his lap a couple of years ago.

"Dad, make her see reason," she said. "I've got homework. I can't do everything. Besides, it's my room."

"Uh-oh," he smiled, taking her hand. "Teenage territoriality on the horizon. I can see we're going to have to make some new rules for your sake."

"Well, why not start now?" she asked.

He sighed. "The trouble with you two," he said, "is that you're too much alike. I can't tell either of you a thing."

"Daddy . . ." Meg's tone was complaining.

He looked from her face to that of her mother, who was standing in the kitchen doorway watching them. He never tired of comparing their faces, so different on the surface and yet lit by the same inner glow. The sparks that sometimes flew between them were merely an outward sign of that unseen bond that made them perhaps closer to each other than to anyone else.

His eyes met Leslie's. Though it was Meg who was on the threshold of young womanhood, Leslie looked as fresh as a girl, standing in the doorway smiling at him. Her slim figure and beautiful hair—still wild, despite the rubber band holding it back in a ponytail while she worked in the kitchen—made her look eternally young. This was all the more exciting to him as he reflected that she was pregnant again. She would give him his fourth child next July. The children had not been told yet. He and Leslie had decided to keep it as a surprise for a few more days.

Daddy.

Now he looked at Meg. Not for the first time he admired the chameleonlike way in which her mood affected her looks. Her sandy hair actually seemed darker now, and her blue-green irises crystallized toward a shadowy violet. Her freckles glimmered against her milky skin in the afternoon light, making her look at once delicate and vibrant.

She shifted her weight slightly. His wound ached for an instant, but he barely felt it. He was admiring Meg's composite essence. Her face was like a magic mirror reflecting in each of its facets the women who had owned places in his heart. One of them was in the kitchen doorway now, smiling with pride in her oldest daughter even as she wondered what bone of contention would put them at odds next.

Another was under the ground in a cemetery in this city, having journeyed bravely through a life as long and tumultuous as a crusade before giving it all up to save this daughter.

The third was buried back home in Pennsylvania, long since forgotten by the world that trumpeted her brother's fame, but still speaking to him in a quiet voice whose truths he never ceased to ponder in the most private part of his mind.

You left yourself behind all along, Jordie. Find yourself now. For me . . .

He had never painted the painting Meg wanted. True, the city around him, like cities everywhere, bore the brush strokes of his vision. Meg had tried to congratulate him on that, as though to make up for what he had lost. On the canvas of history his name would have its place, for a while at least. But he had long since stopped caring about history.

Jordan Lazarus looked at his family. This languid midweek afternoon, punctuated by a rare phone call from work and the occasional skirmish between siblings, was the closest thing to paradise he had ever experienced. He had sacrificed a lot for it, and never regretted the sacrifice for an instant.

It occurred to him that if his sister Meg could see this scene from wherever she was today, she might look at the family he had fathered and decide that only now had Jordan at last taken up her challenge and made her proud.

Be happy . . .

With this thought Jordan looked from the girl in his lap to the mother still standing in the doorway. It seemed that his whole life, from his earliest dreams to his final struggles, hung on the precious invisible line between those two faces.

Time, Jordan Lazarus mused, is a harsh mistress who can use a man's own wishes to lure him far from the best of himself, and even let him die in exile from his own soul. In Jordan's case this capricious goddess had taken pity in the end, and brought him home.

The children were at odds again.

"Dad!" called Mary from the floor.

"Dad," murmured Meg, looking into his eyes with an odd tenderness.

And he glanced at Leslie, whose lips were even now, in silence, pronouncing the magic word.